THE
WALKING
DEAD

THE WALKING DEAD

RISE OF THE GOVERNOR
AND THE ROAD TO WOODBURY

ROBERT KIRKMAN
AND
JAY BONANSINGA

Thomas Dunne Books
St. Martin's Griffin
New York

THOMAS DUNNE BOOKS.
An imprint of St. Martin's Press.

www.thomasdunnebooks.com
www.stmartins.com

ISBN 978-1-250-07309-9 (trade paperback)

First Edition: November 2014

10 9 8 7 6 5 4 3 2 1

Rise of the Governor

To Jeanie-B, Joey, and Bill . . . the loves of my life.
—Jay

For Sonia, Peter, and Collette . . . I promise I'll
work less as soon as college is paid for.
—Robert

ACKNOWLEDGMENTS

Special thanks to Robert Kirkman, Brendan Deneen,
Andy Cohen, David Alpert, Stephen Emery, and all the good
people at Circle of Confusion.
—Jay

Big ups to Jay Bonansinga, Alpert and the rest at Circle
of Confusion, the fine folks at Image Comics, and Charlie Adlard
for steering the ship. Much respect for Rosenman, Rosenbaum,
Simonian, and Lerner. And, of course . . . Brendan Deneen.
—Robert

PART 1

The Hollow Men

There's nothing glorious in dying.
Anyone can do it.

—Johnny Rotten

ONE

It occurs to Brian Blake as he huddles in the musty darkness, the terror constricting his chest, the pain throbbing in his knees: If only he possessed a *second* pair of hands, he could cover his *own* ears, and maybe block out the noise of human heads being demolished. Sadly, the only hands Brian currently owns are busy right now, covering the tiny ears of a little girl in the closet next to him.

The seven-year-old keeps shuddering in his arms, jerking at the intermittent *THWACK-GAHHHH-THUMP* outside the closet. Then comes the silence, broken only by the sticky sound of boot steps on bloody tile, and a flurry of angry whispers out in the vestibule.

Brian starts coughing again. He can't help it. For days he has been fighting this goddamn cold, a stubborn blight on his joints and sinuses that he cannot shake. It happens to him every fall, when the Georgia days start getting dank and gloomy. The dampness gets into his bones, saps his energy, and steals his breath. And now he feels the pounding stab of a fever with each cough.

Doubling over in another hacking, wheezing fit, he keeps his hands pressed down on little Penny's ears as he coughs. He knows the sound of his rasping is attracting all kinds of attention outside the closet door, out in the convolutions of the house, but there's nothing he can do about it. He sees tracings of light with each cough—like tiny filigrees of fireworks across his blind pupils.

The closet—barely four feet wide, and maybe three feet deep—is as dark as an inkwell, and it reeks of mothballs, mouse droppings, and old cedar. Plastic coat bags hang down in the darkness, brushing the sides of Brian's face. Brian's younger brother Philip told him it was okay to cough in the closet. In fact, Brian was free to cough his fucking head off—it would draw out the monsters—but Brian better not give his goddamn cold to Philip's little girl. If he did, Philip would crack *Brian*'s head open.

The coughing fit passes.

Moments later, another pair of lumbering footsteps disturbs the silence outside the closet—another dead thing entering the kill zone. Brian squeezes his hands tighter against Penny's ears, and the child flinches at another rendition of Skull Splitting in D minor.

If asked to describe the racket outside the closet, Brian Blake would probably revert to his days as a failed music store entrepreneur and tell you that the head-cracking sounds are like a percussive symphony they might play in hell—like some trippy outtake from Edgard Varèse or a druggy drum solo from John Bonham—with repeating verses and choruses: the heavy breathing of humans . . . the shambling footsteps of another moving corpse . . . the whistle of an axe . . . the *thunk* of steel sinking into flesh . . .

. . . and finally, the big finale, the splat of moist, dead weight on the slimy parquet.

Another break in the action sends fever chills down Brian's spine. The silence closes in again. Eyes now adjusted to the darkness, Brian sees the first shimmer of thick arterial blood seeping under the bottom of the door. It looks like motor oil. He gently yanks his niece away from the spreading puddle, pulling her back against the boots and umbrellas along the back wall.

The hem of Penny Blake's little denim dress touches the blood. She quickly pulls the fabric away, and frantically rubs at the stain, as if the very absorption of the blood will infect her somehow.

Another convulsive coughing fit doubles Brian over. He fights it. He swallows the broken glass of a sore throat and pulls the little girl into a full-on embrace. He doesn't know what to do or say. He wants to help his niece. He wants to whisper something reassuring to her but cannot think of a single reassuring thing to whisper.

The girl's father would know what to say. Philip would know. He always knows what to say. Philip Blake is the guy who says the things that everybody else *wishes* they had said. He says what needs to be said, and he does what needs to be done. Like right now. He's out there with Bobby and Nick, doing what needs to be done . . . while Brian hunkers here in the dark like a scared rabbit, wishing he knew what to say to his niece.

Considering the fact that Brian Blake is the oldest of the two siblings, it's odd how Brian has always been the runt. Barely five feet seven in his boot heels, Brian Blake is a raw-boned scarecrow of a man scarcely able to fill out his black peg-leg jeans and torn Weezer T-shirt. A mousey goatee, macramé bracelets, and a thatch of dark Ichabod Crane hair complete the picture of a thirty-five-year-old Bohemian waif stuck in Peter Pan limbo, now kneeling in the mothball-scented gloom.

Brian sucks in a hoarse breath and looks down at the doe-eyed Penny, her mute, horrified face ghostly in the darkness of the closet. The child has always been a quiet little girl, with an almost porcelain complexion, like that of a china doll, which has given her face a rather ethereal cast. But since her mother's death she has turned even further inward, becoming more wan and stoic, to the point of appearing almost translucent, with tendrils of raven-black hair obscuring her huge eyes.

For the last three days, she has hardly said a word. Of course, they have been three *extraordinary* days—and trauma works differently on children than it does on adults—but Brian is worried that Penny is perhaps slipping into some kind of shock.

"It's gonna be okay, kiddo," Brian whispers to her with a lame little cough as punctuation.

She says something without looking up at him. She mumbles it, staring down at the floor, a tear pearling on her dirty cheek.

"What was that, Pen?" Brian cradles her against him and wipes her tear.

She says something again, and again, and again, but not exactly to Brian. She says it more like a mantra, or a prayer, or an incantation: *"It's never-ever going to be okay, never-ever-ever-ever-ever."*

"Sshhhhh." He holds her head, pressing it gently against the folds of his T-shirt. He feels the damp heat of her face against his ribs. He covers her ears again as he hears the *THWACK* of another axe blade outside the closet, smashing through the membrane of a scalp, into the hard shell of a skull, through the layers of dura, and into the pulpy gray gelatin of an occipital lobe.

It makes a smacking noise like a baseball bat hitting a wet softball—the ejaculate of blood like a mop head slapping the floor— followed by a ghastly, wet thud. Oddly, that's the worst part for Brian: that hollow, moist thump of a body landing on expensive ceramic tile. The tile is custom made for the house, with elaborate inlay and Aztec designs. It's a lovely house . . . or at least, it once was.

Again the noises cease.

Again the horrible dripping silence follows. Brian stifles a cough, holding it in like a firecracker that's about to pop, so he can better hear the minute changes in breathing outside the closet, the greasy footsteps shuffling through gore. But the place is dead silent now.

Brian feels the child seize up next to him—little Penny girding herself for another salvo of axe blows—but the silence stretches.

Inches away, the sound of a bolt clicking, and the closet doorknob turning, rashes Brian's body with gooseflesh. The door swings open.

"Okay, we're good." The baritone voice, whiskey-cured and smoky, comes from a man peering down into the recesses of the closet. Eyes blinking at the darkness, face shimmering with sweat, flush with the exertion of zombie disposal, Philip Blake holds a grue-slick axe in his workman's hand.

"You sure?" Brian utters.

Ignoring his brother, Philip gazes down at his daughter. "Everything's okay, punkin, Daddy's okay."

"Are you *sure*?" Brian says with a cough.

Philip looks at his brother. "You mind covering your mouth, sport?"

Brian wheezes, "You sure it's clear?"

"Punkin?" Philip Blake addresses his daughter tenderly, his faint Southern drawl belying the bright, feral embers of violence just now fading in his eyes. "I'm gonna need y'all to stay right there for a minute. Awright? You stay right there until Daddy says it's okay to come out. You understand?"

With a slight nod, the pale little girl gives him a feeble gesture of understanding.

"C'mon, sport," Philip urges his older brother out of the shadows. "Gonna need your help with the cleanup."

Brian struggles to his feet, pushing his way through the hanging overcoats.

He emerges from the closet and blinks at the harsh light of the vestibule. He stares and coughs and stares some more. For a brief moment, it looks as though the lavish entryway of the two-story Colonial, brightly lit by fancy copper chandeliers, is in the throes of being redecorated by a work crew afflicted by palsy. Great swaths of eggplant-purple spatters stain the teal green plaster walls. Rorschach patterns of black and crimson adorn the baseboards and moldings. Then the shapes on the floor register.

Six bodies lie akimbo in bloody heaps. Ages and genders are obscured by the wet carnage, the mottled, livid skin tones, and the misshapen skulls. The largest lies in a spreading pool of bile at the foot of the great circular staircase. Another one, perhaps the lady of the house, perhaps once a convivial hostess offering peach cobbler and Southern hospitality, is now splayed across the lovely white parquet floor in a contorted mess, a stringer of wormy gray matter flagging from her breached cranium.

Brian Blake feels his gorge rising, his throat involuntarily dilating.

"Okay, gentlemen, we got our work cut out for us," Philip is saying, addressing his two cronies, Nick and Bobby, as well as his brother, but Brian can barely hear over the sick thump of his own heartbeat.

He sees the other remains—over the last two days, Philip has started calling the ones they destroy "twice-cooked pork"—strewn along the dark, burnished baseboards at the threshold of the living room. Maybe the teenage children who once lived here, maybe visitors who suffered the Southern *in*hospitality of an infected bite, these bodies lie in sunbursts of arterial spray. One of them, his or her dented head lying facedown like a spilled soup pan, still pumps its scarlet fluids across the floor with the profusion of a breached fire hydrant. A couple of others still have small hatchet blades embedded in their crania, sunk down to the hilt, like the flags of explorers triumphantly stuck into once unattainable summits.

Brian's hand flies up to his mouth, as if he might stem the tide rising up his esophagus. He feels a tapping sensation on the top of his skull, as though a moth is ticking against his scalp. He looks up.

Blood drips from the overhead chandelier, a droplet landing on Brian's nose.

"Nick, why don't you go grab some of them tarps we saw earlier in the—"

Brian falls to his knees, hunches forward, and roars vomit across the parquet. The steaming flood of khaki-colored bile sluices across the tiles, mingling with the spoor of the fallen dead.

Tears burn Brian's eyes as he heaves four days of soul-sickness onto the floor.

Philip Blake lets out a tense sigh, the buzz of adrenaline still coursing through him. For a moment he makes no effort to go to his brother's side, but simply stands there, setting down his bloody axe, rolling his eyes. It's a miracle Philip doesn't have a groove worn into the tops of his eye sockets from all the eye rolling he's done over the years on his brother's account. But what else is Philip supposed to do? The poor son of bitch is family, and family is family . . . especially in off-the-scale times such as these.

The resemblance is sure there—nothing Philip can do about *that*. A tall, rangy, sinewy man with the ropy muscles of a tradesman, Philip Blake shares the same dark features as his brother, the same dark almond eyes and coal-black hair of their Mexican-American mother. Mama Rose's maiden name was Garcia, and her features had dominated the lineage over those of the boys' father, a big, coarse alcoholic of Scots-Irish descent named Ed Blake. But Philip, three years younger than Brian, had gotten all the muscle.

He now stands over six feet tall in his faded jeans, work boots, and chambray shirt, with the Fu Manchu mustache and jailhouse tats of a biker; and he is about to move his imposing figure over to his retching brother, and maybe say something harsh, when he stops himself. He hears something he doesn't like coming from across the vestibule.

Bobby Marsh, an old high school pal of Philip's, stands near the base of the staircase, wiping an axe blade on his size XXL jeans. A portly thirty-two-year-old junior college dropout, his long greasy brown hair pulled back in a rattail, Bobby Marsh is not exactly obese, but definitely overweight, definitely the type of guy his Burke County High classmates would call a butterball. He now giggles with nervous, edgy, belly-shivering laughter as he watches Brian Blake vomit. The giggling is colorless and hollow—a sort of tic that Bobby cannot seem to control.

The anxious giggling had started three days ago when one of the first of the undead had lumbered out of a service bay at a gas station near the Augusta airport. Clad in blood-soaked overalls, the grease monkey shuffled out of hiding with a trail of toilet paper on his heel, and the thing had tried to make a meal out of Bobby's fat neck before Philip had stepped in and clobbered the thing with a crowbar.

The discovery that day—that a major blow to the head does the job quite nicely—had led to more nervous chortling on Bobby's part—definitely a defense mechanism—with a lot of anxious chatter about it being "something in the water, man, like the black-fucking-plague." But Philip didn't want to hear about reasons for this shit storm then, and he sure doesn't want to hear about them now.

"Hey!" Philip addresses the heavyset man. "You still think this is *funny*?"

Bobby's laughter dies.

On the other side of the room, near a window overlooking the dark expanse of a backyard, which is currently shrouded in night, a fourth figure watches uneasily. Nick Parsons, another friend from Philip's wayward childhood, is a compact, lean thirty-something with the kind of prep-school grooming and marine-cut hair of an eternal jock. The religious one of the bunch, Nick has taken the longest to get used to the idea of destroying things that were once human. Now his khakis and sneakers are stippled with blood, and his eyes burn with trauma, as he watches Philip approach Bobby.

"Sorry, man," Bobby mutters.

"My daughter's in there," Philip says, coming nose to nose with Marsh. The volatile chemicals of rage and panic and pain can instantly ignite in Philip Blake.

Bobby looks at the blood-slicked floor. "Sorry, sorry."

"Go get the tarps, Bobby."

Six feet away, Brian Blake, still on his hands and knees, expels the last of his stomach contents, and continues to dry-heave.

Philip goes over to his older brother, kneels by him. "Let it out."

"I'm—uh—" Brian croaks, sniffing, trying to form a complete thought.

Philip gently lays a big, grimy, callused hand on his brother's hunched shoulders. "It's okay, bro . . . just let it all out."

"I'm—s-sorry."

"It's all right."

Brian gets himself under control, wipes his mouth with the back of his hand. "Y-you think you got all of them?"

"I do."

"You sure?"

"Yep."

"You searched . . . everywhere? In the basement and stuff?"

"Yes, sir, we did. All the bedrooms . . . even the attic. Last one came out of hiding at the sound of that fucking cough, loud enough to wake the fucking dead. Teenage girl, tried to have one of Bobby's chins for lunch."

Brian gulps down a raw, painful swallow. "These people . . . they . . . *lived* here."

Philip sighs. "Not anymore."

Brian manages to look around the room, then gazes up at his brother. Brian's face is wet with tears. "But they were like . . . a family."

Philip nods, and he doesn't say anything. He feels like giving his brother a shrug—*so fucking what*—but all he does is keep nodding. He's not thinking about the zombified family he just dispatched, or the implications of all the mind-numbing butchery he's already wreaked over the last three days—slaughtering individuals who were recently soccer moms and mailmen and gas station attendants. Yesterday, Brian had gone off on some bullshit intellectual tangent about the difference between morals and ethics in this situation: Morally, one should never kill, *ever*, but ethically, which is subtly different, one should maintain the policy of killing only if it's in self-defense. But Philip doesn't see what they're doing as killing. You can't kill a thing that's already been killed. What you do is squash it like a bug, and move on, and stop *thinking* so much.

The fact is, right now, Philip isn't even thinking about the next move his little ragtag group will make—which is probably going to be entirely up to him (he has become the de facto leader of this bunch, and he might as well face it). Right now, Philip Blake is focused on a single objective: Since the nightmare started less than seventy-two hours ago, and folks started turning—for reasons nobody has yet been able to figure out—all that Philip Blake has been able to think about is protecting Penny. It is why he got the hell out of his hometown, Waynesboro, two days ago.

A small farming community on the eastern edge of central Georgia, the place had gone to hell quickly when folks had started dying and coming back. But it was Penny's safety that had ultimately convinced Philip to fly the coop. It was because of Penny he had enlisted the help of his old high school buddies; and it was because of Penny he had set out for Atlanta, where, according to the news, refugee centers were being set up. It was all because of Penny. Penny is all that Philip Blake has left. She is the only thing keeping him going—the only salve on his wounded soul.

Long before this inexplicable epidemic had broken out, the void in Philip's heart would pang at 3 A.M on sleepless nights. That's the exact hour he had lost his wife—hard to believe it's been nearly four years now—on a rain-slick highway south of Athens. Sarah had been visiting a friend at the University of Georgia, and she'd been drinking, and she lost control of her car on a winding road in Wilkes County.

From the moment he had identified the body, Philip knew he would never be the same. He had no qualms about doing the right thing—taking on two jobs to keep Penny fed and clothed and cared for—but he would never be the same. Maybe that's why all this was happening. God's little gag. When the locusts come, and the river runs red with blood, the guy with the most to lose gets to lead the pack.

"Doesn't matter who they were," Philip finally says to his brother. "Or *what* they were."

"Yeah . . . I guess you're right." By this point, Brian has managed to sit up, cross-legged now, taking deep wheezing breaths. He watches Bobby and Nick across the room, unrolling large canvas tarps and shaking open garbage bags. They begin rolling corpses, still dripping, into the tarps.

"Only thing that matters is we got this place cleaned out now," Philip says. "We can stay here tonight, and if we can score some gas in the morning, we can make it to Atlanta tomorrow."

"Doesn't make any sense, though," Brian mutters now, glancing from corpse to corpse.

"What are you talking about?"

"Look at them."

"What?" Philip glances over his shoulder at the gruesome remains of the matriarch being rolled up in a tarp. "What about 'em?"

"It's just the family."

"So?"

Brian coughs into his sleeve, then wipes his mouth. "What I'm saying is . . . you got the mother, the father, four teenage kids . . . and that's like *it*."

"Yeah, so what?"

Brian looks up at Philip. "So, how the hell does something like this happen? They all . . . *turned together*? Did one of them get bitten and bring it back inside?"

Philip thinks about it for a moment—after all, he's still trying to figure out just exactly what is going on, too, how this madness works—but finally Philip gets tired of thinking about it and says, "C'mon, get off your lazy ass and help us."

It takes them about an hour to get the place cleaned up. Penny stays in the closet for the duration of the process. Philip brings her a stuffed animal from one of the kid's rooms, and tells her it won't be long before she can come out. Brian mops the blood, coughing fit-fully, while the other three men drag the canvas-covered corpses—two large and four smaller ones—out the back sliding doors and across the large cedar deck.

The late-September night sky above them is as clear and cold as a black ocean, a riot of stars shining down, taunting them with their impassive, cheerful twinkling. The breaths of the three men show in the darkness as they drag the bundles across dew-frosted planks. They carry pickaxes on their belts. Philip has a gun stuffed down the back of his belt. It's an old .22 Ruger that he bought at a flea market years ago, but nobody wants to rouse the dead with the bark of gunfire right now. They can hear the telltale drone of walking dead on the wind—garbled moaning sounds, shuffling footsteps—coming from somewhere in the darkness of the neighboring yards.

It's been an unusually nippy early autumn in Georgia, and to-night the mercury is supposed to dip into the lower forties, perhaps even the upper thirties. Or at least that's what the local AM radio station claimed before it petered out in a gust of static. Up to this point in their journey, Philip and his crew have been monitoring TV, radio, and the Internet on Brian's BlackBerry.

Amid the general chaos, the news reports have been assuring people that everything is just peachy-keen—your trusty government is in control of the situation—and this little bump in the road will be smoothed out in a matter of hours. Regular warnings chime in on civil defense frequencies, admonishing folks to stay indoors, and keep out of sparsely populated areas, and wash their hands fre-quently, and drink bottled water, and blah, blah, blah.

Of course, nobody has any answers. And maybe the most omi-nous sign of all is the increasing number of station failures. Thank-fully, gas stations still have gas, grocery stores are still stocked, and electrical grids and stoplights and police stations and all the infra-structural paraphernalia of civilization seem to be hanging on.

But Philip worries that a loss of power will raise the stakes in unimaginable ways.

"Let's put 'em in the Dumpsters behind the garage," Philip says so softly he's almost whispering, dragging two canvas bundles up to the wooden fence adjacent to the three-car garage. He wants to do this swiftly and silently. He doesn't want to attract any zombies. No fires, no sharp noises, no gunshots if he can help it.

There's a narrow gravel alley behind the seven-foot cedar fence, serving the rank and file of spacious garages lining the backyards. Nick drags his load over to the fence gate, a solid slab of cedar planks with a wrought-iron handle. He drops the bundle and opens the gate.

An upright corpse is waiting for him on the other side of the gate.

"LOOK OUT, Y'ALL!" Bobby Marsh cries out.

"Shut the fuck up!" Philip hisses, reaching for the pickaxe on his belt, already halfway to the gate.

Nick recoils.

The zombie lurches at him, chomping, missing his left pectoral by millimeters, the sound of yellow dentures snapping impotently like the clicking of castanets—and in the moonlight, Nick can see that it's an elderly adult male in a tattered Izod sweater, golf slacks, and expensive cleats, the lunar gleam shining in its milky, cataract-filmed eyes: *somebody's grandfather.*

Nick gets one good glimpse at the thing before stumbling backward over his own feet and falling onto his ass on the lush carpet of Kentucky bluegrass. The dead golfer lumbers through the gap and onto the lawn just as a flash of rusty steel arcs through the air.

The business end of Philip's pickaxe lands squarely in the monster's head, cracking the coconutlike shell of the old man's skull, piercing the dense, fibrous membrane of the dura mater and sinking into the gelatinous parietal lobe. It makes a sound like celery snapping and sends a clot of dark brackish fluid into the air. The insectile verve on the grandfather's face instantly dims, like a cartoon whose projection system has just jammed.

The zombie folds to the ground with the inelegant deflation of an empty laundry sack.

The pickaxe, still deeply embedded, pulls Philip forward and down. He yanks at it. The point is stuck. "Shut the motherfucking gate now, shut the gate, and do it quietly, goddamnit," Philip says, still affecting a frenzied stage whisper, slamming his left Chippewa steel-toed logger boot down on the breached skull of the cadaver.

The other two men move as if in some synchronized dance, Bobby quickly dropping his load and rushing over to the gate. Nick struggles to his feet and backs away in a horrified stupor. Bobby quickly latches the wrought-iron lever. It makes a hollow metallic rattle that is so noisy it echoes across the dark lawns.

At last, Philip wrenches the pick from the stubborn crag of the zombie's skull—it comes out with a soft smooch sound—and he is turning toward the remains of the family, his mind swimming with panic, when he hears something odd, something unexpected, coming from the house.

He looks up and sees the rear of the Colonial, the window glass lit brilliantly from within.

Brian is silhouetted behind the sliding glass door, tapping on the pane, motioning for Philip and the others to hurry back, right now. Urgency burns in Brian's expression. It has nothing to do with the dead golfer—Philip can tell—something is wrong.

Oh God, please let it not *have to do with Penny.*

Philip drops the pickaxe and crosses the lawn in seconds flat.

"What about the stiffs?" Bobby Marsh is calling after Philip.

"Leave 'em!" Philip yells, vaulting up the deck steps and rushing to the sliding doors.

Brian is waiting with the slider ajar. "I gotta show you something, man," he says.

"What is it? Is it Penny? Is she okay?" Philip is out of breath as he slips back into the house. Bobby and Nick are coming across the deck, and they too slip into the warmth of the Colonial.

"Penny's fine," Brian says. He's holding a framed photograph. "She's fine. Says she doesn't mind staying in the closet a little while longer."

"Judas Priest, Brian, what the fuck!" Philip catches his breath, his hands balled into fists.

"I gotta show you something. You want to stay here tonight?" Brian turns toward the sliding glass door. "Look. The family died together in here, right? All six of them? Six?"

Philip wipes his face. "Spit it out, man."

"Look. Somehow they all turned *together*. As a family, right?" Brian coughs, then points at the six pale bundles lying near the garage. "There's six of them out there on the grass. Look. Mom and dad and four kids."

"So fucking *what*?"

Brian holds up a portrait in a frame, the family from a happier time, all smiling awkwardly, dressed in their starchy Sunday best. "I found this on the piano," he says.

"And . . . ?"

Brian points at the youngest child in the photo, a boy of eleven or twelve years old, little navy blue suit, blond bangs, stiff smile.

Brian looks at his brother and says very gravely, "There's seven of them in the picture."

TWO

The graceful two-story Colonial that Philip selected for their extended pit stop sits on a manicured side street deep in the tree-lined labyrinth of a gated enclave known as Wiltshire Estates.

Situated off Highway 278, about twenty miles east of Atlanta, the six-thousand-acre community is carved out of a forest preserve of dense longleaf pine and massive, old live oaks. The southern boundary fronts the vast, rolling hills of a thirty-six-hole golf course designed by Fuzzy Zoeller.

In the free brochure, which Brian Blake found on the floor of an abandoned guard shack earlier that evening, a flowery sales pitch makes the place sound like a Martha Stewart wet dream: *Wiltshire Estates provides an award-winning lifestyle with world-class amenities . . . named the "Best of the Best" by* GOLF Magazine Living *. . . also home to the Triple-A Five Diamond Shady Oaks Plantation Resort and Spa . . . full-time security patrols . . . homes from $475,000 to 1 million-plus.*

The Blake party happened upon the fancy outer gates at sunset that day—on their way to the refugee centers in Atlanta—all of them crammed into Philip's rust-pocked Chevy Suburban. In the spill of the headlights, they saw the fancy cast-iron finials and great arched legend with the Wiltshire name hammered in metal across the spires, and they stopped to investigate.

At first, Philip thought the place might serve as a quick pit stop, a place to rest and maybe forage for supplies before completing the last leg of the journey into the city. Perhaps they would find others like them, other living souls, maybe a few good Samaritans who would help them out. But as the five tired, hungry, wired, and dazed travelers made an initial circle of the winding roads of Wiltshire, with the darkness quickly closing in, they realized that the place was, for the most part, *dead*.

No lights burned in any of the windows. Very few cars remained in the driveways or at the curbs. A fire hydrant gushed at one corner, unattended, sending a foamy spray across a lawn. At another corner, an abandoned BMW sat with its shattered front end wrapped around a telephone pole, its twisted passenger door gaping open. People had apparently left in a hurry.

The reason they left, for the most part, could be seen in the distant shadows of the golf course, in the gullies behind the resort, and even here and there on the well-lighted streets. Zombies shambled aimlessly like ghostly remnants of their original selves, their slack, yawning mouths letting out a rusty groan that Philip could hear well enough, even through the sealed windows of the Suburban, as he circumnavigated the maze of wide, newly paved roads.

The pandemic or the act of God—or whatever the hell started it all up—must have hit Wiltshire Estates hard and fast. Most of the undead seemed to be off in the berms and pathways of the golf course. Something must have happened there to speed the process. Maybe golfers are mostly old and slow. Maybe they taste good to the undead. Who the hell knows? But it is apparent, even from hundreds of yards away—glimpsed through trees or over the tops of privacy fences—that scores, maybe hundreds, of undead are congregated in the vast complex of clubhouses, fairways, footbridges, and sand traps.

In the dark of night, they resemble insects lazily swarming a hive.

It's disconcerting to look at, but somehow the phenomenon has left the adjacent community, with its endless circuit of cul-de-sacs and curving lanes, relatively deserted. And the more Philip and his wide-eyed passengers circled the neighborhood, the more they began to long for a small chunk of that award-winning lifestyle, just a taste, for just long enough to replenish themselves and recharge.

They thought that they could maybe spend the night here, get a fresh start in the morning.

They chose the big Colonial at the bottom of Green Briar Lane because it seemed far enough away from the golf course to avoid the attentions of the swarm. It had a big yard with good sight lines, and a high, sturdy privacy fence. It also seemed empty. But when they carefully backed the Suburban across the lawn and up to a side door—leaving the vehicle unlocked, the keys in the ignition—and they sneaked in a window, one by one, the house almost immediately started working on them. The first creaking noises came from the second floor, and that's when Philip had sent Nick back to the Suburban for the assortment of axes stored in the back well.

"I'm telling you, we got 'em all," Philip is saying now, trying to calm his brother down, who sits across the kitchen in the breakfast nook.

Brian doesn't say anything, just stares at his bowl of soggy cereal. A bottle of cough medicine sits nearby, a quarter of which Brian has already chugged down.

Penny sits next to him, also with a bowl of Cap'n Crunch in front her. A little stuffed penguin the size of a pear sits next to her bowl, and every now and then Penny moves her spoon to the toy's mouth, pretending to share her cereal with the thing.

"We checked every inch of this place," Philip goes on as he throws open cabinet after cabinet. The kitchen is a cornucopia, brimming with upper-class provisions and luxuries: gourmet coffees, immersion blenders, crystal goblets, wine racks, handmade pastas, fancy jams and jellies, condiments of every variety, expensive liqueurs, and cooking gadgets of every description. The giant Viking range is spotless, and the massive Sub-Zero refrigerator is packed with expensive meats and fruits and spreads and dairy products and little white Chinese carryout boxes full of still-fresh leftovers. "He might have been visiting a relative or something," Philip adds, making note of a nice single-malt Scotch sitting on a shelf. "Might've been with his grandparents, staying over at a friend's house, whatever."

"Holy freaking Jesus, look at this!" Bobby Marsh exclaims across the room. He stands in front of the pantry, and he's lustily inspecting the goodies inside it. "Looks like Willy-damn-Wonka and the Chocolate Factory in here . . . cookies, lady fingers, and the bread's still fresh."

"The place is safe, Brian," Philip says, pulling the bottle of Scotch down.

"Safe?" Brian Blake stares at the tabletop. He lets out a cough and cringes.

"That's what I said. Matter of fact, I'm thinking—"

"Just lost another one!" a voice pipes in from the other side of the kitchen.

It's Nick. For the past ten minutes, he's been nervously surfing through the TV channels on a little plasma screen mounted under a cabinet to the left of the sink, checking the local stations for updates, and now, at a quarter to twelve Central Standard Time, Fox 5 News out of Atlanta has just crumbled into snow. All that leaves on the cable box—other than national networks showing reruns of nature programs and old movies—is Atlanta's stalwart, CNN, and all *they're* showing at the moment are emergency robo-announcements, the same warning screens with the same bullet points that have been airing for days. Even Brian's BlackBerry is giving up the ghost, the signal very spotty in this area. When it *does* work, the device is full of blind e-mails and Facebook tags and anonymous tweets with cryptic messages such as:

. . . AND THE KINGDOM WILL BE IN DARKNESS . . .

. . . IT'S THE BIRDS FALLING FROM THE SKY, THAT'S WHAT STARTED IT . . .

. . . BURN IT ALL DOWN BURN IT ALL . . .

. . . BLASPHEMIES AGAINST GOD . . .

. . . U SUCK U DIE . . .

. . . THE HOUSE OF THE LORD HAS BECOME A DWELLING PLACE OF DEMONS . . .

. . . DON'T BLAME ME FOR THIS I'M A LIBERTARIAN . . .

. . . EAT ME . . .

"Turn it off, Nick," Philip says gloomily, plopping down on a chair in the breakfast nook with his bottle. He frowns and reaches around to the back of his belt, where his pistol is digging into the small of his back. He lays the Ruger on the table and thumbs the cap off the Scotch, then takes a healthy swig.

Brian and Penny both stare at the gun.

Philip puts the cap back on the bottle, then tosses the Scotch across the kitchen to Nick, who catches it with the aplomb of an all-state second basemen (which he once was). "Tune in to the all-booze channel for a while . . . you need to get some sleep, stop watching screens."

Nick takes a taste. He takes another one, then caps the bottle and tosses it to Bobby.

Bobby nearly drops it. Still standing at the pantry, he is busily wolfing down an entire package of Oreos, the black crust already forming in the corners of his mouth. He washes the cookies down with a big pull of single-malt, and lets out a grateful belch.

Drinking is something Philip and his two friends are accustomed to doing together, and they need to do it tonight more than ever. It started in their freshman year at Burke County, with crème de menthe and watermelon wine in pup tents in each others' back-yards. Later, they graduated to boilermakers after football games. Nobody can hold his liquor like Philip Blake, but the other two men are close rivals in the juicer sweepstakes.

Early in his married life, Philip would go out carousing with his two high school buddies on a regular basis, mostly to remind him-self what it was like to be young and single and irresponsible. But after Sarah's death, the three men drifted apart. The stress of being a single parent, and working days at the muffler shop, and nights driving the freightliner with Penny in the sleeper compartment, had consumed him. The boys' nights out became less and less fre-quent. Once in a while, though—in fact, as recently as last month—Philip still finds time to meet Bobby and Nick down at the Tally Ho or the Wagon Wheel Inn or some other Waynesboro dive for an eve-ning of good-natured debauchery (while Mama Rose watches Penny).

In recent years, Philip had started wondering if he was just going through the motions with Bobby and Nick to remind himself that he was alive. Maybe that was why, this past Sunday—when the feces hit the fan in Waynesboro, and he decided to take Penny and shuffle off to a safer place—he rounded up Nick and Bobby for the journey. They felt like a piece of his past, and that helped somehow.

He had never intended to take Brian along, though. Bumping into Brian had been an accident. That first day on the road, about forty miles west of Waynesboro, Philip had taken a quick detour into Deering, to check on his mom and dad. The elderly couple lived in a retirement community near the Fort Gordon military base. When Philip arrived at his folks' little town house, he found that the entire population of Deering had been moved to the base for safe-keeping.

That was the good news. The bad news was that Brian was there. He was holed up in the deserted town house, huddling in the base-ment crawl space, petrified by the growing number of walking dead in the backcountry. Philip had almost forgotten about his brother's current status: Brian had moved back home after his marriage to that crazy Jamaican girl from Gainesville had gone south—*literally*. The girl had pulled up stakes and had gone back to Jamaica. This, coupled with the fact that every single one of Brian's harebrained business schemes had all crashed and burned—most of them financed with their parents' money (like his latest brilliant idea of opening a music store in Athens, when there was already one on every corner)—made Philip cringe at the thought of having to watch over his brother for any length of time. But what was done was done.

"Hey, Philly," Bobby says from across the room, polishing off the last of the cookies, "you think those refugee centers in the city are still up and running?"

"Who the hell knows?" Philip looks at his daughter. "How you doing, punkin?"

The little girl shrugs. "Okay." Her voice is barely audible, like a broken wind chime in the breeze. She stares at the stuffed penguin. "I guess."

"What do you think of this house? You like it?"

Penny shrugs again. "I don't know."

"What would you say if we stayed here a while?"

This gets everyone's attention. Brian looks up at his brother. All eyes are on Philip now. Nick finally speaks up: "Whattya mean 'a while'?"

"Gimme that hooch," Philip says, motioning at Bobby for the bottle. The bottle comes over and Philip takes a long pull, letting it burn nicely. "Look at this place," he says after wiping his mouth.

Brian is confused. "You said just for the night, right?"

Philip takes a deep breath. "Yeah, but I'm sorta getting over that idea right now."

Bobby starts to say, "Yeah, but—"

"Look. I'm just saying. Might be best for us to lay low for a spell."

"Yeah, but Philly, what about—"

"We could just stay put, Bobby, see what happens."

Nick has been listening intently to this. "Philip, come on, man, they've been saying on the news that the big cities are the safest—"

"The news? Jesus Christ, Nick, blow the wax outta your head. The news is going down the tubes with the rest of the population. Look at this place. You think some government halfway house is gonna have *these* kinds of goodies, beds for everyone, enough food for weeks, twenty-year-old Scotch? Showers, hot water, washing machines?"

"We're so close, though," Bobby says after a moment's thought.

Philip sighs. "Yeah, well . . . close is a relative term."

"It's twenty miles, tops."

"Might as well be twenty *thousand* miles, all them wrecks on the interstate, 278 crawling with those things."

"That ain't gonna stop us," Bobby says. His eyes light up. He snaps his fingers. "We'll build a—whattya call it?—on the front end of the Chevy—a scoop—like in fucking *Road Warrior*—"

"Watch your language, Bobby," Philip says, nodding at the little girl.

Nick speaks up. "Dude, we stay here, and it's only a matter of time until those things out at the—" He stops himself, glancing at the child. Everybody knows what he's talking about.

Penny studies her soggy cereal as though she's not listening.

"These places are solid, Nicky," Philip counters, setting down the bottle, crossing his muscular arms across his chest. Philip has been giving a lot of thought to the problem of those wandering hoards out on the golf course. The key would be keeping quiet, masking out the light at night, not sending up any signals, or smells, or undo commotion. "As long as we got power, and we keep our wits about us, we're golden."

"With one gun?" Nick says. "I mean, we can't even use it without drawing their attention."

"We'll check out the other houses, look for weapons. These rich bastards are big on deer huntin', maybe we can even find a silencer for the Ruger . . . hell, we can make one. You see that workshop downstairs?"

"C'mon, Philip. What are we, gunsmiths now? I mean . . . all we got to defend ourselves right now is a few—"

"Philip's right."

Brian's voice startles everybody—the way it comes out on a hoarse, wheezing tone of certainty. He pushes his cereal away and looks up at his brother. "You're right."

Philip is probably the one who is the most taken aback by the conviction in Brian's nasally voice.

Brian stands up, comes around the table, and stands in the doorway leading into the spacious, well-furnished living room. The lights are off in there, and all the shades are drawn. Brian points toward the front wall. "Basically, the front of the house is the problem. The sides and the back are pretty well protected by that tall fence. The dead don't seem to be able to, like, penetrate barriers and stuff . . . and every house on this block has a fenced-in backyard." For a moment, it looks as if Brian's going to cough but he holds it in, puts his hand to his mouth for a moment. His hand is shaking. He goes on: "If we can, like, borrow materials from the other yards, other houses, maybe we can secure a wall across the front of the house, maybe across the neighbors' houses, too."

Bobby and Nick are looking at each other now, nobody reacting, until Philip finally says with a faint smile, "Leave it to the college boy."

It's been a while since the Blake boys have smiled at each other, but now Philip sees that at least his ne'er-do-well brother wants to be useful, wants to do something for the cause, wants to man up. And Brian seems to be absorbing confidence from Philip's approval.

Nick is unconvinced. "For how long, though? I feel like a sitting duck in this place."

"We don't know what's gonna happen," Brian says, his voice raw and yet somehow manic. "We don't know what caused this thing, how long it's gonna last . . . they could, like, figure this thing out, come up with an antidote or something . . . they could drop chemicals from crop dusters, the CDC could contain it . . . you never know. I think Philip's totally right. We should cool our jets here for a while."

"Damn straight," Philip Blake says with a grin, still sitting with his ropy arms crossed. He gives his brother a wink.

Brian returns the wink with a satisfied little nod, wiping a strand of hair as thick as straw from his eyes. He takes a shallow breath into wheezing lungs and then triumphantly walks over to the bottle of Scotch, which sits on the table next to Philip. Grabbing the bottle with a gusto that he hasn't shown in years, Brian lifts it to his lips and takes a massive gulp with the victorious swagger of a Viking celebrating a successful hunt.

Instantly, he flinches, doubles over, and lets out a fusillade of coughs. Half the liquor in his mouth goes spraying across the kitchen, and he coughs and coughs and coughs and wheezes furiously, and for a moment, the others just stare. Little Penny is thunderstruck, gawking with her huge eyes, wiping droplets of liquor from her cheek.

Philip looks at his pathetic excuse for a brother and then looks at his buddies. Across the room, Bobby Marsh struggles to stifle a laugh. Nick tries to repress his own twitching grin. Philip tries to say something but can't help but start laughing, and the laughter is contagious. The others start chortling.

Soon, everybody is laughing hysterically—even Brian—and for the first time since this whole nightmare kicked in, the laughter is genuine: a release of something dark and brittle lurking in all of them.

That night, they try to sleep in shifts. Each one of them gets their own room on the second floor—the remnants of former inhabitants like eerie artifacts in a museum: a bedside table with a half-full glass of water, a John Grisham novel open to a page that will never be finished, a pair of pompoms hanging off a teenage girl's four-poster bed.

For most of the night, Philip sits watch downstairs, out in the living room, with his gun on a coffee table next to him and Penny tucked under blankets on a sectional sofa beside his chair. The child tries unsuccessfully to fall asleep, and around three in the morning, as Philip finds his mind casting back to those tormented thoughts of Sarah's accident, he notices out of the corner of his eye that Penny is tossing and turning restlessly.

Philip leans over to her and strokes her dark hair and whispers, "Can't sleep?"

The little girl has the covers pulled up to her chin, and she looks up at him. She shakes her head. Her ashen face is almost angelic in the orange light of a space heater, which Philip has rigged next to the couch. Outside, in the distant wind, barely audible over the soft drone of the heater, the dissonant chorus of groaning is relentless, like an infernal series of waves lapping a shore.

"Daddy's here, punkin, don't worry," Philip says softly, touching her cheek. "I'll always be here."

She nods.

Philip gives her a tender smile. He leans down and plants a kiss on her left eyebrow. "Ain't gonna let nothin' happen to you."

She nods again. She has the little penguin lodged snugly in the crook of her neck. She looks at the stuffed animal and frowns. She moves the penguin to her ear, and she acts as though she's listening to the animal whisper a secret. She looks up at her father. "Daddy?"

"Yeah, punkin?"

"Penguin wants to know somethin'."

"What's that?"

"Penguin wants to know if them people are sick."

Philip takes a deep breath. "You tell Penguin . . . yeah, they're sick all right. They're more than sick. That's why we've been . . . puttin' them outta their misery."

"Daddy?"

"Yeah?"

"Penguin wants to know if we're gonna get sick, too."

Philip strokes the girl's cheek. "No, ma'am. You tell Penguin we're gonna stay healthy as mules."

This seems to satisfy the girl enough for her to look away and stare into the void some more.

By four o'clock that morning, another sleepless soul in another part of the house is asking imponderable questions of his own. Lying in a tangle of blankets, his skinny form clad only in T-shirt and briefs, his fever breaking in a film of sweat, Brian Blake stares at the stucco plaster of a dead teenage girl's ceiling and wonders if this is how the world ends. Was it Rudyard Kipling who said it ends "not with a bang but a whimper." No, wait a minute . . . it was *Eliot*. T. S. Eliot. Brian remembers studying the poem—was it 'The Hollow Men'?—in his twentieth century comparative literature class at the U of G. A lot of good *that* degree had done him.

He lies there and broods about his failures—as he does every night—but tonight the ruminations are intercut with carnage, like frames of a snuff film inserted into his stream of consciousness.

The old demons stir, mingling with the fresh fears, wearing a groove into his thoughts: Was there something he could have done or said to keep his ex-wife, Jocelyn, from drifting away, from lawyering up like she did, from saying all those hurtful things before she went back to Montego Bay? And can you kill the monsters with a simple blow to the skull or do you have to destroy the brain tissue? Was there something Brian could have done or begged for or borrowed to keep his music shop open in Athens—the only one of its kind in the South, his brilliant fucking idea of a store that catered to hip-hop artists with refurbished turntables and used bass cabinets and gaudy microphones festooned with Snoop Dogg bling? How fast are the unlucky victims out there multiplying? Is it like an airborne plague, or is it passed in the water like Ebola?

The circular ruminations of his mind keep going back to more immediate matters: the nagging feeling that the seventh member of the family that once lived here is still somewhere in the house.

Now that Brian has closed the deal among his compatriots that they should indeed stay here indefinitely, he can't stop worrying about it. He hears every creak, every faint ticking of the foundation settling, every hushed whirr of the furnace coming on. For some reason that he cannot explain, he is absolutely certain that the blond-haired kid is still here, in the house, waiting, biding his time for . . . what? Maybe the kid is the only one in the family who didn't turn. Maybe he's terrified and hiding.

Before turning in that night, Brian had insisted they check the nooks and crannies of the house one last time. Philip had accompanied him with a pickaxe and a flashlight, and they had checked every corner of the basement, every cabinet, every closet and storage locker. They looked inside the meat freezer in the cellar, and even checked the washer and dryer for unlikely stowaways. Nick and Bobby looked up in the attic, behind trunks, in boxes, in wardrobes. Philip looked under all the beds and behind all the dressers. Coming up empty, they still made some interesting discoveries along the way.

They found a dog's food bowl in the basement, but no sign of the animal. They also found an array of very useful power tools in the workshop: jigsaws, drills, routers, and even a nail gun. The nail gun would be especially handy for building barricades since it is somewhat quieter than a pounding hammer.

In fact, Brian is thinking about other uses for that nail gun when, all at once, he hears a noise that instantly frosts his scantily clothed body in goose bumps.

The sound is coming from above him, on the other side of the ceiling.

It's coming from the attic.

THREE

Upon hearing the noise—almost subconsciously identifying it as something other than the house settling, or the wind in the dormers, or the furnace rattling—Brian sits up on the edge of the bed.

He cocks his head and listens more carefully. It sounds like somebody scratching at something, or the faint sound of fabric tearing in fits and jerks. At first, Brian feels compelled to go get his brother. Philip would be the best one to deal with this. It could be the kid, for God's sake . . . or something worse.

But then, almost as an afterthought, Brian stops himself. Is he going to puss out again . . . as usual? Is he going to run, like always, to his brother—his *younger* brother, for God's sake—the same individual whose hand Brian had once held at the crosswalk every morning when the two of them were grade school kids at Burke County Elementary? No, goddamnit. Not this time. This time, Brian is going to grow a pair.

He takes a deep breath, turns, and searches for the flashlight he had left on the bedside table. He finds it and switches it on.

The narrow beam shoots across the dark bedroom, spreading a silver pool of light on the opposite wall. *Just you and me, Justin,* Brian thinks as he rises to his feet. His head is clear. His senses are crackling.

The truth is, Brian had felt incredibly good earlier that night when he had concurred with his brother's plans, when he had seen the look in Philip's eyes, like maybe Brian is not a hopeless loser after all. Now it's time to show Philip that the moment in the kitchen was not a fluke. Brian can get the job done just as well as Philip.

He moves quietly toward the door.

Before leaving the room, he grabs the metal baseball bat that he found in one of the boys' bedrooms.

The papery rustling noises can be heard more clearly in the hallway, as Brian pauses under the attic hatchway, which is a glorified trapdoor embedded in the ceiling above the second-floor landing. The other bedrooms along the hallway—filled with the deep snores of Bobby Marsh and Nick Parsons—are situated on the other side of the landing, on the east side of the house, out of earshot. That's why Brian is the only one hearing this right now.

A leather strap hangs down, low enough for Brian to jump up and grasp. He pulls the spring-levered hatch open, and the accordion-like stairs unfold with a pinging noise. Brian shines the flashlight up into the dark passage. Dust motes drift in the beam. The darkness is impenetrable, opaque. Brian's heart chugs.

You fucking pussy, he thinks to himself. *Get your pussy ass up there.*

He climbs the steps with the baseball bat under one arm, the flashlight in his free hand, and he pauses when he reaches the top of the ladder. He shines the light on a huge steamer trunk with Magnolia Springs State Park stickers on it.

Now Brian smells the cold putrid odors of must and mothballs. The autumn chill has already seeped into the attic through the seams of the roof. The air is cool on his face. And after a moment, he hears the rustling again.

It's coming from a deeper place in the shadows of the attic. Brian's throat is as dry as bone meal as he climbs to his feet on the threshold. The ceiling is low enough to force him to hunch. Shivering in his underwear, Brian wants to cough but doesn't dare.

The scratching noises stop, and then start again, vigorous and angry sounding.

Brian raises the bat. He gets very still. He's learning the mechanics of fear all over again: When you're really, really scared, you don't shake like in the movies. You grow still, like an animal bristling.

It's only afterward you start shaking.

The beam of the flashlight slowly scans across the dark niches of the attic, the detritus of the well-to-do: an exercise bike laced with cobwebs, a rowing machine, more trunks, barbells, tricycles, wardrobe boxes, water skis, a pinball machine furry with dust. The scratching noises cease again.

The light reveals a coffin.

Brian practically turns to stone.

A *coffin?*

Philip is already halfway up the staircase when he notices, up on the second-floor landing, the attic stepladder hanging down, unfolded.

He pads up to the landing in his stocking feet. He carries an axe in one hand and a flashlight in the other. The .22 pistol is shoved down the back of his jeans. He is shirtless, his ropy musculature shimmering in moonbeams filtering down through a skylight.

It takes him mere seconds to cross the landing and scale the accordion steps, and when he emerges into the darkness of the attic, he sees the silhouette of a figure across the narrow space.

Before Philip even has a chance to shine his flashlight on his brother, the situation becomes clear.

"It's a tanning bed," the voice says, making Brian jump. For the past few seconds, Brian Blake has been paralyzed with terror, standing ten feet away from the dusty, oblong enclosure shoved up against one wall of the attic. The top of the thing is latched shut like a giant clamshell, and something scratches to get out of it.

Brian jerks around and finds in the beam of his flashlight his brother's gaunt, sullen face. Philip stands on the threshold of the attic with the axe in his right hand. "Move away from it, Brian."

"You think it's—"

"The missing kid?" Philip whispers, cautiously moving toward the object. "Let's find out."

The scratching noise, as if stimulated by the sound of voices, surges and rises.

Brian turns toward the tanning bed, braces himself, and raises the baseball bat. "He might have been hiding up here when he turned."

Philip approaches with the axe. "Get outta the way, sport."

"I'll take care of it," Brian says bitterly, moving toward the latch, his baseball bat poised.

Philip gently steps in between his brother and the tanning bed. "You don't have to prove nothing to me, man. Just move outta the way."

"No, goddamnit, I got this," Brian hisses, reaching for the dusty latch.

Philip studies his brother. "Okay, whatever. Go for it, but do it quick. Whatever it is—don't think about it too much."

"I know," Brian says, grasping the latch with his free hand.

Philip stands inches behind his brother.

Brian unlatches the enclosure.

The scuttling noises cease.

Philip raises the axe as Brian throws open the lid.

Two quick movements—a pair of blurs in the darkness—shoot across Philip's sight line: a rustling of fur and the arc of Brian's bat.

It takes a second or two for the animal to register in Philip's heightened senses—the mouse darting out of the glare of the flashlight and scurrying across the fiberglass trough toward a hole gnawed in one corner.

The baseball bat comes down hard, missing the fat, oily-gray rodent by a mile.

Pieces of the bed's switch panel and old toys shatter at the impact. Brian lets out a gasp and recoils at the sight of the mouse vanishing down the hole, slithering back into the inner workings of the bed's base.

Philip lets out a sigh of relief and lowers the axe. He starts to say something when he hears a little metallic tune playing in the shadows next to him. Brian looks down, breathing hard.

A little jack-in-the-box, thrown by the impact of the bat, lies on the floor.

Triggered by the fall, the tinny music plays a few more notes of a circus lullaby.

Then the toy clown pops out—sideways—from the fallen metal container.

"Boo," Philip says wearily, with very little humor in his voice.

Their moods improve slightly the next morning after a huge breakfast of scrambled eggs and slab bacon and grits and ham and griddlecakes and fresh peaches and sweet tea. The fragrant mélange fills with entire house with the welcoming odors of coffee and cinnamon and smoked meats sizzling. Nick even makes his special redeye gravy for the group, which sends Bobby into ecstasy.

Brian finds cold remedies in the master bedroom medicine cabinet and starts feeling a little better after he downs a few DayQuil capsules.

After breakfast, they explore the immediate vicinity—the single square block known as Green Briar Lane—and they get more good news. They find a treasure trove of supplies and building materials: woodpiles for fireplaces, extra planking under decks, more food in the neighbors' refrigerators, cans of gas in the garages, winter coats and boots, boxes of nails, liquor, blowtorches, bottled water, a short-wave radio, a laptop, a generator, stacks of DVDs, and a gun rack in one of the basements with several hunting rifles and boxes of shells.

No silencer; but beggars can't be choosers.

They also get lucky in the undead department. The houses on either side of the Colonial are empty; their residents evidently got the hell out of Dodge before the shit had gone too far down. Two houses away from the Colonial, on the west side, Philip and Nick encounter an elderly couple who have turned, but the oldsters are easily, quickly, and most importantly, *quietly* dispatched with some well-placed hatchet blows.

That afternoon, Philip and company cautiously begin work on

the barricade across the front parkway of the Colonial and its two neighbors—a total span of a hundred and fifty feet for the three lots, and sixty down either side—which sounds to Nick and Bobby like a daunting amount of territory to cover, but with the ten-foot-long prefab sections they find under a neighbor's deck, combined with fencing cannibalized off the place across the street, the work goes surprisingly fast.

By dusk that evening, Philip and Nick are connecting the last sections on the northern edge of the property line.

"I've been keeping an eye on 'em all day," Philip is saying, pressing the forked tip of the nail gun against the bracing of a corner section. He's referring to the swarms out near the golf club. Nick nods as he butts the two support beams against each other.

Philip pulls the trigger, and the nail gun makes a muffled snapping noise—like the crack of a metal whip—sending a six-inch galvanized nail into the boards. The nail gun is baffled with a small piece of packing blanket, secured with duct tape, to dampen the noise.

"I ain't seen a single one of them wander closer," Philip says, wiping the sweat from his brow, moving to the next section of support beams. Nick holds the boards steady, and the tip presses down.

FFFFFUMP!

"I don't know," Nick says skeptically, moving to the next section, the sweat making his satin roadie jacket cling to his back. "I still say it's not *if* . . . but *when*."

FFFFFFFUMP!

"You worry too much, son," Philip says, moving to the next section of planking, tugging on the gun's cord. The extension cable snakes off toward an outlet on the corner of the neighbor's house. Philip had to connect a grand total of six twenty-eight-foot cords to get the thing to reach. He pauses and glances over his shoulder.

About fifty yards away, in the backyard of the Colonial, Brian pushes Penny in a swing. It's taken a little getting used to for Philip, putting his hapless brother in charge of his precious little girl, but right now Brian is the best nanny he's got.

The play set—of course—is deluxe. Rich folks love to spoil their kids with shit like this. This one—more than likely a haunt of the missing kid—has got all the bells and whistles: slide, clubhouse, four swings, climbing wall, jungle gym, and sandbox.

"We got it made here," Philip goes on, turning back to his work. "Long as we keep our heads screwed on straight, we're gonna be fine."

As they position the next section, the rustling sounds of their movements and the creak of the planks mask the telltale noise of shuffling footsteps.

The footsteps are coming from across the street. Philip doesn't hear them until the errant zombie is close enough for its odor to register.

Nick is the first one to smell it: that black, oily, mildewy combination of rotting protein and decay—like human waste cooking in bacon grease. It immediately puts Nick's guard up. "Wait a minute," he says, holding a section of planking. "You smell—"

"Yeah, smells like—"

A fish-belly arm bursts through a gap in the fencing, grabbing a hank of Philip's denim shirt.

The assailant was once a middle-aged woman in a designer running suit, now an emaciated wraith with torn sleeves, blackened, exposed teeth, and the button eyes of a prehistoric fish, her hooked hand clutching Philip's shirttail with the vise grip of frozen dead fingers. She lets out a low groan like a broken pipe organ as Philip spins toward his axe, which lies canted against a wheelbarrow twenty feet away.

Too damn far.

The dead lady goes for Philip's neck with the autonomic hunger of a giant snapping turtle, and across the yard, Nick fumbles for a weapon, but it's all happening too fast. Philip rears backward with a grunt, just now realizing that he still holds the nail gun. He dodges the snapping teeth, and then instinctively raises the muzzle of the nail gun.

In one quick movement, he touches the tip to the thing's brow.

FFFFFFFFFFFUMP!

The lady zombie stiffens.

Icy fingers release their grip on Philip.

He pulls himself free, huffing and puffing, gaping at the thing.

The vertical cadaver teeters for a moment, wobbling as if drunk, shuddering in its soiled velveteen Pierre Cardin warm-up, but it will not go down. The head of the six-inch galvanized nail is visible above the ridge of the lady's nose like a tiny coin stuck there.

The thing remains upright for endless moments, its sharklike eyes turned upward, until it begins to slowly stagger backward across the parkway, its ruined face taking on a strange, almost dreamy expression.

For a moment, it looks as though the thing is remembering something, or hearing some high-pitched whistle. Then it collapses in the grass.

"I think the nail does just enough damage to take 'em out," Philip is saying after dinner, pacing back and forth across the shuttered windows of the lavish dining room, the nail gun in his hand like a visual aid.

The others are sitting at the long burnished oak table, the remnants of dinner lying strewn in front of them. Brian cooked for the group that night, defrosting a roast in the microwave and making gravy with a vintage cabernet and a splash of cream. Penny is in the adjacent family room watching a DVD of *Dora the Explorer*.

"Yeah, but did you see the way that thing went down?" Nick points out, pushing an uneaten gob of meat across his plate. "After you zapped it . . . looked like the damn thing was stoned for a second."

Philip keeps pacing, clicking the trigger of the nail gun and thinking. "Yeah but it *did* go down."

"It's quieter than a gun, I'll give you that."

"And it's a hell of a lot easier than splitting their skulls open with an axe."

Bobby has just started in on his second helping of pot roast and gravy. "Too bad you don't have a six-mile extension cord," he says with his mouth full.

Philip clicks the trigger a few more times. "Maybe we could hook this puppy up to a battery."

Nick looks up. "Like a car battery?"

"No, like something you could carry more easily, something like one of them big lantern batteries or something outta one of them electric mowers."

Nick shrugs.

Bobby eats.

Philip paces and thinks.

Brian stares at the wall, mumbling, "Something to do with their brains."

"Say what?" Philip looks at his brother. "What was that, Bri?"

Brian looks at him. "Those things . . . the sickness. It's basically in the brain, right? It's gotta be." He pauses. He looks at his plate. "I still say we don't even know they're dead."

Nick looks at Brian. "You mean after we take 'em out? After we . . . destroy 'em?"

"No, I mean *before*," Brian says. "I mean, like, the condition they're in."

Philip stops pacing. "Shit, man . . . on Monday, I saw one of 'em get squashed by an eighteen-wheeler and ten minutes later, it's dragging itself along the street with its guts hanging out. They've been saying it on all the news reports. They're dead, sport. They're *way* dead."

"I'm just saying, the central nervous system, man, it's complicated. All the shit in the environment right now, new strains of shit."

"Hey, you want to take one of them things to a doctor for a checkup, be my guest."

Brian sighs. "All I'm saying is, we don't *know* enough yet. We don't know shit."

"We know all we need to know," Philip says, giving his brother a look. "We know there's more of them fucking things every day, and all they seem to want to do is have us for lunch. Which is why we're gonna hang here for a while, let things play out a little."

Brian breathes out a painful, weary sigh. The others are silent.

In the lull, they can hear the faint noises that they've been hearing all night, coming from the darkness outside: the muffled, intermittent thudding of insensate figures bumping up against the makeshift barricade.

Despite Philip's efforts to erect the rampart quickly and quietly, the commotion of the day's construction project has drawn more of the walking corpses.

"How long do you think we're gonna be able to stay here?" Brian asks softly.

Philip sits down, lays the nail gun on the table and takes another sip of his bourbon. He nods toward the family room, where the whimsical voices of children's programming drift incongruously. "She needs a break," Philip says. "She's exhausted."

"She loves that play set out back," Brian says with a weak smile.

Philip nods. "She can live a normal life here for a while."

Everybody looks at him. Everybody silently chews on the concept.

"Here's to all the rich motherfuckers of the world," Philip says, raising his glass.

The others toast without really knowing just exactly what they're toasting . . . or how long it will last.

FOUR

The next day, in the clean autumn sun, Penny plays in the backyard under the watchful gaze of Brian. She plays throughout the morning while the others take inventory and sort through their supplies. In the afternoon, Philip and Nick secure the window wells in the basement with extra planking, and try unsuccessfully to rig the nail gun to DC power, while Bobby, Brian, and Penny play cards in the family room.

The proximity of the undead is a constant factor, swimming shark-like under the surface of every decision, every activity. But for the moment, there's just an occasional stray, an errant wanderer bumping up against the privacy fence, then shambling away. For the most part, the activity behind the seven-foot cedar bulwark on Green Briar Lane has, so far, gone unnoticed by the swarm.

That night, after dinner, with the shades drawn, they all watch a Jim Carrey movie in the family room, and they almost feel normal again. They're all starting to get used to this place. The occasional muffled thump out in the darkness barely registers now. Brian has practically forgotten the missing twelve-year-old, and after Penny goes to bed, the men make long-term plans.

They discuss the implications of staying in the Colonial as long as supplies hold out. They've got enough provisions for weeks. Nick wonders if they should send out a scout, maybe gauge the situation on the roads into Atlanta, but Philip is adamant about staying put.

"Let whoever's out there duke it out among themselves," Philip advises.

Nick is still keeping tabs on the radio, TV, and Internet . . . and like the failing bodily functions of a terminal patient, the media seem to be sparking out one organ at a time. By this point, most radio stations are playing either recorded programming or useless emergency information. TV networks—the ones on basic cable that are still up and running—are now resorting to either twenty-four-hour automated civil defense announcements or inexplicable, incongruous reruns of banal late-night infomercials.

By the third day, Nick realizes that most of the radio dial is static, most of basic cable is snow, and the Wi-Fi in the house is gone. No dial-up connections are working, and the regular phone calls Nick has been making to emergency numbers—which, up to this point, have all played back recordings—are now sending back the classic "fuck you" from the phone company: *The number you have dialed is not available at this time, please try again later.*

By late morning that day, the sky clouds over.

In the afternoon, a dismal, chill mist falls on the community, and everybody huddles indoors, trying to ignore the fact that there's a fine line between being safe and being a prisoner. Other than Nick, most of them are tired of talking about Atlanta. Atlanta seems *farther away* now—as if the more they ponder the twenty-some miles between Wiltshire and the city, the more impassable they seem.

That night, after everybody drifts off to sleep, Philip sits his lonely vigil in the living room next to a slumbering Penny.

The mist has deteriorated into full-blown thunder and lightning.

Philip pokes a finger between two shutter slats, and he peers out into the darkness. Through the gap, he can see—over the top of the barricade—the winding side streets and massive shadows of live oaks, their branches bending in the wind.

Lightning flickers.

Two hundred yards away, a dozen or so humanoid shapes materialize in the strobe light, moving aimlessly through the rain.

It's hard to tell for sure from Philip's vantage point, but it looks as though the things might be moving—in their leaden, retarded fashion, like stroke victims—*this way*. Do they smell fresh meat? Did the noises of human activity draw them out? Or are they simply lumbering around randomly like ghastly goldfish in a bowl?

Right then, for the first time since they arrived at Wiltshire Estates, Philip Blake begins to wonder if their days in this womb of wall-to-wall carpet and overstuffed sofas are numbered.

The fourth day dawns cold and overcast. The pewter-colored sky hangs low over the wet lawns and abandoned homes. Although the occasion goes unspoken, the new day marks a milestone of sorts: the beginning of the plague's second week.

Now Philip stands with his coffee in the living room, peering out through the shutters at the jury-rigged barricade. In the pale morning light, he can see the northeast corner of the fence shuddering and trembling. "Son of a *buck*," he mutters under his breath.

"What's the matter?" Brian's voice snaps Philip out of his stupor.

"There's more of 'em."

"Shit. How many?"

"Can't tell."

"What do you want to do?"

"Bobby!"

The big man trundles into the living room in his sweatpants and bare feet, eating a banana. Philip turns to his portly pal and says, "Get dressed."

Bobby swallows a mouthful of banana. "What's going on?"

Philip ignores the question, looks at Brian. "Keep Penny in the family room."

"Will do," Brian says, and hurries off.

Philip starts toward the stairs, calling out as he goes: "Get the nail gun and as many extension cords as you can carry . . . hatchets, too!"

FFFFFFFOOOMP! Number five goes down like a giant rag doll in tattered suit pants, the dead, milky eyes rolling back in its head as it slides down the other side of the fence, its putrid body collapsing to the parkway. Philip steps back, breathing hard from the exertion, damp with sweat in his denim jacket and jeans.

Numbers one through four had been as easy as shooting fish in a barrel—one female and three males—all of whom Philip had sneaked up on with the nail gun as they bumped and clawed against the weak spot at the fence's corner. At that point, all Philip had to do was stand on the bottom strut with a good angle on the tops of their heads. He put them down quickly, one after another: *FFFFOOOMP! FFFFOOOMP! FFFFOOOMP! FFFFOOOMP!*

Number five had been slippery. Inadvertently jerking out of the line of fire at the last moment, it did a little intoxicated shuffle, then craned its neck upward at Philip, jaws snapping. Philip had to waste two nails—both of which ricocheted off the sidewalk—before he finally sent one home into the suit-wearing asshole's cerebral cortex.

Now Philip catches his breath, doubled over with exhaustion, the nail gun still in his right hand, still plugged into the house with four twenty-five-foot cords. He straightens up and listens. The front parkway is silent now. The fence is still.

Glancing over his shoulder, Philip sees Bobby Marsh in the backyard, about a hundred feet away. The big man is sitting on his fat ass, trying to catch his breath, leaning against a small abandoned doghouse. The doghouse has a little shingle roof and the word LAD-DIE BOY mounted above the opening at one end.

These rich people and their fucking dogs, Philip thinks ruefully, still a little manic and wired. *Probably fed that thing better than most kids.*

Over the back fence, about twenty feet away from Bobby, the limp remains of a dead woman are draped over the crest, a hatchet still buried in her skull where Bobby Marsh put out her lights.

Philip gives Bobby a wave and a hard, questioning look: *Everything cool?*

Bobby returns the gesture with a thumbs-up.

Then . . . almost without warning . . . things begin happening very quickly.

The first indication that something is decidedly *not* cool occurs within a split second of Bobby signaling the thumbs-up sign to his friend and leader and mentor. Drenched in sweat, his heart still pumping with the burden of his huge girth as he sits leaning against the doghouse, Bobby manages to accompany the thumbs-up signal with a smile . . . completely oblivious to the muffled noise coming from inside the doghouse.

For years now, Bobby Marsh has secretly yearned to please Philip Blake, and the prospects of giving Philip the thumbs-up after a messy job well done fills Bobby with a weird kind of satisfaction.

An only child, barely able to make it out of high school, Bobby clung to Philip in the years before Sarah Blake had died, and after that—after Philip had drifted away from his drinking buddies—Bobby had desperately tried to reconnect. Bobby called Philip too many times; Bobby talked too much when they were together; and Bobby often made a fool of himself trying to keep up with the wiry, alpha dog of a ringleader. But now, in a strange way, Bobby feels as though this bizarre epidemic has—among other things—given Bobby a way to bond again with Philip.

All of which is probably why, at first, Bobby doesn't hear the noise inside the doghouse.

When the thump comes—as if a giant heart were beating inside the little miniature shack—Bobby's smile freezes on his face, and his upturned thumb falls to his side. And by the time the realization that there's something inside the doghouse—something moving—manages to travel the synapses of Bobby's brain and register plainly enough for him to move, it's already too late.

Something small and low to the ground bursts out of the doghouse's arched opening.

Philip is already halfway across the yard, running at a full sprint, when it becomes clear that the thing that has just thrust its way out of the doghouse is a tiny human being—or at least a rotting, bluish, contorted *facsimile* of a tiny human being—with leaves and dog shit in its filthy, matted blond bangs, and chains tangled around its waist and legs.

"F-FUH-FFUHHHHK!" Bobby yelps and jerks back away from the twelve-year-old corpse as the thing that was once a boy now pounces on Bobby's ham-hock-sized leg.

Bobby tumbles sideways, ripping his leg free in the nick of time, just as the little contorted face—like a sunken gourd with hollow cavities for eyes—gobbles the grass where Bobby's leg had been one millisecond earlier.

Philip is now fifty feet away, charging toward the doghouse at top speed, raising the nail gun like a divining rod aimed at the miniature monster. Bobby crawls crablike through the damp grass, his ass crack showing pathetically, his gasps high and shrill like those of a little girl.

The pint-sized fiend moves with the graceless energy of a tarantula, scuttling across the grass toward Bobby. The fat man tries to struggle to his feet and run, but his legs get tangled and he tumbles again, backward this time.

Philip is twenty feet away when Bobby starts shrieking in a higher register. The zombie child has hooked a clawlike hand around Bobby's ankle, and before Bobby can wrest his leg away from the thing, it sinks a mouthful of putrefying teeth into Bobby's leg.

"GODDAMNIT!" Philip booms as he approaches with the nail gun.

A hundred feet behind him, the extension cord pulls free of the outlet.

Philip slams the tip of the nail gun down on the back of the thing's skull as the monster latches on to Bobby's quivering, fat body.

The nail gun trigger clicks. Nothing happens. The zombie burrows down into Bobby's flaccid thigh, piranhalike, breaching his femoral artery and taking half his scrotum with it. Bobby's scream deteriorates into a ululating howl as Philip instinctively tosses the gun aside, then lurches at the beast. He tears the thing off his friend as though removing a giant leech and heaves it—head over heels—across the lawn before it has a chance to take another bite.

The dead child flops and rolls twenty feet across the muddy grass.

Nick and Brian burst out of the house, Brian grabbing for the extension cord, Nick roaring across the lawn with a pickaxe. Philip grabs Bobby and tries to stop him from squirming and screaming, because the extra exertion is making the big man hemorrhage faster, the ragged wound already sending up geysers of blood in rhythm with Bobby's quickening pulse. Philip slams his hand down on Bobby's leg, stanching the flow slightly, the blood oozing between Philip's greasy fingers, as other figures move across Philip's peripheral vision. The dead thing is crawling back across the moist ground toward Philip and Bobby, and Nick does not hesitate, approaching at a sprint, raising the axe, eyes wide with panic and rage. The axe sings through the air, the rusty point coming down on the back of the zombie-child's skull, sinking three inches into the cranial cavity. The monster deflates. Philip screams up at Nick something about a *belt*, a *BELT*, and now Nick is hovering, fumbling for his belt. Philip has no formal training in first aid but he knows enough to try and stop the bleeding with some kind of tourniquet. He wraps Nick's belt around the shivering fat man's leg, and Bobby is trying to talk again but he looks like a man experiencing extreme cold, his lips moving, quivering silently. Meantime—as all this is going on—Brian is a hundred feet away, plugging the extension cord back in the outlet, probably because it's all he can think of doing. The nail gun lies in the grass fifteen feet behind Philip. At this point, Philip is shouting at Nick to *GO GET SOME FUCKING BANDAGES AND ALCOHOL AND WHATEVER!!!* Nick hurries off, still carrying the pickaxe, while Brian approaches, staring at the dead thing lying facedown in the grass, its skull stoved in. Brian gives it a wide berth. He picks up the nail gun—just in case—and he scans the hill behind the back fence as Philip now holds Bobby in his arms like a giant baby. Bobby is crying, breathing quick, shallow, rattling breaths. Philip comforts his friend, murmuring encouragement and assuring him that it's all going to be okay . . . but it's clear, as Brian cautiously approaches, that things are definitely not going to be okay.

Moments later, Nick returns with an armful of large sterile cotton bandages from inside, as well as a plastic bottle of alcohol in one back pocket and a roll of cotton tape in the other. But something has changed. The emergency has transformed into something darker—a deathwatch.

"We gotta get him inside," Philip announces, now soaked in his friend's blood. But Philip makes no effort to lift the fat man. Bobby Marsh is going to die. That much is clear to all of them.

It's especially clear to Bobby Marsh, who now lies in a state of shock, staring up at the gunmetal sky, struggling to speak.

Brian stands nearby, holding the nail gun at his side, staring down at Bobby. Nick drops the bandages. He lets out an anguished breath. He looks as though he might start to cry, but instead he simply drops to his knees on the other side of Bobby and hangs his head.

"I—I—n-n-nn—" Bobby Marsh tries desperately to get Philip to understand something.

"Sssshhhhh . . ." Philip strokes the man's shoulder. Philip cannot think straight. He turns, grabs a roll of bandages, and starts dressing the wound.

"Nnn-n-NO!" Bobby pushes the bandage away.

"Bobby, goddamnit."

"NN-NO!"

Philip stops, swallows hard, looks into the watery eyes of the dying man. "It's gonna be okay," Philip says, his voice changing.

"N-no—it ain't," Bobby manages. Somewhere way up in the sky, a crow yammers. Bobby knows what's going to happen. They saw a man in a ditch back in Covington come back in less than ten minutes. "S-ss-stop saying that, Philly."

"Bobby—"

"It's over," Bobby manages in a feeble whisper, and his eyes roll back for a moment. Then he sees the nail gun in Brian's hand. With his big bloody sausage fingers, Bobby reaches for the muzzle.

Brian drops the gun with a start.

"Goddamnit, we gotta get him inside!" Philip's voice is laced with hopelessness as Bobby Marsh blindly reaches for the nail gun. He gets his fat hand around the pointed barrel and tries to lift it to his temple.

"Jesus Christ," Nick utters.

"Get that thing away from him!" Philip waves Brian away from the victim.

Bobby's tears track down the sides of his huge head, cleansing the blood in streaks. "P-please, Philly," Bobby murmurs. "J-just . . . *do* it."

Philip stands up. "Nick!—C'mere!" Philip turns and walks a few paces toward the house.

Nick rises to his feet and joins Philip. The two men stand fifteen feet away from Bobby, out of earshot, their backs turned, their voices low and strained.

"We gotta cut him," Philip says quickly.

"We gotta what?"

"Amputate his leg."

"What!"

"Before the sickness spreads."

"But how do you—"

"We don't know how fast it spreads, we gotta try, we owe the man at least *that*."

"But—"

"I'm gonna need ya to go get the hacksaw from the shed and also bring—"

A voice rings out behind them, interrupting Philip's tense litany: "Guys?"

It's Brian, and from the grim sound of his nasally call, the news is most likely bad.

Philip and Nick turn.

Bobby Marsh is stone-still.

Brian's eyes well up as he kneels next to the fat man. "It's too late."

Philip and Nick come over to where Bobby lies in the grass, his eyes closed. His big, flabby chest does not move. His mouth is slack.

"Oh no . . . Sweet Jesus Christ no," Nick says, staring at his dead pal.

Philip doesn't say anything for quite a long time. No one does.

The immense corpse lies still, there on the wet ground, for endless minutes . . . until something stirs in the man's extremities, in the tendons of his massive legs, and in the tips of his plump fingers.

At first, the phenomenon looks like the typical residual nerve twitches that morticians might see now and again, the dieseling engine of a cadaver's central nervous system. But as Nick and Brian gape, their eyes widening—both of them slowly rising, then slowly beginning to back away—Philip comes closer still, kneeling down, a sullen businesslike expression on his face.

Bobby Marsh's eyes open.

The pupils have turned as white as pus.

Philip grabs the nail gun and presses it to the big man's forehead just above the left eyebrow.

FFFFFFFFUMP!

Hours later. Inside the house. After dark. Penny asleep. Nick in the kitchen, drowning his grief in whiskey . . . Brian nowhere to be found . . . Bobby's cooling corpse in the backyard, covered in a tarp next to the other bodies . . . and Philip now standing at the living room window, gazing out through the slatted shutters at the growing number of dark figures on the street. They shuffle like sleepwalkers, moving back and forth behind the barricade. There are more of them now. Thirty, maybe. Forty even.

Streetlights shine through the cracks in the fence, the moving shadows breaking the beams at irregular intervals, making the light strobe, making Philip crazy. He hears the silent voice in his head— the same voice that first made itself known after Sarah had died: *Burn the place down, burn the whole fucking world down.*

For a moment earlier that day, after Bobby had died, the voice had wanted to mutilate the twelve-year-old's body. The voice had wanted to take that dead thing apart. But Philip tamped it down, and now he's fighting it again: *The fuse is lit, brother, the clock is ticking . . .*

Philip looks away from the window, and he rubs his tired eyes.

"It's okay to let it out," a different voice says now, coming from across the darkness.

Philip whirls and sees the silhouette of his brother across the living room, standing in the archway of the kitchen.

Turning back to the window, Philip offers no response. Brian comes over. He's holding a bottle of cough syrup in his trembling hands. In the darkness his feverish eyes shimmer with tears. He stands there for a moment.

Then he says in low, soft voice, careful not to awaken Penny on the couch next to them, "There's no shame in letting it out."

"Letting *what* out?"

"Look," Brian says, "I know you're hurting." He sniffs, wipes his mouth on his sleeve, his voice hoarse and congested. "All I wanted to say is, I'm really sorry about Bobby, I know you guys were—"

"It's done."

"Philip, c'mon—"

"This *place* is done, it's cooked."

Brian looks at him. "What do you mean?"

"We're getting out of here."

"But I thought—"

"Take a look." Philip indicates the growing number of shadows out on Green Briar Lane. "We're drawing 'em like flies on shit."

"Yeah, but the barricade is still—"

"The longer we stay here, Brian, the more it's gonna get like a prison." Philip stares out the window. "Gotta keep moving forward."

"When?"

"Soon."

"Like tomorrow?"

"We'll start packin' in the morning, get as many supplies in the Suburban as we can."

Silence.

Brian looks at his brother. "You okay?"

"Yeah." Philip keeps staring. "Go to sleep."

At breakfast, Philip decides to tell his daughter that Bobby had to up and go home—"to go take care of his folks"—and the explanation seems to satisfy the little girl.

Later that morning, Nick and Philip dig the grave out back, choosing a soft spot at the end of the garden, while Brian keeps

Penny occupied in the house. Brian thinks they should tell Penny some version of what happened, but Philip tells Brian to stay the hell out of it and keep his mouth shut.

Now, in front of the rose trellis in the backyard, Philip and Nick lift the massive tarp-wrapped body and lower it into the hollowed-out earth.

It takes them quite a while to get the hole filled back up, each man tossing spade after spade of rich, black Georgia topsoil on their friend. While they work, the atonal moaning of the undead drifts on the wind.

It's another blustery, overcast day, and the sounds of the zombie horde carry up across the sky and over the tops of houses. It drives Philip nuts as he sweats in his denims, heaving dirt on the grave. The oily, black, rotten-meat odor is as strong as ever. It makes Philip's stomach clench as he puts the last few shovelfuls of earth on the grave.

Now Philip and Nick pause on opposite sides of the huge mound, leaning on their shovels, the sweat cooling on their necks. Neither says a word for a long moment, each man lost in his thoughts. Finally, Nick looks up, and very softly, very wearily, and with great deference, says, "You want to say something?"

Philip looks across the grave at his buddy. The moaning noises are coming from all directions like the roar of locusts, so loud Philip can barely think straight.

Right then, for some strange reason, Philip Blake remembers the night that the three friends got drunk and sneaked into the Starliter Drive-In Theater out on Waverly Road and broke into the projection booth. Waving his fat little fingers in front of the projector, Bobby had made shadow puppets appear on the distant screen. Philip had laughed so hard that night he thought he was going to puke, watching the silhouettes of rabbits and ducks cavorting across the flickering images of Chuck Norris spin-kicking Nazis.

"Some folks thought Bobby Marsh was a simpleton," Philip says with his head lowered, his gaze down-turned, "but they didn't know the man. He was loyal and he was funny, and he was a goddamn good friend . . . and he died like a man."

Nick is looking down, his shoulders trembling slightly, his voice breaking, his words barely audible over the rising clamor around them: "Almighty God, in your mercy turn the darkness of death into the dawn of new life, and the sorrow of parting into the joy of heaven."

Philip feels tears welling up and he grits his teeth so hard his jaw throbs.

"Through our Savior, Jesus Christ," Nick says in a shaky voice, "who died, rose again, and lives for evermore. Amen."

"Amen," Philip manages in a faint croak that sounds almost alien to his own ears.

The relentless din of the undead swells and surges louder and louder.

"SHUT THE FUCK UP!" Philip Blake bellows at the zombies, the noises coming from all directions now. "YOU DEAD MOTHER-FUCKERS!" Philip turns away from the grave, slowly pivoting: "I WILL SKULL-FUCK EVERY ONE OF YOU CANNIBAL-COCKSUCKERS!!! I WILL RIP EVERY STINKING HEAD OFF EVERY FUCKING ONE OF YOU AND SHIT DOWN YOUR ROTTEN FUCKING NECKS!!!"

Hearing this, Nick starts sobbing as Philip runs out of gas and falls to his knees.

While Nick cries, Philip just stares down at the fresh dirt as though some answer lies there.

If there was ever any doubt about who was in charge—not that there ever was—it is now made abundantly clear that Philip is the alpha and omega.

They spend the rest of that day packing, Philip issuing orders in monosyllables, his voice low and gravelly with stress. "Take the toolbox," he grunts. "Batteries for the flashlights," he mumbles. "And that box of shells," he mutters. "Extra blankets, too."

Nick thinks that maybe they should consider taking two cars.

Although most of the abandoned vehicles in the community are ripe for the picking—many of them late-model luxury jobs, many with the keys still in them—Brian worries about splitting the ragged little group into two. Or maybe he's just clinging to his brother now. Maybe Brian just needs to stay close to the center of gravity.

They decide to stick with the Chevy Suburban. The thing is a tank. Which is exactly what they'll need to get into Atlanta.

His stubborn cold now settling into his lungs, causing a perpetual wheeze that may or may not be early-stage pneumonia, Brian Blake focuses on the task at hand. He packs three large coolers with food stamped with the furthest expiration dates: smoked lunch meats, hard cheeses, sealed containers of juice and yogurt and soda and mayonnaise. He fills a cardboard box with bread and beef jerky and instant coffee and bottled water and protein bars and vitamins and paper plates and plastic utensils. He decides to throw in an array of chef's knives: cleavers, serrated knives, and boning knives—for whatever close encounters they might stumble into.

Brian fills another box with toilet paper and soap and towels and rags. He rifles through the medicine cabinets and takes cold remedies and sleeping pills and pain relievers, and while he's doing this, he gets an idea: something he should do before they depart.

In the basement, Brian finds a small can half full of Benjamin Moore Apple Peel Red and a two-inch horsehair paintbrush. He finds an old three-by-three-foot-square piece of plywood, and quickly but carefully, he writes a message: five simple words in big capital letters, large enough to be seen from a passing vehicle. He nails a couple of short legs on the bottom edge of the sign.

Then he takes the sign upstairs and shows it to his brother. "I think we should leave this outside the gate," Brian says to Philip.

Philip just shrugs and tells Brian it's up to him, whatever he wants to do.

They wait until after dark to make their exit. At the stroke of 7 P.M.—with the cold, metallic sun drooping behind the rooftops—they hurriedly pack the Suburban. Working quickly in the lengthening shadows, while monsters swarm against the barricade, they form a sort of bucket brigade, quickly passing suitcases and containers from the side door of the house to the open hatch of the SUV.

They take their original axes with an assortment of additional picks and shovels and hatchets and saws and cutting blades from the toolshed out back. They bring rope and wire and road flares and extra coats and snow boots and fire-starter blocks. They also pack a siphoning tube and as many extra plastic tanks of gasoline as they can fit into the rear storage well.

The Suburban's tank is currently full—Philip managed to siphon fifteen gallons' worth earlier in the day from an abandoned sedan in a neighbor's garage—as they have no clue about the status of local gas stations.

Over the last four days, Philip had discovered a variety of sporting guns in neighboring homes. Rich folks love their duck season in these parts. They love picking off green heads from the luxury of their heated blinds with their high-powered rifles and purebred hounds.

Philip's old man used to do it the hard way, with nothing but waders, moonshine, and a mean disposition.

Now Philip chooses three guns to stow in vinyl zip-up bags in the rear compartment—one is a .22-caliber Winchester rimfire, and the other two are Marlin Model 55 shotguns. The Marlins are especially useful. They're known as "goose guns." Fast and accurate and powerful, the 55s are designed for killing migratory fowl at high altitudes . . . or, in this case, the bull's-eye of a skull at a hundred-plus yards.

It's almost eight o'clock by the time they get the Suburban packed, and get Penny situated in the middle seat. Bundled in a down coat with her stuffed penguin at her side, she seems oddly sanguine, her pale face drawn and languid, as though she were about to visit the pediatrician.

Doors click open and shut. Philip climbs behind the wheel. Nick takes the front passenger seat, and Brian settles in next to Penny in the middle. The sign sits on the floor, pressed against Brian's knees.

The ignition fires. The growl of the engine carries across the still darkness, making the undead stir on the other side of the barricade.

"Let's do this quick, y'all," Philip says under his breath, slamming it into reverse. "Hold on."

Philip puts the pedal to the floor, and the four-wheel drive digs in.

The gravitational force throws everyone forward as the Suburban roars backward.

In the rearview mirror, the weak spot in the makeshift barricade looms closer and closer until . . . BANG! The vehicle bursts through the cedar planking and into the dim streetlight of Green Briar Lane.

Immediately, the left rear quarter panel collides with a walking corpse as Philip stands on the brakes and jacks it into drive. The zombie launches twenty feet into the air behind them, doing a limp pirouette in a mist of blood, a piece of its moldering arm detaching and pinwheeling in the opposite direction.

The Suburban blasts off toward the main conduit, smashing through three more zombies, sending them flinging off into oblivion. With each impact, the dull thumping sensations traveling through the chassis—as well as the yellowish buglike smears left on the windshield—make Penny cringe and close her eyes.

At the end of the street, Philip yanks the wheel and screeches around the corner, then pushes north toward the entrance.

A few minutes later Philip barks another order: "Okay, do it quick—and I mean QUICK!"

He slams down on the brakes, making everybody lurch forward in their seats again. They've just reached the great entrance gate, visible in a cone of streetlight across a short expanse of shrub-lined gravel.

"This'll just take a second," Brian says, grabbing the sign, clicking his door handle. "Leave it running."

"Just get it done."

Brian slips out of the car, carrying the big three-by-three sign.

In the cold night air, he hastens across the gravel threshold, his ears hyperalert and sensitive to the distant thrum of groaning noises: They're coming this way.

Brian chooses a spot just to the right of the entrance gate, a section of brick wall unobstructed by shrubbery, and he positions the sign against the wall.

He sinks the wooden legs into the soft earth to stabilize the board, and then hurries back to the car, satisfied he's done his part for humanity, or whatever is left of it.

As they drive off, each and every one of them—even Penny—glances back through the rear window at the little square sign receding into the distance behind them:

ALL DEAD
DO NOT
ENTER

FIVE

They head west, slowly, through the rural darkness, keeping their speed down around thirty miles per hour. The four lanes of Interstate 20 are littered with abandoned cars, as the macadam snakes toward the sickly pink glow of the western horizon, where the city awaits like a bruise of light on the night sky. They are forced to weave through the obstacle course of wrecks with agonizing slowness, but they manage to put nearly five miles behind them before things start going wrong.

For most of these five miles, Philip keeps thinking of Bobby and all the things they could have done to save him. The pain and regret are burrowing deep down in the pit of Philip's gut, a cancer metastasizing into something darker and more poisonous than grief. In order to fight the emotions he keeps thinking of that old trucker's adage: *Scan don't stare.* Gripping the wheel with the practiced clench of a longtime hauler, he sits forward in his seat, his gaze alert and fixed on the margins of the highway.

For five miles only a handful of dead brush the ghostly edges of their headlights.

Just outside of Conyers they pass a couple stragglers shuffling along the shoulder of the road like blood-spattered AWOL soldiers. Passing the Stonecrest Mall they see a cluster of dark figures hunkered down in a ditch, apparently feasting on some sort of roadkill, either animal or human, impossible to tell in the flickering darkness. But that has been the extent of it—for five miles, at least—and

Philip keeps his speed at a steady (but safe) thirty miles per hour. Any slower and they risk hooking a stray monster; any faster and they risk sideswiping the growing number of wrecks and abandoned vehicles cluttering the lanes.

The radio is dead, and the others ride in silence, their gazes glued to the passing landscape.

The outer rings of metro Atlanta roll past them in slow motion, a series of pine forests broken by an occasional bedroom community or strip mall. They pass car dealerships as dark as morgues, the endless ocean of new models like coffins reflecting the milky moonlight. They pass deserted Waffle Houses, their windows busted out like open sores, and office parks as barren as war zones. They pass Shoney's, and trailer parks, and Kmarts, and RV Centers, each one more desolate and ruined than the last. Small fires burn here and there. Parking lots look like the dark playrooms of mad children, the abandoned cars strewn across the pavement like toys thrown in anger. Broken glass glitters everywhere.

In less than a week and a half, the plague has apparently savaged the outer exurbs of Atlanta. Here, in the rural nature preserves and office campuses, where middle-class families have emigrated over the years to escape the arduous commutes, backbreaking mortgages, and high-stress urban life, the epidemic has laid waste to the social order in a matter of days. And for some reason, it's the sight of all the devastated churches that bothers Philip the most.

Each sanctuary they pass is in a progressively worse state: The New Birth Missionary Baptist Center outside of Harmon is still smoldering from a recent fire, its charred ruin of a cross rising against the heavens. A mile and a half down the road the Luther Rice Seminary features hastily hand-scrawled signs over its portals warning passers-by that the end is nigh and the rapture is here and all you sinners can kiss your asses good-bye. The Unity Faith Christian Cathedral looks as though it's been ransacked and scoured clean and then pissed upon. The parking lot at the St. John the Revelator Pentecostal Palace resembles a battlefield littered with bodies, many of the corpses still moving with the telltale, somnambulant hunger of the undead. *What kind of God would let this happen? And while we're on the subject: What kind of God would let a simple, innocent good old boy like Bobby Marsh die in such a way? What kind of—*

"Oh shit!"

The voice comes from the backseat, and it shakes Philip out of his dark musings. "What?"

"Look," Brian says, his voice weak from either his cold or the fear, or maybe a little of both. Philip glances at the rearview mirror, and he sees his brother's anxious expression in the green glow of the dash. Brian is pointing toward the western horizon.

Philip gazes back through the windshield, instinctively pumping the brakes. "What? I don't see anything."

"Holy crap," Nick says from the passenger seat. He is staring through a break in the piney woods off to the right, where light shines through the trees.

About five hundred yards ahead of them, the highway banks off in a northwesterly direction, cutting through a stand of pines. Beyond the trees, through clearings in the foliage, flames are visible.

The interstate is on fire.

"God*damnit*," Philip says on a tense sigh. He slows the vehicle to a crawl as they make the turn.

Within moments the overturned tanker truck comes into view, lying jackknifed in a cocoon of flames, like an upended dinosaur. The truck's carcass blocks the two westbound lanes, its cab detached and lying in pieces, tangled with three other cars across the median and both of the eastbound lanes. The scorched shells of other cars lie overturned behind the burning wreckage.

Beyond the wreck the lanes look like a parking lot, with scores of cars, some burning, most of them tangled in the chain reaction.

Philip pulls the Suburban over and brings it to a stop on the shoulder fifty yards from the dwindling flames. "That's just fantastic," he says to no one in particular, wanting to launch a barrage of profanity, but barely containing himself (on account of Penny's ears being inches away).

From this distance—even in the flickering darkness—several things are clear. First, and foremost, it is obvious they are either going to have to find a team of firefighters and heavy-duty towing equip-

ment in order to continue on course or they're going to have to figure out a fucking detour. Second, it looks as though whatever
happened here took place in the very recent past, perhaps earlier
today, perhaps only hours ago. The pavement around the wreck is
blackened and scarred, as though a meteor had punched a hole in it,
and even the trees lining the highway are charred from the shock
waves. Even through the closed windows of the Suburban, Philip
can smell the acrid stench of burning diesel and melted rubber.

"What now?" Brian finally says.

"Gotta turn around," Nick says, looking over his shoulder.

"Just lemme think for a second," Philip says, staring at the overturned truck cab, the roof sheared off it like the lid of a tin can. In the
darkness, charred bodies lie sprawled across the muddy median.
Some of them are twitching with the lazy undulations of snakes
waking up.

"C'mon, Philip, we can't get around it," Nick says.

Brian speaks up. "Maybe we can cut across to 278."

"GODDAMNIT, SHUT UP AND LET ME THINK!"

The sudden flare of rage makes Philip's skull throb with the force
of a splitting migraine, and he grits his teeth, clenching his fists and
stuffing the voice back down inside himself: *Crack it open, do it, tear
it open now, tear the heart out* . . .

"Sorry," Philip says, wiping his mouth, glancing over his shoulder at the frightened little girl huddling in the darkness of the backseat. "I'm real sorry, punkin, Daddy lost it there for a second."

The little girl stares at the floor.

"What do you want to do?" Brian asks softly, and from the forlorn
tone of his voice it sounds as though he would follow his brother
into the flames of hell if Philip thought that was the best option right
now.

"Last exit was—what?—maybe a mile or so back there?" Philip
glances over his shoulder. "I'm thinking that maybe we should—"

The slapping noise comes out of nowhere, cutting Philip off mid-
thought.

Penny shrieks.

"SHIT!"

Nick jerks away from the passenger window, where a charred corpse has materialized out of the darkness.

"Get down, Nick. Now." Philip's voice is flat and unaffected, like a radio dispatcher, as he quickly leans over to the glove box, pops the tiny door, and fishes for something. The thing outside the window presses up against the glass, barely recognizable as human, its flesh blistered to a crisp. "Brian, cover Penny's eyes."

"SHIT! SHIT!" Nick ducks down and covers his head, as though in an air raid. "SHIT! SHIT! SHIT!"

Philip finds the Ruger .22 pistol where he left it, already with a round in the chamber.

In one fluid motion Philip raises the weapon with his right hand, while simultaneously jacking down the power window with his left. The burned zombie reaches through the opening with its scorched, emaciated arm, letting out a guttural moan, but before it can grab hold of Nick's shirt, Philip squeezes off a single shot—point-blank, into the thing's skull.

The bark of the Ruger is enormously loud inside the Subrban's interior, and it makes everybody jump, as the charred corpse whiplashes—a direct hit above its left temple sending brain matter spitting across the inside of the windshield.

The thing slides down the outside of the passenger door, the muffled sound of its body hitting the pavement barely audible over the ringing in Philip's ears.

Twenty-two-caliber semiautos like the Ruger have a unique bark. The blast sounds like a hard flat slap—a two-by-four smacking concrete—and the gun invariably jumps in the shooter's hand.

That night, despite the muffling effect of the interior of the Suburban, that single boom echoed out across the dark landscape, reverberating over treetops and office parks, carrying on the wind.

The slapback could be heard a mile away, piercing the silence of the deep woods, penetrating the mortified auditory canals of shadowy creatures, awakening dead central nervous systems.

"Everybody awright?" Philip looks around the dark interior, setting the hot gun down on the carpeted hump next to him. "Everybody cool?"

Nick is just now rising back up, his eyes wide and hot, taking in all the residue on the inside of the glass. Penny, curled up in Brian's arms, keeps her eyes shut, as Brian frantically looks around, peering through all the windows, looking for any other intruders.

Philip slams the Suburban into reverse, kicking the accelerator as he quickly rolls the window back up. Everybody jerks forward as the vehicle screeches backward—a hundred feet, a hundred and fifty feet, two hundred feet—away from the smoking tanker truck.

Then the Suburban skids to a stop, and they sit there in stunned silence for a moment.

Nothing moves outside in the flickering shadows. Nobody says anything for the longest time, but Philip is convinced he's not the only one, at this moment, wondering if this twenty-mile trek into the city is going to be a lot harder than they originally thought.

They sit there in the idling Suburban for quite some time, debating their best course of action, and this makes Philip very antsy. He doesn't like sitting in one place for very long, especially with the engine running, burning gas and time, with those moving shadows behind the burning trees, but the group cannot seem to come to a consensus, and Philip is trying his hardest to be a benevolent dictator in this little banana republic.

"Look, I still say we try to drive around it." Philip gives a nod toward the darkness to the south.

The far shoulder of the oncoming lanes is littered with smoldering vehicles, but there's a narrow gap—maybe the width of the Suburban, with a few inches to spare—between the gravel shoulder and the thicket of pines along the highway. The recent rains combined with the oil spill from the overturned tanker have turned the land to slop. But the Suburban is a big, heavy vehicle with wide tires, and Philip has driven the thing through far worse conditions.

"It's too steep, Philly," Nick says, wiping the gray matter from the inside of the windshield with a grimy towel.

"Yeah, man, I have to agree," Brian says from the shadows of the backseat, his arm around Penny, the anguished features of his face visible in the flicker of firelight. "I vote for heading back to the last exit."

"We don't know *what* we'll find on 278, though, it could be worse."

"We don't know that," Nick says.

"We gotta keep moving forward."

"But what if it's worse in the city? Seems like it's getting worse the closer we get."

"We're still fifteen, twenty miles away—we don't know shit about what it's like in Atlanta."

"I don't know, Philly."

"Tell you what," Philip says. "Let me take a look."

"What do you mean?"

He reaches for the gun. "I'll just take a quick look."

"Wait!" Brian speaks up. "Philip, come on. We gotta stick together."

"I'm just gonna see what the ground is like, see if we can make it through."

"Daddy—" Penny starts to say something, and then thinks better of it.

"It's okay, punkin, I'll be right back."

Brian looks out the window, unconvinced. "We agreed we'd stick together. No matter what. C'mon, man."

"It'll take two minutes." Philip opens his door, shoving the Ruger into his belt.

The cool air and the sound of crackling flames and the smell of ozone and burning rubber waft into the Suburban like uninvited guests. "You guys sit tight, I'll be right back."

Philip climbs out of the car.

The door slams.

Brian sits in the silent Suburban for a moment, listening to his heart thudding in his chest. Nick is looking through each and every window, scanning the immediate vicinity, which is alive with flickering shadows. Penny gets very still. Brian looks at the little girl. The child looks like she's shrinking into herself, like a little night bloom, contracting into itself, pulling its petals shut.

"He'll be right back, kiddo," Brian says to the kid. He aches for her. This is not right, a child going through this, but on some level Brian knows how she feels. "He's a tough old boy, Philip. He can beat the crap outta any monster comes along, believe me."

From the front seat Nick turns and says, "Listen to your uncle, sweetie. He's right. Your daddy can take care of himself and then some."

"I saw your daddy catch a rabid dog once," Brian says. "He was maybe nineteen, and there was this German shepherd terrorizing the neighbor kids."

"I remember that," Nick says.

"Your daddy chased that thing—foaming mouth and all—down to the dry creek bed, and he wrestled the damn thing into a trash barrel."

"I totally remember that," Nick says. "Grabbed it with his bare hands, threw it halfway across the gully before slamming the trash can down on it like he was catching a fly."

Brian reaches down and tenderly brushes a strand of hair from the little girl's face. "He'll be okay, honey . . . trust me. He's a mean *muchacho*."

Outside the vehicle, a piece of burning wreckage falls to the ground. The clatter makes everybody jump. Nick looks at Brian. "Hey, man . . . you mind reaching back into that zipper bag by the wheel well?"

Brian looks at Nick. "What do you need?"

"One of them goose guns."

Brian stares at him a moment, then turns and leans over the back headrest. He roots out the long, canvas hunting bag wedged between a cooler and a backpack. He unzips it and finds one of the Marlin 55s.

Handing the shotgun across the backseat to Nick in the front, Brian says, "You need the shells, too?"

"I think it's already loaded," Nick says, hinging open the barrel and peering down into the breech.

Brian can tell Nick is handy with the thing, has probably hunted before, although Brian never witnessed it. Brian had never been the type to participate in the manly pursuits of his younger brother and his cronies, although he secretly yearned to do just that. "Two shells in the breech," Nick says, snapping the barrel shut.

"Just be careful with that thing," Brian says.

"Used to hunt feral hogs with one of these babies," Nick says, cocking and locking it.

"Hogs?"

"Yep . . . wild hogs . . . up to Chattahoochee reservation. Used to go on night hunts with my dad and my uncle Verne."

"Pigs you're talking about," Brian says incredulously.

"Yeah, basically. A hog is just a big ol' pig. Maybe they're older, too, I'm not—"

Another loud metallic crash comes from outside Nick's window.

Nick jerks the barrel toward the noise, finger on the trigger, his teeth gnashing with nervous tension. Nothing moves outside the passenger window. Muscles uncoil inside the Suburban, a long sigh of relief from Nick. Brian starts to say, "We gotta get our butts in gear before—"

Another noise.

This time it comes from the driver's side, a shuffling of feet—

—and before Nick can even register the identity of the shadowy figure approaching the Suburban's driver-side window, he swings the Marlin's muzzle up at the window, takes aim, and is about to squeeze off a couple of twenty-gauge greetings, when a familiar voice booms outside the car.

"JESUS CHRIST!"

Philip is visible outside the window just for an instant, before ducking out of the line of fire.

"Oh God, I'm sorry, I'm sorry," Nick says, instantly recognizing his mistake.

Philip's voice outside the window is lower now, more controlled, but still seething with anger. "You want to point that thing away from the goddamn window?"

Nick lowers the barrel. "I'm sorry, Philly, my bad, I'm sorry."

The door clicks and Philip slips back into the car, breathing hard, his face shiny with sweat. He shuts his door and lets out a long breath. "Nick—"

"Philly, I'm sorry . . . I'm a little jumpy."

For a moment Philip looks like he's going to take the other man's head off, then the anger fades. "We're all a little jumpy . . . I get that."

"I'm totally sorry."

"Just pay attention."

"I will, I will."

Brian speaks up. "What did you find out there?"

Philip reaches up to the stick shift. "A way around this damn mess." He flips it into four-wheel drive and slams the lever down. "Everybody hold on."

He turns the wheel, and they slowly roll across a spray of broken glass. The shards crunch under the Suburban's massive wheels, and nobody says anything, but Brian's thinking about the potential for flat tires.

Philip steers the vehicle down across the center median—which is a shallow culvert overgrown with switchgrass, weeds, and cattails—and the rear wheels dig into the rutted earth. As they approach the other side, Philip gives it a little more juice, and the Suburban lurches upward and across the eastbound lanes.

Philip keeps his hands glued to the steering wheel as they approach the far shoulder. "Hold on!" he calls out, as they suddenly plunge down a slope of muddy weeds.

The Suburban pitches sideways like a sinking ship. Brian holds on to Penny, and Nick holds on to the center armrest. Yanking the wheel, Philip kicks the accelerator.

The vehicle fishtails toward a narrow gap in the wreckage. Tree branches scrape the side of the SUV. The rear wheels slide sideways, then chew into the mud. Philip wrestles the wheel. Everybody else holds their respective breaths, as the Suburban scrapes through the opening.

When the car emerges out the other side, a spontaneous cheer rings out. Nick slaps Philip on the back, and Brian whoops and hollers triumphantly. Even Penny seems to lighten up a little, the hint of a smile tugging at the corners of her tulip-shaped lips.

Through the windshield they can see the tangle of vehicles in the darkness ahead of them—at least twenty cars, SUVs, and light trucks in the westbound lanes—most of them damaged in the pileup. All of them abandoned, many of them burned-out shells. The empty vehicles stretch back at least a hundred yards.

Philip puts the pedal to the metal, muscling the SUV back toward the road. He jerks the wheel. The rear of the SUV wags and churns.

Something is wrong. Brian feels the loss of traction beneath them like a buzzing in his spine, the engine revving suddenly.

The cheering dies.

The car is stuck.

For a moment Philip keeps the pedal to the floor, urging the thing forward with his ass cheeks, as if his sheer force of will and white-hot rage—and the tightening of his sphincter muscles—can get the blasted thing to move. But the Suburban keeps drifting sideways. Soon the thing is simply spinning all four wheels, kicking up twin gushers of mud out the back into the moonlit darkness behind them.

"FUCK!—FUCK! FUCK! FUCK!" Philip slams a fist down on the steering wheel, hard enough to make the thing crack and send a splinter of pain up his arm. He practically shoves the foot feed through the floor, the engine screaming.

"Let up on it, man!" Nick hollers over the noise. "It's just digging us in deeper!"

"FUCK!"

Philip lets up on the gas.

The engine winds down, the Suburban leaning to one side, a foundering boat in brackish waters.

"We gotta push it out," Brian says after a moment of tense silence.

"Take the wheel," Philip says to Nick, opening his door and slipping outside. "Give it gas when I tell ya to. Come on, Brian."

Brian opens the rear door, slips outside, and joins his brother in the glow of the taillights.

The rear tires have sunk at least six inches into the greasy muck, each rear quarter panel spattered with mud. The front wheels are no better. Philip places his big, gnarled hands on the wood grain of the tailgate, and Brian moves to the other side, assuming a wide stance in order to get a better purchase in the mud.

Neither of them notices the dark figures lumbering out of the trees on the other side of the highway.

"Okay, Nick, now!" Philip calls out and shoves with all his might.

The engine growls.

The wheels churn, spewing fountains of mud, as the Blake brothers push and push. They push with everything they have, all to no avail, as the slow-moving figures behind them shamble closer.

"Again!" Philip shouts, putting all his weight behind the shoving.

The rear wheels spin, sinking deeper into the mire, as Brian gets sprayed with an aerosol of mud.

Behind him, moving through a fog bank of smoke and shadows, the uninvited close the distance to about fifty yards, crunching through broken glass with the slow, lazy, awkward movements of injured lizards.

"Get back in the car, Brian." Philip's voice has abruptly changed, becoming low and even. "Right now."

"What is it?"

"Just do it." Philip is opening the rear hatch. Hinges squeak as he reaches in and fishes for something. "Don't ask any questions."

"But what about—" Brian's words stick in his throat as he catches a glimpse in his peripheral vision of at least a dozen dark figures—maybe more—closing in on them from several directions.

SIX

The figures approach from across the median, and from behind the flaming debris of the wreck, and from the adjacent woods—all shapes and sizes, faces the color of spackling compound, eyes gleaming like marbles in the firelight. Some are burned. Some are in tatters. Some are so well dressed and groomed they look as though they just came from church. Most have that curled-lip, exposed-incisor look of insatiable hunger.

"Shit." Brian looks at his brother. "What are you gonna do? What are you thinking?"

"Get your ass in the car, Brian."

"Shit—shit!" Brian hurries around to the side door, throws it open, and climbs in next to Penny, who is looking around with a bewildered expression. Brian slams the door, and smashes down the lock. "Lock the doors, Nick."

"I'm gonna help him—" Nick goes for his goose gun and opens his door, but he stops abruptly when he hears the strange sound of Philip's flat, cold, metallic tone through the open rear hatch.

"I got this. Do what he says, Nick. Lock the doors and stay down."

"There's too many of them!" Nick is thumbing the hammers on the Marlin, already with his right leg out the door, his work boot on the pavement.

"Stay in the car, Nick." Philip is digging out a pair of matched log splitters. A few days ago he found the small axes in a garden shed of a mansion at Wiltshire Estates—two matched, balanced implements of razor-sharp carbon steel—and at the time he wondered what in the world some fat rich guy (who probably paid a yard service to split his firewood) would want a pair of small bad-axes for.

In the front seat, Nick pulls his leg back inside the SUV, slams his door, and bangs the lock down. He twists around with his eyes blazing and the gun cradled in his arms. "What the hell? What are you doing, Philly?"

The rear hatch slams.

The silence crashes down on the interior.

Brian looks down at the child. "I'm thinking maybe you ought to get down on the floor, kiddo."

Penny says nothing as she slides down the front of the seat, and then curls into a fetal position. Something in her expression, some glint of knowing in her big soft eyes, reaches out to Brian and puts the squeeze on his heart. He pats her shoulder. "We'll get through this."

Brian turns and peers over the backseat, over the cargo and out through the rear window.

Philip has a bad-axe in either hand, and is calmly walking toward the converging crowd of zombies. "Jesus," Brian utters under his breath.

"What's he doing, Brian?" Nick's voice is high and taut, his hands fingering the Marlin's bolt.

Brian cannot muster a response because he is now held rapt by the terrible sight through the window.

It's not pretty. It's not graceful or cool or heroic or manly or even well executed . . . but it feels good. "I got this," Philip says to himself, under his breath, as he lashes out at the closest one, a heavyset man in farmer's dungarees.

The bad-axe sheers off a grapefruit-sized lobe of the fat one's skull, sending a geyser of pink matter into the night air. The zombie falls. But Philip doesn't stop. Before the next closest one can reach him, Philip goes to work on the big flaccid body on the ground, windmilling the cold steel in each hand down on the dead flesh.

"Vengeance is mine; I will repay, saith the Lord." Blood and tissue fountain. Sparks kick off the pavement with each blow.

"I got this, I got this, I got this," Philip murmurs to no one in particular, letting all the pent-up rage and sorrow come out in a flurry of glancing blows. "I got this, I got this, I got this, I got this, I got this—"

By this point others have closed in—a skinny young man with black fluid dripping off his lips, a fat woman with a bloated, dead face, a guy in a bloody suit—and Philip spins away from the mangled corpse on the ground to go to work on the others. He grunts with each blow—*I GOT THIS!*—cleaving skulls—*I GOT THIS!*—severing carotid arteries—*I GOT THIS!*—letting his anger drive the cold steel through cartilage and bone and nasal cavities—*I GOT THIS!*—the blood and brain matter misting up across his face as he remembers the foaming mouth of rabid fangs coming for him when he was a kid, and God taking his wife Sarah, and the monsters taking his best friend Bobby Marsh—*I GOT THIS!—I GOT THIS!—I GOT THIS!!*

Inside the Suburban, Brian turns away from the scene outside the back window, coughs, and feels his gut rising at the nauseating sounds penetrating the sealed interior of the Suburban. He stifles the urge to vomit. He reaches down and gently puts his hands around Penny's ears, a gesture which, sadly, is becoming a routine.

In the front seat Nick cannot tear his eyes from the carnage behind them. On Nick's face Brian can see a weird mixture of repulsion and admiration—a kind of thank-God-he's-on-our-side type of awe—but it only serves to tighten Brian's gut. He will not throw up, goddamnit, he will be strong for Penny.

Brian slips down on the floor and holds the girl close to him. The child is limp and damp. Brian's brain swims with confusion.

His brother is everything to him. His brother is the key. But something is happening to Philip, something horrible, and it's beginning to gnaw at Brian. What are the rules? These walking abominations deserve every fucking thing Philip is dishing out . . . but what are the rules of engagement?

Brian is trying to put these thoughts out of his mind when he realizes the killing noises have ceased. Then he hears the heavy boot
steps of a person outside the driver's side door. The door clicks.

Philip Blake slips back inside the Suburban, dropping the bloody
hand-axes on the floor in front of Nick. "There'll be more of 'em," he
says, still winded, his face beaded with perspiration. "The gunshot
woke 'em up."

Nick peers out the back window at the battlefield of bodies visible
in the firelight on the slope, his voice coming out in a monotone, a
combination of awe and disgust: "Home run, man . . . grand slam
home run."

"We gotta get outta here," Philip says, wiping a pearl of sweat
from his nose, catching his breath, and glancing up at the rearview
mirror, searching for Penny in the shadows of the backseat as if
he doesn't even hear Nick.

Brian speaks up. "What's the plan, Philip?"

"We gotta find a safe place to stay for the night."

Nick looks at Philip. "What do you mean exactly? You mean
other than the Suburban?"

"It's too dangerous out here in the dark."

"Yeah, but—"

"We'll push it out of the mud in the morning."

"Yeah, but what about—"

"Grab whatever you need for the night," Philip says, reaching for
the Ruger.

"Wait!" Nick grabs Philip's arm. "You're talking about leaving
the car! Leaving all our shit out here?"

"Just for the night, come on," Philip says, opening his door and
climbing out.

Brian lets out a sigh and looks up at Nick. "Shut up and help me
with the backpacks."

They camp that night about a quarter of a mile west of the overturned
tanker, inside an abandoned yellow school bus, which sits on the
shoulder, well illuminated by the cold glow of a sodium vapor light.

The bus is still fairly warm and dry, and it's high enough off the pavement to give them good sight lines on the woods on either side of the interstate. It has two doors—one in the front and one off the rear—for easy escape. Plus the bench seats are padded and long enough for each of them to stretch out for some semblance of rest. The keys are still in the ignition, and the battery still has juice.

Inside the bus it smells like the inside of a stale lunchbox, the ghosts of sweaty, rambunctious kids with their wet mittens and body odors lingering in the fusty air.

They eat some Spam and some sardines and some expensive pita crackers that were probably meant to adorn party trays at golf outings. They use flashlights, careful not to shine them off the windows, and eventually they spread their sleeping bags on the bench seats for some shut-eye, or at least some facsimile of sleep.

They each take turns sitting watch in the cab with one of the Marlins, using the huge side mirrors for unobstructed views of the bus's rear end. Nick takes the first shift and tries unsuccessfully for nearly an hour to raise a station on his portable weather radio. The world has shut down, but at least this section of Interstate 20 is equally still. The edges of the woods remain quiet.

When it's Brian's turn to sit watch—up to this point he has only managed a few minutes of fitful dozing on a squeaky bench seat in back—he gladly takes his place in the cab with all the levers and the dangling pine tree air fresheners and the laminated photograph of some long-lost driver's baby son. Not that Brian is very comfortable with the prospects of being the only one awake, or for that matter, having to fire the goose gun. Still, he needs some time to think.

At some point just before dawn, Brian hears Penny's breathing—just barely audible over the faint whistle of the wind through the ranks of sliding windows—becoming erratic and hyperventilated. The child has been dozing a few seats away from the cab, next to her father.

Now the little girl sits up with a silent gasp. "Oh . . . I got it . . . I mean . . ." Her voice is barely a whisper. "I got it, I think."

"Ssshhh," Brian says, rising from his seat, creeping back down the cabin to the little girl, whispering, "It's okay, kiddo . . . Uncle Brian's here."

"Um."

"It's okay . . . ssshhhh . . . let's not wake your dad." Brian glances over at Philip, who is tangled in a blanket, his face contorted with troubling dreams. He took half a pint of brandy before bed to knock himself out.

"I'm okay," Penny utters in her mousey little voice, looking down at the stuffed penguin in her small hands, squeezing it like a talisman. The thing is soiled and threadbare, and it breaks Brian's heart.

"Bad dreams?"

Penny nods.

Brian looks at her and thinks it over. "Got an idea," he whispers. "Why don't you come up and keep me company for a while."

The little girl nods.

He helps her up, and then, draping a blanket around her and taking her hand, he silently leads her back up to the cab. He flips down a little jump seat next to the driver's perch, and says, "There ya go." He pats the worn upholstery. "You can be my copilot."

Penny settles into the seat with her blanket pulled tightly around her and the penguin.

"See that?" Brian points to a filthy little video monitor above the dash, about the size of a paperback book, on which a grainy black-and-white image reveals the highway behind them. The wind rustles through the trees, the sodium lights gleaming off the roofs of wrecked cars. "That's a security camera, for backing up, see?"

The girl sees it.

"We're safe here, kiddo," Brian says as convincingly as possible. Earlier in his shift he had figured out a way to turn the ignition key to the accessory position, lighting up the dash like an old pinball machine coming to life. "Everything's under control."

The girl nods.

"You want to tell me about it?" Brian says softly a moment later.

Penny looks confused. "Tell you about what?"

"The bad dream. Sometimes it helps to like . . . *tell* someone . . . you know? Makes it go away . . . *poof*."

Penny gives him a feeble little shrug. "I dreamed I got sick."

"Sick like . . . those people out there?"

"Yes."

Brian takes a long, anguished, deep breath. "Listen to me, kiddo. Whatever these people have, you are not going to catch it. Do you understand? Your daddy will not let that happen, never in a million years. *I* will not let that happen."

She nods.

"You are very important to your daddy. You are very important to *me*." Brian feels an unexpected hitch in his chest, a catching of his words, a burning sensation in his eyes. For the first time since he departed his parents' place over a week and half ago, he realizes how deeply his feelings go for this little girl.

"I got an idea," he says after getting his emotions in check. "Do you know what a code word is?"

Penny looks at him. "Like a secret code?"

"Exactly." Brian licks his finger, and then wipes a stain of dirt from her cheek. "You and I are going to have this secret code word."

"Okay."

"This is a very special code. Okay? From now on, whenever I say this secret word, I want you to do something for me. Can you do that? Can you, like, always remember to do something for me whenever I give you the secret code word?"

"Sure . . . I guess."

"Whenever I say the code word, I want you to hide your eyes."

"Hide my eyes?"

"Yeah. And cover your ears. Until I tell you it's okay to look. All right? And there's one more thing."

"Okay."

"Whenever I give you the secret code . . . I want you to remember something."

"What?"

"I want you to remember that there's gonna come a day when you won't have to hide your eyes anymore. There's gonna come a day when everything's all better, and there won't be any more sick people. Got that?"

She nods. "Got it."

"Now what's the word gonna be?"

"You want me to pick it?"

"You bet . . . it's your secret code . . . you should pick it."

The little girl wrinkles up her nose as she ponders a suitable word. The sight of her contemplating—so intently that she looks as though she's calculating the Pythagorean theorem—presses down on Brian's heart.

Finally the child looks up at Brian, and for the first time since the plague had begun, a glimmer of hope kindles in her enormous eyes. "I got it." She whispers the word to her stuffed animal, then looks up. "Penguin likes it."

"Great . . . don't keep me in suspense."

"*Away*," she says. "The secret code word's gonna be *away*."

The gray dawn comes in stages. First, an eerie calm settles around the interstate, the wind dying in the trees, and then a luminous pale glow around the edges of the forest wakes everybody up and gets them going.

The sense of urgency is almost immediate. They feel naked and exposed without their vehicle, so everybody concentrates on the task at hand: packing up, getting back to the Suburban, and getting the damn thing unstuck.

They make the quarter-mile hike back to the SUV in fifteen minutes, carrying their bedrolls and excess food in backpacks. They encounter a single zombie on the way, a wandering teenage girl, and Philip easily puts out her lights by quickly and quietly chopping a furrow into her skull, while Brian whispers the secret word to Penny.

When they reach the Suburban, they work in silence, ever mindful of the shadows of adjacent woods. First they try to apply weight to the rear end by putting Nick and Philip on the tailgate, and having Brian give it gas from the driver's seat, pushing with one leg outside the door. It doesn't work. Then they search the immediate area for something to build traction under the wheels. It takes them an hour but they eventually unearth a couple of broken pallets scattered along a drainage ditch, and they bring them back, and wedge them under the wheels.

This also fails.

Somehow the mud beneath the SUV is so saturated with moisture and runoff and oil and God knows what else that it just keeps sucking the vehicle deeper, the leaning Suburban slipping progressively backward down the slope. But they refuse to give up. Driven by a relentless anxiety over unexplained noises in the adjacent pine forest—twigs snapping, low concussive booms in the distance—as well as the constant unspoken dread of having all their worldly possessions and supplies lost with the foundering Suburban, nobody is willing to face the encroaching hopelessness of the situation.

By mid-afternoon, after working for hours, and breaking for lunch, and then going back at it for a couple more hours, all they have succeeded in doing is causing the SUV to drift nearly six feet farther down the muddy incline, while Penny sits inside the vehicle, alternately playing with Penguin and pressing her morose face to the window.

At that point, Philip steps back from the mud pit and gazes at the western horizon.

The overcast sky has begun its fade toward dusk, and the prospect of nightfall suddenly puts a pinch on Philip's gut. Covered with sludge, soaked in sweat, he pulls a bandana and wipes his neck.

He starts to say something, when another series of noises from the neighboring trees yank his attention to the south. For hours now the crackling, snapping noises—maybe footsteps, maybe not—have been getting closer.

Nick and Brian—both wiping their hands with rags—join Philip. None of them says anything for a moment. Each of their expressions reflects the hard reality, and when another snap from the trees crackles—as loud as a pistol shot—Nick speaks up: "Writing's on the wall, ain't it."

Philip shoves his handkerchief back in his pocket. "Night's gonna fall soon."

"Whattya think, Philly?"

"Time for plan B."

Brian swallows hard, looking at his brother. "I wasn't aware there *was* a plan B."

Philip gazes at his brother, and for a moment, Philip feels a bizarre mixture of anger, pity, impatience, and affection. Then Philip looks at the old, rust-pocked Suburban, and feels a twinge of melancholy, as though he's about to say good-bye to another old friend. "There is now."

They siphon gas from the Suburban into plastic tanks they brought from Wiltshire. Then they get lucky enough to find a big, late-model Buick LeSabre, the keys still in it, left for dead on the side of the road, about an eighth of a mile west of there. They commandeer the Buick and roar back to the foundered SUV. They fill the Buick with gas and transfer as many supplies as they can squeeze into the car's huge trunk.

Then they take off toward the setting sun, each of them glancing back at the swamped SUV, receding into the distance like a shipwreck sinking into oblivion.

Indications of the looming apocalypse appear on either side of the interstate with alarming frequency now. As they draw nearer and nearer to the city, weaving with increasing difficulty through abandoned wreckage—the trees thinning and giving way to a growing number of residential enclaves, shopping plazas, and office parks—the telltale signs of doom are everywhere. They pass a dark, deserted Walmart, the windows broken, a sea of clothes and merchandise strewn across the parking lot. They notice more and more power outages, entire communities as dark and silent as tombs. They pass strip malls ravaged by looting, biblical warnings scrawled on exhaust chimneys. They even see a small single-engine plane, tangled in a giant electrical tower, still smoking.

Somewhere between Lithonia and Panthersville, the Buick's rear end starts vibrating like a son of bitch, and Philip realizes the thing has two blown tires. Maybe they were already flat when they acquired the car. Who knows? But there is no time to try and fix the infernal things, and no time to debate the matter.

Night is pressing in again, and the closer they get to the outskirts of metro Atlanta, the more the roads are knotted with the carcasses of mangled wrecks and abandoned cars. Nobody says it out loud, but they are all beginning to wonder whether they could get into the city faster on foot. Even the neighboring two-lanes like Hillandale and Fairington are blocked with empty cars, lined up like fallen dominoes in the middle of the road. At this rate, it will take them a week to get into town.

Which is why Philip makes the executive decision at that point to leave the Buick where it sits, pack up every last thing they can possibly carry, and set out on foot. Nobody's crazy about the idea, but they go along with it. The alternative of searching the frozen traffic jam in the pitch-darkness for spare tires or a suitable replacement vehicle doesn't seem viable right now.

They quickly dig their necessities out of the Buick's trunk, stuffing duffel bags and backpacks with supplies, blankets, food, weapons, and water. They are getting better at communicating with whispers, hand gestures, and nods—hyperaware now of the distant drone of dead people, the sounds waxing and waning in the darkness beyond the highway, percolating in the trees and behind buildings. Philip has the strongest back, so he takes the largest canvas duffel. Nick and Brian each strap on an overloaded backpack. Even Penny agrees to carry a knapsack filled with bedding.

Philip takes the Ruger pistol, the two bad-axes—one shoved down each side of his belt—and a long machetelike tool for cutting underbrush, which he shoves down the length of his spine between the duffel and his stained chambray shirt. Brian and Nick each cradle a Marlin 55 shotgun in their arms, as well as a pickaxe strapped to the sides of their respective backpacks.

They start walking west, and this time, not a single one of them looks back.

A quarter of a mile down the road, they encounter an overpass clogged with a battered Airstream mobile home. Its cab is wrapped around a telephone pole. All the streetlights have flickered out, and in the full dark, a muffled banging noise is heard inside the walls of the ruined trailer.

This makes everybody pause suddenly on the shoulder beneath the viaduct.

"Jesus, it could be somebody—" Brian stops himself when he sees his brother's hand shoot up.

"Sssshhhhh!"

"But what if it's—"

"Quiet!" Philip cocks his head and listens. His expression is that of a cold stone monument. "This way, come on!"

Philip leads the group down a rocky slope on the north edge of the interchange, each of them descending the hill gingerly, careful not to slip on the wet pea gravel. Brian brings up the rear, wondering again about the rules, wondering if they just deserted one of their fellow human beings.

His thoughts are quickly subsumed by the plunge into the darker territory of countryside.

They follow a narrow blacktop two-lane called Miller Road northward through the darkness. For about a mile, they encounter nothing more than a sparsely commercialized area of desolate industrial parks and foundries, their signs as dark as hieroglyphs on cave walls: Barloworld Handling, Atlas Tool and Die, Hughes Supply, Simcast Electronics, Peachtree Steel. The rhythmic shuffle of their footsteps on the cold asphalt mingles with the thrumming of their breaths. The silence starts working on their nerves. Penny is getting tired. They hear rustling noises in the woods off to their immediate right.

At last Philip raises his hand and points toward a sprawling, low-slung plant stretching back into the distance. "This place will do," he says in a low flat whisper.

"Do for *what*?" Nick says, pausing next to Philip, breathing hard.

"For the night," Philip says. There is no emotion in his voice.

He leads the group past a low, unlighted sign that says GEORGIA PACIFIC CORPORATION.

Philip gets in through the office window. He has everybody huddle in the shadows outside the entrance while he makes his way through empty, littered corridors toward the warehouse in the center of the building.

The place is as dark as a crypt. Philip's heart beats in his ears as he strides along with the bad-axes at his side. He tries one of the light switches to no avail. He barely notices the pungent aroma of wood pulp permeating the air—a gluey, sappy odor—and when he reaches the safety doors, he slowly shoves them open with the toe of his boot.

The warehouse is the size of an airplane hanger, with giant gantries hanging overhead, the rows of huge scoop lights dark, the odor of paper must as thick as talc. Thin moonlight shines down through gargantuan sky windows. The floor is sectioned off into rows of enormous paper rolls—as big around as redwood trunks—so white they seem to glow in the darkness.

Something moves in the middle distance.

Philip shoves the bad-axes down either side of his belt, then grasps the hilt of the Ruger. He draws out the gun, snaps back the slide, and raises the muzzle at a dark figure staggering out from behind a stack of pallets. The factory rat comes through the shadows toward Philip slowly, hungrily, the front of his dungarees dark with dried blood and bile, his long, slack face full of teeth gleaming in the moonbeams coming through the skylight.

One shot puts the dead thing down—the blast bouncing back like a kettledrum in the cavernous warehouse.

Philip makes a sweep of the remaining length of the warehouse. He finds a couple more of them—an older fat man, a former night watchman from the looks of his soiled uniform, and a younger one—each dragging his dead ass out from behind shelving units.

Philip feels nothing as he pops each one in the skull at point-black range.

On his way back toward the front entrance he discovers a fourth one in the shadows, caught between two massive paper rolls. The bottom half of the former forklift operator is wedged between the blinding white cylinders, crushed beyond recognition, all his fluids pooled and dried on the cement floor beneath him. The top half of the creature convulses and flails, its milk-stone eyes stupidly awake.

"What's up, bubba?" Philip says as he approaches with the gun at his hip. "Another day, another dollar . . . huh?"

The zombie chomps impotently at the air between its face and Philip.

"Lunch break overdue?"

Chomp.

"Eat this."

The .22-caliber blast echoes as the slug smashes through the forklift operator's orbital bone, turning the milky eye black, and sending a chunk of the parietal hemisphere flying. The spray—a mixture of blood, tissue, and cerebrospinal fluid—spatters the rows of pristine white paper, as the top half of the dead thing wilts like a noodle.

Philip admires his work of art—the scarlet tendrils on that field of heavenly white—for quite a long time before going to get the others.

SEVEN

They spend the night in a glass-encased foreman's office, high above the main floor of the Georgia Pacific warehouse. They use their battery-powered lanterns and they move the desks and chairs aside, and they spread their bedrolls on the linoleum tiles.

The previous occupant must have practically lived in the little two-hundred-square-foot crow's nest, because there are CDs, a stereo, a microwave, a small refrigerator (the food inside it mostly spoiled), drawers full of candy bars, work orders, half-full liquor bottles, office supplies, fresh shirts, cigarettes, check stubs, and porn.

Philip hardly says a word the whole night. He just sits near the window overlooking the warehouse floor, occasionally taking a swig of whiskey from the pint bottle he found in the desk, while Nick sits on the floor in the opposite corner, silently reading a small Concordance Bible by the light of a lantern. Nick claims he carries the little dog-eared leather-bound book wherever he goes; but the others have rarely seen him reading it . . . until now.

Brian forces down some tuna fish and saltine crackers, and he tries to get Penny to eat something but she won't. She seems to be drawing further into herself, her eyes now displaying a permanent glaze that looks vaguely catatonic to Brian. Later, Brian sleeps next to her, while Philip dozes in the swivel chair by the greasy wire-mesh window, through which past foremen have kept their eyes peeled for loafers. This is the first time Brian has seen his brother too consumed by his own thoughts to sleep next to his daughter, and it does not bode well.

The next morning, they awaken to the sounds of dogs barking somewhere outside.

The dull, pale light floods in through the high windows, and they pack quickly. Nobody has any appetite for breakfast so they use the bathroom, tape their feet to ward against blisters, and put on extra socks. Brian's heels are already sore from the few miles they've trekked, and there's no telling how far they will go today. They each have one change of clothes, but nobody has the energy to put on anything clean.

On their way out, each one of them—except Philip—studiously avoids looking at the bodies lying in pools of gore in the warehouse.

Philip seems galvanized by the sight of corpses illuminated by daylight.

Outside, they discover the source of the barking. About a hundred yards west of the warehouse a pack of strays—mostly mutts—are fighting over something pink and ragged on the ground. As Philip and the others approach, the dogs scatter, leaving the object of their attentions in the mud. Brian identifies the object as they pass, and softly gives Penny the code word: *away.*

The thing is a severed human arm, chewed so badly it looks like it belongs to a wet rag doll.

"Don't look, punkin," Philip mutters to his daughter, and Brian pulls Penny next to him, covering the girl's eyes.

They trudge westward, moving silently, their footsteps furtive and careful like thieves creeping through the morning sun.

They follow a road called Snapfinger Drive, which runs parallel to the interstate. The blacktop ribbon winds through barren forest preserves, abandoned residential villages, and ransacked strip malls. As they move through increasingly populated areas, the side of the road holds horrors that no little girl should ever see.

A high school football field is strewn with headless torsos. A mortuary has been hastily boarded and nailed shut *from the outside*—the horrible muffled sounds of the recently risen scratching and clawing to get out. Philip fervidly searches for a suitable vehicle to highjack, but most of the cars along Snapfinger lie in ditches like burned husks or sit on the gravel shoulder with two or three tires blown. Traffic lights, most of them either blinking yellow or completely black, hang over clogged intersections.

The highway—visible up along a ridge a hundred yards to their left—crawls with the dead. Every so often the tattered remains of a person will cross through the distant pale rays of the rising sun, causing Philip to motion for everybody to get the hell down and stay quiet. But despite the arduous process of ducking behind trees or wreckage every time they sense another presence looming nearby, they cover quite a bit of ground that day.

They encounter no other survivors.

Late that afternoon, the weather turns clear and sunny—ironically, a fine early autumn afternoon in any other context—the temperature in the low sixties. By five o'clock, the men are sweating, and Penny has tied her sweatshirt around her waist. Philip calculates their progress, subtracting a thirty-minute rest for lunch, and he figures that they've averaged about a mile an hour—crossing nearly eight miles of suburban wilderness.

Still, none of them realizes how close they are to the city until they come upon a muddy hillock rising out of the pines just west of Glenwood, where a Baptist church sits on a ridge, smoldering from a recent conflagration, its steeple a smoking ruin.

Exhausted, drained, and hungry, they follow the winding road up the grade to the top of the hill; and when they reach the church parking lot, they all stand there for a moment, gazing out at the western horizon, frozen with a sort of unexpected awe.

The skyline, only three miles away, looks almost radiant in the fading light.

For boys growing up within a couple hundred miles of the great capital of the New South, Philip and Brian Blake have spent precious little time in Atlanta. For the two and half years that he drove trucks for Harlo Electric, Philip occasionally made deliveries there. And Brian has seen his share of concerts at the Civic Center, the Earl, the Georgia Dome, and the Fox Theater. But neither man knows the town well.

As they stand on the edge of that church parking lot, with the acrid smell of the apocalypse in their sinuses, the skyline in the hazy distance reflects back at them a sort of unattainable grandeur. In the dreamy light they can see the capitol spire with its golden-clad dome, the mirrored monoliths of the Concourse Complex, the massive Peachtree Plaza towers, and the pinnacle of the Atlantic building, but it all seems to give off an air of *mirage*—a sort of Lost-City-of-Atlantis feeling.

Brian is about to say something about the place being so close and yet so far—or perhaps make a comment about the unknowable condition of the streets down below—when he sees a blur out of the corner of his eye.

"Look!"

Penny has darted away, unexpectedly and quickly, her voice shrill with excitement.

"PENNY!"

Brian starts after the little girl, who is scurrying across the western edge of the church parking lot.

"GRAB HER!" Philip calls out, chasing after Brian, who is charging after the girl.

"Lookit! Lookit!" Penny's little legs are churning frantically as she darts toward a side street, which winds along the far side of the hill. "It's a policeman!" She points as she runs. "He'll save us!"

"PENNY, STOP!"

The little girl scurries around an exit gate and down the side road. "He'll save us!"

Brian clears the end of the fence at a dead run, and he sees a squad car about fifty yards away, parked on the side of the road under a massive live oak. Penny is approaching the royal blue Crown Victoria—the Atlanta Police decal on the door, the trademark red swoosh, and the light bar mounted on the roof—a silhouette hunched behind the wheel.

"Stop, honey!"

Brian sees Penny pausing suddenly outside the driver's door, panting with exertion, staring in at the man behind the wheel.

By this point, Philip and Nick have caught up with Brian, and Philip zooms past his brother. He charges up to his little girl and scoops her off the ground as though pulling her out of a fire.

Brian reaches the squad car and looks in the half-open driver's side window.

The patrolman was once a heavyset white man with long sideburns.

Nobody says anything.

From her father's arms, Penny gapes through the car window at the dead man in uniform straining against his shoulder strap. From the looks of his badge and his garb, as well as the word TRAFFIC emblazoned on the front quarter panel of the vehicle, he was once a low-level officer, probably assigned to the outer regions of the city, feeding stray cars to the impound lots along Fayetteville Road.

Now the man twists in his seat, imprisoned by a seat belt he cannot fathom, openmouthed and drooling at the fresh meat outside his window. His facial features are deformed and bloated, the color of mildew, his eyes like tarnished coins. He snarls at the humans, snapping his blackened teeth with feral appetite.

"Now that's just plain pathetic," Philip says to no one in particular.

"I'll take her," Brian says, stepping closer and reaching for Penny.

The dead cop, catching the smell of food, snaps his jaws toward Brian, straining the belt, making the canvas harness creak.

Brian jerks back with a start.

"He can't hurt ya," Philip says in a low, alarmingly casual tone. "He can't even figure out the goddamn seat belt."

"You're kidding me," Nick says, looking over Philip's shoulder.
"Poor dumb son of a bitch."

The dead cop growls.

Penny climbs into Brian's arms, and Brian steps back, holding the child tightly. "C'mon, Philip, let's go."

"Wait a minute, hold your horses." Philip pulls the .22 from the back of his belt.

"C'mon, man," Nick pipes in, "the noise is gonna draw more of 'em . . . let's get outta here."

Philip points the gun at the cop, who grows still at the sight of the muzzle. But Philip doesn't pull the trigger. He simply smiles and makes a childlike shooting noise: *psssh-psssh-pssssh.*

"Philip, come on," Brian says, shifting Penny's weight in his arms. "That thing doesn't even—"

Brian stops and stares.

The dead cop is transfixed by the sight of that Ruger in his face. Brian wonders if his rudimentary central nervous system is some-how sending a signal to some far-off muscle memory buried deep in his dead brain cells. His expression changes. The monstrous abomination of a face falls like a rotten soufflé, and the thing almost looks sad. Or maybe even scared. It's hard to tell behind that beastly snarling mouth and mask of necrotic tissue, but something in those Buffalo-nickel eyes flickers then: a trace of dread?

An unexpected tide of emotion rises in Brian Blake, and it takes him by surprise. It's hard to put a name to it—it's partly repulsion, partly pity, partly disgust, partly sorrow, and partly rage. He sud-denly puts Penny down, and he gently turns her around so that she's facing the church.

"This is an *away* moment, kiddo," Brian says softly, and then turns to face his brother.

Philip is taunting the zombie. "Just relax and follow the bouncing ball," he says to the drooling creature, waving the barrel slowly back and forth.

"I'll do it," Brian says.

Philip freezes. He turns and gives his brother a look. "Say what?"

"Give me the gun, I'll finish it off."

Philip looks at Nick, and Nick looks at Brian. "Hey, man, you don't want to—"

"Give me the gun!"

The smile that twitches at the corners of Philip's lips is complex, and humorless. "Be my guest, sport."

Brian takes the gun and without hesitation steps forward, pokes it in the car, presses the muzzle against the dead cop's head, and starts to squeeze off a single shot . . . but his finger will not respond. His trigger finger will not obey the command his brain is giving it.

In the awkward pause the zombie drools as though waiting for something.

"Gimme the gun back, sport." Philip's voice sounds far away to Brian.

"No . . . I got this one." Brian grits his teeth and tries to pull the trigger. His finger is a block of ice. His eyes burn. His stomach clenches.

The dead cop snarls.

Brian begins to tremble as Philip steps forward.

"Gimme the gun back."

"No."

"Come on, sport, give it back."

"I got it!" Brian wipes his eyes with his sleeve. "Damnit, I got it!"

"Come on." Philip reaches for the gun. "Enough."

"God*damn*it," Brian says, lowering the gun, the tears welling in his eyes. He can't do it. He might as well face it. He gives the gun to his brother, and steps back with his head lowered.

Philip puts the policeman out of his misery with a single pop that sends a spray of blood mist across the inside of the prowler's windshield. The bark echoes up and out over the ruined landscape.

The dead cop slumps over the wheel.

A long moment passes as Brian fights his tears and tries to hide his trembling. He gazes through the car window at the cop's remains. He feels like saying he's sorry to the dead officer but decides against it. He just keeps staring at the limp body still held in place by the shoulder strap.

The faint sound of a child's voice, like the flutter of broken wings, comes from behind them. "Dad . . . Uncle Brian . . . Uncle Nick? Um . . . something bad is happening."

The three men whirl around almost simultaneously. Their gazes rise across the church parking lot, to the place toward which Penny is staring and pointing. "Son of a *bitch*," Philip says, seeing the worst-case scenario unfolding before his very eyes.

"Oh my God," Nick says.

"Shit, shit—shit!" Brian feels his spine go cold as he sees the front of the church.

"Come on, punkin, this way." Philip goes over to the child and tugs her gently back toward the cruiser. "We're gonna borrow this nice policeman's car." He reaches inside the driver's door, unlatches it, kicks it open, unsnaps the seat belt, and yanks the limp body from the vehicle—the zombie sprawling to the pavement with the ceremonial splat of an overripe gourd.

"Everybody in—quick! Throw your shit in the back! And get in!"

Brian and Nick circle around to the other side, throw open the doors, toss in their backpacks, and get in.

Philip slides Penny over the center hump, setting her on the passenger seat and climbing behind the wheel. The keys are in the ignition.

Philip turns the key.

The engine ticks.

The dashboard barely lights, just a dull ember of power left.

"Damnit to hell! DAMNIT!" Philip glances out the window at the church. "Okay. Wait a minute. Wait . . . wait." He shoots a quick glance through the windshield, and he sees that the road ahead banks into a steep downgrade, which leads under a train trestle. He looks at Brian and Nick. "You two. Get out. Now!"

Brian and Nick look at each other, stunned. What they see emerging from the church—most likely aroused by the commotion of voices and the pistol shot—would most likely burn itself into their memories for some time to come. Unfortunately it would also linger in Penny's imagination, probably more vividly: dead things materializing behind gaping holes in stained-glass portals and half-open doorways, some of them still clad in ragged, blood-soaked clerical vestments, some of them in Sunday-go-to-meeting suits and crepe dresses drenched with gore. Some of them are gnawing on severed human appendages, while others carry body parts at their sides, the organs still dripping from the gruesome orgy inside the chapel. There are at least fifty, maybe more, and they move side by side with a lurching purpose toward the police car.

For a single instant, before throwing open his door and joining Nick outside the car, Brian finds his mind flashing on a strange thought: *They are moving as one—even in death, still a tightly knit congregation—like puppets of some great overmind.* But the notion quickly flies from his thoughts as he hears the call of his brother from behind the wheel of the cop car.

"PUSH THE SON OF THE BITCH WITH EVERYTHING YOU GOT AND THEN HOP ON!"

Now Brian joins Nick behind the car and then, without really even thinking about it, begins to push. By this point Philip has jammed the thing into neutral, and has his door open, and his leg outside the car, and is shoving the thing with his boot with all his might.

It takes them a few moments to build up steam—the churchgoing hoard behind them approaching steadily, dropping their ghastly treasures amid the promise of fresh meat—but soon the cruiser is coasting rapidly down the hill, faster and faster, to the point where Brian and Nick have to hop on board. Nick grasps the whip antenna for purchase. Brian gets halfway inside the flapping rear door, but can't get himself the rest of the way inside without falling, so he holds tightly to the door's frame.

By this point the car is halfway down the hill, putting distance between them and the scores of undead shambling after them. The weight of the vehicle is building inertia. The Crown Victoria now feels as though it's a runaway train, bumping down the cracked pavement toward the intersection at the bottom of the hill. The wind whips Brian's dark hair as he holds on for dear life.

Nick hollers something, but the noise of the wind and the thumping wheels drown out his voice. At the bottom of the hill lies a defunct Conrail switchyard, its maze of ancient rails fossilized into the Georgia earth, its ramshackle sheds and office buildings as black and decayed as prehistoric ruins. Philip is yelling something that Brian cannot hear.

They reach the bottom of the hill and the steering wheel locks up.

The squad car bangs over the track and careens into the switchyard. Philip cannot turn the wheel. The car skids. The wheels cut into the cinders, the undercarriage sparking off the iron.

Brian and Nick hold on tight as the cruiser skuds to a halt in a cloud of black dust.

"Grab your shit! Everybody! Now!" Philip already has his door open and he's already pulling Penny out. Brian and Nick hop off the rear end and join Philip, who hefts his duffel onto one shoulder and lifts his daughter onto the other. "This way!" He nods toward a narrow street to the west.

They hurry out of the switchyard.

A row of boarded storefronts and burned-out buildings stretches down a perpendicular cobblestone road.

They move quickly along, staying tight under a row of awnings on the south side of the street, their shoulders brushing graffiti-stained doors and Rust-Oleum-flecked windows. The dusk is closing in and shadows are lengthening, burying them in gloom.

The sense of being surrounded is overwhelming, although at the moment they don't see any creatures, just a long corridor of shitty, obsolete businesses once serving this corroded, forsaken part of Atlanta's outskirts: pawnshops, currency exchanges, bail bondsmen, auto parts places, taverns, and junk shops.

As they move along the scarred storefronts, huffing and puffing with the weight of their loads, not daring to speak or make any unnecessary noise, the urgency of getting inside somewhere begins to work on them. Night is falling again, and this place will be the dark side of the moon in less than an hour. They have no map, no GPS, no compass, no sense of where they are other than the misty landmark of the skyline miles to the west.

Brian feels the anxiety on the back of his neck like a cold finger. They turn a corner.

Brian sees the mechanic's shop first, but Philip sees it a split second later and motions toward it with a nod. "Up there on the corner, see it?"

Nick sees it now. "Yeah, yeah . . . looks good."

It does *indeed* look good: On the southwest corner of a deserted intersection one block away, Donlevy's Autobody and Repair appears to be the only business in this godforsaken area that has any life still in it—although it currently appears closed for the season.

They hasten toward the building.

As they approach, they see that the half-acre lot is recently repaved. The two islands of gas pumps out front, clean and apparently operational, sit under a giant Chevron sign. The building itself—lined with columns of new tires, fronted on one side by a pair of massive double garage doors—is a gleaming slab of silver metal siding and reinforced glass. There's even a second floor, housing either an office or more retail space.

Philip leads them around back. The rear of the place is tidy, with newly painted garbage Dumpsters shoved up against the cinderblock back wall. They search for a door or window but find neither.

"What about the front door?" Brian says in a breathless whisper as they pause next to the Dumpsters. They can hear the congregation coming down the street, the shuffling, groaning chorus of fifty-plus zombies.

"I'm sure it's locked," Philip says, his gaunt, hard face shiny from the labors of carrying his daughter and his duffel. Penny is compulsively, nervously sucking her thumb against his shoulder.

"How do you know?"

Philip shrugs. "Guess it's worth a try."

They creep around the far side of the building, and they stay in the shadows under the Chevron awning, as Philip sets Penny and duffel down and hurries up to the entrance door. He yanks the handle.

It's open.

EIGHT

They huddle for some time inside the repair center's front office, under the cashier's counter, next to a spinner rack of candy bars and potato chips.

Philip locks the door and crouches next to the others in the shadows, watching the parade of undead out on the street, passing by the shop, oblivious to the whereabouts of their prey, stupidly scanning with their button eyes like dogs hearing high-pitched whistles.

From this vantage point, gazing through the meshed, reinforced windows, Brian gets a chance to scrutinize the dead clergy and ragged parishioners as they awkwardly promenade past the service station. How did this church full of true believers turn en masse? Did they gather as frightened Christians after the plague had broken out, cleaving to each other for succor and comfort? Did they hear fire-and-brimstone sermons from the preachers about the Revelation to John? Did the pastors furiously cant warning parables: "'And the fifth angel blew his trumpet, and I saw a star fallen from heaven to earth, and he was given the key to the shaft of the bottomless pit!'"

And how did the first one turn? Was it somebody in a back pew having a heart attack? Was it a ritual suicide? Brian imagines one of those old black ladies—her system clogged with cholesterol, her plump, gloved hands waving with the spirit—suddenly clutching her massive bosom at the first twinge of a coronary. And minutes later—maybe in an hour or so—the woman rises, her porcine face full of a *new religion*, a singular, savage faith.

"Fucking Holy Rollers," Philip grumbles from across the cashier's counter. Then he turns to Penny and swallows contritely. "Sorry for the language, punkin."

They explore the repair center. The place is spotless and secure, cold but clean, the floors swept, the shelves well ordered, the cool air redolent with the odors of new rubber and the vaguely pleasant chemical fragrance of fuels and fluids. They realize they can stay here for the night, but it is not until they investigate the large repair garage that they make their most fortuitous discovery.

"Holy crap, it's a tank," Brian says, standing on the cold cement, shining a flashlight at the black beauty parked under canvas tarps in one corner.

The others gather around the sole vehicle standing in the darkness. Philip whips off the tarp. It's a late-model Cadillac Escalade in cherry condition, its onyx finish gleaming in the yellow light.

"Probably belonged to the owner," Nick ventures.

"Christmas comes early," Philip says, kicking one of the massive tires with his muddy work boot. The luxury SUV is enormous, with huge molded bumpers, giant vertical headlights, and big, shiny chrome wheels. It looks like the kind of vehicle a secret government agency would have in its fleet, the sinister tinted windows reflecting the bloom of the flashlight back at them.

"There's nobody inside it, right?" Brian shines the beam off the opaque glass.

Philip pulls the .22 from his belt, clicks a door open, and points the muzzle in at the empty, showroom-clean interior, with its wood trim, leather seats, and console that looks like a control center for an airliner.

Philip says, "Bet you a dollar to a doughnut there's keys in a drawer somewhere."

The whole incident with the cop and the church seems to have pushed Penny into a deeper stupor. She sleeps that night curled into a fetal ball on the floor of the repair area, covered in blankets, her thumb in her mouth.

"Haven't seen her do that in a coon's age," Philip remarks nearby, sitting on his bedroll with the last of the whiskey. He wears a sleeveless T-shirt and filthy jeans, his boots sitting next to him. He takes a sip and wipes his mouth.

"Do what?" Brian is sitting cross-legged, bundled in his blood-spattered coat, on the other side of the little girl, careful not to speak too loudly. Nick dozes over by a workbench, zipped in a sleeping bag. The temperature has plunged into the forties.

"Suck her thumb like that," Philip says.

"She's dealing with a lot."

"We all are."

"Yeah." Brian stares into his lap. "We'll make it, though."

"Make it where?"

Brian looks up. "The refugee center. Wherever it is . . . we'll find it."

"Yeah, sure." Philip kills the rest of the bottle and sets it down. "We'll find the place and the sun'll come out tomorrow and all the orphans will find good homes and the Braves will win the fucking pennant."

"Something bothering you?"

Philip shakes his head. "Jesus Christ, Brian, open your eyes."

"Are you mad at me?"

Philip stands and stretches his sore neck. "Now why the fuck would I be mad at *you*, sport? It's business as usual. No big deal."

"What does that mean?"

"Nothing . . . just get some sleep." Philip walks over to the Escalade, kneels down, and looks under the chassis for something.

Brian climbs to his feet, his heart racing. He feels dizzy. His sore throat is better, and he stopped coughing after a few days of rest and rejuvenation in the Wiltshire house, but he still does not feel a hundred percent. Who does? He goes over and stands behind his brother. "What do you mean by 'business as usual'?"

"It is what it is," Philip mutters, checking the SUV's underbelly.

"You're mad about the cop," Brian says.

Philip stands up slowly, turns, and comes face-to-face with his brother. "I said go to sleep."

"Maybe I have a harder time shooting something that was once human—so sue me."

Philip grabs Brian by the nape of the T-shirt, spins him around, and slams him back against the side of the Escalade. The impact nearly knocks the breath out of Brian, and the noise wakes up Nick, and it even makes Penny stir. "You listen to me," Philip growls in a threatening, husky voice that's both sober and drunk at the same time. "Next time you take a gun from me, you make sure you're ready to put it to good use. That cop was harmless, but who knows about next time, and I ain't gonna be the one babysitting you with nothin' but my gonads in my hand, you understand? You read me?"

Brian is nodding, his throat dry with terror. "Yes."

Philip increases the pressure on Brian's shirt. "You better get past your namby-pamby bullshit sheltered life and start carrying your weight around here and stoving some heads in because it sure as hell is gonna get worse before it gets better!"

"I understand," Brian says.

Philip doesn't let go, his eyes glinting with rage. "We're gonna survive this thing, and we're gonna do it by being bigger monsters than they are! You understand? There ain't no rules anymore! There ain't no philosophy, there ain't no grace, there ain't no mercy, there's only us and them, and all they wanna do is *eat* our ass! So we're gonna fucking eat *them*! We're gonna chew 'em up and spit 'em out, and we're gonna survive this thing or I will blow a hole through this whole fucked-up world! You follow me? You FOLLOW ME!"

Brian nods like crazy.

Philip lets him go and walks away.

By this point Nick is awake and sitting up, and staring agape.

Penny's eyes are wide and she furiously sucks her thumb, watching her father storm across the repair floor. He walks over to the massive reinforced garage doors, pauses, and stares out at the night though the slatted burglar bars, his big gnarly fists clenched.

Across the floor, still pinned against the side of the Escalade, Brian

Blake wages a silent battle to keep from crying like a namby-pamby-bullshit-sheltered-baby.

The next morning, in the lambent daylight filtering into the shop, they hurry through a breakfast of cereal bars and bottled water, and then pour the contents of three five-gallon jugs of gas into the Escalade's tank. They find the keys in a drawer in the office, and they pack all their belongings in the SUV's cargo area. The tinted windows are fogged with condensation from the cold. Brian and Penny settle into the backseat while Nick stands at the garage door awaiting Philip's signal. Since the power is down—seemingly everywhere now—they are forced to spring the manual latch on the automated door opener.

Now Philip climbs behind the wheel of the Escalade and fires it up. The huge six-point-two-liter V-8 hums. The console lights up. Philip jacks it into gear and edges forward, giving Nick the signal.

Nick yanks the closest garage door, and the casters squeak, as the thing rises on its tracks. The light and air of the day explode through the windshield, as Nick hustles around to the passenger side door and climbs into the shotgun seat. The door slams.

Philip pauses for a moment, looking down at the dash.

"What's the matter?" Nick says in a shaky voice, still a little nervous about questioning anything Philip does. "Shouldn't we maybe get moving?"

"One second," Philip says, reaching down to a pull-out drawer.

Inside a spring-loaded map case he finds about two dozen CDs, neatly organized by the former owner—Calvin R. Donlevy of 601 Greencove Lane S.E. (according to the registration in the glove box). "Here we go," Philip says, rifling through the discs. Calvin R. Donlevy of Greencove Lane is apparently a lover of classic rock, judging by all the Zeppelin, Sabbath, and Hendrix in his collection. "A little somethin' to help with the concentration."

All at once a Cheap Trick disc goes in and Philip puts the hammer down.

The gravitational thrust of four hundred fifty horses pushes them against the seats, as the wide-body Escalade blasts off through the opening, barely making it through the gap without sideswiping the metal trusses. Daylight floods the interior. The buzz-saw guitar intro of the party anthem "Hello There" leaps out of the Bose 5.1 surround sound system, as they boom across the lot and into the street.

Cheap Trick's lead singer asks if all the ladies and gentlemen are ready to rock.

Philip roars around the corner and heads north on Maynard Terrace. The street widens. Lower-income homes blur by on either side of the vehicle. A wandering zombie in a torn raincoat looms off to the right, and Philip veers toward the thing.

The sickening thump is barely audible above the roar of the engine (and the thunderous drumbeats of Cheap Trick). In back Brian sinks down lower in his seat, feeling sick to his stomach and worrying about Penny. She slumps in her seat next to him, staring straight ahead.

Brian reaches over and buckles her in and tries to give her a smile.

"Gotta be an entrance ramp north of here," Philip is saying over the noise, but the sound of his voice is almost completely drowned by the growl of the engine and the music. Two more walking dead loom off to their left, a man and woman in tatters, maybe homeless people, scuttling along the curb, and Philip happily swerves and takes them both down like soggy bowling pins.

A severed ear sticks to the windshield, and Philip puts the wipers on.

They reach the north end of Maynard Terrace, the entrance ramp straight ahead. Philip slams the brakes. The Escalade screams to a stop in front of a six-car pileup at the foot of the ramp, a cluster of upright corpses circling the wreckage like lazy buzzards.

Philip snaps the lever into reverse. The pedal goes down, the rock music thundering. The gravitational force sucks everybody forward. Brian braces Penny against her seat.

A yank of the wheel, and the Escalade does a one-eighty, then charges back down McPherson Avenue—which runs parallel to the interstate.

They cross a mile of real estate in a couple of minutes, with kick drum and bass providing syncopated beats to the horrible thumping of errant dead, too slow to get out of the way, colliding with the massive quarter panels and launching into the air like giant flailing birds. More and more of them are emerging from the shadows and trees, awakened by the bellowing growl of the muscle car.

Philip's jaws tense with grim determination as they near another entrance ramp.

The brakes lock up at Faith Avenue, where a Burger Win burns out of control, the whole area fogbound with greasy smoke. This ramp is blocked worse than the last. Philip yells a garbled curse, and then slams the thing into reverse, rocketing backward.

The Escalade swerves over to an adjacent side street. Another yank of the steering wheel. Another kick of the pedal. Now they're burning rubber again, moving westward, weaving around roadblocks, heading toward the skyscrapers in the distance, which loom larger and larger like apparitions in the haze.

The increasing number of blocked streets, debris, ruined cars, and wandering dead seem insurmountable, but Philip Blake will not be denied. He sits hunched over the wheel, breathing thickly, eyes fixed on the horizon. He passes a Publix grocery store that looks as though it's been bombed in a blitzkrieg, its lot infested with dead.

Philip increases his speed in order to plow through a file of zombies in the street.

The tide of gore splashing up across the SUV's huge hood is spectacular—a lurid display of morbid tissue spraying up and blossoming across the windshield. Wipers swish and streak the gruesome remains.

In the backseat Brian turns to his niece. "Kiddo?" No answer. "Penny?"

The child's vacant stare is fixed on the Technicolor display across the windshield. She doesn't seem to hear Brian over the din of rock and roll and the rumble of the car, or perhaps she chooses *not* to hear him, or perhaps she's too far gone to hear anything.

Brian gently taps her shoulder, and she snaps her gaze at him.

Then Brian reaches across her, and carefully writes a single word on the inside of her fogged window:

AWAY

Brian remembers reading somewhere that the Atlanta metro area was up to almost six million people. He remembers being surprised at the number. Atlanta always seemed to Brian to be a sort of miniature metropolis, a mere token of Southern Progress, isolated in a sea of sleepy little redneck burgs. The few visits he had taken to the city at ground level gave him the impression that the town was one giant suburb. Sure, it had its midtown canyon of tall buildings—it had Turner and Coke and Delta and the Falcons and all the rest— but mostly it seemed like a little sister to the great northern cities. Brian had been to New York once, visiting his ex-wife's family, and that vast, grimy, claustrophobic antfarm had seemed like a *real* city to Brian. Atlanta seemed like a *simulacrum* of a city. Maybe part of it was the town's history, which Brian remembers learning about in a college survey course: During Reconstruction, after Sherman had torched the place, the planners decided to let the old historic landmarks go the way of the dodo bird; and over the next century and a half Atlanta got tarted up in steel and glass. Unlike other Southern towns like Savannah and New Orleans—where the flavor of the Old South still proudly permeates—Atlanta turned to the bland surfaces of modern expressionism. *Look, Ma,* they seemed to say, *we're progressive, we're cosmopolitan, we're cool, not like those bumpkins in Birmingham.* But to Brian it always seemed like the Lady Atlanta "doth protested too much." To Brian, Atlanta had always been a pretend city.

Until now.

Over the course of those next horrible twenty-five minutes, as Philip relentlessly zigzags down desolate side streets and across leprous vacant lots running parallel to the interstate, carving their way closer and closer to the heart of town, Brian sees the real Atlanta like a flickering slide show of forensic crime scene photos outside the tinted windows of the hermetically sealed SUV. He sees blind alleys choked with wreckage, flaming trash heaps, housing projects plundered and abandoned, windows blown out everywhere, stained sheets hanging out of buildings scrawled with desperate pleas for help. This is *indeed* a city—a primeval necropolis—overcrowded and malodorous with death. And the worst part of it is, they are not yet to the border of the downtown area.

At approximately 10:22 A.M. Central Standard Time, Philip Blake manages to find Capital Avenue, a wide six-lane thoroughfare that wends past Turner Field and then downtown. He turns the stereo off. The silence booms in their ears as they turn onto Capital and then slowly proceed north.

The road is cluttered with abandoned cars, but they're spaced far enough apart for the Escalade to weave in between them. The spires of skyscrapers—off to the left—are so close now they seem to glow in the haze like the mainsails of rescue ships.

Nobody says a thing as they roll past oceans of cement on either side of the street. The stadium parking lots are mostly empty. A few golf carts overturned here and there. Vending trucks sit in the corners, all closed up and defaced with graffiti. Scattered dead, way in the distance, wander the gray barrens in the cold autumn daylight.

They look like stray dogs about to fall over from malnutrition.

Philip rolls down his window and listens. The wind whistles. It has an odd smell to it—a mélange of burning rubber, melted circuits, and something oily and hard to identify like rotting tallow—and something chugs in the distance, vibrating the air like a vast engine.

A realization twists in Brian's gut. If the refugee centers are open somewhere to the west—somewhere in the ventricles of the city—wouldn't there be emergency vehicles out here? Signs? Checkpoints? Armed marshals somewhere? Police helicopters? Wouldn't there be some indication—this close to the downtown area—that relief is in sight? Up to this point, over the course of their journey into the city, they have seen only a few potential signs of life. Back on Glenwood

Avenue they thought they saw someone on a motorcycle flash by but they couldn't be sure. Later, on Sydney Street, Nick said he saw someone darting across a doorway but he wouldn't swear to it.

Brian pushes the thoughts out of his mind when he sees the vast tangle of highways forming a cloverleaf about a quarter of a mile away.

This sprawling interchange of major arteries marks the eastern border of Atlanta's urban area—the place where Interstate 20 meets up with 85, 75, and 403—and now it sits baking in the cold sun like a forgotten battlefield, clogged with wrecks and overturned semis. Brian feels the Escalade beginning to ascend a steep upgrade.

Capital Avenue rises on massive pilings over the interchange. Philip takes the incline slowly, snaking through an obstacle course of deserted wrecks at about fifteen miles an hour.

Brian feels a tapping on his left shoulder, and he realizes that Penny is trying to get his attention. He turns and looks at her.

She leans over and whispers something to him. It sounds like, "I can't see."

Brian looks at her. "You can't see?"

She shakes her head and whispers it again.

This time, Brian understands. "Can you hold it for a minute, kiddo?"

Philip hears this, and he glances in the rearview. "What's the matter?"

"She has to pee."

"Oh boy," Philip says. "Sorry, punkin, you're gonna have to cross your legs for a few minutes."

Penny whispers to Brian that she really, really, *really* has to go.

"She's gotta go, Philip," Brian informs his brother. "Really bad."

"Just hold it for a little bit, punkin."

They are approaching the zenith of the hill. At night, the view from this part of the city, as a motorist crosses Capital Avenue, must be gorgeous. There's a moment coming, about a hundred yards in the distance now, when the Escalade will clear the shadow of a tall building to the west. At night, the luminous constellations of city lights come into view at this point, providing a breathtaking panorama of the capitol dome in the foreground, and the sparkling cathedral of skyscrapers behind it.

They clear the shadow of the building, and they see the city spread out before them in all its glory. Philip slams on the brakes.

The Escalade lurches to a stop.

They sit there for an endless moment, all of them stricken speechless.

The street to the left runs along the front of the venerable old marble edifice of the capitol building. It is one-way going the wrong way, completely choked with abandoned cars. But that is not why everyone in the SUV is suddenly thunderstruck. The reason why nobody can muster a word—the silence lasting only a second, but seeming to go on for an eternity—is because of what they see coming at them down Capital Avenue from the north.

Penny wets herself.

The greeting party, as copious as a Roman army and as slapdash as a swarm of giant arachnids, comes from Martin Luther King Drive, a little over a block away. They come from the cool shadows where government buildings block out the sun, and there are so many of them that it takes a moment for the human eye to simply register what it is seeing. All shapes and sizes and stages of deterioration, they emerge from doorways and windows and alleys and wooded squares and nooks and crannies, and they fill the street with the profusion of a disordered marching band, drawn to the noise and smell and advent of a fresh automobile filled with fresh meat.

Old and young, black and white, men and women, former businessmen, housewives, civil servants, hustlers, children, thugs, teachers, lawyers, nurses, cops, garbage men, and prostitutes, each and every one of their faces uniformly pale and decomposed, like an endless orchard of shriveled fruit rotting in the sun—a thousand pairs of lifeless gunmetal-gray eyes locking in unison onto the Escalade, a thousand feral, primordial tracking devices fixing themselves hungrily on the newcomers in their midst.

Over the course of that single instant of horror-stricken silence,

Philip makes a number of realizations with the speed of a synapse firing.

He realizes he can smell the telltale odor of the horde coming through the open window, and possibly even the air vents in the dash: that sickening, rancid bacon-and-shit stench. But more than that, he realizes that the strange drone he heard earlier, when he rolled down his window—that vibrating hum in the air like the twanging of a million high-tension wires—is the sound of a city full of the dead.

Their collective groaning, as they now labor as one giant multi-faceted organism toward the Escalade, makes Philip's skin crawl.

All of which leads to one final realization that strikes Philip Blake between the eyes with the force of a ball-peen hammer. It occurs to him—considering the sight unfolding in almost dreamy slow motion in front of him—that the quest to find a refugee center in this town, not to mention anyone still alive, is fast becoming about as prudent as the boy looking for a pony in a pile of horseshit.

In that microsecond of dread—that minuscule soupçon of frozen stillness—Philip realizes that the sun will probably not be coming out tomorrow, and the orphans will stay orphans, and the Braves will never again win the fucking pennant.

Before jerking the shift lever he turns to the others and in a voice laced with bitterness says, "Show of hands, how many y'all still hot to find that refugee center?"

PART 2

Atlanta

He who fights too long against dragons becomes a dragon
himself; and if you gaze too long into the abyss,
the abyss will gaze into you.

—Nietzsche

NINE

Very few production cars on the road—in the U.S., at least—are capable of attaining any kind of speed in reverse. First of all, there's the gear problem. Most cars, vans, pickups, and sport-utility vehicles that come off the line have five or six forward gears but only one for reverse. Second of all, most vehicles have front suspensions designed to go forward not backward. This prevents drivers from getting up a head of steam in reverse. Third of all, in reverse you're usually steering by looking over your shoulder, and pushing cars to top speeds in this fashion usually terminates in spectacular spinouts.

On the other hand, the vehicle that Philip Blake is currently commandeering is a 2011 Platinum Cadillac Escalade with all-wheel drive and tricked-out torsion bars for any off-road applications that ace mechanic Calvin R. Donlevy of Greencove Lane might have endeavored to undertake in the backwaters of Central Georgia (in happier times). The vehicle weighs in at nearly four tons, and is close to seventeen feet long, with a StabiliTrak electronic stability control system (standard on all Platinum models). Best of all, it's equipped with a rearview camera that displays on a generous seven-inch navigation screen built into the dash.

Without hesitation, his nervous system wired to his right hand, Philip slams the lever into reverse, and keeps his gaze riveted to that flickering yellow image materializing on the navigation screen. The image shows the partly cloudy sky over the horizon line of pavement behind them: *the top of the overpass.*

Before the oncoming regiment of zombies have a chance to get within fifty yards, the Escalade rockets backward.

The g-forces suck everybody forward—Brian and Nick each twisting around to gaze out the tinted rear window at the overpass rushing toward them—as the tail end of the Escalade shimmies slightly, the vehicle building speed. Philip pushes it hard. The engine screams. Philip doesn't turn around. He keeps his gaze locked onto that screen, the little glowing yellow picture showing the top of the overpass growing larger and larger.

One slight miscalculation—a single foot-pound of pressure on the steering wheel in either direction—and the Escalade goes into a spin. But Philip keeps the wheel steady, and his foot on the gas, and his eyes on the screen, as the vehicle tears backward faster and faster— the engine now singing high opera, somewhere in the vicinity of C sharp. On the monitor Philip sees something change.

"Aw shit . . . look!"

Brian's voice pierces the noise of the engine but Philip doesn't have to look. In the little yellow square of video he sees a series of dark figures appearing a couple hundred feet away, directly in their path, at the top of the overpass, like the pickets of a fence. They're moving slowly, in a haphazard formation, their arms opening to receive the vehicle now hurtling directly at them. Philip lets out an angry grunt.

He slams both work boots down on the brake pad, and the Escalade skids and smokes to a sudden stop on the sloping pavement.

At this point Philip realizes—along with everybody else—that they have one chance, and the window of that opportunity is going to close very quickly. The dead things coming at them from the front are still a hundred yards off, but the hordes behind them, shambling over the crest of the viaduct from the projects and vacant lots around Turner Field, are closing in with alarming speed, considering their ponderous, leaden movements. Philip can see in a side mirror that an adjoining street called Memorial Drive is accessible between two overturned trailers, but the army of zombies that are looming close and closer in his rearview will be reaching that cross street very soon themselves.

He makes an instantaneous decision, and bangs down on the accelerator.

The Escalade roars backward. Everybody holds on. Philip backs it straight toward the crowd of shuffling corpses. On the video monitor the image shows the columns of zombies excitedly reaching out, mouths gaping, as they grow larger and larger on the screen.

Memorial Drive comes into view on the camera, and Philip stomps on the brake.

The rear of the Escalade bowls over a row of the undead with a nauseating, muffled drumming noise, as Philip rips the shift lever back into drive, his logger boot already pushing the pedal to the floor. They all sink into the upholstery as the SUV lunges forward, Philip taking a sharp left, threading the needle between two ruined trailers.

Sparks jump in the air as the SUV swipes a side rail, and then it's through the gap and fleeing down the relatively clear and blessedly zombie-free lanes of Memorial Drive.

Hardly a minute goes by before Brian hears the scraping noise. It's a coarse, wet, keening sound coming from under the chassis. The others hear it, too. Nick looks over his shoulder. "What the hell is that noise?"

"Something's caught under the wheels," Brian says, trying to see the side of the car out his window. He can't see anything.

Philip is silent, his hands welded to the steering wheel, his jaw set and tense.

Nick is looking out at the side mirror. "One of those things is stuck under the wheel!"

"Oh *great*," Brian says, twisting in his seat. He notices a tiny fan of blood droplets across the back window. "What are we gonna—"

"Let it ride along," Philip says flatly, not taking his eyes off the street. "It'll be pulp in a few minutes."

They get about six blocks, bumping across a set of railroad tracks—getting deeper into the city—before encountering much more than a few isolated wrecks and roaming dead. The grid of streets threading between the buildings is choked with debris, the remnants of explosions, burned cars filled with charred skeletons, windows blown out, and piles of trash and detritus drifted up against storefronts. Somewhere along the way, the scraping noises cease, although nobody sees what has happened to the hanger-on.

Philip decides to take a north-south street into the heart of the city, but when he turns right—swerving around a mangled delivery truck on its side in the center of the intersection—he hits the brakes. The Escalade jerks to a stop.

They sit there for a moment, the engine idling. Philip doesn't move, his hands still white-knuckling the wheel, his eyes squinting as he gazes into the distant shadows of tall buildings straight ahead.

At first, Brian can't see what the problem is. He cranes his neck to glimpse the litter-strewn city street stretching many blocks before them. Through the tinted glass, he sees high-rises on either side of the four-lane avenue. Trash swirls in the September wind.

Nick is also puzzled by the sudden stop. "What's wrong, Philip?"

Philip doesn't respond. He keeps staring straight ahead with that uneasy stillness, his teeth clenching, his jaws working.

"Philip?"

No response.

Nick turns back to the windshield and stares out at the street. His expression tightens. He sees now what Philip sees. He gets very still.

"Will somebody tell me what's going on?" Brian says, leaning forward to see better. For a moment, all he can make out is the distant canyon of high-rises, and many blocks of debris-littered pavement. But he realizes soon enough that he's seeing a still life of a desolate city beginning to rapidly change like a giant organism reacting to the intrusion of foreign bacteria. What Brian sees through that shaded window glass is so horrible that he begins moving his mouth without saying anything.

In that single instant of brain-numbing awe, Brian Blake flashes back to a ridiculous memory from his childhood, the madness of the moment gripping his mind. One time, his mom took him and

Philip to the Barnum and Bailey Circus in Athens. The boys were maybe thirteen and ten respectively, and they reveled in the high-wire acts, the tigers jumping through flaming rings, the men shooting out of cannons, the acrobats, the cotton candy, the elephants, the sideshows, the sword swallower, the human dart board, the fire-eaters, the bearded ladies, and the snake charmer. But the memory that sticks with Brian the most—and what he thinks of right at this moment—is the clown car. That day in Athens, at the height of the show, a little goofy car pulled out across the center ring. It was a cartoonish sedan with painted windows, about the size of a station wagon, built low to the ground and painted in a patchwork of Day-Glo colors. Brian remembers it so vividly—how he laughed his head off at the clowns piling out of the car, one after another, and how at first it was just funny, and then it became kind of amazing, and finally it was just downright bizarre, because the clowns kept coming: six, eight, ten, twenty—big ones, little ones—they kept climbing out of that car as though it was a magic container of freeze-dried clowns. Even as a thirteen-year-old, Brian was transfixed by the gag, knowing full well there had to be a trick to it, maybe a trapdoor embedded in the sawdust beneath the car, but it didn't matter because the very sight of it was mesmerizing.

That exact phenomenon—or at least a perverted facsimile of it—is now unfolding right before Brian's eyes along an urban thorough-fare in the lower bowels of midtown Atlanta. He gapes silently at it for a moment, trying to put the gruesome spectacle into words.

"Turn around, Philip." Brian's voice sounds hollow and reedy in his own ears as he stares at the countless throngs of undead awak-ening in every corner of the city before them. If the horde they en-countered only moments ago on their way into town was a regiment of a Roman army, this—*this*—is the whole empire.

As far as the eye can see, down the narrow channel of the four-lane street, the undead emerge from buildings, from behind cars, from within wreckage, from the shadows of alleys, from busted-out display windows, from the marble porticos of government build-ings, from the spindly planters of decorative trees, and from the tattered remains of sidewalk cafés. They are even visible in the far distance, where the vanishing point of the street blurs into the shadows of skyscrapers, their ragged silhouettes appearing like a myriad of slow-moving bugs roused from the darkness of an overturned rock. Their number defies logic.

"We gotta get outta here," Nick says in a rusty squeak of a voice.

Philip, still stoic and silent, works his clenched fingers on the steering wheel.

Nick nervously shoots a glance over his shoulder. "We gotta go back."

"He's right, Philip," Brian says, putting a hand gently on Penny's shoulder.

"What's the matter, what are you doing?" Nick looks at Philip. "Why aren't you turning around?"

Brian looks at the back of his brother's head. "There's too many of them, Philip. There's too many of them. There's too many."

"Oh my God, we're fucked . . . we're *fucked*," Nick says, transfixed by the ghastly miracle building across their path. The closest ones are maybe half a block away, like the leading edge of a tsunami—they look like office dwellers of both genders, still clad in corporate attire that appears shredded and chewed up and dipped in axle grease—and they stagger this way like snarling sleepwalkers.

Behind them, for blocks and blocks, countless others stumble along the sidewalks and down the center of the street. If there is a "rush hour" in hell, it most certainly can't hold a candle to *this*. Through the Escalade's air vents and windows, the tuneless symphony of a hundred thousand moans raises the hackles on the back of Brian's neck, and he reaches over and taps his brother on the shoulder. "The city's gone, Philip."

"Yeah, yeah, he's right, the place is toast, we gotta turn around," Nick babbles.

"One second." Philip's voice is ice cold. "Hold on."

"Philip, come on," Brian says. "This place belongs to them now."

"I said hold on."

Brian stares at the back of his brother's head and a cold sensation trickles down Brian's spine. He realizes that what Philip means by the phrase *hold on* is not "hold on a second while I think this over" or "hold on for a minute while I figure this thing out."

What Philip Blake means by *hold on* is—

"Y'all got your seat belts on?" he asks rhetorically, making Brian's skin turn cold.

"Philip, don't—"

Philip kicks the foot feed. The Escalade erupts into motion. He steers the vehicle straight into the teeming mob, cutting off Brian's thoughts and pressing everybody into their seats.

"PHILLY, NO!"

Nick's warning cry dissolves into a salvo of muffled thumps, like the beating of a giant tom-tom drum, as the Escalade jumps the sidewalk and mows down at least three dozen zombies.

Tissue and fluids rain across the car.

Brian is so unnerved that he ducks down against the floor and joins Penny in that place called *away*.

The smaller ones go down like ducks in a shooting gallery, bursting apart under the wheels and leaving a trail of rotting innards. The larger ones bounce off the quarter panels and hurtle through the air, smacking the sides of buildings and coming apart like overripe fruit.

The dead seem to have no capacity to learn. Even a moth will flitter away once it flies too close to a flame. But this vast society of walking corpses in Atlanta apparently have no clue as to why they can't eat the shiny black thing roaring at them—the same thundering piece of metal that just an instant ago turned their fellow zombies into blood pudding—so they just keep coming.

Hunched over the wheel, teeth gnashing, knuckles white, Philip uses the wipers, with periodic sprays of cleaning solution, to keep the windshield clean enough to see through as he chews his way north, plowing the 8,300 pounds of Detroit iron through the moving sea of zombies. Varying his speed between thirty and fifty miles an hour, he carves a path toward the center of town.

At times, he is literally cutting a swath through a crowd so dense that it's like blazing a trail through a thick forest of blood fruit, the flailing arms and curled fingers like tree limbs, clawing at the side windows as the Escalade digs through the walking excrement. At other times, the SUV crosses short sections of clear street, with only a few zombies trundling along on a sidewalk or at the edges of the pavement, and this gives Philip a chance to get his speed up, and to swerve to the right to a pick a few off, and then to the left for a few more, and then he'll hit another wall-to-wall mob, and that's probably the most fun, because that's when the shit really flies.

It's almost as though the viscera is raining down from above, from the sky, rather than from under the wheels or along the frame or over the top of the big front grill as the Escalade shears through the bodies. The wet matter streaks across the glass, again and again, with the rhythm of a giant pinwheel, a kaleidoscope of color, the palette like a rainbow of human tissue—oxblood red, pond-scum green, burnt-ocher yellow, and pine-tar black—and it's almost kind of beautiful to Philip.

He roars around a corner and plunges into another mass of zombies coming down the street.

The strangest part is the continual repetitive flashes of similar tissues and organs—some of them recognizable, some of them not so recognizable. Entrails fly in all directions, splashing the windshield and sliding across the hood. Little kernels of teeth periodically gather in the wiper blades, and something else, something pink, like little pearls of fish roe, keeps collecting in the seams of the hood.

Philip glimpses dead face after dead face, each one flashing in his window—visible one moment, gone the next—and he's in a zone now, he's somewhere else, not in the SUV, not behind the wheel, but *inside* the mob, inside the city of undead, chewing through their ranks, devouring the motherfuckers. Philip is the baddest monster of them all, and he's going to make it through this ocean of shit if he has to tear down the entire universe.

Brian realizes what is happening before he even looks. Ten excruciating minutes after they started mowing through the sea of zombies—

after making it across nearly twenty-three city blocks—the Escalade goes into a spin.

The centripetal force tugs Brian against the floor, and he pops his head up—peering over the seat—as the SUV slides sideways on the grease of fifty thousand corpses. He has no time to yell or do anything about what is happening. He can only brace himself and Penny against the seat backs for the inevitable impact.

Wheels slick with gore, the SUV does a three-sixty, the rear end windmilling through the last few stray cadavers. The city blurs outside the windows, and Philip fights the wheel, tries to straighten it, but the tires are hydroplaning on a sheet of intestines and blood and spoor.

Brian lets out a strangled yelp—part warning and part inarticulate cry—as the vehicle spins toward a row of storefronts.

In the frenzied moments before the crash, Brian glimpses a row of derelict shop windows: hatless busts of bald mannequins, empty jewelry displays, frayed wires growing out of vacant floorboards, all of it blurred behind the wire-meshed display windows. But it's just a vague impression of these things, Brian's vision distorted by the violent spinning of the SUV.

And that's when the right side of the Escalade collides with the display window.

The crash has that suspension-of-time feeling for Brian, the store window turning to stardust, the noise of shattering glass like a wave slamming a breakwater as the Escalade punctures the burglar bars and plunges sideways into the dark shadows of the Goldberg Fine Jewelry Center of Atlanta.

Counters and display cases explode in all directions, a sparkling, silver sleet of debris as the gravitational forces yank all passengers to the right. The Escalade's airbags deploy in tiny explosions—great heaving balloons of white nylon filling the interior before it has a chance to collapse—and Nick is thrown sideways into the white fabric. Philip is flung sideways into Nick, and Penny is thrown across the rear floor into Brian.

The SUV skids sideways for an eternity through the empty store.

The vehicle finally comes to rest after slamming hard into a weight-bearing pillar in the center of the store, shoving everybody hard against the padded lining of the airbags, and for a moment, nobody moves.

White, feathery debris snows down through the dark, dusty air of the jewelry store, and the sounds of something collapsing behind them creaks in the sudden silence. Brian glances through the cracked rear window and sees the front of the store, a pile of fallen girders blocking the hole in the window, a cloud of dust obscuring the street.

Philip is twisting around in his seat, his face ashen and wild with panic. "Punkin? Punkin? You okay? Talk to me, little girl! You all right?"

Brian turns to the child, who is still on the floor, looking woozy and maybe in some kind of shock, but otherwise unharmed. "She's good, Philip, she's good," Brian says, feeling the back of the child's head for any blood, any sign of injury. She seems fine.

"Everybody else okay?" Philip looks around the dust motes of the dark interior. A thin ray of daylight filtering across the store is the only illumination. In the gloom, Brian can see the other men's faces: sweaty, stone-still with terror, eyes glinting.

Nick raises a thumb. "I'm good."

Brian says he is, too.

Philip already has his door open, and is struggling out from behind the airbag. "Get everything you can carry," he tells them, "but make sure you get the shotguns and all the shells. You hear me?"

Yes, they hear him, and now Brian and Nick are climbing out of the SUV. Over the course of a mere minute, Brian makes a series of observations—most of them, apparently, already calculated by Philip—beginning with the front of the store.

From the chorus of moaning noises and thousands of shuffling feet, it is clear to Brian that the zombie horde is closing in on the accident scene. The Escalade is finished, its front end nearly totaled, its tires blown, its entire length shellacked with gore.

The rear of the store leads toward a hallway. Dark, narrow, lined with drywall, the corridor may or may not lead to an exit. There's no time to investigate. All they have time to do is grab their packs, their duffels, and their weapons. Dazed from the collision, dizzy with panic, bruised and battered, ears ringing, Brian and Nick each grab a goose gun, and Philip takes as many bladed tools as he can stow on his body, a bad-axe in each side of his belt, the Ruger and three extra magazines.

"Come on, kiddo, we gotta skeedaddle," Brian says to Penny, but the child looks lethargic and confused. He tries to pull her from the mangled interior, but she hangs on to the back of the seat.

"Carry her," Philip says, coming around the front of the SUV.

"Come on, sweetie, you can ride piggyback," Brian tells the girl.

Penny reluctantly climbs out, and Brian lifts her onto his back.

The four of them quickly creep through the jewelry store's back hall.

They get lucky. Just past the glass doorway of a back office, they find an unmarked metal door. Philip throws the bolt, and he cracks the door open a few inches, peering out. The smell is incredible—a black, greasy stench that reminds Brian of the time his sixth-grade class took a field trip to the Turner stockyards outside Ashburn. The smell on the abattoir floor was like this. Philip raises a hand, motioning for everybody to stop.

Over Philip's shoulder, Brian can see a long, narrow, dark alley lined with overflowing garbage Dumpsters. But it's the actual *content* of the receptacles that registers most sharply in Brian's brain: pale human arms dangling over the sides, ragged, ulcerated legs, matted hair hanging down, and pools of old blackened blood dried beneath them.

Philip motions to the others. "Y'all follow me, and do exactly what I say," he says, snapping the cocking mechanism on the Ruger—eight rounds of .22-caliber bullets ready to rock—and then he's moving.

They follow him out.

As quietly and quickly as possible, they make their way through the stench and shadows of the deserted slaughterhouse of an alley toward a side street visible at one end. Weighed down by the duffel bag over one shoulder, and the child clinging to his back, Brian limps along in between Philip and Nick—Penny's sixty-five pounds never feeling as heavy as they do now. Nick, who is bringing up the rear, walks with his Marlin 20-gauge cradled in his arms. Brian has his own shotgun wedged underneath his backpack—not that he has any idea how to use the damn thing.

They reach the end of the alley, and they are about to slip out and make their way down the deserted side street, when Philip accidentally steps on a human hand protruding from under a garbage Dumpster.

The hand—connected to a zombie with some fight still in it—instantly recoils under the container. Philip jerks backward with a start.

"DUDE!" Nick cries out, and the hand shoots back out and grabs Philip's ankle.

Philip sprawls to the ground, his Ruger spinning off across the pavement.

The dead man—an ashy-skinned, bearded homeless person in bloodstained rags—crabs toward Philip with the speed of a giant spider.

Philip claws for his gun. The others fumble for their weapons, Brian going for his shotgun while trying to balance the child on his back. Nick thumbs back the hammers on his Marlin.

The dead thing clutches Philip's leg and opens its jaws with the rigor-mortis creak of rusty hinges as Philip fumbles for his axe.

The zombie is about to take a chunk out of Philip's lower calf when the barrel of Nick's goose gun presses down on the back of the thing's skull.

The blast rips through the zombie's brain, sending half its face through the air on a geyser of blood and matter, the booming echo of the shotgun reverberating through the canyons of steel and glass.

"Now we're screwed," Philip says, struggling to his feet, scooping up the Ruger.

"What's the matter?" Brian says, adjusting the weight of the little girl on his back.

"Listen," Philip says.

In the brittle silence, they hear the ocean-wave sound of moaning suddenly change, altering its course as though on a shifting wind, the masses of undead drawn by the boom of the shotgun.

"So, we'll go back inside," Nick says in a strident, tense voice. "Back inside the jewelry store—there's gotta be a second floor."

"Too late," Philip says, checking the Ruger, looking down into its breech. He's got four rounds of hollow tips left in the hilt, and three mags of eight each in his back pockets. "I'm bettin' they're already flooding in the front of the place."

"What do you suggest?"

Philip looks at Nick, and then at his brother. "How fast you think you can run with all that weight?"

They take off at a moderate clip, Philip in the lead, Brian hobbling along after him, Nick bringing up the rear, past caved-in storefronts and petrified, charred funeral pyres of bodies burned by enterprising survivors.

Brian can't tell for sure but it seems like Philip is madly looking for a safe exit off the streets—a clean doorway, a fire escape ladder, something—but he's distracted now by an increasing number of moving corpses appearing around every corner.

Philip blasts the first one at fifty paces, sending a slug through its forehead, dropping it like a bad habit. The second one surprises him at closer range, lurching out of a shadowy doorway, and Philip puts it down with his second shot. More of them are materializing from porches and gaping store windows. Nick puts the goose gun and two decades of boar hunting to good use, taking down at least a dozen of them in the space of two blocks.

The blasts echo up over the skyline like sonic booms in the stratosphere.

They turn a corner and hurry down a narrower side road of herringbone brick, perhaps a landmark antebellum street that once rang with buckboards and horses, now bordered on either side by boarded condominiums and office buildings. The good news is that they seem to be moving away from the congested area, encountering fewer and fewer walking dead with each passing block.

The bad news is that they feel trapped now. They sense the city closing in around them, swallowing them whole in its glass-and-steel gullet. By this point, the sun has begun its afternoon descent, and the shadows thrown by the massive skyline have begun to lengthen.

Philip sees something in the distance—maybe a block and a half away—and instinctively ducks under the canopy of a torn awning.

The others hunker down with him against the boarded window of a former dry cleaner, and they crouch in the shadows to catch their breaths.

Brian is panting with exertion, little Penny still clinging soporifically to his back, like some kind of sleepy, traumatized monkey. "What is it, what's the matter?" Brian asks, realizing that Philip is craning his neck to see something in the distance.

"Tell me I'm seeing things," Philip says.

"What is it?"

"Gray building up there on the right," Philip says, nodding to the north. "See it? 'Bout two blocks away? See the doorway?"

In the distance, a three-story apartment building rises out of a row of dilapidated two-story condominiums. A massive postwar pile of chalk-colored brick and jutting balconies, it's the largest building on the block, the top of it reaching out of the shadows and reflecting the cold, pale sunlight off its array of antennas and exhaust stacks.

"Oh my God, I see it," Brian utters, still balancing Penny on his sore back as he kneels. The child clutches at his shoulders with a desperate grip.

"That ain't no mirage, Philly," Nick comments, a trace of awe coloring his voice.

They all stare at the human figure in the distance, too far away to identify as a man or a woman, adult or child, but there it is . . . *waving at them.*

TEN

Philip approaches cautiously from the opposite side of the street, the .22 at his side, cocked and ready, but not exactly raised. The others follow along behind him in a single file, all of their hackles up, their eyes wide open and prepared for anything.

The young woman across the street calls to them in a low, hissing whisper: "Hurry up already!"

She appears to be in her late twenties, maybe early thirties, with long dishwater-blond hair pulled back in a tight ponytail. She wears jeans and a loose-fitting cable-knit sweater that's severely stained, the red smudges and spatters visible even from this distance as she waves them over with a small-caliber revolver, maybe a police .38, swinging it like it's an air traffic control baton.

Philip wipes his mouth, thinking, catching his breath, trying to get a bead on the woman.

"C'mon!" she yells. "Before they smell us!" She's obviously anxious for them to follow her inside, and it's very likely she means them no harm; the way she's swinging the gun, it would not surprise Philip if it wasn't even loaded. She calls out: "And don't let any of those Biters see you come inside!"

Philip is wary, guarded, and he pauses on the curb before crossing the street. "How many of you *are* there?" he calls out to her.

Across the street, the blond woman lets out an exasperated sigh. "For God's sake, we're offering you food and shelter, come on!"

"How many?"

"Jesus, do you want help or not?"

Philip tightens his grip on the Ruger. "You're gonna answer my question first."

Another nervous sigh. "Three! Okay? There's three of us. You happy now? This is your last opportunity because if y'all don't come now, I'm going to go back inside, and then you're gonna be shit outta luck." She speaks with the faint drawl of a native Georgian, but has some big city in her voice, too. Maybe even a little bit of the North.

Philip and Nick exchange glances. The distant choir of rusty moaning drifts closer on the wind like a coming storm. Brian nervously readjusts Penny's weight on his back, and then shoots a jittery glance over his shoulder at the end of the block. He looks at Philip. "What other options do we have, Philip?"

"I agree, Philly," Nick whispers under his breath, swallowing his fear.

Philip looks at the young lady across the street. "How many men, how many women?"

She hollers back at him, "You want me to fill out a questionnaire? I'm going back inside. Good luck with everything—you're gonna need it!"

"Wait!"

Philip nods at the others, and then cautiously leads them across the street.

"You got any cigarettes?" the young woman asks, leading the group into the building's outer vestibule, securing the door behind her with a makeshift cross-brace. "We're down to our last bent butts."

She's a little beat-up, with scars on her chin, bruises on the side of her face, and one eye that's so bloodshot it looks like a mild hemorrhage. Beyond those rough edges, though, she strikes Philip as a fine-looking woman, with cornflower-blue eyes, and the kind of sun-kissed skin you might see on a farm girl—a sort of easy, low-maintenance beauty. But from the defiant tilt of her head, and the zaftig curves hidden under her bulky clothes, she gives off the air of an earth mother, and one does not fuck with earth mothers.

"Sorry, no smokers," Philip says, holding the door for Brian.

"Y'all look like you got banged up out there," the woman says, leading them across a reeking, littered chamber lined on one side with eighteen pairs of mailboxes and buzzers. Brian gently puts Penny down. The little girl staggers for a moment, getting her bearings. The air smells of must and zombie. The building does not feel safe.

The young woman kneels down by Penny. "Aren't you a sweet one."

Penny doesn't say anything, just looks down.

The woman looks up at Brian. "She yours?"

"She's mine," Philip says.

The woman brushes a strand of matted black hair from Penny's face. "My name's April, honey, what's yours?"

"Penny."

The voice that comes out of the child is so meek and nerve-racked it sounds like the mewl of a kitten. The woman named April smiles and strokes the girl's shoulder, then rises and looks at the men. "Let's get inside before we draw more of those things." She goes over to one of the intercoms and thumbs the button. "Dad, let us in."

Through a burst of static, a voice replies, *"Not so fast, little girl."*

Philip grabs her arm. "You got *power* in there? You got electricity?"

She shakes her head. "Afraid not . . . intercom's on a battery." She pokes the button. "Dad, come on."

Through the crackling static: *"How do we know we can trust these yahoos?"*

Click: "You gonna let us in or what?"

Crackle: *"You tell 'em to give up their guns."*

She lets out another anguished sigh and turns to Philip, who is shaking his head, giving her a no-way-in-hell kind of look.

Click: "They got a little girl, for chrissake. I'll vouch for 'em."

Crackle: *"And Hitler painted roses . . . we don't know these folks from Adam."*

Click: "Dad, open the damn lock!"

Crackle: *"You saw what happened up to Druid Hills."*

April slams her hand down on the intercom: "This ain't Druid Hills! Now let us in, goddamnit, before we grow moss on our asses!"

A harsh, metallic buzz is followed by a loud clunk as the auto-latch on the inner security door springs open. April leads them through the doorway, and then down a shopworn, sour-smelling hallway with three apartment doors on either side. At the far end of the corridor stands a metal door marked STAIRS, with criss-crossing boards nailed over it.

April knocks on the last door on the right—Apartment 1C—and within moments, a heavier, older, coarser version of April opens the door. "Oh my God, what an adorable little girl," the big gal says, seeing Penny, who is now holding Brian's hand. "Come on in, folks . . . can't tell ya how good it is to finally see people who can keep their drool in their mouths."

April's sister, who introduces herself as Tara, is plump and rough around the edges. She smells of smoke and cheap shampoo, and is dressed in a faded floral-print muumuu to hide her excess flesh. Her cleavage rises like bread dough out of the top of her dress, a little Woody Woodpecker tattoo on the crest of one bosom. She has the same striking blue eyes as her younger sister, but keeps them heavily lined and decorated with steel-blue eye shadow. Her long Lee press-on nails look like they could open a tin can.

Philip enters the apartment first, the Ruger still in his hand at his side.

The others follow.

At first, Philip barely notices the cluttered living room, the chairs draped with clothing, the battered luggage along one wall, and the oddly shaped musical instrument cases leaning against the boarded sliding door. He hardly notices the small kitchenette off to the left, the peach crates of provisions and the sink full of dirty dishes. The smell of cigarette smoke and stale fabric and dried sweat hanging in the air barely registers in Philip's nostrils.

Right now, all he can focus on is the barrel of a 12-gauge shotgun pointed directly at him from a rocking chair across the room.

"That's far enough," says the old man with the shotgun. A lanky, weathered old duffer, he has the farmer-tanned face of a cigar-store

Indian, with an iron-gray flattop haircut and ice-chip blue eyes. The slender tube of an oxygen rig is clipped under his buzzard's beak of a nose, the tank sitting next to him like a faithful pet. He barely fits into his stovepipe jeans and flannel shirt, his white, hairy ankles showing above the tops of his shit-kickers.

Philip instinctively raises the .22, instantly going into Mexican showdown mode. He aims it at the old man and says, "Sir, we got enough trouble out there, we don't need any in here."

The others freeze.

April pushes her way past the men. "For God's sake, Dad, put that thing down."

The old man waves the girl aside with the barrel. "You hush now, little girl."

April stands there with her hands on her hips, a disgusted look on her face.

Across the room, Tara says, "Can we all just dial it down a little bit?"

"Where'd you folks come from?" the old man asks Philip, the shotgun still raised and ready.

"Waynesboro, Georgia."

"Never heard of it."

"It's in Burke County."

"Hell, that's almost South Carolina."

"Yessir."

"You on drugs? Speed, crack . . . something like that?"

"No, sir. Why the hell would you think that?"

"Something going on behind them eyes, they look all jacked up on speed."

"I don't do drugs."

"How'd you end up on our doorstep?"

"Heard there was some kinda refugee center set up here, but it ain't lookin' too good."

"You got that right," says the old man.

April chimes in, "Sounds like we all got something in common."

Philip keeps his eyes on the old man, but says to the girl, "How's that?"

"That's the same reason *we* ended up in this godforsaken place," she says. "Looking for that damned refugee center everybody was talking about."

Philip stares at the shotgun. " 'Best laid plans,' I guess."

"Damn straight," says the old man, the faint whistle of oxygen seeping from the tank. "I don't suppose you realize what you done to us."

"I'm listening."

"You got them Biters all stirred up. By sundown, there's gonna be a goddamn convention of them things outside our door."

Philip sniffs. "I'm sorry about that but it ain't like we had a choice."

The old man sighs. "Well now . . . I suppose that's true."

"Your daughter's the one pulled us off the street . . . we had no bad intentions. Hell, we had no intentions at all . . . other than keepin' from getting bit."

"Yeah, well . . . I can see your point there."

A long beat of silence follows. Everybody waits. The two firearms begin to lower.

"What are them cases for?" Philip finally asks, nodding toward the row of tattered instrument cases across the rear of the living room. His gun is still raised but the fight-or-flight juice has drained from him. "You got tommy guns in them things?"

The old man finally lets out a flinty laugh. He lays his gun on his lap, crosswise, letting up on the hammers, all the tension draining out of his gaunt face. The oxygen tank pings. "My friend, you're lookin' at what's left of the World Famous Chalmers Family Band, stars of stage, screen, and state fairs across the South." The old man sets the gun down on the floor with a grunt. He looks up at Philip. "I apologize for the ornery reception." He struggles to his feet, rising to his full height until he looks like a withered Abe Lincoln. "Name's David Chalmers, mandolin, vocals, and father of these two ragamuffins."

Philip shoves his gun back behind his belt. "Philip Blake. This is my brother Brian. And that wallflower over there is Nick Parsons . . . and I thank you kindly for saving our asses out there."

The two patriarchs shake hands, and the tension goes out of the room with the suddenness of an off switch being thrown.

It turns out there *was* a fourth member of the Chalmers Family Band—Mrs. Chalmers—a portly little matron from Chattanooga who sang high soprano on the group's bluegrass and old-timey numbers. According to April, it was a blessing in disguise that the matriarch of the family succumbed to pneumonia five years earlier. If she had lived to see this horrible shit inflicting the human race, she would have been crushed, would have seen it as the end-time, and probably would have walked right off the pier at Clark's Hill Lake.

So it was that the Chalmers Family Band became a trio, and went on with the act, playing the carny circuit across the tristate area, with Tara on bass, April on guitar, and Daddy on mandolin. As a single father, the sixty-six-year-old David had his hands full. Tara was a pothead, and April had her mother's temper and single-mindedness.

When the plague broke out, they were in Tennessee at a bluegrass festival, and they made their way back home in the band's camper. They got as far as the Georgia border before the camper broke down. From there, they got lucky enough to find an Amtrak train that was still running between Dalton and Atlanta. Unfortunately, the train deposited them smack-dab in the middle of the southeast side, at King Memorial Station, which was now lousy with the dead. Somehow, they managed to work their way north without getting attacked, traveling at night in stolen cars, searching for the mythical refugee center.

"And that's how we ended up here in our little low-rent paradise," April tells Philip in a soft voice late that night. She sits on the end of a tattered sofa, while Penny dozes restlessly next to her in a wad of blankets. Philip sits nearby.

Candles are lit on the coffee table. Nick and Brian are asleep on the floor across the room, while David and Tara are each snoring in a different musical key in their respective rooms.

"We're too petrified to go upstairs, though," April adds with a trace of regret in her voice. "Even though we could use whatever supplies are still up there. Batteries, canned goods, whatever. Jesus, I'd give my left tit for some toilet paper."

"Never give *that* up for a little toilet paper," Philip says with a grin, sitting barefoot in his stained T-shirt and jeans at the other end of the sofa, his belly full of rice and beans. The Chalmerses' supplies are running low, but they still had half of the ten-pound bag of rice that they pilfered from a broken shop window a week ago, and enough beans to make dinner for everyone. April cooked. The grub wasn't bad, either. After dinner, Tara rolled cigarettes with the last of her Red Man tobacco and a few buds of skunkweed. Philip partook in a few puffs, even though he had sworn off pot years ago—it usually made him hear things in his head that he didn't want to hear. Now his brain feels woolly and thick in the strange afterglow.

April manages a sad smile. "Yeah, well . . . so close and yet so far."

"What do you mean?" Philip looks at her, and then slowly looks up at the ceiling. "Oh . . . right." He remembers hearing the noise earlier, and making note of it. They've quieted down now, but the shuffling, creaking noises from the higher floors have intermittently been crossing the ceiling all evening, moving with the insidious, invisible presence of termites. The fact that Philip almost forgot about these noises is a testament to how desensitized he's becoming to the prospects of such proximity to the dead. "What about the other ground-floor apartments?" he asks her.

"We picked them clean, got every last bit of usable stuff out of them."

"What happened in Druid Hills?" he asks after a moment of silence.

April lets out a sigh. "Folks told us there was a refugee center up there. There wasn't."

Philip looks at her. "And?"

April shrugs. "We got there and found a whole bunch of people hiding out behind the gates of this big scrap-metal place. People just like us. Scared, confused. We tried to talk some of them into leaving with us. Strength in numbers, all that gung-ho shit."

"So, what happened?"

"I guess they were too scared to leave and too scared to stay." April looks down, her face reflecting the candlelight. "Tara and Dad and I found a car that would run, and we gathered up some supplies and took off. But we heard the motorcycles coming when we were pulling away."

"Motorcycles?"

She nods, rubs her eyes. "We got about a quarter of a mile down the road—maybe not even that far—and we round this hill and all of a sudden we hear, way in the distance behind us, these screams. And we look back across the valley, where this dusty old salvage yard is, and it's like . . . I don't know. Fucking *Road Warrior* or something."

"It's what?"

"This motorcycle gang is tearing the place apart, running people down, entire families, God knows what else. It was pretty damn ugly. And the weird thing is, it wasn't the near-miss that got to us. It wasn't the bullet we dodged. I think it was the guilt. We all wanted to go back and help, and be good upstanding citizens and all that, but we didn't." She looks at him. "Because we ain't good upstanding citizens; there ain't any of those left."

Philip looks at Penny. "I can see why your daddy wasn't crazy about the idea of taking in boarders."

"Ever since that scrap-yard fiasco, he's been real paranoid about running across any survivors—maybe more paranoid than he is about the Biters."

"*Biters* . . . I heard you say that before. Who came up with that one?"

"That's my dad's term; it kinda stuck."

"I like it." Philip smiles at her again. "And I like your daddy. He takes care of business, and I don't blame him for not trusting us. He seems like a tough old nut, and I respect that. We need more like him."

She sighs. "He's not as tough as he used to be, I'll tell you that."

"What's he got? Lung cancer?"

"Emphysema."

"That's not good," Philip says, and then he sees something that stops him cold.

April Chalmers has her hand on Penny's shoulder and is almost absently stroking the little girl as she sleeps. It's such a tender, unexpected gesture—so natural—that it reaches down into Philip and awakens something inside him that's long been dormant. He can't understand the feeling at first, and his confusion must be showing on his face because April looks up at him.

"You okay?"

"Yeah, I'm . . . I'm good." He touches the Band-Aid on his temple where he smacked himself in the collision earlier that day. The Chalmerses dug out their first-aid kit and patched everybody up before dinner. "Tell you what," Philip says. "You go get some sleep, and in the morning, the boys and I will clear out the upstairs."

She looks at him for a moment like she's wondering whether or not to trust him.

The next morning, after breakfast, Philip shows April that his word is good. He enlists Nick, and he grabs extra magazines for the Ruger and a box of shells for one of the Marlins. He shoves the bad-axes down either side of his belt, and gives a small pickaxe to Nick for close encounters.

Pausing by the door, Philip crouches down to tighten the laces of his logger boots, which are so spattered with mud and gore that they look like they're embroidered with black and purple thread.

"Y'all be careful up there," old David Chalmers says, standing in the doorway of the kitchenette. He looks gray and washed out in the morning light, leaning on the metal caddy in which his oxygen tank is mounted. The tube under his nose softly whistles with each breath. "Y'all don't know what you're gonna find."

"Always," Philip says, tucking his denim shirt inside his jeans, checking the axes for quick and easy access. Nick stands over him, waiting with the goose gun on his shoulder. There's a taut expression on Nick's face, a combination of grim determination and excitement.

"Most of 'em will be on the second floor," the old man adds.

"We'll clear 'em on out."

"Just watch yer backs."

"Will do," Philip says, rising to his feet and checking the axes.

"I'm coming."

Philip whirls around to see Brian standing there with a clean T-shirt on—an REM logo on the front, the pride of Athens—and a dour, purposeful expression on his face. He's cradling one of the shotguns in his arms like it's a living thing.

"You sure?"

"Hell yeah."

"What about Penny?"

"The gals will watch her."

"I don't know."

"Come on," Brian says. "You need an extra pair of eyes up there. I'm up for it."

Philip thinks it over. He glances across the living room and sees his daughter sitting Indian-style on the floor between the two Chalmers women. The ladies are playing crazy eights with a tattered deck of cards, making Penny periodically smile and slap down a card. It's been a long time since the little girl has smiled. Philip turns to his brother and offers a grin. "That's the spirit."

They get up there via the stairs at the end of the first-floor corridor— the elevators at the other end as dead as the zombies—but first they have to tear the wooden bracings off the door. The noise of axe blows and nails squeaking out seems to stimulate movement above them, in the dark chambers behind apartment doors. At one point, Philip passes gas with all the exertion, a reminder of April's bean dinner from the night before.

"That fart's gonna wipe out more zombies than any twenty-gauge shell," Nick comments.

"Hardy-har-har," Philip says and tears off the last of the bracing planks

On their way up the dark stairwell, Philip says, "Remember, y'all—*be quick*. They are slippery motherfuckers but they're slow as shit, and dumber than Nick here."

"Hardy-har, back atcha," Nick says, expertly injecting a pair of .20-gauge shells into his goose gun.

They reach the top landing, and find the fire door to the second floor shut tightly. They pause. Brian is shaking.

"Calm down, sport," Philip tells his brother, noticing the barrel of the shotgun is wavering, trembling slightly. Philip gently pushes the muzzle away from the general vicinity of his ribs. "And try not to accidentally send a ball of that bird shot into one of *us*."

"I got it under control," Brian retorts in a shaky, tense voice, revealing that he obviously has *nothing* under control.

"Here we go," Philip says. "And remember, go at them hard and quick."

A single, fierce kick with the shank of his boot heel sends the door lurching open.

ELEVEN

For a millisecond, they stand there with hearts beating like trip-hammers. Other than a few scattered candy wrappers and empty, broken pop bottles, and one hell of a lot of dust, the second-floor hall—identical to the ground-floor corridor—is empty. Dim daylight shines through the far windows and laces through streaks of dust motes, which cant down across the closed doors: 2A, 2C, and 2E along one side, 2B, 2D, and 2F along the other.

Nick whispers, "They're all locked inside their places."

Philip nods. "Gonna be like shooting fish in a damn barrel."

"Come on, let's do it," Brian says unconvincingly. "Let's get it done."

Philip glances at his brother, then glances at Nick. "John Rambo here."

They go over to the first door on the right—2F—and raise the business ends of their guns. Philip snaps the slide on the Ruger.

Then he kicks the door in.

A giant ball of stink punches them in their faces. It is the first thing that registers: a hideous stew of human degradation, urine and feces—and zombie stench—vying for dominance over the sharper odors of rancid food and moldy bathrooms and mildewed clothes. It is so overwhelming and unbearable that it literally drives the men back a half step each.

"Jesus wept," Nick says in a choked utterance, involuntarily averting his face, as if the stench is a wind blowing at him.

"Still think my fart stinks?" Philip says as he takes a careful step into the reeking shadows of the apartment. He raises the .22.

Nick and Brian follow with shotguns at the ready, eyes wide and shiny with tension.

A moment later, they find four of them in repose, on the floor of a ransacked living room, each one slumped in a corner, slack jawed and catatonic, growling languidly at the sight of intruders, but too stupid or sick or demented to move, as though they have grown weary of their hellish fate and now have forgotten how to use furniture. It's hard to tell in the gloomy light, especially with their faces all bloated and blackened with mortified flesh, but it looks as though it's another family: mom and dad and two grown kids. The walls have weird patches of scratch marks, like a giant abstract painting, showing evidence that the things were following some flickering instinct to claw their way out.

Philip goes over to the first one, its shark eyes glimmering as the Ruger looms. The blast sends its brains across the Jackson Pollock of scratch marks behind it. The thing sinks to the floor. Meanwhile, Nick is across the room putting another one out of its misery, the boom of the Marlin like a great dry paper sack popping. Brain matter paints the walls. Philip takes the third one down as it is slowly rising, Nick moving toward the fourth—BOOM!—and the sounds of fluids spattering surfaces are buffered by the ringing in their ears.

Brian is standing ten paces behind them, his gun poised, his spirit drowning inside him on a rising tide of repulsion and nausea. "This is—this is not—" he starts to say, but a flash of movement to his left cuts off his words.

The errant zombie comes at Brian from the depths of a side hallway, plunging out of the shadows like a monstrous clown with a black fright wig and candy eyes. Before Brian even has a chance to identify it as a daughter or girlfriend, dressed in a torn robe with one shriveled breast exposed like a flap of chewed meat, the thing pounces on him with the force of a defensive back making a tackle.

Brian sprawls backward to the floor, and it all happens so fast that Philip and Nick have no time to intercede. They are too far away.

The moving cadaver lands on top of Brian, the thing snarling with black, slimy teeth and—in that split instant before Brian realizes that he is still holding the shotgun—the zombie opens its jaws so wide it looks as though its skull is about to unhinge.

Brian gets one horrible glimpse down the recesses of the thing's throat—an endless black well straight down into hell—before he instinctively jerks the shotgun up. Almost by accident, the muzzle lodges itself in the gaping hole of the thing's mouth, and Brian screams out a garbled cry as he squeezes off a single blast.

The back of the thing's skull explodes, sending up a cloud of blood mist and tissue. The backwash hits the ceiling in deep purple arterial matter, and Brian is thunderstruck for a moment, his back pinned to the floor. The thing's head is still skewered on the shaft of the shotgun. He blinks. The silver eyes of the girlfriend or daughter, or *whoever* she was, are frozen now and fixed on Brian.

He coughs and turns away as the girl's head slowly slides down the length of the barrel, a giant shish kebob, the dead eyes still locked on Brian. He feels the moist slime of her face on his hands. He closes his eyes. He can't move. His right hand still glued to the trigger, his left still welded to the stock, he grimaces with horror.

Cold laughter brings him back around. "Look who just scored his first touchdown," Philip Blake says, standing over his brother in a cloud of cordite smoke, grinning from ear to ear with mirthless delight.

Nick is the one who finds the egress to the roof, and Philip is the one who gets the idea to deposit all the rotting carcasses up there so they don't stink up the place any further (or make the scavenger hunt through the upper floors any more unpleasant than it has to be).

It takes them a little over an hour to drag all the inhuman remains up the stairwell to the third floor, and then up through a narrow stairwell to the fire door. They have to shoot the lock off, and have to work in a sort of modified bucket brigade, dragging the smelly flesh sacks down the hallways and up two flights of stairs to the roof, leaving leech trails of gore on the cabbage-rose carpet runners.

They manage to get every last one of them—they terminated fourteen of them altogether, going through two entire clips of .22-caliber rounds, as well as half a box of shells—up the passageway and onto the roof.

"Look at this place," Nick marvels as he puts the last carcass down on the tarpaper warning track along the east side of the roof, the wind whipping his pant legs and tossing his hair. The corpses lie in a row like cordwood lined up for the winter. Brian stands at the opposite end of the file, gazing down at the dead things with a strange, implacable expression on his face.

"Pretty cool," Philip says, walking over to the edge of the roof.

At this height, he can see the distant buildings of the exclusive Buckhead area, Peachtree Plaza, and the glass cathedral of skyscrapers to the west. The frozen spires of the city rise in pristine summits, impassive, stoic in the sunlight, untouched by the apocalypse. Down below, Philip sees the scattered wandering dead moving in and out of shadows like broken toy soldiers come to life.

"Cool place to hang out," Philip says, turning and surveying the rest of the roof. Around a giant conglomeration of antennae, rent stracks, and heating and air-conditioning machinery, now cold and powerless, an apron of pea gravel offers enough space to play a touch football game. A forgotten tangle of lawn furniture leans against an air duct. "Grab a chair and take a load off."

They drag tattered chaise lounges over to the edge of the roof.

"I could get used to this place," Nick says, settling down on a lounger facing the skyline.

Philip sits down next to him. "You mean the roof or this place in general?"

"All of it."

"Copy that."

"How do you do it?" Brian says, standing behind them, fidgeting with nerves. He refuses to sit down, refuses to relax. He's still wired from his encounter with the impaled head.

"Do what?" Philip says.

"I don't know, like, the killing and stuff, and then the next minute you're—"

Brian stops himself, unable to put it into words, and Philip turns and looks at his brother. He sees the man's hands shaking. "Sit down, Bri, you did good down there."

Brian pulls a chair over, sits down, wrings his hands, ruminating. "I'm just saying—"

Again, he can't articulate what he's "just saying" and he falters.

"It ain't killing, sport," Philip says. "Soon as you get that straight, you're gonna be fine."

"What is it then?"

Philip shrugs. "Nicky, what would you call it?"

Nick is staring out at the skyline. "God's work?"

Philip has a big laugh at that one, and then says, "I got an idea."

He gets up and goes over to the closest corpse, one of the smaller ones.

"Check this out," he says, and drags the thing over to the edge of the roof.

The other two join Philip at the ledge. The rancid wind tosses their hair as they gaze over the ledge at the street thirty-five feet below them.

Philip shoves the cadaver with the toe of his boot until it slips over the side.

The thing seems to fall in slow motion, its limp appendages flopping like broken wings. It strikes the cement parkway down below, in front of the building, and comes apart with the sound, color, and texture of a very ripe watermelon erupting in a starburst of pink tissue.

In the master bedroom of the first-floor apartment, David Chalmers is sitting in his wifebeater T-shirt and boxer shorts, sucking on an inhaler, trying to get enough Atrovent into his lungs to quell the wheezing, when he hears the commotion outside the boarded sliding-glass doors of the rear portion of the apartment.

The sound instantly raises the hairs on his neck, and he quickly fumbles himself into his clothes, including the breathing tube, which he gets halfway on, one side dangling under a hairy nostril.

He storms across the room on creaking knees, yanking the oxygen tank along on its castors like a stubborn child being pulled by an impatient nanny.

Crossing the living room, he catches a glimpse out of the corner of his eye of three figures standing rapt and terrified at the threshold of the kitchen. April and Tara had been making cookies with the little girl—using up the last of their flour and sugar—and now the three females stand there, gaping in the direction of the noise.

David hobbles over to the boarded, meshed, burglar-barred sliding doors.

Through a narrow gap in the plywood planks, in between the branches of skeletal trees, he can just barely see the far end of the courtyard, and beyond that a slice of the street running parallel to the front of the apartment building.

Another body rains down as if dropped by God himself, hitting the pavement, making a wet, lurid, smacking sound not unlike a giant water balloon popping. But that's not the noise that's getting to David Chalmers right now. That's not the noise that's penetrating the apartment, coming in waves, a vast, distant, tuneless symphony.

"Sweet jumpin' Jesus," he mutters in a breathy wheeze, whirling around so fast he nearly tips over the tank in its caddy.

He drags the thing toward the door.

On the roof, Philip and Nick pause after heaving the fifth body off the ledge.

Panting from the effort and a sort of morbid giddiness, Philip comments: "They blow up good, don't they?"

Nick is trying unsuccessfully not to laugh. "This is ten kinds of wrong but I gotta admit it feels good."

"You got that right."

"What's the point, guys?" Brian wants to know, standing behind them.

"The point is, there *is* no point," Philip says without looking at his brother.

"What is that, like a Zen saying?"

"It is what it is."

"Okay, now you lost me. I mean, I don't see how throwing these things off the roof is *accomplishing* anything."

Philip turns and gives his brother a look. "Lighten up, sport. You bagged your first trophy today. It wasn't pretty but it got the job done. We're just blowing off a little steam."

Nick sees something in the distance that he hadn't noticed until now. "Hey, check out—"

"I'm just saying," Brian interrupts. "We gotta keep our wits about us and shit." He has his hands in his pockets, nervously kneading the change and the penknife that he has stashed in there. "April and her family are good people, Philip, we gotta behave ourselves."

"Yes, Mom," Philip says with a cold smile.

"Hey, you guys, check out that building down there on the corner."

Nick is pointing at a squat, ugly brick edifice on the northeast corner of the closest intersection. Blackened around the edges with the fumes of the city, the faded letters painted above the first-floor display windows say DILLARD'S HOME FURNISHINGS.

Philip sees it. "What about it?"

"Look at the front corner of the building, there's a pedestrian thing."

"A what?"

"A walkway or a breezeway or whatever you call it. See it?"

Sure enough, Philip sees a grimy glass bridge spanning the adjacent street, connecting the office building catty-corner to them to Dillard's second floor. The glass-encased footbridge is empty and sealed at either end. "What are you thinking, Nicky?"

"I don't know." Nick stares at the pedestrian bridge, pondering. "Could be—"

"Gentlemen!" The husky boom of the old man's voice interrupts.

Brian turns and sees David Chalmers trundling toward them from the open stairwell door. Urgency burns in the old man's eyes, and he drags his oxygen tank along with a practiced limp. Brian takes a step toward him. "Mr. Chalmers, did you get all the way up here by yourself?"

The old man is breathing hard as he approaches. Through his wheezing, rattling breaths, he says, "I may be old and sick, but I ain't helpless . . . and call me David. I see y'all cleaned out them floors real nice and tidy, and for that I thank you, I truly do."

Philip and Nick turn and face the man. "Is there a problem?" Philip asks.

"Hell yeah, there's a problem," the old man says, eyes flashing with anger. "What you been doin' up here, pitchin' them bodies off the roof like that? You're just cutting off your own *feet*!"

"What do you mean?"

The old man lets out a grunt. "Y'all deaf or somethin'? You can't hear that?"

"Hear what?"

The old man shuffles out to the edge of the roof. "Take a gander." He points a gnarled finger at two buildings in the distance. "You see what you done?"

Philip gazes off to the north, and all at once he realizes why he's been hearing that infernal noise of a thousand and one moans for the past fifteen minutes. Legions of zombies are migrating toward their building, most likely drawn to the noise and spectacle of bodies hitting the pavement.

Maybe ten or twelve blocks away now, they move with the undulating slither of blood clots traveling down arteries. For a moment, Philip can't tear his eyes away from the hideous migration.

They're coming from all directions. Percolating through the shadows, oozing out of alleys, choking the main drags, they meet up and multiply at intersections like a great amoeba growing in size and strength, inexorably drawn to the catalyst of humans in their midst. Philip looks away finally and pats the old man on the shoulder. "Our bad, David . . . our bad."

That night, they try to eat dinner and pretend that it's just an ordinary meal among friends, but the persistent clawing noises outside the building keep killing the conversation. The sounds are a constant reminder of their exile, of the mortal threat just outside their door, of their isolation. They tell each other their life stories, and they try to make the best of it, but the menacing noises keep everybody on edge.

Considering there are seventeen other apartments in the building, they had expected to harvest a bounty of provisions from the upper floors that day. But all they found was a few dry goods in the pantries, some cereal and hard pasta, maybe half a dozen cans of soup, a bunch of stale crackers, and a few bottles of cheap grocery store wine.

It had been weeks now since the building lay abandoned, without power, infested with the dead, and all the food had rotted. Maggots crawled in most refrigerators, and even the bedding and the clothes and the furniture had mildewed and soured with the stink of zombies. Maybe folks took their essentials with them when they fled. Maybe they took all the bottled water and batteries and flashlights and wooden matches and weapons.

They left their medicine cabinets untouched, though, and Tara manages to collect a shoe box full of pills: tranquilizers like Xanax and Valium, stimulants like Adderall and Ritalin, blood pressure meds, diet pills, beta-blockers, antidepressants, and cholesterol medications. She also finds a couple of bottles of bronchodilators that will serve the old man well. Philip gets a kick out of Tara's flimsy pretense of being concerned for everybody's health when he knows full well she is mostly interested in anything that will provide her with a recreational buzz. And who the hell can blame her? Pharmaceutical relief in this situation is as good an escape as any.

The truth is, by that second night, despite the constant din of the undead outside their windows, the Chalmers family has begun to grow on Philip. He likes them. He likes their Bohemian-country style, he likes their pluck, and he just plain likes being with other survivors. Nick also seems reenergized by the union of the two families, and Penny is actually talking again, her eyes clear for the first time in weeks. The presence of other females, in Philip's estimation, is just what the doctor ordered for his daughter.

Even Brian, his chest cold almost completely gone now, seems stronger, more confident. He still has a long way to go, in Philip's humble opinion, but he seems galvanized by the possibility of some kind of community, no matter how small and ragged.

The next day, they begin settling into a routine. From the roof Philip and Nick keep track of the zombie quotient on the streets, while Brian checks the weak spots around the first floor—the windows, the fire escapes, the courtyard, the front foyer. Penny is getting to know the Chalmers sisters, and David mostly keeps to himself. The old man is battling his lung disease as best he can. He naps and takes his inhaler and visits with the newcomers as much as possible.

In the afternoon, Nick starts working on a makeshift catwalk, which he plans to run between the roof of the apartment building and the roof of the neighboring structure. He's got it in his head that he can make it to the pedestrian bridge at the corner without ever having to set foot on ground level. Philip thinks he's crazy but tells him to go ahead and waste his time if he wants to.

Nick believes this maneuver is actually the key to their survival, especially since they are all secretly concerned—you can see it on the face of anyone who goes into the kitchen—that they will soon run out of supplies. The water is turned off in the building, and carrying bucketfuls of human waste from the bathroom to the back window overlooking the courtyard (for dumping) is the least of their problems. They have a limited supply of water, and *that* has everybody very worried.

After dinner that night, at a little after about eight o'clock, when an awkward silence in the conversation reminds everybody of the unrelenting noises coming from the dark outside, Philip gets an idea. "Why don't y'all play something for us," he says. "Drown those bastards out."

"Hey," Brian says, his eyes lighting up. "That's a great idea."

"We're a little rusty," the old man says from his rocker. He looks tired and drawn tonight, the sickness working on him. "If you want to know the truth, we haven't strummed a note since this all started up."

"Chicken," Tara remarks from the couch, rolling a number with the flecks of tobacco, seeds, and stems at the bottom of her little Band-Aid canister. The others sit around the living room, ears perking up at the prospect of hearing the World Famous Chalmers Family Band.

"Come on, Daddy," April chimes in. "We can play 'The Old Rugged Cross' for 'em."

"Naw, they don't want to hear no religious claptrap, occasion such as this."

Tara is already maneuvering her portly self across the room toward her gigantic bass fiddle case, her makeshift cigarette dangling from her lip. "You name it, Daddy, I'll slap a bass line to it."

"Aw, what could it hurt?" David Chalmers relents as he levers his creaking body out of the rocker.

The Chalmers dig their instruments out of their cases, and then tune up. When they're ready, they seem to position themselves in a tight formation before they begin, as synchronized as a marine drill team, with April in front, on guitar, and David and Tara on the flanks in back, on mandolin and bass respectively. Philip can just imagine them on the stage at the Grand Ole Opry, and he can see Brian soaking it all in across the room. One thing about Brian Blake, he knows his music. Philip has always marveled at his brother's depth of knowledge on the subject, and now, with this unexpected boon, Philip figures that Brian must be delighted.

They start playing.

Philip gets very still.

It feels as though his heart is suddenly being inflated with helium.

It's not just the stark and unexpected beauty of their music—that first number a lovely old Irish jig, with a sad, thumping bass line and a rolling guitar pattern that sounds like a hundred-year-old hurdy-gurdy. Nor is it the fact that sweet little Penny seems suddenly transported by the melody as she sits on the floor, her eyes going all dreamy. Nor is it the fact that a simple, delicate tune in the face of all this ugliness practically breaks Philip's heart. It's the moment when April begins to sing that floods Philip's soul with electric honey:

There's a shadow on my wall, but it don't scare me at all
I'm happy all night long in my dreams

As clean and crisp as a glass bell, with perfect pitch, April's spectacular, velvety alto voice rings in the room. It caresses the notes, and even has a hint of the church in it, a slight soulful sauciness that reminds Philip of a choir singer in a country chapel:

In my dreams, in my dreams
I'm happy all night long in my dreams
I'm safe here in my bed, happy thoughts are in my head
And I'm happy all night long in my dreams

The voice awakens an aching desire in Philip—something he hasn't felt since Sarah died. He has X-ray vision all of a sudden. He can see little things about April Chalmers as she strums her six-string and warbles joyously that he hadn't noticed before. He sees a tiny anklet chain around her ankle, and a small tattoo of a rose inside the crook of her arm, and the pale half-moons of her breasts—as white as mother-of-pearl—between the bunched buttons of her blouse.

The song comes to an end and everybody applauds—Philip's clapping the most vigorous of all.

The next day, after a meager breakfast of stale cereal and powdered milk, Philip notices April, off to herself, near the front door, putting on her hiking boots, and wrapping the sleeves of her sweatshirt with duct tape.

"Thought you might like a second cup," Philip says to her innocently, coming up to her with a cup of coffee in each hand. "It's instant but it ain't half bad." He notices her wrapping her ankles with tape. "What the hell are you doing?"

She looks at the coffee. "You use the rest of that gallon jug for that?"

"I guess so."

"We got one more gallon to last the seven of us until the twelfth of never."

"What do you got in that head of yours?"

"Don't make a big deal out of it." She zips up her sweatshirt, and tightens the rubber band on her ponytail, tucking it into the hood. "I've been planning this for a while, and I want to do it by myself."

"Planning what?"

She reaches into the front coat closet and pulls out a metal baseball bat. "We found this thing in one of the apartments, knew it'd be useful one day."

"What are you doing, April?"

"You know that fire escape ladder on the south side of the building?"

"You're not going out there by yourself."

"I can slip out 3F, climb down the ladder, and draw the Biters away from the building."

"No . . . *no.*"

"Draw them away long enough to go get supplies and slip back in."

Philip sees his own filthy logger boots by the door, where he left them the night before. "Mind handing me those boots?" he says. "If your mind's made up, you sure as shit ain't doing this alone."

TWELVE

Once again, it's the smell that first jabs him sharply in the face as he leans out the south window of apartment 3F—a coppery gumbo of human waste slow cooked in bacon fat—an odor that is so horrendous it makes Philip flinch. His eyes start watering as he shimmies through the opening. He doesn't think he will *ever* get used to that smell.

He climbs out onto a rusty, ramshackle cast-iron landing. The platform, which is connected to a ladder that zigzags down three floors to a side street, wobbles under Philip's weight. His stomach lurches with the sudden shift in gravity, and he braces himself against the rails.

The weather has turned dreary and damp, the sky the color of asphalt, with a northeast wind curling through the distant concrete canyons. Luckily, down below, a minimum number of Biters are roaming the narrow side street running along the south side of the apartment building. Philip glances at his watch.

In roughly one minute and forty-five seconds, April is going to be risking her life in front of the building, and this urgency gets Philip going. He quickly climbs down the first flight, the rickety ladder groaning with his weight, trembling with each step.

As he descends, he senses the silver eyes of dead things noticing him, drawn by the metallic rattle of the ladder, their primitive senses tracking him, smelling him, sensing his vibrations like spiders sensing a fly in their web. Dark silhouettes, glimpsed in his peripheral vision, start lazily shuffling toward him, more and more of them coming around the front of the building to investigate.

They ain't seen nothing yet, he thinks as he drops to the ground and then runs across the street. Sixty-five seconds. The plan is to get in and get out quickly, and Philip moves along the boarded storefronts with the stealth of a Delta Force marine. He reaches the east end of the block and finds an abandoned Chevy Malibu with out-of-state plates.

Thirty-five seconds.

Philip can hear the shuffling footsteps closing in on him as he crouches behind the Malibu and quickly slips his backpack off. His hands do not shake as he digs out the sixteen-ounce bottle of Coke filled with gasoline (April had found a spare plastic tank of gas in the apartment building's basement maintenance room).

Twenty-five seconds.

He twists the cap, stuffs in the gas-soaked rag, and shoves the pointed end in the Malibu's tailpipe, letting a twelve-inch length of rag dangle. Twenty seconds. He digs out a Bic lighter, sparks it, and sets the rag alight. Fifteen seconds. He runs away.

Ten seconds.

He makes it across the street, brushing past a cluster of Biters, and into a dark alcove, diving behind a row of garbage cans, before he hears the *WHOOMP* of that first eruption—the bottle catching in the tailpipe—followed by a much bigger explosion.

Philip ducks and covers as a sonic boom shakes the street and sends up a fireball that turns the shadows into well-lighted places.

Right on time, April thinks as she crouches down in the shadows of the foyer, the concussion blast rattling the glass door. The light popping overhead is like an unseen photographer's strobe. She peers out through the bottom half of the barred door and glimpses the sea change in the ocean of dead.

Like a moving tide of ragged, livid faces, shifting with the gravitational tug of the moon, they start following the noise and light, heading in a disorganized mass toward the south side of the building.

Tinsel shimmering in the sun couldn't attract a flock of sparrows better than this explosion works on these Biters. Within a minute or so, the street in front of the building is practically deserted.

April girds herself. She takes a deep breath. She secures the straps of her duffel bags. She closes her eyes. She says a quick, silent prayer . . . and then she springs up, yanks the cross-brace, and shoves the door open.

She creeps outside. The wind tosses her hair, and the stench strangles her. She stays low as she darts across the street.

The sensory overload threatens to distract her—the smells, the proximity of the horde half a block away, the thunderous beating of her heart—as she frantically moves from dark storefront to dark storefront. Thankfully, she is familiar enough with the neighborhood to know where the convenience store is located.

If measured by the clock, it only takes April Chalmers eleven minutes and thirty-three seconds to slip through the jagged maw of broken glass and visit the ransacked interior of the convenience store. Only eleven and half minutes to fill one and a half canvas bags with enough food and water and miscellaneous stuff to keep them going for quite a while.

But to April Chalmers, those eleven and half minutes feel suspended in time.

She grabs nearly twenty pounds of groceries from the convenience store—including a small canned ham with enough preservatives to keep until Christmas, two gallons of filtered water, three cartons of Marlboro reds, lighters, beef jerky, vitamins, cold remedies, antibacterial ointment, and six extra large rolls of blessed, blessed toilet paper—throwing it all in her duffel bag with lightning speed.

The back of her neck prickles as she works with constant awareness of the ticking clock. The street will fill up again soon and the army of Biters will block her path if she doesn't get back within minutes.

Philip goes through another half a clip of .22-caliber rounds, working his way back around the rear of the apartment building. The majority of the Biters are now clustered around the flaming debris of the Malibu, a riot of moving corpses like June bugs drawn to the light. Philip clears a path around the back of the courtyard by squeezing off two shots. One of them cracks open the cranium of a lumbering cadaver dressed in a running suit, the zombie dropping like a puppet whose strings have been cut. Another blast opens a trough in the top of a skull belonging to what looks like a former homeless woman, her geode eyes flickering out as she falls.

Before the other Biters have a chance to close in on him, he vaults over the rear fence of the courtyard and charges across the leprous brown grass.

He climbs up the back wall of the building, using an awning as a foothold. A second fire escape ladder is folded halfway up the stucco wall of the first story, and Philip gets a grip on it and starts to pull himself the rest of the way up.

But all at once, he pauses, and has second thoughts about the plan.

April reaches the critical point in her mission—twelve minutes have elapsed since she emerged—but she risks visiting one more merchant.

Half a block south, an Ace Hardware store sits empty, its display windows broken, its burglar gates loose enough for a smallish woman to negotiate. She slips through the gap and enters the dark store.

She fills the remainder of the second canvas bag with water filters (for making the standing water in toilets drinkable), a box of nails (to replenish their supply, which they used securing the barricades), markers and rolls of large-format paper (for making signs to alert any other survivors), light bulbs, batteries, a few cans of Sterno, and three small flashlights.

On her way back toward the front of the store, now lugging nearly forty pounds of merchandise in two bulging duffels, she passes a figure slumped at the end of a side aisle stacked with fiberglass insulation.

April pauses. The dead girl on the floor, slumped and leaning against the far wall, is missing one leg. From the snail-trail of gore leading across the floor, it's clear that the thing dragged itself here. The dead girl is not much older than Penny. April gapes for a moment.

She knows she has to get out of there but she can't tear her gaze from the pathetic, ragged corpse sitting in its own juices, which have obviously leaked out of the blackened stump where its right leg used to be.

"Oh God, I can't," April says under her breath, to herself, uncertain what it is she can't do: Put the thing out of its misery, or leave it to suffer for eternity in this deserted hardware store.

April pulls the metal bat from her belt and sets down her packs. She approaches cautiously. The dead thing on the floor hardly moves, just slowly gazes up with the trembling stupor of a fish dying on the deck of a boat.

"I'm sorry," April whispers, and buries the end of the bat in the girl's skull. The blow makes the wet, snapping noise of green wood breaking.

The zombie folds silently to the floor. But April stands there, closing her eyes for a moment, trying to will the image from her mind, an image that will probably haunt her for the rest of her life.

Seeing the shank of the bat cleave open a skull is bad enough, but what April just saw in the horrible brief instant before she brought the bat down, as she was drawing it back, winding up, was this: Either through some meaningless flicker of deadened nerves, or through some deeper understanding, the dead girl turned her face away in that moment before the bat arced down.

A noise near the front of the store gets her attention and she hurries back to her duffel bags, throws the straps over her shoulders, and starts toward the exit. But she doesn't get far. She slams on the brakes when she sees a *second* young girl blocking her path.

It stands fifteen feet away, just inside the mangled burglar screens, in the identical soiled dress as that of the girl April just dispatched.

At first, April thinks her eyes are playing tricks. Or maybe it's the ghost of the girl she just put down. Or maybe April is losing her mind. But as the second dead girl starts shuffling down the aisle toward April with black drool falling off its cracked lips—this one has both its legs—April realizes that it's a *twin*.

It's the other girl's identical twin.

"Here we go," April says, drawing back the bat, dropping her load, preparing to fight her way out.

She takes one step toward the pint-sized monster, raising the bat, when a dry popping blast rings out behind the twin, and April blinks.

The bullet shatters a corner of the front window and takes off the top of the twin's head. April flinches back at the kick of blood mist, as the girl collapses in a heap. April lets out a pained sigh of relief.

Philip Blake stands outside the store, out in the middle of the empty street, clicking a new magazine into his .22-caliber Ruger.

"You in there?" he calls.

"I'm here! I'm okay!"

"I know it ain't polite to rush a lady but they're comin' back!"

April grabs her treasures, and then leaps over the bloody remains blocking the aisle and slips through the burglar gate and out into the street. Instantly, she sees the problem: The throng of zombies is returning, coming around the corner with the collective fervor of a demented chorus line moving in haphazard formation.

Philip grabs one of the bags and they both make a run for the apartment building.

They cross the street in seconds flat, with at least fifty Biters on either flank.

Brian and Nick are peering out the reinforced glass of the outer vestibule door when they see the situation in the street rapidly changing.

They see wolf packs of zombies coming down the street from both directions, returning from wherever the hell they had just gone. In the midst of all this, two human beings, one male and one female, like ball carriers in some obscure, surreal, twisted sport, come charging toward the apartment building with duffel bags slung and bouncing against their backs. Nick perks up.

"There they are!"

"Thank God," Brian says, lowering the Marlin shotgun until the butt rests on the floor. He's shaking. He shoves his left hand in his pocket, and he tries to get a grip on himself. He does not want his brother to see him shaking.

"Let's get the door open," Nick says, leaning his shotgun in the corner.

He gets the door open just as Philip and April are roaring up the walk, a multitude of Biters on their heels. April roars through the doorway first, shaking and hyperventilating with adrenaline.

Philip follows her in, his dark eyes aglow with testosterone-fueled mania. "That's what I'm talkin' about!"

Nick slams the door just in time. Three Biters crash into the outer glass, rattling the steel-impregnated door, their drooling mouths leaving streaks. Several pairs of milky-white eyes gaze in through the greasy glass at the people in the foyer. Dead fingers claw at the door. Other Biters are staggering up the walk.

Brian has his shotgun raised at the figures outside the door. He backs away. "What the hell is going on, man! Where were you guys?"

Nick ushers them through the inner door and into the foyer. April drops her bulging duffel. "That was—that was—*Jesus,* that was close!"

Philip sets down his pack. "Girl, you got some *cojones,* I'll give you that."

Nick steps up. "What's the idea, Philly! You guys just disappear without telling anybody?"

"Talk to *her,*" Philip says with a grin, shoving his Ruger inside his belt.

"We were totally freaking out!" Nick rants. "We were about one second away from going outside to look for you!"

"Calm down, Nicky."

"Calm down? Calm *down!* We were turning the place upside down looking for you! Tara was about to have a shit fit!"

"It's my fault," April says, wiping the grime from her neck.

"Look at our take, man!" Philip indicates the loot stuffed into the bags.

Nick has his fists clenched. "Then we hear a fucking *explosion*? What are we supposed to think? Was that *you* guys? Did you have something to do with that?"

Philip and April exchange a glance, and Philip says, "That idea was kinda both of ours."

April cannot stifle her victorious grin as Philip takes a step toward her, raising his hand. "How about a high five, darlin'?"

They high-five each other, with Nick and Brian staring in disbelief. Nick is about to say something else when a figure appears on the other side of the foyer, pushing through the inner door.

"Oh my God!" Tara storms into the room and goes to her sister. She pulls April into a bear hug. "Oh my God, I was so freaked! Thank God you're okay! Thank God! Thank *God*!"

April pats her sister. "I'm sorry, Tara, it was something I had to do."

Tara lets go, her face flashing with anger. "I ought to beat the *shit* outta you. Seriously! I'm telling that little girl you're just upstairs, but she's getting as freaked as I am! What am I supposed to do? That was a goddamn stupid, irresponsible thing to do! Which is so goddamn typical of you, April!"

"What the hell does that mean?" April gets into her sister's face. "Why don't you say what you mean for once?"

"You fucking *bitch*." Tara winds up like she's going to slap the younger woman when Philip suddenly steps in between them.

"Whoa there, Tonto!" Philip gives Tara a reassuring pat. "Hold on a second. Take a deep breath, sis." Philip nods toward the duffel bags. "I want to show you something. Okay? Just cool your pits for a second."

He kneels down and unzips the bags, displaying the contents.

The others stare silently at the supplies. Philip straightens back up and looks Tara in the eyes. "That 'fucking bitch' there saved our asses today—there's food and water in there. That 'fucking bitch' risked her ass, not knowing if she'd be able to pull it off and not wanting anybody else to get hurt. You ought to be kissing that 'fucking bitch's' feet."

Tara looks away from the duffel bags and looks down at the floor. "We were worried, that's all," she says in a feeble, low voice.

Nick and Brian are now both kneeling by the duffel bags, looking through the treasures. "Philly," Nick says, "I have to admit: You guys kicked *ass*."

"You guys rock," Brian mutters almost under his breath with awe as he rifles through the toilet paper and the beef jerky and the water filters. The emotional atmosphere in the room begins to shift with the slow certainty of clouds parting. Smiles appear on all their faces.

Soon, even Tara is throwing grudging glances over their shoulders at the contents of the duffel bags. "Any cigarettes in there?"

"Here's three cartons of Reds," April says, leaning down and digging out the cigarettes. "Enjoy them, you fucking bitch."

With a good-natured smile, she hurls the cartons at her sister.

Everybody laughs.

Nobody sees the small figure standing across the room, in the inner doorway, until Brian glances up. "Penny? You okay, kiddo?"

The little girl pushes the door open and walks into the foyer. She is still dressed in her pajamas, and her little peaches-and-cream face is chiseled with seriousness. "That man in there? Mr. Chah-merz? He just fell down."

They find David Chalmers on the floor of the master bedroom, amid a litter of tissues and medications. Granules of broken glass from a fallen aftershave bottle sparkle like a halo around his trembling head.

"Jesus!—Daddy!" Tara kneels by the fallen man, pulling his oxygen tube free. David's grizzled face is the color of nicotine as he involuntarily gasps for air, a fish out of water trying to breathe the poisonous atmosphere.

"He's choking!" April hurries around to the other side of the bed, checking the oxygen tank, which lies on the floor on its side near the window, tangled in its tubing. The old man must have pulled it off the bedside table when he fell.

"Daddy? Can you hear me?" Tara gives the man's ashen face a series of quick, light slaps.

"Check his tongue!"

"Daddy? Daddy?"

"Check his tongue, Tara!" April rushes back around the bed, the oxygen tank and a coil of tubing in her hands. While she does this, the others—Philip, Nick, Brian, and Penny—watch from the doorway. Philip feels helpless. He doesn't know whether to jump in or just watch. The girls seem to know what they're doing.

Tara gently levers open the old man's mouth, looking down his gullet. "It's clear."

"Dad?" April kneels on the other side of him, positioning the tiny breathing apparatus under his hooked nose. "Daddy, can you hear me?"

David Chalmers keeps silently gasping, the back of his throat clucking painfully like a record skipping. His eyelids—as ancient and translucent as a mayfly's wings—begin fluttering. Tara frantically feels under the back of his skull for signs of injury. "I don't see any bleeding," she says. "Daddy?"

April feels his forehead. "He's ice-cold."

"Is the oxygen running?"

"Full blast."

"Daddy?" April gently repositions the old man so he's lying supine with the oxygen tube across his upper lip. Again they give him little slaps. "Daddy? Daddy? Daddy, can you hear us? Daddy?"

The old man coughs, eyes fluttering. He blinks. He tries to get a good lungful of air, but his shallow breaths keep hitching in his throat. His eyes are rolled back in his head, and he appears to be only semiconscious.

"Daddy, look at me," April says, her hand gently turning his face toward hers. "Can you see me?"

"Let's get him on the bed," Tara suggests. "Fellas, you mind giving us a hand?"

Philip, Nick, and Brian step into the room. Philip and Nick take one side of the old man, and Tara and Brian the other, and on the count of three, they carefully lift the old man off the floor and lay him on the bed, making the springs squeak and tangling the tube on one side.

Moments later, they have the tube clear and the old man covered in blankets. Only his pale, sunken face is visible above the linens, his eyes shut, his mouth lolled open, and his breathing coming in fits and starts. He sounds like a combustion engine that refuses to turn over. Every few moments, his eyelids flutter and something flickers behind them—lips stretched into a grimace—but then his face goes slack. He is still breathing . . . barely.

Tara and April sit on either side of the bed, stroking the lanky form under the blankets. For a long while, nobody says anything. But chances are, they're all thinking the same thing.

"You think it's a stroke?" Brian asks softly, minutes later, sitting out by the sliding glass doors.

"I don't know, I don't know." April paces the living room, chewing her fingernails, while the others sit around the room, watching her. Tara is in the bedroom, at her father's bedside. "Without medical attention, what chance does he have?"

"Has anything like this ever happened before?"

"He's had trouble breathing before but nothin' like this." April stops pacing. "God, I knew this day was gonna come." She wipes her eyes, which are moist with tears. "We're on the last tank of oxygen."

Philip asks about medication.

"We got his medicine, sure, but that ain't gonna do him much good now. He needs a doctor. Stubborn old coot blew off his last appointment a month ago."

"What do we have in the way of medical supplies?" Philip asks her.

"I don't know, we got some shit from upstairs, antihistamines and shit." April paces some more. "We got first-aid kits. Big deal. This is serious. I don't know what we're gonna do."

"Let's stay calm and think this thing through." Philip wipes his mouth. "He's resting peacefully now, right? His airways are clear. You never know, something like this . . . he could bounce back."

"But what if he doesn't?" She stops moving and looks at him. "What if he doesn't bounce back?"

Philip gets up and goes over to her. "Listen. We gotta keep our heads clear." He pats her shoulder. "We'll keep a close watch on him, we'll figure something out. He's a tough old bird."

"He's a tough old bird who's dying," April says, a single tear tracking down her face.

"You don't know that," Philip says, wiping the tear from her cheek.

She looks at him. "Good try, Philip."

"Come on."

"Good try." She looks away, her crestfallen expression as desolate as a death mask. "Good try."

That night, the Chalmers girls sit watch at their father's bedside, their chairs drawn up on either side of the bed, a battery-powered lantern painting the old man's pallid face in pale light. The apartment is as cold as a meat locker. April can see Tara's breath across the room.

The old man lies there for most of the night in stony repose, his hollow cheeks contracting periodically with his labored breathing. The grizzled whiskers of his chin look like metal filings, shifting in a magnetic field, moving occasionally with the tics of his stricken nervous system. Every once in a while his dry, cracked lips will begin to work impotently, trying to form a word. But other than little dry puffs of air, nothing comes out.

At some point in the wee hours, April notices that Tara has dozed off, her head down on the edge of the bed. April grabs a spare blanket and carefully drapes it over her sister. She hears a voice.

"Lil?"

It's coming from the old man. His eyes are still closed, but his mouth is working furiously, his expression furrowed with anger. Lil is short for Lillian, David's late wife. April hasn't heard the nickname in years.

"Daddy, it's April," she whispers, touching his cheek. He recoils, his eyes still closed. His mouth is contorted, his voice slurred and drunken with nerve damage on one side of his face.

"Lil, get the dogs in! There's a storm comin'—a big one—a nor'easter!"

"Daddy, wake up," April whispers softly. Emotion wells up inside her.

"Lil, where are you?"

"Daddy?"

Silence.

"Daddy?"

At this point, Tara is sitting up, blinking, startled at the sound of her father's strangled voice. "What's going on?" she says, rubbing her eyes.

"Daddy?"

The silence continues, the old man's breaths coming hard and fast now.

"Da—"

The word sticks in April's throat as she sees something horrible crossing the old man's face. His eyelids flick open to half-mast, the whites of his eyes showing, and he begins to speak in an alarmingly clear voice: "The devil has plans for us."

In the gloomy half-light of the lantern, the two sisters exchange mortified glances.

The voice that comes out of David Chalmers is low and gravelly, an engine dieseling: "The day of reckoning is drawing near . . . the Deceiver walks among us."

He falls silent, his head lolling to one side of the pillow as if the wires to his brain have been abruptly cut.

Tara checks his pulse.

She looks at her sister.

April looks at her father's face, his expression now slackened and relaxed into a sanguine, tranquil mask of deep and endless sleep.

With the morning's light, Philip stirs in his sleeping bag on the living room floor. He sits up and rubs his sore neck, his joints stiff from the cold. For a moment, he lets his eyes adjust to the gloomy light, and he orients himself to his surroundings. He sees Penny on the sofa, cocooned in blankets, sound asleep. He sees Nick and Brian across the room, also encased in blankets, also asleep. The memory of the previous evening's deathwatch returns to Philip in stages, the agonizing, hopeless struggle to help the old man and to assuage April's fears.

He glances across the room. In the shadows of the adjacent hallway, the door to the master bedroom is visible in the gloom, still closed.

Climbing out of his sleeping bag, Philip hurriedly and silently gets dressed. He pulls on his pants and pushes on his boots. He runs fingers through his hair and goes into the kitchen to rinse his mouth out. He hears the murmur of voices behind the walls. He goes over to the bedroom door and listens. He hears Tara's voice.

She's praying.

Philip knocks softly.

A moment later, the door clicks open and April is standing there, looking as though someone threw acid in her eyes. They are so bloodshot and wet that they look scourged. "'Morning," she says in a low whisper.

"How's he doing?"

Her lips tremble. "He ain't."

"What?"

"He's gone, Philip."

Philip stares at her. "Aw God . . ." He swallows hard. "I'm real sorry, April."

"Yeah, well."

She starts to cry. After an awkward moment—a wave of contrary emotions punching through Philip's gut—he pulls her into an embrace. He holds her, and he strokes the back of her head. She trembles in his arms like a lost child. Philip doesn't know what to say. Over April's shoulder, he can see into the room.

Tara Chalmers is kneeling by the deathbed, praying silently, her head down on the tangled linen. One of her hands is lying on the cold, gnarled hand of her late father. For some reason that Philip can't figure out, he finds it difficult to take his eyes off the sight of the girl's hand caressing the bloodless fingers of the dead.

"I can't get her to come out of there." April is sitting at the kitchen table, sipping a cup of weak, tepid tea brewed on a Sterno can. Her eyes are clear for the first time since she came out of the death room that morning. "Poor thing . . . I think she's trying to pray him back to life."

"No shame in that," Philip says. He sits across the table from her, a half-eaten bowl of rice in front of him. He has no appetite.

"Have you thought about what you want to do?" Brian asks from across the kitchen. He stands at the sink where he's pouring water, which was collected from some of the toilets upstairs, into filter canisters.

The sounds of Nick and Penny playing cards in the other room drift in.

April looks up at Brian. "Do about what?"

"Your father . . . you know . . . like, burialwise?"

April sighs. "You've been through this before, haven't you?" she says to Philip.

Philip looks at his uneaten rice. He has no idea if she's talking about Bobby Marsh or Sarah Blake, both of whose deaths Philip recounted to April the other night. "Yes, ma'am, that's true." He looks at her. "Whatever you want to do, we'll help you do it."

"Of *course* we'll bury him." Her voice breaks a little bit. She looks down. "I just never pictured myself doing it in a place like this."

"We'll do it together," Philip says. "We'll do it right and proper."

April looks down, a tear falling into her tea. "I hate this."

"We gotta stick together," Philip says without much conviction. He says it because he doesn't know what else to say.

April wipes her eyes. "There's a patch of ground out back under the—"

A sharp noise from the hallway interrupts, and all heads turn.

A muffled thump is followed by a crash, the sound of furniture overturning.

Philip is out of his chair before the others even realize that the noise is coming from behind the closed door of the master bedroom.

THIRTEEN

Philip kicks the door open. Advent candles on the floor. The carpet burning in places. The smoky air vibrating with screams. A blur of movement smears across the darkness and it takes breathless nanoseconds for Philip to realize what he's looking at in the flickering shadows.

The overturned dresser—the source of the crashing noise—has landed inches away from Tara, who's on the floor, crawling with animal instinct, trying desperately to pull herself free of the vise grip of dead fingers on her legs.

Dead fingers?

At first, just for an instant, Philip figures something got in through a window, but then he sees the withered form of David Chalmers—completely turned now—on the floor, on top of Tara's legs, digging yellowed fingernails into her flesh. The old man's sunken face is livid now, the color of mold, his eyes frosted with glassy-white cataracts. He snarls with a ravenous guttural groan.

Tara manages to extricate herself and struggles to her feet, and then slams sideways into the wall.

Right then, many things happen at once: Philip realizes what's going on, and that he left his gun in the kitchen, and that he has a limited amount of time to eradicate this threat.

That is the key—the fact that the kindly old mandolin player is long gone—and what *this* is, this hulking mass of dead tissue rising up and growling a garbled, drooling cry, is a *threat*. More than the flames licking across the carpet, more than the smoke—already forming a nightmarish haze in the room—this *thing* that has materialized inside their sanctuary is the biggest threat.

A threat to all of them.

At this same moment, before Philip has a chance to even move, the others arrive, filling the open doorway. April lets out an anguished yelp—not really a scream, more like a shriek of pain, like an animal getting gut shot. She pushes her way into the room, but Brian grabs her and holds her back. April writhes in his arms.

All this happens in the space of an instant as Philip sees the bat.

In all the excitement on the previous night, April had left her Hank Aaron autographed metal baseball bat in the corner by the barred window. Now it sits gleaming in the flickering flames, maybe fifteen feet away from Philip. There is no time to consider the distance or even map out a maneuver in his mind. All he has time to do is make a lunge across the room.

By this point, Nick has whirled around and is racing across the apartment for his gun. Brian tries to pull April out of the room, but she's strong and she's frantic and she's screaming now.

It takes Philip mere seconds to cover the distance between the door and the bat. But in that brief span of time, the thing that was once David Chalmers goes for Tara. Before the large woman can get her bearings and flee the room, the dead man is upon her.

Cold, gray fingers ply themselves awkwardly toward her throat. She slams back against the wall, flailing at it, trying to push it away. Rotting jaws part, rancid breath wafting up in her face. Blackened teeth gape open. The thing goes for the pale, fleshy curve of her jugular.

Tara shrieks, but before the teeth have a chance to make contact, the bat comes down.

Up until this moment—especially for Philip—the act of vanquishing a moving corpse had become an almost perfunctory deed, as mechanical and obligatory as stunning a pig for the slaughter. But this feels different. It takes only three sharp blows.

The first one—a hard crack to the back temporal region of David Chalmers's skull—stiffens the zombie and arrests its progress toward Tara's neck. She slips to the floor in a paroxysm of tears and snot.

The second blow strikes the side of the skull as the thing is involuntarily turning toward its attacker, the tempered steel of the bat caving in the parietal bone and part of the nasal cavity, sending threads of pink matter into the air.

The third and final whack totals the entire left hemisphere of its skull as the thing is falling—the sound like a head of cabbage smashed in a drill press. The monster that was David Chalmers lands in a wet heap on one of the spilled candles, the ribbons of drool, blood, and gluey gray tissue hitting the flames and sizzling across the floor.

Philip stands over the body, out of breath, his hands still welded to the bat. Almost as punctuation to the horror, a high-pitched beeping noise begins to shrill. Battery-operated fire alarms across the first floor are loudly chirping, and it takes Philip a second to identify the sounds in his ringing ears. He drops the bloody bat.

And *that* is when he notices the difference. *This* time, after *this* extermination, nobody moves. April stares from the doorway. Brian releases his grip on her, and he *too* gapes. Even Tara, sitting up against the wall across the room, gripped in tears of revulsion and agony, settles into an almost catatonic stare.

The strangest thing is, rather than staring at the bloody heap on the floor, they are all staring at Philip.

In due course, they put out all the fires, and they clean the place up. They wrap the body and move it out into the corridor where it will be safe until burial.

Luckily, Penny witnessed very little of the debacle in the room. She *heard* enough of it, though, to make her withdraw back into her mute, invisible shell.

In fact, for quite a long time, nobody *else* has much to say, either, and the edgy silence continues throughout the rest of that day.

The sisters seem to be in some kind of shocked stupor, just going through the motions of the cleanup, not even talking to each other. They have each cried their eyes dry. But they keep staring at Philip; he can feel it like cold fingers on the back of his neck. What the hell did they expect? What did they want him to do? Let the monster feed on Tara? Did they want Philip to try and *negotiate* with the thing?

At noon the following day, they hold a makeshift memorial service in a section of the courtyard surrounded by a security fence. Philip insists on digging the grave himself, refusing assistance from even Nick. It takes hours. The Georgia clay is stubborn in this portion of the state. But by mid-afternoon, Philip is drenched in sweat and ready.

The sisters sing David's favorite song—"Will the Circle Be Unbroken"—at his graveside. This reduces both Nick and Brian to tears. The sound of it is heartrending, especially as it carries up into the high blue sky and mingles with the omnipresent choir of groaning noises coming from outside the fence.

Later, they all sit around the living room, sharing the liquor that they had recovered from one of the apartments (and were saving for God knows what). The Chalmers sisters tell stories of their old man, his childhood, his early days in the Barstow Bluegrass Boys Band, and his time as a deejay on WBLR out of Macon. They speak of his temper, and his generosity, and his womanizing, and his devotion to Jesus.

Philip lets them talk and just listens. It's good to finally hear their voices again, and the tension of the past day seems to be easing a little bit. Maybe it's all part of their process of letting go, or maybe they just need to let it set in.

Later that night, Philip is in the kitchen, alone, refilling his glass with the last couple of fingers of sour mash whiskey, when April comes in.

"Look . . . I wanted to talk to you . . . about what happened and stuff."

"Forget it," Philip says, looking down into the caramel liquid in his glass.

"No, I should have . . . I should have said something sooner, I guess I was in shock."

He looks at her. "I'm sorry it went down like it did, I truly am. I'm sorry you had to see that."

"You did what you had to do."

"And I thank you for saying that." Philip pats her shoulder. "I took an instant liking to your daddy, he was a great piece of work. Lived a long good life."

She chews the inside of her cheek, and Philip can tell she's fighting the urge to cry. "I thought I was prepared for losing him."

"Nobody's ever prepared."

"Yeah, but like *this* . . . I'm still trying to wrap my brain around it."

Philip nods. "Hell of a thing."

"I mean . . . a person doesn't . . . you just don't have any reference point for this kinda shit."

"I know what you mean."

She looks at her hands, which are shaking. Maybe the memory of Philip bashing her father's skull in is still lingering. "I guess all I wanted to say is . . . I ain't blaming you for what you done."

"Appreciate that."

She looks at his drink. "We got any more of that cheap wine left?"

He finds a little bit left in one of the bottles and pours it for her. They drink in silence for a long while. Philip finally says, "What about your sis?"

"What about her?"

"She doesn't seem to be . . ." His voice trails off, the proper words escaping him.

April nods. "In a forgiving kind of mood?"

"Something like that."

April gives him a bitter smile. "She still blames me for stealing her lunch money back at Clark's Hill Elementary."

Over the next few days, the new blended family solidifies as the Chalmers sisters go through their grieving process, sometimes arguing over nothing, sometimes giving everybody else the silent treatment, sometimes holing up in their rooms for extended periods of crying or brooding.

April seems to be handling the transition better than her sister. She clears out her father's things and moves into the master bedroom, giving Philip the room she originally occupied. Philip sets up a nice area for Penny with shelves and some coloring books he found upstairs.

The child is becoming attached to April. They spend hours together, exploring the upper floors, playing games, and experimenting with ways to stretch their meager provisions into nominal yet creative dinners cooked on Sterno flames, such as crumbled jerky stir-fry, peach and raisin casserole, and canned vegetable surprise (the surprise, sadly, turning out to be more shredded pieces of beef jerky).

Gradually, the hordes of undead drift away from the immediate area, leaving behind only a few stragglers, giving the Blakes and Nick a chance to test the limits of their reconnaissance missions to neighboring buildings. Philip notices that Brian is getting bolder, willing to venture out of the building now and again on quick trips. But it's Nick Parsons who truly seems to be taking to this place.

Nick sets up a room for himself in a studio apartment on the second floor—number 2F—at the east end of the corridor. He finds books and magazines in other apartments, and drags spare furniture into the studio. He spends time hanging out on the balcony, sketching pictures of the neighboring streets, mapping out the immediate area, reading his Bible, starting a garden for winter vegetables, and thinking a lot about what has happened to the human race.

He also completes his ramshackle catwalk between the two adjacent buildings.

The narrow walkway is hewn out of plywood and paint ladders lashed together with rope and duct tape (and more than a little praying). The footbridge extends off the back of the roof, spanning a twenty-five-foot gap over an alley, and connecting up with the top rail of a fire escape on the adjacent roof.

The completion of the catwalk marks a turning point for Nick. Getting up his courage one day, he shimmies across the rickety structure and—just as he had predicted—he makes it all the way to the southeast corner of the block without walking outside. From there, he figures out how to get into the pedestrian bridge to the department store. When he comes back that night with armfuls of goodies from Dillard's, he is greeted like a returning war hero.

He brings them fancy gourmet candy and nuts; warm clothing; new shoes and embossed stationery; expensive pens; a collapsible camp stove; satin sheets and luxurious three-hundred-thread-count linens; and even stuffed animals for Penny. Even Tara lightens up at the sight of the European cigarettes with the pastel wrappers. And Nick is doing something else on these solo runs, something that he keeps to himself at first.

On the one-week anniversary of David Chalmers's death, Nick talks Philip into tagging along on a little reconnaissance mission so Nick can reveal what he's been doing. Philip is not crazy about crossing the ladder-bridge—he claims he's worried about it breaking under his weight, but the thing that truly bothers Philip is his secret fear of heights. Nick persuades him by piquing his curiosity. "You gotta see this, Philly," Nick enthuses on the roof. "This whole area is a goldmine, man. I'm tellin' you it's perfect."

With great reluctance, Philip goes ahead and drags himself across the catwalk, on his hands and knees behind Nick, grumbling all the way (and secretly petrified). Philip doesn't dare look down.

They reach the other side, hop down, descend a fire escape ladder, and then slip into the adjacent building through an open window.

Nick leads Philip through the deserted hallways of an accounting firm, the floors littered with forgotten forms and documents like so many fallen leaves. "Not much farther now," Nick says, ushering Philip down a staircase and across a desolate lobby strewn with overturned furniture.

Philip is hyperaware of their echoing footsteps, crunching over cinders of debris. He feels the blind spots and empty spaces in his solar plexus, he hears every snap and every tick as though something might lumber out at them at any moment. He keeps his hand on the stock of the .22 thrust into his jeans. "Over here, right off the parking garage," Nick says, pointing to an alcove at the end of the lobby.

Around a corner. Past an overturned vending machine. Up a short flight of steps. Through an unmarked metal door, and suddenly, almost without warning, the entire world opens up for Philip.

"Holy mother-of-pearl," Philip marvels as he follows Nick across the pedestrian bridge. The enclosed walkway is filthy, scattered with trash and reeking of urine, the thick, reinforced Plexiglas walls so filmed with grime they distort the surrounding cityscape. But the view is spectacular. The passageway is flooded with light, and it feels like you can see for miles.

Nick pauses. "Pretty cool, huh?"

"Pretty fucking outstanding." Thirty feet above the street, the wind buffeting the structure, Philip can look down and see scattered zombies wandering underneath them like exotic fish drifting below a glass-bottom boat. "If it wasn't for those ugly motherfuckers, I'd show this to Penny."

"That's what I wanted to show *you*." Nick walks over to the south side of the walkway. "You see that bus? About half a block down there?"

Philip sees it—a hulking silver MARTA bus sitting at the curb.

Nick says, "Look above the bus's front door, by the mirror, on the right side, you see the mark?"

Sure enough, Philip sees a hand-drawn symbol above the passenger entrance—a hastily scrawled five-point star—done in red spray paint. "What am I looking at?"

"It's a safe zone."

"A what?"

"Been working my way down that street and up this one back here," Nick tells him with the innocent pride of a kid showing a soapbox derby model to his dad. "There's a barber shop over there, clean as a whistle, secure as a bank, the door unlocked." He points farther up the street. "There's an empty semitrailer up there a ways, in good shape, just sitting there, with a good, strong—whattya call 'em—*accordion door*? On the back end."

"What's the point here, Nicky?"

"Safe zones. Places you can duck into. If you're on a supply run and you get in trouble or whatever. I'm finding them farther and farther down the street. Putting marks on 'em so we don't miss 'em. There's all sorts of cubbyholes out there, you wouldn't believe it."

Philip looks at him. "You've been going all the way down to the end of that street by yourself?"

"Yeah, you know—"

"God*damn*it, Nick. You shouldn't be goin' all the way out there without any backup."

"Philly—"

"No, no . . . don't just 'Philly' me on this, man. I'm serious. I want you to be more careful. You understand? I'm serious about this."

"Okay, okay. You're right." Nick gives Philip a good-natured punch in the arm. "I hear you."

"Good."

"You gotta admit, though, this place rocks. Considering the situation we're in?"

Philip shrugs, looking down through the grimy glass at the cannibal fish circling. "Yeah, I guess."

"It could be a lot worse, Philly. We're not in the tall buildings, it's flat enough around here for you to see your way around. We got plenty of room to spread out at the apartment building, we got stores with supplies within walking distance. I'm even thinking we could find a generator somewhere, maybe hot-wire a car to get it back. I could see us staying here, Philly . . . I don't know . . . for a long time." He thinks about it some more. "Indefinitely . . . you know?"

Philip gazes through the filthy glass at the necropolis of empty buildings, and the ragged monsters meandering in and out of view. "*Everything*'s indefinite nowadays, Nicky."

That night, Brian's cough returns. The weather is getting colder and damper by the day, and it is taking a toll on Brian's immune system.

After dark, the apartment is freezing. By morning, it's an icebox, the floor like a skating rink on the soles of Brian's stocking feet. He's taken to wearing three layers of sweaters and a knit scarf that Nick procured from Dillard's. With his fingerless gloves and his thatch of unruly black hair and his hollow Edgar Allan Poe eyes, Brian is starting to look like a waif from a Charles Dickens novel.

"I think this place is really good for Penny," Brian says to Philip that night on a second-floor balcony. The Blake brothers are having an after-dinner drink—more of the cheap wine—and gazing out at the desolate skyline. The cool evening air rustles their hair, and the zombie stink wafts just under the smell of rain.

Brian stares out at the distant silhouettes of dark buildings as if in a trance. For a person in twenty-first-century America, it is almost incomprehensible to see a great metropolis completely dark. But that's exactly what the Blakes are looking at: a skyline so dead and black it looks like a mountain range on a moonless night. Every few moments, Brian thinks he sees the faint glint of a fire or a light twinkling in the black void. But it could very easily be his imagination.

"I think that gal *April* is the thing that's doin' the most good for Penny," Philip says.

"Yeah, she's really good with her." Brian is also growing fond of April, and he's been noticing that Philip may very well have a bit of a crush on her as well. Nothing would make Brian happier than to have Philip find a little peace right now, a little stability with a girlfriend.

"That other one's a slice, though, ain't she?" Philip says.

"Tara? Yeah. Not a happy camper."

For the past few days, Brian has been generally avoiding Tara Chalmers—she is a walking ulcer, always irritable, paranoid, still in the throes of grief over her dad. But Brian figures she'll eventually work her way through it. She seems like a decent person.

"The girl does not realize I saved her fucking life," Philip says.

Brian lets out a series of dry coughs. Then he says, "I've been meaning to talk to you about that."

Philip looks at him. "What."

"The old man turning like that?" Brian measures his words. He knows he's not the only one worrying about this. Ever since David Chalmers came back from the dead and tried to devour his oldest daughter, Brian has been ruminating about the phenomenon, and the implications of what happened, and the rules of this savage new world, and maybe even the prognosis for the entire human race. "Think about it, Philip. He didn't get bit. Right?"

"No, he didn't."

"So, why did he turn?"

For a moment, Philip just stares at Brian, and the darkness seems to expand around them. The city seems to stretch into infinity like the landscape of a dream. Brian feels gooseflesh on his arms as though the very act of putting it into words—saying it out loud—has unleashed a malevolent genie from a bottle. And they will never, ever be able to put that genie back.

Philip sips his wine. In the darkness, his face is grim and set. "Hell of lot we don't know. Maybe he got infected with something earlier, maybe came into contact with just enough of it to start working on his system. The old man was on his way out anyway."

"If that's true, then we all—"

"Hey, professor. Give it a rest. We're all healthy and we're gonna stay that way."

"I know. I'm just saying . . . maybe we ought to think about taking more precautions."

"What precautions? I got your precautions right here." He touches the stock of his .22-caliber Ruger stuffed behind his belt.

"I'm talking about washing up better, sterilizing stuff."

"With what?"

Brian lets out a sigh and looks up at the overcast night sky, a low canopy of haze as dark as black wool. Autumn rains are brewing. "We got the water upstairs in the toilets," he says. "We got the filters and the propane, and we got access to cleaning products down the street, soaps and cleansers and shit."

"We're already filtering the water, sport."

"Yeah, but—"

"And we're washing up with that contraption Nicky found." The so-called contraption is an outdoor camp shower that Nick found in Dillard's sporting goods department. About the size of a small cooler, it has a collapsible five-gallon tank and a shower hose that operates off a battery-powered pump. For five days now, they've each been enjoying the periodic luxury of a brief shower, recycling the water as much as possible.

"I know, I know . . . I'm just saying, maybe it's like, better to go overboard right now with the cleanliness. That's all. Until we know more."

Philip gives him a hard look. "And what if there ain't nothing more to learn?"

Brian has no answer for that one.

The only response comes from the city, humming darkly back at them, with a blast of foul-smelling wind and a big, silent fuck you.

Maybe it's the alarming conglomeration of unappetizing ingredients concocted that night by April and Penny for dinner—a mixture of canned asparagus, Spam, and crumbled potato chips cooked over a propane flame—sitting like a dropped anchor in the pit of Philip's stomach. Or perhaps it's the cumulative effect of all the stress and rage and sleeplessness that does it. Or maybe it's the conversation he had on the balcony with his brother. But regardless of the cause, after he turns in for the night, and drifts off into an uneasy sleep, Philip Blake experiences an elaborate and lurid dream.

He has the dream in his newly established private quarters (April's former bedroom was apparently once somebody's home office—while clearing out the owner's things, Philip and April found stacks of Mary Kay Cosmetics order forms and makeup samples). But now, lying on the queen-sized bed shoved against the wall, Philip writhes in semiconsciousness, drifting in and out of a feverish horror show. It's the kind of dream that has no shape. It has no beginning, middle, or end. It just keeps spinning in its rut of circular terror.

He finds himself back in his childhood home in Waynesboro—the shabby little bungalow on Farrel Street—in the back bedroom he used to share with Brian. Philip is not a child in the dream, he is an adult, and somehow the plague has time-traveled back to the 1970s. The dream is almost three-dimensionally vivid. There's the lily of the valley wallpaper, and the Iron Maiden posters, and the scarred school desk, and Brian is somewhere in the house, unseen, screaming, and Penny is also there, in some adjacent room, crying for her daddy. Philip runs through the hallways, which form an endless labyrinth. Plaster is cracking. The zombie horde is outside, clamoring to get in. The boarded windows are trembling. Philip has a hammer and tries to secure the windows with nails, but the head of the hammer falls off. Crashing noises. Philip sees a door cracking open and he rushes over to it, and the doorknob comes off in his hand. He searches drawers and cabinets for weapons, and the facings fall off the cabinets, and plaster sifts down from the ceiling, and his boot breaks through a hole in the floor. The walls are collapsing, and the linoleum is buckling, and the windows are falling from their frames, and Philip keeps hearing Penny's desperate, shrieking voice calling for him: "DADDY!"

Skeletal arms thrust through crumbling window casements, blackened, curled fingers groping.

"DADDY?"

Bone-white skulls burst up through the floor like gruesome periscopes.

"DADDY!"

Philip lets out a silent scream as the dream shatters apart like spun glass.

FOURTEEN

Philip gasps awake with a start. He jerks forward on the bed, blinking and squinting at the pale morning light. Someone stands at the foot of his bed. No. Two people. He sees them now—one tall and one short.

"Good morning, sunshine," April says with her hand around Penny's shoulder.

"Jesus." Philip sits up against the headboard in his wifebeater and sweatpants. "What the hell time is it?"

"It's like almost noon."

"Holy Christ," Philip utters, getting his bearings. His entire sinewy form is filmed with cold sweat. His neck aches and his mouth tastes like a litter box. "I can't believe it."

"We gotta show you something, Daddy," the little girl tells him, her big eyes ablaze with excitement. The sight of his daughter looking so happy sends a soothing wave of relief through Philip, driving the last remnants of the dream from his feverish brain.

He gets up and gets dressed, telling the two ladies to calm down. "Gimme a second to put my face on," he says in a hoarse, whiskey-cured grunt, running fingers through his greasy hair.

They take him up to the roof. When they emerge from the fire door and plunge into the cool air and light, Philip balks at the glare. Despite the fact that the day is overcast and dark, Philip is hungover and the light makes his eyeballs throb. He squints up at the sky and sees the foreboding storm clouds churning and roiling into the area from the north. "Looks like rain," he says.

"That's good," April says, giving Penny a wink. "Show him why, honey."

The little girl grasps her father's hand and drags him across the roof. "Look, Daddy, me and April made a garden to grow stuff in."

She shows him a small makeshift planter in the center of the roof. It takes a moment for Philip to realize that the garden is constructed out of four wheelbarrows, their wheels removed, their housings taped together. A six-inch layer of soil fills each of the four cavities, a few unidentified shoots of green already transplanted into each barrow. "This is pretty damn fine," he says, giving the child a squeeze. He looks at April. "Pretty damn fine."

"It was Penny's idea," April says with a little gleam of pride in her eyes. She points at a row of buckets. "We're gonna collect the rain, too."

Philip drinks in April Chalmers's beautiful, slightly bruised face, her sea-foam blue eyes, her ashy blond hair undone and hanging over the collar of her scroungy cable-knit sweater. He can't take his eyes off her. And even as Penny starts jabbering happily about all the things she wants to grow—cotton candy plants, bubblegum bushes— Philip cannot help but extrapolate: The way April kneels down next to the child, listening intently with her hand on Penny's back, the look of affection on the woman's face, the easy rapport between the two, the sense of connection—all of it suggests something deeper than mere survival.

Philip can barely allow himself to think the word, and yet it comes to him right then, on that windy precipice, in a rush: *family.*

"Excuse me!"

The gruff voice comes from the fire door behind them, on the other side of the roof. Philip whirls. He sees Tara in one of her stained muumuus and one of her patented moods in the open doorway. She holds a bucket. Her heavily jowled face and Maybelline eyes look even more lined and surly than usual. "Would it be too much to ask for a little help?"

April rises and turns. "I told you I'd help you in a minute."

Philip can see that Tara has been collecting water from toilet basins. He considers getting in the middle of this but decides against it.

"That was half an hour ago," Tara says. "Meantime, I been lugging water while you've been lollygaggin' up here in Mr. Rogers's neighborhood."

"Tara, just . . . calm down." April sighs. "Gimme a second, I'll be right there."

"Fine—whatever!" Tara turns in a huff and swishes angrily back down the inner stairs, leaving the sour vibration of contempt in her slipstream.

April looks down. "I'm sorry about that, she's still dealing with . . . you know . . . *stuff.*"

By the downtrodden expression on April's face, it's clear that it would take too much energy for her to run down the litany of what's needling at her sister. Philip's no dummy. He knows it's complicated and it has something to do with jealousy and sibling rivalry, and maybe even the fact that April seems to be going through her grieving period with someone other than Tara.

"No need to apologize," Philip tells her. "There *is* somethin' I want you to know, though."

"What's that?"

"Just want you to know how grateful I am, the way you been treatin' my daughter."

April smiles. "She's a great kid."

"Yes, ma'am . . . she is . . . and you ain't so bad yourself."

"Why, thank you." She leans over and gives Philip a peck on the cheek. Nothing fancy, just a quick little kiss. But it makes an impression. "Now I gotta get back before my sister shoots me."

April walks off, leaving Philip thunderstruck and reeling in the wind.

As kisses go, it wasn't anything special. Philip's late wife, Sarah, had been a blue ribbon kisser. Hell, Philip had encountered prostitutes over the years since Sarah's death who had given up more in the kissing department. Even hookers have feelings, and Philip would usually ask at the beginning of a session if they would mind terribly if he slipped in a few kisses, just for good measure, just to pretend there was love involved. But this little smooch of April's is more like hors d'oeuvres, a hint of things to come. Philip wouldn't call it a tease. Nor would he call it the platonic kind of kiss a sister might give a brother. It exists in that irresistible limbo between two extremes. It is—from Philip's perspective—a knock on the door, an attempt to see if anyone's home.

That afternoon, Philip expects the rain to come but it doesn't. It's already mid-October—he has no idea what day it is—and everybody keeps expecting the gulley-washers that traditionally sweep through central Georgia this time of year to roll in, but something keeps them at bay. The temperature is dropping, and the air buzzes with latent moisture, but still the rain doesn't come. Maybe the drought has something to do with the plague. But for whatever reason, the unsettled sky, with its dark underbelly of storm clouds, seems to reflect the strange, inexplicable tension building in Philip.

Late in the day, he asks April to go with him on a quick trip down the street.

It takes some convincing—despite the fact that the zombie quotient has thinned dramatically since the last time they went out. Philip tells April he needs help scouting the vicinity for a Home Depot or a Lowe's that might have generators lying around. It's getting colder and colder, especially at night, and they're going to need power soon in order to survive. He says he needs somebody who knows the area.

He also tells her that he wants to show her the safe routes Nick has been carving out. Nick offers to go along but Philip says it would be better if he stuck around and kept watch on the place with Brian.

April is up to the task, and is willing to go, but she's a little dubious about the rickety, homemade catwalk. What if it starts raining when they're on the ladders? Philip assures her it's a piece of cake, especially for a little drink of water her size.

They get their coats on and get their weapons ready—April brings along one of the Marlins this time—and they prepare to embark. Tara is seething with anger at them, disgusted by what she calls "a stupid, dangerous, immature, retarded waste of time." Philip and April politely ignore her.

"Don't look down!"

Philip is halfway across the makeshift ladder-bridge over the back alley. April is ten feet behind him, holding on for dear life. Gazing over his shoulder at her, he smiles to himself. Major *cojones* on this girl.

"I'm cool," she says, crabbing along with white knuckles and clenched jaw. The wind tousles her hair. Thirty feet beneath her, a pair of moving cadavers dumbly gaze around the air for the source of the voices.

"Almost home free," Philip urges as he reaches the other side.

She crabs the remaining twenty feet. He helps her down onto the fire-escape landing. The cast-iron grating squeaks under their weight.

They find the open window and slip inside the former home of Stevenson and Sons Accounting and Estate Planning. The office corridors are darker and colder than they were the last time Philip traversed their length. The storm front has brought dusk to the area earlier than usual tonight.

They cross the empty hallways. "Don't worry," Philip assures her as they crunch across debris and crumpled tax returns, "This place is as safe as you can get, this day and age."

"That's not very reassuring," she says, cradling the shotgun, thumbing the hammer nervously.

Dressed in tattered fleece and jeans, April has her arms and lower legs wrapped with gaffer's tape. Nobody else does this. Philip asked her about it once and she told him she saw an animal trainer do it on TV—a last-resort defense against a bite breaking the skin.

They cross the lobby and find the access stairs just past the ruined vending machines.

"Get a load of this," Philip says as he leads her up the single flight
to the unmarked door. He pauses before opening the door. "You remember Captain Nemo?"

"Who?"

"That old flick *Twenty Thousand Leagues Under the Sea*? That old
loony captain, playing his organ in that submarine, while the giant
squids swim across them big picture windows?"

"Never saw it."

Philip smiles at her. "Well, you're about to."

The last thing April Chalmers expects is for something other than
horrific violence to take her breath away, but that's pretty much what
happens when she follows Philip through the unmarked door and
onto the pedestrian bridge. She pauses on the threshold and just
stares.

She's been in these urban breezeways before—maybe even this
very bridge—but somehow, tonight, the gauzy light and space of
the thing, as it stretches across the intersection, thirty feet above the
streets, connecting up with the second floor of Dillard's, seems almost miraculous. Through the glass roof, veins of lightning flicker
and thread across the storm clouds. Through the transparent walls,
the darkening shadows of the city teem with wandering zombies.
Atlanta looks like a vast game board in chaotic disarray.

"I see what you mean," she says. Her voice comes out in a murmur, as she takes it all in, feeling a weird mixture of emotions—
giddiness, fear, excitement.

Philip strolls down the center of the bridge, pausing by one wall
and shrugging off the straps of his duffel bag. He nods to the south.
"Want you to see something," he says. "C'mere."

She joins him, putting down her shotgun and backpack against
the glass wall.

Philip points out the marks on the abandoned vehicles and

doorways left by Nick Parsons. Philip explains the theory of "safe zones" and he talks about how cunning Nick has become. "I think he's got something really good going here," Philip concludes.

April agrees. "We could use those hiding places when we find that generator everybody's talking about."

"You got that right, sister."

"Nick's a good guy."

"That he is."

The encroaching darkness is drawing down over the city, and in the bluish shadows of the bridgeway, Philip's rugged face looks even craggier to April than usual. With his inky black Fu Manchu whiskers and dark eyes nested in laugh lines, he reminds April of a cross between a young Clint Eastwood and . . . who? Her dad as a young man? Is that why she's feeling these twinges of attraction toward the big, lanky redneck? Is April so retarded that she's attracted to a man just because he's the doppelgänger of her father? Or does this pathetic puppy love have something to do with the stress of fighting to survive in a world suddenly doomed with extinction? This is the guy who cracked open her daddy's skull, for God's sake. But maybe that's unfair. That was *not* David Chalmers back there. Her daddy's spirit, as the song goes, had flown away. His soul had departed long before he climbed out of his bed and tried to make a meal out of his eldest daughter.

"I gotta tell you," Philip is saying, gazing out at the ragged figures, like stray dogs, roaming the streets for scraps. "We get a few things in place, and we could stay for a long time in that apartment building."

"I think you're right. All we gotta do is figure out a way to slip some Valium into Tara's oatmeal."

Philip laughs—a good, clean laugh—which shows a side of him that April has not yet seen. He looks at her. "We got an opportunity here, we can make this work. We can do more than just survive. And I'm not just talking about getting a generator."

April looks up into his eyes. "Whaddaya mean?"

He turns toward her. "Met a lotta girls in my day, ain't never run across one quite like you. Tough as nails . . . but the tenderness you show toward my kid? Never seen Penny take to somebody like she's taken to you. Hell, you saved our asses, pulling us off the streets. You're a very special lady, you know that?"

All at once April feels her skin flush hot with chills, and her midsection weaken, and she realizes Philip is looking at her in a new way. His eyes shimmer with emotion. She knows now that he's been thinking the same thing that she has. She looks down, embarrassed. "Your standards must be low," she mutters.

He reaches out and gently puts one of his big, callused workman's hands on the curve of her jaw. "I got the highest standards of anybody I know."

A clap of thunder booms outside the glass, rattling the bridge and making April jump.

Philip kisses her on the lips.

She pulls back. "I don't know, Philip . . . I mean . . . I don't know if this is . . . you know."

Second thoughts and third thoughts and fourth thoughts flow through April in the space of an instant. If she takes this to the next level, what will happen with Tara? How will it fuck up the dynamics at the apartment? How will it complicate things? How will it affect their safety, their chances of survival, their future (if they even have one)?

Philip's expression brings her back—the way he's looking at her, his gaze almost glassy with emotion, his mouth slack with desire.

He leans in and kisses her again, and this time she finds herself putting her arms around him and returning the kiss, and she doesn't even notice the droplets of rain beginning to ping off the glass over her head.

She feels her body go limp in Philip's forceful embrace. Their lips part, and electricity flows through April as they explore each other with their tongues, the taste of coffee and spearmint gum and Philip's musky odor filling her senses. Her nipples harden under her sweater.

A flash of blue lightning turns the dusk to brilliant silver daylight.

April loses track of herself. She loses track of *everything*. Her head is spinning. She doesn't notice the rain slapping against the glass roof. She doesn't even notice the fact that Philip is gently lowering both of them to the floor of the walkway. Their lips locked and working sensually, Philip's big hands caressing April's breasts, he carefully lays her back against the glass wall, and before April knows what is happening, he is on top of her.

The storm unleashes its fury. The rain comes down now in sheets against the roof. Thunder rolls and lightning crackles and sparks like static electricity in the anxious air as Philip fumbles April's sweater up across her bare midriff, exposing her bra in the blue light.

Gnarled fingers wrestle open belt buckles. Thunder booms. April feels the urgent nudge of Philip's loins burrowing between her legs. Lightning flickers. Her jeans are halfway down her legs, her breasts free now.

The edge of a fingernail brushes her belly, and all at once, like a switch flipping inside her—accompanied by a single volley of thunder—she thinks, *WAIT.*

BOOOOOOOM!

WAIT!

A tidal wave of desire carries Philip Blake off on its roaring currents.

He can barely hear April's voice coming from somewhere far away, telling him to *Stop, wait, hold on, listen, listen, this is too much, I'm not ready for this, please, please, stop right now, stop.* None of it registers in Philip's brain as it swims with lust and passion and pain and loneliness and a desperate need to *feel something,* because now his entire being is wired to his groin, all his pent-up emotion coursing through him.

"God, I'm begging you to stop!" the faraway voice pleads, April's body stiffening.

Philip rides the writhing woman beneath him as if surfing a pipeline of white noise, knowing that she secretly wants him, *loves him,* despite what she's saying. So, he keeps shoving himself into her, again and again, in great magnesium-bright flashes of lightning and raw energy, filling her, taking her, nourishing her, transforming her, until she goes limp beneath him, limp and silent now.

The soft white explosion of pleasure erupts like a skyrocket launching inside Philip.

He slides off her, landing on the floor next to her, staring straight up at the rain—momentarily oblivious to the shadowy, desecrated souls thirty feet below them, captured in the flicker-show of lightning like monstrous figures in a silent movie.

Philip takes April's silence as a sign that maybe, just maybe, everything's going to be okay. As the storm settles into a steady deluge, its muffled jet-engine roar filling the walkway, the two of them pull their clothes back on and lie there side by side for a long time, not saying a word, staring up at the strafing sheets of rain crashing off the glass roof.

Philip is in a state of shock, his heart racing, his skin clammy and cold. He feels like a broken mirror, as if a shard of his own soul has fractured off and reflected back the face of a monster. What did he just do? He knows he did something wrong. But it almost feels like somebody else did it.

"Got a little carried away there," he says at last, after many minutes of terrible silence.

She doesn't say a word. He glances over at her, and sees her face in the darkness, reflecting the liquid shadows of rain streaming down the sides of the glass walkway. She looks semiconscious. Like she's having a waking dream.

"Sorry about that," he says, the words sounding tinny and hollow in his own ears. He shoots another glance at her, trying to gauge her mood. "You okay?"

"Yes."

"You sure?"

"Yes."

Her voice has a mechanical quality to it, completely colorless, barely audible above the noise of the rain. Philip is about to say something else when a volley of thunder interrupts his thought. The rumbling reverberates through the iron framework of the walkway, a teeth-rattling vibration that makes Philip cringe.

"April?"

"Yes."

"We ought to get back."

The return trip is shrouded in silence. Philip walks a few paces behind April through the deserted lobby, up a staircase, and down the empty, litter-strewn corridors. Every now and then, Philip considers saying something, but he doesn't. He figures it's probably best to let it ride right now. Let her work through it. Anything Philip says might make it worse. April walks ahead of him with the shotgun on her shoulder, looking like a tired soldier returning from a rough patrol. They reach the top floor of the accounting firm and find the gaping window, the rain blowing in past jagged, broken glass. Only a few words are spoken—"You go first" and "Watch your step"—as Philip helps her climb out and cross the rain-swept fire escape. The pounding wind and rain that lashes down on them as they shimmy across the treacherous makeshift catwalk almost feels good to Philip. It braces him and wakes him up and gives him hope that maybe he can repair whatever damage has been done here tonight with this woman.

By the time they get back to the apartment—both of them soaked to the bone, exhausted, and dazed—Philip is confident he can fix this.

Brian is in the office bedroom with Penny, putting her to sleep on her cot. Nick is in the living room, working on his map of safe zones. "Hey, how'd it go?" he asks, looking up from his papers. "You guys look like drowned rats; you find any Home Depots out there?"

"Not this time," Philip replies, heading for the bedroom, not even pausing to take off his shoes.

April says nothing, doesn't even meet Nick's gaze as she heads toward the hallway.

"Look at you two," Tara says, coming out of the kitchen with a surly expression and a lit cigarette dangling out of the corner of her mouth. "Just like I thought—a wild fucking goose chase!"

She stands there with her hands on her hips as her sister vanishes without a word into her room at the end of the hall. Tara gives Philip a look, and then storms away, following her sister.

"I'm going to bed," Philip says flatly to Nick and then adjourns to his room.

The next morning, Philip stirs awake just before dawn. The rain still pounds the streets outside. He can hear it drumming off the window. The room is dark and cold and dank, and smells of mold. He sits on the edge of the bed for the longest time, looking at Penny, who slumbers across the room on her cot, her tiny body all balled up in a fetal position. The half-formed memories of a dream cling to Philip's woozy brain, as well as the sickening sensation that he doesn't know where the nightmares end and the episode with April the previous evening begins.

If only he had *dreamed* those events in the pedestrian walkway instead of actually acting them out. But the hard, sharp edge of reality comes back to him in that dark room in a series of flash frames in his mind, as though he's watching someone else perpetrate the crime. Philip hangs his head, trying to push the feelings of dread and guilt from his mind.

Running fingers through his hair, he talks himself into being hopeful. He can work through this with April, figure out a way to move forward, put it behind them, apologize to her, make it up to her.

He watches Penny sleep.

In the two and a half weeks since Philip's little cadre joined up with the Chalmers, Philip has noticed his daughter coming out of her shell. At first, he detected little things: the way Penny had begun to look forward to concocting their god-awful dinners, and the way she lit up every time April walked into a room. With each passing day, though, the child has become more and more talkative, remembering things from before the "turn," commenting on the strange weather patterns, asking questions about the "sickness." Can animals get the disease? Does it wear off? Is God mad at them?

Philip's chest hitches with emotion as he gazes at the slumbering child. There has to be a way to make a life for his daughter, make a family, make a home—even in the midst of this waking nightmare—there has to be a way.

For a brief instant, Philip imagines a desert island and a little cottage nestled in a grove of coconut trees. The plague is a million light-years away. He imagines April and Penny on a swing set, playing together out by a vegetable garden. He imagines himself sitting on a back porch, healthy, brown from the sun, happily watching the two ladies in his life sharing contented moments. He imagines all this while he watches his daughter sleep.

He gets up and pads over to her, kneeling and lightly putting a hand on the downy softness of her hair. She needs to bathe. Her hair is matted and greasy, and she has a faint body odor. That smell somehow reaches out to Philip and pinches his gut. His eyes well up. He has never loved anyone other than this child. Even Sarah—whom he adored—came in second. His love for Sarah was—like that of all married people—complicated, conditional, and fluid. But when he first laid eyes on his baby girl as a blotchy little newborn, seven and half years ago, he learned what it means to love.

It means to be afraid, to be vulnerable for the rest of your life.

Something catches Philip's attention across the room. The door is half ajar. He remembers shutting it before turning in. He remembers that very clearly. Now it's cracked open about six inches.

At first, this doesn't really make much of an impression or worry him all that much. Maybe he accidentally neglected to latch the door, and the thing drifted open on its own. Or maybe he got up to piss in the middle of the night and forgot to close it. Or maybe *Penny* had to pee and left it open. Hell, maybe he's a sleepwalker and doesn't even know it. But then, just as he's turning back to continue gazing down at his daughter, he notices something else.

Things are missing from the room.

Philip's heart starts thumping. He left his backpack—the one he was wearing when he arrived here over two weeks ago—leaning against the wall in the corner, but now it's gone. His gun is missing as well. He left the .22 pistol on top of the dresser with the last magazine of bullets beside it. The ammo is gone, too.

Philip springs to his feet.

He looks around. The gloomy dawn is just beginning to lighten the room, the window shade projecting tears of rain, the ghostly reflections of water sluicing down the glass outside it. His boots are not where he left them. He left them on the floor by the window, but now they're gone. Who the hell would take his boots? He tells himself to calm down. There has to be a simple explanation. No reason to get all jacked up. But the absence of the gun is what troubles him the most. He decides to take this one step at a time.

Silently, careful not to awaken Penny, he crosses the room and slips out the open door.

The apartment is silent and still. Brian dozes in the living room on the pull-out bed. Philip pads into the kitchen, lights up the propane stove, and makes himself a cup of instant coffee with some rainwater left in a bucket. He splashes some of the cold water on his face. He tells himself to stay calm, take some deep breaths.

When the coffee is hot, he takes the cup and walks down the hallway to April's room.

Her door is also ajar.

He looks in and sees that the room is empty. His pulse quickens.

A voice says, "She ain't here."

He whirls and comes face-to-face with Tara Chalmers, who holds the Ruger pistol, the muzzle raised and aimed directly at Philip.

FIFTEEN

"All right . . . go easy, sis." Philip makes no move. He just stands there, frozen in the hallway, with his free hand raised, and the coffee in his other hand, jutting out to the side like he's interested in offering it to her. "Whatever it is, we can work it out."

"*Really . . . ?*" Tara Chalmers glowers at him with her painted eyes flaring. "Ya think?"

"Look . . . I don't know what's going on—"

"What's going on," she says without a trace of nerves or fear, "is that we're changing the lineup around here."

"Tara, whatever you're thinking—"

"Let's get something straight." Her voice is steady and flatlined of emotion. "I need you to shut the fuck up and do what I say, or I will blow you the fuck away and don't think I won't."

"This ain't—"

"Put the cup down."

Philip obliges, slowly setting the cup on the floor. "Okay, sis. Whatever you say."

"Stop calling me that."

"Yes, ma'am."

"Now we're gonna go get your brother, your friend, and your kid."

Philip buzzes with adrenaline. He doesn't think Tara has the balls to do any real harm, and he considers making a move for the weapon—a distance of six to eight feet lies between him and the barrel of the Ruger—but he resists the temptation. Better to comply at this point and try and get her talking.

"May I say somethin'?"

"MOVE!"

Her sudden cry shatters the stillness, loud enough to not only awaken Penny and Brian, but probably be heard up on the second floor where Nick—an early riser—is likely already up and about. Philip takes a step toward her. "If you'd just give me a chance to—"

The Ruger barks.

The blast goes wide—maybe on purpose, maybe not—chewing a divot in the wall eighteen inches from Philip's left shoulder. The roar of the gun is enormous in the enclosed space of the hallway, and Philip's ears are ringing as he realizes a particle of the plaster wall has stuck to his cheek.

He can barely see Tara through the blue smoke of cordite. She is either grinning or grimacing, it's hard to tell at this point.

"The next one goes in your face," she tells him. "Now, you gonna be a good boy or what?"

Nick Parsons hears the gunfire just after opening his Concordance Bible for his morning read. Sitting in bed, with his back against the headboard, he jumps at the noise, the Bible flying out of his hands. It was open to the Revelation to John, Chapter 1 Verse 9, the part where John says to the church, "I am John your brother who shares with you in Jesus the tribulation and the kingdom and patient endurance."

Leaping out of bed, he goes to the closet where his Marlin shotgun is supposed to be resting against the wall in the corner, except it's not there. Panic vibrates down through Nick's spine, and he spins, and he looks around his room at all the missing gear. His knapsack—gone. His boxes of shotgun shells—gone. His tools, his pickaxe, his boots, his maps—all gone.

At least his jeans are still there, neatly folded over the back of a chair. He yanks them on and charges out of the room. Through the studio apartment. Out the door. Down the corridor. Down a flight

202 | Kirkman & Bonansinga

of steps and out onto the first floor. He thinks he hears the sound of a voice raised in anger but he's not sure. He rushes toward the Chalmers's apartment. The door is unlocked and he pushes his way inside.

"What's going on? What's going on?" Nick keeps repeating as he slams to a stop in the living room. He sees something that doesn't make any sense. He sees Tara Chalmers with the Ruger pointed at Philip, and Philip with this weird look on his face, and Brian standing a few feet away with Penny drawn close to him, his arms around the little girl in a protective posture. And weirder still: Nick sees their belongings piled on the floor in front of the sofa.

"Move over there," Tara says, brandishing the gun, and directing Nick toward Philip, Brian, and Penny.

"What's wrong?"

"Never mind, just do what I say."

Nick slowly complies but his mind is swimming with confusion. What in God's name happened here? Almost involuntarily, Nick looks at Philip, looks into the big man's eyes for answers, but for the first time since Nick has known Philip Blake, the big guy looks almost sheepish, almost blank with indecision and frustration. Nick looks at Tara. "Where's April? What happened?"

"Never mind."

"What are you doing? What's the idea putting of all our stuff in a—"

"Nicky," Philip chimes in. "Let it go. Tara's gonna tell us what she wants us to do. And we're gonna do it, and everything's gonna be okay."

Philip says this to Nick but as he's saying it, he's looking at Tara.

"Listen to your pal here, Nick," Tara says, and she too says this to Nick but doesn't take her gaze off Philip. Her eyes practically glow with contempt and anger and vengeance and something else—something incomprehensible to Nick, something that feels disturbingly intimate.

Now it's Brian's turn to pipe in: "What is it you want us to do exactly?"

Tara still doesn't take her eyes off Philip as she says, "Get out."

At first, this simple imperative sentence sounds to Nick Parsons like a rhetorical statement. To his stunned ears, it sounds as though she's not exactly telling them to do something as much as she's making some kind of a point. But this initial reaction—and maybe hopeful thinking—is immediately short-circuited by the look on Tara Chalmers's face.

"Hit the road."

Philip keeps staring at her. "Where I come from, that's called murder."

"Call it whatever you want. Just take your shit and go."

"You're gonna send us out there without weapons."

"I'm gonna do more than that," she says. "I'm gonna climb up on that roof with one of them high-powered pigeon guns and I'm gonna make *sure* you leave."

After a long, horrible moment of silence, Nick looks at Philip.

And finally, Philip tears his gaze away from the stout, buxom girl with the pistol. "Get your stuff," he says to Nick, and then to Brian he says, "There's a rain poncho in my pack, put it on Penny."

The amount of time it takes them to get dressed and ready to leave is nominal—mere minutes, with Tara Chalmers standing guard like a stone sentry—but it gives Brian Blake plenty of time to wildly ruminate to himself about what could have happened. Tying his boots, and putting the slicker on Penny, he realizes that all indications point to some kind of sick triangle going on. April's absence speaks volumes. As does Tara's unmitigated, righteous anger. But what *caused* it? It couldn't be something Philip said or did. What could offend the girls this deeply?

For a crazy instant, Brian's mind casts back to his insane ex-wife. Compulsive, volatile, flaky Jocelyn had done stuff like this. She would vanish without a trace for weeks. One time, while Brian was at night school, she actually put all his shit out on the stairs of their tenement building, as though she were removing a stain from her life. But *this*. This is different. The Chalmers girls have shown no previous signs of being irrational or nuts.

The thing that bothers Brian the most is the way his brother is behaving. Beneath the surface of his simmering anger and frustration, Philip Blake almost seems *resolved,* maybe even hopeless. This is a clue. This is important. But the problem is, there's no time to figure it out.

"Come on, let's roll," Philip says, his backpack slung over his shoulder. He has his denim jacket on now—the black, oily grime and gore from their earlier journey still visible all over it—and he's heading toward the door.

"Wait!" Brian says. He turns to Tara. "At least let us take some food. For Penny's sake."

She just levels her gaze at him and says, "I'm letting you walk outta here alive."

"Come on, Brian." Philip pauses in the doorway. "It's over."

Brian looks at his brother. Something about that deeply lined, weathered face is galvanizing to Brian. Philip is family, he's blood. And they've come a long way. They've survived too many jams to die now like homeless pets abandoned on the side of the road. Brian feels a strange sensation building in the base of his spine, filling him with an unexpected strength. "Fine," he says. "If this is the way it has to be . . ."

He doesn't finish the sentence—there is nothing more to say—he simply puts an arm around Penny and ushers her out behind her father.

The rain is both a blessing and a curse. It bullwhips across their faces as they emerge from the building's front entrance, but as they crouch under spindly trees along the parkway to get their bearings, they see that the storm has apparently driven the Biters off the streets. The sewers are flooding, the roads streaming with overflow, and the gray sky hangs low.

Nick squints into the distance to the south, the streets relatively clear. "That way's best! Most of the safe zones are down there!"

"Okay, we'll head south," Philip says and turns to Brian. "Can you piggyback her again? I'm countin' on you, sport. Watch her back."

Brian wipes moisture from his face and gives his brother a thumbs-up.

Turning to the child, Brian starts to go about the business of gently lifting her onto his back, but he abruptly stops. For the briefest instant, he just stares in amazement at the little girl. She is also giving a thumbs-up sign. Brian glances at his brother, and the two men acknowledge something beyond words.

Penny Blake just stands there, waiting, chin jutting defiantly. Her soft little eyes are blinking away the rain, and the look on her face is reminiscent of the expression her late mother would often display when impatient with male nonsense. Finally, the child says, "I'm not a baby . . . can we go now?"

They make their way to the corner, staying low, slipping on the slimy walk, the rain a constant drag on their progress. It gets in their faces and in their clothes and into their joints almost immediately. It's an icy, needling autumn rain with no signs of slowing down.

Up ahead, a few shabby, cadaverous zombies cluster near an abandoned bus stop, their greasy heads of hair like moss matted across their dead faces. They look like they're waiting for a bus that will never come.

Philip leads his group across the corner and under an awning. Nick points the way to the first safe zone—the city bus sitting in mothballs half a block south of the pedestrian bridge. A quick hand gesture from Philip, and now they hurry along the storefronts toward the bus.

"I say we go back," Nick Parsons is grumbling as he crouches down on the floor of the bus and fishes through his backpack. The rain makes a muffled tommy-gun noise on the bus's roof. Nick finds a T-shirt, pulls it out, and wipes the moisture from his face. "We're talking about a single girl here—we can take the place back from her—I say we go back and kick her the hell out."

"Think we can take it from her, huh?" Philip is up in the pilot area, searching the compartments for things left behind by the driver. "You got a bulletproof vest in that backpack of yours?"

The bus—a thirty-foot fuselage of molded seats facing inward along either side—reeks with the ghostly secretions of former passengers, a sort of wet dog-fur smell. In the rear of the bus, resting on the second-to-last seat, with Penny in the seat next to him, Brian shivers in his wet sweatshirt and jeans. He has a bad feeling, and it's not only because of their exposure to the stormy, urban wilderness of Atlanta.

Brian's sense of doom has more to do with the mystery of what happened back at the apartment building last night. He can't stop wondering just exactly what transpired between the hours of 5 P.M. (when Philip and April embarked on their mission) and 5 A.M. the following morning (when everything suddenly blew up in their faces). From the gravelly tension in his brother's voice and the cold determination on his face, it's becoming clear to Brian that it may already be a moot point. Their immediate priority is now survival. But Brian can't stop thinking about it. The mystery speaks to something deeper, something gnawing at Brian to which he can't quite put words.

Lightning flashes outside the bus, as brilliant as a photographer's strobe.

"We had a good thing going at that place," Nick goes on, his voice whiny and unsteady. He stands up, grabbing a hand strap for purchase. "Those are our guns, man. All the work we did? That's our stuff as much as theirs!"

"Stay down, Nick," Philip says flatly. "I don't want any of them pus bags seeing us in here."

Nick ducks down.

Philip sits down in the driver's seat, the springs squeaking. He checks a map case on the dash and finds nothing useful. The keys are in the ignition. Philip turns it over and gets nothing but a clicking noise. "I'm not going to say it again. That place is *over* for us."

"Why, though? Why can't we take it back, Philly? We can take that fat bitch. The three of us?"

"Let it go, Nick," Philip says, and even Brian, all the way in the back of the bus, hears the icy warning tone in Philip's voice.

"I just don't get it," Nick complains under his breath. "How something like this could happen—"

"Bingo!" At last, Philip has found something useful. The four-foot-long steel rod—about the width and heft of a short length of iron rebar—is attached to clips under the driver's side window. Hooked on one end, the tool is likely used to reach across the cab to the accordion door (in order to manually pull it shut). Now, as Philip wields the thing in the gloomy light, it looks like an excellent makeshift weapon. "This'll do," he murmurs.

"How did this happen, Philly?" Nick persists, crouching down in the flickering stutter of lightning.

"GODDAMNIT!"

Philip suddenly slams the iron rod against the dash, sending shards of plastic flying and making everybody jump. He smacks it again, cracking the two-way radio. He strikes it again and again with all his might, caving in the controls and shattering the fare box, sending coins flying. He keeps striking the console until the dashboard is totaled.

Finally, with the veins in his neck bulging, his face livid with rage, he turns and burns his gaze into Nick Parsons. "Would you please shut the fuck up!"

Nick stares.

In the rear of the bus, sitting next to Brian, Penny Blake turns away and gazes out the window, the dirty rain tracking down in rivulets. Her expression hardens as though she's working out a complicated mathematical problem that's far too complex for her grade level.

Meanwhile, up front, Nick is frozen with shock. "Take it easy, Philly . . . I'm just . . . babbling. You know? Didn't mean anything. The place just kinda grew on me."

Philip licks his lips. The fire in his eyes dwindles. He takes a deep breath and lets out a pained exhalation. He puts the rod down on the driver's seat. "Look . . . I'm sorry . . . I understand how you feel. But it's better this way. Without electricity, that place is going to be a walk-in freezer by mid-November."

Nick keeps looking down. "Yeah . . . I guess I see your point."

"It's better this way, Nicky."

"Sure."

At this point, Brian tells Penny he'll be right back, and he pushes himself off his seat.

He moves up the aisle, staying low, moving just beneath the level of the sliding windows, until he joins Nick and his brother. "What's the plan, Philip?"

"We'll find someplace we can build fires. Can't build fires in an apartment building."

"Nick, how many more of these 'safe zones' have you got mapped out?"

"Enough to get outta this part of town, if we catch a break or two."

"Sooner or later, we're gonna have to find a car, though," Brian says.

Philip grunts. "No shit."

"You think there's gas in this bus?"

"Deisel, probably."

"Guess it doesn't matter *what* it is. We got no way to siphon it."

"And no way to store it," Philip reminds him.

"And no way to move it," Nick adds.

"That metal thing over there?" Brian points at the metal reacher on the driver's seat. "You think that thing's sharp enough to puncture the gas tank?"

"On the bus?" Philip glances at the steel rod. "I suppose. What good's that gonna do?"

Brian swallows hard. He has an idea.

One by one, they each quickly slip through the accordion door and into the rain, which has now settled into a low, cold drizzle. The daylight is muddy. Philip carries the steel rod, Nick the three brown Miller Light bottles that Brian found wedged under the rear seats. Brian keeps Penny close—there are dark figures visible in all directions, the closest ones maybe a block away—and the clock is ticking.

Every few moments, the lightning turns the city magnesium bright—illuminating the dead coming from either end of the street. Some of the Biters have noticed humans scurrying around the back of the bus, and those zombies approach now with a more defined purpose in their lumbering gait.

Philip knows the location of the gas tank from his days as a truck driver.

He crouches down near the massive front tire, and he quickly feels under the chassis for the bottom edge of the tank as the rain drips off his chin. This bus has two separate reservoirs, each one containing a hundred gallons of fuel.

"Hurry, man, they're coming!" Nick kneels behind Philip with the bottles.

Philip slams the pointed end of the steel rod into the bottom of the forward tank, but it only dents the iron enclosure. He cries out a garbled howl of white-hot anger and drives the point again into the reservoir.

This time, the point punctures the skin of the tank and a thin stream of yellow, oily liquid suddenly shoots out all over Philip's arms and hands. Nick leans in and quickly fills the first twelve-ounce bottle.

Thunder pounds the sky, followed by another salvo of lightning. Brian glances over his shoulder and sees an entire regiment of walking corpses—closer now in the flash of heavenly daylight, only twenty-five yards away—many of their faces clearly discernible in the photostrobe radiance.

One of them is missing a jaw, another one walking along with a streamer of intestines lolling out of a gaping hole in its stomach.

"Hurry, Nick! Hurry!" Brian has pieces of a torn shirt ready to go in one hand, the lighter in the other. He fidgets restlessly next to Penny, who is trying her best to be brave, clenching her little fists, chewing her lip as she keeps tabs on the advancing army of upright cadavers.

"There's one—go, GO!" Nick hands the first bottle of fuel to Brian.

Brian stuffs the rag into it, then quickly turns the bottle upside down until the cloth is soaked. This procedure only encompasses a few seconds, but Brian can feel the time running out, the presence of hundreds of Biters closing in. A flick of the lighter produces a flame that is instantly extinguished by the wind.

"C'mon, sport . . . c'mon, c'mon!" Philip is turning to the oncoming horde, raising his steel implement. Behind him, Brian cups his hands around the wick and finally gets it lit. The rag flares, the flames curling down the side of the bottle, feeding off the fumes and spill.

Brian hurls the Molotov cocktail at the leading edge of the crowd.

The bottle shatters five feet away from the closest zombies and blooms in a yellow sunburst of fire, making a crackling sound in the mist. Several corpses stagger backward at the unexpected light and heat, some of them bumping into their counterparts, knocking them over like dominoes. The sight of these monsters tumbling would ordinarily be almost funny, but not now.

Now Philip grabs the second full bottle, and stuffs the rag in. "Gimme the lighter!" Brian hands over the Bic. "Now get moving!" Philip commands, lighting the rag and hurling the flaming bottle at the army of monsters coming from the opposite direction.

This time, the bottle lands in their midst, erupting in their ranks, setting ablaze at least a dozen Biters with the ferocity of napalm.

Brian doesn't look back as he scoops Penny off the ground and follows Nick in a desperate run for the barbershop.

Brian, Penny, and Nick get halfway to the next safe zone when they realize that Philip is lagging behind them.

"What the hell's he doing!" Nick's voice is shrill and frantic as he ducks into the doorway of another boarded storefront.

"Hell if I know!" Brian says, ducking into the doorway with Penny, gazing back at his brother.

A hundred yards away, Philip is yelling something obscene and inarticulate at the monsters, swinging his iron weapon at an attacker. The flaming zombie comes at him in a wreath of smoke and sparks.

"Oh my God!" Brian shields Penny's face. "Get down—GET DOWN!"

In the distance, Philip Blake is backing away from the mob with the lighter raised in one hand and the bloody iron raised in the other, some kind of Viking brazenness taking over now, all his pent-up rage coming out in a series of big, portentous gestures.

He pauses and lights a spreading pool of fuel seeping out from underneath the bus, and then turns and flees the scene with the full-tilt abandon of a ball carrier charging toward open field.

Behind him, the puddle of fuel catches and spreads, the blue flames billowing toward the massive steel girth of the bus. Philip traverses about fifty yards of wet pavement, cracking the skulls of half a dozen Biters along the way, while the fire crawls up the side of the bus.

A low, subsonic thump rises above the rain and moaning noises. Philip can't see Brian and the others in the mist ahead of him.

"PHILIP! IN HERE!"

Brian's howl is a beacon, and Philip dives toward the sound of it as the explosion rocks the ground and turns a dark, gray afternoon into the surface of the sun.

None of them gets a good look at it. They are all slammed against a door inside the boarded alcove, shielding their faces from the flaming shrapnel—pieces of the bus, jagged shards of metal bulwark, and fountains of glass—flying past the doorway. Brian manages to glimpse a reflection off the glass of a store window across the street: The explosion, half a block away, has launched twenty tons of bus straight up, a mushroom cloud of dazzling, horrifying fire, the force of the blast bursting open the cabin, the molten hot shock wave punching through multitudes of dead with the violent brilliance of a supernova—countless bodies swept away on the wave, incinerated in the furnace, some of them torn to pieces by the flying debris, the mortified body parts flying up into the storm-lashed sky like a flock of birds attempting to escape.

A flaming piece of fender lands fifteen feet from the doorway.

Everybody jumps at the clanging noise, their eyes wide with shock. "Fuck! FUCK!" Nick exclaims, hands shielding his face. Brian

holds Penny in a locked embrace, speechless, momentarily paralyzed.

Philip wipes his face with the back of his hand and gazes around
the doorway with the stupor of a sleepwalker just coming awake.
"Awright then." He glances over his shoulder, and then back at Nick.
"Where's this barber shop?"

SIXTEEN

Half a block south—in the darkness of a festering, airless tile room, among scattered remnants of *True Detective* magazines, plastic combs, dust bunnies of human hair, and tubes of Brylcreem—they dry their faces with towels and barber smocks, and then find more ingredients for homemade Molotov cocktails.

Bottles of hair tonic get emptied, and then filled with alcohol and plugged with wads of cotton. They also find an old, scarred Louisville Slugger hidden under the cash register. The baseball bat probably once warded off unruly customers or neighborhood punks looking to boost the day's receipts. Now Philip gives the nascent weapon to Nick and tells him to use it wisely.

They scavenge for any other supplies they might be able to use. An old vending machine in back yields a handful of candy bars, a couple of Twinkies, and an ancient sausage stick. As they stuff their knapsacks, Philip tells them not to get too comfortable. He can hear noises outside—more dead encroaching on the area, drawn to the explosion. The rain is slowing down. Noises are carrying. They have to keep moving if they're going to get out of the city before dark. "C'mon, c'mon," Philip says. "Let's get our asses in gear and get to that next zone—Nicky, you take the lead."

Reluctantly, Nick leads them out of the barbershop, into the drizzle, and down another row of storefronts. Philip brings up the rear with the iron bar ready to rock, keeping a watchful eye on Penny, who clings with simian instinct to Brian's back.

Halfway to the next safe zone, a stray corpse lurches out from behind a wreck, shuffling menacingly toward Brian and Penny. Philip
lashes out at the back of its head with the hooked end of the iron
prod—hitting it just above the six cervical vertebrae—so hard that
the cranium detaches and hangs down across its chest as it collapses
to the wet paving stones. Penny averts her gaze.

More cadavers are materializing in the mouths of alleys and the
shadows of doorways.

Nick finds the next painted symbol, near the corner of two cross
streets.

The star is scrawled above the glass door of a small shop of some
sort. The store's façade is draped in iron burglar screens, and other
than a few frayed wires, broken neon tubes, and wads of gaffer's
tape, the display windows are empty. The door is shut but unlocked
(just as Nick had left it three days earlier).

Yanking the door open, Nick waves everybody inside, and they
enter in a hurry.

In fact, they slip inside so quickly that nobody notices the shop's
sign over the door's lintel, the letters formed by dark, cold neon
script: TOM THUMB'S TINY TOY SHOPPE.

The front of the store, barely five hundred square feet, is littered
with brightly colored debris. Overturned shelves have spilled their
inventory of dolls and race cars and trains across the soiled tiles. A
tornado of destruction has swirled through the shop. Wires dangle
where mobiles once hung, the shattered plastic remains of LEGO
sets and planes piled here and there. The feathery stuffing of ripped
plush toys stirs like dead leaves in the slipstream of the visitors slamming the door behind them.

For a moment, they stand in the vestibule, dripping, catching their
collective breaths, gaping at the startling ruins strewn before them.
Nobody moves for the longest time. Something about the wreckage
mesmerizes them, and keeps them glued to the threshold.

"Everybody stay put," Philip finally says, pulling a handkerchief
and wiping moisture from his neck. He sidesteps a mangled stuffed

bear, and then he cautiously moves deeper into the shop. He sees an unmarked rear exit, maybe a stockroom, maybe a way out. Brian gently puts Penny down, and checks her for any signs of injury.

Penny stares at the sad rubble of decapitated Barbies and disemboweled stuffed animals.

"When I ran across this place," Nick is saying from across the room, looking for something, "I was thinking they might have stuff we could use, gadgets, walkie-talkies, flashlights . . . *something*." He moves around the end of the cashier's counter, up a few steps, and over to a perch behind the register. "Place like this, in this part of town . . . hell, they might even have a gun."

"What's back there, Nicky?" Philip shoots a thumb at a curtained doorway in the rear of the store. The black privacy drape hangs down to the floor. "You get a chance to check it out?"

"Stockroom is my guess. Be careful, Philly. It's dark back there."

Philip pauses by the curtain, shrugs off his backpack and fishes in it for the small penlight he keeps in the side pocket. He flips it on, and he pushes his way through the drape . . . vanishing into the gloom.

Across the store, Penny is transfixed by the broken dolls and eviscerated teddy bears. Brian watches her closely. He aches to help her, aches to get everybody back on track, but all he can do right now is kneel next to the child and try to keep her distracted. "You want one of those candy bars?"

"Nope." It comes out of her like the crackle of a pull-string doll, her eyes fixed on all the busted toys.

"You sure?"

"Yep."

"We got Twinkies," Brian tells her, trying to fill the silence, trying to keep her talking, trying to keep her occupied. But right now, all Brian can think about is the look on Philip's face, and the violence in his eyes, and the whole world—*their world*—falling apart.

"No, I'm okay," Penny says. She sees a little Hello Kitty backpack lying in a pile of trash, and she goes over to it. She picks it up, inspects it. "You think anybody would get mad if I took some of these things?"

"What things, kiddo?" Brian looks at her. "You mean the toys?" She nods.

A stab of sorrow and shame cleaves Brian's midsection. "Go for it," he says.

She starts gathering up pieces of trampled dolls and tattered stuffed animals. It looks almost like a ritual to Brian, like a rite of passage for the little girl, as she selects Barbies with missing limbs and teddy bears with torn seams. She slips the injured toys into the knapsack with the care of someone performing triage at a clinic. Brian lets out a sigh.

Right then, Philip's voice calls out from somewhere deep in the guts of the back hallway, cutting off Brian's thoughts—he was about to fecklessly offer Penny the sausage stick—and now Brian springs to his feet. "What did he say?"

Across the shop, behind the cash register, Nick perks up. "I don't know—I didn't hear."

"Philip!" Brian starts toward the back curtain, his flesh crawling with nervous tension. "You okay?"

Hasty footsteps shuffle inside the draped doorway, and all at once, the curtain flaps open and Philip is peering out at them with a wild expression contorting his face, somewhere between excitement and mania. "Grab your shit, we just won the Irish fucking sweep-stakes!"

Philip takes them down a narrow, dark corridor, past shelves of un-opened toys and games, around a corner, and through a security door apparently left unlocked amid the previous occupants' hurried exo-dus. Down another narrow hallway, guided by the thin beam of Philip's penlight, and they come to a fire escape. The metal door is slightly ajar, the shadows of a passageway visible on the other side.

"Get a load of what's on the other side of our little toy store." Philip pushes the fire door open with his boot. "Our ticket out of this hellhole."

The metal door swings wide, and Brian finds himself staring

across another narrow hallway at the mirror image of the first fire door.

The metal door across the hall is also ajar, and through the gap Brian sees, cloaked in shadows, rows of gleaming spoked wheels. "Oh my God," he utters. "Is that what I think it is?"

The space is huge—encompassing the entire corner of the adjacent building's first floor—lined with reinforced window glass on three sides. Visible through the windows is the street corner outside, where shadowy forms wander aimlessly, drifting through the rain like doomed souls, but *inside*—in the shiny, happy world of Champion Cycle Center, Atlanta's premier motorcycle dealership—all is warm and tidy and polished to a high sheen.

The showroom appears to be untouched by the plague. In the wan, overcast light filtering in through the massive display windows, motorcycles of all makes and models are lined up in four neat rows extending from one end of the dealership to the other. The air smells of new rubber and oiled leather and finely honed steel. The edges of the showroom are carpeted with logo-embroidered pile as lush and new as a fancy hotel lobby. Powerless neon signs hang down at junctures with product legends: Kawasaki, Ducati, Yamaha, Honda, Triumph, Harley-Davidson, and Suzuki.

"You think any of them have gas in them?" Brian turns in a slow three-sixty, taking in the whole of the showroom.

"We got our pick of the litter, sport." Philip nods toward the rear of the room, past the sales counter and desks and shelves brimming with parts. "They got a workspace back there with a garage out back . . . we can siphon fuel into any one of them things easy enough."

Penny stares emotionlessly at the banquet of chrome and rubber. She has the Hello Kitty pack strapped securely to her tiny shoulders.

Brian's head is swimming. Contrary emotions crash up against each other like whitecaps—excitement, anxiety, hope, fear. "Only one problem," he utters under his breath, the weight of his anguish and uncertainty pressing down on his shoulders.

Philip looks at his brother. "What the hell's the problem now?"

Brian wipes his mouth. "I have no idea how to work one of those things."

They all have a much-needed laugh—nervous, brittle laughter, perhaps, but laughter nonetheless—at the expense of Brian. Philip assures his brother that it doesn't make one lick of difference that Brian has never ridden a motorcycle—a "retard" could learn it in two minutes. More importantly, both Philip and Nick have owned hogs over the years, and the last time Philip checked, there was only four of them, so the two nonoperators can ride along on the saddles.

"Faster we get outta A-T-L, the better chances we got with no guns," Philip says minutes later, rifling through a rack of leathers in the rear corner of the store—jackets, trousers, vests, and accessories. He chooses a bomber-brown Harley jacket and a pair of heavy-duty black boots. "I want everybody changed outta their wet clothes and ready to go in five minutes—Brian, you help Penny."

They get changed as the rain eases up outside the big windows. The street corner crawls with shambling figures now—scores of frayed, tattered souls, some of them scorched from the explosion, others in advanced stages of decomposition. Faces are starting to cave in, some of them dripping with parasites and blackening into moldy masks of putrefied flesh. None of them, however, notices the movement inside the dark showroom.

"You see them Biters gathering out there?" Nick says to Philip under his breath. Nick already has dry clothes on, and is zipping up a black leather jacket. He gives a little nod toward the gray light of the storefront. "Some of them things are pretty ripe."

"So?"

"Some of them got—what?—three, four weeks on 'em?"

"At least." Philip thinks about it for a moment, changing out of his wet denims. His underwear is stuck to him and he has to practically peel it off. He turns away so that Penny doesn't see his package. "Whole thing broke out over a month ago . . . so what?"

"They're rotting."

"Huh?"

Nick lowers his voice so that he doesn't catch Penny's ear; the little girl is busying herself across the showroom with a size small winter coat, which Brian is trying to figure out how to snap. "Think about it, Philly. The normal course of affairs, a dead body is dust in a year or so." He lowers his voice further. "Especially one that's exposed to the elements."

"What are you saying, Nick? All we gotta do is wait out the clock? Let the maggots do the work?"

Nick shrugs. "Well, yeah, I guess I just thought—"

"Listen to me." Philip jabs a finger in Nick's face. "Keep your theories to yourself."

"I didn't mean to—"

"They ain't going away, Nicky. Get that through your thick fucking skull. I don't want my daughter hearing any of this shit. They eat the living, and they reproduce, and when they rot away, there's gonna be more of them to take their place, and judging from the fact that old man Chalmers turned without even getting bit, the whole goddamn world's days are numbered, so drink up, bubba, it's later than y'all think."

Nick looks down. "All right, man, I get it . . . cool down, Philly."

At this point, Brian has Penny bundled up, and the two of them come over. "We're as ready as we'll ever be."

"What time you got?" Philip asks Brian, who looks semiridiculous in a Harley leather jacket that's a size and half too big for him.

He looks at his watch. "Almost noon."

"Good . . . gives us a good six, seven hours of daylight to get the hell outta Dodge."

"You guys pick out your bikes?" Brian asks.

Philip gives him a cold smile.

They choose two of the biggest metal masterpieces in the place— a couple of Harley-Davidson Electra Glides, one in pearl blue and the other in midnight black. They choose them for the size of the engines, the roominess of the seats, the cubic inches of storage space, and also because—hey—they're fucking Harleys. Philip decides that Penny will ride with him, and Brian will ride with Nick. The gas tanks are empty but several bikes in the repair garage in the rear have fuel in them so they siphon as much as they can into the Harleys.

Over the course of the fifteen minutes it takes them to get the bikes ready and find helmets that fit and transfer all their belongings into the luggage carriers, the street outside the front of the place grows hectic with dead. Hundreds of Biters crowd the intersection now, wandering aimlessly in the gray drizzle, brushing against the glass, groaning their rusty groans, drooling their black bile, fixing their pewter-colored eyes on the moving shadows inside the windows of Champion Cycle Center.

"It's busy out there," Nick mumbles to no one in particular as he rolls the massive two-wheeler toward the side exit, where a small vertical garage door faces the parking lot along the side of the dealership. He straps on his helmet.

"Element of surprise," Philip says, pushing his black Harley over to the door. His stomach growls with hunger and nerves as he puts on his helmet. He hasn't eaten in nearly twenty-four hours. None of them has. He shoves the iron rod from the bus into a seam between the handlebars and windscreen (for quick and easy access). "C'mon, punkin, hop on," he says to Penny, who stands sheepishly nearby with a kiddie helmet on. "Gonna take a little spin, get outta this place."

Brian helps the child climb up onto the rear seat, a padded perch above the black lacquer luggage compartment. There's a safety belt in one of the side compartments, and Brian snaps it around the little girl's waist. "Don't worry, kiddo," he says softly to her.

"Gonna head south and then west, y'all," Philip says as he mounts the iron beast. "Nicky, you follow me."

"Copy that."

"Everybody ready?"

Brian goes over to the door and gives a nervous nod. "Ready."

Philip kicks the Harley to life, the engine howling and filling the dark showroom with noise and fumes. Nick kicks his bike on. The second engine sings a noisy aria in dissonant unison with the first. Philip revs the throttle and gives Brian the high sign.

Brian jacks the manual lock on the door and then throws it open, letting in the wet wind. Philip kicks the gear and takes off.

Brian leaps onto the back of Nick's bike and they blast off after Philip.

"OH SHIT! OH GOD! PHILIP! PHILIP! LOOK DOWN! LOOK DOWN, MAN! PHILIP, LOOK DOWN!"

Brian's frantic wail is muffled by his helmet and drowned by the noise of the cycles.

It happens mere moments after they slam through a mass of Biters choking the intersection, the ragged bodies bouncing off their fenders. After making a hard left turn and zooming south on Water Street, leaving the throngs in their dust and fumes, Brian sees the mangled corpse dragging along the pavement behind Philip's bike.

The bottom half of the thing is torn away, its intestines like electrical wiring flagging in the wind, but the torso still has fight left in it, its moldering head still intact. With its two dead arms, it clings to the rear fenders, and it starts pulling itself up the side of the Harley.

The worst part is, neither Philip nor Penny seem to be aware of it.

"PULL ALONGSIDE HIM! NICK, PULL UP!" Brian screams, his arms clutched around Nick's midsection.

"I'M TRYING!"

At this point, roaring down the deserted, wet side street, the bike hydroplaning on slick pavement, Penny notices the creature stuck to the bike, clawing its way toward her, and she starts screaming. From Brian's vantage point, thirty feet behind her, the child's scream is inaudible—like an exaggerated gesture of a silent-movie actress.

Nick opens up the throttle. His Harley closes the distance.

"GRAB THE BAT!" he screams over the din, and Brian tries to root the baseball bat out from beneath the luggage carrier behind him.

Up ahead, almost without warning, Philip Blake notices the thing attached to the back of his bike. Philip's helmet cocks around quickly as he gropes for his weapon.

By this point, Nick is within five or six feet of the black Harley's taillights, but before Brian can intercede with the bat, he sees Philip drawing the iron rod from its makeshift scabbard on the front of his bike.

With a quick and violent motion, which causes the black Harley to veer slightly off course, Philip twists around in his seat—one-handing the handlebars—and thrusts the hooked end of the metal rod into the zombie's mouth.

The skewered head of the monster gets stuck inches below Penny, the rod wedged between the gleaming exhaust pipes. Philip draws his right leg up and—with the force of a battering ram—he kicks the corpse (rod and all) off the bike. The thing tumbles and rolls, and Nick has to swerve suddenly to avoid it.

Philip increases his speed, staying on course, heading south, not even bothering to look back.

They continue on, zigzagging through the south side of town, avoiding the congested areas. A mile down the road, Philip manages to find another main artery that's relatively clear of wreckage and roaming dead, and he leads them down it. They are now three miles from the Atlanta city limits.

The horizon line is clear, the sky lightening slightly to the west.

They have enough gas to get four hundred miles without refueling.

Whatever awaits them out there in the gray rural countryside has to be better than what they suffered through in Atlanta.

It *has* to be.

PART 3

Chaos Theory

No man chooses evil because it is evil; he only mistakes
it for happiness, the good he seeks.

—Mary Wollstonecraft

SEVENTEEN

Around Hartsfield airport, the rain lets up, leaving behind a scoured, metallic sky of low clouds and dismal cold. It feels terrific, however, to get this far in less than an hour. Highway 85 has far less wreckage blocking its lanes than Interstate 20, and the population of dead has thinned considerably. Most roadside buildings are still intact, their windows and doors battened and secured. The stray dead walking about here and there almost seem like part of the landscape now—blending into the skeletal trees like a ghastly fungus infecting the woods. The land itself seems to have turned. The towns *themselves* are dead. Riding through this area leaves one with more of an impression of *desolation* than the end of the world.

The only immediate problem is the fact that every abandoned filling station or truck stop is infested with Biters, and Brian is getting very concerned about Penny. At every pit stop—either to take a leak or to forage for food or water—her face seems more drawn, her tiny little tulip lips more cracked. Brian is worried she's getting dehydrated. Hell, he's worried they're *all* getting dehydrated.

Empty stomachs are one thing (they can go without food for extended lengths of time), but the lack of water is becoming a serious issue.

Ten miles southwest of Hartsfield, as the landscape begins to transition into patchworks of pine forests and soy bean farms, Brian is wondering if they could drink the water from the motorcycles' radiators, when he sees a green directional sign looming up ahead with a blessed message: REST AREA—1 MI. Philip gives them a signal to pull off, and they take the next exit ramp.

As they roar uphill and into the lot, which is bordered by a small wood-framed tourist center, the relief spreads through Brian like a salve: The place is mercifully deserted, free of any signs of the living *or* the dead.

"What really happened back there, Philip?" Brian sits on a picnic table situated on a small promontory of grass behind the rest area shack. Philip paces, sucking down a bottle of Evian that he wrested from a broken vending machine. Nick and Penny are fifty yards away, still within view. Nick is gently spinning Penny on a ramshackle old merry-go-round under a diseased live oak. The girl just sits on the thing, joylessly, like a gargoyle, staring straight out as she turns and turns and turns.

"I told you once already to give that a rest," Philip grumbles.

"I think you like owe me an answer."

"I don't owe you shit."

"Something happened that night," Brian persists. He isn't afraid of his brother anymore. He knows Philip could beat the shit out of him at any moment—the potential for violence between the Blakes seems more imminent now than ever—but Brian doesn't care anymore. Something deep within Brian Blake has shifted like a seismic plate changing with the landscape. If Philip wants to wring Brian's throat, so be it. "Something between you and April?"

Philip gets very still and looks down. "What the fuck difference does it make?"

"It makes a big difference—it does to *me*. Our lives are on the line here. We had a pretty fair chance of surviving back there at that place, and then, just like that . . . poof?"

Philip looks up. His eyes fix themselves on his brother, and something very dark passes between the two men. "Drop it, Brian."

"Just tell me one thing. You seemed so hell-bent to get outta there—do you have a plan?"

"Whaddaya mean?"

"Do you have, like, a strategy? Any idea where the hell we're headed?"

"What are you, a fuckin' tour guide?"

"What if the Biters get thick again? We basically got a piece of wood to fight 'em with."

"We'll find something else."

"Where are we going, Philip?"

Philip turns away and lifts the collar of his leather bomber, staring out at the ribbon of pavement snaking off into the western horizon. "Another month or so, winter's gonna set in. I'm thinking we stay moving, heading southwest . . . toward the Mississippi."

"Where's that gonna get us?"

"It's the easiest way to go south."

"And?"

Philip turns and looks at Brian, a mixture of purpose and anguish crossing Philip's deeply lined face, as though he doesn't really believe what he's saying. "We'll find a place to live—long-term—in the sun. Someplace like Mobile or Biloxi. New Orleans, maybe . . . I don't know. Someplace warm. And we'll live there."

Brian lets out an exhausted sigh. "Sounds so easy. Just head south."

"You got a better plan, I'm all ears."

"Long-term plans are like a luxury I haven't even thought about."

"We'll make it."

"We gotta find some food, Philip. I'm really worried about Penny getting some nourishment."

"You let me do the worrying about my daughter."

"She won't even eat a Twinkie. You believe that? A kid who doesn't want a Twinkie."

"Cockroach food." Philip grunts. "Can't say I blame her. We'll find something. She's gonna be okay. She's a tough little thing . . . like her mother."

Brian can't argue with that. Lately, the little girl has shown miraculous spirit. In fact, Brian has started wondering whether Penny might actually be the glue that's holding them all together, keeping them from self-destructing.

He glances across the rest area and sees Penny Blake dreamily spinning on that rusty merry-go-round in the little scabrous playground area. Nick has lost his enthusiasm for turning it and now just gives it little incremental nudges with his boot.

Beyond the playground, the land rises up to an overgrown wooded knoll, where a small windswept cemetery sits in the pale sun.

Brian notices that Penny is talking to Nick, grilling him about something. Brian wonders what the two of them are talking about that has the girl looking so worried.

"Uncle Nick?" Penny's little face is tight with concern as she slowly turns on the merry-go-round. She has called Nick "Uncle" for years, even though she knows very well he is not her real uncle. The affectation has always given Nick a secret twinge of longing—the desire to be somebody's *real* uncle.

"Yes, honey?" A leaden feeling of doom presses down on Nick Parsons as he absently pushes Penny on the merry-go-round. He can see the Blake brothers in his peripheral vision, arguing about something.

"Is my dad mad at me?" the little girl asks.

Nick does a double take. Penny looks down as she slowly spins. Nick measures his words. "Of course not. He's not mad at you. Whaddaya mean? Why would you even think that?"

"He don't talk to me as much as he used to."

Nick gently pulls the merry-go-round to a stop. The little girl jerks slightly back against the bar. Nick tenderly pats her on the shoulder. "Listen. I promise you. Your daddy loves you more than anything else in the world."

"I know."

"He's under a lot of pressure. That's all."

"You don't think he's mad at me?"

"No way. He loves you something fierce, Penny. Believe me. He's just . . . under a lot of pressure."

"Yeah . . . I guess so."

"We all are."

"Yeah."

"I'm sure *none* of us have been talking all that much lately."

"Uncle Nick?"

"Yes, sweetie?"

"Do you think Uncle Brian's mad at me?"

"God, no. Why would Uncle Brian be mad at you?"

"Maybe 'cause he's gotta carry me all the time?"

Nick smiles sadly. He studies the look on the girl's face, her little brow all furrowed with seriousness. He strokes her cheek. "Listen to me. You are the bravest little girl I ever met. I mean that. You are a Blake girl . . . and that's something to be proud of."

She thinks about this and smiles. "You know what I'm gonna do?"

"No, honey. Tell me."

"I'm gonna fix all them broken dolls. You'll see. I'm gonna fix 'em."

Nick grins at her. "That sounds like a plan."

The little girl's smile is something that Nick Parson's wondered if he would ever see again.

A moment later, on the other side of the rest area, among the picnic tables, Brian Blake sees something out of the corner of his eye. A hundred yards away, beyond the playground, amid the crumbling headstones, long-faded markers, and tattered plastic flowers, something moves.

Brian locks his gaze on three distant figures emerging from the shadows of the trees. Shuffling along in haphazard formation, they approach like lazy bloodhounds smelling the kill. It's hard to tell at this distance but they look as though their clothes have been fed through a reaper, their mouths hanging open in perpetual torment.

"Time to get our asses in gear," Philip says with very little urgency, and he starts toward the playground with a kind of heavy, mechanical stride.

As he hurries after him, it occurs to Brian, just for an instant, that the way his brother is walking, his muscular arms limp at his sides, the weight of the world on his shoulders, he could very easily—from a distance—be mistaken for a zombie himself.

They put more miles behind them. They skirt small towns as empty and still as dioramas in a vast museum. The blue light of dusk starts pulling its shade down on the overcast sky, the wind turning bitter against their visors as they weave around wrecks and deserted trailers, working their way west on 85. Brian starts thinking that they need to find a place to spend the night.

Perched on the saddle behind Nick, his eyes watering, his ears deafened by the wind and the roar of the Harley's twin-cam engine, Brian has plenty of time to imagine the perfect place for the weary traveler in the land of the dead. He imagines an enormous, sprawling fortress with gardens and walks and impenetrable moats and security fences and guard towers. He would give his left nut for a steak and French fries. Or a bottle of Coke. Or even some of the Chalmerses' mystery meat—

A reflection off the inside of his helmet visor interrupts the flow of his thoughts.

He glances over his shoulder.

Strange. For the briefest instant there, at the precise same moment he saw a dark blot blur across the inside of his visor, he thought he felt something on the back of his neck, a faint sensation, like the kiss of cold lips. It might just be his imagination, but he also thought he saw something flicker across the side mirror. Just for an instant. Right before they began banking to the south.

He gazes over his shoulder and sees nothing behind them but empty lanes tumbling away, receding into the distance and then vanishing around the curve. He shrugs and turns back to his rambling, chaotic thoughts.

They venture deeper into the rural hinterlands, until they see nothing but miles and miles of broken-down farms and unincorporated boonies. The rolling hills of bean fields plunge down steep moraines on either side of the highway. This is old land—prehistoric, tired, worked to death by generations. Carcasses of old machinery lie dormant everywhere, buried in kudzu and mud.

Dusk starts settling into night, the sky fading from pale gray to a deep indigo. It's after seven o'clock now and Brian has completely forgotten about the peculiar flash of movement reflecting off the inside of his visor. They need to find cover. Philip's headlamp comes on, flinging a shaft of silver light into the gathering shadows.

Brian is about to shout something about finding a hideout when he sees Philip signaling up ahead—a stiff wave, and then a gloved finger jabbing to the right. Brian glances off to the north and sees what his brother is pointing at.

Way off in the distant rolling farmland, rising above a prominence of trees, the silhouette of a house is visible—so far away, it looks like a delicate cutout of black construction paper. If Philip had not pointed it out, Brian never would have noticed it. But now he sees why it has sunk a hook into Philip: It looks like a grand old relic of the nineteenth century, maybe even the eighteenth century, probably once a plantation house.

Brian sees another flicker of dark movement out of the corner of his eye, flashing across the side mirror, something behind them, passing just for a fraction of a second through the outer edges of his vision.

Then it's gone, vanishing as Brian twists around in his seat to gaze over his shoulder.

They take the next exit and boom down a dusty dirt road. As they close in on the house—which sits all by its lonesome at the crest of a vast foothill at least half a mile off the highway—Brian shivers in the cold. He has a terrible feeling all of sudden, despite the fact that the closer they get to the farmhouse, the more inviting it looks. This area of Georgia is known for its orchards—peaches, figs, and plums—and as they roar up a winding drive that leads to the house, they see that it's an aging beauty.

Surrounded by peach trees, which spread off into the distance like the spokes of a wheel, the central building is a massive two-story brick pile with ornate garrets and dormers rising off the roof. It has the flavor of an old, decrepit Italian villa. The porch is a fifty-foot-long portico with columns, balustrades, and mullioned windows choked with vines of brown ivy and bougainvillea. In the fading light, it looks almost like a ghost ship from some pre–Civil War armada.

The noise and fumes of the Harleys swirl in the dusty air as Philip leads them across the front lot, which is bordered by a massive, decorative fountain made of marble and masonry. Apparently fallen into disrepair, the fountain has a film of scum across its basin. Several outbuildings—stables, perhaps—lie off to the right. A tractor lies half-buried in crabgrass. To the left of the front façade sits a massive carriage house, big enough for six cars.

None of this antique opulence registers with Brian as they cautiously pull up to a side door between the garage and the main house.

Philip brings his Harley to a stop in a thunderhead of dust, revving the motor for a moment. He kills the engine and sits there, staring up at the salmon-colored brick monstrosity. Nick pulls next to him and snaps down his kickstand. They don't say a word for the longest time. Finally, Philip lowers his stand, dismounts, and says to Penny, "Stay here for a second, punkin."

Nick and Brian dismount.

"You got that baseball bat handy?" Philip says without even looking at them.

"You think there's anybody in there?" Nick asks.

"Only one way to find out."

Philip waits for Nick to go around the back of his Electra Glide and fetch the bat, which is sheathed down one side of his luggage carrier. He brings it back and hands it over.

"You two stay with Penny," Philip says, and starts toward the portico.

Brian stops him, grabbing his arm.

"Philip—" Brian is about to say something about dark shapes flashing across his side mirror back on the highway, but he stops himself. He's not sure he wants Penny to hear this.

"The hell's the matter with you?" Philip says.

Brian swallows air. "I think there's somebody following us."

The former occupants of the villa are long gone. In fact, the inside of the place looks as though it's been sitting empty since long before the plague broke out. Yellowed sheets cover the antique furniture. The many rooms are empty, dusty chambers frozen in time. A grandfather clock still ticks stubbornly in a parlor. Niceties of a bygone era festoon the house: ornate moldings and French doors and circular staircases and two separate and massive fireplaces with hearths the size of walk-in closets. Under one sheet sits a grand piano, under another a Victrola, under another a wood-burning stove.

Philip and Nick sweep the upper floors for Biters and find nothing other than more dusty relics of the Old South: a library, a corridor of oil paintings of Confederate generals in gilded frames, a nursery with a dusty old cradle dating back to Colonial times. The kitchen is surprisingly small—another holdover from the nineteenth century when only servants dirtied their hands with cooking—but the enormous pantry has shelves brimming with dusty canned goods. The dry grains and cereals are all mealy and crawling with worms, but the array of fruits and vegetables is staggering.

"You're seeing things, sport," Philip says under his breath that night in front of a crackling fire in the front parlor. They found piles of cordwood in the backyard by the barn and now they've managed to warm their bones for the first time since leaving Atlanta. The warmth and shelter of the villa—as well as the nourishment of canned peaches and okra—caused Penny to instantly doze off. She now slumbers on a luxurious down comforter in the nursery on the second floor. Nick sleeps in the room next to her. But the two brothers have insomnia. "Who the hell would bother following *us* anyway?" Philip adds, taking another sip of the expensive cooking sherry he found in the pantry.

"I'm telling you, I saw what I saw," Brian says, nervously rocking on a bentwood chair on the other side of the fire. He's got a dry shirt on and a pair of sweatpants, and he feels almost human again. He looks over at his brother, and sees that Philip is staring intensely at the fire as though it holds a secret coded message.

For some reason, the sight of Philip's gaunt, troubled face, reflecting the flicker of firelight, breaks Brian's heart. He flashes back to epic childhood journeys into the woods, overnight stays in pup tents and cabins. He remembers having his first beer with his brother, back when Philip was only ten and Brian was thirteen, and he remembers Philip being able to drink him under the table even then.

"It might have been a car," Brian goes on. "Or maybe a van, I'm not sure. But I swear to God, I saw it back there just for a second . . . and it sure as hell seemed like it was tailing us."

"So what if there *is* somebody following us, who gives a rat's ass?"

Brian thinks about it for a second. "The only thing is . . . if they were friendly . . . wouldn't they, like, catch up with us? Signal to us?"

"Who knows . . ." Philip stares at the fire, his thoughts elsewhere. "Whoever they are . . . if they're out there, chances are, they're as fucked up as us."

"That's true, I guess." Brian thinks about it some more. "Maybe they're just . . . scared. Maybe they're like . . . checking us out."

"Ain't nobody gonna be able to sneak up on us up here, I'll tell you that."

"Yeah . . . I guess."

Brian knows exactly what his brother is talking about. The location and position of the villa is ideal. Situated on a rise that overlooks miles of thinning trees, the house has sight lines that would give them plenty of warning. Even on a moonless night, the orchards are so still and quiet that nobody would be able to creep up on them without being heard or seen. And Philip is already talking about setting booby-trap wires around the periphery to alert them to intruders.

On top of that, the place offers them all sorts of benefits that could sustain them for quite a while, maybe even into the winter.

There is a well out back, gas in the tractor, a place to hide the Harleys, miles of fruit trees still bearing edible albeit frost-shriveled fruit, and enough wood to keep the stoves and fireplaces going for months. The only problem is their lack of weapons. They scoured the villa and only found a few implements in the barn—a rusty old scythe, a pitchfork—but no firearms.

"You okay?" Brian says after a long stretch of silence.

"Fit as a fucking fiddle."

"You sure?"

"Yes, Grandma." Philip stares into the fire. "We're all gonna be fit as fucking fiddles after a few days in this place."

"Philip?"

"What is it now?"

"Can I say something?"

"Here it comes." Philip doesn't take his eyes off the fire. He wears his wifebeater and a dry pair of jeans. His socks have holes in them, his big toe showing through one of them. The sight of this in the firelight—Philip's gnarled toenail sticking out—is heartrending for Brian. It makes his brother seem, maybe for the first time ever, almost vulnerable. It is highly unlikely that any of them would be alive right now if it weren't for Philip. Brian swallows back his emotion.

"I'm your brother, Philip."

"I'm aware of that, Brian."

"No, what I'm saying is . . . I don't judge you, I never will."

"What's your point?"

"My point is . . . I appreciate what you've been doing . . . risking your ass protecting us. I want you to know this. I appreciate it."

Philip doesn't say anything, but the way he's staring at that fire begins to change a little bit. He starts gazing *beyond* it, the flames making his eyes glimmer with emotion.

"I know you're a good person," Brian goes on. "I *know* this." A brief pause here. "I can tell something is eating at you."

"Brian—"

"Wait a minute, just hear me out." The conversation has crossed a Rubicon, now beyond the point of no return. "If you don't want to tell me what happened back there with you and April, that's fine. I'll never ask you again." There's a long pause. "But you can tell me, Philip. You can tell me because I'm your brother."

Philip turns and looks at Brian. A single tear tracks down Philip's chiseled, leathery face. It makes Brian's stomach clench. He can't remember ever having seen his brother cry, even as a child. One time, their daddy whipped a twelve-year-old Philip unmercifully with a hickory switch, raising so many welts on Philip's backside that he had to spend nights sleeping on his stomach, but he never cried. Almost out of spite, he refused to cry. But now, as he meets Brian's gaze in the flickering shadows, Philip's voice is drained as he says, "I fucked up, sport."

Brian nods, says nothing, just waits. The fire crackles and sizzles.

Philip looks down. "I think I sorta fell for her." The tear drips on him. But his voice never breaks, it just remains flat and weak: "Ain't gonna say it was love but what the fuck is love anyway? Love is a fucking disease." He cringes at some demon twisting in him. "I fucked up, Brian. Could've had something with her. Could've had something solid for Penny, something good." He grimaces as though holding off a tide of sorrow, tears welling up in his eyes until every time he blinks, they run down his face. "I couldn't stop myself. She said stop but I couldn't do it. I couldn't stop. See . . . the thing is . . . it felt so goddamn good." Tears dripping. "Even when she was pushing me away, it felt good." Silence. "What the fuck is wrong with me?" More silence. "I know there ain't no excuse for it." Pause. "I'm not stupid . . . I just didn't think I would ever . . . I didn't think I could . . . I didn't think . . ."

His voice crumbles until there's nothing but the crackle of the fire and the huge dark silence outside the villa. At length, after an interminable period of time, Philip looks up at his brother.

In the dancing light, Brian sees that the tears are spent. Nothing but barren anguish remains on Philip Blake's face. Brian doesn't say a word. He simply nods.

————

The next few days take them into November, and they decide to stay put and see what the weather does.

A freezing sleet sweeps across the orchards one morning. On another day, a killer frost grips the fields and takes down much of the fruit. But for all the signs of winter rolling in, they feel no compulsion to leave just yet. The villa might be their best bet to wait out the harsh days on the horizon. They've got enough canned goods and fruit—if they're careful—to keep them going for months. And enough wood to keep them warm. And the orchards seem relatively free of Biters, at least in the immediate vicinity.

In some ways, Philip seems to be doing better now that the burden of his guilt has been off-loaded. Brian keeps the secret to himself, thinking about it often, but never broaching the subject again. The two brothers are less edgy with each other, and even Penny seems to be settling in nicely to this new routine that they are carving out for themselves.

She finds an antique dollhouse in an upper parlor, and stakes out a little place for herself (and all her broken, misfit toys) at the end of the second-floor hallway. Brian comes up there one day and finds all the dolls lying in neat little rows on the floor, all the severed appendages lying next to their corresponding bodies. He stares for quite a long while at the strange miniature morgue before Penny snaps him out of his daze. "C'mon, Uncle Brian," she says. "You can be a doctor . . . help me put them back together."

"Yeah, that's a good idea," he says with a nod. "Let's put them back together."

On another occasion, early in the morning, Brian hears a sound coming from the first floor. He goes down into the kitchen and finds Penny standing on a chair, covered in flour and gunk, fiddling with pots and pans, her hair matted with makeshift pancake batter. The kitchen is a disaster area. The others arrive, and the three men just stand there, in the doorway of the kitchen, staring. "Don't be mad," Penny says, glancing over her shoulder. "I promise I'll clean up the mess."

The men look at each other. Philip, grinning now for the first time in weeks, says, "Who's mad? We ain't mad. We're just hungry. When's breakfast gonna be ready?"

As the days pass, they take precautions. They decide to burn firewood only at night, when the smoke cannot be seen from the highway. Philip and Nick construct a perimeter of baling wire stretched between small wooden stakes at each corner of the property, placing tin cans at key junctures, to alarm them of possible intruders—Biters and human alike. They even find an old antique double-barrel 12-gauge in the villa's attic.

The shotgun is filmed in dust and engraved with cherubs, and looks as if it might blow up in their faces if they tried to fire the thing. They don't even have any shells for it—the gun looks like the kind of thing somebody would hang in their study on the wall next to old photographs of Ernest Hemingway—but Philip sees some value in having it around. It looks threatening enough—on a galloping horse, as his dad used to say.

"You never know," Philip says one night, leaning the shotgun against the hearth and settling back to numb himself with more cooking sherry.

The days continue to slip away with shapeless regularity. They catch up on their sleep, and they explore the orchards, and they harvest fruit. They set box traps for stray critters and one day they even catch a scrawny jackrabbit. Nick volunteers to clean the thing, and he ends up making a fairly decent braised rabbit on the woodstove that night.

They have only a few encounters with Biters during this time. One day, Nick is halfway up a tree, reaching for some withered plums, when he sees a walking corpse in farmer's overalls way off in the shadows of a neighboring grove. He calmly climbs down and sneaks up on the thing with his pitchfork, skewering the back of its head as though popping a balloon. On another occasion, Philip is siphoning gas from a tractor when he notices a mangled corpse in a nearby drainage ditch. Legs smashed and contorted underneath it, the woman-thing looks like it dragged itself miles to get here. Philip chops off its head with the scythe, and burns the remains with a squirt of gas and a spark of a Bic.

Piece of cake.

All the while, the villa seems to be adopting them as much as they are adopting it. With all the sheets removed from the opulent old furniture, it seems almost like a place they could call home. They each have their own room now. And although they're each still plagued by nightmares, there's nothing more soothing than coming down to an old elegant kitchen with the November sun streaming through French windows, and the fragrance of a coffeepot that's been simmering all night.

In fact, if it weren't for the periodic feelings of being watched, things would be pretty close to perfect.

The feelings began to intensify for Brian as early as the second night they were there. Brian had just moved into his own bedroom on the second floor—an austere sewing parlor with a quaint little four-poster bed and an eighteenth-century armoire—when he sprang awake in the middle of the night.

He had been dreaming that he was a castaway, adrift on a make-shift raft on a sea of blood, when he saw a flash of light. In the dream, he thought it might be a distant lighthouse on some distant shore, summoning him, rescuing him from this endless plague of blood, but when he awakened, he realized he had just seen *actual* light in the *waking* world—just for a second—a rectangular slice of light, sliding across the ceiling.

In a blink, it was gone.

He wasn't even sure he had actually seen it, but every fiber of his being told him to get up and go to the window. He did, and gazing out at the black void of the night, he could have sworn he caught a glimpse of a car, a quarter mile away, turning around at the point where the highway met the farm road. Then the thing vanished, sliding into nothingness.

Brian found it exceedingly difficult to get any more sleep that night.

When he told Philip and Nick about it the next morning, they simply wrote it off as a dream. Who the hell would pull off the highway, and then turn around and take off?

But the suspicion grew in Brian over that next week and a half. At night, he kept catching glimpses of slowly moving lights out on the highway or on the far side of the orchard. Some nights, in the wee hours, he could swear that he was hearing the crunch of tires on gravel. The furtive, fleeting quality of these sounds was the worst part. It gave Brian the feeling that somehow the villa was being *cased*. But he got so tired of having his paranoid suspicion dismissed by the others that he simply stopped reporting it. Maybe he *was* imagining all of it.

He didn't say another word on the matter until the two-week anniversary of their stay in the villa, when, at a point just before dawn, the sound of tin cans rattling stirred him from a deep sleep.

EIGHTEEN

"What the hell?" Brian snaps awake in the darkness of his room. He fumbles for one of the kerosene lanterns on his bedside table, knocking over the hurricane glass and spilling fluid. He gets up and goes to the window, the floor icy on the soles of his bare feet.

Moonlight shines down from a crystalline cold autumn night sky, lining every shape outside with a luminous halo of silver. Brian can still hear the tin cans on the trip wires rattling out there somewhere. He can also hear the others stirring in their bedrooms behind him, down the hall. Everybody is up now, awakened by the jangling cans.

The strangest part is—and Brian wonders if he's imagining this—the rattling sounds are coming from all directions. Tin cans are clattering in the groves *behind* the villa as well as in front of it. Brian is craning his neck to see better when his bedroom door bursts open.

"Sport! You up?" Philip is shirtless, wearing jeans and logger boots that he hasn't had a chance to tie yet. He holds the old shotgun with one hand, his eyes wide open with alarm. "I'm gonna need you to go get that pitchfork in the back hallway—pronto!"

"Is it Biters?"

"Just get moving!"

Brian gives a nod and hurries out of the room, his brain swimming with panic. He wears only his sweatpants and a sleeveless T-shirt. As he pads through the darkness of the house—down the stairs, across the parlor, and into the back hall—he senses movement outside the windows, the presence of others closing in on them from outside.

Grabbing the pitchfork, which leans against the back door, Brian whirls and heads back to the front room.

By this point, Philip, Nick, and even Penny have reached the bottom of the steps. They go to the front bay window, which offers a wide-angle view of the surrounding yards, the sloping drive down to the adjacent road, and even the edge of the closest orchard. Immediately they see dark shapes—low to the ground—sliding across the property from three different directions.

"Are those cars?" Nick utters in barely a whisper.

As their eyes adjust to the moonlit night, they each realize that yes, indeed, those *are* cars moving slowly across the property toward the villa. One comes up the winding drive, another one from the north end of the orchard, a third just visible to the south, crunching slowly over the gravel path leading out of the trees.

Almost with perfect synchronous timing, each vehicle suddenly stops at an equidistant point from the house. They sit there for a second, each one maybe fifty feet away, their windows too dark to reveal their occupants. "This ain't no welcome wagon," Philip murmurs, the understatement of the evening.

Again, almost in perfect concurrence, each pair of headlights suddenly snaps on. The effect is fairly dramatic—almost theatrical, in fact—as the beams strike the windows of the villa, filling the dark interior with cold chromium light. Philip is about to go outside and make a stand with the defunct shotgun when the sound of a crash is heard, coming from the rear of the villa.

"Punkin, you stay with Brian," Philip says to Penny. Then he shoots a glance at Nick. "Nicky, I want you to see if you can slip out a side window, take the machete, double back on 'em if you can. You follow me?"

Nick understands exactly what he's saying, and he takes off down the side hallway.

"Stay behind me, but stay close." Philip raises the shotgun, the butt against his shoulder. Carefully and focused with cobralike calm,

Philip shuffles commando-style toward the sound of footsteps on broken glass now coming from the kitchen.

"Nice and easy does it, hoss," the home invader says in a cheerful Tennessee twang, raising the barrel of a nine-millimeter Glock as Philip enters the kitchen with the shotgun also raised.

Before being so rudely interrupted, the intruder had been calmly looking around the kitchen as though he had just climbed out of bed for a midnight snack. Headlamps, coming from outside, pierce the room with harsh radiance. The pane of glass above the door-knob behind the man is busted in, and the faint light of dawn is just beginning to glow.

Well over six feet tall, dressed in shopworn camo-pants, muddy jackboots, and a blood-soaked Kevlar flak vest, the home invader is completely bald, with a scarred, missile-shaped head and eyes like craters cut by tiny meteors. On closer scrutiny, he looks sick, like he's been exposed to radiation, his jaundiced skin mottled with sores.

Philip points the worthless antique shotgun at the bald man's cranium—about eight feet between the two men—and Philip concentrates on pretending—maybe even believing—that the shotgun is loaded. "I'll give y'all the benefit of the doubt," Philip says. "I'll assume you thought the place was empty."

"That's exactly right, hoss," the bald man says, his voice calm, maybe medicated, like that of a dreamy disc jockey. His teeth are capped in gold, and they shimmer dully as he smiles a reptilian smile. "So, we'll thank y'all to just leave us be—no harm, no foul."

The man with the Glock apes a hurt frown. "Now, that ain't too neighborly of you." The man has a slight tremor, a tic, percolating with latent violence. "I see y'all got a cute little thang back there."

"Never mind that." Philip stands his ground. He can hear the front door squeak, footsteps crossing the parlor. His brain crashes with panic and warring impulses. He knows the next few seconds are critical, maybe even mortally so. But all he can think of doing is to stall. "We don't want any bloodshed, and brother, I guarantee you, no matter what happens, yours and mine's gonna be the first blood that's shed."

"Smooth talker." The bald man calls out suddenly to one of his comrades in the dark. "Shorty?"

A voice answers from outside the back door. "Got him, Tommy!"

Almost on cue, Nick appears outside the jagged window of the back door, a large Bowie knife held against his windpipe. His captor, a skinny kid with pimples and a marine jarhead haircut, pushes open the door and shoves Nick into the kitchen.

"I'm sorry, Philly," Nick says as he is shoved against the cabinets—hard enough to steal his breath. The slender young man with the crew cut holds the knife against Nick's Adam's apple, a machete thrust down the young man's belt. A jittery, bony specimen with fingerless Carnaby gloves on his hands, the skinny kid looks like an escapee from a marine brig. His fatigue jacket has the sleeves torn off, and his long bare arms are riddled with jailhouse hieroglyph.

"Hold on, now," Philip says to the bald man. "There's no reason to—"

"Sonny!" The bald man calls out to another accomplice at the precise same moment Philip hears the footsteps creaking across the hundred-year-old hardwood floor out in the front parlor. Philip keeps the shotgun raised and aimed, but shoots a quick side glance back over his shoulder. Brian and Penny huddle in the shadows directly behind Philip, maybe five feet off his heels.

Two more figures have suddenly appeared behind Brian and Penny, making the little girl jump.

"Got it covered, Tommy!" says one of the figures as the steel-plated barrel of a large-caliber revolver—maybe a .357 Magnum, maybe an Army .45—becomes visible for all to see, pressing against the back of Brian Blake's skull. Brian stiffens like a cornered animal.

"Hold on now," Philip says.

In his peripheral vision, he can see that the two figures holding guns on Brian and Penny are a man and a woman . . . although he would use the word *woman* loosely in this case. The gal clutching a piece of Penny's collar is an androgynous marionette of skin and bones, clad in leather pants and layers of mesh, with lampblack eyeliner, spikey hair, and the slightly greenish pallor of a junkie. She nervously taps the barrel of a .38 police special against the shank of her beanpole thigh.

The man next to her—the one apparently named Sonny—also looks as though he's no stranger to the needle. His sunken eyes stare out from a pockmarked mask of ignorance and meanness, his emaciated form clad in army-surplus rags.

"I want to thank you, brother," the bald man says, shoving his nine-millimeter back into its belt sheath, acting like the showdown has now officially ended. "You dug up quite a spot here. I'll give you that." He goes over to the sink and calmly helps himself to the jug of well water sitting on the counter, quaffing down an entire glassful. "This'll do nicely as a home base."

"That's all well and good," Philip says, not making any move to lower his faux weapon. "Only problem is, we can't take on any more people."

"That's okay, brother."

"Then what exactly are you planning to . . . ? What are your intentions?"

"Our *intentions*?" The bald man enunciates the word with mock profundity. "Our intentions are to take this place from y'all."

Somebody that Philip can't see snickers with great amusement.

Philip's brain is a fractured chessboard, pieces moving now in herky-jerky motion. He knows that it's likely that these hardened road rats mean to kill him and everybody else in the house. He knows they're parasites, and they've most likely been circling the place like buzzards for weeks—Brian wasn't hearing things, it turns out.

Even now, Philip can hear others outside—low voices, twigs snapping—and he does the quick mental arithmetic: There are at least six of them, maybe more, and at least four vehicles, and each one seems to be heavily armed, with plenty of ammo—Philip can see mags and speed-loaders clipped to some of the belts—but the one thing they seem to lack that maybe, just maybe, Philip can work with, is the appearance of intelligence. Even the big bald guy—who seems to be the honcho—has the look of a dull stoner in his eyes.

There won't be any appeals to mercy, no appeals to the better angels here. Philip has only one chance at survival.

"You mind if I say something?" he asks. "Before y'all do anything rash."

The bald man raises his glass as though giving a toast. "You got the floor, friend."

"We got two ways this can go down, is all I'm trying to say."

This seems to pique the bald man's curiosity. He sets down his glass and turns to Philip. "Only two ways?"

"One way is, we start blazing and I can tell you how that's gonna play out."

"Do tell."

"Your folks will overpower us and that'll be that, but the only thing is, I promise you one thing and—I'll be honest with you—I've never been so sure of anything in my life."

"And what's that?"

"No matter what, I know that I'll be able to get off a single shot, and I say this with no disrespect, but I will make damn sure that the overwhelmin' majority of these steel beads go into the top half of your body. Now, sir, do you want to hear option two?"

The bald man has lost his sense of humor. "Keep talkin'."

"Option two is you let us walk outta here alive, and you take our place with our compliments, and nobody has to clean up no messes and you get to keep the top half of your body."

For quite a while, things proceed in a very orderly fashion (on the bald man's orders). The junkie couple—in his stricken brain, Philip is coming to think of them as Sonny and Cher—simply back away slowly from Brian and Penny, allowing Brian to lift the child off the floor and carry her across the front parlor to the door.

The agreement—if you can call it that—is for Philip and his group to simply walk away from the villa, leaving all their things, and that's that. Brian watches Philip backing out of the house with the shotgun still raised. *Thank God for that piece of shit antique.* Nick follows.

The two of them join Brian and Penny in the doorway, and Brian nudges the door open with Penny in his arms.

They shuffle outside, the shotgun still aimed at the intruders inside.

A number of things flood Brian's senses—the cool wind, the pale light of dawn rising behind the orchards, the silhouettes of two additional gunmen on either flank of the house, the cars angled with their high beams still on like theatrical spotlights heralding the next act of a nightmarish play.

The bald man's voice calls out from inside: "Boys! Let 'em pass!"

The two accomplices outside, dressed in ragged military fatigues and wielding heavy artillery—each man cradles a sawed-off pistol-grip shotgun—watch with the baleful interest of predatory birds as Brian carefully transfers Penny onto his shoulders, piggyback style. Philip whispers low, "Stay close, and follow me. They still mean to kill us. Just do what I say."

Brian follows Philip—who is still bare-chested and still has that ridiculous gun raised commando-style—across the yard, past one of the watchful gunmen, and toward the neighboring grove of peach trees.

It takes an excruciating amount of time for Philip to get everybody across the property and into the shadows of the closest orchard—mere seconds by the clock, but an eternity for Brian Blake—because now the methodical transfer of ownership has begun to fall apart.

Brian can hear troubling things behind him as he hurriedly carries Penny toward the tree line. Brian is still barefoot, and the soles of his feet sting from the brambles and stones. Voices raised in anger drift out of the villa, footsteps, movement across the front porch.

The first shot rings out just as Philip and his group are plunging into the trees. The blast shatters the air, and chews through a branch six inches from Brian's right shoulder, spitting bark at the side of his face and making Penny yelp. Philip shoves Brian—still with Penny on his back—forward into the deeper shadows. "RUN!" he orders them. "RUN, BRIAN! NOW!"

For Brian Blake, the next five minutes pass with the chaotic blur of a dream. He hears more gunfire behind him, bullets sizzling through the foliage as he hurtles through the woods, the watery light of dawn not yet driving away the deeper shadows of the orchards. Brian's bare feet—getting more and more chewed up by the second—dig into the soft undercarpet of leaves and fruit slime, his brain sparking with roman candles of panic. Penny bounces along on his back, hyperventilating with terror. Brian has no idea how far to go, where to go, or when he can stop. He just keeps churning deeper into the shadows of the orchard.

He crosses about two hundred yards of wooded shadows before reaching a huge deadfall of rotting timber, and he ducks behind it.

Gasping to get air into his lungs, his breath visible in the chilled atmosphere, his heart thumping in his ears, he gently shrugs Penny off his back. He sits her down next to him in the weeds.

"Stay down low, kiddo," he whispers. "And be very, very, very quiet—quiet as a mouse."

The orchard vibrates with movement in all directions—the gunfire momentarily ceasing—and Brian risks peering over the top of the deadfall to get a better view. Through thick columns of peach trees, Brian can see a figure about a hundred yards away, coming toward him.

Brian's eyes have adjusted to the wan shadows well enough to see that it's one of the dudes from outside the house, the pistol-grip shotgun jutting up and ready to rock. Others are threading through the trees behind him, a shadowy figure coming toward the dude at a right angle.

Ducking back behind the rotted timbers, Brian frantically weighs his options. If he runs, they'll hear him. If he stays put, they'll stumble upon him for sure. Where the hell is Philip? Where is Nick?

Right then, Brian hears the rhythmic snapping of twigs in another part of the grove speeding up, somebody moving quickly toward the gunman.

Peering over the top of the deadfall, Brian sees the silhouette of his brother—fifty yards away—creeping low through the undergrowth, coming at a right angle toward the shooter. Brian's spine goes cold with dread, his stomach clenching.

Nick Parsons appears in the shadows on the other side of the gunman with a rock in his hand. He pauses and then hurls the stone—which is the size of a grapefruit—a hundred feet across the orchard.

It bangs off a tree, making an enormous clapping sound, which startles the gunman.

The dude whirls and squeezes off a wild shot at the noise, the sonic boom waking up the orchard and making Penny jump. Brian ducks down, but not before witnessing, almost simultaneously, a blur of movement streaking toward the gunman before the dude even has a chance to pump another shell into the breech.

Philip Blake bursts out of the foliage with the old double-barrel already in midswing. The petrified wooden stock strikes the gunman square on the back of his skull, hitting him so hard that he nearly flies out of his jackboots. The pistol-grip shotgun flies. The gunman lurches and sprawls to the mossy earth.

Brian looks away, covering Penny's eyes, as Philip quickly—savagely—finishes the job with four more tremendous blows to the fallen gunman's skull.

Now the balance of power subtly shifts. Philip finds a throw-down pistol—a snub-nose .38—behind the fallen gunman's belt. A pocketful of shells and a speed-loader give Philip and Nick another boost. Brian watches all this from the deadfall fifty yards away.

A surge of relief courses through Brian, a glimmer of hope. They can get away now. They can start over. They can survive another day.

But when Brian signals to his brother from behind the deadfall, and Philip and Nick come over to the hiding place, the look on

Philip's face in the pale light sends a sharp dagger of panic through Brian's gut. "We're gonna take these motherfuckers out," he says. "Each and every last one of them."

"But Philip, what if we just—"

"We're gonna get this place back, it's ours, and they're going down."

"But—"

"Listen to me." Something about the way Philip locks his eyes on to Brian's makes Brian's skin crawl. "I need you to keep my daughter out of harm's way, no matter what. Do you understand what I'm saying?"

"Yeah, but—"

"That's all I need you to do."

"Okay."

"Just keep her safe. Look at me. Can you do that for me?"

Brian nods. "Yeah. Absolutely, Philip. I will. Just don't go and get yourself killed."

Philip doesn't say anything, doesn't react, just stares as he pumps a shell into the pistol-grip 20-gauge, then gives Nick a look.

In a matter of moments, the two men have sprung back into action, vanishing into the grove of trees, leaving Brian to sit in the weeds, weaponless, petrified with fear, frantic with indecision, his bare feet bleeding. Did Philip want him to stay put? Was that the plan?

A gunshot thunders. Brian jumps. Another one answers, the echo boomeranging across the cold heavens above the treetops. Brian clenches his fists hard enough to draw blood. Is he supposed to sit here?

He pulls Penny close as another gunshot rings out, closer, the muffled, strangled sound of a watery death gasp reverberating after it. Brian's thoughts begin to race again, the tremors rocking through him.

Footsteps crunch toward the hiding place. Brian ventures another quick peek over the top of the timbers, and he sees the creepy bald dude with the nine-millimeter Glock weaving quickly through the trees, coming this way, his scarred face burning with killing rage. The crumpled body of the skinny kid named Shorty lies in the mud a hundred feet to the north, half his head blown away.

Another blast makes Brian duck down, his heart in his throat. He's not sure if the bald man is down or if the blast just came from the bald man's weapon.

"Come on, kiddo," Brian says to a nearly catatonic Penny, who is curled up in the undergrowth, covering her head. "We gotta get outta here."

He pries her out of the weeds and takes her hand—it's too dangerous to carry her anymore—and he drags her away from the firefight.

They creep along behind the shadows of peach trees, staying under the cover of thickets, avoiding the footpaths radiating through the orchards. The bottoms of his feet almost numbed now by the pain and the cold, Brian can still hear voices behind him, scattered gunfire, and then nothing.

For a long time, Brian hears nothing but wind in the branches, and maybe a series of frantic footsteps now and again, he's not sure, his heart is beating too loudly in his ears. But he keeps going.

He gets another hundred yards or so before ducking down behind an old broken-down hay wagon. Catching his breath, he holds Penny close. "You okay, kiddo?"

Penny manages to give him a thumbs-up, but her expression is crumbling with terror.

He inspects her clothes, her face, her body, and she seems physically unharmed. He pats her and tries to comfort her but the adrenaline and fatigue are making Brian shake so badly, he can barely function.

He hears a sound and freezes. He hunches down and peers through the slats of the rotted wagon. About fifty yards away, a figure skulks through the shadows of a gulley. The figure is tall and rangy, and is carrying a pistol-grip shotgun, but is too far away to identify.

"Daddy—?"

Penny's voice startles Brian, coming out of her barely on a whisper, but loud enough to give them away. Brian grabs the child. He puts his hand over her mouth. Then Brian cranes his neck to see over the wagon. He catches a glimpse of the figure coming up the slope of the gulley.

Unfortunately, the figure coming toward them is not the little girl's daddy.

The blast practically vaporizes half the wagon, as Brian is thrown to the ground in a whirlwind of dust and debris. He eats dirt, and he claws for Penny, and he gets a hold of a piece of her shirt, and he drags her toward the deeper woods. He crawls several yards, yanking Penny along, and then he manages to finally struggle to his feet, and now he's dragging Penny toward the deeper shadows, but something's wrong.

The little girl has gone limp in his grasp, as though she has passed out.

Brian can hear the crunch of boot steps behind him, the clang of the pump, as the gunman closes in on them for the kill shot. Frantically lifting Penny onto his shoulder, Brian hobbles as quickly as possible toward the cover of trees, but he doesn't get far before he realizes he is covered in blood. The blood is streaming down the front of his shirt, soaking him, pulsing in rivulets.

"Oh God no, God no, God no no no—" Brian lowers Penny to the soft earth, laying her on her back. Her bloodless face is the color of a bed sheet. Her eyes are glassy and fixed on the sky as she makes hiccup noises, a tiny rivulet of blood leaking from the corner of her mouth.

Brian hardly hears the gunman now, pounding toward him, the snap of the pump injecting another shell. Penny's little shirt, a cotton T-shirt, is soaked with deep scarlet, the ragged exit tear at least six inches in diameter. Grains of deer shot propelled by a 20-gauge shell are powerful enough to penetrate steel, and it looks like the child took at least half the expanding cloud of shot through her back and out the side of her tummy.

The gunman closes in.

Brian lifts the child's shirt and lets out an almost primal moan of anguish. His hand can't stanch the profuse bleeding, the gaping wound a crescent-shaped mess. Brian presses his hand down on the wound. The blood bubbles. He rips a piece of his shirttail and tries to plug the jagged hole in her midsection, but the blood is everywhere now. Brian stammers and cries and tries to talk to her as the oily blood seeps through his fingers, and the gunman draws near: "It's okay, you're gonna be okay, we're gonna get you fixed up, it's gonna be fine, you're gonna be all better . . ."

Brian's arms and waist are baptized in the warmth of her life force draining out of her. Penny utters a single feeble whisper: ". . . *away* . . ."

"No, Penny, no, no, don't do that . . . don't go away yet, not now . . . don't go away . . . !"

At this point, Brian hears the twig snap directly behind him.

A shadow falls across Penny.

"Goddamn shame," a gravelly voice murmurs behind Brian, the cold end of a shotgun muzzle pressing down on the back of Brian's neck. "Take a good look at her."

Brian twists around and glances up at the gunman, a tattooed, bearded man with a beer belly, aiming the shotgun directly at Brian's face. Almost as an afterthought, the man growls, "Look at her . . . she's the last thing you're gonna ever see."

Brian never takes his hand off Penny's wound, but he knows it's too late.

She's not going to make it.

Brian is ready now . . . ready to die.

The boom has a dreamlike quality, as though Brian has suddenly flown out of his body and is now high above the orchard, witnessing things from the perspective of a disembodied spirit. But almost instantly, Brian—who instinctively jerked forward at the boom—jerks back in shock. Blood mists across his arms and across Penny.

Was the impact of the point-blank blast so catastrophic that it was painless? Is Brian already dead and not even aware of it?

The shadow of the gunman begins falling, almost in slow motion, like an old redwood giving up the ghost.

Brian whirls around in time to see that the bearded man has been shot from behind, the top of his skull a mass of red pulp, his beard matted in blood. Eyes rolling back in his head, he collapses. Brian stares. Like a curtain dropping, the falling man reveals two figures behind him, charging toward Brian and Penny.

"GODDAMNIT NO!" Philip throws the pistol-grip shotgun—still smoking hot—to the ground and races through the trees. Nick follows on his heels. Philip roars up to Brian and shoves him aside. "NO! NO!"

Philip drops to his knees by the dying child, who is now asphyxiating, drowning in her own blood. He scoops her up and tenderly touches the gaping wound as though it's just a boo-boo, just a scrape, just a little bump. He draws her into an embrace, her blood soaking him.

Brian lies on the ground a few feet away, breathing the musty earth, a curtain of shock pulling down over his eyes. Nick stands nearby. "We can stop the bleeding, right? We can fix her up? Right?"

Philip cradles the bloody child.

Penny expires in his arms in a breathy little death rattle, which leaves her face as white and cold as porcelain. Philip shakes her. "C'mon, punkin . . . stay with us . . . stay with us now. Come on . . . stay with us . . . please stay with us . . . Punkin? Punkin? Punkin?"

The terrible silence hangs in the air.

"Sweet Jesus," Nick utters to himself, his gaze going down to the ground.

For the longest time, Philip holds the child while Nick stares into the dirt, silently praying. For most of that time, Brian lies prone on the ground, five feet away, crying into the moist earth, babbling softly, more to himself than to anyone else: "I tried . . . happened so fast . . . I couldn't . . . it was . . . I can't believe it . . . I can't . . . Penny was—"

All at once, a big, gnarled hand wrenches down on the back of Brian's shirt.

"What did I say?" Philip snarls, a guttural growl, as he yanks his brother off the ground, and then slams Brian against the trunk of a nearby tree. Brian goes limp. He sees stars.

"Philly, no!" Nick tries to step in between the two brothers, but Philip shoves Nick away hard enough to send the smaller man sprawling to the ground. Philip still has his right hand locked around his brother's throat.

"What did I say?" Philip slams Brian against the trunk. The back of Brian's skull bounces off the bark, sending veins of light and pain through his field of vision, but he makes no effort to fight back or escape. He wants to die. He wants to die at the hands of his brother.

"WHAT DID I SAY?" Philip heaves Brian away from the tree. The ground flies up at Brian like a battering ram, smashing one shoulder and the side of his face, and then a fusillade of kicks descends upon Brian as he rolls involuntarily across the ground. One kick from the steel-toed logger boot strikes him in the jaw hard enough to crack his mandible. Another one fractures three ribs, sending white-hot pain up his side. Yet another strikes the small of his back, dislocating vertebra and nearly puncturing his kidney. Shiny, bright pain splinters his tailbone. And after a while, Brian can hardly feel the pain anymore, he can only watch it all unfold from way up above his mangled body, as he surrenders to the beating as a supplicant surrenders to a high priest.

NINETEEN

The next day, Philip spends an hour in the toolshed out behind the villa, going through the collection of weapons taken from the intruders, as well as all the bladed tools and farm implements left by the former inhabitants. He knows what he has to do, but choosing the mode of execution is agonizing for him. At first, he decides on the nine-millimeter semiauto. It'll be the fastest and the cleanest. But then he has second thoughts about using a gun. It just seems unfair somehow. Too cold and impersonal. Nor can he bring himself to use an axe or a machete. Too messy and uncertain. What if his aim is off by half an inch and he botches the job?

At last he decides on the nine-millimeter Glock, shoving a fresh mag of rounds into the hilt and snapping back the cocking slide.

He takes a deep breath, and then goes over to the shed's door. He pauses and braces himself. Scratching noises sporadically travel across the exterior walls of the shed. The villa's property buzzes with Biter activity, scores of the things drawn to the commotion of the previous day's firefight. Philip kicks the door open.

The door bangs into a middle-aged female zombie in a stained pinafore dress who was sniffing around the shed. The force of the impact sends her skeletal form stumbling backward, arms pinwheeling, a ghastly moan rising out of her decomposed face. Philip walks past her, casually raising the Glock, hardly even breaking his stride as he quickly squeezes off a single shot into the side of her skull.

The roar of the Glock echoes as the female corpse whiplashes sideways in a cloud of scarlet mist, then folds to the ground.

Philip marches across the rear of the villa, raising the Glock and taking out another pair of errant Biters. One of them is an old man dressed only in yellowed underwear—maybe an escapee from a nursing home. Another one is most likely a former fruit grower, his bloated, blackened body still clad in its original sappy dungarees. Philip puts them down with a minimum of fuss—a single shot each— and he makes a mental note to clear the remains later that day with one of the snow-shovel attachments on the riding mower.

Almost a full day has passed since Penny died in his arms, and now the new dawn is rising clear and blue, the crisp autumn sky high and clean over the acres of peach trees. It's taken Philip nearly twenty-four hours to work up the nerve to do what he has to do. Now he grips the gun with a sweaty palm as he enters the orchard.

He has five rounds left in the magazine.

In the shadows of the woods, a figure writhes and moans against an ancient tree trunk. Bound with rope and duct tape, the prisoner strains with futile desperation to escape. Philip approaches and raises the gun. He points the barrel between the figure's eyes, and for just an instant, Philip tells himself to get it over with quickly: *Lance the wound, remove the tumor, get it done.*

The muzzle wavers, Philip's finger freezing up on the trigger pad, and he lets out a tormented sigh. "I can't do it," he utters under his breath.

He lowers the gun and stares at his daughter. Six feet from him, tied to the tree, Penny growls with the feral hunger of a rabid dog. Her china doll face has narrowed and sunken into a rotted white gourd, her soft eyes hardened into tiny silver coins. Her once inno-cent tulip-shaped lips are now blackened and curled away from slimy teeth. She doesn't recognize her father.

This is the part that tears the biggest chunk out of Philip's soul. He can't stop remembering the look in Penny's eyes each time he would pick her up at the day care center or at her aunt Nina's house at the end of a long, hard work day. The spark of recognition and excitement—and hell yes, unadulterated *love*—in those big, brown doelike eyes each time Philip returned was enough to keep Philip going no matter what. Now that spark is gone forever—cemented over with the gray film of the undead.

Philip knows what he has to do.

Penny snarls.

Philip's eyes burn with agony.

"I can't do it," he murmurs again, looking down, not really addressing Penny or even himself. Seeing her like this sends a bolt of electric rage down through his system, arcing like the pilot of a welding torch, touching off a secret flame deep within him. He hears the voice: *Tear the world open, tear it apart, rip open its fucking heart . . . do it now.*

He backs away from the horror in the orchard, his brain roiling with fury.

The villa's property—now basking in a mild autumn morning—is a half-moon-shaped plot of land, the main house at its center. Several outbuildings rise along the gentle curve behind the house: the carriage house, a small storage shed for the riding mower and tractor, a second shed for tools, a coach house on elevated pilings for guests, and a large wood-sided barn with a huge weather vane and cupola on top. This last structure, the worm-eaten wood siding faded to a sun-bleached pink, is where Philip now heads.

He needs to drain off this poisonous current coursing through him; he needs to vent.

The main entrance of the barn is a double door at one end, latched with a giant timber across its center. Philip walks up and throws open the plank, the doors squeaking apart, revealing the dust motes floating in shadows inside. Philip enters, closing the double doors behind him. The air smells of horse piss and moldy hay.

Two more figures wriggle and squirm in the corner, gripped in their own brand of hellish torment, bound and gagged with duct tape: *Sonny and Cher.*

The twosome tremble against each other on the floor of the barn, their mouths taped, their backs pressed against the door of an empty horse stall, their bodies in the throes of some kind of withdrawal. Either heroin or crack or something else, it doesn't really matter to Philip. The only thing that matters now is that these two have no idea how much worse life is about to get for them.

Philip walks over to the dynamic duo. The skinny gal is trembling with spasms, her painted eyes caked with dried tears. The man is breathing hard through his nostrils.

Standing in a narrow beam of sunlight teeming with dust and hay dander, Philip stares down at them like an angry god. "You," he says to Sonny. "Gonna ask you a question . . . and I know it's hard to nod with your head taped up and shit, so just blink once for yes, twice for no."

The man looks up through raw, watery, sunken eyes. He blinks once.

Philip looks at him. "You like to watch?"

Two blinks.

Philip reaches down to his belt buckle and starts to unfasten it. "That's a shame, because I'm gonna give one hell of a show."

Two blinks.

Again . . . two blinks.

Two blinks, two blinks, two blinks.

"Easy, Brian, not so fast," Nick says to Brian the next night, up in the second-floor sewing room. In the light of kerosene lanterns, Nick is helping Brian drink water through a straw. Brian's mouth is still swollen and clumsy, and he dribbles on himself. Nick has been doing everything he can to help Brian recover, and keeping food down him is paramount. "Try some more of the vegetable soup," Nick suggests.

Brian has a few spoonfuls. "Thanks, Nick." Brian's voice is choked, thick with pain. "Thanks for everything." His words are slightly slurred, his soft palate still inflamed. He speaks tentatively, haltingly. Lying in bed, he has rags wrapped snugly around his broken ribs, Band-Aids on his face and neck, his left eye puffy with a purplish bruise. Something might be wrong with his hip; neither of them can tell for sure.

"You're gonna be fine, man," Nick says. "Your brother is another story."

"What do you mean?"

"He's lost it, man."

"He's been through a lot, Nick."

"How can you say that?" Nick sits back, lets out a pained sigh. "Look what he did to you. And don't say it's because he lost Penny—we've all lost people we love. He came very close to taking you out."

Brian looks at his own mangled feet sticking out of the bottom of the blankets. With great effort, he says, "I deserve everything I got."

"Don't say that! It wasn't your fault, what happened. Your brother's turned a corner with this thing. I'm really worried about him."

"He'll be okay." Brian looks at Nick. "What's wrong? Something else is bothering you."

Nick takes a deep breath and wonders whether he should confide in Brian. The Blake brothers have always had a complex relationship, and over the years, Nick Parsons has often felt that *he* was more of a brother to Philip Blake than his biological sibling. But there's always been an X factor with the Blakes, a bond of blood that runs deep within the two men.

Nick finally says, "I know you aren't exactly the religious type. I know you think I'm a Holy Roller."

"That's not true, Nick."

Nick waves it off. "Doesn't matter . . . my faith is strong, and I don't judge a man by his religion."

"Where you going with this?"

Nick looks at Brian. "He's keeping her alive, Brian . . . or maybe *alive* is not the right word."

"Penny?"

"He's out there with her now."

"Where?"

Nick explains what's been going on over these last two days since the firefight. While Brian has been recovering from the beating, Philip's been busy. He's keeping two of the intruders—the only ones who survived the firefight—locked up in the barn. Philip claims he's questioning them about possible human settlements. Nick is worried he's torturing them. But that's the least of their worries. The fate of Penny Blake is what's eating at Nick. "He's got her chained to a tree like a pet," Nick says.

Brian frowns. "Where?"

"Out in the orchard. He goes out there at night. Spends time with her."

"Oh God."

"Listen, I know you think this is bullshit, but the way I was brought up, there's a force in the universe called Good and a force called Evil."

"Nick, I don't think this is—"

"Wait. Let me finish. I believe that all this—the plague or whatever you want to call it—is the work of what you would call the Devil or Satan."

"Nick—"

"Just let me say my piece. I've been thinking about it a lot."

"Go ahead, I'm listening."

"What's the thing Satan hates the most? The power of love? Maybe. Somebody being born again. Yeah, probably. But I kinda think it's when a person passes, and their spirit flies up to Paradise."

"I'm not following you."

Nick looks into Brian's hollow gaze. "That's what's going on here, Brian. The Devil's figured out a way to keep people's souls trapped here on earth."

A moment passes as Brian absorbs this. Nick doesn't expect Brian to believe any of this, but maybe, just maybe, Nick can get him to understand.

In that brief silence, the north wind whistles in the shutters. The weather is turning. The villa creaks and moans. Nick lifts the collar of his mothball-scented sweater—days ago, they found some warm clothes in the villa's attic—and now he shivers in the frigid air of the second floor. "What your brother's doing is wrong, it's against God," Nick says then, and the statement hangs in the gloom.

At that moment, out in the darkness of the orchard, a small campfire crackles and flickers on the ground. Philip sits on the cold earth in front of the fire, his shotgun next to him, a musty little book he found in the villa's nursery open on his lap. " 'Let me in, Let me in, Little Pig,' " Philip reads aloud in a stiff, labored singsong voice. " 'Or I'll huff and I'll puff and blow your house in!' "

Three feet away, tied to the tree trunk, Penny Blake snarls and drools at every word, her tiny jaws snapping impotently.

" 'Not by the hair of my chinny chin chin,' " Philip recites, turning a delicate page of onionskin. He pauses and glances up at the thing that used to be his daughter.

In the flicker of firelight, Penny's small face contorts with unyielding hunger, as wrinkled and bloated as a jack-o'-lantern. Her midsection, wound with baling wire, strains against the tree. She reaches out with curled, clawlike fingers and clutches at the air— yearning to break free and make a meal of her father.

" 'But of course,' " Philip continues, his voice breaking, " 'the wolf *did* blow the house in.' " An agonizing pause before Philip says in a shattered voice, filled with equal parts sorrow and madness, " 'And he ate the pig.' "

Over the remainder of that week, sleep does not come easily for Philip Blake. He tries to get a few hours each night but the nervous energy keeps him tossing and turning until he has to get up and do something. Most nights, he goes out to the barn and works off some of his rage on Sonny and Cher. They are the ostensible reasons Penny has turned, and it is up to Philip to make sure they suffer like no man or woman has ever suffered. The delicate process of keeping them just this side of death is not easy. Every once in a while, Philip has to give them water to make sure they don't die on him. He also has to be careful they don't kill themselves in order to escape their torments. Like a good jailer, Philip keeps the ropes tight, and all sharp objects out of their grasp.

On *this* night—Philip thinks it's a Friday—he waits until Nick and Brian are asleep before he slips out of his room, pulls on his denim jacket and boots, and makes his way out the back door and across the moonlit grounds to the weather-beaten barn on the northeast corner of the property. He likes to announce himself as he arrives.

"Daddy's home," he murmurs in a convivial tone, his breath showing in puffs of vapor as he pulls the padlock and pushes open the double doors.

He flips on a battery-powered lantern.

Sonny and Cher are slumped in the shadows where he left them, two ragged creatures trussed up like suckling pigs, side by side, sitting in a spreading pool of their own blood, piss, and shit. Sonny is barely awake, his head lolled to one side, his heavy-lidded junkie eyes rimmed in red. Cher is unconscious. She lies next to him, her leather pants still down around her ankles.

Each of them bear the festering marks of Philip's tools of punishment—needle-nosed pliers, barbed wire, two-by-fours with exposed rusty nails, and various blunt objects that occur to Philip in the heat of the moment.

"Wake up, sis!" Philip reaches down and flips the woman onto her back, the restraints cutting into her wrists, the rope around her neck keeping her from squirming too much. He slaps her. Her eyes flutter. Philip slaps her again. She comes awake now, the muffled cries dampened by the hank of duct tape over her mouth.

At some point in the night, she managed to pull her bloody panties back up and over her privates.

"Let me once again remind you," Philip says, yanking her panties back down to her knees. He stands over her, wrenching her legs apart with his boots as though clearing a path for himself. She writhes and wriggles below him as if she might be able to squirm out of her own skin. "Y'all are the ones took my daughter from me—so we're all gonna go to hell together."

Philip unbuckles his belt, and drops his pants, and it doesn't require much imagination for him to instantly produce an erection—his rage and hate burn so warmly in his solar plexus, it feels like a battering ram. He drops to his knees between the woman's trembling legs.

The first thrust is always the trigger—the voice in his brain abruptly chiming out, taunting him, urging him on with fragments of old biblical nonsense that his daddy used to mumble while drunk: *Vengeance is mine, vengeance is mine sayeth the Lord!*

But tonight, after the third or fourth thrust into the limp woman, Philip stops.

A combination of things steals his focus, hooks his attention. He hears footsteps outside, crunching across the rear of the property, and he even sees, through the slatted siding, the shadow of a figure blurring past the barn. But what gets Philip to draw back and stand up, and hurriedly pull his pants back on, is the fact that this figure is moving toward the orchard.

Toward the place where Penny resides.

Philip exits the barn and instantly sees a figure plunging into the shadows of the orchard. The figure is a compact, trim man in his thirties clad in a sweater and jeans, carrying a huge rusty spade over his shoulder.

"Nick!"

Philip's warning cry goes unheeded. Nick has already vanished into the trees.

Drawing the nine-millimeter from behind his belt, Philip charges toward the orchard. He snaps a round into the chamber as he plunges into the woods. Darkness gives way to the beam of a flashlight.

Fifty feet away, Nick Parsons is shining a light on the livid face of the Penny-thing.

"NICK!"

Nick whirls suddenly with the shovel raised, and the flashlight tumbles out of his hand. "It's gone too far, Philly, it's gone too far."

"Put the shovel down," Philip says as he approaches with the gun raised. The flashlight beam shines up into the leaves, casting an eerie, pale glow over everything, like a grainy black-and-white film.

"You can't do this to your daughter, you don't realize what you're doing."

"Put it down."

"You're keeping her soul from entering heaven, Philly."

"Shut up!"

Twenty feet away, the Penny-thing yanks on its bonds in the shadows. The cockeyed beam of the flashlight highlights her monstrous features from below. Her eyes reflect the dry silver light.

"Philly, listen to me." Nick lowers the shovel, his voice unsteady with emotion. "You have to let her die . . . she's one of God's children. Please . . . I'm begging you as a Christian . . . please let her go."

Philip aims the Glock directly at Nick's forehead. "If she dies . . . you die next."

For a moment, Nick Parsons looks crestfallen, absolutely beaten.

Then he drops the shovel, hangs his head, and walks back toward the villa.

Throughout all this, the Penny-thing keeps its sharklike gaze on the man it once called father.

Brian continues to heal. Six days after the beating, he feels strong enough to get out of bed and limp around the house. His hip twinges with every step, and the dizziness comes in waves whenever he goes up and down the stairs, but on the whole, he's doing pretty well. His bruises have faded and the swelling has gone down, and he feels his appetite returning. He also has a good talk with Philip.

"I miss her something fierce," Brian says to his brother late one night in the kitchen, each man suffering from severe insomnia. "I'd trade places with her in a heartbeat if it meant bringing her back."

Philip looks down. He has developed a series of very subtle tics, which emerge when he's under pressure—sniffing, pursing his lips, clearing his throat. "I know, sport. It ain't your fault . . . what happened out there. I never should have done that to you."

Brian's eyes moisten. "I probably would have done the same thing."

"Let's put it behind us."

"Sure." Brian wipes his eyes. He looks at Philip. "So, what's the deal with the people in the barn?"

Philip looks up. "What about 'em?"

"The whole thing has Nick on edge . . . and you can hear things out there . . . at night, I'm talking about. Nick thinks you're, like . . . pulling their fingernails off."

A cold smile twitches at the corner of Philip's mouth. "That's sick."

Brian isn't smiling. "Philip, whatever you're doing out there, it's not going to bring Penny back."

Philip looks down again. "I know that . . . don't you think I know that?"

"Then I'm begging you to stop. Whatever it is you're doing . . . *stop*." Brian looks at his brother. "It's not serving any purpose."

Philip looks up with embers of emotion in his eyes. "That trash out there in the barn stole everything that mattered to me . . . that bald motherfucker and his crew . . . them two junkies . . . they destroyed the life of a beautiful innocent little girl and they did it outta sheer meanness and greed. Ain't nothing I could do to them would suffice."

Brian sighs. Further protest seems futile, so he simply stares at his coffee.

"And you're wrong about it not serving any purpose," Philip concludes, after a moment of thought. "It serves the purpose of making me feel better."

The next night, after the lanterns go out, and the fires in the three separate fireplaces dwindle down to coals, and the northeasterly wind begins toying with the dormers and loose shingles, Brian is lying in bed in the sewing room, trying to lull himself into a troubled sleep, when he hears the door latch click and sees the silhouette of Nick Parsons slipping into his room. Brian sits up. "What's going on?"

"Sssshhh," Nick whispers, coming across the room and kneeling by the bed. Nick has his coat on, his gloves, and a bulge on his hip that looks like the grip of a handgun. "Keep it down."

"What is it?"

"Your brother's asleep . . . finally."

"So what?"

"So we gotta do a—whaddaya callit—an intervention."

"What are you talking about? Penny? You're talking about trying to take Penny out again?"

"No! The barn, man! The barn!"

Brian moves to the edge of the bed and rubs his eyes, stretches his sore limbs, shakes the cobwebs off. "I don't know if I'm ready for this."

They slip out the back, each one of them armed with a handgun. Nick has the bald man's .357 steel-plated revolver, Brian has a snub-nose that belonged to one of the thug gunmen. They steal across the property to the barn, and Brian shines a flashlight on the padlock. They find a piece of timber in a woodpile, and they use it to pry open the rotted doors, making as little noise as possible.

Brian's heart hammers in his chest as they slip inside the dark barn.

The stench of mold and urine fills their senses as they work their way back through the fetid shadows to the rear of the barn, where two dark heaps lie on the floor in puddles of blood as black as oil. At first, the shapes don't even look human, but when the beam of Brian's flashlight falls on a pale face, Brian lets out a gasp.

"Holy fucking shit."

The man and woman are still alive, barely, their faces disfigured and swollen, their midsections exposed like raw meat. A thin tendril of steam rises from festering, sucking wounds. Both captives are semiconscious, their parboiled eyes fixed on the rafters. The woman is brutalized, a broken doll with legs akimbo and blood patterns covering her pasty, tattooed flesh.

Brian begins to tremble. "Holy shit . . . what have we . . . ? Holy *fucking shit* . . ."

Nick kneels by the woman. "Brian, get some water."

"What about—"

"Get it from the well! Hurry!"

Brian hands over his flashlight, spins, and hustles back the way he came.

Nick shines the light on the constellation of wounds and sores—some old and infected, some fresh—across a hundred percent of their twisted bodies. The man's chest rises and falls quickly, convulsively, with shallow breaths. The woman struggles to fix her rheumy gaze on Nick. She is blinking wildly.

Her lips move beneath the duct tape. Nick starts to carefully peel the gag away from her mouth.

"P-p-pleeee . . . kuhhh . . ." She's trying to say something urgent but Nick can't understand her.

"It's okay, we're gonna get you outta here, it's okay, you're gonna make it."

"K-khhh . . ."

"Cold?" Nick tries to pull her pants back on her. "Try to breathe, try to—"

"K-khhlll."

"What? I can't—"

The woman tries to swallow, and again she says, "K-kill uss . . . p-please . . ."

Nick stares. His guts go cold. He feels something softly nudging his hip and he looks down and sees the woman's scabby hand fumbling at the pistol grip sticking out of his belt. Nick feels all the fight go out of him. His heart sinks down through the floor.

He pulls the .357 from his belt and stands up and gazes down at the abominations on the floor of the barn for a long time.

He says a prayer: the Twenty-third Psalm.

Brian is on his way back to the barn with a plastic pail of well water when he hears the two muffled pops from inside the barn. Like firecrackers bursting inside tin cans, the blasts are short and sharp. The sound of them makes Brian freeze in his tracks, the water sloshing over the rim of the bucket. He sucks in a startled breath.

Then he sees, out of the corner of his eye, a faint light flickering on in one of the villa's second-floor windows: Philip's room. A flash-light up there plays across the window, then vanishes. This is fol-lowed by a series of muffled footsteps banging down the stairs and through the house, hard and fast, and this gets Brian moving again.

He drops the pail. He charges back across the property to the barn. He slams through the doorway, plunging into the dark. Then he hurtles through the shadows, toward the silver beam of light on the floor in the rear. He sees Nick standing over the captives.

A ribbon of cordite smoke rises from the muzzle of the .357 in Nick's right hand, now hanging at his side as he stares down at the bodies.

Brian joins Nick and starts to say something when all at once Brian looks down and sees the head wounds: blossoms of gore bloom up the stall door—shimmering in the horizontal light beam.

The man and the woman are stone-cold dead, each one of them now lying supine in their drying fluids, their faces at peace, re-leased from their contortions of misery. Again, Brian tries to say something.

He can't get out any words.

A moment later, in the darkness across the barn, the double doors burst open and Philip storms in. Fists clenched at his sides, face chis-eled with rage, eyes flashing with white-hot madness, he marches toward the light. He looks as though he's going to devour some-body. He has a pistol shoved down the side of his belt and a machete banging on one hip.

He gets about halfway across the barn before he starts to slow down.

Nick has turned away from the bodies and is now standing his ground, staring at Philip as he approaches. Brian steps back, a tidal wave of shame crashing down over him. He feels like his soul is be-ing ripped in half. He stares at the floor as his brother approaches slowly now, warily, glancing nervously from the dead bodies to Nick, and then to Brian, and then back at the dead bodies.

For the longest time, nobody can think of anything to say. Philip keeps looking at Brian, and Brian keeps trying to conceal the paralyzing shame spreading through him, but the more he tries to conceal it, the more it drags him down.

If Brian only had the guts for it, he would put the barrel of the snub-nose in his mouth right now and put *himself* out of his misery. In some strange way, he feels responsible for this—for all of it—but he's too much of a coward to kill himself like a man.

He can only stand there and look away in abject shame and humiliation.

And like an invisible chain reaction, the pathetic, gruesome tableau of desecrated bodies—combined with the unyielding silence of his brother and his friend—begins to break Philip down.

He fights the tears pooling in his eyes and juts his quivering chin out in a mixture of defiance and self-loathing. He works his mouth like he's got something important to impart, and it takes a huge effort to speak, but he finally manages to say in a choked mutter, "Whatever."

Nick looks mortified, staring at Philip in disbelief. " *'Whatever'?"*

Philip turns and walks away, pulling the Glock from his belt as he goes. He snaps the slide and fires into the wall of the barn—BOOOOMMMMMM!—the recoil kicking in his hand, the loud bark making Brian jump. BOOOOOMMMM! Another blast flashes in the darkness, taking a chunk of the door. BOOOOOMMMM! The third shot puts a chink in the rafter and rains debris down on the floor.

Philip angrily kicks the doors open and storms out of the barn.

The silence left behind seems to ripple for a moment with afterimages of Philip's fiery wrath. Brian hasn't taken his eyes off the floor throughout all this, and he continues to hang his head and stare miserably at the moldy matted hay. Nick takes one last look at the bodies, and then lets out a long, pained, unsteady breath. He looks at Brian, and he shakes his head. "There you have it," he says.

But something behind his words—the subtle tone of dread in his voice—tells Brian that things have now irrevocably changed in their little dysfunctional family.

TWENTY

"What the fuck is he doing?" Nick stands at the villa's front window, staring out at the overcast morning.

Across the front of the property, at the top of the driveway, Philip has Penny on a modified dog leash, assembled from spare parts found in the toolshed—a long length of copper pipe with a spiked collar threaded through one end. He drags her toward a Ford S-10 pickup parked on the grass. The truck is one of the vehicles owned by the bald man's crew, and Philip has now loaded its cargo bed with canned goods, guns, provisions, and bedding.

Penny sputters and growls as she is yanked along, grabbing at the pipe leashed to her neck, biting at the air. In the diffuse, watery light, her dead face looks like a living Halloween mask, sculpted out of wormy-gray modeling clay.

"That's what I've been trying to tell you," Brian says, standing next to Nick, gazing out at the bizarre scene unfolding in the front yard. "He got up this morning convinced we can't stay here anymore."

"And why's that?"

Brian shrugs. "I don't know . . . after all that's happened . . . I guess the place is like poison for him, full of ghosts . . . I don't know."

Brian and Nick have been up all night, guzzling coffee and discussing their situation. Nick has been dancing around the fact that he thinks Philip has gone off his spindle, succumbing to the stress of losing Penny, and to the cumulative pressure of protecting them.

Although Nick has stopped short of verbalizing it, he has alluded to the possibility that the Devil has gotten his hooks into Philip. Brian is too exhausted to argue metaphysics with Nick, but there is no denying the fact that things have become dire.

"Let him go," Nick says finally, turning away from the window.

Brian looks at him. "What do you mean? You mean you're staying?"

"Yeah, I'm staying, and you should, too."

"Nick, come on."

"How can we keep following him . . . after all this shit . . . the stuff that's gone down?"

Brian wipes his mouth and thinks about it. "Look. I'll say it again. What he did to those people is, like, *beyond awful*. He lost his way. And I'm not sure I'll ever be able to look at him the same way again . . . but this is about survival now. We can't split up. Our best shot is sticking together no matter what."

Nick glances back out the window. "You really think we're gonna make it to the Gulf Coast? That's like four hundred miles and change."

"Our best shot is doing it together."

Nick fixes his gaze on Brian. "He's got his dead daughter on a fucking leash. He pretty near beat you to death. He's a loose cannon, Brian, and he's gonna blow up in our faces."

"That loose cannon got us all the way across Georgia from Waynesboro in one piece," Brian says, a flare of anger burning in his gut. "So, he's nuts, he's volatile, he's possessed by demons, he's the prince of fucking darkness . . . he's still my brother and he's our best chance of survival."

Nick looks at him. "Is that what we're calling it now? Survival?"

"You want to stay here, be my guest."

"Thanks, I'll do that."

Nick walks away, leaving Brian to turn back to the window and nervously watch his brother.

Utilizing a radiator hose as a siphon, they consolidate all the fuel on the property—from tractors, from vehicles, even from the Harleys—

into the Ford S-10. All told, they're able to top off the seventeen-gallon tank and then some. Philip arranges a place for Penny in the rear cargo bay by moving the boxes of supplies around into a semi-circle and laying blankets down on the deck. He chains her to a U-bolt so she can't get herself into any mischief or fall over the side.

Nick watches all this from his second-floor window, pacing the room like a caged animal. The reality of the situation starts to set in. He'll be alone in this big old drafty villa. He'll spend nights alone. He'll spend the whole winter alone. He'll hear the north winds shrieking through the gutters and the distant moaning of Biters wandering the orchards . . . all while biding his time alone. He'll wake up alone and eat alone and forage for food alone and dream of better days alone and pray to God for deliverance . . . all by himself. As he watches Philip and Brian finish up the last of the preparations for departure, a twinge of regret tightens Nick's midsection—*seller's remorse*. He crosses the room to his closet.

It takes him a matter of seconds to stuff his essentials into a duffel bag.

He rushes out of the room and takes the stairs two at a time.

Brian is just settling into the passenger seat, and Philip is just putting the truck in gear, just beginning to pull away from the villa, when the sound of the front door ripping open reaches their ears.

Brian glances over his shoulder and sees Nick with a duffel bag slung over his shoulder, running across the front parkway, waving them back.

It's hard to believe that Philip would neglect to check under the pickup's hood. Had he taken three minutes to make sure everything was in working order, he would have found the perforated hose. But Philip Blake is not exactly a hundred percent these days. His mind is a shortwave radio tuned to different stations now.

But regardless of whether it was a deliberate cut made by the home invaders after the firefight broke out (to ensure that nobody escaped), or it was a piece of flak that had pierced the truck's grill, or it was simply a coincidental failure, the pickup begins to smoke and sputter less than five miles from the villa.

At a point approximately fifty miles southwest of Atlanta, in a place most folks around these parts call the Middle of Nowhere, the pickup hobbles off the highway and onto the gravel shoulder, where it stutters to a stop, all the warning lights across the dash flickering on. White vapor seeps out from under the hood, and the ignition won't turn over. Philip lets out an alarming barrage of profanity, nearly kicking his logger boot through the floor. The other two men look down, silently waiting for the squall to pass. Brian wonders if this is what a battered wife feels like: too afraid to escape, too afraid to stay.

At length, Philip's tantrum passes. He gets out and opens the hood.

Brian joins him. "What's the verdict?"

"Screwed and tattooed."

"No hope of fixing it?"

"You got a radiator hose on you?"

Brian glances over his shoulder. The side of the road slopes down to a ravine filled with old tires, weeds, and rubbish. Movement draws his gaze to the far end of the ravine—about a quarter of a mile away—where a cluster of Biters mill about in the garbage. They stumble around and root for flesh in the rocks like trufflenuzzling pigs. They haven't yet noticed the disabled vehicle now smoking on the side of the road three hundred yards away.

In the rear of the pickup, Penny yanks at her chain. The chain is threaded through her dog collar and bolted to the corrugated deck. The proximity of other upright corpses seems to be tweaking her, exciting her, disturbing her.

"What do you think?" Brian finally asks his brother, who has carefully lowered the hood and clicked it shut with a minimum of noise.

Nick is climbing out of the cab. He joins them. "What's the plan?"

Brian looks at him. "The plan is . . . we're fucked."

Nick chews his fingernail, glancing back over his shoulder at the zombie conclave slowly working its way down the ravine, getting closer every minute. "Philip, we can't sit here. Maybe we can find another car."

Philip exhales a pained sigh. "All right, you fellas know the drill . . . grab your shit, I'll get Penny."

They light out with Penny on the leash, their backs laden with supplies. They hug the shoulder, following the highway. Brian limps along without complaint, despite the stabbing pain in his hip. Around Greenville, they have to take a detour due to an inexplicable pileup of wrecked vehicles, the scorched tangle of metal spanning across both northbound and southbound lanes, the area crawling with zombies. From a distance, it looks as though the earth itself has split open and vomited up hundreds of walking corpses.

They decide to take a two-lane—Rural Route 100—which wends its way southward, through Greenville, and around the congestion. And they get maybe a mile or two before Philip puts his hand up and stops.

"Hold on a second," he says, frowning. He cocks his head. "What is that?"

"What is *what*?"

"That noise."

"What noise?"

Philip listens. They all listen. Philip turns in a slow circle, trying to pinpoint the direction from which the sound is coming. "Is that an engine?"

Brian hears it now. "Sounds like a fucking tank."

"Or maybe a bulldozer," Nick ventures.

"What the fuck." Philip narrows his eyes as he listens. "That can't be too far away."

They continue on. Less than a mile down the road, they come upon a dented sign:

WOODBURY—1 MI.

They continue on down the road, all eyes on the smoke-clogged western sky.

"Whoever they are, they got fuel," Nick says.

Brian sees a cloud of dust on the horizon. "You think they're friendly?"

"I ain't taking any chances," Philip says. "C'mon . . . we'll find a back way in, take it one step at a time."

Philip leads them across the shoulder, then down a weedy slope.

They scuttle across an adjacent farm field, a vast and fallow valley of soft earth. Their boots sink into the mire as they go. The chill wind lashes at them, and it takes them an interminable amount of time to circumnavigate the outskirts before the remnants of an abandoned town begin to materialize ahead of them.

A Walmart sign rises above a stand of ancient live oaks. The golden arches of a McDonald's are visible not far beyond the Walmart. Litter tumbles down empty streets, past postwar brick buildings and cookie-cutter condos. But on the north side of the town, within a maze of cyclone fences, the sounds of engines and hammering and the occasional voice reveal the presence of humans.

"Looks like they're building a wall or somethin'," Nick says as they pause under the cover of trees. In the distance, about two hundred yards away, a handful of figures labor over a tall wooden rampart closing off the north edge of town. The barricade already stretches nearly two blocks.

"Rest of the place looks dead," Philip comments. "Can't be many survivors."

"What the hell is that?" Brian is pointing at a semicircle of high stanchions a few blocks west of the barricade. Clusters of arc lights point down at a large open space, obscured behind buildings and fences.

"Football field for the high school maybe?" Philip is reaching for his Glock. He pulls it out and checks the remaining rounds in the magazine. He's got six hollow-points left.

"What are you thinking, Philip?" Nick looks anxious, jittery.

Brian wonders if Nick is worried about walking into another trap. Or maybe he's just edgy around Philip. The truth is, Brian isn't too keen on waltzing uninvited into this little ragtag community, especially considering the fact that they have a moldering zombie in tow, and a father of said zombie so tightly wound he seems capable of almost anything at any moment. But what choice do they have? Dark clouds are gathering on the western horizon again, and the temperature is plummeting.

"What do you got there, sport?" Philip nods toward the gun bulging out the side of Brian's belt. "The .38?"

"Yeah."

"And you got the .357?" Philip says to Nick, who nods nervously. "Okay . . . here's what we're gonna do."

They enter from the northeast corner of town, from the trees along the railroad tracks. They come slowly, with their hands raised in a nonthreatening gesture. At first, they're surprised by how far they get—in plain sight of at least a dozen humans—before anyone even notices strangers strolling into town.

"Hey!" A hefty, middle-aged man in a black turtleneck sweater hops off a bulldozer, pointing at the newcomers. "Bruce! Look! We got company!"

Another worker—a tall black man in a peacoat with a glistening shaved head—pauses his hammering. He looks up and his eyes widen. He goes for a shotgun leaning against a nearby cooler.

"Take it easy, fellas!" Philip approaches slowly across a dusty truck lot, his hands raised. His expression is an approximation of calm, as mild and friendly as he can muster. "Just passin' through . . . not lookin' for any drama."

Brian and Nick follow closely on Philip's heels, each with their hands up.

The two men come over with shotguns. "You boys packin' heat?" the black man wants to know.

"The safety's on," Philip says, pausing to carefully reach for his Glock. "I'm gonna show you the piece, nice and easy like."

He shows them the nine-millimeter.

"What about you two?" The man in the turtleneck addresses Brian and Nick.

They each show their guns.

"Is it just the three of ya?" The man wearing the turtleneck has a Northern accent. His close-cropped blond hair is peppered with gray, and he has a wrestler's neck and a stevedore's barrel chest. His big porcine belly hangs over his belt.

"Just us three," Philip says, and it's essentially the truth. He left Penny tied to a tree in the shadows of the hickory grove a hundred yards outside the barricade. Philip secured her with extra rope and put a bandana around her mouth so she wouldn't make any noise. It killed him to gag her like that, but until he knows what he's dealing with here, he figures it's best to keep her out of sight.

"What happened to you?" the turtleneck guy says to Brian, nodding at his wounds.

"He had a bad time fightin' off some Biters," Philip explains.

The man in the turtleneck lowers his shotgun. "You boys from Atlanta?"

"No, sir. Little hole-in-the-wall called Waynesboro."

"You seen any National Guard out there?"

"No, sir."

"You been traveling on your own?"

"Pretty much." Philip puts his gun back. "We just need to rest up and we'll be on our way."

"You got food?"

"Nope."

"Any cigarettes?"

"No, sir." Philip indicates his companions. "If we could just get a roof over our head for a short spell, we won't bother anybody. You fellas okay with that?"

For a moment, the two workmen give each other a glance like they're sharing a private joke. Then the black man bursts out laughing. "Boys, this is the wild fucking west . . . nobody gives two pieces of a rat's ass *what* you do."

It turns out that the black man was understating the situation in Woodbury.

Over the remaining hours of that day, Philip, Brian, and Nick get the lay of the land and it's not exactly Mayberry RFD. There are about sixty inhabitants clinging to the secure sector on the north side of town, keeping to themselves mostly, eking out an existence on scraps, most of them so paranoid and mistrustful of each other that they rarely even come out of their private hovels. They live in deserted condos and empty stores, and they have no organized leadership whatsoever. It's amazing that any of them had the initiative to begin building a wall. In Woodbury, it's every man, woman, and child for themselves.

All of which suits Philip, Brian, and Nick just fine. After scouting the edges of town, they decide to hole up in an abandoned two-unit apartment building on the southern border of the safe zone, near the uninhabited commercial district. Somebody has moved school buses and empty semitrailers into rows around the periphery of town, forming a makeshift bastion to keep out the Biters.

For now, the place seems relatively safe.

That night, Brian can't sleep, so he decides to sneak out and explore the town. Walking isn't easy—his ribs are still bothering him, and his breathing is labored and wheezy—but it feels good to get out and clear his head.

In the diamond-chip moonlight, the sidewalks lie desolate and barren, threading through what was once a typical little blue-collar burg. Trash blows willy-nilly across deserted playgrounds and squares. Storefronts housing the requisite small-town merchants—the local dentist, DeForest's Feed and Seed, a Dairy Queen, the Piggly Wiggly—are all dark and boarded. Evidence of the "turn" lies everywhere—in the lime pits at Kirney's Salvage Yard, where bodies have been recently deposited and torched, and in the community gazebo at Robert E. Lee Square, where bloodstains from some grue-some battle still glisten like black tar in the moonlight.

Brian isn't surprised to learn that the open field in the center of town—which he first glimpsed from the neighboring farm field—is an old dirt racetrack. Apparently, the residents have enough fuel to keep generators going around the clock; and as Brian soon discovers, every so often, in the dark of night, the huge arc lights over the racetrack flare on for no good reason. On the far side of the track, Brian passes a semitrailer pulsing like a great steel heart with the muffled vibrations of combustion engines—the cables snaking out the back and tying into neighboring buildings.

By the time dawn starts to glow on the eastern horizon, Brian decides he better head back to the two-flat. He crosses a deserted parking lot, and then takes a shortcut down a litter-strewn alley. He reaches the adjacent street and passes a group of old men huddled around a flaming trash barrel, warming their hands against the chill and passing around a bottle of Thunderbird.

"Watch your back, sonny," one of the men says to Brian as he passes, and the two other men chuckle humorlessly. The three men are ancient, grizzled, spavined codgers in moth-eaten Salvation Army coats. They look like they've been hunkered around this bar-rel for eternity.

Brian pauses. He has the snub-nosed .38 pistol wedged behind his belt, under his jacket, but he feels no compulsion to brandish it. "Got Biters in the area?"

"Biters?" one of the other men says. This one has a long white beard and his wrinkled eyes narrow with confusion.

"He means them dead things," says the third old derelict, the fat-test of the three.

"Yeah, Charlie," says the first old man. "You remember . . . them walkin' pus bags that ate Yellow Mike . . . the reason we're stuck in this shitheel town?"

"I know what he's talkin' about!" snaps the bearded codger. "Just never heard 'em called such a thing before."

"You new in town, son?" The fat one is giving Brian the once-over.

"As a matter of fact, yeah . . . I am."

The fat old man shows a grin full of rotten, green teeth. "Welcome to hell's waiting room."

"Don't listen to him, son," the first old man says, putting a bony, arthritic arm around Brian's shoulder. Then, in a low, mucousy voice, the old guy says confidentially: "It ain't the dead things you gotta be mindful of around here . . . it's the living."

The next day, Philip tells Brian and Nick to keep their mouths shut while they're in Woodbury, stay under the radar, avoid any contact with other residents, refrain from even telling people their names. Thankfully, the apartment serves them well as a temporary refuge. Built in the 1950s, with furnishings at least that old—chipped mirror tile on one wall, a moth-eaten sleeper sofa in the living room, a huge rectangular fish tank next to the TV, brimming with scum and the tiny floating corpses of neglected goldfish—the place has three bedrooms and running water. It smells like rancid cat shit and rotting fish, but as Brian's dad used to say, "Beggars can't be choosers." They find canned goods in the pantries of both apartments, and they decide to stay for a while.

Much to Brian's amazement, the townspeople leave them alone, as though they are ghosts. Brian can tell that word has spread among the inhabitants of newcomers in their midst, but still, it's as though the Blakes and Nick are apparitions haunting the broken-down apartment. Which is not too far from the truth. Nick keeps to himself and reads his Bible and doesn't say much. Philip and Brian, still edgy around each other, also go about their business with minimal conversation. It doesn't even occur to them to find a vehicle and continue on their southward journey. It feels to Brian like they've given up . . . on getting to the coast, on the future, maybe on each other.

Brian continues to heal, and Philip tends to his own obsession with Penny, stealing away to the hickory grove every chance he gets.

Late one night, Brian hears the apartment door clicking open and shut.

He lies there in bed, listening for nearly an hour, when finally he hears Philip returning in a flurry of shuffling steps and gurgling noises. This is the third night in a row Philip has silently slipped out of the apartment—presumably to check on Penny while the townspeople are asleep—but up until tonight, his return has been as quiet and discreet as his departure. But now Brian can hear Philip breathing heavily out in the living room, murmuring something that is drowned out by watery groaning sounds and the clank of a chain.

Brian climbs out of bed and goes into the living room. He freezes when he sees Philip dragging Penny on her leash, yanking her across the floor like a whipped dog.

For a brief instant, Brian is speechless. All he can do is stare at the little moving corpse in her pigtails and muddy pinafore dress, her feet tracking filth across the apartment floor, and hope that she's a temporary visitor and not—God forbid—a new roommate.

TWENTY-ONE

"What the hell are you doing?" Brian asks his brother as the dead girl claws at the air with stupid hunger. She fixes her milky eyes on Brian.

"It'll be okay," Philip says, yanking his dead daughter toward the back hall.

"You're not—"

"Mind your own goddamn business."

"But what if somebody—"

"Nobody saw me," he says, kicking open the door to the laundry room.

It's a small, claustrophic chamber of linoleum tile and corkboard walls with a broken-down washer and dryer, and ancient cat litter ground into the seams of the floor. Philip drags the drooling, snarling thing into the corner and attaches her leash to the exposed water pipes. He does this with the firm yet gentle hand of an animal trainer.

Brian watches from the hall, appalled at what he's seeing. Philip has blankets spread out on the floor and duct-taped to the sharp edges of the washing machine to prevent the Penny-thing from making noise or hurting herself. It's obvious he's been preparing for this for a while now. He's been thinking about it a lot. He rigs a makeshift leather halter—fashioned from a belt and pieces of the leash—around her head, attaching it to the pipes.

Philip goes about his business with the gentle rigor of a caretaker securing a wheelchair for a handicapped child. With the steel separator, he holds the tiny monster at arm's length and carefully secures the restraints to the wall. All through this, the thing that was once a child snarls and slavers and yanks at her restraints.

Brian stares. He can't decide whether to turn away, cry, or scream. He gets the feeling that he's stumbled upon something disturbingly intimate here, and for a brief instant, his racing thoughts cast back to the time he was eighteen years old and visiting the nursing home in Waynesboro to say good-bye to his dying grandmother. He'll never forget the look on her caretaker's face. On an almost hourly basis, that male nurse had to clean the shit from the old lady's backside, and the expression on his face while he did so, with relatives in the room, was horrible: a mixture of disgust, stoic professionalism, pity, and contempt.

That same weird expression is now contorting Philip Blake's features as he buckles straps around the monster's little head, carefully avoiding the danger zone around her snapping jaws. He sings softly to her as he works on her shackles—some sort of off-key lullaby that Brian can't identify.

Eventually, Philip is satisfied with the restraints. He tenderly strokes the top of the Penny-thing's head, and then kisses her forehead. The girl's jaws snap at him, missing his jugular by centimeters.

"I'll leave the light on, punkin," Philip says to her, speaking loudly, as though addressing a foreigner, before calmly turning and walking out of the laundry room, shutting the door securely behind him.

Brian stands there in the hall, his veins running cold. "You want to talk about this?"

"It'll be okay," Philip reiterates, avoiding eye contact as he walks away, heading toward his room.

The worst part is that the laundry room is next door to Brian's bedroom, and from that moment on, he hears the Penny-thing every night, clawing, moaning, straining against her bonds. She's a constant reminder of . . . what? Armageddon? Madness? Brian doesn't even have the vocabulary for what she represents. The smell is a thousand times worse than cat urine. And Philip spends a lot of time locked inside that laundry room with the dead girl, doing God-knows-what, and it drives the wedge deeper between the three men. Still in the throes of grief and shock, Brian is torn between pity and repulsion. He still loves his brother, but this is too much. Nick has no comment on the matter, but Brian can tell that Nick's spirit is broken. The silences grow longer between the men, and Brian and Nick begin spending more time outside the apartment, wandering the safe zone, getting to know the dynamics of the inhabitants better.

Keeping a low profile, roaming the periphery of the little frontier enclave, Brian learns that the town is basically broken into two social castes. The first group—the one with the most power—includes anyone with a useful trade or vocation. Brian discovers that this first group features two bricklayers, a machinist, a doctor, a gun-store owner, a veterinarian, a plumber, a barber, an auto mechanic, a farmer, a fry cook, and an electrician. The second group—Brian thinks of them as the Dependents—features the sick, the young, and all the white-collar workers with obscure administrative backgrounds. These are the former middle managers and office drones, the paper pushers and corporate executives who once pulled down six-figure incomes running divisions of huge multinationals—now just taking up space, as obsolete as cassette tapes. With echoes of old sociology courses banging around the back of his mind, Brian wonders if this tenuous, rickety assemblage of desperate souls can ever develop into anything like a community.

The sand in the works appears to be three members of the National Guard, who wandered into Woodbury from a nearby Guard Station a couple of weeks ago and started pushing people around. This little rogue clique—which Brian thinks of as the Bullies—is led by a gung-ho former marine with a flattop haircut and icy blue eyes who goes by the name of Gavin (or "the Major," as his underlings call him). It only takes a couple of days for Brian to peg Gavin as a socio-path with designs on power and plunder. Maybe the plague made Gavin flip his wig, but over the course of that first week in Woodbury, Brian observes Gavin and his weekend warriors snatching provisions out of the hands of helpless families and taking advantage of several women at gunpoint out behind the racetrack at night.

Brian keeps his distance, and keeps his head down, and as he makes these silent observations about Woodbury's pecking order, he keeps hearing the name Stevens.

From what Brian can glean from scattered conversations with townspeople, this Stevens gentleman was once an ear, nose, and throat man with his own practice in a suburb of Atlanta. After the turn, Stevens set out for safer pastures—apparently alone, some believe due to a divorce. The good doctor quickly stumbled upon the motley group of survivors in Woodbury. Seeing the ragged inhabitants gripped by sickness, malnourished, and many of them nursing injuries, Stevens decided to offer his services. He's been busy ever since, operating out of the former Meriwether County Medical Center three blocks from the racetrack.

On the afternoon of his seventh day in Woodbury, still wheezing, every breath a stab of pain in his side, Brian finally gets up the nerve to visit the squat, gray-brick building on the south end of the safe zone.

"You're lucky," Stevens says, snapping an X-ray into its clip at the top of a light panel. He points at a milky image of Brian's ribs. "No serious breaks . . . just three minor fractures to the second, fourth, and fifth pectorals."

"Lucky, huh?" Brian mutters, sitting shirtless on the padded gurney. The room is a depressing tile crypt in the basement of the medical center—once the pathology lab—now serving as Stevens's examination room. The air reeks of disinfectant and mold.

"Not a word I've used that often in recent days, I will admit," Stevens says, turning toward a stainless steel cabinet next to the light panel. He's a tall, trim, smartly groomed man in his late forties with designer steel-frame eyeglasses riding low on the bridge of his nose. He wears a lab coat over his wrinkled oxford shirt and has a sort of weary, professorial intelligence in his eyes.

"And the wheezing?" Brian asks.

The doctor fishes through a shelf of plastic vials. "Early stage pleurisy due to the damage to the ribs," he mumbles as he searches the medication. "I would encourage you to cough as much as possible . . . it's going to hurt, but it'll prevent secretions from pooling in the lungs."

"And my eye?" The stabbing pain in Brian's left eye, radiating up from his bruised jaw, has worsened over the last few days. Every time he looks in the mirror, his eye seems more bloodshot.

"Looks fine to me," the doctor says, pulling a pill bottle from the shelf. "Your mandible on that side has a nasty contusion, but that should heal up in time. I'm gonna give you some naproxen for the pain."

Stevens hands the vial over and then stands there with arms crossed against his chest.

Brian almost involuntarily reaches for his wallet. "I'm not sure if I have—"

"There's no payment for services rendered here," the doctor says with a raised brow, somewhat bemused by Brian's innate gesture. "There's no staff, there's no infrastructure, there's no follow-up, and for that matter, there isn't a decent cup of espresso or a half-assed daily newspaper to read."

"Oh . . . right." Brian puts the pills in his pocket. "What about the hip?"

"Bruised but intact," he says, flipping off the light panel and closing the cabinet. "I wouldn't worry. You can put your shirt back on now."

"Good . . . thanks."

"Not a big talker, are you?" The doctor washes his hands at a wall sink, dries them on a dirty towel.

"I guess not."

"Probably better that way," the doctor says, wadding the towel and tossing it into the sink. "You probably don't even want to tell me your name."

"Well . . ."

"It's okay. Forget it. You'll be known in the records as the Bohemian Fellow with the Cracked Ribs. You want to tell me how it happened?"

Brian shrugs as he buttons his shirt. "Took a fall."

"Fighting off the specimens?"

Brian looks at him. "Specimens?"

"Sorry . . . clinical-speak. Biters, zombies, pus bags, whatever they're calling them nowadays. That how you got injured?"

"Yeah . . . something like that."

"You want a professional opinion? A prognosis?"

"Sure."

"Get the hell outta here while you still can."

"Why's that?"

"Chaos theory."

"Excuse me?"

"Entropy . . . empires fall, stars wink out . . . the ice cubes in your drink melt."

"I'm sorry, I'm not following."

The doctor pushes his glasses up his nose. "There's a crematorium in the sublevel of this building . . . we destroyed two more men today, one of them the father of two children. They were attacked on the north side yesterday morning. They reanimated last night. More Biters are getting through . . . the barricade's a sieve. Chaos theory is the impossibility of a closed system remaining stable. This town is doomed. There's nobody at the controls . . . Gavin and his cronies are getting bolder . . . and you, my friend, are simply another piece of fodder."

For the longest time, Brian doesn't say anything, he just stares past the doctor.

At last, Brian pushes himself off the table and extends his hand. "I'll keep that in mind."

That night, woozy from the painkillers, Brian Blake hears a knock at his bedroom door. Before he even has a chance to get his bearings and turn on a light, the door clicks open and Nick sticks his head in. "Brian, you awake?"

"Always." Brian grunts as he climbs out of the blankets and sits up on the side of the bed. Only a few of the apartment's wall outlets are live with generated power. Brian's room is a dead circuit. He switches on a battery-operated lantern and sees Nick pushing into the room, fully dressed, his expression tight with alarm.

"You gotta see something," Nick says, going to the window, peering through the blinds. "I saw him last night, same deal, didn't think much of it."

Still groggy, Brian joins Nick at the window. "What are we looking at?"

Through the slat, out in the darkness of a vacant lot, Philip's silhouette can be seen emerging from the far trees. He looks like a stick figure in the darkness. Since Penny's death, he's been losing weight, going without sleep, hardly eating a thing. He looks sick, broken, like his faded denims are the only things holding his long, lanky limbs together. He carries a bucket, and he walks with a strange, wooden kind of purpose, like a sleepwalker or an automaton.

"What's with the bucket?" Brian asks under his breath, almost rhetorically.

"Exactly." Nick nervously scratches himself. "He had it last night, too."

"Just take it easy, Nick. Stay in here." Brian turns the lantern out. "Let's just see what happens."

A few moments later, the sound of the front door clicking open reverberates through the dark apartment. Philip's shuffling footsteps can be heard crossing the living room and making their way down the hall.

The click of the laundry room door is followed by the sound of Penny becoming agitated, the chain clanking, the garbled sounds of groaning—noises to which Brian and Nick have almost grown accustomed. Then something reaches their ears that they haven't heard before: the wet slosh of something hitting the tiles . . . followed by the strange, animalistic, gooey noises of a zombie feeding.

"What the fuck is he doing?" In the half-light, Nick's face is a pale gibbous moon of terror.

"Holy Christ," Brian whispers. "He can't be—"

Brian doesn't even get a chance to finish the thought, because Nick is on his way to the door with a full head of steam, heading for the hallway.

Brian chases after him. "Nick, don't—"

"This isn't happening." Nick barrels down the hallway, moving toward the laundry room. He knocks hard on the door. "Philip, what's going on?"

"Go away!"

The sound of Philip's muffled voice is clogged with emotion.

"Nick—" Brian tries to get in between Nick and the door but it's too late.

Nick turns the knob. The door is unlocked. Nick enters the laundry room.

"Oh God."

Nick's mortified reaction reaches Brian's ears a split second before Brian can get a good look at what's going on in the laundry room.

Brian pushes his way into the narrow enclosure and sees the dead girl eating a human hand.

Brian's initial reaction is not one of repulsion or disgust or outrage (which, as it happens, is exactly the combination of emotions currently twisting Nick's features as he gapes at the feeding in progress). Instead, Brian is overcome by a wave of sadness. He says nothing at first, simply looks on as his brother crouches down in front of the tiny upright corpse.

Ignoring the presence of the other men, Philip calmly pulls a severed human ear from the bucket, and waits patiently for the Penny-thing to finish consuming the hand. She gobbles the middle-aged male fingers with unbridled gusto, chewing the bloodless hairy knuckles as though they were delicacies, the stringers of pink, foamy saliva dangling from her lips.

She hardly pauses long enough to swallow before Philip places the human ear within range of her blackened teeth, offering the morsel to the child with the care and concern of a priest proffering a wafer to a communicant. The Penny-thing devours the cartilage and gristly rolls of human skin with mindless abandon.

"I'm outta here," Nick Parsons finally manages to blurt, pivoting and storming out of the room.

Brian enters and crouches down next to his brother. He doesn't raise his voice. He doesn't accuse Philip of anything. Brian is drowning in sorrow right now and all he can think of saying is, "What's going on, man?"

Philip hangs his head. "He was already dead . . . they were gonna burn him . . . found his body in a bag out behind the clinic . . . he died of something else . . . I just took a few pieces . . . nobody'll notice . . ."

The Penny-thing finishes the ear, and starts groaning for more.

Philip feeds her a dripping, severed foot, the jagged bone exposed at the ankle like a slimy tusk of ivory.

"You think this is . . . ?" Brian searches for words. "You think this is a good idea?"

Philip looks down at the floor as the sticky, wet noises of the feeding frenzy fill the laundry room. The girl-thing gnaws at the bone as Philip's voice drops an octave, beginning to crack with emotion. "Think of him as an organ donor . . ."

"Philip—"

"I can't let go of her, Brian . . . I can't . . . she's all I got."

Brian takes a deep breath and fights his own tears. "The thing of it is . . . she's not Penny anymore."

"I know that."

"Then why—"

"I see her and I try to remember . . . but I can't . . . I can't remember . . . I can't remember anything but this shit storm we're living in . . . and them road rats that shot her . . . and she's all I got . . ." The pain and grief choking his voice start to thicken, hardening into something darker. "They took her from me . . . my whole universe . . . new rules now . . . new rules . . ."

Brian can't breathe. He watches the Penny-thing gnawing on that pasty severed foot. He looks away. He can't take it anymore. His stomach is clenched with nausea, his mouth watering. He can feel the heat rising in his gorge, and he struggles to his feet. "I have to . . . I can't stay in here, Philip . . . I have to go."

Whirling around, Brian stumbles out of the laundry room and gets halfway down the hall when he drops to his knees and roars vomit.

His stomach is relatively empty. What comes out of him is mostly bile. But it comes on spasms of agony. He retches and retches, the acids spattering a six-foot length of carpet between the hallway and the living room. He upchucks his guts, which instantly makes a cold sweat break out all over his body and sends him into a paroxysm of coughing. The fit goes on for endless minutes, each cough throbbing painfully in his ribs. He coughs and coughs until he finally collapses into a heap on the floor.

Fifteen feet away, in the light of a battery-powered lantern, Nick Parsons packs his knapsack. He shoves in a change of clothes, a couple of cans of beans, blankets, a flashlight, some bottled water. He searches the cluttered coffee table for something.

Brian manages to sit up, wiping his mouth with the back of his hand. "You can't leave, man . . . not now."

"Hell I can't," Nick says, finding his Bible under a pile of candy wrappers. He puts the Bible in the backpack. The muffled feeding noises drift down the hallway, fueling Nick's anxiety.

"I'm begging you, Nick."

Nick zips the knapsack shut. He doesn't look at Brian as he says, "You don't need me . . ."

"That's not true." Brian swallows the bitter taste of bile. "I need you now more than ever . . . I need your help . . . to keep things together."

"*Together?*" Nick looks up. He slings the backpack over his shoulder, and then he walks over to where Brian is slumped on the floor. "Things haven't been *together* around here for a long time."

"Nick. Listen to me—"

"He's too far gone, Brian."

"Listen. I understand what you're saying. Give him one more chance. Maybe this is like a one-time thing. Maybe . . . I don't know . . . it's grief. One more chance, Nick. We got a much better shot at survival if we stay together."

For a long, agonizing moment, Nick considers all this. Then, on a weary, exasperated sigh, which seems to deflate his very spirit, he drops the knapsack.

The next day, Philip vanishes. Brian and Nick don't even bother looking for him. They stay inside for most of the day, hardly speaking to each other, feeling like zombies themselves, moving silently from bathroom to kitchen to living room, where they sit staring out the barred window at the blustery sky, trying to come up with an answer, a way out of this downward spiral.

Around five o'clock that afternoon, they hear a strange buzzing noise coming from outside—like a cross between a chain saw and a boat motor. Worried that it might have something to do with Philip, Brian goes to the back door, listens, then pushes his way outside and takes a few steps across the cracked cement of the back porch.

The noise is louder now. In the distance, on the north side of town, a thundercloud of dust rises into the steel-gray sky. The howl of engines sputters and waxes and wanes on the breeze, and with a surge of relief, Brian realizes that it's merely somebody maneuvering race cars around the dirt track arena. Every so often, the sound of cheers warbles and echoes on the wind.

For a moment, Brian panics. Don't these idiots realize all this noise is going to draw every Biter within a fifty-mile radius? At the same time, though, Brian is transfixed by that buzz-saw sound drifting on the breeze. Like a wandering radio signal, it touches something sore inside him, an ache for preplague times, a series of painful memories of lazy Sunday afternoons, a good night's sleep, walking into a goddamn grocery store and buying a fucking gallon of milk.

He goes back inside, puts his jacket on, and tells Nick he's going for a walk.

The entrance to the racetrack borders the main drag, a high cyclone fence stretched between two brick piles. As Brian approaches, he sees drifts of trash and old tires scattered across the meager box office, which is boarded by graffiti-stained planks.

The noise rises to ear-piercing levels—the winding scream of motors and caterwauling crowds—tainted by the odors of gasoline and burning rubber. The sky is choked with a haze of dust and smoke.

Brian finds a gap in the fence, and he heads for it, when he hears a voice.

"Hey!"

He pauses, turns, and sees three men in ratty camo-fatigues coming toward him. Two of the men are in their twenties, with greasy long hair and assault rifles pinned up high against their shoulders patrol-style. The oldest of the three—a crew-cut hard-ass, his olive drab jacket buttoned up with a bullet bandolier across his chest—walks out front, obviously in command.

"Admission is forty bucks or the equivalent in trade," says the commander.

"Admission?" Brian says, taken aback. He sees a name patch on the older man's breast pocket: maj. gavin. Up to this point, Brian has only stolen glimpses of the vicious National Guardsman, but now, at this proximity, Brian can see a glint of crazy in the man's frosty blue eyes. His breath smells of Jim Beam.

"Forty bucks for an adult, son—you an adult?" The other men chuckle. "Kids get in free, of course, but you look over eighteen to me. Just barely."

"You're taking *money* from people?" Brian is confused. "Times like these?"

"You're free to trade, friend. You got a chicken? Some *Penthouse* magazines you been jackin' off to?"

More snickers.

Brian's gut goes cold with anger. "I don't have forty bucks."

The smile disappears from the Major's face like a switch has been thrown. "Then have a nice day."

"Who gets the money?"

This gets the attention of the other two Guardsmen. They move in closer. Gavin comes nose to nose with Brian, and says in a soft, threatening grunt, "It's for the Commons."

"The what?"

"The Commons . . . the collective . . . community improvements and what-not."

Brian feels a surge of rage twisting inside him. "You sure it's not for the collective of *you three*?"

"I'm sorry," the Major says in a flat, icy tone, "I must have missed the memo that says you're the new city clerk. You boys get the memo stating that this peckerwood is the new Woodbury city clerk?"

"No, sir," says one of the greasy-haired minions. "Didn't get that memo."

Gavin pulls a .45 semiauto from his belt holster, thumbs off the safety, and presses the barrel against Brian's temple. "You need to study up on group dynamics, son. You flunk civics class in high school?"

Brian says nothing. He stares into the Major's eyes, and a red lens draws down over Brian's vision. Everything goes red. Brian's hands tingle, his head spins.

"Say ahh," the Major says.

"What?"

"I SAID OPEN YOUR GODDAMN MOUTH!" Gavin bellows, and the other two Guardsmen swing their assault rifles into ready positions, the muzzles trained on Brian's skull. Brian opens his mouth, and Gavin inserts the cold barrel of the .45 between Brian's teeth like a dentist checking for cavities.

Something breaks inside Brian. The steel muzzle tastes like old coins and bitter oil. The entire world turns the deepest shade of scarlet.

"Go back to where you came from," the Major says. "Before you get yourself hurt."

Brian manages a nod.

The muzzle slips out of his mouth.

Moving as if in a dream, Brian slowly backs away from the Guardsmen, turns, and walks stiffly back the way he came, now traveling through an invisible mist of crimson.

Around seven o'clock that evening, Brian is back at the apartment, alone, still bundled in his jacket, standing at the barred window in the rear of the living room, gazing out at the dwindling daylight, his racing thoughts like contrary waves crashing against a breakwater. He covers his ears. The muffled thumping noises of the miniature zombie in the next room fuel his stupor—a phonograph needle skipping on a record—driving Brian further and further inward.

At first, he barely registers the sound of Nick returning from who-knows-where, the shuffling footsteps, the click of the closet door. But when he hears the muted mutterings drifting down the hallway, he snaps out of his trance and goes to investigate.

Nick is digging in the closet for something. His tattered nylon coat is damp, his sneakers muddy, and he's murmuring under his breath, "'I will lift my eyes up to the hills . . . And from whence comes my help? . . . My help comes from the Lord . . . Who made heaven and earth.'"

Brian sees Nick pull the pistol-grip shotgun from the closet.

"Nick, what are you doing?"

Nick doesn't answer. He snaps open the gun's pump mechanism, and checks the breech. It's empty. He madly searches the floor of the closet, and he finds the single box of shells, which they managed to spirit all the way from the villa to Woodbury. He keeps muttering, "'The Lord shall preserve us from all evil . . . He shall preserve our souls . . .'"

Brian takes a step closer. "Nick, what the hell is going on?"

Still no answer. Nick tries to load the shells with shaky hands and he drops one. It rolls across the floor. Nick fumbles another one into the breech, and then pumps it home with a clang. "'Behold he who keeps Israel shall neither slumber nor sleep . . .'"

"Nick!" Brian grabs the man's shoulder and spins him around. "What the fuck is *wrong* with you?"

For a moment, it almost looks like Nick is about to swing the shotgun up and blow Brian's head off—the look of unadulterated fury contorts Nick's face. Then he gets himself under control, and swallows, and looks at Brian and says, "This can't go on."

Then, without another word, Nick turns and marches across the room and out the front door.

Brian grabs his .38, shoves it down the back of his belt, and hurries after Nick.

TWENTY-TWO

The purple light of dusk settles over the landscape. Icy winds toss the trees along the edges of the woods bordering Woodbury. The air swirls with the odors of wood smoke and carbon monoxide, as well as the unceasing whine of dirt racers emanating from the center of town. The back streets are fairly deserted, most of the inhabitants at the track . . . but still, it's a miracle nobody sees Brian and Nick stumbling across the vacant lot bordering the safe zone.

Nick prays furiously as he heads for the woods, carrying the pistol-grip shotgun on his shoulder like some kind of holy bludgeon. Brian keeps grabbing at Nick, trying to slow him down, trying to get him to stop his goddamn praying for one second and talk like a normal person, but Nick is driven by some feverish objective.

At last, as they approach the tree line, Brian yanks at Nick's coat so hard, he nearly knocks him over. "What the fuck are you doing?"

Nick spins and gives Brian a hard look. "I saw him dragging a girl out here." Nick's voice is brittle and on the verge of tears.

"Philip?"

"It can't go on, Brian—"

"What girl?"

"Someone from town, he took her by force. Whatever he's doing, it has to stop."

Brian studies Nick's quivering chin. Nick's eyes fill up with tears. Brian takes a deep breath. "Okay, calm down for a second, just calm down."

"He's got the darkness in him, Brian. Let go of me. It's gotta stop."

"You saw him take a girl but you didn't—"

"Let go of me, Brian."

For a moment, Brian just stands there, clutching at Nick's sleeve. Gooseflesh ripples down Brian's back, his midsection going cold. He refuses to accept this. There has to be a way to get things back on track, get things under control.

Finally, after an agonizing pause, Brian looks at Nick and says, "Show me."

Nick takes Brian down a narrow, untrimmed footpath that snakes through a copse of pecan trees. Overgrown with hemlock and iron-weed, the path is already lousy with shadows. Magic hour is closing in, the temperature nose-diving.

Brambles and thorns tear at their jackets as they hasten toward a break in the foliage.

To their right, through a latticework of leaves, they can see the southernmost edge of the construction site, where a new section of the wooden barricade is going up. Piles of timber lie nearby. The bull-dozer sits in the gloom. Nick indicates a clearing up ahead.

"There he is," Nick whispers as they approach a deadfall on the threshold of the clearing. He drops down behind the logs, looking almost like a hysterical little boy playing army. Brian joins him, crouching down and peering over the top of the rotting timber.

About twenty yards in the distance, in a natural basin of mossy earth, shrouded by a canopy of ancient live oaks and longleaf pine, Philip Blake is visible. The ground is carpeted in matted pine needles, fungus, and weeds, and a low faint glow of methane clings to the forest floor, a ghostly magenta haze that gives the clearing an almost mystical cast. Nick raises the shotgun. "'Dear Lord,'" he mumbles under his breath, "'please cleanse us of all this unrighteousness—'"

"Nick, stop it," Brian whispers.

"'I renounce all sins,'" Nick drones on, gaping at the horror in the clearing. "'They offend thee, O Lord—'"

"Shut up, just *shut up!*" Brian is trying to make sense of it all. In the shadows, it's hard to make out exactly what they're looking at. At first glance, it looks like Philip is out there, kneeling down in the weeds, hog-tying a pig. His denim jacket soaked in sweat, covered in cockleburs, he winds rope around the wrists and ankles of a writhing figure beneath him.

A frigid blast of horror swirls through Brian when he realizes it is *indeed* a young woman on the ground, her blouse torn, her mouth gagged with nylon rope. "Jesus Christ, what the hell is he—"

Nick keeps babbling under his breath: "'Forgive me, Lord, for what I'm about to do, and with the help of Thy grace I serve Thy will—'"

"Shut the fuck up!" Brian's brain is chugging, seizing up with panic, racing with frantic assumptions: Philip is either going to rape this poor woman or kill her and feed her to Penny. Something has to be done, and it has to be done quickly. Nick is right. He was right all along. There has to be a way to stop this before—

A blur of movement next to Brian.

Nick is vaulting over the deadfall, pushing his way through the briars and into the clearing.

"Nick, wait!" Brian gets halfway through the brambles when he sees the deadly tableau taking shape in the shadowy clearing like an arrangement of players on a surreal chessboard, coming together in dreamy slow motion.

Nick stumbles out into the open with his shotgun raised at Philip, and Philip, startled by the sudden sound of Brian's warning cry, springs to his feet. Weaponless, glancing nervously from the wriggling women to the duffel bag lying in the toadstools next to her, Philip raises his hands. "Put that goddamn thing down, Nicky."

Nick raises the bead of the muzzle until it's trained directly on Philip. "Devil's got his hooks in you, Philip. You've sinned against God . . . desecrated His name. It's in the hands of the Lord now."

Brian is staggering into the clearing, fumbling for his .38, hyperventilating with adrenaline. "Nick, don't!—DON'T DO IT!" Brian's mind races as he comes to a halt ten feet behind Nick.

By this point, the girl on the ground has managed to roll over—still bound and gagged—and she's crying into the moist earth, as if wishing it would open up and let her climb in and die. Meanwhile, Nick and Philip are standing six feet away from each other, their gazes locked.

"What are you, the avenging angel?" Philip asks his longtime friend.

"Maybe I am."

"This doesn't concern you, Nicky."

Nick is trembling with emotion, his eyes blinking away tears. "There's a better place for you and your daughter, Philly."

Philip stands as still as a stone monument, his narrow, weathered face looking positively grotesque in the gloomy light. "And I suppose you're the one who's gonna send me and Penny to Glory?"

"Somebody's gotta stop this, Philly. Might as well be me." Nick raises the sight to his eye and mutters, " 'Lord, please forgive—' "

"Nick, wait!—Please, please! *Listen to me!*" Brian circles around with the .38 pointed up in the air like he's a referee. He comes within inches of Nick, who still has his sight fixed on Philip. Brian babbles: "All the years of bumming around Waynesboro, all the laughs you shared, all the miles we put behind us—doesn't that count for something? Philip saved our lives! Things have gotten out of hand, yeah. But things can be put back together. Put the gun down, Nick. I'm begging you."

Nick shakes. He keeps the sight fixed. Sweat beads on his forehead.

Philip takes a step closer. "Don't worry about it, Brian. Nicky's always been a talker. He ain't got the stones to shoot somebody who's still alive."

Nick trembles furiously.

Brian watches, frozen with indecision.

Philip calmly reaches down to the girl, grabs her by the scruff of her collar, and yanks her up like a stray piece of luggage. He turns and starts dragging the squirming girl toward the far side of the clearing.

Nick's voice drops into a lower register. "Have mercy on us all."

The shotgun ratchets suddenly.

And the muzzle roars.

A 12-gauge shotgun is a blunt instrument. The lethal .33-caliber pellets can spread as wide as a foot or more in a short distance, tearing through its target with enough force to penetrate a cinder block.

The buckshot that hits Philip in the back punches through the meat of his shoulder blades and the cords of his neck, sending half his brain stem out through the front of his throat. The grains also take the side of the girl's scalp off, killing her instantly. The two bodies are launched in a cloud of pink mist.

The pair tumble forward in a tangled clench before sprawling side by side on the forest floor, their arms and legs akimbo. The girl is already stone-still dead but Philip twitches in his death throes for several agonizing seconds. His face is upturned, frozen in a mask of utter surprise. He tries to breathe but the damage to his brain is shutting everything down.

The shock of what has just happened drives Nick Parsons to his knees, his finger still frozen on the trigger pad, the shotgun sizzling hot.

His vision tunnels as he gapes at the damage inflicted on the two human bodies in the path of the blast. He drops the shotgun in the weeds and moves his mouth but makes no sound. What has he done? He feels himself contracting inward like a seed pod, cold and desolate, the clanging noise of Armageddon ringing in his ears, the scalding tears of shame coming now in rivulets down his face: What has he done? What has he done? What has he done?

Brian Blake turns to ice. His pupils dilate. The sight of his brother lying in a bloody heap on the ground next to the dead girl stamps itself forever on his brain. All other thoughts drain out of his mind.

Only the noise of Nick's keening wails penetrate Brian's stupor.

Howling with sobs now, Nick is still on his knees next to Brian.

All reason and sanity have drained out of Nick Parsons's face, and he caterwauls at the sight of the carnage. Bursts of gibberish come out of him in stringers of snot—part prayer, part insane pleading—his breath showing in the chill twilight. He looks up at the heavens.

Brian raises the .38 without thinking—a jolt of psychotic rage driving him—and he squeezes off a single shot, point-blank, into the side of Nick Parsons's skull.

The battering ram drives Nick over in a jet of red fluid, the slug ripping through his brain, coming out the other side and chewing through a tree. Nick folds, eyes rolling back, brain already dead.

He lands with the profound surrender of a child going to sleep.

The passage of time loses all meaning. Brian doesn't see the dark silhouettes of figures approaching through the distant trees, drawn to the noise. Nor does he have any awareness of moving across the clearing to the mangled pair of bodies. But somehow, without even being conscious of it, Brian Blake ends up on the ground next to Philip, cradling his younger brother's bloody form in his lap.

He gazes down at Philip's grizzled face, now as pale as alabaster, stippled with blood.

A flicker of life still glints in Philip's eyes, as the two brothers meet each other's gaze. For a brief instant, Brian flinches at the glacier of sorrow cutting through him, the connection between the two siblings as thick as blood, as deep as the earth, now fracturing Brian's soul with the power of shifting tectonic plates. The weight of their common history—the endless tedium of grammar school, the blessed summer vacations, the passing of late-night whispers from one bunk bed to the other, their first beers on that ill-fated Appalachian camping trip, their secrets, their fights, their small-town dreams foiled by life's cruel equations—all of it slices through his soul.

Brian weeps.

His cries—as shrill and keen as that of an animal in a trap—rise up into the darkening sky, blending with the distant whining of race cars. He sobs so hard he doesn't even notice Philip's passing.

When Brian looks back down at his brother, Philip's face has hardened into a marble-white sculpture.

The foliage trembles twenty feet away. At least a dozen Biters of all shapes and sizes are forcing their way through the thicket.

The first one, an adult male in tattered work clothes, pops through the branches with arms reaching at the nothingness, shoe-button eyes scanning the clearing. The thing fixes its gaze on the closest meal: Philip's cooling corpse.

Brian Blake rises to his feet and turns away. He can't watch. He knows this is the best option. The *only* option. Let the zombies clean up the mess.

He shoves the .38 back behind his belt and heads for the construction site.

Brian finds a perch on top of a truck cab to wait out the feeding frenzy.

His brain is a television tuned to many stations all at once. He draws his pistol and clutches it like a security blanket.

The cacophony of voices, the fragments of half-formed images, all crackle and flicker inside Brian's skull. The twilight has passed into full-bore darkness, the closest vapor light hundreds of yards off. But Brian sees the world around him in photo-negative brilliance now, his fear as keen as a knife edge. He is alone now . . . as alone as he has ever been . . . and it eats at him deeper than any zombie.

The wet, gurgling, sucking noises coming from the clearing are barely audible above the constant buzzing of dirt track racers. Somewhere in the back of Brian's hectic thoughts, he knows that the din of the racetrack is drowning the commotion in the clearing—probably part of Philip's plan, his abduction of the girl going unheard, unseen.

Through the lacing of brambles and foliage, Brian can see the silhouettes of monsters tearing into the human remains left in the clearing. Clusters of zombies hunch over their quarry, apelike, gorging on hunks of flesh, detached bones dripping with gore, flaps of skin, torn scalps, unidentified appendages, and sopping organs still warm and steaming in the chill air. More of them crowd in, clumsily shoving each other aside, grunting for a morsel.

Brian closes his eyes.

For a moment, he wonders if he should pray. He wonders if he should offer a silent eulogy for his brother, for Nick and the woman, for Penny, for Bobby Marsh, for David Chalmers, for the dead, for the living, and for this whole fucked-up, broken, godforsaken world. But he doesn't. He simply sits there as the zombies feed.

Some time later—God only knows when—the Biters drift away from the flensed, excoriated remains now lying strewn across the clearing.

Brian slips off the roof of the truck cab and makes his way back through the darkness to the apartment.

That night, Brian sits in the empty apartment, in the living room, in front of the empty, scummy fish tank. It's the end of the programming day in Brian's brain. The national anthem has been sung, the broadcast has signed off, and now only a blizzard of white noise blankets his thoughts.

Still clad in his filthy jacket, he sits staring through the fish tank's rectangular glass side—which is filmed in green mold, and mottled with specks of chum—as though watching some monotonous still life being broadcast from hell. He sits this way, staring trancelike into the vacuous heart of that fish tank, for endless minutes. The minutes turn into hours. His mind-screen is a blank cathode-ray tube boiling with electronic snow. The coming of daylight barely registers. He doesn't hear the commotion outside the apartment, the troubled voices, the sounds of vehicles.

The day drags on—time now meaningless—until the next evening draws its curtain of darkness down over the apartment. Brian sits in the dark, oblivious to the passage of time, continuing to stare with catatonic interest at the invisible broadcast originating from the empty shell of the fish tank. The next morning comes and goes.

At some point that next day, Brian blinks. The flicker of a message sparks and sputters across the blank screen of his mind. At first, it's faint and garbled, like a poorly transmitted signal, but with each passing second, it grows stronger, clearer, louder: GOOD-BYE.

Like a depth charge in the center of his soul, the word implodes in a convulsion of white-hot energy, jerking him forward in the shopworn armchair, sitting him bolt upright, forcing open his eyes.

—*GOOD-BYE*—

He's dehydrated and stiff, his stomach empty, his pants soaked through with his own urine. For nearly thirty-six hours, he sat in that chair, comatose, as still as a divining rod, and moving isn't easy at first, but he feels cleansed, scourged, as clearheaded as he's ever been. He limps into the kitchen and finds little in the cupboard other than a couple of cans of peaches. He tears one open and wolfs the whole thing down, the juice running across his chin. Peaches have never tasted so good. In fact, it occurs to him that perhaps he has never tasted peaches before. He goes into the bedroom and changes out of his disgusting clothes . . . puts on his only other pair of jeans and his only other shirt (an AC/DC silk-screened tee). He finds his spare Dr. Martens boots and slips them on.

Mounted on the back of the door is a cracked, floor-length mirror.

A wiry, disheveled, compact ferret of a man stares back at him. The crack in the looking glass bisects his narrow visage and his thatch of long, unruly black hair. His face is fringed with straggly whiskers, his eyes sunken and rimmed in dark circles. He hardly recognizes himself.

"Whatever," he says to the mirror, and walks out of the room.

He finds his .38 in the living room, along with one last speed-loader—the last six rounds in his possession—and he shoves the gun down the back of his belt, the speed-loader into his pocket.

Then he visits Penny.

"Hey there, kiddo," he says with great tenderness as he enters the laundry room. The narrow chamber of linoleum reeks of the dead. Brian barely notices the smell. He goes over to the little creature, who growls and sputters at his presence, straining against her chains. She's the color of cement, her eyes like smooth stones.

Brian crouches down in front of her, looks in her bucket. It's empty.

He looks up at her. "You know I love you, right?"

The Penny-thing snarls.

Brian strokes the side of her delicate little ankle. "I'm going to go get some supplies, sweetheart. I'll be back before you know it, don't worry."

The little dead thing cocks its head and lets out a groan that sounds like air running through rusty pipes. Brian pats her on the leg—out of the range of her rotting incisors—and then rises to his feet.

"See ya soon, sweetie."

The moment that Brian slips unnoticed from the side door of the apartment, and starts north, striding through the raw winds of the afternoon, his head down, his hands in the pockets of his jacket, he can tell something is going on. The racetrack is silent. A couple of townspeople run past him, their eyes aglow with alarm. The air reeks of the dead. Off to the left, behind the barricade of buses and semis, scores of walking corpses wander along the barrier, sniffing for a way in. Up ahead, black smoke pours out of the clinic's incinerator. Brian quickens his pace.

As he closes in on the town square, he can see, way in the distance, at the north end of the safe zone, where the fence is under construction, men standing on wooden parapets with rifles and binoculars. They don't look happy. Brian hurries along. All his pain—the stiffness in his joints, the throb in his ribs, all of it—vanishes amid the high-voltage current of his adrenaline.

Woodbury keeps its food rations in a brick warehouse across from the old courthouse. Brian pauses in front of the warehouse when he sees the old derelict juicers loitering across the street in front of the flagstone government building with its chipped Romanesque columns. Other folks stand on the stone steps, nervously smoking cigarettes, while others crowd the entranceway. Brian crosses the intersection and approaches the gathering.

"What's going on?" he asks the fat old man in the Salvation Army coat.

"Trouble in River City, son," the old codger says, jerking a greasy thumb at the courthouse. "Half the town's in there havin' a pow-wow."

"What happened?"

"Found three more residents out in the woods yesterday, picked clean as chicken bones . . . place is crawlin' with roamers now, drawn by the racetrack most likely. Damn fools makin' all that noise."

For a moment, Brian considers his options. He could very easily avoid this mess, pack up, and move on. He could boost one of the four-wheelers and take Penny in the back and be gone in a flash.

He doesn't owe these people anything. The safest bet is to not get involved, just get the fuck out of Dodge. That's the smartest way to play it. But something deep inside Brian makes him reconsider. What would Philip do?

Brian stares at the crowd of townspeople milling about the entrance to the courthouse.

TWENTY-THREE

"Does anybody even know what their names were?" A woman in her late sixties with a halo of fright-wig gray hair stands up in the back of the community room on the first floor of the courthouse building, the veins in her neck wattle pulsing with tension.

The thirty or so beleaguered residents of Woodbury gathered around her—town elders, heads of small families, former merchants, and passers-through who landed here almost by mistake—fidget on folding chairs in tattered coats and muddy boots, facing the front of the narrow conference room. The space has an end-of-world feel to it, with crumbling plaster, overturned coffee urns, exposed wiring, and litter strewn across the parquet floor.

"What the fuck difference does it make?" barks Major Gene Gavin from the front of the room, his minions behind him with their M4 assault rifles on their hips like faux gangbangers. It feels right and proper to the Major to be standing at the head of this little town hall meeting right now, near the flagpoles displaying the American and Georgia State flags. Like MacArthur taking over Japan, or Stonewall Jackson at Bull Run, the Major relishes the opportunity to finally make his stand as the leader pro tem of this miserable town full of chickenshits and rejects. Ramrod tough in his green fatigues and jarhead brush cut, the Major has been waiting for this moment, biding his time for weeks.

No stranger to whipping pussies into shape, Gavin knows he

needs respect in order to lead, and in order to be respected, he needs to be feared. Which is exactly how he used to deal with the weekend warriors under his command at Camp Ellenwood. Gavin was a survival instructor with the 221st Military Intelligence Battalion, and he used to torment those lily-livered weaklings on overnight bivouacs up to Scull Shoals by shitting in their duffels and giving them the rubber hose treatment for the smallest infractions. But that might as well have been a million years ago. *This* situation is Code *Fucked*, and Gavin is going to take every advantage to stay on top of things.

"It was just a couple of them new guys," Gavin adds as an afterthought. "And some slut from Atlanta."

An elderly gentlemen in the front stands up, his bony knees trembling: "All due respect . . . that was Jim Bridges's daughter, and she weren't no slut. Now, I think I speak for everybody when I say we need protection, maybe a curfew . . . keep people in after dark. Maybe we could take a vote."

"Sit down, old man . . . before you hurt yourself." Gavin gives the old geezer his best menacing look. "We got bigger problems to deal with now—there's a goddamn convention of them Biters closing in on us."

The old man takes his seat, grumbling to himself. "All that noise from the damn dirt races . . . that's the reason them Biters is surroundin' us."

Gavin unsnaps the holster on his hip, exposing the grip of his .45, and takes a threatening step toward the old man. "I'm sorry, I don't recall opening the floor to comments from the nursing home." Gavin jabs a finger at the old man. "My advice is for you to shut the fuck up before you get yourself in trouble."

A younger man springs to his feet two chairs away from the old man. "Take it easy, Gavin," the younger man says. Tall, olive-skinned, his hair tucked under a bandana, he wears a sleeveless shirt that reveals heavily muscled arms. His dark eyes gleam with street-level smarts. "This ain't some John Wayne movie, take it down a notch."

Gavin turns to the man in the bandana, brandishing the .45 with menace. "Shut your mouth, Martinez, and put your spic ass back in your chair."

Behind Gavin, the two Guardsmen tense up, swinging the muzzles of their M4s up and into ready positions, their eyes scanning the room.

The man named Martinez just shakes his head, and sits back down.

Gavin lets out a frustrated sigh.

"You people don't seem to grasp the seriousness of this situation," he says, holstering the .45 as he moves back to the front of the room, speaking with the cadence of a drill instructor. "We're sittin' ducks here, we don't do somethin' about them barricades. Got a bunch of freeloaders takin' up space. Expecting everybody else to carry the weight. No discipline! I got news for ya, your little vacation is over. Gonna be some new rules, and you're all gonna pitch in, and you're gonna do what you're told, and you're gonna keep your fucking mouths shut! Am I making myself clear?"

Gavin pauses, daring somebody to object.

The townspeople sit in silence, looking like children who've been sent to the principal's office. In one corner, Stevens, the physician, sits next to a young woman in her twenties. Dressed in a stained smock, the girl has a stethoscope draped around her neck. Stevens looks like a man smelling something that's been rotting for a long time. He raises his hand.

The Major rolls his eyes and lets out an exasperated sigh. "What is it now, Stevens?"

"Correct me if I'm wrong," the doctor says, "but we're stretched thin already. We're doing our best."

"What's your point?"

The doctor gives him a shrug. "What is it you want from us?"

"I WANT YOUR GODDAMN OBEDIENCE!"

The booming response barely registers on Stevens's thin, cunning features. Gavin takes long, even breaths, getting himself back under control. Stevens pushes his eyeglasses up the bridge of his nose and looks away, shaking his head. Gavin gives his men a look.

The Guardsmen nod in unison at the Major, trigger fingers on trigger pads.

This isn't going to be as easy as Gavin thought.

Brian Blake stands in the back of the room, in the shadow of a dusty, bankrupt vending machine, his hands in his pockets, listening, taking it all in. His heart thumps. And he hates himself for it. He feels like a laboratory rat in a maze. The crippling fear—an old nemesis—is back with a vengeance. He can feel the speed-loader like a tumor in his pocket, the bulge cold against his thigh. His throat is tight and dry, his tongue two sizes too big for his mouth. What the fuck is wrong with him?

At the front of the room, Gavin keeps pacing in front of the gallery of town founders displayed in shopworn frames across the room's front wall. "Now, I don't care what you call this cluster fuck we find ourselves in, I call it war . . . and right now, this little shit-heel town is officially under marshal-fucking-law."

Tense murmurings spread through the group. The old man is the only one brazen enough to speak up. "What does that mean, exactly?"

Gavin walks over to the old man. "That means y'all are going to follow orders, be good little boys and girls." He pats the top of the codger's bald pate like he's petting a rabbit. "Y'all behave yourselves, do what you're told, and we just might survive this shit storm."

The old man swallows hard. Most of his fellow townspeople look down at the floor. It's clear to Brian, observing from the back of the room, that the inhabitants of Woodbury are trapped in more ways than one. The hatred in the room is thick enough to paint the walls. But the fear is thicker. It exudes from the very pores of everybody present, including Brian, who is hard at work fighting it. He shoves his terror back down his throat.

Somebody murmurs something near the front of the room, over by the window. Brian is too far away to make out the words, and he gazes over the tops of heads to see who it is.

"You got something you want to say, Detroit?"

Near the window, a middle-aged black man in greasy dungarees and gray beard is sulking in his seat, looking gloomily out the window. His long, tawny fingers are caked with axle grease. The town mechanic, a transplant from up North, he mumbles something to himself, not looking at the Major.

"Speak up, homeboy." The Major approaches the black man. Towering over him, Gavin says, "What's *your* beef? You don't like the program?"

Almost inaudibly, the black man says, "I'm outta here."

He gets up to make his exit, when suddenly the Major reaches for his gun.

With almost involuntary instinct, the black man reaches a big, callused hand down to the revolver shoved into his belt. But before he can draw the weapon or even give it a second thought, Gavin draws on him. "Please go for it, Detroit," Gavin snarls, pointing the .45 at the man. "So I can blow the back of your nappy fuckin' head off."

The other soldiers move in behind the Major, raising their assault rifles, fixing their eyes on the black man.

Hand still on the hilt of his pistol, eyes locked with Gavin, the black man named Detroit murmurs, "It's bad enough we gotta fight off them dead things . . . now we gotta deal with you pushin' us around?"

"Sit. The fuck. Down. Now." Gavin puts the barrel on Detroit's forehead. "Or I will take you down. And that is a promise."

With an exasperated sigh, Detroit flops back down.

"That goes for the rest of you!" The Major turns to the others. "You think I'm doin' this for my health? You think I'm runnin' for dog catcher? This ain't no democracy. This is life and fucking death!" He begins pacing across the front of the room. "You want to keep from being dog food, you'll do what you're told. Let the professionals mind the store, and keep your fuckin' pie holes shut!"

Silence hangs in the room like a poisonous gas. In back, Brian feels the skin on the back of his neck prickle. His heart is going to break through his sternum, it's hammering so hard in his chest. He can't breathe. He wants to rip this tin soldier's head off but his body is going into some kind of fight-or-flight paralysis. His brain crackles with flickering fragments of memory, sights and sounds from a lifetime driven by fear, avoiding bullies on the playground at Burke County Elementary, skirting the parking lot of the Stop-and-Go to avoid a group of leather thugs, running away from a gang of toughs at a Kid Rock concert, wondering where Philip is . . . where the hell is Philip when you need him . . .

A noise from the front of the room shakes Brian out of his rumination.

The man named Detroit is getting up. He's had enough. His chair squeaks as he rises to his full height—well over six feet—and turns to walk away.

"Where the hell are *you* going?" Gavin watches the black man move down the aisle toward the front exit. "HEY! I ASKED YOU A QUESTION, DETROIT! WHERE THE FUCK DO YOU THINK YOU'RE GOING!"

Detroit doesn't even look back, he just waves dismissively, mumbling, "I'm outta here . . . good luck, y'all . . . you're gonna need it with these motherfuckers."

"YOU SIT YOUR BLACK ASS BACK DOWN RIGHT NOW OR I WILL BLOW YOU AWAY!"

Detroit keeps walking.

Gavin pulls his sidearm.

There is an audible intake of air among the townspeople as Gavin draws a bead on the back of Detroit's head.

The blast sucks the air out of the room—so loud, it rattles the walls, accompanied by a scream from one of the older women—as a single round goes into the back of the black man's skull. Detroit is thrown forward into the vending machine next to Brian. Brian jerks. The black man bounces off the steel panel and then folds to the floor, his blood spray-painting the Coke display, the wall above the machine, and even part of the ceiling.

Many things happen in the aftermath of that blast, even before the ringing echoes of screams have had a chance to fade away. Almost immediately, three separate townspeople—two middle-aged men, and a woman in her thirties—dart toward the exit, and Brian watches as if in a dream, his ears ringing, his eyes flash-blind. He can barely hear the strangely calm voice of Major Gavin—void of regret, void of any feeling whatsoever—ordering his two Guardsmen—Barker and Manning—to go get the fleeing townspeople, and while they're at it, round up anyone else who's "still out there hiding like goddamn cockroaches," because Gavin wants every soul who's still got a pulse to hear what he has to say. The two Guardsmen hurry out of the room, leaving behind the stunned, petrified group of twenty-five residents, the Major . . . and Brian.

The room seems to turn on its axis for Brian as Gavin holsters his gun, looking down at the body of the black man sprawled on the floor as though it was a hunting trophy. Gavin turns and saunters back toward the front. He's got everybody's attention now like never before, and he seems to be enjoying every minute of it. Brian can barely hear the Major droning on now about making an example out of any cocksucker who thinks they can endanger the lives of Woodbury's residents by being a lone wolf, by bucking the system, by being a smart-ass know-it-all who thinks they can go it alone and keep their shit to themselves. These times, according to Gavin, are special times. Foretold in the Bible. Prophesied. Matter of fact, these times are maybe, just maybe, the end-time. And from now on, every last son of a bitch in this town needs to get used to the fact that this may very well be the last battle between man and Satan, and as far as the fine folks of Woodbury, Georgia, are concerned, Gavin has been hereby appointed, by default, the goddamn Messiah.

This maniacal lecture lasts for perhaps a minute—maybe two minutes at the most—but in that brief span of time, Brian Blake goes through a metamorphosis.

Frozen against the side of the vending machine, the fallen man's blood seeping under the soles of his shoes, Brian realizes he will have no chance in this world if he lets his natural inclinations drag him down. Brian's instincts—to shrink away from violence, to skirt dangers, to avoid confrontation—fill him with shame, and he finds himself casting his racing thoughts back to the very first encounter he had with the walking dead, back in Deering, at his parents' place, a million light-years away. They came out of the toolshed in back, and Brian was trying to talk to them, reason with them, warning them to stay away, throwing stones at them, running back into the house, boarding up windows, pissing his pants, behaving like the weakling he always was and always will be. And in the space of that single terrible instant—as Gavin pontificates to the townspeople—Brian is gripped with a flickering flash-frame series of visions of his cowardice and indecision along the road to western Georgia, as if he'd learned nothing along the way: huddling in the closet at Wiltshire Estates, bagging his first zombie almost by accident in the Chalmerses' building, bellyaching to his brother about this and that, always weak and scared and useless. Brian realizes suddenly—with the convulsive pain of an embolism exploding in his heart—that there is no way he can survive on his own. No way in hell. And now, as Major Gavin starts barking orders at the traumatized residents from the front of the council room, assigning arduous duties and rules and procedures, Brian feels his consciousness disconnecting, detaching from his body like a butterfly leaving its cocoon. It starts with Brian wishing that Philip were there to protect him, as he'd done since the beginning of the ordeal. How would Philip handle Gavin? What would Philip do? Soon, this simple longing transforms into agonizing pain and loss over Philip's death—the torture like an open wound—the sharp edge of grief slicing through Brian and tearing him in two. Bracing himself against that blood-spattered vending machine, Brian feels his center of gravity rising, his spirit breaking away from his body, like a primordial chunk of the earth tearing away to form the moon. Dizziness threatens to drive him to the floor but he fights it, and before he can even register what is going on, Brian has risen out of his body. His consciousness now floats above his body, a ghostly onlooker, gazing down at himself in that airless, reeking, crowded community room in the old Woodbury courthouse.

Brian sees himself grow still.

Brian sees the target at the front of the room, twenty-five feet away.

Brian sees himself take a single step away from the vending machine, reaching behind his belt, grasping hold of the beavertail grip of the .38-caliber pistol, while Gavin continues hollering orders up front, oblivious, pacing across stoic portraits of Woodbury's forefathers.

Brian sees himself taking three more tactical steps, moving down the center aisle, while simultaneously drawing the .38 from his belt in one smooth instinctual movement. He holds the gun at his side as he completes the fourth additional stride—coming within fifteen feet of Gavin, finally getting Gavin's attention, causing the Major to pause and look up—and that's when Brian raises the muzzle and empties the entire cylinder of lethal, hollow-point Glaser Safety Slugs into the general vicinity of Gavin's face.

This time, the townspeople jerk in their seats at the noise but, oddly, nobody screams.

No one is more shocked by Brian's actions than Brian, and he stands frozen for one excruciating moment in the center aisle, the .38 still raised and empty, his arm locked in the shooting position, the spectacle of Major Gavin's remains slumped on the floor against the front wall. Gavin's upper body is riddled, his face and neck pumping deep red arterial blood in oily bubbles.

The spell is broken by the sound of squeaking chairs, the shuffle of people rising. Brian lowers the gun to his side. He looks around. Some of the townspeople are moving to the front of the room. Others are staring at Brian. One of the men kneels by Gavin's body, but he doesn't bother feeling for a pulse or looking too closely. The one named Martinez comes over to Brian.

"Don't take this personally, brother," Martinez says, his voice a low, grave murmur. "But you better get your ass outta here."

"No." Brian feels as though his center of gravity has returned, his very soul rebooting like a computer powering back up.

Martinez stares. "Gonna be hell to pay when those goons get back."

"It'll be okay," Brian says, reaching into his pocket for the speed-loader. He dumps the empty shells, then fumbles the fresh round into the pistol. He's unskilled at the maneuver but his hands are rock steady. He has stopped shaking. "We outnumber them ten to one."

Some of the townspeople are gathered by the vending machine, clustered around the body of the one named Detroit. Dr. Stevens is feeling for a pulse as the sound of someone softly crying reaches Brian's ears. He turns toward the group gathered there.

"Who's armed in here?" he asks.

A few hands go up.

"Stay close," Brian says, then weaves his way through the stunned, milling townspeople to the exit. He stands inside the door, gazing out through the panes of safety glass at the blustery, overcast autumn day.

Even through the door's window glass, the unmistakable drone of zombies can be heard way off in the distance, under the wind. They now sound different somehow to Brian's ears. Segregated behind makeshift barricades, sectioned off from the stubborn little enclave of survivors by thin membranes of wood and metal, the low, ubiquitous symphony of moaning noises—as ugly and dissonant as wind chimes fashioned from human bones—no longer whisper of doom. They now speak of opportunity. They sound to Brian like an invitation to a new way of life, a new paradigm that is just now forming within Brian like the birth of a new religion.

A voice next to Brian snaps him out of his trance. He turns and sees Martinez, giving him an inquisitive look. "I'm sorry," Brian says. "What did you say?"

"Your name . . . I didn't catch it before."

"My name?"

Martinez nods. "I'm Martinez . . . and you are . . . ?"

Brian pauses for the slimmest of moments before replying, "Philip . . . Philip Blake."

Martinez reaches out to shake Brian's hand. "Pleasure to meet you, Philip."

With a firm grip, the two men clasp hands, and in that single gesture a new order begins to take shape.

The Road to Woodbury

Dedicated to Jilly (*L'amore della mia vita*)
—Jay Bonansinga

For all the people who have made me look far
more talented than I actually am over the years:
Charlie Adlard, Cory Walker, Ryan Ottley, Jason Howard,
and of course . . . mister Jay Bonansinga
—Robert Kirkman

ACKNOWLEDGMENTS

Special thanks to Robert Kirkman, David Alpert, Brendan Deneen, Nicole Sohl, Circle of Confusion, Andy Cohen, Kemper Donovan, and Tom Leavens.

—Jay Bonansinga

For my father, Carl Kirkman, who taught me the value of working for yourself and showed me what someone can accomplish if they work hard and focus on what they want to achieve. And for my father-in-law, John Hicks, who gave me the confidence to take the plunge and quit my day job and strike out on my own. I owe a lot to both of you.

—Robert Kirkman

PART 1

Red Day Rising

Life hurts a lot more than death.

—Jim Morrison

ONE

No one in the clearing hears the biters coming through the high trees.

The metallic ringing noises of tent stakes going into the cold, stubborn Georgia clay drown the distant footsteps—the intruders still a good five hundred yards off in the shadows of neighboring pines. No one hears the twigs snapping under the north wind, or the telltale guttural moaning noises, as faint as loons behind the treetops. No one detects the trace odors of putrid meat and black mold marinating in feces. The tang of autumn wood smoke and rotting fruit on the midafternoon breeze masks the smell of the walking dead.

In fact, for quite a while, not a single one of the settlers in the burgeoning encampment registers any *imminent* danger whatsoever—most of the survivors now busily heaving up support beams hewn from found objects such as railroad ties, telephone poles, and rusty lengths of rebar.

"Pathetic . . . look at me," the slender young woman in the ponytail comments with an exasperated groan, crouching awkwardly by a square of paint-spattered tent canvas folded on the ground over by the northwest corner of the lot. She shivers in her bulky Georgia Tech sweatshirt, antique jewelry, and ripped jeans. Ruddy and freckled, with long, deep-brown hair that dangles in tendrils wound with delicate little feathers, Lilly Caul is a bundle of nervous tics, from the constant yanking of stray wisps of hair back behind her ears to the compulsive gnawing of fingernails. Now, with her small hand she clutches the hammer tighter and repeatedly whacks at the metal stake, grazing the head as if the thing is greased.

"It's okay, Lilly, just relax," the big man says, looking on from behind her.

"A two-year-old could do this."

"Stop beating yourself up."

"It's not *me* I want to beat up." She pounds some more, two-handing the hammer. The stake goes nowhere. "It's this stupid stake."

"You're choked up too high on the hammer."

"I'm what?"

"Move your hand more toward the end of the handle, let the tool do the work."

More pounding.

The stake jumps off hard ground, goes flying, and lands ten feet away.

"Damn it! *Damn it!*" Lilly hits the ground with the hammer, looks down and exhales.

"You're doing fine, babygirl, lemme show you."

The big man moves in next to her, kneels, and starts to gently take the hammer from her. Lilly recoils, refusing to hand over the implement. "Give me a second, okay? I can handle this, I *can*," she insists, her narrow shoulders tensing under the sweatshirt.

She grabs another stake and starts again, tapping the metal crown tentatively. The ground resists, as tough as cement. It's been a cold October so far, and the fallow fields south of Atlanta have hardened. Not that this is a bad thing. The tough clay is also porous and dry—for the moment at least—hence the decision to pitch camp here. Winter's coming, and this contingent has been regrouping here for over a week, settling in, recharging, rethinking their futures—if indeed they *have* any futures.

"You kinda just let the head fall on it," the burly African-American demonstrates next to her, making swinging motions with his enormous arm. His huge hands look as though they could cover her entire head. "Use gravity and the weight of the hammer."

It takes a great deal of conscious effort for Lilly not to stare at the black man's arm as it pistons up and down. Even crouching in his sleeveless denim shirt and ratty down vest, Josh Lee Hamilton cuts an imposing figure. Built like an NFL tackle, with monolithic shoulders, enormous tree-trunk thighs, and thick neck, he still manages to carry himself quite gently. His sad, long-lashed eyes and his deferential brow, which perpetually creases the front of his balding pate, give off an air of unexpected tenderness. "No big deal . . . see?" He shows her again and his tattooed bicep—as big as a pig's belly—jumps as he wields the imaginary hammer. "See what I'm sayin'?"

Lilly discreetly looks away from Josh's rippling arm. She feels a faint frisson of guilt every time she notices his muscles, his tapered back, his broad shoulders. Despite the amount of time they have been spending together in this hell-on-earth some Georgians are calling "the Turn," Lilly has scrupulously avoided crossing any intimate boundaries with Josh. Best to keep it platonic, brother-and-sister, best buds, nothing more. Best to keep it strictly business . . . especially in the midst of this plague.

But that has not stopped Lilly from giving the big man coy little sidelong grins when he calls her "girlfriend" or "babydoll" . . . or making sure he gets a glimpse of the Chinese character tattooed above Lilly's tailbone at night when she's settling into her sleeping bag. Is she leading him on? Is she manipulating him for protection? The rhetorical questions remain unanswered.

For Lilly the embers of fear constantly smoldering in her gut have cauterized all ethical issues and nuances of social behavior. In fact, fear has dogged her off and on for most her life—she developed an ulcer in high school, and had to be on antianxiety meds during her aborted tenure at Georgia Tech—but now it simmers constantly inside her. The fear poisons her sleep, clouds her thoughts, presses in on her heart. The fear makes her do things.

She seizes the hammer so tightly now it makes the veins twitch in her wrist.

"It's not rocket science *ferchrissake!*" she barks, and finally gets control of the hammer and drives a stake into the ground through sheer rage. She grabs another stake. She moves to the opposite corner of the canvas, and then wills the metal bit straight through the fabric and into the ground by pounding madly, wildly, missing as many blows as she connects. Sweat breaks out on her neck and brow. She pounds and pounds. She loses herself for a moment.

At last she pauses, exhausted, breathing hard, greasy with perspiration.

"Okay . . . that's one way to do it," Josh says softly, rising to his feet, a smirk on his chiseled brown face as he regards the half-dozen stakes pinning the canvas to the ground. Lilly says nothing.

The zombies, coming undetected through the trees to the north, are now less than five minutes away.

Not a single one of Lilly Caul's fellow survivors—numbering close to a hundred now, all grudgingly banding together to try and build a ragtag community here—realizes the one fatal drawback to this vacant rural lot in which they've erected their makeshift tents.

At first glance, the property appears to be ideal. Situated in a verdant area fifty miles south of the city—an area that normally produces millions of bushels of peaches, pears, and apples annually—the clearing sits in a natural basin of seared crabgrass and hard-packed earth. Abandoned by its onetime landlords—probably the owners of the neighboring orchards—the lot is the size of a soccer field. Gravel drives flank the property. Along these winding roads stand dense, overgrown walls of white pine and live oak that stretch up into the hills.

At the north end of the pasture stands the scorched, decimated remains of a large manor home, its blackened dormers silhouetted against the sky like petrified skeletons, its windows blown out by a recent maelstrom. Over the last couple of months, fires have taken out large chunks of the suburbs and farmhouses south of Atlanta.

Back in August, after the first human encounters with walking corpses, the panic that swept across the South played havoc with the emergency infrastructure. Hospitals got overloaded and then closed down, firehouses went dark, and Interstate 85 clogged up with wrecks. People gave up finding stations on their battery-operated radios, and then started looking for supplies to scavenge, places to loot, alliances to strike, and areas in which to hunker.

The people gathered here on this abandoned homestead found

each other on the dusty back roads weaving through the patchwork tobacco farms and deserted strip malls of Pike, Lamar, and Meriwether counties. Comprising all ages, including over a dozen families with small children, their convoy of sputtering, dying vehicles grew . . . until the need to find shelter and breathing room became paramount.

Now they sprawl across this two-square-acre parcel of vacant land like a throwback to some depression-era Hooverville, some of them living in their cars, others carving out niches on the softer grass, a few of them already ensconced in small pup tents around the periphery. They have very few firearms, and very little ammunition. Garden implements, sporting goods, kitchen equipment—all the niceties of civilized life—now serve as weapons. Dozens of these survivors are still pounding stakes into the cold, scabrous ground, working diligently, racing some unspoken, invisible clock, struggling to erect their jury-rigged sanctuaries—each one of them oblivious to the peril that approaches through the pines to the north.

One of the settlers, a lanky man in his midthirties in a John Deere cap and leather jacket, stands under the edge of a gigantic field of canvas in the center of the pasture, his chiseled features shaded by the gargantuan tent fabric. He supervises a group of sullen teenagers gathered under the canvas. "C'mon, ladies, put your backs into it!" he barks, hollering over the din of clanging metal filling the chilled air.

The teens grapple with a massive wooden beam, which serves as the center mast of what is essentially a large circus tent. They found the tent back on I-85, strewn in a ditch next to an overturned flatbed truck, a faded insignia of a giant paint-chipped clown on the vehicle's bulwark. Measuring over a hundred meters in circumference, the stained, tattered canvas big top—which smells of mildew and animal dung—struck the man in the John Deere hat as a perfect canopy for a common area, a place to keep supplies, a place to keep order, a place to keep some semblance of civilization.

"Dude . . . this ain't gonna hold the weight of it," complains one of the teens, a slacker kid in an army fatigue coat named Scott Moon. His long blond hair hangs in his face and his breath shows as he huffs and struggles with the other tattooed, pierced goth kids from his high school.

"Stop your pissin' and moanin'—it'll hold the thing," the man in the cap retorts with a grunt. Chad Bingham is his name—one of the family men of the settlement—the father of four girls: a seven-year-old, nine-year-old-twins, and a teenager. Unhappily married to a meek little gal from Valdosta, Chad fancies himself a strict disciplinarian, just like his daddy. But his daddy had boys and never had to deal with the nonsense perpetrated by females. For that matter, Chad's daddy never had to deal with rotting pus pockets of dead flesh coming after the living. So now Chad Bingham is taking charge, taking on the role of alpha male . . . because, just as his daddy used to say, *Somebody's gotta do it.* He glares at the kids. "Hold it steady!"

"That's as high as it's gonna go," one of the goth boys groans through clenched teeth.

"You're high," Scott Moon quips through a stifled little giggle.

"Keep it steady!" Chad orders.

"What?"

"I said, hold the dad-blamed thing *STEADY!*" Chad snaps a metal cotter pin through a slot in the timber. The outer walls of the massive canvas pavilion shudder in the autumn wind, making a rumbling noise, as other teens scurry toward the far corners with smaller support beams.

As the big top takes shape, and the panorama of the clearing becomes visible to Chad through the tent's wide opening at one end, he gazes out across the flattened brown weeds of the pasture, past the cars with their hoods up, past the clusters of mothers and children on the ground counting their meager caches of berries and vending-machine detritus, past the half-dozen or so pickups brimming with worldly possessions.

For a moment, Chad locks gazes with the big colored dude thirty yards away, near the north corner of the property, standing guard over Lilly Caul like a gigantic bouncer at some outdoor social club. Chad knows Lilly by name, but that's about it. He doesn't know much else about the girl—other than the fact that she's "some chick friend of Megan's"—and he knows less about the big man. Chad has been in proximity with the giant for weeks and can't even remember his name. Jim? John? Jack? As a matter of fact, Chad doesn't know anything about *any* of these people, other than the fact that they're all pretty goddamn desperate and scared and crying out for discipline.

But for a while now, Chad and the big black dude have been sharing loaded glances. Sizing each other up. Taking the measure of each other. Not a single word has been exchanged but Chad feels challenges being issued. The big man could probably take Chad in a hand-to-hand situation but Chad would never let it come to that. Size doesn't matter to a .38 caliber bullet, which is conveniently chambered in the steel-plated Smith & Wesson Model 52 tucked down the back of Chad's wide Sam Browne belt.

Right now, though, an unexpected current of recognition arcs across the fifty yards between the two men like a lightning bolt. Lilly continues to kneel in front of the black man, angrily beating the crap out of tent stakes, but something dark and troubling glints in the black dude's gaze suddenly as he stares at Chad. The realization comes quickly, in stages, like an electrical circuit firing.

Later, the two men will conclude, independently, that they—along with everybody else—missed two very important phenomena occurring at this moment. First, the noise of the tent construction in the clearing has been drawing walkers for the last hour. Second, and perhaps more importantly, the property is hampered by a single critical shortcoming.

In the aftermath, the two men will realize, privately, with much chagrin, that due to the natural barrier provided by the adjacent forest, which reaches up to the crest of a neighboring hill, any natural sound behind the trees is dampened, muffled, nearly deadened by the topography.

In fact, a college marching band could come over the top of that plateau, and a settler would not hear it until the cymbals crashed right in front of his face.

Lilly Caul remains blissfully unaware of the attack for several minutes—despite the fact that things begin unfolding at a rapid rate all around her—the noise of the clanging hammers and voices are replaced by the scattered screams of children. Lilly continues angrily driving stakes into the ground—mistaking the yelps of the younger ones for play—right up until the moment Josh grabs the nape of her sweatshirt.

"What—" Lilly jerks with a start, twisting around toward the big man with eyes blinking.

"Lilly, we gotta—"

Josh barely gets the first part of a sentence out when a dark figure stumbles out of the trees fifteen feet away. Josh has no time to run, no time to save Lilly, no time to do anything other than snatch the hammer out of the girl's hand and shove her out of harm's way.

Lilly tumbles and rolls almost instinctively before getting her bearings and rising back to her feet, a scream stuck in the back of her throat.

The trouble is, the first corpse that comes staggering into the clearing—a tall, pasty-colored walker in a filthy hospital smock with half his shoulder missing, the cords of his tendons pulsing like worms—is followed by two other creatures. One female and one male, each one with a gaping divot for a mouth, their bloodless lips oozing black bile, their shoe-button eyes fixed and glazed.

The three of them trundle with their trademark spasmodic gait, jaws snapping, lips peeling away from blackened teeth like piranhas.

In the twenty seconds it takes the three walkers to surround Josh, the tent city undergoes a rapid and dramatic shift. The men go for their homemade weapons, those with iron reaching down to their improvised holsters. Some of the more brazen women scramble for two-by-fours and hay hooks and pitchforks and rusty axes. Caretakers sweep their small children into cars and truck cabs. Clenched fists slam down on door locks. Rear loading gates clang upward.

Oddly, the few screams that ring out—from the children, mostly, and a couple of elderly women who may or may not be in early-stage senility—dwindle quickly, replaced by the eerie calm of a drill team or a provisional militia. Within the space of that twenty seconds, the noise of surprise quickly transitions into the business of defense, of repulsion and rage channeled into controlled violence. These people have done this before. There's a learning curve at work here. Some of the armed men spread outward toward the edges of the camp, calmly snapping hammers, pumping shells into shotgun breeches, raising the muzzles of stolen gun-show pistols or rusty family revolvers. The first shot that rings out is the dry pop of a .22 caliber Ruger—not the most powerful weapon by any means, but accurate and easy to shoot—the blast taking off the top of a dead woman's skull thirty yards away.

The female barely gets out of the trees before folding to the ground in a baptism of oily cranial fluid, which pours down over her in thick rivulets. This takedown occurs seventeen seconds into the attack. By the twentieth second, things begin happening at a faster clip.

On the north corner of the lot Lilly Caul finds herself moving, rising up on the balls of her feet, moving with the slow, coiled stiffness of a sleepwalker. Instinct takes over, and she finds herself almost *involuntarily* backing away from Josh, who is quickly surrounded by three corpses. He has one hammer. No gun. And three rotting mouths full of black teeth closing in.

He pivots toward the closest zombie while the rest of the camp scatters. Josh drives the sharp end of the hammer through Hospital Smock's temple. The cracking noise brings to mind the rending of an ice-cube tray. Brain matter fountains, the puff of pressurized decay released in an audible gasp, as the former inpatient collapses.

The hammer gets stuck, wrenched out of Josh's big hand as the walker folds.

At the same time, other survivors fan out across all corners of the clearing. On the far edge of the trees Chad gets his steel-plated Smith up and roaring, hitting the eye socket of a spindly old man missing half his jaw, the dead geriatric spinning in a mist of rancid fluids, pinwheeling into the weeds. Behind a line of cars a tent pole skewers a growling female through the mouth, pinning her to the trunk of a live oak. On the east edge of the pasture an axe shears open a rotting skull with the ease of a pomegranate being halved. Twenty yards away the blast of a shotgun vaporizes the foliage as well as the top half of a decaying former businessman.

Across the lot, Lilly Caul—still backing away from the ambush engulfing Josh—jerks and quakes at the killing racket. The fear prickles over her flesh like needles, taking her breath away and seizing up her brain. She sees the big black man on his knees now, clawing for the hammer, while the other two walkers scuttle spiderlike across the fallen tent canvas toward his legs. A second hammer lies in the grass just out of his reach.

Lilly turns and runs.

It takes her less than a minute to cover the ground between the row of outer tents and the center of the pasture, where two dozen weaker souls are huddled among the crates and provisions stashed under the partially erected circus tent. Several vehicles have fired up, and are now pulling next to the huddling throng in clouds of carbon monoxide. Armed men on the back of a flatbed guard the women and children as Lilly ducks down behind a battered steamer trunk, her lungs heaving for air, her skin crawling with terror.

She stays like that for the duration of the attack, her hands over her ears. She doesn't see Josh near the tree line, getting his hand around the hammer embedded in the fallen cadaver, wrenching it free at the last possible instant and swinging it toward the closest attacker. She doesn't see the blunt end of the hammer striking the male zombie's mandible, staving in half the rotting skull with the tremendous force of Josh's blow. And Lilly misses the last part of the struggle; she misses the female nearly getting her black incisors around Josh's ankle before a shovel comes down on the back of her head. Several men have reached Josh in time to dispatch the final zombie, and Josh rolls away, unharmed and yet trembling with the adrenaline and tremors of a near miss.

The entire attack—now vanquished and fading away in a soft drone of whimpering children, dripping fluids, and the escaping gases of decomposition—has encompassed less than one hundred and eighty seconds.

Later, dragging the remains off into a dry creek bed to the south, Chad and his fellow alpha dogs count twenty-four walkers in all—a totally manageable threat level . . . for the time being, at least.

"Jesus, Lilly, why don't you just suck it up and go apologize to the man?" The young woman named Megan sits on a blanket outside the circus tent, staring at the untouched breakfast in front of Lilly.

The sun has just come up, pale and cold in the clear sky—another day in the tent city—and Lilly sits in front of a battered Coleman stove, sipping instant coffee from a paper cup. The congealed remnants of freeze-dried eggs sit in the camp skillet, as Lilly tries to shake the guilt-ridden ruminations of a sleepless night. In this world there is no rest for the weary *or* the cowardly.

All around the great and tattered circus tent—now fully assembled—the bustle of other survivors drones on, almost as if the previous day's attack never happened. People carry folding chairs and camp tables into the great tent through the wide opening at one end (probably once the entrance for elephants and clown cars), as the tent's outer walls palpitate with the shifting breezes and changes in air pressure. In other parts of the encampment more shelters are going up. Fathers are gathering and taking inventory of firewood, bottled water, ammunition, weapons, and canned goods. Mothers are tending to children, blankets, coats, and medicine.

Upon closer scrutiny a keen observer would see a thinly veiled layer of anxiety in every activity. But what is uncertain is which danger poses the greatest threat: the undead or the encroaching winter.

"I haven't figured out what to say yet," Lilly mutters finally, sipping her lukewarm coffee. Her hands haven't stopped shaking. Eighteen hours have passed since the attack, but Lilly still stews with shame, avoiding contact with Josh, keeping to herself, convinced that he hates her for running and leaving him to die. Josh has tried to talk to her a few times but she couldn't handle it, telling him she was sick.

"What is there to say?" Megan fishes in her denim jacket for her little one-hit pipe. She tamps a tiny bud of weed into the end and sparks it with a Bic, taking a healthy toke. An olive-skinned young woman in her late twenties with loose henna-colored curls falling around her narrow, cunning face, she blows the green smoke out with a cough. "I mean look at this dude, he's huge."

"What the hell does that mean?"

Megan grins. "Dude looks like he can take care of himself, is all I'm saying."

"That has nothing to do with it."

"Are you sleeping with him?"

"What?" Lilly looks at her friend. "Are you serious?"

"It's a simple question."

Lilly shakes her head, lets out a sigh. "I'm not even going to dignify that with—"

"You're not . . . are you? Good-Little-Doobie-Lilly. Good to the last drop."

"Would you stop?"

"Why, though?" Megan's grin turns to a smirk. "Why have you not climbed on top of that? What are you waiting for? That body . . . those guns he's got—"

"Stop it!" Lilly's anger flares, a sharp splitting pain behind the bridge of her nose. Her emotions close to the surface, her trembling returning, she surprises even her*self* with the volume of her voice. "I'm not like you . . . okay. I'm not a social butterfly. Jesus, Meg. I've lost track. Which one of these guys are you with now?"

Megan stares at her for a second, coughs, then loads up another one-hit. "You know what?" Megan offers the pipe. "Why don't you take it down a little bit? Chill?"

"No, thanks."

"It's good for what ails ya. It'll kill that bug you got up your ass."

Lilly rubs her eyes, shakes her head. "You are a piece of work, Meg."

Megan gulps another hit, blows it out. "I'd rather be a piece of work than a piece of shit."

Lilly says nothing, just keeps shaking her head. The sad truth is, Lilly sometimes wonders if Megan Lafferty is not exactly that—a piece of shit. The two girls have known each other since senior year at Sprayberry High School back in Marietta. They were inseparable back then, sharing everything from homework to drugs to boyfriends. But then Lilly got designs on a career, and spent two years of purgatory at Massey College of Business in Atlanta, and then on to Georgia Tech for an MBA she would never get. She wanted to be a fashionista, maybe run a clothing design business, but she got as far as the reception area of her first interview—a highly coveted internship with Mychael Knight Fashions—before chickening out. Her old companion, fear, put the kibosh on all her plans.

Fear made her flee that lavish lobby and give up and go home to

Marietta and resume her slacker lifestyle with Megan, getting high, sitting on couches, and watching reruns of *Project Runway*.

Something had changed between the two women in recent years, however, something fundamentally chemical—Lilly felt it as strong as a language barrier. Megan had no ambition, no direction, no focus, and was okay with that. But Lilly still harbored dreams—stillborn dreams, perhaps, but dreams nonetheless. She secretly longed to go to New York or start a Web site or go back to that receptionist at Mychael Knight and say, "Oops, sorry, just had to step out for a year and a half . . ."

Lilly's dad—a retired math teacher and widower named Everett Ray Caul—always encouraged his daughter. Everett was a kind, deferential man who took it upon himself, after his wife's slow death from breast cancer back in the midnineties, to raise his only daughter with a tender touch. He knew she wanted more out of life, but he also knew she needed unconditional love, she needed a family, she needed a home. And Everett was all she had. All of which made the events of the last couple of months so hellish for Lilly.

The first outbreak of walkers hit the north side of Cobb County hard. They came from blue-collar areas, the industrial parks north of Kennesaw woods, creeping into the population like malignant cells. Everett decided to pack Lilly up and flee in their beat-up VW wagon, and they got as far as U.S. 41, before the wreckage slowed them down. They found a rogue city bus a mile south of there—careening up and down the back streets, picking survivors up—and they almost made it onboard. To this day, the image of her father pushing her through the bus's folding door as zombies closed in haunts Lilly's dreams.

The old man saved her life. He slammed that accordion door behind her at the last possible instant, and slid to the pavement, already in the grip of three cannibals. The old man's blood washed up across the glass as the bus tore out of there, Lilly screaming until her vocal cords burned out. She went into a kind of catatonic state then, curled into a fetal position on a bench seat, staring at that blood-smeared door all the way to Atlanta.

It was a minor miracle that Lilly found Megan. At that point in the outbreak, cell phones still worked, and she managed to arrange a rendezvous with her friend on the outskirts of Heartsfield Airport. The two women set out together on foot, hitchhiking south, flopping in deserted houses, just concentrating on survival. The tension between them intensified. Each seemed to be compensating for the terror and loss in different ways. Lilly went inward. Megan went the other direction, staying high most of the time, talking constantly, latching on to any other traveler who crossed their path.

They hooked up with a caravan of survivors thirty miles southwest of Atlanta—three families from Lawrenceville, traveling in two minivans. Megan convinced Lilly there was safety in numbers, and Lilly agreed to ride along for a while. She kept to herself for the next few weeks of zigzagging across the fruit belt, but Megan soon had designs on one of the husbands. His name was Chad and he had a bad-ass good-old-boy way about him, with his Copenhagen snuff under his lip and his navy tattoos on his wiry arms. Lilly was appalled to see the flirting going on amid this waking nightmare, and it wasn't long before Megan and Chad were stealing off into the shadows of rest stop buildings to "relieve themselves." The wedge between Lilly and Megan burrowed deeper.

It was right around this time that Josh Lee Hamilton came into the picture. Around sunset one evening the caravan had gotten pinned down by a pack of the dead in a Kmart parking lot, when the big African-American behemoth came to the rescue from the shadows of the loading dock. He came like some Moorish gladiator, wielding twin garden hoes with the price tags still flagging in the wind. He easily dispatched the half-dozen zombies, and the members of the caravan thanked him profusely. He showed the group a couple of brand-new shotguns in the back aisles of the store, as well as camping gear.

Josh rode a motorcycle, and after helping load the minivans with provisions, he decided to join the group, following along on his bike as the caravan made their way closer to the abandoned orchards patchworking Meriwether County.

Now Lilly had begun to regret the day she agreed to ride on the back of that big Suzuki. Was her attachment to the big man simply a projection of her grief over the loss of her dad? Was it a desperate act of manipulation in the midst of unending terror? Was it as cheap and transparent as Megan's promiscuity? Lilly wondered if her act of cowardice—deserting Josh on the battlefield yesterday—was a sick, dark, subconscious act of self-fulfilling prophecy.

"Nobody said you're a piece of shit, Megan," Lilly finally says, her voice strained and unconvincing.

"You don't have to say it." Megan angrily taps the pipe on the stove. She levers herself to her feet. "You've totally said enough."

Lilly stands. She has grown accustomed to these sudden mood swings in her friend. "What is your problem?"

"You . . . you're my problem."

"The hell are you talking about?"

"Forget it, I can't even handle this anymore," Megan says. The rueful tone of her voice is filtered by the hoarse buzz of the weed working on her. "I wish you luck, girlie-girl . . . you're gonna need it."

Megan storms off toward the row of cars on the east edge of the property.

Lilly watches her pal vanish behind a tall trailer loaded with cartons. The other survivors take very little notice of the tiff between the two girls. A few heads turn, a few whispers are exchanged, but most of the settlers continue busying themselves with the gathering and accounting of supplies, their somber expressions tight with nervous tension. The wind smells of metal and sleet. There's a cold front creeping in.

Gazing out across the clearing, Lilly finds herself momentarily transfixed by all the activity. The area looks like a flea market crowded with buyers and sellers, people trading supplies, stacking cordwood, and chatting idly. At least twenty smaller tents now line the periphery of the property, a few clotheslines haphazardly strung between trees, blood-spattered clothing taken from walkers, nothing wasted, the threat of winter a constant motivator now. Lilly sees children playing jump rope near a flatbed truck, a few boys kicking a soccer ball. She sees a fire burning in a barbecue pit, the haze of smoke wafting up over the roofs of parked cars. The air is redolent with bacon grease and hickory smoke, an odor that, in any other context, might suggest the lazy days of summer, tailgate parties, football games, backyard cookouts, family reunions.

A tide of black dread rises in Lilly as she scans the bustling little settlement. She sees the kids frolicking . . . and the parents laboring to make this place work . . . all of them zombie fodder . . . and all at once Lilly feels a twinge of insight . . . a jolt of reality.

She sees clearly now that these people are doomed. This grand plan to build a tent city in the fields of Georgia is not going to work.

TWO

The next day, under a pewter-colored sky, Lilly is playing with the Bingham girls in front of Chad and Donna Bingham's tent, when a grinding noise echoes over the trees along the adjacent dirt access road. The sound stiffens half the settlers in the area, faces snapping toward the noise of an approaching engine, which is groaning through its low gears.

It could be anyone. Word has spread across the plagued land of thugs pillaging the living, bands of heavily armed rovers stripping survivors of everything including the shoes on their feet. Several of the settlers' vehicles are currently out on scavenging reconnaissance but you never know.

Lilly looks up from the girls' hopscotch court—the squares have been etched in a little bare patch of brick-red clay with a stick—and the Bingham girls all freeze in mid-skip. The oldest girl, Sarah, shoots a glance at the road. A skinny tomboy in a faded denim jumper and down vest with big inquisitive blue eyes, fifteen-year-old Sarah, the whip-smart ringleader of the four sisters, softly utters, "Is that—"

"It's okay, sweetie," Lilly says. "Pretty sure it's one of ours."

The three younger sisters start craning their necks, looking for their mom.

Donna Bingham is presently out of view, washing clothes in a galvanized tin drum out behind the family's large camping tent, which Chad Bingham lovingly erected four days ago, equipping it with aluminum cots, racks of coolers, vent stacks, and a battery-operated DVD player with a library of children's fare such as *The Little Mermaid* and *Toy Story 2*. The sound of Donna Bingham's shuffling footsteps can be heard coming around the tent as Lilly gathers up the children.

"Sarah, get Ruthie," Lilly says calmly yet firmly as the engine noises close the distance, the vapor of burning oil rising above the tree line. Lilly rises to her feet and quickly moves over to the twins. Nine-year-old Mary and Lydia are identical cherubs in matching peacoats and flaxen pigtails. Lilly herds the little ones toward the tent flap while Sarah scoops up the seven-year-old Ruthie—an adorable little elf with Shirley Temple curls hanging over the collar of her miniature ski jacket.

Donna Bingham appears around the side of the tent just as Lilly is ushering the twins into the enclosure. "What's going on?" The mousy woman in the canvas jacket looks as though a stiff wind might blow her over. "Who is it? Is it rovers? Is it a stranger?"

"Nothing to worry about," Lilly tells her, holding the tent flap open as the four girls file into the shadows. In the five days since the contingent of settlers arrived here, Lilly has become the de facto babysitter, watching over various groups of offspring while parents go out scavenging or go on walks or just grab some alone time. She's happy for the welcome distraction, especially now that the babysitting can provide an excuse to avoid all contact with Josh Lee Hamilton. "Just stay in the tent with the girls until we know who it is."

Donna Bingham gladly shuts herself inside the enclosure with her daughters.

Lilly whirls toward the road and sees the grill of a familiar fifteen-forward-speed International Harvester truck materializing in a haze of wood smoke at the far end of the road—coming around the bend in gasps of exhaust—sending a wave of relief through Lilly. She smiles in spite of her nerves and starts toward the bare ground on the west edge of the field, which serves as a loading area. The rust-bucket truck clatters across the grass and shudders to a stop, the three teenagers riding in the back with the roped-down crates nearly tumbling forward against the pockmarked cab.

"Lilly Marlene!" the driver calls out the open cab window as Lilly comes around the front of the truck. Bob Stookey has big greasy hands—the hands of a laborer—wrapped around the wheel.

"What's on the menu today, Bob?" Lilly says with a wan smile. "More Twinkies?"

"Oh, we got a full gourmet spread with all the trimmings today, little sis." Bob cocks his deeply lined face toward the crew in back. "Found a deserted Target, only a couple of walkers to deal with . . . made out like bandits."

"Do tell."

"Let's see . . ." Bob jerks the shift lever into park and kills the rumbling engine. His skin the color of tanned cowhide, his droopy eyes rimmed red, Bob Stookey is one of the last men in the New South still using pomade to grease his dark hair back over his weathered head. "Got lumber, sleeping bags, tools, canned fruit, lanterns, cereal, weather radios, shovels, charcoal—what else? Also got a bunch of pots and pans, some tomato plants—still with a few warty little tomaters on the vines—some tanks of butane, ten gallons of milk that expired only a couple of weeks ago, some hand sanitizer, Sterno, laundry soap, candy bars, toilet paper, a Chia Pet, a book on organic farming, a singing fish for my tent, and a partridge in a pear tree."

"Bob, Bob, Bob . . . no AK-47s? No dynamite?"

"Got something better than that, smarty pants." Bob reaches over to a peach crate sitting on the passenger seat next to him. He hands it through the window to Lilly. "Be a darlin' and put this in my tent while I help these three stooges in back with the heavy stuff."

"What is it?" Lilly looks down at the crate full of plastic vials and bottles.

"Medical supplies." Bob opens his door and climbs out. "Need to keep 'em safe."

Lilly notices half a dozen pint bottles of liquor wedged in between the antihistamines and codeine. She gazes up at Bob and gives him a look. "Medical supplies?"

He grins. "I'm a very sick man."

"I'll say," Lilly comments. She knows enough about Bob's background by now to know that aside from being a sweet, genial, somewhat lost soul, as well as being a former army medic—which makes him the only inhabitant of the tent city with any medical training—he is also an inveterate drunk.

In the early stages of their friendship, back when Lilly and Megan were still on the road, and Bob had helped them out of a jam at a rest stop crawling with zombies, Bob had made feckless attempts to hide his alcoholism. But by the time the group had settled here in this deserted pastureland five days ago, Lilly had begun regularly helping Bob stagger safely back to his tent at night, making sure nobody robbed him—which was a real threat in a group this large and varied and filled with so much tension. She liked Bob, and she didn't mind babysitting *him* as well as the little ones. But it also added an additional layer of stress that Lilly needed as much as she needed a high colonic.

Right now, in fact, she can tell he needs something else from her. She can tell by the way he's wiping his mouth thoughtfully with his dirty hand.

"Lilly, there's something else I wanted to—" He stops and swallows awkwardly.

She lets out a sigh. "Spit it out, Bob."

"It's none of my business . . . all right. I just wanted to say . . . aw, hell." He takes a deep breath. "Josh Lee, he's a good man. I visit with him now and again."

"Yeah . . . and?"

"And I'm just saying."

"Go on."

"I'm just . . . look . . . he ain't doing too good right about now, all right? He thinks you're sore at him."

"He thinks I'm what?"

"He thinks you're mad at him for some reason, and he ain't sure why."

"What did he say?"

Bob gives her a shrug. "It's none of my beeswax. I ain't exactly privy to . . . I don't know, Lilly. He just wishes you wasn't ignoring him."

"I'm not."

Bob looks at her. "You sure?"

"Bob, I'm telling you—"

"All right, look." Bob waves his hand nervously. "I ain't telling you what to do. I just think two people like y'all, good folks, it's a shame something like this, you know, in these times . . ." His voice trails off.

Lilly softens. "I appreciate what you're saying, Bob, I do."

She looks down.

Bob purses his lips, thinks it over. "I saw him earlier today, over by the log pile, chopping wood like it was going outta style."

The distance between the loading area and the stack of cordwood measures less than a hundred yards, but crossing it feels like the Bataan Death March to Lilly.

She walks slowly, with her head down, and her hands thrust in the pockets of her jeans to conceal the trembling. She has to weave through a group of women sorting clothes in suitcases, circle around the end of the circus tent, sidestep a group of boys repairing a broken skateboard, and give wide berth to a cluster of men inspecting a row of weapons spread out on a blanket on the ground.

As she passes the men—Chad Bingham included in their number, holding court like a redneck despot—Lilly glances down at the tarnished pistols, eleven of them, different calibers, makes, and models, neatly arrayed like silverware in a drawer. The pair of 12-gauge shotguns from Kmart lie nearby. Only eleven pistols and the shotguns, and a limited number of rounds—the sum total of the settlers' armory—now standing as a thin tissue of defense between the campers and calamity.

Lilly's neck crawls with gooseflesh as she passes, the fear burning a hole in her guts. The trembling increases. She feels as though she's running a fever. The shaking has always been an issue for Lilly Caul. She remembers the time she had to deliver a presentation to the admission committee at Georgia Tech. She had her notes on index cards and had rehearsed for weeks. But when she got up in front of those tenured professors in that stuffy meeting room on North Avenue, she shook so much she dropped the stack of cards all over the floor and completely choked.

She feels that same kind of nervous tension right now—amplified by a factor of a thousand—as she approaches the split-rail fence along the western edge of the property. She feels the trembling in her facial features, and in her hands inside her pockets, so intense now it feels like the tremors are about to seize up her joints and freeze her in place. "Chronic anxiety disorder," the doctor back in Marietta called it.

In recent weeks, she has experienced this kind of spontaneous palsy in the immediate aftermath of a walker attack—a spell of shuddering that lasts for hours afterward—but now she feels a deeper sense of dread flooding through her that comes from some inchoate, primal place. She is turning inward, facing her own wounded soul, twisted by grief and the loss of her father.

She jumps at the crack of an axe striking timber, her attention yanked toward the fence.

A group of men stand in a cluster around a long row of dry logs. Dead leaves and cottonwood swirl on the wind above the tree line. The air smells of wet earth and matted pine needles. Shadows dance behind the foliage, tweaking Lilly's fear like a tuning fork in her brain. She remembers nearly getting bitten back in Macon three weeks ago when a zombie lurched out at her from behind a garbage Dumpster. To Lilly, right now, those shadows behind the trees look just like the passageway behind that Dumpster, rotten with menace and the smell of decay and horrible miracles—the dead coming back to life.

Another axe blow makes her start, and she turns toward the far end of the woodpile.

Josh stands with his shirtsleeves rolled up, his back to her. An oblong sweat stain runs down his chambray shirt between his massive shoulder blades. His muscles rippling, the skin folds in his brown nape pulsing, he works with a steady rhythm, swinging, striking, yanking back, bracing, swinging again with a *thwack*!

Lilly walks up to him and clears her throat. "You're doing it all wrong," she says in a shaky voice, trying to keep things light and casual.

Josh freezes with axe blade in midair. He turns and looks at her, his sculpted ebony face pearled with sweat. For a moment, he looks shell-shocked, his twinkling eyes belying his surprise. "You know, I figured somethin' wasn't working right," he says finally. "I've only been able to split about a hundred logs in fifteen minutes."

"You're choked down way too low on the handle."

Josh grins. "I knew it was somethin' like that."

"You have to let the logs do the work for ya."

"Good idea."

"You want me to demonstrate?"

Josh steps aside, hands her the axe.

"Like this," Lilly says, trying her best to appear charming and witty and brave. Her trembling is so bad the axe head quivers as she makes a feeble attempt to split a log. She swings and the blade side-swipes the wood, then sticks into the ground. She struggles to pull it free.

"Now I get it," Josh says with an amused nod. He notices her shaking, and his grin fades. He moves next to her. He puts his huge hand over hers, which is white-knuckling the axe handle as she struggles to pull it out of the clay. His touch is tender and soothing. "Everything's gonna be okay, Lilly," he says softly.

She lets go of the axe and turns to face him. Her heart races as she looks into his eyes. Her flesh goes cold, and she tries to put her feelings into words, but all she can do is look away in shame. Finally she manages to find her voice. "Is there someplace we can go and talk?"

"How do you do it?"

Lilly sits with her legs crossed Indian-style, on the ground under the massive branches of a live oak, which dapple the carpet of matted leaves around her with a skein of shadows. She reclines against the gigantic tree trunk as she speaks. Her eyes remain fixed on the swaying treetops in the middle distance.

She has a faraway look that Josh Lee Hamilton has seen now and again on the faces of war veterans and emergency room nurses—the gaze of perpetual exhaustion, the haggard look of the shell-shocked, the thousand-yard stare. Josh feels the urge to take her delicate, slender body into his arms and hold her and stroke her hair and make everything all better. But he senses somehow—he knows—now is not the time. Now is the time to listen.

"Do what?" he asks her. Josh sits across from her, also cross-legged, wiping the back of his neck with a damp bandanna. A box of cigars sits on the ground in front of him—the last of his dwindling supply. He is almost hesitant to go through the last of them—a superstitious twinge that he'll be sealing his fate.

Lilly looks up at him. "When the walkers attack . . . how do you deal with it without being . . . scared shitless?"

Josh lets out a weary chuckle. "If you figure that out, you're gonna have to teach me."

She stares at him for a moment. "Come on."

"What?"

"You're telling me you're scared shitless when they attack?"

"Damn straight."

"Oh, please." She tilts her head incredulously. "You?"

"Let me tell you something, Lilly." Josh picks up the package of cigars, shakes one loose, and sparks it with his Zippo. He takes a thoughtful puff. "Only the stupid or the crazy ain't scared these days. You ain't scared, you ain't paying attention."

She looks out beyond the rows of tents lined along the split-rail fence. She lets out a pained sigh. Her narrow face is drawn, ashen. She looks as though she's trying to articulate thoughts that just stubbornly refuse to cooperate with her vocabulary. At last she says, "I've been dealing with this for a while. I'm not . . . proud of it. I think it's messed up a lot of things for me."

Josh looks at her. "What has?"

"The wimp factor."

"Lilly—"

"No. Listen. I need to say this." She refuses to look at him, her eyes burning with shame. "Before this . . . outbreak happened . . . it was just sort of . . . inconvenient. I missed out on a few things. I screwed some things up because I'm a chickenshit . . . but now the stakes are . . . I don't know. I could get somebody killed." She finally manages to look up into the big man's eyes. "I could totally ruin things for somebody I care about."

Josh knows what she's talking about, and it puts the squeeze on his heart. From the moment he laid eyes on Lilly Caul he had felt feelings that he hadn't felt since he was a teenager back in Greenville—that kind of rapturous fascination a boy can fix upon the curve of a girl's neck, the smell of her hair, the spray of freckles along the bridge of her nose. Yes, indeed, Josh Lee Hamilton is smitten. But he is *not* going to screw this relationship up, as he had screwed up so many before Lilly, before the plague, before the world had gotten so goddamn bleak.

Back in Greenville, Josh developed crushes on girls with embarrassing frequency, but he always seemed to muck things up by rushing it. He would behave like a big old puppy licking at their heels. Not this time. This time, Josh was going to play it smart . . . smart and cautious and one step at a time. He may be a big old dumb-ass hick from South Carolina but he's not stupid. He's willing to learn from his past mistakes.

A natural loner, Josh grew up in the 1970s, when South Carolina was still clinging to the ghostly days of Jim Crow, still making futile attempts to integrate their schools and join the twentieth century. Shuffled from one ramshackle housing project to another with his single mom and four sisters, Josh put his God-given size and strength to good use on the gridiron, playing varsity ball for Mallard Creek High School with visions of scholarships in his eyes. But he lacked the one thing that sent players up the academic and socioeconomic ladders: *raw aggression.*

Josh Lee Hamilton had always been a gentle soul . . . to a fault. He let far weaker boys pick on him. He deferred to all adults with a "yessim" or "yessir." He simply had no fight in him. All of which is why his football career eventually petered out in the mid-eighties. That was right around the time his mother, Raylene, got sick. The doctors said it was called "lupus erythematosus," and it wasn't terminal, but for Raylene it was a death sentence, a life of chronic pain and skin lesions and near paralysis. Josh took it upon himself to be his mom's caretaker (while his sisters drifted away to bad marriages and dead-end jobs out of state). Josh cooked and cleaned and took good care of his mama, and within a few years he got good enough at cooking to actually get a job in a restaurant.

He had a natural flair for the culinary, especially cooking meat, and he moved up the ranks at steakhouse kitchens across South Carolina and Georgia. By the 2000s, he had become one of the most sought-after executive chefs in the Southeast, supervising large teams of sous-chefs, catering upscale social events, and getting his picture in *Atlanta Homes and Lifestyles*. And all the while he managed to run his kitchens with kindness—a rarity in the restaurant world.

Now, amid these daily horrors, beset with all this unrequited love, Josh longed to cook something special for Lilly.

Up until now, they had subsisted on things like canned peas and Spam and dry cereal and powdered milk—none of which would provide the proper backdrop for a romantic dinner or a declaration of love. All the meat and fresh produce in the area had gone the way of the maggots weeks ago. But Josh had designs on a rabbit, or a wild boar that might be roaming the neighboring woods. He would make a ragout, or a nice braise with wild onions and rosemary and some of that Pinot Noir that Bob Stookey had scavenged from that derelict liquor store, and Josh would serve the meat with some herbed polenta, and he would add extra special touches. Some of the ladies in the tent city had been making candles from the suet they found in a bird feeder. That would be nice. Candles, wine, maybe a poached pear from the orchard for dessert, and Josh would be ready. The orchards were still lousy with overripe fruit. Maybe an apple chutney with the pork. Yes. Absolutely. Then Josh would be ready to serve Lilly dinner and tell her how he feels about her, how he wants to be with her and protect her and be her man.

"I know where you're going with this, Lilly," Josh finally says to her, tamping his cigar's ash on a stone. "And I want you to know two things. Number one, there's no shame in what you did."

She looks down. "You mean running away like a whipped dog when you were under attack?"

"Listen to me. If the shoe was on the other foot, I would've done the same damn thing."

"That's bullshit, Josh, I didn't even—"

"Let me finish." He snubs out the cigar. "Number two, I *wanted* you to run. You didn't hear me. I hollered for you to get the Sam Hell outta there. Makes no sense—only one of them hammers within grasp, both of us trying to mix it up with them things. You understand what I'm saying? You don't need to feel any shame for what you done."

Lilly takes a breath. She keeps looking down. A tear forms and rolls down the bridge of her nose. "Josh, I appreciate what you're trying to—"

"We're a team, right?" He leans down so he can see her beautiful face. "Right?"

She nods.

"The dynamic duo, right?"

Another nod. "Right."

"A well-oiled machine."

"Yeah." She wipes her face with the back of her hand. "Yeah, okay."

"So let's keep it that way." He throws her his damp bandanna. "Deal?"

She looks at the do-rag in her lap, picks it up, looks at him and manages a grin. "Jesus Christ, Josh, this thing is totally gross."

Three days pass in the tent city without an attack of any note. Only a few minor incidents sully the calm. One morning, a group of kids stumble upon a quivering torso in a culvert ditch along the road. Its gray, wormy face cocked toward the treetops in perpetual, groaning agony, the thing looks as though it recently tangled with a mechanical reaper, and has ragged stumps where its arms and legs once were. Nobody can figure out how the limbless thing got there. Chad puts the creature down with a single hatchet blow through its rotting nasal bone. On another occasion, out by the communal toilets, an elderly camper realizes, with heart-skipping dismay, that during his afternoon bowel movement, he is unwittingly shitting on a zombie. Somehow the roamer got itself stuck down in the sewage trough. The thing is easily dispatched by one of the younger men with a single thrust of a post-hole digger.

These prove to be isolated encounters, though, and the middle of the week progresses uneventfully.

The respite gives the inhabitants time to organize, finish erecting the last of their shelters, stow supplies, explore the immediate area, settle into a routine, and form coalitions and cliques and hierarchies. The families—ten of them in all—seem to carry more weight in the decision-making process than do single people. Something about the gravitas of having more at risk, the imperative of protecting children, maybe even the symbolism of carrying the genetic seeds of the future—all of it adding up to a kind of unspoken seniority.

Among the patriarchs of the families, Chad Bingham emerges as the de facto leader. Each morning, he leads the communal powwows inside the circus tent, assigning duties with the casual authority of a Mafia capo. Each day, he struts along the edges of the camp with his snuff defiantly bulging under his cheek, his pistol in full view. With winter in the offing, and troubling noises behind the trees at night, Lilly worries about this ersatz figurehead. Chad has been keeping his eye on Megan, who has been shacking up with one of the other fathers, in plain view of everybody including the man's pregnant wife. Lilly worries that the whole semblance of order here rests on top of a tinderbox.

Lilly's tent and Josh's tent sit a mere ten yards away from each other. Each morning, Lilly awakens and sits facing the zippered end of her tent, gazing out at Josh's tent, drinking her instant Sanka and trying to sort out her feelings for the big man. Her cowardly act still gnaws at her, haunts her, festers in her dreams. She has nightmares of the bloody folding door on that rogue bus back in Atlanta, but now, instead of her father being devoured, sliding down that smeared glass, Lilly sees Josh.

His accusing eyes always wake her up with a start, the cold sweat soaked through her nightclothes.

On these dream-racked nights, lying sleepless in her moldy sleeping bag, staring at the mildewed roof of her tiny tent—she acquired the used pup tent on a raid of a deserted KOA camp, and it reeks of smoke, dried semen, and stale beer—she inevitably hears the noises. Faint, off in the distant darkness beyond the rise, behind the trees, the sounds mingle with the wind and crickets and rustling foliage: unnatural snapping noises, jerky shuffling sounds, which remind Lilly of old shoes tumbling and banging inside a dryer.

In her mind's eye, mutated by terror, the distant noises conjure images of terrible black-and-white forensic photos, mutilated bodies blackened by rigor mortis and yet still moving, dead faces turning and leering at her, silent snuff films of dancing cadavers jitterbugging like frogs on a hot skillet. Lying wide awake each night, Lilly ruminates about what the noises might actually mean, what is going on out there, and when the next attack will come.

Some of the more thoughtful campers have been developing theories.

One young man from Athens named Harlan Steagal, a nerdy grad student with thick horn-rims, begins holding nightly philosophy salons around the campfire. Jacked up on pseudoephedrine, instant coffee, and bad weed, the half a dozen or so social misfits grope for answers to the imponderable questions tormenting everybody: the origins of the plague, the future of mankind, and perhaps the timeliest issue of them all, the walkers' patterns of behavior.

The consensus among the think tank is that there are only two possibilities: *(a)* zombies have no instinct, purpose, or behavioral pattern other than involuntary feeding. They are merely sputtering nerve endings with teeth, bouncing off each other like deadly machines that simply need to be "turned off." Or *(b)* there is a complex pattern of behavior going on here that no survivor has figured out yet. The latter begs the question of how the plague is transmitted from the dead to the living—is it only through the bite of a walker?—as well as questions of horde behavior, *and* of possible Pavlovian learning curves, *and* even larger-scale genetic imperatives.

In other words—to put it in the patois of Harlan Steagal: *"Are the dead things like playing out some weird, fucked-up, trippy evolutionary thing?"*

Lilly overhears much of this rambling discourse over those three days and pays it little heed. She has no time for conjecture or analysis. The longer the tent city goes on without being assailed by the dead, the more Lilly feels vulnerable, despite the safety precautions. With most of the tents now erected and a barricade of vehicles parked around the periphery of the clearing, things have quieted down. People are settled in, keeping to themselves, and the few campfires or cooking stoves that are employed for meals are quickly extinguished for fear of errant smoke or odors attracting unwanted intruders.

Still, Lilly becomes exceedingly nervous each night. It feels as though a cold front is moving in. The night sky gets crystalline and cloudless, a new frost forming each morning on the matted ground and fencing and tent canvases. The gathering cold reflects Lilly's dark intuition. Something terrible seems imminent.

One night, before turning in, Lilly Caul pulls a small leather-bound paper calendar from her backpack. In the weeks since the advent of the plague, most personal devices have failed. The electrical grid has gone down, fancy batteries have run their course, service providers have vanished, and the world has reverted to the fundamentals: bricks, mortar, paper, fire, flesh, blood, sweat, and whenever possible, *internal combustion*. Lilly has always been an analog girl—her place back in Marietta brims with vinyl records, transistor radios, windup clocks, and first editions crammed into every corner—so she naturally starts keeping track of the plague days in her little black binder with the faded American Family Insurance logo embossed in gold on the cover.

On this night, she puts a big X on the square marked Thursday, November 1.

The next day is November 2—the day her fate, as well as that of many others, will irrevocably change.

Friday dawns clear and bitingly cold. Lilly stirs just after sunrise, shivering in her sleeping bag, her nose so cold it feels numb. Her joints ache as she hurriedly piles on the layers. She pushes herself out of her tent, zipping her coat and glancing at Josh's tent.

The big man is already up, standing beside his tent, stretching his massive girth. Bundled in his fisherman's sweater and tattered down vest, he whirls, sees Lilly, and says, "Cold enough for ya?"

"Next stupid question," she says, coming over to his tent, reaching for the thermos of steaming instant coffee gripped in his huge, gloved hand.

"Weather's got people panicked," he says softly, handing the thermos over. With a nod, he indicates the three trucks idling along the road across the clearing. His breath shows in puffs of vapor as he talks. "Bunch of us heading up into the woods, gathering as much firewood as we can load."

"I'll come with."

Josh shakes his head. "Talked to Chad a minute ago, I guess he needs you to watch his kids."

"Okay. Sure. Whatever."

"You keep that," Josh says, gesturing toward the thermos. He grabs the axe that sits canted against his tent and gives her a grin. "Should be back by lunchtime."

"Josh," she says, grabbing his sleeve before he can turn away. "Just be careful in the woods."

His grin widens. "Always, babydoll . . . always."

He turns and marches off toward the clouds of visible exhaust along the gravel road.

Lilly watches the contingent hopping into cabs, jumping up onto running boards, climbing into cargo bays. She doesn't realize at this point the amount of noise they're making, the commotion caused by three large trucks embarking all at once, the voices calling to each other, doors slamming, the fog bank of carbon monoxide.

In all the excitement, neither Lilly, nor anyone else for that matter, realizes how far the racket of their departure is carrying out over the treetops.

Lilly senses danger first.

The Binghams have left her inside the circus tent, in charge of the four girls, who now frolic across the floor of matted grass, scampering amid the folding tables, stacks of peach crates, and tanks of butane. The interior of the circus tent is illuminated by makeshift skylights—flaps in the ceiling pulled back to let in the daylight—and the air in there smells of must and decades of moldy hay impregnated into the canvas walls. The girls are playing musical chairs with three broken-down lawn chairs scattered across the cold earthen floor.

Lilly is supposed to be the music.

"Duh-do-do-do . . . duh-da-da-da," Lilly croons halfheartedly, murmuring an old Top 40 hit by the Police, her voice thin and weak, as the girls giggle and circle the chairs. Lilly is distracted. She keeps glancing through the loading entrance at one end of the pavilion, a large swath of the tent city visible in the gray daylight. The grounds are mostly deserted, those who are not away scavenging now hiding in their tents.

Lilly swallows her terror, the cold sun slanting down through the far trees, the wind whispering through the big-top tent. Up on the rise, shadows dance in the pale light. Lilly thinks she hears shuffling sounds up there somewhere, behind the trees maybe; she's not sure. It might be her imagination. Sounds inside the fluttering, empty tent play tricks on the ears.

She turns away from the opening and scans the pavilion for weapons. She sees a shovel leaning against a wheelbarrow filled with potting soil. She sees a few garden implements in a dirty bucket. She sees the remains of the breakfast dishes in a plastic garbage can— paper plates crusted with beans and Egg Beaters, wadded burrito wrappers, empty juice boxes—and next to it a plastic storage container with dirty silverware. The silverware came from one of the retrofitted camper/pickups, and Lilly makes note of a few sharp knives in the container but mostly she sees plastic "sporks" sticky with food gunk. She wonders how effective a spork would be against a monstrous drooling cannibal.

She silently curses the camp leaders for not leaving firearms.

Those who remain on the property include the older settlers—Mr. Rhimes, a couple of spinsters from Stockbridge, an eighty-year-old retired teacher named O'Toole, a pair of geriatric brothers from an abandoned nursing home in Macon—as well as a couple dozen adult women, a good portion of them too busy now with laundry duty and philosophical chatter along the back fence to notice anything amiss.

The only other souls currently present in the tent city are children—ten sets of them—some still huddling against the cold in their private tents, others kicking a soccer ball around in front of the derelict farmhouse. Each gaggle of kids has an adult woman in charge of them.

Lilly looks back out the exit and sees Megan Lafferty, way in the distance, sitting perched on the porch of the burned-out house, pretending to be babysitting and not smoking pot. Lilly shakes her head. Megan is supposed to be watching the Hennessey kids. Jerry Hennessey, an insurance salesman from Augusta, has been carrying on with Megan for days now in a not-too-discreet fashion. The Hennessey kids are the second-youngest kids in the encampment—at ages eight, nine, and ten respectively. The youngest children in the settlement are the Bingham twins and Ruthie, who at this moment pause in their play to stare impatiently at their nervous babysitter.

"C'mon, Lilly," Sarah Bingham calls out with her hands on her hips, catching her breath near a stack of fruit crates. The teenager wears an adorable, stylish imitation-angora sweater that breaks Lilly's heart. "Keep singing."

Lilly turns back to the children. "I'm sorry, sweetie, I just—"

Lilly stops herself. She hears a noise coming from outside the tent, from up in the trees. It sounds like the creaking bulwark of a listing ship . . . or the slow squeak of a door in a haunted house . . . or, more likely, the weight of a zombie's foot on a deadfall log.

"Girls, I'm—"

Another noise cuts off Lilly's words. She spins toward the tent's opening at a loud rustling sound, which rings out from the east, shattering the stillness a hundred yards away, coming from a thicket of wild rose and dogwood.

A flock of rock pigeons suddenly takes flight, the swarm bursting out of the foliage with the inertia of a fireworks display. Lilly stares, transfixed for a single instant, as the flock fills the sky with a virtual constellation of gray-black blots.

Like controlled explosions, along the far edge of the camp, another two flocks of pigeons erupt. Cones of fluttering specks punch up into the light, scattering and re-forming like ink clouds undulating in a clear pool.

The rock pigeons are plentiful in this area—"sky rats" they're called by the locals, who claim the pigeons are actually quite delicious if boned and grilled—but their sudden appearance in recent weeks has come to signify something darker and more troubling than a possible food source.

Something has stirred the birds from their resting place and is now making its way toward the tent city.

THREE

"Girls, listen to me." Lilly quickly shuffles over to the youngest Bing-ham girl and scoops her up in her arms. "I'm gonna need you to come with me."

"Why?" Sarah gives Lilly that patented teenage sulk. "What's wrong?"

"Don't argue with me, sweetie, please," Lilly says softly, and the look in Lilly's eyes straightens the teenager with the power of a cattle prod. Sarah hastily turns and takes the twins by their hands, then starts shepherding them toward the exit.

Lilly stops in her tracks in the middle of the tent's opening when she sees the first zombie burst out of the trees forty yards away—a big male with a hairless scalp the color of a bruise and eyes like milk glass—and all at once Lilly is shoving the kids back into the pavil-ion, clutching Ruthie in her arms and uttering under her breath, "Change in plans, girls, change in plans."

Lilly quickly urges the kids back into the dim light and moldy air of the empty circus tent. She sets the seven-year-old down on the matted weeds by a steamer trunk. "Everybody be very quiet," Lilly whispers.

Sarah stands with a twin on either side of her, the teenager's face aghast, wide-eyed with terror. "What's going on?"

"Just stay there and be quiet." Lilly hurries back to the tent open-ing and wrestles with the massive flap, which is cinched ten feet up with rope ties. She yanks at the ropes, until the tent flap falls across the gap.

The original plan—which flickered instantaneously across Lilly's mind—was to hide the kids in a vehicle, preferably one with its keys still in its ignition, in case Lilly had to make a quick escape. But now, all Lilly can think of doing is huddling silently in the empty pavilion and hoping that the other campers fend off the assault.

"Let's all play a different game now," Lilly says when she returns to the huddling girls. A scream rings out from somewhere across the property. Lilly tries to stanch her trembling, a voice resonating in her head, *Goddammit, you stupid bitch, you gotta grow some balls for once in your life, for these kids.*

"A different game, right, right, a different game," Sarah says, her eyes glittering with fear. She knows now what's going on. She clutches the small hands of her twin sisters and follows Lilly between two high stacks of fruit crates.

"Gonna play hide-and-seek," Lilly says to little Ruthie, who is mute with horror. Lilly gets the four girls situated in the shadows behind the crates, each child crouched down low now and breathing hard. "Have to stay very still—and very, very, very quiet. Okay?"

Lilly's voice seems to comfort them temporarily, although even the youngest knows now this is no game, this is not make-believe.

"I'll be right back," Lilly whispers to Sarah.

"No! Wait! NO, DON'T!" Sarah clutches at Lilly's down jacket, holding on to her for dear life, the teenager's eyes pleading.

"I'm just going to grab something across the tent, I'm not leaving."

Lilly extricates herself and scuttles on her hands and knees across the carpet of pressed grass to the pile of buckets near the long central table. She grabs the shovel that leans against the wheelbarrow, then crawls back to the hiding place.

All the while, terrible sounds layer and build outside the wind-blown walls of the pavilion. Another scream pierces the air, followed by frantic footsteps, and then the sound of an axe sinking into a skull. Lydia whimpers, Sarah shushes her, and Lilly crouches down in front of the girls, her vision blurring with terror.

The frigid wind tosses the skirt of the tent's walls, and for a brief moment, under the momentary gap, Lilly glimpses the onslaught in progress. At least two dozen walkers—only their shuffling, muddy feet visible like a brigade of upright stroke victims—converge on the tent-strewn field. The running feet of survivors, mostly women and elderly, are fleeing in all directions.

The spectacle of the attack temporarily distracts Lilly from the noise behind the girls.

A bloody arm lurches under the tent flap only inches away from Sarah's legs.

Sarah shrieks as a dead hand clamps down on her ankle, its blackened fingernails digging in like talons. The arm is gouged and tattered, clad in the ripped sleeve of a burial suit, and the girl convulses in shock. Moving on instinct, the teenager crawls away—the force of her movement yanking the rest of the zombie inside the tent.

A dissonant chorus of squeals and shrieks rings out from the sisters as Lilly springs to her feet with the shovel clutched tightly in sweaty palms. Instinct kicks in, Lilly spinning and cocking the shovel high. The dead man bites at the air with snapping-turtle fury, as the teenager writhes and crawls across the cold ground, crying out garbled yelps of terror, dragging the zombie with her.

Before the rotting teeth get a chance to penetrate, Lilly brings the shovel down hard on the zombie's skull, the impact making a flat clanging noise like the chime of a broken gong. The crack of the cranium vibrates up Lilly's wrists and makes her cringe.

Sarah breaks free of the cold fingers and struggles to her feet.

Lilly brings the shovel down again . . . and again . . . as the iron scoop rings its flat church-bell clang and the dead thing deflates in a rhythmic black gush of arterial blood and rotting gray matter. By the fourth blow, the skull caves in, making a wet cracking noise, the black spume bubbling across the matted grass.

By this point, Sarah has joined her sisters, each girl clinging to the other, each bug-eyed and whimpering with horror as they back toward the exit, the great canvas flap billowing noisily in the wind behind them.

Lilly turns away from the mangled corpse in the tattered pin-striped suit and starts toward the opening twenty-five feet away, when all at once she freezes in place, grabbing Sarah's sleeve. "Wait, Sarah, wait—WAIT!"

At the other end of the circus tent, the giant tarpaulin flap furls upward in the wind, revealing at least half a dozen walkers crowding in on the exit. They shuffle spastically into the tent—all adults, both male and female, clad in torn, blood-spattered street clothes, bunched together in an awkward grouping—their wormy cataract-filmed eyes fixing on the girls.

"This way!" Lilly yanks Sarah toward the opposite end of the circus tent—maybe a hundred and fifty feet away—and Sarah scoops the tike up into her arms. The twins scurry after them, slipping on the wet, matted grass. Lilly points at the bottom of the canvas wall—now a hundred feet away—and whispers breathlessly, "Gonna sneak under the tent."

They get halfway to the opposite wall when another walker appears in their path.

Apparently this slimy, mutilated corpse in faded denim dungarees—with half its face torn away on one side in a ragged starburst of red pulp and teeth—got in under the tarp and now comes straight for Sarah. Lilly steps between the zombie and the girl and swings the shovel as hard as she can, making contact with the mangled cranium and sending the thing staggering sideways.

The zombie slams into the center pillar, and the raw inertia and deadweight knocks the timber out of its mooring. Guidelines snap. There's a cracking noise like a ship breaking through ice and three of the four Bingham girls let out ululating shrieks as the massive big top collapses into itself, snapping the smaller rigging posts like matchsticks and pulling stakes out of the ground around it. The conical ceiling sinks like a vast soufflé.

The tent falls on the girls and the world goes dark and airless and full of slithering movement.

Lilly flails at the heavy fabric and struggles to get her bearings, still grasping the shovel, the tarpaulin pressing down on her with the sudden weight of an avalanche. She hears the muffled squealing of the children and she sees daylight fifty feet away. She crabs under the tent toward the light with the shovel in one hand.

At last she brushes a foot against Sarah's shoulder. Lilly cries out: "Sarah! Take my hand! Grab the girls with the other and PULL!"

———

At this point, for Lilly, the passage of time—as it often does in catastrophes-in-progress—begins to retard, as several things transpire almost simultaneously. Lilly reaches the end of the tent and bursts out from under the deflated canvas, and the wind and cold wake her up, and she yanks Sarah out with all her might, and two of the other girls get dragged out behind Sarah—their voices shrieking like teakettles on the boil.

Lilly springs to her feet and helps Sarah up with the other two little girls.

One girl—Lydia, the youngest of the twins by a "good half an hour," as Sarah claims—is missing. Lilly pushes the other girls away from the tent and tells them to stay back but stay close. Then Lilly whirls toward the tent and sees something that stops her heart.

Shapes are moving under the fallen circus tent. Lilly drops the shovel. She stares. Her legs and spine seize up into blocks of ice. She can't breathe. She can only stare at the small lump of fabric undulating madly twenty feet away—little Lydia struggling to escape—the sound of the child's scream dampened by the tarp.

The worst part—the part that encases Lilly Caul in ice—is the sight of the *other* lumps tunneling steadily, molelike, toward the little girl.

At that moment, the fear pops a fuse in Lilly's brain, the cleansing fire of rage traveling through her tendons and down her marrow.

She lurches into action, the burst of adrenaline driving her to the edge of the fallen tent, the rocket fuel of anger in her muscles. She yanks the canvas up and over her head, crouching down and reaching for the girl. *"LYDIA, SWEETIE, I'M RIGHT HERE!! COME TO ME, SWEETIE!!"*

Lilly sees in the pale diffuse darkness under the tarpaulin the little flaxen-haired girl, fifteen feet away, frog-kicking and scrambling to escape the clutches of the canvas. Lilly hollers again and dives under the tarp and reaches out and gets a piece of the little girl's jumper. Lilly pulls with all her might.

That's when Lilly sees the ragged arm and bloodless blue face appearing in the dark only inches behind the child, making a drunken grab for the little girl's Hello Kitty sneaker. The rotting, jagged fingernails claw the sole of the child's tennis shoe just as Lilly manages to yank the nine-year-old out from under the folds of reeking fabric.

Both Lilly and child tumble backward into the cold light of day.

They roll a few feet, and then Lilly manages to pull the little girl into a bear hug. "It's okay, baby, it's okay, I got you, you're safe."

The child sobs and gasps for breath but there's no time to comfort her. The din of voices and rustling canvas rises around them as the camp is attacked.

Lilly, still on her knees, waves the other girls over to her. "Okay, girls, listen to me, listen, we have to be quick now, quick, stay close, and do exactly as I say." Lilly huffs and puffs as she stands. She grabs the shovel, turns, and sees the chaos spreading across the tent city.

More walkers have descended upon the camp. Some of them move in clusters of three and four and five, growling and drooling with rabid, feral hunger.

Amid the screams and pandemonium—settlers fleeing in all directions, car engines firing up, axes swinging, clotheslines collapsing—some of the tents shudder with violent struggles going on *inside*, the assailants burrowing through gaps, ferreting out the paralyzed inhabitants. One of the smaller tents falls onto its side, legs scissoring out one end. Another enclosure quakes in a feeding frenzy, the translucent nylon walls displaying silhouettes of blood mist like ink blots.

Lilly sees a clear path leading to a row of parked cars fifty yards away and turns to the girls. "I need you all to follow me . . . okay? Stay very close and don't make a sound. All right?"

After a series of frantic, silent nods, Lilly yanks the girls across the lot . . . and into the fray.

The survivors of this inexplicable plague have quickly learned that the biggest advantage a human enjoys over a reanimated corpse is speed. Under the right circumstances, a human can easily outrun even the stoutest walking cadaver. But this physical superiority is overwhelmed in the face of a swarm. The danger increases exponentially with each additional zombie . . . until the victim is engulfed in a slow-moving tsunami of ragged teeth and blackened claws.

Lilly learns this harsh reality on her way to the closest parked car.

The battered, gore-streaked silver Chrysler 300 with the luggage cap on the roof sits on the gravel shoulder of the access road less than fifty yards from the circus tent, parked at an angle in the shade of a locust tree. The windows are up, but Lilly still has reason to believe they can at least gain access, if not start the car. The odds are about even that the keys are in the ignition. People have been leaving keys in cars for a while now for quick escapes.

Unfortunately, the property now teems with the dead, and Lilly and the girls barely traverse ten yards of weed-whiskered turf before several attackers move in on each flank. "Stay behind me!" Lilly cries out to her charges, and then swings the shovel.

The rusty iron bangs into the mottled cheek of a female in a blood-spattered housecoat, sending the walker careening into a pair of nearby males in greasy dungarees, who tumble like bowling pins to the ground. But the female stays upright, staggering at the blow, flailing for a moment, then coming back for more.

Lilly and the girls get another fifteen yards closer to the Chrysler when another battery of zombies blocks their path. The shovel zings through the air, smashing through the bridge of a younger walker's nose. Another blow hits the mandible of a dead woman in a filthy mink coat. Yet another blow cracks the skull of an old hunched crone with intestines showing through her hospital smock, but the old dead lady merely staggers and backpedals.

At last, the girls reach the Chrysler. Lilly tries the passenger door and finds it—blessedly—unlocked. She gently but quickly shoves Ruthie into the front seat as the pack of walkers closes in on the sedan. Lilly sees the keys dangling off the slot in the steering column—another stroke of luck. "Stay in the car, honey," Lilly says to the seven-year-old, and then slams the door.

By this point, Sarah reaches the right rear passenger door with the twins.

"SARAH, LOOK OUT!"

Lilly's keening scream rises above the primordial din of growling that fills the air, as a dozen or so dead loom behind Sarah. The teenager yanks open the rear door, but has no time to get the twins inside the car. The two smaller girls trip and sprawl to the grass.

Sarah screams a primal wail. Lilly tries to get in between the teen and the attackers with the shovel, and Lilly manages to bash in another skull—the huge cranium of a putrified black man in a hunting jacket—sending the attacker staggering back into the weeds. But there are too many walkers now, lumbering in from all directions to feed.

In the ensuing chaos, the twins manage to crawl into the car and slam the door.

Her sanity snapping, her eyes filling with white-hot rage, Sarah turns and lets out a garbled cry as she shoves a slow-moving walker out of her way. She finds an opening, pushes her way through it, and flees.

Lilly sees the teenager racing toward the circus tent. "SARAH, DON'T!!"

Sarah gets halfway across the field before an impenetrable pack of zombies closes in on her, blocking her path, latching on to her back and overpowering her. She goes down hard, eating turf, as more of the dead swarm around her. The first bite penetrates her imitation-angora sweater at the midriff, taking a chunk of her torso, sparking an earsplitting shriek. Festering teeth sink into her jugular. The dark tide of blood washes across her.

Twenty-five yards away, near the car, Lilly fights off a growing mass of gnashing teeth and dead flesh. Maybe twenty walkers in all now—most of them exhibiting the grotesque buzzing adrenaline of a feeding frenzy as they surround the Chrysler—their blackened mouths working and smacking voraciously, while behind blood-smeared windows, the faces of three little girls look on in catatonic horror.

Lilly swings the shovel again and again—her efforts futile against the growing horde—as the cogs and gears of her brain seize up, mortified by the grisly sounds of Sarah's demise on the ground across the property. The teenager's shrieking deteriorates and sputters into a watery series of caterwauls. At least a half-dozen walkers are on her now, burrowing in, chewing and tearing at her gushing abdomen. Blood fountains from her shuddering form.

Over by the row of cars, Lilly's midsection goes icy cold as she slams the shovel into another skull, her mind crackling and flickering with terror, ultimately fixing on a single course of action: *Get them away from the Chrysler.*

The silent dog-whistle urgency of that single imperative—*get them away from the children*—galvanizes Lilly and sends a jolt of energy down her spine. She turns and swings the shovel at the Chrysler's front quarter panel.

The clang rings out. The children inside the car jerk with a start. The livid blue faces of the dead turn toward the noise.

"C'MON! C'MON!!" Lilly lunges away from the Chrysler, moving toward the nearest car lined up in the haphazard row of vehicles—a beat-up Ford Taurus with one window covered in cardboard—and she strikes the edge of the roof as hard as she can, making another harsh metallic clang that gets the attention of more of the dead.

Lilly darts toward the next car in line. She bangs the scoop against the front left quarter panel, issuing another dull clang.

"C'MON!! C'MON!! C'MON!!"

Lilly's voice rises above the clamor like the bark of a sick animal, stretched thin with horror, hoarse with trauma, toneless, a touch of madness in it. She slams the shovel against car after car, not really knowing exactly what she's doing, not really in control of her actions anymore. More zombies take notice, their lazy, awkward movements drawn to the noise.

It takes Lilly mere seconds to reach the end of the row of vehicles, slamming the shovel into the last vehicle—a rust-pocked Chevy S-10 pickup—but by that point, most of the assailants have latched on to her clarion call, and now slowly, stupidly, clumsily wander toward the sound of her traumatized shouts.

The only walkers that remain are the six that continue to devour Sarah Bingham on the ground in the clearing by the great, billowing circus tent.

"C'MON!! C'MON!! C'MON!! C'MON!! C'MON!! C'MON!! C'MON!! C'MONNNNN!!!!!" Lilly vaults across the gravel road and dashes up the hill toward the tree line.

Pulse racing, vision blurred, lungs heaving for air, she drops the shovel and digs her hiking boots into the mire as she ascends the soft forest floor. She plunges into the trees. Her shoulder bangs against the trunk of an ancient birch, the pain flaring in her skull, stars shooting across her line of vision. She moves instinctively now, a horde of zombies coming up the rise behind her.

Zigzagging through the deeper woods, she loses her sense of direction. Behind her, the pack of walkers has slowed and lost her scent.

Time loses all meaning. As though in a dream, Lilly feels motion slow down, her screams refusing to come out, her legs bogging down in the invisible quicksand of nightmares. The darkness closes in as the forest thickens and deepens.

Lilly thinks of Sarah, poor Sarah, in her sweet little pink angora sweater, now bathed in her own blood, and the tragedy drags Lilly down, yanking her off her feet and throwing her down to the soft floor of matted pine needles and decaying matter and endless cycles of death and regeneration. Lilly lets out a paroxysm of pain on a breathless sob, her tears rolling down her cheeks and moistening the humus.

Her weeping—heard by no one—goes on for quite some time.

The search party finds Lilly late that afternoon. Led by Chad Bingham, the group of five men and three women—all heavily armed—see Lilly's light blue fleece jacket behind a deadfall log a thousand yards due north of the tent city, in the gelid darkness of the deep woods, in a small clearing under a canopy of loblolly branches. She appears to be unconscious, lying in a patch of brambles. "Careful!" Chad Bingham calls out to his second-in-command, a skinny mechanic from Augusta by the name of Dick Fenster. "If she's still movin', she might've turned already!"

Nervous breaths showing in the chill air, Fenster cautiously goes over to the clearing with his snub-nosed .38 drawn and ready, hammer back, trigger finger twitching. He kneels down by Lilly, takes a good long look, and then turns back to the group. "She's all right! She's alive . . . ain't bit or nothing . . . still conscious!"

"Not for long," Chad Bingham utters under his breath as he marches toward the clearing. "Chickenshit fucking whore gets my baby killed—"

"Whoa! Whoa!" Megan Lafferty steps between Chad and the deadfall. "Hold on a second, hold on."

"Get outta my way, Megan."

"You gotta take a deep breath."

"Just gonna talk to her."

An awkward pause seems to weigh down on everybody present. The other members of the search party stand back in the trees, looking down, their drawn, exhausted faces reflecting the day's horrible work. Some of the men are red-eyed, stricken with loss.

Returning from their firewood-gathering expedition, the noise of their engines and axes still ringing in their ears, they were shocked to find the tent city in ghastly disarray. Both human and zombie alike littered the blood-soaked grounds, sixteen settlers slaughtered, some of them devoured—nine of them children. Josh Lee Hamilton did the dirty work of finishing off the remaining walkers and the unfortunate humans whose remains were left intact. Nobody else had the heart to shoot their friends and loved ones in the head to ensure their eternal rest. The incubation period—strangely—seems to be more and more unpredictable lately. Some victims reanimate within minutes after a bite. Others take hours—even days—to turn. At this moment, in fact, Josh is still back at camp, supervising a disposal crew, preparing the victims for mass burial. It'll take them another twenty-four hours to get the circus tent back up.

"Dude, listen, seriously," Megan Lafferty says to Chad, her voice lowering and becoming softly urgent. "I know you're torn up and all but she saved three of your girls. . . . I told you I saw it with my own eyes. She drew the walkers away, she fucking risked her life."

"I just—" Chad looks as though he's either going to cry or scream. "I just . . . want to talk."

"You got a wife back at camp's gonna lose her mind with grief . . . she needs you."

"I just—"

Another awkward beat of silence. One of the other fathers starts to softly weep in the shadows of the trees, his handgun falling to the ground. It's nearly five o'clock and the cold is squeezing in, the puffs of vapor wafting in front of all of their tortured faces. Across the clearing, Lilly sits up and wipes her mouth, and tries to get her bearings. She looks like a sleepwalker. Fenster helps her to her feet.

Chad looks down. "Fuck it." He turns and walks away, his voice trailing after him. "Fuck it."

The next day, under a frigid overcast sky, the tent dwellers have an improvised graveside service for their fallen friends and loved ones.

Nearly seventy-five survivors gather in a large semicircle around the mass burial site on the east edge of the property. Some of the mourners hold candles flickering stubbornly against the October winds. Others clutch at each other in convulsive grief. The searing pain on some of the faces—especially those of grieving parents—reflects the agonizing randomness of this plague world. Their children were taken with the arbitrary suddenness of a lightning bolt, and now the mourners' faces sag with desolation, their parboiled eyes shimmering in the unrelenting silver sunlight.

The cairns are set into the clay, stretching up the gentle rise of bare ground beyond the split-rail fence. Small piles of stones mark each of the sixteen graves. Some markers have hanks of wildflowers carefully wedged between the rocks. Josh Lee Hamilton made sure Sarah Bingham's marker got adorned with a lovely bouquet of little white Cherokee roses, which grow in profusion along the edges of the orchards. The big man had grown fond of the feisty, whip-smart teenager . . . and her death has wrenched his heart in two.

"God, we ask that you take our lost friends and neighbors into your hands," Josh says now from the edge of the fence, the wind buffeting his olive-drab army coat stretched across his massive shoulders. His deeply etched face glistens with tears.

Josh grew up Baptist, and although he lost most of his religion over the years, he asked his fellow survivors earlier this morning if he might say a few words. Baptists don't put much stock in prayers for the dead. They believe the righteous instantly go to heaven at the time of death—or, if you're a nonbeliever, you instantly go to hell—but Josh still felt obliged to say something.

He saw Lilly earlier in the day, and he held her for a moment, whispering words of comfort to her. But he could tell something was wrong. Something was going on inside her beyond mere grief. She felt limp in his enormous arms, her slender form trembling ceaselessly like a wounded bird. She said very little. Only that she needed to be alone. She didn't show up for the burial service.

"We ask that you take them to a better place," he goes on, his deep baritone voice cracking. The work of body disposal has taken its toll on the big man. He struggles to hold it together but his emotions are strangling his vocal chords. "We ask that you—you—"

He can't go on. He turns away, and he bows his head and lets the silent tears come. He can't breathe. He can't stay here. Barely aware of what he's doing, he finds himself moving away from the crowd, away from the soft, horrible sound of weeping and praying.

Among the many things he has missed today in his daze of sadness is the fact that Lilly Caul's decision to avoid the burial service is not the only conspicuous absence. Chad Bingham is also missing.

"Are you okay?" Lilly keeps her distance for a moment, standing on the edge of the clearing, wringing her hands nervously, about fifteen feet away from Chad Bingham.

The wiry man in the John Deere cap says nothing for the longest time. He just stands on the edge of the tree line, his head bowed, his back to her, his shoulders slumped as though carrying a great weight.

Minutes before the burial service began, Chad Bingham surprised Lilly by showing up at her tent and asking her if they could talk privately. He said he wanted to set things right. He said he didn't blame her for Sarah's death, and from the heartbreaking look in his eyes, Lilly believed him.

Which is why she followed him up here to a small clearing in the dense grove of trees lining the northern edge of the property. Barely two hundred square feet of pine-needle-matted ground, bordered by mossy stones, the clearing lies under a canopy of foliage, the gray sunlight filtering down in beams of thick dust motes. The cool air smells of decay and animal droppings.

The clearing is far enough away from the tent city to provide privacy.

"Chad—" Lilly wants to say something, wants to tell him how sorry she is. For the first time since she met the man—initially appalled by his willingness to conduct a dalliance with Megan right under his wife's nose—Lilly now sees Chad Bingham as simply human . . . imperfect, scared, emotional, confused, and devastated by the loss of his little girl.

In other words, he's just some good old boy—no better or worse than any of the other survivors. And now Lilly feels a wave of sympathy washing over her. "You want to talk about it?" she asks him at last.

"Yeah, I guess . . . maybe not . . . I don't know." His back still turned, his voice comes out like a leaky faucet, in fits and starts, as faint as water dripping. The sorrow knots his shoulder blades, makes him tremble slightly in the shadows of the pines.

"I'm so sorry, Chad." Lilly ventures closer to him. She has tears in her eyes. "I loved Sarah, she was such a wonderful girl."

He says something so softly Lilly cannot hear it. She moves closer.

She puts her hand gently on the man's shoulder. "I know there's nothing anybody can say . . . a time like this." She speaks to the back of his head. The little plastic strap on the back of his cap says SPALDING. He has a small tattoo of a snake between the cords of his neck. "I know it's no consolation," Lilly adds then, "but Sarah died a hero—she saved the lives of her sisters."

"Did she?" His voice rises barely above a whisper. "She was such a good girl."

"I know she was . . . she was an amazing girl."

"You think so?" His back still turned. Head bowed. Softly shuddering shoulders.

"Yes I do, Chad, she was a hero, she was one in a million."

"Really? You think so?"

"Absolutely."

"Then why didn't you do your *FUCKING JOB*!" Chad turns around and strikes Lilly so hard with the back of his hand that she bites through her tongue. Her head whiplashes, and she sees stars.

Chad hits her again and she stumbles backward, tripping over an exposed root and tumbling to the ground. Chad looms over her, his fists clenching, his eyes blazing. "You stupid, worthless bitch! All you had to do is protect my girls! Fucking chimpanzee could do that!"

Lilly tries to roll away but Chad drives the steel toe of his work boot into her hip, tossing her sideways. Pain stabs her midsection. She gasps for air, her mouth filling with blood. "P-please duh—"

He reaches down and yanks her back to her feet. Holding her up by the front of her sweatshirt, he hisses at her, his sour breath hot on her face, "You and your little slutty friend think this is a party? You smoking dope last night? Huh? HUH?"

Chad smashes a right hook into Lilly's jaw, cracking her teeth and sending her back to the ground. She lands in a heap of agony, two of her ribs cracked, the blood choking her. She can't breathe. Icy cold spreads through her and blurs her vision.

She can barely focus on Chad Bingham's ropy, compact form hovering over her, dropping down on her with tremendous weight, straddling her, the drool of uncontrollable rage leaking out of the corner of his mouth, his spittle flying. "Answer me! You been smoking weed when you're with my kids?"

Lilly feels Chad's powerful grip closing around her throat, the back of her head banging off the ground now. "ANSWER ME, YOU FFFUHHHH—"

Without warning, a third figure materializes behind Chad Bingham—pulling him off Lilly—the identity of this rescuer barely visible.

Lilly only sees a blur of a man so enormous he blots out the rays of the sun.

Josh gets two good handfuls of Chad Bingham's denim jacket and then yanks with all his might.

Either through a sudden spike of adrenaline coursing through the big man, or simply due to Chad's relatively scrawny girth, the resulting heave-ho makes Chad Bingham look like a human cannonball. He soars across the clearing in a high arc, one of his boots flying off, his cap spinning into the trees. He slams shoulder first into an enormous ancient tree trunk. His breath flies out of him, and he flops to the ground in front of the tree. He gasps for breath, blinking with shock.

Josh kneels by Lilly and gently raises her bloody face. She tries to speak but can't get her bleeding lips around the words. Josh lets out a pained breath—a sort of gut-shot moan. Something about seeing that lovely face—with its sea-foam eyes and delicately freckled cheeks, now stippled with blood—sends him into a rage that draws a gauzy filter down over his eyes.

The big man rises, turns, and marches across the clearing to where Chad Bingham lies writhing in pain.

Josh can see only the milky-white blur of the man on the ground, the pale sunlight beaming down through the musty air. Chad makes a feeble attempt to crawl away but Josh easily catches the man's retreating legs, and with a single decisive yank, Chad's body is wrenched back in front of the tree. Josh stands the wiry man up against the trunk.

Chad stammers with blood in his mouth. "This ain't—it ain't none of your—pleeeease—m-my brother—you don't have to DDUHHH—!"

Josh slams the man's flailing body against the bark of the hundred-year-old black oak. The impact cracks the man's skull and dislocates his shoulder blades with the violent abruptness of a battering ram.

Chad lets out a garbled, mucusy cry—more primal and involuntary than conscious—his eyes rolling back in his head. If Chad Bingham were repeatedly hit from behind by a massive battering ram, the series of impacts would not rival the force with which Josh Lee Hamilton now begins slamming the sinewy man in denim against the tree.

"I'm not your brother," Josh says with eerie calm, a low velvety voice from some hidden, inaccessible place deep within him, as he bangs the rag doll of a man against the tree again and again.

Josh rarely loses control like this. Only a handful of times in his life has it happened: Once, on the gridiron when an opposing offensive tackle—a good old boy from Montgomery—called him a nigger . . . and on another occasion when a pickpocket in Atlanta grabbed his mother's purse. But now the quiet storm inside him rages harder than ever before—his actions unmoored and yet somehow controlled—as he repeatedly slams the back of Chad Bingham's cranium against the tree.

Chad's head flops with each impact, the sick thud getting more and more watery now as the back of the skull caves. Vomit roars out of Chad—again an involuntary phenomenon—the particles of cereal and yellow bile looping down, unnoticed, across Josh Lee Hamilton's ham-hock forearms. Josh notices Chad's left hand groping for the grip of his steel-plated Smith & Wesson tucked inside the back of his belt.

Josh easily tears the pistol out of Chad's pants and tosses the weapon across the clearing.

With his last scintilla of strength, his brain sputtering from multiple concussions and the hemorrhage leaking out the back of his fractured skull, Chad Bingham makes a futile attempt to drive a knee up into the big man's groin, but Josh quickly and handily blocks the knee with one forearm, and then delivers an extraordinary blow—a great winding backhand slap, a surreal echo of the slap delivered moments ago to Lilly—which sends Chad Bingham hurling sideways.

Chad sprawls to the ground fifteen feet away from the tree trunk.

Josh can't hear Lilly stumbling across the clearing. He can't hear her strangled voice, "Josh, NO! NO! JOSH, STOP, YOU'RE GOING TO KILL HIM!!"

All at once, Josh Lee Hamilton wakes up, and blinks as though discovering that he's been sleepwalking and has found himself naked and wandering down Peachtree Boulevard during rush hour. He feels Lilly's hands on his back, clawing at his coat, trying to yank him back and away from the man lying in a heap on the ground.

"You're gonna kill him!"

Josh whirls. He sees Lilly—bruised and battered, her mouth full of blood, barely able to stand or breathe or speak—directly behind him, her watery gaze locked on to his. He pulls her into an embrace, his eyes welling with tears. "Are you okay?"

"I'm fine . . . please, Josh . . . you have to stop before you kill him."

Josh starts to say something else but stops himself. He turns and looks down at the man on the ground. Over the course of that terrible, silent pause—as Josh moves his lips but is unable to make a sound or put a thought into words—he sees the deflated body on the ground, lying in a pool of its own fluids, as still and lifeless as a bundle of rags.

FOUR

"Hold still, honey." Bob Stookey gently turns Lilly's head so he can get a better angle on her fat lip. He carefully dabs a pea-sized amount of antibiotic on the split, scabbed flesh. "Almost done."

Lilly jerks at the pain. Bob kneels next to her, his first-aid kit open on the edge of the cot on which Lilly lies prone, staring up at the canvas ceiling. The tent glows with the pale rays of late-afternoon sun, which shine through the stained fabric walls. The air is cold and smells of disinfectant and stale liquor. Lilly has a blanket draped across her bare midriff and bra.

Bob needs a drink. He needs one badly. His hands are shaking again. Lately, he's been flashing back to his days in the U.S. Marine Hospital Corps. One tour in Afghanistan eleven years ago, emptying bedpans at Camp Dwyer—it seems like a million light years away—could never have prepared him for *this*. He was on the sauce back then as well, barely made it out of Medical Education and Training in San Antonio due to the drinking, and now the war has come home for Bob. The shrapnel-riddled bodies he patched in the Middle East were nothing compared to the battlefields left behind in the wake of *this* war. Bob has dreams of Afghanistan sometimes— the walking dead mingling and infecting the ranks of the Taliban in Grand Guignol fashion—the cold, dead, gray arms sprouting from the walls of mobile surgical suites.

But patching Lilly Caul is an altogether different proposition for Bob—far worse than being a battlefield medic or cleaning up the aftermath of a walker attack. Bingham did a number on her. Best Bob can tell, she has at least three busted ribs, a major contusion to her left eye—which may or may not involve a vitreous hemorrhage or even retinal detachment—as well as a nasty series of bruises and lacerations to her face. Bob feels ill-equipped—both in technique and medical supplies—to even *pretend* to treat her. But Bob is the only game in town around here, and so he has now jury-rigged a splint of bedsheets, hardback book covers, and elastic bandages around Lilly's midsection and has applied his dwindling supply of antibiotic cream to her superficial wounds. The eye worries him the most. He needs to watch it, make sure it heals properly.

"There we go," he says, applying the last daub of the cream to her lip.

"Thanks, Bob." Lilly's speech is impeded by the swelling, a slight lisp on the *s*. "You can send your bill to my insurance company."

Bob lets out a humorless chuckle and helps her pull her coat back over her bandaged midsection and bruised shoulders. "What the hell happened out there?"

Lilly sighs, sitting up on the cot, gingerly zipping the coat and cringing at the stabbing pains. "Things got a little . . . carried away."

Bob finds his dented flask of cheap hooch, sits back on his folding chair, and takes a long medicinal swig. "At the risk of stating the obvious . . . this ain't good for anybody."

Lilly swallows as though trying to digest broken glass. Tendrils of her auburn hair dangle in her face. "You're telling me."

"They're meeting right now in the big top about it."

"Who is?"

"Simmons, Hennessey, some of the older guys, Alice Burnside . . . you know . . . sons and daughters of the revolution. Josh is . . . well, I've never seen him like this. He's pretty messed up. Just sitting on the ground outside his tent like a sphinx . . . ain't saying a word . . . just staring into space. Says he'll go along with whatever they decide."

"What does that mean?"

Bob takes another healthy sip of his medicine. "Lilly, this is all new. Somebody murdered a living person. These people ain't dealt with anything like this before."

"*'Murdered'?*"

"Lilly—"

"That's what they're calling it now?"

"I'm just saying—"

"I gotta go talk to them." Lilly tries to stand but the pain drives her back to the edge of the cot.

"Whoa there, Kemo sabe. Take it easy." Bob leans over and gently steadies her. "I just gave you enough codeine to calm a Clydesdale."

"Goddammit, Bob, they're not going to lynch Josh for this, I'm not gonna let that happen."

"Let's just take it one step at a time. You ain't goin' nowhere right now."

Lilly lowers her head. A single tear wells up and drips from her good eye. "It was an accident, Bob."

Bob looks at her. "Maybe let's just focus on healing right now, huh?"

Lilly looks up at him. Her busted lip is swollen to three times its normal size, her left eye shot with red, the socket already blackened and bruised. She pulls the collar of her thrift shop overcoat tighter and shivers against the cold. She wears a number of oddball accessories that catch Bob's eye: macramé bracelets and beads and tiny feathers woven into the tendrils of amber locks falling across her devastated face. It's curious to Bob Stookey how a girl can still pay attention to fashion in this world. But that is part of Lilly Caul's charm, part of the fiber of her being. From the little fleur-de-lis tattoo on the back of her neck to the meticulous rips and patches in her jeans, she is one of those girls who can make ten dollars and an afternoon at a secondhand store stretch into an entire wardrobe. "This is all my fault, Bob," she says in a hoarse, somnolent voice.

"That's a load of crap," Bob Stookey counters after taking another pull off the tarnished flask. Maybe the liquor has begun to loosen Bob's lips, because he feels a twinge of bitterness. "My guess is, knowin' that Chad character, he'd been asking for this for a while now."

"Bob, that's not—"

Lilly stops herself when she hears the crunch of footsteps outside the tent. The shadow of a leviathan falls across the canvas. The familiar silhouette pauses for a moment, lurking awkwardly outside the zippered front flap of Bob's tent. Lilly recognizes the figure but says nothing.

A huge hand gently folds back the tent flap and a large, deeply lined brown face peers in. "They said I could—they gave me three minutes," Josh Lee Hamilton says in a choked, sheepish baritone.

"What are you talking about?" Lilly sits up and stares at her friend. "Three minutes for what?"

Josh kneels in front of the tent flap, looking at the ground, struggling to tamp down his emotions. "Three minutes to say good-bye."

"*Good-bye?*"

"Yeah."

"What do you mean, *'good-bye'*? What happened?"

Josh lets out a pained sigh. "They took a vote . . . decided the best way to deal with what happened was to send me packing, kick me outta the group."

"*What!*"

"I suppose it's better than gettin' hung from the highest tree."

"You didn't—I mean—it was completely accidental."

"Yeah, sure," Josh says, staring at the ground. "Poor fella accidentally bumped into my fist a whole bunch of times."

"Under the circumstances, though, these people know what kind of man—"

"Lilly—"

"No, this is wrong. This is just . . . wrong."

"It's over, Lilly."

She looks at him. "Are they letting you take any supplies? One of the vehicles maybe?"

"I got my bike. It'll be okay, I'll be awright . . ."

"No . . . no . . . this is just . . . *ridiculous.*"

"Lilly, listen to me." The big man pushes his way partially into the tent. Bob glances away out of respect. Josh crouches down, reaches out and gently touches Lilly's wounded face. From the way Josh's lips are pressed together, the way his eyes are shimmering, the lines deepening around his mouth, it's clear he's holding in a tidal wave of emotion. "This is how it's gotta play out. It's for the best. I'll be fine. You and Bob hold the fort down."

Lilly's eyes well up. "I'll go with you, then."

"Lilly—"

"There's nothing for me here."

Josh shakes his head. "Sorry, babydoll . . . it's a single ticket."

"I'm coming with you."

"Lilly, I'm real sorry but that ain't in the cards. It's safer here. With the group."

"Yeah, it's real stable here," she says icily. "It's a regular love fest."

"Better here than out there."

Lilly looks at him through ravaged eyes, tears beginning to track down her battered face. "You can't stop me, Josh. It's my decision. I'm coming along and that's all there is to it. And if you try and stop me, I will hunt you down, I will stalk you, I will find you. I'm coming with you and there's nothing you can do about it. You can't stop me. Okay? So just . . . deal with it."

She buttons up her coat, slips her feet into her boots, and starts gathering up her things. Josh watches in dismay. Lilly's movements are tentative, interrupted by intermittent flinches of pain.

Bob exchanges a glance with Josh, something unspoken yet powerful passing between the two men, as Lilly gets all her stray items of clothing stuffed into a duffel bag and pushes her way out of the tent.

Josh lingers in the mouth of the tent for a moment, looking back in at Bob.

Bob finally shrugs and says with a weary smile: *"Women."*

Fifteen minutes later, Josh has the saddlebags of his onyx Suzuki street bike brimming with tins of Spam and tuna fish, road flares, blankets, waterproof matches, rope, a rolled-up pup tent, a flashlight, a small camp stove, a collapsible fishing rod, a small .38 caliber Saturday night special, and some paper plates and spices cribbed from the common area. The day has turned blustery, the sky casting over with ashy dark clouds.

The threatening weather adds another layer of anxiety to the proceedings as Josh secures the luggage bags and glances over his shoulder at Lilly, who stands ten feet away on the edge of the road, shrugging on an overstuffed backpack. She cringes at a sharp pain in her ribs as she tightens the straps on the pack.

From across the property, a handful of self-proclaimed community leaders look on. Three men and a middle-aged woman stand stoically watching. Josh wants to holler something sarcastic and withering to them but holds his tongue. Instead, he turns to Lilly and says, "You ready?"

Before Lilly can answer a voice rings out from the east edge of the property.

"Hold on, folks!"

Bob Stookey comes trundling along the fence with a large canvas duffel slung over his back. The clanking rattle of bottles can be heard—Bob's private stock of "medicine," no doubt—and there's a strange look on the old medic's face, a mixture of anticipation and embarrassment. He approaches cautiously. "Before y'all ride off into the sunset, I got a question for ya."

Josh gives the man a look. "What's going on, Bob?"

"Just answer me one thing," he says. "You got any medical training?"

Lilly comes over, her brow furrowed with confusion. "Bob, what do you need?"

"It's a simple question. Do either of you yahoos got any legitimate medical credentials?"

Josh and Lilly share a glance. Josh sighs. "Not that I know of, Bob."

"Then let me ask you something else. Who in the flying fuck's gonna watch that eye for infection?" He gestures toward Lilly's hemorrhaged eye. "Or keep tabs on them fractured ribs for that matter?"

Josh looks at the medic. "What are you trying to say, Bob?"

The older man shoots a thumb at the row of vehicles parked along the gravel access road behind him. "As long as y'all are gallivanting off into the wild blue yonder, wouldn't it make more sense to do it with a certified U.S. Marine Medical Corpsman?"

They put their stuff in Bob's king cab. The old Dodge Ram pickup is a monster—pocked with rust scars and dents—with a retrofitted camper top on the extended cargo bay. The camper's windows are long and narrow and as opaque as soap glass. Lilly's backpack and Josh's saddlebags go in through the rear hatch, and get wedged between piles of dirty clothes and half-empty bottles of cheap whiskey. There's a pair of rickety cots back there, a large cooler, three battered first-aid kits, a tattered suitcase, a pair of fuel tanks, an old leather doctor's bag that looks like it came from a pawnshop, and a phalanx of garden implements shoved against the firewall in front—shovels, a hoe, a few axes, and a nasty-looking pitchfork. The vaulted ceiling rises high enough to accommodate a slouching adult.

As he stows his bags, Josh sees scattered pieces of a disassembled 12-gauge shotgun, but no sign of any shells. Bob carries a .38 snubnose, which probably couldn't hit a stationary target at ten paces with no wind—and that's if and only if Bob is sober, which is rarely the case. Josh knows they will need firearms and ammunition if they want a fighting chance of survival.

Josh slams the hatch and feels somebody else watching them from across the property.

"Hey, Lil!"

The voice sounds familiar, and when Josh turns around, he sees Megan Lafferty, the girl with the ruddy brown curls and unhinged libido, standing a couple of car lengths away, next to the gravel shoulder. She holds hands with the stoner kid—what's his name?—with the stringy blond hair in his face and the ratty sweater. Steve? Shawn? Josh can't remember. All Josh remembers is putting up with the girl's bed-hopping all the way from Peachtree City.

Now the two slacker kids stand there, watching with buzzard-like intensity.

"Hey, Meg," Lilly says softly, somewhat skeptically, as she comes around the back of the truck and stands next to Josh. The sound of Bob banging around under the truck's hood can be heard in the awkward silence.

Megan and the stoner kid approach cautiously. Megan measures her words as she addresses Lilly: "Dude, I heard you were like taking off for higher ground."

Next to Megan the stoner giggles softly. "Always up for getting *higher*."

Josh shoots the kid a look. "What can we do for you fine young people?"

Megan doesn't take her eyes off Lilly. "Lil, I just wanted to say . . . like . . . I hope you're not like pissed at me or anything."

"Why would I be pissed at *you*?"

Megan looks down. "I said some things the other day, I wasn't really thinking straight . . . I just wanted to . . . I don't know. Just wanted to say I was sorry."

Josh glances over at Lilly, and in that brief moment of silence before she responds, he sees the essence of Lilly Caul in a single instant. Her bruised face softens. Her eyes fill with forgiveness. "You don't have to be sorry for anything, Meg," Lilly tells her friend. "We're all just trying to keep our shit together."

"He really fucked you up bad," Megan says, pondering the ravages of Lilly's face.

"Lilly, we gotta get going," Josh chimes in. "Gonna be dark soon."

The stoner kid whispers to Megan, "You gonna ask them or what?"

"Ask us what, Meg?" Lilly says.

Megan licks her lips. She looks up at Josh. "It's totally fucked up, the way they're treating you."

Josh gives her a terse nod. "Appreciate it, Megan, but we really have to be taking off."

"Take us with you."

Josh looks at Lilly, and Lilly stares at her friend. Finally Lilly says, "Um, see, the thing is . . ."

"Safety in fucking numbers, man," the stoner kid enthuses with his dry little nervous pot giggle. "We're like totally in *warrior mode*—"

Megan shoots her hand up. "Scott, would you put a cork in it for *two minutes*." She looks up at Josh. "We can't stay here with these fascist assholes. Not after what happened. It's a fucking mess here, people don't trust each other anymore."

Josh crosses his big arms across his barrel chest, looking at Megan. "You've done your share to stir things up."

"Josh—" Lilly starts to intercede.

Megan suddenly looks down with a crestfallen expression. "No, it's okay. I deserve that. I guess I just . . . I just forgot what the rules are."

In the ensuing silence—the only sounds the wind in the trees and the squeaking noises of Bob futzing under the hood—Josh rolls his eyes. He can't believe what he's about to agree to. "Get your stuff," he says finally, "and be quick about it."

Megan and Scott ride in back. Bob drives, with Josh on the passenger side and Lilly in the narrow enclosure in the rear of the cab. The truck has a modified sleeping berth behind the front seat with smaller side doors and a flip-down upholstered bench that doubles as a bed. Lilly sits on the tattered bench seat and braces herself on the handrail, every bump and swerve coaxing a stabbing pain in her ribs.

She can see the tree line on either side of the road darkening as they drive down the winding access road that leads out of the orchards, the shadows of late afternoon lengthening, the temperature plummeting. The truck's noisy heater fights a losing battle against the chill. The air in the cab smells of stale liquor, smoke, and body odors. Through the vents, the scent of tobacco fields and rotting fruit—the musk of a Georgia autumn—is faintly discernible, a warning to Lilly, a harbinger of cutting loose from civilization.

She starts looking for walkers in the trees—every shadow, every dark place a potential menace. The sky is void of planes or birds of any species, the heavens as cold, dead, and silent as a vast gray glacier.

They make their way onto Spur 362—the main conduit that cuts through Meriwether County—as the sun sinks lower on the horizon. Due to the proliferation of wrecks and abandoned cars, Bob takes it nice and easy, keeping the truck down around thirty-five miles an hour. The two-lane turns blue-gray in the encroaching dusk, the twilight spreading across the rolling hills of white pine and soybeans.

"What's the plan, captain?" Bob asks Josh after they've put a mile and a half behind them.

"Plan?" Josh lights a cigar and rolls down the window. "You

must be mistaking me for one of them battlefield commanders you used to sew up in Iraq."

"I was never in Iraq," Bob says. He has a flask between his legs. He sneaks a sip. "Did a nickel's worth in Afghanistan, and to be honest with ya, that place is looking better and better to me."

"All I can tell ya is, they told me to get outta town, and that's what I'm doin'."

They pass a crossroads, a sign that says FILBURN ROAD, a dusty, desolate farm path lined with ditches, running between two tobacco fields. Josh makes note of it and starts thinking about the wisdom of being on the open road after dark. He starts to say, "I'm startin' to think, though, maybe we shouldn't stray too far from—"

"Josh!" Lilly's voice pierces the rattling drone of the cab. "Walkers— look!"

Josh realizes that she's pointing at the distant highway ahead of them, at a point maybe five hundred yards away. Bob slams on the brakes. The truck skids, throwing Lilly against the seat. Sharp pain like a jagged piece of glass slices through her ribs. The muffled thump of Megan and Scott slamming into the firewall in back penetrates the cab.

"Son of a buck!" Bob grips the steering wheel with weathered, wrinkled hands, his knuckles turning white with pressure as the truck idles noisily. "Son of a five-pointed *buck*!"

Josh sees the cluster of zombies in the distance, at least forty or fifty of them—maybe more, the twilight can play tricks—swarming around an overturned school bus. From this distance, it looks as though the bus has spilled clumps of wet clothing, through which the dead are sorting busily. But it quickly becomes clear the lumps are human remains. And the walkers are feeding.

And the victims are children.

"We could just ram our way through 'em," Bob ventures.

"No . . . no," Lilly says. "You serious?"

"We could go around 'em."

"I don't know." Josh tosses the cigar through the vent, his pulse quickening. "Them ditches on either side are steep, could roll us over."

"What do you suggest?"

"What do you have in the way of shells for that squirrel gun you got back there?"

Bob lets out a tense breath. "Got one box of pigeon shot, 25-grain, about a million years old. What about that peashooter?"

"Just what's in the cylinder, I think there's five rounds left and that's it."

Bob glances in the rearview mirror. Lilly sees his deeply lined eyes sparking with panic. Bob is looking at Lilly when he says, "Thoughts?"

Lilly says, "Okay, so even if we take out most of them, the noise is gonna draw a swarm. You ask me, I say we avoid them altogether."

Right then, a muffled thudding noise makes Lilly jump. Her ribs twinge as she twists around. In the narrow little window on the back wall of the cab, Megan's pale, anxious face hovers. She pounds her palm on the glass and mouths the words *What the fuck?*

"Hold on! It's okay! Just hold on!" Lilly yells through the glass, then turns to Josh. "Whaddaya think?"

Josh looks out his window at the long, rust-dimpled mirror. In the oblong reflection, he sees the lonely crossroads about three hundred yards back, barely visible in the dying light. "Back up," he says.

Bob looks at him. "Say what?"

"Back up . . . hurry. We're gonna take that side road back there."

Bob jacks the lever into reverse and steps on it. The truck lurches.

The engine whines, the gravitational tug pulling everybody forward.

Bob bites his lower lip as he wrestles the steering wheel, using the side mirror to guide him, the truck careening backward, the front end fishtailing, the gears screaming. The rear end approaches the crossroads.

Bob locks up the brakes and Josh slams into his seat as the truck's rear end skids off the far shoulder of the two-lane, tangling with a knot of wild dogwood, cattails, and mayapple, sending up a cloud of leaves and debris. No one hears the shuffling sounds of something dead stirring behind the scrub brush.

No one hears the faint scrape of the dead thing lumbering out of the foliage and clamping its dead fingers around the king cab's rear bumper until it's too late.

Inside the rear camper compartment, each of them tumbling to the floor in the violent pitching motions of the truck, each of them giggling hysterically, Megan and Scott are oblivious to the zombie now attached to the running board in the rear. As the Dodge Ram slams into drive and blasts down the perpendicular dirt road, they each climb back onto their makeshift seats fashioned out of peach crates, each still giggling furiously.

The air inside the cramped camper is blue from the haze of an entire bowl of sativa weed, which Scott fired up ten minutes ago. He's been conserving his stash, nursing it, dreading the inevitable day he would run out and would have to figure out how to grow it in the sandy clay.

"You just farted when you fell," Scott chortles at Megan, his eyes already dreamy and blistered with a major buzz humming behind his eyes.

"I most certainly did not," she counters in her uncontrollable giggle, trying to balance herself on the crate. "That was my fucking shoe scraping the fucking floor."

"Bullshit, dude, you *so* farted."

"Did not."

"You did, you *so did*—you just ripped one, and it was such a girl fart."

Megan roars with laughter. "What the fucking hell is a girl fart?"

Scott guffaws. "It's—it's kinda like—kinda like a cute little toot. Like a little train engine. *Toot-toot.* The little fart that could . . ."

They both bend over with an uncontainable spasm of hilarity as a livid, milky-eyed face rises up like a small moon in the dark surface of the window at the rear of the camper. This one is male and middle-aged and nearly bald, its scalp mapped with deep blue veins and wisps of mildew-gray hair.

Neither Megan nor Scott sees it at first. They don't see the wind blowing its mossy strands of thinning hair, or its greasy lips peeling back to expose blackened teeth, or the fumbling of insensate, rotting fingers as they push through the gap in the partially sprung hatch.

"OH, SHIT!" Scott blurts the words out on a stutter of sputtering laughter when he sees the intruder boarding. "OH, SHIT!!"

Megan now doubles over with convulsive laughter as Scott spins and falls on his face and then scuttles madly across the narrow floor space on his hands and knees toward the garden implements. He's not laughing anymore. The zombie is already halfway inside the camper. The sound of its buzz-saw snarl and the stench of its decomposed tissues fill the air. Megan finally sees the intruder and she starts to cough and wheeze, her laughter garbling slightly.

Scott reaches for the pitchfork. The truck swerves. The zombie—all the way inside now—stumbles drunkenly sideways and slams into the wall. A stack of crates tumbles. Scott gets the pitchfork up and moving.

Megan scuttles backward, sliding along on her ass, burrowing into the far corner. The terror in her eyes seems incongruous with her high-pitched, hiccupping giggles. Like a motor that won't stop turning, her garbled, deranged laughter continues as Scott stands up on wobbling knees and lunges with the pitchfork as hard as he can in the general direction of the moving corpse in front of him.

The rusty tines strike the side of the thing's face as it's turning.

One of the spikes impales the zombie's left eye. The other points go into the mandible and jugular. Black blood ejaculates across the camper. Scott lets out a war cry and pulls the implement free. The zombie staggers backward toward the windblown hatch—which is flapping now—and for some reason, the second blow gets a huge, convulsive, crazed laugh out of Megan.

The tines sink into the thing's skull.

This is so goddamn hilarious to Megan: the funny dead man shuddering as though electrocuted, with the fork sunk in his skull, his arms reaching impotently at the air. Like a silly circus clown in whiteface, with big goofy black teeth, the thing staggers backward for a moment, until the wind pressure pulls it out of the flapping rear hatch.

The pitchfork slips free of Scott's grasp and the zombie tumbles off the truck. Scott falls on his ass, landing in a pile of clothes.

Both Megan and Scott crack up now at the absurdity of the

zombie careening to the road with the pitchfork still planted in its skull. They both scuttle on hands and knees to the rear hatch and gaze out at the human remains receding into the distance behind them—the pitchfork still sticking straight out of its head like a mile marker.

Scott pulls the hatch shut and they both crack up again in spasms of stoned laughter and frenzied coughing.

Still giggling, her eyes wet, Megan turns toward the front of the camper. Through the cab window, she can see the backs of Lilly's and Josh's heads. They look preoccupied—oblivious to what just occurred only inches away from them. They appear to be pointing at something in the distance, way up on the crest of an adjacent hill.

Megan can't believe that nobody in the cab heard the commotion in the rear camper. Was the road noise that loud? Was the struggle drowned out by the sound of giggling? Megan is about to bang on the glass when she finally sees what all the pointing is about.

Bob is turning off the road and heading up a steep dirt path toward a building that may or may not be abandoned.

FIVE

The deserted gas station sits at the top of a hill overlooking the surrounding orchards. Bordered on three sides by weed-whiskered
clapboard fencing and scattered garbage Dumpsters, the place has a
hand-painted sign over its twin fuel islands—one diesel and three
gas pumps—which says FORTNOY'S FUEL AND BAIT. The single-story
building features a flyspecked office, a retail store, and a small service garage with a single lift.

When Bob pulls in to the cracked cement lot—his lights off in
order to avoid detection—night has fallen into full darkness, and
the king cab's tires crunch on broken glass. Megan and Scott peer
out of the rear hatch, taking in the shadows of the abandoned property, as Bob pulls the truck around behind the garage area, out of
the line of vision of any nosy passersby.

He parks the truck between the carcass of a wrecked sedan and a
pillar of tires. A moment later, the engine cuts off and Megan hears
the squeak of the passenger door and the heavy thud of Josh Lee
Hamilton stepping out and coming around the back of the camper.

"Y'all stay put for a second," Josh says softly, evenly, after opening the camper door and seeing Megan and Scott crouched near the
hatch like a couple of owls. Josh doesn't notice the blood spatters on
the walls. He checks the cylinder of his .38, the blue steel gleaming
in the darkness. "Gonna check this place for walkers."

"I don't mean to be rude but *what the fuck*?" Megan says, her buzz
completely gone now, replaced by a kind of jagged adrenaline surge.

"Didn't you guys see what happened back here? Didn't you hear what was going on?"

Josh looks at her. "All I heard was a couple of potheads partying to beat the band—smells like Mardi Gras in a whorehouse back here."

Megan tells him what happened.

Josh gives Scott a look. "Surprised you had the wherewithal . . . your brain scrambled like that." Josh's expression softens. He lets out a sigh and smiles at the kid. "Congratulations, junior."

Scott gives him a cockeyed little grin. "My first kill, boss."

"Chances are it won't be your last," Josh says, snapping the cylinder shut.

"Can I just like ask one more thing?" Megan says then. "What're we *doing* here? I thought we had enough gas."

"It's too hairy out there for night travel. Best to hunker down till morning. Gonna need you two to stay put until you get the all clear."

Josh walks off.

Megan shuts the door. In the darkness, she feels Scott's gaze on her. She turns and looks at him. He has a weird look in his eyes. She grins at him. "Dude, I gotta admit, you *are* pretty damn handy with the garden tools—pretty goddamn bad-ass with that pitchfork."

He grins back at her. Something changes in his eyes, as though he sees her for the first time—despite the darkness—and he licks his lips. He wipes a strand of dirty blond hair from his eyes. "It was nothing."

"Yeah, right." For a while now, Megan has been marveling at how much Scott Moon resembles Kurt Cobain. The resemblance seems to radiate off him with atavistic magic, his face shimmering in the darkness, his scent—patchouli oil and smoke and sweet-leaf and bubble gum—casting out and swirling in Megan's brain.

She grabs him and mashes her lips on top of his, and he pulls her hair, and grinds his mouth into hers, and soon their tongues are intertwined and their midsections are gnashing against each other.

"Fuck me," she whispers.

"Here?" he utters. "Now?"

"Maybe not," she says, looking around, breathless. Her heart races. "Let's wait until he's done inside and we'll find a place."

"Cool," he says, and he reaches out and fondles her through her torn Grateful Dead T-shirt. She jams her tongue in his mouth. Megan needs him now, this instant—she needs relief, badly.

She pulls away. In the darkness, the twosome stare at each other, breathing hard, like wild animals that would kill each other if they weren't the same species.

Megan and Scott find a place to consummate their lust only moments after Josh issues the all clear.

The two stoners don't fool anybody, in spite of their perfunctory attempts to be discreet: Megan feigns exhaustion and Scott suggests that he fix her a place to sleep on the floor of the storeroom in the rear of the retail shop. The cramped storage area—two hundred square feet of mildewed tile and exposed plumbing—reeks of dead fish and cheese bait. Josh tells them to be careful and rolls his eyes as he walks away, disgusted, and maybe, just maybe, a little jealous.

The thumping sounds start up almost immediately, even before Josh returns to the office, where Lilly and Bob are unpacking a knapsack full of supplies for the night. "What the hell is that?" Lilly asks the big man when he returns.

Josh shakes his head. The muffled thudding noises of two bodies going at it in the other room reverberate through the tight quarters of the filling station. Every few moments, a gasp or a moan swells above the rhythmic fucking sounds. "Young love," he says with exasperation.

"You gotta be kidding me." Lilly stands shivering in the dark front office as Bob Stookey nervously unpacks bottled water and blankets from a crate, pretending not to hear the carnal noises. Lilly holds herself as though she might disintegrate at any moment. "So this is what we have to look forward to?"

The power at Fortnoy's is down, the fuel reservoirs empty, and the air in the building as cold as a walk-in refrigerator. The retail shop appears to be picked clean. Even the filthy refrigerator is emptied of earthworms and minnows. The front office features a dusty rack of magazines, a single vending machine running low on stale candy bars and bags of chips, rolls of toilet paper, a few overturned plastic contour chairs, a shelf of antifreeze and car deodorizers, and a scarred wooden counter on which sits a cash register that looks like it belongs in the Smithsonian. The register's drawer is open and empty.

"Maybe they'll get it out of their systems." Josh checks his last cigar, which sits partially burned down in his jacket pocket. He glances around the office for a smoke rack. The place looks ransacked. "Looks like the Fortnoy boys left in a hurry."

Lilly touches her bruised eye. "Yeah, I guess the looters got here before we did."

"How you holdin' up?" Josh asks her.

"I'll live."

Bob glances up from his crate of supplies. "Have a seat, Lillygirl." He positions one of the contour chairs against the window. The light of the harvest moon shines in and stripes the floor in silver dusty shadows as Bob cleans his hands with a sterile wipe. "Let's check them bandages."

Josh watches as Lilly takes a seat and Bob opens a first-aid kit.

"Hold still now," Bob admonishes softly as he carefully dabs an alcohol wipe around the crusty edges of Lilly's injured eye. The skin under her brow has swollen to the size of a hardboiled egg. Lilly keeps flinching, and that bothers Josh. He bites back the urge to go to her, to hold her, to stroke her downy soft hair. The sight of those wavy mahogany tendrils dangling down across her narrow, delicate, bruised face is killing the big man.

"Ouch!" Lilly cringes. "Go easy, Bob."

"Got a nasty shiner there, but if we can keep it clean, you oughtta be good to go."

"Go where?"

"That's a damn good question." Bob carefully unhooks the Ace bandage around her ribs, gently palpates the bruised areas with his fingertips. Lilly flinches again. "Ribs ought to heal on their own, as long as you don't get into any wrestling matches or marathon races."

Bob replaces the elastic bandage around her midriff, then puts a fresh butterfly bandage on her eye. Lilly gazes up at the big man. "What are you thinking, Josh?"

Josh looks around the place. "We'll spend the night here, take turns keeping watch."

Bob tears off a piece of surgical tape. "Gonna get colder than a witch's boob in here."

Josh sighs. "Saw a generator in the garage, and we got blankets. Place is pretty secure and we're up high enough on this ridge to see any large numbers of them things forming out there before they get to us."

Bob finishes up and closes the first-aid kit. The muffled sounds of fornication dwindle in the other room, a momentary break in the action. In that brief stretch of silence, over the sound of the wind rattling the signage out front, Josh hears the distant a cappella of the dead—that faint telltale throb of dead vocal cords—like a broken pipe organ, moaning and gurgling in atonal unison. The noise stiffens the tiny hairs on the back of his neck.

Lilly listens to the distant chorus. "They're multiplying, aren't they?"

Josh shrugs. "Who knows."

Bob reaches into the pocket of his tattered down coat. He roots out his flask, thumbs off the cap, and takes a healthy swig. "You think they smell us?"

Josh goes over to the grimy front window and gazes out at the night. "I think all the activity at Camp Bingham's been drawing 'em out of the woodwork for weeks now."

"How far from base camp *are* we, ya think?"

"Not much more than a mile or so, as the crow flies." Josh gazes out over the pinnacles of distant pines, their swaying ocean of boughs as dense as black lace. The sky has cleared, and now the heavens are spangled with a riot of icy-cold stars.

Across the needlework of constellations rise wisps of wood smoke from the tent city.

"Been thinking about something . . ." Josh turns and looks at his companions. "This place ain't the Ritz but if we can do a little scavenging, maybe find some more ammunition for the guns . . . we might be better off staying put for a while."

The notion hangs in the silent office for a moment, sinking in.

————

The next morning, after a long, restless night sleeping on the cold cement floor of the service bay—making do with threadbare blankets and taking shifts standing guard—they have a group meeting to decide what to do. Over cups of instant coffee prepared on Bob's Coleman stove, Josh convinces them that the best thing to do is stay holed up there for the time being. Lilly can heal up, and if necessary, they can steal provisions from the nearby tent city.

By this point, nobody puts up much of a fight. Bob has discovered a stash of whiskey under a counter in the bait shop, and Megan and Scott alternate between getting high and "spending quality time" in the back room for hours on end. They work hard that first day to secure the place. Josh decides against running the generator indoors for fear of gassing them to death with the fumes, and worries about running it outdoors for fear of drawing unwanted attention. He finds a wood-burning stove in the storeroom and a pile of lumber scraps out behind one of the Dumpsters.

Their second night at Fortnoy's Fuel and Bait, they get the temperature up to tolerable levels in the service area by keeping the stove going full blast, and Megan and Scott noisily keep each other warm in the back room under layers of blankets. Bob gets drunk enough not to notice the cold, but he seems disturbed by the muffled bumping sounds coming from the storeroom. Eventually, the older man gets so loaded he can barely move. Lilly helps him into his bedroll as though putting a child down for the night. She even sings a lullaby to him—a Joni Mitchell song, "The Circle Game"—as she tucks the mildewed blanket around his aging, wattled neck. Oddly, she feels responsible for Bob Stookey, even though *he's* the one who's supposed to be nursing *her*.

Over the next few days, they reinforce the doors and windows, and they wash themselves in the big galvanized sinks in the rear of the garage. They settle into a sort of grudging routine. Bob winterizes his truck, cannibalizing parts off some of the wrecks, and Josh supervises regular reconnaissance missions to the outer edges of the tent city a mile to the west. Under the campers' noses, Josh and Scott are able to steal firewood, fresh water, a few discarded tent rolls, some canned vegetables, a box of shotgun shells, and a case of Sterno. Josh notices the fabric of civilized behavior straining at the seams in the tent city. He hears more and more arguments. He sees fistfights among some of the men, and heavy drinking going on. The stress is taking its toll on the settlers.

During the darkness of night, Josh keeps a tight lid on Fortnoy's Fuel and Bait. He and the others stay inside, keeping as quiet as possible, burning a minimum number of emergency candles and lanterns, jumping at the intermittent noises caused by the increasing winds. Lilly Caul finds herself wondering which is the deadlier menace—the zombie hordes, her fellow human beings, or the encroaching winter. The nights are getting longer and the cold is setting in. It's forming rimes of frost on the windows and getting into people's joints, and although no one talks about it much, the cold is the silent menace that could actually destroy them far easier and more efficiently than any zombie attack.

In order to fight the boredom and constant undercurrents of fear, some of the inhabitants of Fortnoy's develop hobbies. Josh begins rolling homemade cigars out of tobacco leaves that he harvests from neighboring fields. Lilly starts a diary, and Bob finds a treasure trove of old fishing lures in an unmarked trunk in the bait shop. He spends hours in the ransacked retail shop, perched at a workbench in back, compulsively winding fly-fishing lures for future use. Bob plans to bag some nice trout, redfish, or walleyes in the shallows of a nearby river. He keeps the bottle of Jack Daniel's under the bench at all times, tippling from it day and night.

The others notice the rate at which Bob is going through the hooch, but who can blame him? Who can blame anybody for drowning his nerves in this cruel purgatory? Bob is not proud of his drinking. In fact, he's downright ashamed of it. But that's why he needs the medicine—to stave off the shame, and the loneliness, and the fear, and the horrible night terrors of blood-spattered bunkers in Kandahar.

On Friday of that week, in the wee hours of the night—Bob notes in his paper calendar that the date is November 9—he finds himself back at the workbench in the rear of the shop, winding flies, getting shit-faced as usual, when he hears the shuffling noises coming from the storeroom. He hadn't noticed Megan and Scott slipping away earlier that evening, nor had he detected the telltale odors of marijuana residue cooking in a pipe, nor had he heard the muffled giggling coming through the thin walls. But now he notices something else that had eluded his attention that day.

He stops fiddling with the lures and glances across the rear corner of the room. Behind a large, battered propane tank, a gaping hole in the wall is clearly visible in the flickering light of Bob's lantern. He pushes himself away from the bench and goes over to the tank. He shoves it aside and kneels down in front of a six-inch patch of missing wallboard. The hole looks like it was formed by water damage, or perhaps the buckling of plaster during the humid Georgia summers. Bob glances over his shoulder, making sure he's alone. The others are fast asleep in the service area.

The groans and gasps of wild sex draw Bob's attention back to the damaged wall.

He peers through the six-inch gap and into the storeroom, where the dim light of a battery-operated lantern throws moving shadows up and across the low ceiling. The shadows pump and thrust in the darkness. Bob licks his lips. He leans in closer to the hole, nearly falling over in his drunken state, bracing himself against the propane tank. He can see a small portion of Scott Moon's pimpled ass rising and falling in the yellow light, Megan beneath the young man, legs spread, her toes curling with ecstasy.

Bob Stookey feels his heart pinch in his chest, his breath sticking in his craw.

The thing that mesmerizes him the most is not the naked abandon with which the two lovers are going at each other, nor is it the animalistic grunts and mewls filling the air. The thing that holds Bob Stookey rapt is the sight of Megan Lafferty's olive skin in the lamplight, her russet curls splayed across the blanket beneath her head, her hair as lustrous and shiny as honey. Bob can't stop gaping at her, the longing welling up inside him.

He can't tear his gaze from her, even when a floorboard creaks behind him.

"Oh—Bob—I'm sorry—I didn't . . ."

The voice comes from the shadows of the doorway across the retail shop, from the passageway into the front office, and when Bob jerks away from the hole in the wall, whirling around to face his inquisitor, he nearly falls over. He has to hold on to the propane tank. "I wasn't trying to—this ain't—I—I ain't—"

"It's okay—I was just—I wanted to make sure you were okay." Lilly stands in the doorway dressed in her sweatshirt, knit scarf, and sweatpants—her sleeping attire—averting her bandaged face, looking away, her eyes filled with an awkward combination of pity and disgust. The bruising around her eyes has gone down quite a bit. She's moving around a lot better, her ribs healing.

"Lilly, I wasn't—" Bob staggers toward her, holding his big hands up in a gesture of contrition, when he trips on a loose floorboard. He tumbles, sprawling to the floor and letting out a gasp. Amazingly, the carnal noises continue unabated in the adjacent room—an arrhythmic cadence of huffing and slapping flesh.

"Bob, are you okay?" Lilly rushes over to him, kneels, and tries to help him up.

"I'm fine, I'm fine." He gently pushes her away. He rises drunkenly to his feet. He can't look her in the eye. He doesn't know what to do with his hands. He glances across the room. "I thought I heard something suspicious coming from outside."

"Suspicious?" Lilly gazes at the floor, at the wall—anywhere but at Bob. "Oh . . . okay."

"Yeah, it was nothing."

"Oh . . . that's good." Lilly slowly backs away. "Just wanted to make sure you were okay."

"I'm good, I'm good. It's getting late, I'm thinking I'll turn in."

"Good, Bob. You do that."

Lilly turns and makes a hasty exit, leaving Bob Stookey alone in the lantern light. He stands there for a moment, staring at the floor. Then he moves slowly across the room to the bench. He finds the bottle of Jack, thumbs off the cap, and raises it to his lips.

He downs the remaining fingers of booze in three breathless gulps.

"I'm just wondering what's gonna happen when he runs out of booze."

Bundled in her ski jacket and knit beret, Lilly follows Josh down a narrow path winding between columns of pines. Josh makes his way through the foliage, the 12-gauge cradled in his huge arms, moving toward a dry creek bed strewn with boulders and dead-fall. He wears his ratty lumberjack coat and stocking cap, his breath showing as he talks. "He'll find some more . . . don't worry about old Bob . . . juicers always manage to find more juice. To be honest, I'm more worried about us running out of food."

The woods are as silent as a chapel as they approach the banks of the creek. The first snow of the season filters down through the high boughs above them, swirling on the wind, sticking to their faces.

They've been at Fortnoy's for almost two weeks now, and have gone through over half the supply of drinking water and nearly all the canned goods. Josh has decided it's probably best to use up their single box of shotgun shells on killing a deer or a rabbit rather than defending themselves against a zombie attack. Besides, the camp-fires, noise, and activity at the tent city have drawn most of the walker activity away from the gas station in recent days. Josh is now calling upon his childhood memories of hunting with his uncle Vernon up on Briar Mountain in order to get the scent back, get the old skills back. Once upon a time, Josh was an eagle-eyed hunter. But now, with this broken-down squirrel gun and frozen fingers . . . who knows?

"I worry about him, Josh," Lilly says. "He's a good man but he's got issues."

"Don't we all." Josh glances over his shoulder at Lilly coming down the hill, carefully stepping over a fallen log. She looks strong for the first time since the incident with Chad Bingham. Her face has healed nicely, barely showing any discoloration. The swelling has gone down around her eye, and she's no longer limping or fa-voring her right side. "He sure fixed you up nice."

"Yeah, I'm feeling a lot better."

Josh pauses on the edge of the creek and waits for her. She joins him. He sees tracks in the hard-packed mud at the bottom of the creek bed. "Looks like we got a deer crossing here. I'm thinkin' we follow the creek, ought to meet up with a critter or two."

"Can we take a quick rest first?"

"You bet," Josh says, motioning for her to have a seat on a log. She sits. He joins her, holding the shotgun across his lap. He lets out a sigh. He feels a tremendous urge to put his arm around her. What is *wrong* with him? Stricken with puppy love like some stupid teenager in the midst of all these horrors?

Josh looks down. "I like the way you take care of each other, you and old Bob."

"Yeah, and you take care of all of us."

Josh lets out a sigh. "Wish I could have taken better care of my mama."

Lilly looks at him. "You never told me what happened."

Josh takes a deep breath. "Like I told you, she was pretty sick for quite a few years . . . thought I was gonna lose her a few times . . . but she lived long enough to—" He stops, the sorrow ratcheting his insides, swelling up in him, surprising him with its suddenness.

Lilly sees the pain in his eyes. "It's okay, Josh, if you don't want to—"

He makes a feeble gesture, a wave of his big brown hand. "I don't mind telling you what happened. I was still trying to get into work each morning at that point, still trying to get a paycheck in the early days of the Turn, just a few biter sightings back then. I ever tell you what I do? My profession?"

"You told me you were a cook."

He gives her a nod. "Pretty serious one, if I do say so myself." He looks at her, his voice softening. "Always wanted to fix you a proper dinner." His eyes moisten. "My mama taught me the basics, rest her soul, taught me how to make a bread pudding that would bring tears to your eyes and joy to your belly."

Lilly smiles at him, then her smile fades. "What happened to your mom, Josh?"

He stares at the dusting of snow on the matted leaves for quite some time, marshaling the energy to tell the story. "Muhammad Ali's got nothing on my mama . . . she was a fighter, she fought that sickness like a champ, for years. But *sweet*? She was sweet as the day is long. Shaggy dogs and misfits—she would take anybody in, the raggiest-ass individuals, hardened panhandlers, homeless, it didn't matter. She would take 'em in and call 'em 'honey child' and make them corn bread and sweet tea until they stole from her or got in a fight in her front parlor."

"Sounds like she was a saint, Josh."

Another shrug. "Wasn't the best living conditions for me and my sisters, I'll be honest with ya. We moved around a lot, different schools, and every day we would come home and find our place filled with strangers, but I loved the old gal."

"I can see why."

Josh swallows hard. Here it comes. The bad part, the part that haunts his dreams to this day. He gazes at the snow on the leaves. "It happened on a Sunday. I knew my mama was failing, wasn't thinking straight. One doctor told us it was Alzheimer's comin' on. At this point, the dead was getting into the projects, but they still had the warning sirens comin' on, announcements and shit. Our street was blocked off that day. When I left for work, Mama was just sittin' at the window, staring out at them things slipping through the cordons, getting picked off by them SWAT guys. I didn't think anything of it. I figured she'd be okay."

He pauses, and Lilly doesn't say anything. It's clear to both of them that he has to share this with another human being or it will continue to eat away at him. "I tried to call her later that day. Guess the lines were down. Figured no news was good news. I think it was about five-thirty when I knocked off that day."

He swallows the lump in his throat. He can feel Lilly's gaze on him.

"I was rounding the corner at the top of my street. I flash my ID at the guys at the roadblock when I notice a lot of activity down the block. SWAT guys coming and going. Right in front of my building. I pull up. They holler at me to get the hell outta there and I tell them, hey, man, ease on back, I live here. They let me through. I see the front door to our apartment building wide open. Cops coming out and going in. Some of them carrying . . ."

Josh chokes on the words. He breathes. Braces himself. Wipes moisture from his eyes. "Some of them was carrying—*whattyacallem*—specimen containers? For human organs and such? I run up the stairs two at a time. I think I knocked over one of them cops. I get to our door on the second floor and there's these dudes in hazmat suits blocking the entrance and I shove 'em aside and go in and I see . . ."

Josh feels the sorrow creeping up his gorge, strangling him. He pauses to take a breath. His tears burn and track down his chin.

"Josh, you don't have to—"

"No, it's awright, I need to . . . what I saw in there . . . I knew right off the bat what had happened. I knew the second I saw that window open and the table set. Mama had her wedding dishes out. You would not *believe* the blood. I mean, the place was painted in it." He feels his voice cracking, and he swims against the tide of tears. "There was at least six of them things on the floor. SWAT guys must've took 'em out. There was . . . not much left of Mama." He chokes. Swallows. Flinches at the searing pain in his chest. "There was . . . pieces of her on the table. With the good china. I saw . . . I saw . . . her fingers . . . all chewed up next to the gravy boat . . . what was left of her body . . . slumped in a chair . . . her head was all lolled over to one side . . . neck opened up—"

"Okay . . . Josh, you don't need to . . . I'm sorry . . . I'm so sorry."

Josh looks at her as though seeing her face in a new light, hovering there in the diffuse, snowy radiance, her eyes far away, as though in a dream.

Through her tears, Lilly Caul meets the big man's gaze and her heart clenches. She wants to hold him, she wants to comfort this gentle colossus, stroke his massive shoulders and tell him it's all going to be all right. She has never felt this close to another human being and it's killing her. She doesn't deserve his friendship, his loyalty, his protection, his love. What does she say? Your mama's in a better place now? She refuses to diminish this terribly profound moment with stupid clichés.

She starts to say something else when Josh speaks up again in a low, drained, defeated voice, not taking his eyes off her. "She invited them things in for corn bread and beans . . . she took them in . . . like shaggy dogs . . . because that's what she does. Loves all God's creatures." The big man slumps and his shoulders tremble as tears drip off his grizzled jaw and onto the front of his Salvation Army lumber jacket. "Probably called them 'honey-child' . . . right up until the moment they ate her."

Then the big man lowers his head and lets out an alarming sound—half sob, half insane laughter—as the tears stream down his enormous, sculpted brown face.

Lilly moves closer. She puts her hand on his shoulder. She says nothing at first. She touches his gigantic hands, which are clasped around the shotgun across his lap. He looks up at her, his expression a mask of emotional ruin. "Sorry I'm so . . ." he utters in barely a whisper.

"It's okay, Josh. It's okay. I'm here for you always. I'm with you now."

He cocks his head, wipes his face, and manages a broken smile. "I guess you are."

She kisses him—quickly, but on the lips—a little more than a friendly smack. The kiss lasts maybe a couple of seconds.

Josh drops the gun, puts his arms around her, and returns the gesture, and the contrary emotions flow through Lilly as the big man lets his lips linger on hers. She feels herself floating on the windswept snow. She can't sort out the undercurrent of feelings making her dizzy. Does she pity this man? Is she manipulating him again? He tastes like coffee and smoke and Juicy Fruit gum. The cold snow touches Lilly's eyelashes, the warmth of Josh's lips melting the chill. He has done so much for her. She owes him her life ten times over. She opens her mouth, presses her chest against his, and then he pulls away.

"What's wrong?" She looks up at him, searches his big sad brown eyes. Did she do something wrong? Did she step over a line?

"Nothing at all, babydoll." He smiles and leans down and kisses her cheek. It's a warm kiss—soft, tender, a promise of more to come. "Timing, you know," he says then. He picks up the shotgun. "Not safe here . . . don't feel right."

For a moment, Lilly can't figure out whether he's referring to the woods not being right, or if he's talking about the two of them. "I'm sorry if I—"

He gently touches her lips. "I want it to be just right . . . when the time comes."

His smile is the most guileless, clean, sweet smile Lilly has ever seen. She returns his smile, her eyes misting over. Who would have thought, in the midst of all this horror—a perfect gentleman?

Lilly starts to say something else when a sharp noise grabs their attention.

Josh hears the faint drumming of hooves first, and gently shoves Lilly back behind him. He raises the squirrel gun's rusty single barrel. The pounding noises rise. Josh thumbs the hammer back.

At first, he thinks he's seeing things. Above them, coming down the embankment, throwing leaves and debris in their wake, a pack of animals—impossible to identify at first, just a blur of fur—charge through the foliage directly toward them. "Get down!" Josh yanks Lilly back behind a deadfall log on the edge of the creek bed.

"What is it?" Lilly crouches down behind the worm-eaten wood.

"Dinner!" Josh raises the gun's back sight to his eyes and aims at the oncoming deer—a small cluster of does with bushy ears pinned, and eyes as wide as billiard balls—but something stops Josh from firing. His heart throbs in his chest, his skin flushing with gooseflesh—the realization exploding in his brain.

"Josh, what's the matter?"

The deer roar past Josh, snapping twigs and throwing stones as he sidesteps the stampede.

Josh swings the gun up at the darker shadows coming behind the animals. "Run, Lilly!"

"What?—No!" She rises up behind the log, watching the deer vault across the riverbed. "I'm not leaving you!"

"Cross the creek, I'm right behind you!" Josh aims the shotgun up at the shapes coming down the hill, weaving through the undergrowth.

Lilly sees the horde of zombies lumbering toward them, at least twenty, sideswiping trees and bumping into each other. "Oh, shit."

"GO!"

Lilly scrambles across the gravelly trough and plunges into the shadows of the adjacent forest.

Josh backs away, aiming the front sight at the leading edge of the swarm coming toward him.

All at once, in that single instant before he fires, he sees oddly shaped bodies and garb, strange burned faces and costumes mutilated practically beyond recognition, and Josh realizes what happened to the previous owners of the lost three-ring circus tent—the unfortunate members of the Cole Brothers' Family Circus.

SIX

Josh squeezes off a shot.

The blast cracks open the sky, the pigeon grain punching a divot through the forehead of the closest midget. Twenty feet away, the little rotting corpse convulses backward, banging into three other dwarfs in bloody clown face and snarling black teeth. The little zombies—as stunted and deformed as sickly gnomes—scatter sideways.

Josh takes one last glance at the surreal intruders closing in on him.

Behind the midgets, stumbling down the embankment, comes a motley assortment of dead performers. A giant strong man with a handlebar mustache and musculature torn open in bloody gouges lumbers alongside a morbidly obese female cadaver, half nude, her fat rolls dangling over her genitals, her milky eyes buried in a face as lumpy as stale dough.

Bringing up the rear, a haphazard assortment of dead carnies, freaks, and contortionists follow stupidly. Encephalitic pinheads, their tiny mouths snapping, stumble along beside ragged trapeze artists in garish sequins and gangrenous faces, followed by multiple amputees trundling along spasmodically. The pack moves in fits and starts, as feral and hungry as a school of piranhas.

Josh lurches away, vaulting across the dry creek bed in a single leap.

He scuttles up the opposite bank and plunges into the neighboring woods with the shotgun over his shoulder. There is no time to reload another shell. He can see Lilly in the distance, sprinting toward the denser trees. He catches up with her in a matter of seconds and directs her to the east.

The two of them vanish into the shadows before what remains of the Cole Brothers' Family Circus even has a chance to stagger across the creek.

On their way back to the gas station, Josh and Lilly run into a smaller herd of deer. Josh gets lucky and bags one of the juvenile does with a single blast. The booming report echoes up across the sky—far enough from Fortnoy's to avoid drawing attention, but close enough to lug the trophy back home—and the whitetail goes down gasping and twitching.

Lilly has trouble taking her eyes off the carcass as Josh rigs his belt around its hindquarters and drags the steaming remains nearly half a mile back to Fortnoy's. In this Plague World, death in any context—human or animal—has taken on new implications.

That night, the mood lightens among the inhabitants of the gas station.

Josh dresses the deer in the back of the service area, in the same galvanized sinks in which they've been bathing, and he slaughters enough of the animal to last them weeks. He keeps the excess meat outside, in the deepening cold of the back lot, and he prepares a feast of organ meat, ribs, and belly, slow cooked in the broth of some instant chicken soup that they found in the bottom drawer of Fortnoy's office desk, along with shavings of wild meadow garlic and nettle stems. They have some canned peaches to accompany the braised deer, and they gorge themselves.

The walkers leave them alone for most of the evening—no sign of the circus dead or any other enclave. Josh notices during dinner that Bob cannot take his eyes off Megan. The older man seems taken with the girl, and for some reason this worries Josh. For days now, Bob has been very cold and brusque toward Scott (not that the kid has noticed anything in his constant state of flakiness). Nevertheless, Josh feels the volatile chemical bonds of their little tribe being tested, stressed, altered.

Later, they sit around the woodstove and smoke Josh's home-made cigars and share a few ounces of Bob's whiskey stash. For the first time since leaving the tent city—perhaps since the advent of the plague—they feel almost normal. They talk of escape. They speak of desert islands and antidotes and vaccines and finding happiness and stability again. They reminisce about the things they took for granted before the plague broke out: shopping in grocery stores and playing in parks and going out for dinner and watching TV shows and reading the newspaper on Sunday mornings and going to clubs to hear live music and sitting at Starbucks and shopping at Apple stores and using Wi-Fi and getting mail through that anachronistic thing known as the postal service.

They each have their pet pleasures. Scott bemoans the extinction of good weed, and Megan longs for the days when she could hang out at her favorite bar—Nightlies in Union City—and enjoy the free cucumber shooters and shrimp skewers. Bob pines for ten-year-old bourbon the way a mother might yearn for a lost child. Lilly remembers her guilty pleasures of haunting secondhand stores and thrift shops for the perfect scarf or sweater or blouse—the days when finding cast-off clothing wasn't a matter of survival. And Josh recalls the number of gourmet food shops he could find in the Little Five Points area of Atlanta—everything from good kimchi to rare pink truffle oil.

Either through some vagary of the wind, or perhaps the combined noise of their laughter—as well as the ticking and rattling of the woodstove—the troubling noises drifting out over the trees from the tent city go unnoticed that night for hours.

At one point—after the little dinner party breaks up and each of them finds their way back to their bedroll on the floor of the service area—Josh thinks he hears something strange echoing under the sound of the breeze tapping against the glass doors. But he simply passes it off as the wind and his imagination.

Josh offers to take the first shift, sitting watch in the front office, so he can make sure the noises are nothing. But hours go by before he hears or sees anything out of the ordinary.

The front office has a large, filthy plate-glass window across its front façade, much of the glass blocked by shelving, racks of maps and travel guides, and little pine deodorizers. The dusty merchandise blocks any sign of trouble rising up and over the distant sea of pines.

The wee hours pass, and eventually Josh dozes off in his chair.

His eyes remain shut until 4:43 A.M., at which point the first faint sound of engines coming up the hill jar him awake with a start.

Lilly stirs awake to the sound of heavy boot steps pounding through the office doorway. Sitting up against the garage wall, her ass freezing, she doesn't notice that Bob is already awake in his tangled nest of blankets across the garage.

Sitting up and looking around the service bay, Bob Stookey apparently heard the engine noises mere seconds after they had awakened Josh out in the office. "The hell is going on?" he mumbles. "Sounds like the Indy 500 out there."

"Everybody up," Josh says, storming into the garage, frantically looking around the greasy floor, searching for something.

"What's wrong?" Lilly rubs the sleep from her eyes, her heart starting to thump. "What's going on?"

Josh comes over to her. He kneels and speaks softly yet urgently. "Something's going down out there, vehicles moving fast, real reckless and shit—I don't want to get caught unawares."

She hears the roar of engines, the pinging of gravel flying. The noises are getting closer. Lilly's mouth goes dry with panic. "Josh, what are you looking for?"

"Get dressed, babydoll, quick." Josh glances across the room. "Bob—you see that box of .38 caliber slugs we brought back?"

Bob Stookey torques himself up to a standing position, awkwardly pulling his work trousers over his long underwear, a slice of moonlight coming through the skylight and striping his deeply-lined features. "I put it over on the workbench," he says. "What's the deal, captain?"

Josh hurries over and grabs the box of ammo. He reaches under his lumberjack coat, pulls the .38 snubbie from his belt, flicks open the cylinder, and loads it while he talks. "Lilly, you go get the lovebirds. Bob, I'm gonna need you to get that pigeon gun of yours and meet me out front."

"What if they're friendly, Josh?" Lilly pulls her sweater on, steps into her muddy boots.

"Then we got nothing to worry about." He whirls back toward the doorway. "Get moving, both of you." He lurches out of the room.

Heart racing, flesh prickling with terror, Lilly hurries across the garage, charges through the archway, and then down the narrow aisle of the retail store. A single hanging lantern lights her way.

"You guys! Wake up!" she says after reaching the storeroom door and pounding loudly.

Shuffling noises, bare feet on cold floorboards, then the door clicks partially ajar. Megan's drowsy, dazed face peers out on a cloud of skunk-weed smoke. "¿Qué pasa? dude—what the fuck?"

"Get up, Megan, we got trouble."

The girl's face goes instantly taut and alarmed. "Walkers?"

Lilly shakes her head emphatically. "I don't think so, unless they've learned how to drive cars."

Minutes later, Lilly joins Bob and Josh out in front of Fortnoy's—in the frigid, crystalline, predawn air—while Scott and Megan huddle behind them in the office doorway with blankets wrapped around themselves. "Oh, my God," Lilly utters, almost to herself.

A little less than a mile away, over the crest of the neighboring trees, a vast miasma of smoke rises up and blots out the stars. The horizon behind it glows a sickly pink, and it looks as though the black ocean of pines is on fire. But Lilly knows it's not the forest that's burning.

"What have they done?"

"This ain't good," Bob murmurs, the shotgun clutched in his cold hands.

"Get back," Josh says, thumbing the hammer back on the .38 police special.

The engine noises close in, maybe a few hundred yards away now, coming up the winding farm road—the sources of the noise still obscured behind a veil of night and the trees bordering the property—their headlights creating wildly arcing beams. Tires skid and career through gravel. Rays of light shoot up into the sky, then across the tops of trees, then back across the road.

One of the headlights flares across the Fortnoy's sign and Josh mutters, "What the hell is wrong with them?"

Lilly stares at the first vehicle that comes into view—a late-model sedan—swerving up the snaking gravel road, then going into a skid. "What the fuck?"

"They ain't stoppin'! THEY AIN'T STOPPIN'!!" Bob starts backing away from the twin beams of deadly halogen light.

The car skids into the lot, roaring out of control across the fifty yards of pea gravel bordering Fortnoy's property, the rear end raising a thunderhead of dust in the indigo predawn chill.

"LOOK OUT!"

Josh springs into action, grabbing Lilly by the sleeve and pulling her out of harm's way, while Bob spins toward the office and screams at the top of his lungs at the two lovers huddling wide-eyed in the open doorway.

"GET OUTTA THERE!!"

Megan yanks her stoner boyfriend out of the door and across the apron of cracked cement flanking the fuel islands. The sedan—revealing itself, as it looms closer and closer, to be a battered Cadillac DeVille—screeches and fishtails toward the building. Bob lunges toward Megan. Scott lets out a garbled cry.

Another vehicle—a battered SUV with a broken luggage carrier—comes squealing and careening into the lot. Bob grabs Megan and gently shoves her toward the soft weeds beyond the service doors. Scott dives for cover behind a Dumpster. Josh and Lilly duck behind a wreck near the front sign.

The sedan mows down the closest fuel pump and keeps going, its engine whining furiously. The other vehicle goes into a spin. Lilly watches in shock from about fifty feet away, behind the wreck, as the sedan crashes into the front window.

The sickening crunch of glass and metal makes Lilly jerk with a start. Debris and sparks go flying as the sedan penetrates the front of the building.

The car keeps going, rear wheels keening and spinning on the floor, destroying half the building with the force of a giant wrecking ball. Lilly puts her hand to her mouth. The front half of Fortnoy's roof collapses on the sedan as it comes to rest in the retail store.

The SUV slams sideways into the diesel pump, setting the fumes alight. Fire booms upward in a sheath and licks at the rising vapors. The windows of the SUV flicker a dull yellow from something burning *inside* it. Lilly silently thanks God that the fuel reserves are empty, or she and her friends would be vaporized by now.

The SUV comes to rest at an angle under the awning, its high beams still shining brightly, illuminating the building like stage lights in a hallucinatory play.

For a moment, the silence crashes down on the property until the crackle of flames and the sizzle of fluids are all that can be heard.

Josh cautiously moves out from behind the wreck, still clutching his .38 revolver. Lilly joins him and is about to say something like, *What the hell just happened,* when she notices the headlights of the SUV are shining directly into the building, a wide pool of light falling directly on the rear of the sedan.

Inside the car's rear window—fractured by huge starbursts of broken glass—something moves. Lilly sees the back of someone's shoulders, slowly turning, pivoting awkwardly, revealing a pale, discolored face.

All at once, Lilly knows exactly what happened.

Moments later, things at Fortnoy's start unraveling at a rapid rate as Josh calls out to the others in a frantic whisper. *"Get away from the building!"*

Across the lot, Bob, Megan, and Scott still crouch in the weeds behind the Dumpster. They slowly rise and start to answer.

"SSSSSHHHHHHHHH!!" Josh points at the building, indicating the dangers inside, and whispers loud enough to get them moving. *"Hurry up! Get over here!!"*

Bob understands instantly, and he takes Megan's hand and creeps around the flickering flames of the diesel pump. Scott follows.

Lilly stands next to Josh. "What are we gonna do? All our stuff's in there."

The front of the station and half its interior are totaled, the sparks still sputtering, the water mains still flooding the cold floors.

In the glare of the SUV's headlight beams, one of the sedan's flapping rear doors suddenly creaks open wider, a decomposed leg clad in rags stepping out in fitful, spastic movements.

"The place is gone, babydoll," Josh says under his breath. "S-O-L . . . forget it."

Bob and the others join Josh and Lilly, and for a brief instant they stand there, still in shock, catching their collective breaths. Bob still clutches the shotgun in his sweaty palms. Megan looks sick. "What the fuck happened?" she mutters almost rhetorically.

"Folks must have tried to get away," Josh speculates. "Must've had a passenger that got bit, and they turned in the car."

Inside the wrecked building, a zombie emerges from the sedan like a deformed fetus being born.

"Bob, you got your keys on ya?"

Bob looks at Josh. "They're in the truck."

"In the ignition?"

"Glove box."

Josh turns to the others. "I want y'all to wait here, keep your eye on that walker, might be more in there. I'm gonna get the truck."

Josh turns away but Lilly grabs him. "Wait! Wait!! You're telling me we're just gonna leave all our stuff in there, all our supplies?"

"No choice."

He heads around the left side of the smoking pumps while the others stand there stunned and speechless. Twenty-five feet away, the SUV thumps, a half-ajar door creaking open, the firelight blooming. Lilly jerks. Megan gasps as another dead thing pushes its way out of the vehicle.

Bob fiddles a shotgun shell into the breech with shaking hands.

The others back away toward the road, Scott mumbling hysterically, "Shit, man, shit . . . shit . . . shit . . . shit . . . shit . . . shit . . . shit . . ."

The thing that emerges from the SUV, burned beyond recognition, staggers toward them, its mouth gaping with black drool. The back of its collar and part of its left shoulder still crackle with tiny flames, the smoke around its skull like a halo. Apparently an adult male, half the skin of its face burned off, it barely remains upright as it shuffles slowly toward the smell of humans.

Bob can't get the shell seated properly, his shakes are so bad now.

No one sees the flare of taillights across the lot behind the row of wrecks, and no one hears the rumble of the king cab's engine firing up or the squeal of its rear tires digging in as the engine roars.

The burning zombie approaches Megan, who turns to run and trips on a patch of loose gravel. She sprawls to the pavement as Scott cries out and Lilly tries to help her up and Bob struggles with the shotgun.

The walker gets within inches of them when the blur of metal appears.

Josh backs the Ram directly into the zombie, and the impact of the protruding trailer hitch impales the thing, sending the charred corpse flying in a cloud of sparks. The thing breaks apart in the middle, the torso flinging off one way, the lower extremities spinning in the other.

One of the blackened, sizzling organs strikes Megan in the back, splattering her with hot, oily bile and fluids. She lets out a scream.

The pickup skids to a stop next to them, and they pile in, yanking a hysterical Megan in through the back hatch. Josh floors it.

The truck barrels out of the lot and down the winding access road.

All told, a mere three and a half minutes have elapsed since the onslaught . . . but in that time, the destinies of all five survivors have irrevocably changed.

They decide to head down the hill and turn north, weaving through the forest toward the tent city. They proceed cautiously, with their lights off and eyes wide open. In the rear camper, Scott and Megan peer through the firewall window, while Bob and Lilly, side by side in the cab next to Josh, scan the landscape with feverish concentration. No one says a word. They all harbor the unspoken dread of investigating the extent of the damage to the tent city—the resources of the vast encampment now paramount to their survival.

By this point, dawn has broken, the edges of the horizon—pale blue behind the trees—already beginning to drive the shadows from the gullies and culverts. The air is bitter cold and scented with the char of recent fires. Josh keeps both hands on the wheel as the pickup snakes through the cool shadows rising above the tent city.

"STOP! JOSH! STOP!"

Josh stomps on the brakes at the zenith of a hill overlooking the southern edge of the camp. The pickup scrapes to a halt.

"Oh, my God."

"Christ Almighty."

"Let's turn around." Lilly chews on her fingernail, gazing through a break in the foliage. She can see what's left of the tent city in the distance. The air reeks of burned flesh and something worse, something deathly foul, like a mass infection. "There's nothing we can do here."

"Hold on a second."

"Josh—"

"What in God's name happened down there?" Bob murmurs to nobody in particular, staring through the gap in the trees that opens like a proscenium above the meadow fifty yards below. Early-morning sunbeams shoot down through scrims of smoke, making the devastation look almost unreal, like footage from a silent movie. "Looks like Godzilla attacked the place."

"You think somebody went crazy?" Lilly keeps staring at the smoking ruins.

"I don't think so," Josh says.

"You think walkers caused this?"

"I don't know, maybe there was a big old swarm of 'em and a fire started."

Down in the meadow, along the edges of the encampment, flaming cars sit in disarray. Scores of smaller tents still burn, sending up black gouts of smoke into the acrid sky. In the center of the field, the circus tent has been reduced to a smoldering endoskeleton of metal poles and guide wires. Even the hard-packed ground burns in places, as though someone spooned out dollops of liquid flames. Smoking bodies litter the grounds. For a brief, surreal moment, Josh

is reminded of the *Hindenburg* disaster, the flaming debris of the air-
ship in its catastrophic death throes.

"Josh . . ."

The big man turns and looks at Lilly, whose face is turned away
now, scanning the edges of the forest on either side of the king cab.
Her voice lowers several registers until she sounds almost groggy
with terror. "Josh . . . um . . . we have to get out of here."

"What is it?"

"Holy fuckin' Jesus." Bob sees what Lilly sees, and the air in the
cab crackles with tension. "Get us outta here, captain."

"What are you—"

Then Josh sees the problem: the countless shadowy figures
emerging from the trees—almost in synchronous marching order—
like a vast school of fish stirred from the depths. Some of them still
smolder with thin wisps of smoke leaching off their tattered rags.
Others trundle along with robotic hunger, their curled claws out-
stretched. Hundreds and hundreds of cataract-white eyes reflect the
pale light of dawn as they lock on to the lone vehicle in their midst.
The hairs on Josh's thick neck stiffen.

"JOSH, GO!"

He yanks the steering wheel and slams the pedal down, and the
three hundred and sixty cubic inches roar. The truck lurches into a
one-eighty, plowing through a dozen zombies and taking down a
small pine in the process. The noise is incredible, the wet wrenching
of dead limbs and snapping of timbers as the debris and blood kick
up across the front quarter panel. The rear end wags violently, smashing into a cluster of walkers and tossing Megan and Scott around the
camper. Josh pulls back onto the road and floors it, booming back
down the hill in the direction from which they just came.

They barely make it to the adjacent road at the bottom of the hill
before they realize at least three zombies have attached themselves,
barnaclelike, to the pickup.

"Shit!" Josh sees one in his side mirror, clinging to the vehicle on
the driver's side, near the rear quarter panel, feet on the running

board, tangled in strapping ropes, its tattered clothing caught in the camper's metal trim. "Stay cool, everybody—we got some hangers-on!"

"*What!*" Lilly turns toward the passenger window and sees a dead face pop up across the glass like a jack-in-the-box. The face twitches and snarls at her, its inky drool flagging in the wind. Lilly lets out a startled gasp.

Josh concentrates on the road, making a wild turn, then heading north at a steady forty-five miles an hour, moving toward the main two-lane, purposely swerving in an attempt to fling the zombies off the pickup.

Two of the walkers have clamped on to the driver's side, one on the passenger side—and they hold fast—either caught on the truck, or strong enough in their spastic hunger to hold on. "Bob! You got any more of them shells in the cab?"

"They're in the back!"

"Shit!"

Bob shoots a glance at Lilly. "Darlin,' I believe there's a crowbar on the floor behind the passenger seat—"

The truck swerves. One of the walkers tears free, tumbling to the road and pinwheeling down an embankment. Muffled screams come from the back. The sound of glass breaking comes through the wall. Lilly finds the greasy three-foot length of iron with the hooked end on the rear floor. "Found it!"

"Give it to me, honey!"

Josh looks out at the side mirror and sees a second zombie slip free of its mooring and fall to the rushing pavement beneath the wheels. The truck bumps over the corpse and keeps barreling.

Bob hollers in his gravelly wheeze, twisting around toward the sleeper window, raising the crowbar. "Get back, Lilly, cover your face!"

Lilly cowers, shielding herself, as Bob strikes out at the zombie in the window.

The curved end of the crowbar slams against the window but merely chips a divot out of the reinforced safety glass. The zombie snarls, tangled in bungee cords—its toneless growl a Doppler echo on the wind.

Bob lets out a cry and then slams the crowbar into the window again and again, as hard as he can, until the curved tip breaks through the safety glass and plunges into the dead face. Lilly turns away.

The crowbar impales the cadaver through the roof of its mouth and gets stuck. Bob gapes in horror. Behind the mosaic of fractured glass the skewered head hangs suspended in the wind for a moment, the dull glow behind its sharklike button eyes still animated, the mouth still pulsing around the iron as if trying to eat the crowbar.

Lilly can't look. She presses back against the corner, shaking convulsively.

Josh swerves again, and the zombie finally tears loose in the wind, falling to the pavement and vanishing under the wheels. The rest of the window blows away, a tissue of shattered glass imploding and swirling into the cab. Bob flinches, awash in adrenaline, and Josh keeps barreling forward as Lilly curls into a fetal position in back.

They finally reach the main access road and Josh heads south, picking up speed, calling out loud enough for the folks in the back to hear: "Everybody hold on!"

Without another word, Josh accelerates, hands welded to the steering wheel, weaving and lurching around pockets of wrecked, abandoned vehicles for another couple of miles, keeping an eye on the side mirror, making sure they are clear and safely out of range of the swarm.

They put five miles between them and the cataclysm before Josh applies the brakes and stops on the gravel shoulder of a deserted stretch of rural wasteland. The silence that descends on the truck is unreal. Only the sound of their heartbeats in their ears and the high, lonesome whistle of the wind can be heard.

Josh glances over his shoulder at Lilly. The look on her faintly bruised face, the way she's curled up in the corner of the floor, hugging her bended knees against her chest, shivering as though suffering from hypothermia—all of it worries him. "You okay, babydoll?"

Lilly manages to swallow the lump of terror in her throat and gives him a look. "Just peachy."

Josh gives her a nod, then hollers loud enough to be heard back in the camper. "Everybody okay back there?"

Megan's face in the window says it all. Her ruddy features screwed up with nervous tension, she grudgingly gives them a noncommittal thumbs-up.

Josh turns and gazes through the windshield. He breathes hard, as though recovering from a sprint. "Damn things are definitely multiplying."

Bob rubs his face, breathing hard, fighting the shakes. "Getting more brazen, too, you ask me."

After a pause Josh says, "Must've happened fast."

"Yeah."

"Poor bastards didn't know what hit 'em."

"Yeah." Bob wipes his mouth. "Maybe we oughtta go back, try and draw them things away from the camp."

"What for?"

Bob chews the inside of his cheek. "I don't know . . . could be survivors."

Another long pause hangs in the cab, until Lilly finally says, "Not likely, Bob."

"Could be supplies left over we could use."

"Too risky," Josh says, scanning the landscape. "Where the hell are we, anyway?"

Bob roots a map out of a cluttered door pocket. He unfolds it with shaking hands and traces his nail across the tiny capillaries of unmarked farm roads. He still labors to catch his breath. "Best I can tell, we're somewhere south of Oakland—tobacco country." He tries to hold the map steady in his shaking hands. "Road we're on ain't on the map—at least it ain't on *this* map."

Josh stares into the distance. The morning sun hammers down on the narrow two-lane. The unmarked road, which is fringed in weeds and littered with an abandoned wreck every twenty yards or so, snakes along a plateau between two tobacco farms. On either side of the unmarked two-lane, the fields have overgrown with neglect, the weeds and kudzu twining up the slats of weather-beaten guardrails. The shaggy, ramshackle nature of the fields reflects the months that have transpired since the plague broke out.

Bob folds up the map. "What now?"

Josh shrugs. "Ain't seen a farmhouse for miles, seems like we're far enough out in the boonies to avoid another swarm of them things."

Lilly climbs back onto the bench. "What are you thinking, Josh?"

He puts the truck into drive. "I'm thinking we keep heading south."

"Why south?"

"For one, we'll be moving away from the population centers."

"And . . . ?"

"And maybe, if we keep movin' . . . we can keep the cold weather in our rearview."

He gives it some gas and starts to pull back onto the road when Bob grabs his arm.

"Not so fast, captain."

Josh stops the truck. "What is it now?"

"Don't mean to be the bearer of bad news." Bob points at the gas gauge. "But I just put the last drops of my reserves in her last night."

The needle is riding just below *E*.

SEVEN

They search the area for tanks to siphon or gas stations to plunder, and they come up empty. Most of the wrecks along this desolate stretch of farm road are burned to crisps or abandoned with bone-dry tanks. They notice only scattered dead roaming the distant farmlands—lone cadavers wandering aimlessly, far enough away to easily elude.

They decide to sleep in the Ram that night, taking shifts sitting watch and rationing their canned goods and fresh water. Being this far out in the boonies proves to be a blessing as well as a curse. The worrisome lack of fuel and provisions is offset by the lack of walker activity.

Josh admonishes everybody to keep their voices down and make as little noise as possible during their exile in this barren hinterland.

As darkness closes in that first night, and the temperature nose-dives, Josh runs the engine as long as possible, then resorts to running the heater off the battery. He knows he can't keep this up for long. They cover the broken sleeper window with cardboard and duct tape.

They each sleep fitfully that night in the cramped quarters of the truck—Megan, Scott, and Bob in the camper, Lilly in the rear of the cab, and Josh in the front, barely able to stretch his massive body out across the two large bucket seats.

The next day, Josh and Bob get lucky and find an overturned panel van a mile to the west, its rear axle broken but the rest of it intact, its gas tank almost full. They siphon eighteen gallons into three separate containers, and make it back to the Ram before noon. They take off and make their way southeast—crossing another twenty miles of fallow farmland—before stopping for the night under a desolate train trestle, where the wind sings its constant mournful aria through the high-tension wires.

In the darkness of the reeking truck, they argue about whether they should keep moving or find a place to light. They bicker about petty things—sleeping arrangements, rationing, snoring, and stinky feet—and they generally get on each other's nerves. The floor space inside the camper is less than a hundred square feet, much of it covered with Bob's cast-off detritus. Scott and Megan sleep like sardines against the back hatch while Bob tosses and turns in his semisober delirium.

They live like this for almost a week, zigzagging in a southwesterly direction, following the tracks of the West Central Georgia Railway, scavenging fuel when they can. Tempers strain to the breaking point. The camper walls close in.

In the dark, the troubling noises behind the trees get closer every night.

One morning, while Scott and Megan slumber in back, Josh and Lilly sit on the Ram's front bumper, sharing a thermos of instant coffee in the early-morning light. The wind feels colder, the sky lower—the smell of winter in the air. "Feels like more snow's coming," Josh softly observes.

"Where's Bob gone off to?"

"Says he saw a creek off to the west, not far, took his fishing rod."

"Did he take the shotgun?"

"Hatchet."

"I'm worried about him, Josh. He's shaking all the time now."

"He'll be okay."

"Last night I saw him sucking down a bottle of mouthwash."

Josh looks at her. Lilly's injuries have almost completely healed, her eyes clear now for the first time since the beating. Her bruises have all but faded, and she removed the bandages around her ribs the previous afternoon to find that she could walk almost normally without them. But the pain of losing Sarah Bingham still gnaws at her—Josh can see sorrow etched on her sleeping face, late at night. From the front seat, Josh has been watching her sleep. It's the most beautiful thing he has ever seen. He longs to kiss her again but the situation hasn't warranted such luxuries. "We'll all be doing a lot better when we find some real food," Josh says then. "I'm getting mighty tired of cold Chef Boyardee."

"Water's getting low, too. And there's something else I've been thinking about that's not exactly giving me a warm, cozy feeling."

Josh looks at her. "Which is?"

"What if we run into another swarm? They could push the damn truck over, Josh. You know it as well as I do."

"All the more reason to keep moving, keep heading south, below the radar."

"I know, but—"

"More likely to find supplies, we keep moving."

"I understand that but—"

Lilly stops when she sees the silhouette of a figure way off in the distance, maybe three hundred yards away, up on the train trestle, moving this way, following the tracks. The figure's long, narrow shadow, outlined in the dust motes of morning sunlight, flickers down through the slatted ties and crossbeams—moving too fast to be a zombie.

"Speak of the devil," Josh says when he finally recognizes the figure.

The older man approaches, carrying an empty bucket and collapsible fishing rod. He trundles along quickly between the rails, urgency burning on his face. "Hey, y'all!" he calls down breathlessly to them as he reaches the stepladder near the overpass.

"Keep it down, Bob," Josh cautions him, walking over to the base of the trestle, Lilly at his side.

"Wait'll you see what I found," Bob says, descending the ladder.

"Catch a big one, did ya?"

He hops to the ground. He catches his breath, his eyes shimmering with excitement. "No, sir, didn't even find the goddamn crick." He manages a gap-toothed grin. "But I did find something better."

The Walmart sits at the intersection of two rural highways, a mile north of the train tracks, its tall interstate sign with its trademark blue letters and yellow starburst visible from the elevated trestles along the woods. The closest town is miles away, but these isolated big box stores have proven to be lucrative retail outlets for farming communities, especially ones this close to a major interstate like U.S. 85—the Hogansville exit only seven miles to the west.

"All right . . . here's what I'm thinking," Josh says to the others, after pulling up to the lot entrance, which is partially blocked by an abandoned flatbed truck, its front end wrapped around a sign pole. The cargo—mostly lumber—lies strewn across the wide lanes leading into the vast parking lot, which is littered with wrecks and abandoned vehicles. The massive low-slung superstore in the distance looks deserted but looks can be deceiving. "We check out the lots first, make a few circles, just get the lay of the land."

"Looks pretty empty, Josh," Lilly comments as she chews on her thumbnail in the rear berth. For the entire fifteen-minute journey across dusty back roads, Lilly has chewed every available fingernail down to the quick. Now she gnaws on a cuticle.

"Hard to tell just by looking," Bob pipes in.

"Keep your eyes peeled for walkers or any other movement," Josh says, putting the truck into gear and slowly bumping over the spilled lumber.

They circle the property twice, paying closest attention to the shadows of loading docks and entranceways. The cars in the lot are all empty, some burned to blackened husks. Most of the store's glass doors are blown out. A carpet of broken shards glistens in the cold afternoon sun across the front entrance. The store inside is as dark as a coal mine. Nothing moves. Inside the vestibule, a few bodies litter the floor. Whatever happened here happened a while ago.

After his second sweep, Josh pulls up to the front of the store, puts the truck in park, leaves the engine idling, and checks the last three rounds nestled in the cylinder of his .38 police special. "Okay, I don't want to leave the truck untended," he says and turns to Bob. "You got how many shells left?"

Bob snaps open the squirrel gun with trembling hands. "One in the breech, one in my pocket."

"Okay, here's what I'm thinking—"

"I'm going with you," Lilly says.

"Not without a weapon you aren't, not until we know it's safe in there."

"I'll grab a shovel from the back," she says. She glances over her shoulder and sees Megan's face in the window, owlish and expectant as she cranes her neck to see through the windshield. Lilly looks back at Josh. "You're gonna need another pair of eyes in there."

"Never argue with a woman," Bob mumbles, jacking open the passenger door and stepping out into the windy, raw air of the late-autumn afternoon.

They go around back, open the camper's rear hatch, and tell Megan and Scott to stay in the cab with the truck idling until the all-clear signal comes; and if they see any trouble, they should blast the horn like crazy. Neither Megan nor Scott puts up much of an argument.

Lilly grabs one of the shovels, and then follows Josh and Bob across the cement threshold of the store's front façade, the sounds of their footsteps crackling over broken glass drowned by the wind.

Josh forces one of the automatic doors open and they enter the vestibule.

They see the old man without a head lying on the stained parquet near the entrance in a dried pool of blood—now as black as obsidian— the ragged threads of his viscera blossoming out of his neck. Pinned to the little blue greeter's vest, the name tag, which is askew and partially visible, says WALMART on the top, and ELMER K on the bottom. The big yellow happy face insignia is stippled with blood. Lilly stares at poor headless Elmer K for quite some time as they make their way deeper into the empty store.

The air is almost as cold as outside and smells of coppery mold and decay and rancid proteins like those of a giant compost pile. Constellations of bullet holes crown the lintel above the hair care center to the left, while garish Rorschach patterns of arterial spray mark the doorway of the vision center on the right. Shelves either stand empty—already plundered—or overturned on the floor.

Josh raises one of his huge hands and orders his cohorts to stop for a moment as he listens to the silence. He scans the acres of retail space, much of which is littered with headless bodies, unidentifiable streaks of carnage, overturned shopping carts, and trash. The rows of checkout conveyors on the right stand silent and stained with blood. The pharmacy center, cosmetics counter, and health and beauty on the left are also riddled with bullet holes.

Signaling to the others, Josh cautiously continues on, his gun at the ready, his heavy boot steps crunching over debris as he moves deeper into the reeking shadows.

The farther they get from the entrance doors, the darker the aisles become. The pale daylight barely penetrates the far grocery aisles on the right, with its spills and broken glass mingling with human remains, or the home and office and fashion sections on the left, with their scattered clothing and dismembered mannequins. The departments in the rear of the store—toys, electronics, sporting goods, and shoes—lie in utter darkness.

Only the dry silver beams of battery-powered emergency lights illuminate the shadowy depths of the far aisles.

They find flashlights in the hardware department, and shine the beams into the far reaches of the store, making note of all the useful provisions and tools. The more they investigate, the more excited they become. By the time they've circled the entire fifteen thousand square feet of retail space—finding only a few scattered human remains in the early stages of decomposition, innumerable overturned shelves, and rats scurrying from the sounds of their footsteps—they are convinced that the store is safe—picked over, certainly, but *safe*.

At least for the moment.

"Pretty sure we got the place to ourselves," Josh says at last as the threesome returns to the diffuse light of the front vestibule.

They lower their weapons and flashlights. "Looks like some shit went down in here," Bob says.

"I ain't no detective." Josh gazes around the walls and floors awash in bloodstains that could pass for Jackson Pollock paintings. "But I'd say some folks turned in here a while back, and then you got layers of people comin' in and helpin' themselves to what was left."

Lilly looks at Josh, her expression still tight with nervous tension. She glances at the headless greeter. "You think we could clean the place up, maybe stay here a while?"

Josh shakes his head. "We'd be sitting ducks, place is way too tempting."

"It's also a gold mine," Bob pipes in. "Plenty of stuff on the high shelves, maybe stockrooms in back with merchandise, could be damn useful to us." His eyes twinkle, and Josh can tell the older man has taken careful accounting of the top shelves of the liquor department, still brimming with unopened bottles of hooch.

"I saw some wheelbarrows and hand dollies in the garden department," Josh says. He looks at Bob, then he looks at Lilly and grins. "I think our luck just changed for the better."

They load up three wheelbarrows with down coats, winter boots, thermal underwear, stocking caps, and gloves from the fashion department. They throw in a pair of walkie-talkies, tire chains, towlines, a socket-wrench kit, road flares, motor oil, and antifreeze. They get Scott to help them, leaving Megan in the truck to watch for intruders.

From the grocery department—where most of the meats, produce, and dairy products are either missing or have long since spoiled—they procure boxes of instant oatmeal, raisins, protein bars, ramen noodles, jars of peanut butter, beef jerky, cans of soup, spaghetti sauce, juice boxes, cartons of dry pasta, canned meats, sardines, coffee, and tea.

Bob raids what is left of the pharmacy. Most of the barbiturates, painkillers, and antianxiety meds are long gone, but he finds enough leftovers to open a private practice. He takes some Lanacane for first aid, amoxicillin for infections, epinephrine for kicking a heart back to life, Adderall for keeping alert, lorazepam for calming the nerves,

Celox for stanching blood loss, naproxen for pain, loratadine for opening air passages, and a good assortment of vitamins.

From other departments, they acquire irresistible luxury items— items that aren't exactly paramount to their survival but might none- theless bring momentary relief from the grim business of staying alive. Lilly chooses an armful of hardcover books—novels mostly— from the newsstand area. Josh finds a collection of hand-rolled Costa Rican cigars behind the courtesy desk. Scott discovers a battery- operated DVD player and selects a dozen movies. They take a few board games, some playing cards, a telescope, and a small digital voice recorder.

They make a trip out to the truck, stuffing the camper to the gills with the goodies, before returning and starting in on the treasure trove of useful items in the darkness at the rear of the store.

"Shine it over to the left, babydoll," Josh asks Lilly from the aisle outside the sporting goods department. Josh holds two large heavy- duty duffel bags appropriated from the luggage department.

Scott and Bob stand nearby, watching expectantly, as Lilly sweeps the narrow beam of her flashlight across the disaster area that once trafficked in soccer balls and Little League bats.

The yellow shaft of light crosses mangled displays of tennis rack- ets and hockey sticks, cannibalized bicycles and heaps of workout clothes and baseball gloves strewn across the blood-spattered floor. "Whoa . . . right there, Lilly," Josh says. "Hold it steady."

"Shit," Bob says from behind Lilly. "Looks like we're too late."

"Somebody beat us to 'em," Josh grumbles as the flashlight plays across the shattered glass display case to the left of the fish- ing poles and tackle. The case is empty, but from the look of the in- dentations and hooks left behind, it's obvious the enclosure housed a wide variety of hunting rifles, target pistols, and street-legal hand- guns. The racks on the wall behind the display are also empty. "Shine it on the floor for a second, honey."

In the dull cone of light, a few stray shells and bullets are visibly scattered across the floor.

They walk over to the gun counter and Josh drops the duffel

bags, then squeezes his massive form behind the case. He takes the flashlight and shines it down along the floor. He sees a few stray boxes of ammunition, a bottle of gun oil, a receipt pad, and a blunt silver object peeking out from under the case. "Hold on a second . . . *hold the phone.*"

Josh kneels. He reaches under the counter and pulls the blunt steel end of a muzzle out from under the bottom of the case.

"Now we're talking," he says, holding the gun up in the light for all to see.

"Is that a Desert Eagle?" Bob steps in closer. "Is that a .44?"

Josh grips the gun like a boy on Christmas morning. "Whatever the hell it is, it's heavy as shit. Thing must weigh ten pounds."

"May I?" Bob takes the gun. "Holy Christ . . . this is the goddamn howitzer of handguns."

"Now all we need are bullets."

Bob checks the clip. "Manufactured by bad-ass Hebrews, gas-operated . . . the only semiauto of its kind." Bob looks up at the high shelves. "Shine that light up yonder . . . see if they got any .50 caliber express up there."

A moment later, Josh finds a stack of cartons marked "50-C-R" on the top shelf. He boosts himself up and grabs half a dozen cartons.

Meanwhile, Bob thumbs the release and the magazine falls into his greasy hand. His voice goes soft and low, as though he's speaking to a lover. "Nobody designs firearms like the Israelis . . . not even the Germans. This bad boy can penetrate tank armor."

"Dude," Scott says finally, standing behind Bob with a flashlight. "You planning on shooting that thing or fucking it?"

After an awkward moment, they all burst out laughing—even Josh can't resist chuckling—and despite the fact that their laughter is brittle and fraught with nerves, it serves to break the tension in that silent warehouse of blood and looted shelves. They have had a good day. They've hit the jackpot here in this temple of discount consumerism. More importantly, they've acquired something here far more valuable than mere provisions: They have found a glimmer of hope that they'll make it through the winter . . . that they just may come out the other side of this nightmare.

Lilly hears the noise first. Her laughter instantly dies and she looks around as though waking with a start from a dream. "What was that?"

Josh stops laughing. "What's the matter?"

"Did you hear that?"

Bob looks at her. "What's wrong, darlin'?"

"I heard something." Her voice is low and taut with panic.

Josh turns his flashlight off and looks at Scott. "Turn the flashlight off, Scott."

Scott extinguishes the light and the rear of the store is plunged into darkness.

Lilly's heart thumps as they stand there in the shadows for a moment, listening. The store is silent. Then another creaking noise penetrates the stillness.

It comes from the front of the store. A wrenching sound, like rusty metal squeaking, but faint, so faint it's impossible to identify.

Josh whispers, "Bob, where's the shotgun?"

"Left it up front, with the wheelbarrows."

"Great."

"What if it's Megan?"

Josh thinks about it. He gazes out at the stillness of the store. "Megan! That you?"

No answer.

Lilly swallows air. Dizziness courses over her. "You think walkers could push the door open?"

"A stiff breeze could blow it open," Josh says, reaching behind his belt for the .38. "Bob, how handy are you with that bad-ass pistol?"

Bob already has one of the ammo boxes open. He fishes for bullets with trembling, filthy fingers. "Way ahead of you, captain."

"All right, listen—"

Josh starts to whisper instructions when another noise fills the air—muffled but distinct—clearly the sound of frozen hinges rasping somewhere near the entrance. Someone or some *thing* is pushing itself into the store.

Bob fiddles bullets into an empty magazine, his hands shaking. He drops the magazine, the clip hitting the floor and spilling rounds.

"Dude," Scott comments under his breath, nervously watching Bob on his hands and knees retrieving the stray bullets like a little boy madly gathering marbles.

"Listen up," Josh hisses at them. "Scott, you and Bob take the left flank, head toward the front of the store through the grocery department. Babydoll, you follow me. We'll grab an axe from home and garden on the way."

Bob, on the floor, finally manages to get the bullets into the clip, then slams the magazine into the pistol and levers himself back to his feet. "Gotcha. C'mon, junior. Let's do it."

They split off and move through the darkness toward the pale light.

Lilly follows Josh through the shadows of the auto care center, past ransacked shelves, past heaps of litter strewn across the tile flooring, past home and office, past crafts. They move as quietly as possible, staying low and close together, Josh communicating with hand gestures. He has the .38 in one hand, the other hand coming up suddenly and signaling for Lilly to stop.

From the front of the store, the sound of shuffling footsteps can now clearly be heard.

Josh points at a fallen display in the do-it-yourself department. Lilly creeps around behind a display of lightbulbs and finds the floor littered with rakes and pruning shears and three-foot-long axes. She grabs one of the axes and comes back around the lightbulbs, her heart hammering, her flesh crawling with terror.

They approach the front entrance. Lilly can see an occasional flash of movement on the other side of the store as Scott and Bob close in along the west wall of the grocery department. By this point, whatever it is that's slithering into the Walmart seems to have fallen silent and still. Lilly can't hear a thing other than her chugging heart.

Josh pauses behind the pharmacy counter, crouching down. Lilly joins him. Josh whispers to her, "You stay behind me, and if one of them things gets past me, give it a good whack in the center of the head with that thing."

"Josh, I know how to kill a zombie," Lilly retorts in a harsh whisper.

"I know, honey, all I'm saying . . . just make sure you whack it hard enough the first time."

Lilly nods.

"On three," Josh whispers. "You ready?"

"Ready."

"One, two—"

Josh stops cold. Lilly hears something that doesn't compute.

Josh grabs her and holds her steady against the bottom of the pharmacy counter. Paralyzed with indecision, they crouch there for a moment, a single incongruous thought screaming in Lilly's brain.

Zombies don't talk.

"Hello?" The voice echoes across the empty store. "Anybody home?"

Josh hesitates behind the counter for another brief moment, weighing his options, his brain swimming with panic. The voice sounds friendly . . . sort of . . . definitely male, deep, maybe a little bit of an accent.

Josh glances over his shoulder at Lilly. She's holding the axe like a baseball bat, poised to strike, her lips quivering with terror. Josh holds his huge hand up—making a "give me a second" gesture—and he's about to make his move, letting up on the pistol's hammer, when another voice rings out, instantly changing the dynamic.

"LET HER GO, YOU SONS OF BITCHES!"

Josh lunges out from behind the counter with his .38 raised and ready to fire.

Lilly follows with the axe.

A group of six men—all heavily armed—stand in the vestibule.

"Easy . . . easy, easy, easy . . . *whoa!*" The leader, the guy standing out in front of the pack—a high-powered assault rifle in his arms, the muzzle raised menacingly—looks to be in his late twenties, early thirties at the most. Tall, rangy, dark complexioned, he wears a do-rag on his head. The sleeves of his flannel shirt are scissored off. His arms are heavily muscled.

At first, things are happening almost too quickly for Josh to track as he stands his ground with the barrel of his .38 pinned on Bandanna Man.

From behind the checkout lanes, Bob Stookey charges toward the intruders with his Desert Eagle gripped in both hands, commando-style, his red-rimmed eyes wide with drunken heroism. "LET HER GO!" The object of his pique stands behind the bandanna dude, held captive by a younger member of the raiding party. Megan Lafferty squirms angrily in the grip of a wild-eyed black kid, a greasy hand across her mouth, keeping her quiet.

"BOB—DON'T!" Josh bellows at the top of his lungs, and the booming authority of his voice seems to slam the brakes on Bob's gallantry. The older man falters at the end of the checkout lanes, stuttering to a stop a mere twenty feet from the guy holding Megan prisoner. Breathing hard, the old juicer stares helplessly at Megan. Josh can see the emotions all stirred up in the older man.

"Everybody chill!" Josh orders his people.

Scott Moon appears behind Bob with the old squirrel gun raised.

"Scott, cool it with the shotgun!"

The man in the bandanna doesn't lower his AK-47. "Let's dial it down, folks, come on—we're not looking to get into any O.K. Corral–type situation here."

Behind the dark-skinned dude stand five other men with heavy-duty weaponry. Mostly in their thirties, some black, some white, some in hip-hop street attire, others in ragged army fatigues and down vests, they look rested and well fed and maybe even a little high. Most importantly to Josh, they look as though they would just as soon start blasting as engage in any kind of diplomacy.

"We're cool," Josh says, but he's fairly certain that the tone of his voice, the set of his jaw, and the fact that he too has refrained from lowering his gun—all of this probably sends a countervailing message to Bandanna Man. "Aren't we, Bob? Aren't we cool?"

Bob mumbles something inaudible. The Desert Eagle remains in its upright, locked position, and for a brief and awkward moment, the two groups stand each other off with guns pointed at key pieces of anatomy. Josh doesn't like the odds—the intruders are packing enough firepower to take down a small garrison—but on the other hand, Josh's side has three working firearms all pointed, at the moment, directly at the raiding party's leader, whose loss might put a serious kink in this little posse's group dynamic.

"Let the girl go, Haynes," Bandanna Man orders his underling.

"But what about—"

"I said let her go!"

The wild-eyed black kid shoves Megan toward her comrades, and Megan stumbles for a moment, nearly falling, but then manages to stay upright and stagger over to Bob. "What a bunch of fucking dicks!" she grumbles.

"You okay, sweetie?" Bob asks, putting his free arm around her, but not taking his eyes (or the barrel of the magnum) off the intruders.

"Assholes snuck up on me," she says, rubbing her wrists, glowering back at them.

Bandanna Man lowers his gun and addresses Josh. "Look, we can't take any chances these days, we didn't know you from Adam . . . we're just looking after our own."

Unconvinced, Josh keeps the .38 beaded directly on Bandanna Man's chest. "What does that have to do with snatching that girl outta the truck?"

"Like I said . . . we didn't know how many of you we were dealing with . . . who she was gonna warn . . . we didn't know anything."

"You own this place?"

"No . . . whaddaya mean? No."

Josh gives him a cold smile. "Then lemme make a suggestion . . . as to where we go from here."

"Go ahead."

"There's plenty of stuff left in here . . . why don't y'all let us pass and you can have the rest."

Bandanna Man turns to his gang. "Guns down, guys. Come on. Step it on back. Come on."

Almost reluctantly the rest of the intruders comply and lower their weapons.

Bandanna Man turns back to Josh. "Name's Martinez . . . I'm sorry we got off on the wrong foot."

"Name's Hamilton and it's nice to meet you and I'd appreciate it if you'd let us pass."

"No problema, mi amigo . . . but can I just make a suggestion to *you* before we conclude our business together?"

"I'm listening."

"First off, is there any way you could stop pointing those guns at us?"

Josh keeps his eyes on Martinez as he lowers his gun. "Scott, Bob . . . go ahead . . . it's okay."

Scott puts the shotgun on his shoulder and leans against a checkout belt to listen. Bob reluctantly lowers the muzzle of the Desert Eagle, shoves it behind his belt, and keeps his arm around Megan.

Lilly sets her axe—head down—on the floor, leaning it against the pharmacy counter.

"Thanks, I appreciate it." Martinez takes a deep breath and lets out a sigh. "What I'm wondering is this. You seem like you got your head screwed on straight. You got the right to take all that merchandise outta here . . . but can I ask where you're taking it?"

"Truth is, we ain't taking it anywhere," Josh says. "We're getting it to go."

"You folks living on the road?"

"What difference does it make?"

Martinez shrugs. "Look, I know you got no reason to trust me, but the way things are, folks like us . . . we can be mutually beneficial to each other. You know what I'm saying?"

"To be honest, no . . . I don't have a fuckin' clue as to what you're saying."

Martinez sighs. "Let me lay my cards on the table. We could part ways right here and now, no harm no foul, wish each other the best . . ."

"Sounds good to me," Josh says.

"We got a better option, though," the man says.

"Which is?"

"A walled-in place, just up the road, people just like you and me, trying to make a place to live."

"Go on."

"No more running, is what I'm saying. We secured part of a town. It ain't much . . . yet. We got some walls up. Place to grow food. Generators. Heat. We definitely got room for five more."

Josh doesn't say anything. He looks at Lilly. He can't read her face. She looks exhausted, scared, confused. He looks at the others. He sees Bob's wheels turning. Scott looks at the floor. Megan stares balefully out at the intruders through tendrils of curly hair.

"Think about it, man," Martinez goes on. "We could split up what's left in this place and call it a day or we could join forces. We need good strong backs. If I wanted to rob you, fuck with you, mess you up . . . wouldn't I have done it already? I got no reason to make trouble. Come with us, Hamilton. Whaddaya say? There's nothing out there on the road but more shit and winter rolling in. Whaddaya say, man?"

Josh looks at Martinez for a long moment, until finally Josh says, "Give us a second."

They gather over by the checkout counters.

"Dude, you gotta be fucking kidding me," Megan says to Josh in a low, tense whisper. The others huddle around the big man in a semi-circle. "You're thinking about going somewhere with these scumbags?"

Josh licks his lips. "I don't know . . . the more I look at these dudes, the more they look just as scared and freaked out as we are."

Lilly chimes in. "Maybe we could just check the place out, see what it's like."

Bob looks at Josh. "Compared with livin' in tents on the ground with a bunch of hotheads? How bad could it be?"

Megan groans. "Is it just me, or have you people lost your fucking minds?"

"Megan, I don't know," Scott says. "I'm like thinking what do we have to lose?"

"Shut up, Scott."

"Okay, look," Josh says, holding up a huge hand and cutting off the debate. "I don't see any harm in following them, checking the place out. We'll keep our guns, keep our eyes open, and we'll decide when we see the place." He looks at Bob, then looks at Lilly. "Cool?"

Lilly takes a deep breath. Then gives him a nod. "Yeah . . . cool."

"Terrific," Megan grumbles, following the others back toward the entrance.

It takes another hour and the combined efforts of the two groups to go through the rest of the store for heavy items required by the town. They raid the lawn and garden center and home repair for lumber, fertilizer, potting soil, seeds, hammers, and nails. Lilly senses an edgy quality to the uneasy truce between the two contingents. She keeps tabs on Martinez out of the corner of her eye, and she notices an unspoken hierarchy to the ragtag raiding party. Martinez is definitely the honcho, ruling the others with simple gestures and nods.

By the time they get Bob's Ram and the two vehicles from the walled-in town—a panel van and flatbed truck—loaded to the gills, twilight is closing in. Martinez gets behind the wheel of the van, and tells Bob to follow along behind the flatbed . . . and the convoy starts out for the town.

As they wend their way out of the dusty Walmart lot and start up the access road toward the highway, Lilly sits in the back sleeper compartment, gazing through the bug-streaked windshield, as Bob concentrates on keeping up with the exhaust-belching flatbed. They pass tangles of wreckage and dense forests on either side of the farm road, behind which shadows are deepening. A fine mist of sleet rolls in on the north wind.

In the steel-gray twilight, Lilly can barely see the lead vehicle— several car lengths ahead of them—a glimpse of Martinez in the side mirror, his tattooed arm resting on the outer edge of the open window as he drives.

It could be Lilly's imagination, but she is almost positive she sees the bandanna-clad head of Martinez turning toward his passengers, saying something, sharing some intimate tidbit, and then getting a huge reaction from his comrades.

The men are laughing hysterically.

PART 2

This Is How the World Ends

The evil that men do lives after them; the good is often
interred with their bones.

—William Shakespeare

EIGHT

The convoy makes two stops on their way to the walled-in town—the first at the junction of Highways 18 and 109, where an armed sentry consults with Martinez for a moment before waving the vehicles on. A heap of human remains lies in a nearby ditch, still smoldering from a makeshift funeral pyre. They make the second stop at a roadblock near the town sign. By this point the sleet has turned to a wet snow, spitting across the macadam on angular gusts, a very rare phenomenon for Georgia this early in December.

"Looks like they got some serious firepower," Josh comments from the driver's seat, as he waits for the two men in olive-drab camo suits and M1 rifles to finish chatting with Martinez three car lengths ahead of the Ram. Shadows thrown by the headlights obscure the distant faces as they talk, the snow swirling, the Ram's windshield wipers beating out a sullen rhythm. Lilly and Bob remain silent and fidgety as they watch the exchange.

Full darkness has fallen, and the lack of a power grid and the bad weather give the outer rings of the town a medieval quality. Flames burn here and there in oil drums, and the signs of a recent skirmish mar the wooded vales and pine groves circling the town. In the distance the scorched rooftops, bullet-riddled trailers, and torn power lines reflect a series of past upheavals.

Josh notices Lilly studying the rust-pocked green sign up ahead, visible in the wash of headlamp beams, the signpost planted in the white, sandy earth.

WELCOME TO
WOODBURY
POPULATION 1,102

Lilly turns to Josh and says, "How are you feeling about all this?"

"Jury's still out. But it looks like we're about to get further orders."

Up ahead, in luminous motes of snow passing through the headlight beams, Martinez turns away from the confab, lifts his collar, and starts trudging back toward the Ram. He walks with a purpose, but still has that congenial smile plastered over his dark features. He lifts his collar against the cold as he approaches Josh's window.

Josh rolls down the window. "What's the deal?"

Martinez smiles. "Gonna need you to hand over your firearms for the time being."

Josh stares at him. "Sorry, brother, but that ain't gonna happen."

The convivial smile lingers. "Town rules . . . you know how it is."

Josh slowly shakes his head. "Ain't gonna happen."

Martinez purses his lips thoughtfully, then smiles some more. "Can't say I blame you, walking into something like this. Tell you what. Can you leave the rabbit gun in the truck for now?"

Josh lets out a sigh. "I guess we could do that."

"And you mind keeping the sidearms tucked away? Out of sight?"

"We could do that."

"Okay . . . if you want the nickel tour I could ride along with you folks. You got room for one more?"

Josh turns and gives Bob a nod. With a shrug the older man unsnaps his safety belt and gets out, then turns and squeezes into the rear enclosure next to Lilly.

Martinez comes around the passenger side and climbs into the cab. He smells of smoke and machine oil. "Take it nice and slow, cousin," he says, wiping the moisture from his face, gesturing toward the panel van ahead of them. "Just follow the dude in the van."

Josh gives the Ram some gas and they follow the van through the roadblock.

They bump over a series of railroad tracks and enter the town from the southeast. Lilly and Bob remain silent in the rear enclosure, as Josh scans the immediate area. To his right a busted sign reading PIGGLY IGGLY stands over a parking lot littered with dead bodies and broken glass. The grocery store is caved in on one side as though blasted by dynamite. Tall cyclone fencing, gouged and punched out in places, runs along the road known alternately as Woodbury Highway or Main Street. Grisly lumps of human carnage and twisted, scorched metal litter patches of exposed ground—the white, sandy earth practically glowing in the snowy darkness—an eerie sight reminiscent of a desert war zone smack-dab in the middle of Georgia.

"Had a pretty big dustup a few weeks ago with a flock of biters." Martinez lights a Viceroy and opens his window a few inches. The smoke curls out into the wind-lashed snow, vanishing like ghosts. "Things got outta hand for a while, but luckily cooler heads prevailed. Gonna be taking a hard left up here in a second."

Josh follows the van around a hairpin and down a narrower section of road.

In the dark middle distance, behind a veil of windswept sleet, the heart of Woodbury comes into view. Four square blocks of turn-of-the-century brick buildings and power lines crowd a central intersection of merchants, wood-frame homes, and apartment buildings. Much of it is laced with cyclone fences and idle construction sites that appear to be recent additions. Josh remembers when they used to call these places "wide spots in the road."

Woodbury's width seems to extend about half a dozen blocks in all directions, with larger public areas carved out of the wooded wetlands to the west and north. Some of the rooftop chimneys and vent stacks sprout columns of thick black smoke, either from generator exhaust or woodstoves and fireplaces. Most of the street lamps are dark, but some glow in the darkness, apparently running on emergency juice.

As the convoy approaches the center of town, Josh notices the van pulling up to the edge of a construction site. "Been working on the wall for months," Martinez explains. "Pretty near got two square blocks completely protected, and we plan on expanding it—moving the wall back farther and farther as we go."

"Not a bad idea," Josh mutters, almost under his breath, as he ponders the massive high wall of wooden timbers and planks, cannibalized pieces of cabin logs, siding, and two-by-fours, at least fifteen feet tall, extending along the edge of Jones Mill Road. Portions of the barricade still bare the scars of the recent walker attacks, and even in the snow-swept dark the claw marks and patched areas and ricochet holes and bloodstains, as black as tar, call out to Josh.

The place vibrates with latent violence, like some throwback to the Wild West.

Josh brings the truck to a stop, as the van's rear doors jack open and one of the Young Turks hops out the back and then goes over to a seam in the fortification. He pulls open a hinged section, swinging the gate wide enough for the two vehicles to pass through. The van rumbles through the gap, and Josh follows.

"Got about fifty people and change," Martinez continues, taking a deep drag off the Viceroy and blowing it out the window. "Place over there, on the right, that's kind of a food center. Got all our supplies, bottled water, medicine stashed in that place."

As they pass, Josh sees the faded old sign—DEFOREST'S FEED AND SEED—its storefront fortified and reinforced with burglar bars and planking, two armed guards standing out front smoking cigarettes. The gate closes behind them as they roll slowly along, venturing deeper into the secure zone. Other denizens stand around, watching them pass—people bundled up on boardwalks, standing in vestibules—shell-shocked expressions behind scarves and mufflers. Nobody looks particularly friendly or happy to see them.

"Got a doctor on board, working medical center and whatnot." Martinez tosses his cigarette butt out the window. "Hope to expand the walls at least another block by the end of the week."

"Not a bad setup," Bob comments from the backseat, his watery eyes taking it all in. "If ya don't mind my asking, what the hell is that?"

Josh sees the top of the massive edifice a few blocks beyond the walled-in area, toward which Bob is now pointing a greasy finger.

In the hazy darkness it looks like a flying saucer has landed in the middle of a field beyond the town square. Dirt roads circle the thing, and dim lights twinkle in the snow above its circular rim.

"Used to be a dirt racetrack." Martinez grins. In the green glow of the dashboard lights the smirk looks almost lupine, devilish. "Hillbillies love their races."

" 'Used' to be?" Josh asks.

"Boss laid down the law last week, no more races, too much noise. Racket was drawing biters."

"There's a boss here?"

The smirk on Martinez's face curdles into something unreadable. "Don't worry, cousin. You'll be meeting him soon enough."

Josh sneaks a glance at Lilly, who is busily gnawing on her fingernails. "Not sure we're gonna be sticking around very long."

"It's up to you." Martinez gives a noncommittal shrug. He slips on a pair of fingerless, leather Carnaby gloves. "Keep in mind, though, those mutual benefits I was talking about."

"I'll do that."

"Our apartments are all filled up but we still got places you can stay in the center of town."

"Good to know."

"I'm telling you, once we get that wall expanded, you'll have your pick of places to live."

Josh says nothing.

Martinez stops smirking and all at once, in the dim green light, he looks as though he's remembering better days, maybe a family, maybe something painful. "I'm talking about places with soft beds, privacy . . . picket fences and trees."

A long pause of awkward silence.

"Lemme ask you something, Martinez."

"Shoot."

"How did *you* end up here?"

Martinez lets out a sigh. "God's honest truth, I don't really remember."

"How's that?"

He gives another shrug. "I was alone, ex-wife got bit, my kid up and disappeared. I guess I didn't give a shit about much of anything anymore but killing biters. Went on kind of a rampage. Put down a whole slew of those ugly motherfuckers. Some locals found me passed out in a ditch. Took me here. Swear to God that's about all I remember." He cocks his head as though reconsidering. "I'm glad they did, though, especially now."

"What do you mean?"

Martinez looks at him. "This place ain't perfect but it's safe, and it's only gonna get safer. Thanks in no small part to the guy we got in charge now."

Josh looks at him. "This is the 'boss' guy I assume you're talking about?"

"That's right."

"And you say we're gonna get a chance to meet this guy?"

Martinez holds up a gloved hand as if to say, *Just wait*. He pulls a small two-way radio from the breast pocket of his flannel shirt. He thumbs the switch and speaks into the mouthpiece. "Haynes, take us to the courthouse . . . they're waiting for us over there."

Another loaded glance passes between Josh and Lilly as the lead vehicle pulls off the main road and heads across the town square, a statue of Robert E. Lee guarding a kudzu-covered gazebo. They approach a flagstone government building on the far edge of the park, its stone steps and portico ghostly pale in the snow-veiled darkness.

The community room lies at the rear of the courthouse building, at the end of a long, narrow corridor lined with glass doors leading into private offices.

Josh and company gather in the cluttered meeting room, their boots dripping on the parquet floor. They are exhausted and in no mood to meet the Woodbury Welcome Wagon but Martinez tells them to be patient.

Snow ticks against the high windows as they wait. The room, warmed by space heaters and dimly lit with Coleman lanterns, looks as though it has seen its share of heated exchanges. The crumbling plaster walls bare the scars of violence. The floor is strewn with overturned folding chairs and littered with wadded documents. Josh notices blood streaks on the front wall, near a tattered

Georgia state flag. Generators thrum in the bowels of the edifice, vibrating the floor.

They wait a little over five minutes—Josh pacing, Lilly and the others sitting on folding chairs—before the sound of heavy boots echo out in the corridor. Someone is whistling as the footsteps approach.

"Welcome, folks, welcome to Woodbury." The voice that emanates from the doorway is low and nasally, and filled with faux conviviality.

All heads turn.

Three men stand in the doorway with smiles on their faces that don't match their cold, lidded stares. The man in the middle radiates a weird kind of energy that makes Lilly think of peacocks and fighting fish. "We can always use more good people around here," he says, and steps into the room.

Lean and rawboned in his ratty fisherman's sweater, his cinder-black hair shapeless and shaggy, he sports a five o'clock shadow of whiskers on his face that he's already trimming and styling into the beginnings of a Fu Manchu mustache. He has a strange nervous tic that is hardly noticeable—he blinks a lot.

"Name's Philip Blake," he says, "and this is Bruce over here, and that's Gabe."

The other two men—both older—follow on the younger man's heels like guard dogs. Not much of a greeting from these two—other than a few grunts and nods—as they stand slightly behind the man named Philip.

Gabe, on the left, the Caucasian, is a fireplug of a man with a thick neck and jarhead crew cut. Bruce, on the right, is a dour black man with an onyx shaved head. Each of these men holds an impressive automatic assault rifle across his chest, fingers on the trigger pads. For a moment Lilly cannot take her eyes off the guns.

"Sorry about the heavy artillery," Philip says, indicating the weaponry behind him. "We had a little dustup in town last month, got kinda hairy for a while. Can't take any chances now. Too much at stake. Your names are . . . ?"

Josh introduces the group, going around the room and ending on Megan.

"You look like somebody I knew once," Philip informs Megan, the man's eyes all over her now. Lilly does not like the way this guy is looking at her friend. It's very subtle but it bothers her.

"I get that a lot," Megan says.

"Or maybe it's somebody famous. Doesn't she look like somebody famous, guys?"

The "guys" behind him have no opinion. Philip snaps his fingers. "That chick from *Titanic!*"

"Carrie Winslet?" the one named Gabe speculates.

"You stupid fucking idiot, it's not Carrie, it's *Kate . . . Kate . . .* Fucking *Kate* Winslet."

Megan gives Philip a cockeyed smile. "I've been told Bonnie Raitt."

"I *love* Bonnie Raitt," Philip enthuses. " 'Let's Give 'Em Something to Talk About.' "

Josh speaks up. "So you're 'the boss' we've been hearing about?"

Philip turns to the big man. "Guilty as charged." Philip smiles and goes over to Josh and extends a hand. " 'Josh' was it?"

Josh shakes the man's hand. The expression on Josh's face remains noncommittal, polite, deferential. "That's right. We appreciate you taking us in for a while. Not sure how long we'll be staying."

Philip smiles at him. "You just got here, friend. Relax. Check the place out. You won't find a safer place to live. Believe me."

Josh gives a nod. "Looks like you got the walker problem under control."

"We get our share, I won't lie to you. Pack of 'em comes through every few weeks. Had a bad situation a couple of weeks ago but we're getting the town squared away."

"Looks like it."

"Basically we run on the barter system." Philip Blake looks around the room, regarding each of these newcomers as a coach might size up a new team. "I understand you folks scored big at a Walmart today."

"We did all right."

"You're all welcome to take what you need in trade."

Josh looks at him. "Trade?"

"Goods, services . . . whatever you got to contribute. As long as you respect your fellow citizens, keep your noses clean, abide by the rules, pitch in . . . you can stay as long as you like." He looks at Josh. "Gentleman of your . . . *physical endowment* . . . we can use around here."

Josh thinks it over. "So you're some kind of 'elected official'?"

Philip glances at his guards, and the other men grin, and Philip bursts out laughing. He wipes his mirthless eyes and shakes his head. "I'm more like—what's the phrase?—'pro tem'? President pro tem?"

"I'm sorry?"

Philip waves off the question. "Put it this way, not long ago this place was under the thumb of some power-hungry assholes, got too big for their britches. I saw the need for leadership and I volunteered."

"Volunteered?"

Philip's smile fades. "I stepped up, friend. Times like these. Strong leadership is a necessity. We got families here. Women and children. Old people. You got to have somebody watching the door, somebody . . . decisive. You understand what I'm saying?"

Josh nods. "Sure."

Behind Philip, Gabe, still smirking, mumbles, "President Pro Tem . . . I like that."

From across the room, Scott, perched on a windowsill, chimes in: "Dude, you sure *look* like a president . . . with those two Secret Service dudes."

An awkward moment of silence presses down on the group as Scott's breathy little weed-giggle fades and Philip turns to glance at the stoner across the room. "What's your name again, sport?"

"Scott Moon."

"Well, Scott Moon, I don't know about president. Never saw myself as the chief executive type." Another cold smile. "I'd be governor at best."

They spend that night in the gymnasium of the local high school. The aging brick building, situated outside the walled-in zone, sits on the edge of a vast athletic field riddled with shallow graves.

Cyclone fences bear the damage of a recent walker attack. Inside the gym, makeshift cots crowd the varnished basketball court. The air smells of urine and body odors and disinfectant.

The night drags for Lilly. The fetid corridors and breezeways connecting the dark schoolrooms creak and moan in the wind all night, while strangers toss and turn across the dark gymnasium, coughing, wheezing, murmuring feverish ruminations. Every few moments a child cries out.

At one point Lilly glances at the cot next to her, on which Josh slumbers fitfully, and she sees the big man jerking awake from a nightmare.

Lilly reaches over and offers her hand, and the big man takes it.

The next morning, the five newcomers sit in a huddle around Josh's cot, as the ashen sunlight slants down through dust motes and stripes the sick and wounded as they hunch on their meager, stained bedsheets. Lilly is reminded of Civil War encampments and jury-rigged morgues. "Is it just me," she says softly, under her breath to her fellow travelers, "or does this place have a weird vibe?"

"That's putting it lightly," Josh says.

Megan yawns and stretches. "It sure beats sleeping in Bob's little dungeon-on-wheels."

"You got that right," Scott concurs. "I'll take a shitty cot in a stinky gym any day of the week."

Bob looks at Josh. "Gotta admit, captain . . . you could make an argument for staying here for a while."

Josh laces his boots, pulls on his lumberjack coat. "Not sure about this place."

"What's on your mind?"

"I don't know. I'm thinking we take this one day at a time."

"I agree with Josh," Lilly says. "Something about this place bothers me."

"What's not to like?" Megan combs fingers through her hair, scrunching her curls. "It's safe, they got supplies, they got guns."

Josh wipes his mouth thoughtfully. "Look. I can't tell any of you folks what to do. Just be careful. Watch each other's backs."

"Duly noted," Bob says.

"Bob, for the time being, I'm thinking we ought to keep the truck locked up."

"Copy that."

"Keep your .44 handy."

"Gotcha."

"And we ought to all remember where the truck is at all times, you know, just in case."

They all agree, and then they agree to split up that morning and investigate the rest of the town—get a feel for the place in the light of day. They will meet back up that afternoon at the high school and they will reassess at that point whether to go or stay.

The harsh light of day shines down on Lilly and Josh as they exit the high school, turning up their collars against the wind. The snow has blown over, and the weather has turned blustery. Lilly's stomach growls. "You feel like getting some breakfast?" she proffers to Josh.

"Got some of that stuff from Walmart in the truck, if you can stand beef jerky and Chef Boyardee again."

Lilly shudders. "I don't think I can look at another can of SpaghettiOs."

"I got an idea." Josh feels the breast pocket of his flannel jacket. "Come on . . . I'm buying."

They turn west and make their way down the main drag. In the bitter gray daylight the seams of the town reveal themselves. Most of the storefronts sit empty, boarded or barred, the pavement scarred with skid marks and oil spills. Some of the windows and signs show the marks of bullet holes. Passersby keep to themselves. Here and there, bare patches of ground reveal dirty white sand. It seems the whole village is built on sand.

No one offers a greeting as Lilly and Josh pass through the walled area. Most of those who are out at this hour carry building materials or bundles of supplies, and seem to be in a hurry to get where they're going. There's a sullen, prisonlike atmosphere in the air. Quadrants of the town are sectioned off with huge, temporary cyclone fences. The growl of bulldozers drifts on the breeze. On the eastern horizon, a man with a high-powered rifle paces along the top edge of the racetrack arena.

"Morning, gentlemen," Josh says to three old codgers sitting on barrels outside the feed and seed store, watching Lilly and Josh like buzzards.

One of the old men—a wizened, bearded troll in a tattered overcoat and slouch hat—shows a smile full of rotten teeth. "Mornin', big fella. Y'all are the newbies, ain't ya?"

"Just got in last night," Josh tells him.

"Lucky you."

The three coots share a garbled chuckle as if enjoying a private joke.

Josh smiles and lets the joke pass. "Understand this is the food center?"

"You could call it that." More mucusy chuckling. "Keep an eye on your woman."

"I'll do that," Josh says, taking Lilly's hand. They climb the steps and go inside.

In the dim light a long, narrow retail store stretches before them, smelling of turpentine and must, gutted of its shelves, packed with crates up to the ceiling: dry goods, toilet paper, gallon jugs of water, bed linen, and unidentified cartons of merchandise. The single customer present—an older woman bundled in down and scarves—sees Josh and brushes past him, hurrying out the door, averting her eyes. The cool air vibrates with the artificial warmth of space heaters and the crackle of human tension.

In the rear corner of the store, among sacks of seed stacked to the rafters, sits a makeshift counter. A man in a wheelchair is positioned behind the counter, flanked by two armed guards.

Josh walks up to the counter. "How y'all doin' this morning?"

The man in the wheelchair looks up through lidded eyes. "Holy shit, you're a big one," he comments, his long, straggly beard twitching. He wears faded army dungarees, and a headband cinches his greasy, iron-gray ponytail. His face is a map of degradation, from his rheumy red-rimmed eyes to his ulcerated beak of a nose.

Josh ignores the comment. "Just wondering if y'all have any fresh produce? Or maybe some eggs we might take off your hands in trade?"

The man in the wheelchair stares. Josh can feel the suspicious gazes of the armed guards. The gunmen are both young, black, dressed in quasi-gang colors. "Whaddaya have in mind?"

"The thing is, we just brought in a whole slew of items from Walmart with Martinez . . . so I'm wondering if we can work something out."

"That's between you and Martinez. What else you got for me?"

Josh starts to answer when he notices all three men are staring at Lilly, and the way they're staring at her puts Josh's hackles up.

"What'll this buy me?" Josh says finally, shooting his cuff, fiddling with the buckle of his watchband. He snaps it off and lays the sports watch on the counter. It's not a Rolex but it's no Timex, either. The chronograph set him back three hundred bucks ten years ago when his catering job was bringing in decent money.

Wheelchair Man looks down his blemished nose at the shiny thing on the counter. " 'The tarnation is that?"

"It's a Movado, worth five hundred easy."

"Not around here it ain't."

"Give us a break, will ya? Been eating outta cans for weeks."

The man picks up the watch and inspects it with a sour expression as though it's covered in feces. "I'll give ya fifty dollars' worth of rice and beans, slab bacon, and them Egg Beaters."

"C'mon, man. Fifty dollars?"

"Got some white peaches in back, too, just came in from the road, I'll throw those in. That's all I can do."

"I don't know." Josh looks at Lilly, who stares back at him with a shrug. Josh looks at Wheelchair Man. "I don't know, man."

"That'll keep the two of you going for a week."

Josh sighs. "That's a Movado, man. That's a fine piece of craftsmanship."

"Lookit, I ain't gonna argue with—"

A baritone voice from behind the guards rings out, interrupting the man in the wheelchair. "What the fuck's the problem?"

All heads turn toward a figure coming around the corner of

the stockroom, wiping his bloody hands in a towel. The tall, gaunt, weathered man wears a horribly stained butcher's apron, the fabric mottled with blood and marrow. His chiseled, sunburned face, set off by ice-chip blue eyes, glowers at Josh. "There a problem here, Davy?"

"Everything's hunky-dory, Sam," the man in the wheelchair says, not taking his eyes off Lilly. "These folks were somewhat dissatisfied with my offer, and they were just leaving."

"Hold on a second." Josh raises his hands in a contrite gesture. "I'm sorry if I offended you but I didn't say I was—"

"All offers are final," Sam the Butcher announces, throwing his grisly-looking towel on the counter and glaring at Josh. "Unless . . ." He seems to change his mind. "Forget it, never mind."

Josh looks at the man. "Unless what?"

The man in the apron looks at the others, then purses his lips thoughtfully. "See . . . what most folks do around here is work off their debts, pitching in on the wall, patching fences, stacking sandbags and such. You'll definitely get more bang for your buck offering up them big muscles of yours in trade." He gives Lilly a look. "'Course there's all kinds of services a person could provide, all kinds of ways to get more *bang*." He grins. "Especially a person of the female persuasion."

Lilly realizes the men behind the counter are all looking at *her* now, each of them grinning lasciviously. At first she's taken by surprise, and she just stands there blinking. Then she feels all the blood rushing out of her face. She gets dizzy. She wants to kick over the table, or storm out of that musty-smelling chamber, knocking over the shelves and suggesting that they all fuck themselves. But the fear, the throat-closing fear—her old nemesis—holds her paralyzed, her feet nailed to the floor. She wonders what the hell is wrong with her. How did she survive this long without getting devoured? All she's been through and she can't even deal with a few sexist pigs?

Josh speaks up. "Okay, you know what . . . this is not necessary."

Lilly looks at the big black man and sees his huge, square jaw tensing. She wonders whether Josh is talking about the concept of Lilly trading sexual services not being necessary or these thugs making crude, chauvinist comments not being necessary. The store gets very quiet. Sam the Butcher levels his gaze at Josh.

"Don't be so quick to judge, Big Hoss." An ember of contempt smolders in the butcher's humorless blue eyes. He wipes his slimy hands on the apron. "Little lady with a body like that on her, you could be swimming in steak and eggs for a month."

The smirks on the other men turn to laughter. But the butcher barely smiles. His impassive stare seems to be locked on to Josh with the intensity of an arc welder. Lilly feels her heart racing.

She puts a hand on Josh's arm, which is pulsing under his lumberjack coat, tendons as coiled as telephone cable. "C'mon, Josh," she says, almost under her breath. "It's okay. Get your watch and let's go."

Josh smiles respectfully at the laughing men. "Steak and eggs. That's a good one. Listen. Keep the watch. We'll take you up on them beans and Egg Beaters and the rest."

"Go get 'em their food," the butcher says, still with those pale blue eyes fixed on Josh.

The two guards disappear in the back for a moment, gathering up the items. They return with a crate filled with oil-spotted brown paper sacks. "Appreciate it," Josh says softly, taking the food. "We'll let you fellas get back to your business. Have a good day."

Josh ushers Lilly toward the door, Lilly hyperaware now of the gazes of the men on her backside the whole way out.

That afternoon, a commotion in one of the vacant lots on the northern edge of the village draws the attention of the townspeople.

Outside one of the cyclone fences, behind a wooded grove, a series of nauseating shrieks echoes on the wind. Josh and Lilly hear the screaming, and they race along the edge of the construction zone to see what's going on.

By the time they reach a high mound of gravel and climb to the top to see into the distance, three gunshots have rung out over the treetops a hundred and fifty yards away.

Josh and Lilly crouch down in the dying sun, the wind in their faces, as they peer around a pile of debris and notice five men in the distance, near a hole in the fence. One of the men—Blake, the self-proclaimed Governor—wears a long coat and holds what appears to be an automatic pistol in his hand. The scene crackles with tension.

On the ground in front of Blake, tangled in the jagged, torn chain-link fence, a teenage boy, bleeding from bite wounds, claws at the dirt, trying frantically to extricate himself from the fence and return home.

In the shadows of the forest, directly behind the boy, three dead walkers lie in heaps, their skulls breached by gunfire, and the narrative of what has just happened coalesces in Lilly's mind.

The boy apparently lit out by himself to explore the woods, and he was attacked. Now, badly wounded and infected, the boy, trying to return to safety, writhes in pain and terror on the ground, as Blake stands emotionlessly over him, gazing down with the impassive stare of an undertaker.

Lilly jumps when the boom of the 9-millimeter in Philip Blake's hand echoes. The boy's head erupts, and the body sags immediately.

"I don't like this place, Josh, not even a little." Lilly sits on the Ram's rear bumper, sipping tepid coffee from a paper cup.

Darkness has fallen on their second evening in Woodbury and already the town has absorbed Megan, Scott, and Bob into its folds like a multicelled organism living off fear and suspicion, acquiring new life-forms on a daily basis. The town leaders have offered the newcomers a place to live—a studio apartment above a boarded-up drugstore at the end of Main Street—well outside the walled-in area but high enough above street level to be safe. Megan and Scott have already moved much of their stuff up there and have even bartered their sleeping bags for a nickel's worth of locally grown weed.

Bob has stumbled upon a working tavern inside the safe zone, and already has traded half his rations of Walmart products for a few drink tickets and a little drunken camaraderie.

"I'm not crazy about this place myself, babydoll," Josh concurs as he paces behind Bob's camper, his breath showing in the cold. His huge hands are oily with bacon grease from the dinner he just prepared on the camper's Coleman stove, and he wipes them on his lumberjack coat. He and Lilly have been sticking close to the Ram all day, trying to decide what to do. "But we ain't looking at a lot of options right now. This place is better than the open road."

"Really?" Lilly shivers in the cold and clutches at the collar of her down coat. "You sure about that?"

"At least it's safe."

"Safe from what? It's not the walls and the fences keeping things out I'm worried about . . ."

"I know, I know." Josh lights a stogie and puffs a few swirls of smoke. "It's wound pretty tight around here. But it's pretty much like this everywhere you go nowadays."

"Jesus." Lilly shivers some more and sips her coffee. "Where's Bob, anyway?"

"Hanging out with them geezers at the taproom."

"Jesus Christ."

Josh goes over to her, puts a hand on her shoulder. "Don't worry about it, Lil. We'll rest up, we'll stockpile some stuff . . . I'll do some work in trade . . . and we'll get outta here by the end of the week." He tosses his stogie and sits next to her. "I won't let anything happen."

She looks at him. "Promise?"

"Promise." He kisses her cheek. "I'll protect you, girlie-girl. Always. Always . . ."

She kisses him back.

He puts his arms around her and kisses her on the lips. She wraps her arms around his thick neck and things begin to happen. His enormous tender hands find the small of her back, and their kiss turns to something hotter, more desperate. They intertwine, and he urges her back inside the camper, into the private darkness.

They leave the rear hatch open, oblivious to everything but each other, as they begin to make love.

It's better than either one of them dreamed it would be. Lilly loses herself in the murky dark, the light of an icy harvest moon shining in through the gap, as Josh lets all his lonely desire pour out in a series of heaving gasps. He sheds his coat, gets his undershirt off—his skin looks almost indigo in the moonlight. Lilly peels her bra up and over herself, the soft weight of her breasts splaying across her rib cage. Gooseflesh spreads down her tummy as Josh gently enters her and builds steam.

They make feverish love. Lilly forgets everything, even the savage environment outside the camper.

A minute, an hour—time is meaningless now—all of it passes in a blur.

Later, they lie among the detritus of Bob's camper, legs intertwined, Lilly's head against the massive curve of Josh's bicep, a blanket covering them, staving off the chill. Josh presses his lips against the soft convolutions of Lilly's ear and whispers, "Gonna be okay."

"Yeah," she murmurs.

"We're gonna make it."

"Absolutely."

"Together."

"You got that right." She lays her right arm across Josh's massive chest, and she looks into his sad eyes. She feels strange. Buoyant, woozy. "Been thinking about this moment for a long time."

"Me, too."

They let the silence engulf them, carrying them away, and they lie there like that for some time, unaware of the dangers lying in wait . . . unaware of the brutal outside world tightening its grasp.

Most important, they are unaware of the fact that they are being watched.

NINE

On their third day in town, the winter rains roll in, drawing a dark gray pall of misery down over Woodbury. It's already early December and Thanksgiving has come and gone without so much as a wishbone being snapped, and now the dampness as well as the cold starts getting into people's joints. The sandy lots along Main Street turn to wet plaster and the sewers swell and overflow with tainted runoff. A human hand bubbles out of one of the gratings.

That day Josh decides to trade his best chef's knife—a Japanese Shun—for bed linens and towels and soap, and he convinces Lilly to move her things into the apartment over the dry cleaner, where they can take sponge baths and find temporary refuge from the cramped quarters of the camper. Lilly stays indoors most of the day, fervently writing diary entries on a roll of wrapping paper and planning her escape. Josh keeps a close eye on her. Something feels wrong—more wrong than he can articulate.

Scott and Megan are nowhere to be found. Lilly suspects that Megan, already growing bored with Scott, is prostituting herself for dope.

That afternoon Bob Stookey finds a couple of kindred spirits in the bowels of the racetrack, where a labyrinth of cinder-block storage facilities and service areas has been turned into a makeshift infirmary. While the cold-steel rain pummels the metal beams and stanchions of the arena above them—sending a dull, hissing, incessant drone down through the bones of the building—a middle-aged man and a young woman give Bob the grand tour.

"Alice here has been a quick study as a neophyte nurse, I have to say," the man in the wire-frame reading glasses and stained lab coat comments, as he leads Bob and the young lady through an open doorway and into a cluttered examination room. The man's name is Stevens, and he's a trim, intelligent, wry sort who seems out of place to Bob in this feral town. The ersatz nurse, also in a hand-me-down lab coat, looks younger than her years. Her dishwater-blond hair is braided and pulled back from her girlish face.

"I'm still working at it," the girl says, following the men into the dimly lit room, the floor humming with the vibrations of a central generator. "I'm stuck somewhere in the middle of second-year nursing school."

"Both y'all know a lot more than I do," Bob admits. "I'm just an old battle tech."

"She had her baptism of fire last month, God knows," the doctor says, pausing next to a battered X-ray machine. "Business was brisk down here for a while."

Bob looks around the room, sees the bloodstains and the signs of chaotic triage, and he asks what happened.

The doctor and the nurse share an uneasy glance. "Changeover in power."

"Excuse me?"

The doctor sighs. "Place like this, you see a kind of natural selection going on. Only the pure sociopaths survive. It's not pretty." He takes a breath, and then smiles at Bob. "Still, it's good to have a medic around."

Bob wipes his mouth. "Not sure how much help I'd be, but I gotta admit, it sure would be nice to lean on the skills of a real doctor for once." Bob motions at one of the old, battered machines. "I see y'all got an old Siemens machine there, used to truck one of those around Afghanistan."

"Yeah, well, we're not exactly Bellevue but we've got the basics, scavenged them from area clinics . . . got infusion pumps, IV drips, a couple monitors, ECG, EEG . . . we're light on the pharmacy, though."

Bob tells them about the medicine he scavenged from Walmart. "You're welcome to any or all of it," he says. "I got a couple of spare doctor's bags full of the usual. Got extra dressings, you name it. It's yours, you need it."

"That's great, Bob. Where you from?"

"Vicksburg originally, was living in Smyrna when the Turn came. How about you folks?"

"Atlanta," Stevens replies. "Had a small practice in Brookhaven before everything went to hell."

"Also from Atlanta," the girl chimes in. "Was going to school at Georgia State."

Stevens has a pleasant look on his face. "You been drinking, Bob?"

"Huh?"

Stevens gestures toward the silver flask partially visible in Bob's hip pocket. "You been drinking today?"

Bob lowers his head, crestfallen, ashamed. "Yessir, I have."

"You drink every day, Bob?"

"Yes, sir."

"Hard liquor?"

"Yes, sir."

"Bob, I don't mean to put you on the spot." The doctor pats Bob's shoulder. "It's none of my business. I'm not judging you. But can I ask how much you're putting away every day?"

Bob's chest tightens with humiliation. Alice gazes elsewhere for a moment, out of respect. Bob swallows his shame. "I have no earthly idea. Sometimes a couple of pints, sometimes a whole fifth when I can get it." Bob looks up at the slender, bespectacled doctor. "I'll understand if you don't want me getting near your—"

"Bob, relax. You don't understand. I think it's fantastic."

"Huh?"

"Keep drinking. Drink as much as possible."

"I'm sorry?"

"You mind sharing a sip?"

Bob slowly pulls the flask, not taking his eyes off the doctor.

"Appreciate it." Stevens takes the flask, nods a thank-you, and takes a pull. He wipes his mouth and offers it to Alice.

The girl waves it off. "No, thanks, it's a little early in the day for me."

Stevens takes another sip and hands the flask back. "You stay here for any length of time you're gonna need to drink heavily."

Bob puts the flask back in his pocket. He doesn't say anything.

Stevens smiles again, and there's something heartbreaking behind the smile. "That's my prescription, Bob. Stay as drunk as possible."

On the other side of the racetrack complex, beneath the north end of the arena, a wiry, tightly coiled individual emerges from an unmarked metal door and gazes up at the sky. The rain has ceased for the moment, leaving behind a low ceiling of sooty clouds. The wiry gentleman carries a small bundle wrapped in a threadbare woolen blanket the color of dead grass, gathered at the top with rawhide.

The wiry man crosses the street and starts down the sidewalk, his raven-black hair slick with moisture and pulled back in a ponytail today.

As he walks, his preternaturally alert gaze is everywhere, practically all at once, taking in everything that goes on around him. In recent weeks the emotions that have plagued him have subsided, the voice in his head silent now. He feels strong. This town is his raison d'être, the fuel that keeps him keen and sharp.

He is about to turn the corner at the intersection of Canyon and Main when he notices a figure in his peripheral vision. The older guy—the drunk who came in a few days ago with the nigger and the girls—is emerging from the warehouse at the south end of the racetrack. The weathered old dude pauses for a moment to take a gulp from his flask, and the look on his face after swallowing and cringing at the burn is apparent to the wiry man even a block away.

In the distance, the older dude grimaces as the alcohol streams down his gullet, and the grimace is weirdly familiar to the wiry man. The grimace—full of shame and desolation—makes the wiry man feel strange and sentimental, almost tender. The older man puts the flask away and starts trundling toward Main Street with that trademark gait—half limp, half drunken amble—which many homeless people get after years of struggling on the street. The wiry man follows.

Minutes later, the wiry man cannot resist calling out to the juicer. "Hey, sport!"

Bob Stookey hears the voice—gravelly, lightly accented with a trace of Southern small town, echoing on the breeze—but he cannot locate the source.

Bob pauses at the edge of Main Street and looks around. The town is mostly deserted today, the rains driving denizens indoors.

"'Bob' is it?" the voice says, closer now, and Bob finally sees a figure approaching from behind.

"Oh, hi . . . how ya doin'?"

The man saunters up to Bob with a forced smile. "I'm doing great, Bob, thanks." Wisps of coal-black hair dangling in front of the man's chiseled face, he carries a bundle that seems to be leaking moisture, dripping on the pavement. People around town have started to call this man "the Governor"—the name has stuck—which is fine and dandy with this guy. "How you settling in to our little hamlet?"

"Real good."

"You meet Doc Stevens?"

"Yes, sir. Good man."

"Call me 'the Governor.'" The smile softens a bit. "Everybody else seems to be calling me that. What the hell? Kinda like the ring of it."

"The Governor it is," Bob says, and glances down at the bundle in the man's grip. The blanket leaks blood. Bob glances away quickly, alarmed by it, but feigning ignorance. "Looks like the rains have blown over."

The man's smile remains stamped on his face. "Walk with me, Bob."

"Sure."

They start down the cracked sidewalk, moving toward the temporary wall that stands between merchant's row and the outer streets. The sound of nail guns snapping can be heard above the wind. The wall continues expanding along the southern edge of the business district. "You remind me of somebody," the Governor says after a long pause.

"It ain't Kate Winslet, I'm betting." Bob has had enough alcohol to loosen his tongue. He chuckles to himself as he trundles along. "Or Bonnie Raitt, neither."

"Touché, Bob." The Governor glances down at his package, notices the droplets of blood leaving little coin-sized marks on the sidewalk. "What a mess I'm making."

Bob looks away, scrambles to change the subject. "Ain't y'all worried about all that pounding racket over there drawing walkers?"

"We got it under control, Bob, don't you worry about that. Got men posted out on the edge of the woods, and we try and keep the pounding down to a minimum."

"That's good to hear . . . got things figured out pretty good around here."

"We try, Bob."

"I told Doc Stevens, he's welcome to any medical supplies I got in my stash."

"You a doctor, too?"

Bob tells the man about Afghanistan, patching marines, getting an honorable discharge.

"You got kids, Bob?"

"No, sir . . . for the longest time it was just me and Brenda, my old lady. Had a little trailer outside of Smyrna, not a bad life."

"You're looking at my little bundle, aren't ya, Bob?"

"No, sir . . . whatever it is, it's none of my beeswax. Doesn't concern me."

"Where's your wife?"

Bob slows down a bit, as though the mere subject of Brenda Stookey weighs him down. "Lost her to a walker attack shortly after the Turn."

"Sorry to hear that." They approach a gated section of the wall. The Governor pauses, knocks a few times, and the seam opens. Litter swirls as a workman pulls the gate back and nods at the Governor, letting the twosome pass. "My place is just up the road a piece," the Governor says with a tilt of his head toward the east side of town. "Little two-story apartment building . . . come on over, I'll fix you a drink."

"The Governor's mansion?" Bob jokes. He can't help it. The nerves and the booze are working on him. "Ain't you got laws to pass?"

The Governor pauses, turns and smiles at Bob. "I just figured out who you remind me of."

In that brief instant, standing in that gray overcast daylight, the wiry man—who from this point on shall think of himself as "the Governor"—experiences a seismic shift within his brain. He stands there staring at a coarse, deeply lined, alcoholic good old boy from Smyrna who is the spitting image of Ed Blake, the Governor's old man. Ed Blake had that same pug nose, prominent brow, and crow's-feet around red-rimmed eyes. Ed Blake was a big drinker, too, like this guy, with the same sense of humor. Ed Blake would toss off sarcastic one-liners with the same drunken relish, cutting to the quick with his words when he wasn't slapping his family around with the back of his big, callused hands.

All at once, another part of the Governor bubbles up to the surface—a deeply buried part of him—on a wave of sentimental longing, which almost makes him dizzy as he remembers big Ed Blake in happier times, a simple hillbilly laborer who tried to fight his demons long enough to be a loving father. "You remind me of somebody I used to know a long time ago," the Governor says finally, his tone softening as he looks Bob Stookey in the eyes. "C'mon, let's go get a drink."

For the rest of their journey across the safe zone, the two men talk quietly, openly, like old friends.

At one point the Governor asks Bob what happened to his wife.

"Place we lived, this mobile home park . . ." Bob says slowly, heavily, as he hobbles along, remembering dark days. "We got overrun one day with walkers. I was out trying to scrounge up some supplies when it happened . . . by the time I got back they had gotten into our place."

He pauses and the Governor says nothing, just walks in silence, waiting.

"They were tearing into her, and I fought 'em off best I could . . . and . . . I guess they only ate enough of her that she came back."

Another agonizing pause. Bob licks his dry lips. The Governor can see that the man needs a drink badly, needs his medicine to stanch the memories.

"I couldn't bring myself to finish her off." This comes out of Bob on a choked wheeze. His rheumy eyes well up. "I ain't proud of the fact that I left her. Pretty sure she got some folks after that. Her arm and her lower body was pretty mangled but she could still get around. Them people she got, their deaths are my fault."

A pause.

"It's hard to let go sometimes," the Governor ventures at last, glancing down at his ghastly little bundle. The dripping has diminished somewhat, the blood thickening to the consistency of blackstrap molasses. Right then the Governor notices Bob pondering the blood droplets, his brow furrowed in thought. He looks almost sober.

Bob gestures at the gruesome bundle. "You got somebody turned on ya, don't ya?"

"You're not so dumb . . . are ya, Bob?"

Bob wipes his mouth pensively. "Never thought about feeding Brenda."

"C'mon, Bob, I want to show you something."

They reach the two-story brick edifice at the end of the block, and Bob follows the Governor inside.

"Stand behind me for a second, Bob." The Governor fiddles a key into a dead bolt, the door at the end of a second-floor hallway. The door clicks, and the sound of a low growl seeps out. "I would appreciate it, Bob, if you kept what you're about to see to yourself."

"No problem . . . lips are sealed."

Bob follows the Governor into a two-bedroom unit with spartan furnishings that reeks of spoiled meat and disinfectant, the windows painted over with black Rust-Oleum. A floor-length mirror near the front vestibule is covered with newspaper and masking tape. The mirror in the bathroom—visible through an open doorway—is missing, its absence evident in the pale oval outline above the sink. All the mirrors in this place have been removed.

"She's everything to me," the Governor says. Bob follows the man across the living room, down a short hallway, and through a doorway into a cramped laundry room, where the upright corpse of a little girl is chained to a U-bolt drilled into the wall.

"Oh, Lord." Bob keeps his distance. The dead girl—still in pigtails and pinafore dress, as if dressed for church—snarls and spits and flails, her chain straining at its mooring. Bob takes a step back. "Oh, Lord."

"Calm down, Bob."

The Governor kneels in front of the pint-sized zombie and lays the bundle on the floor. The girl bites at the air, blackened teeth clacking. The Governor unwraps a human head, its cranial cavity gaping on one side from a close-range gunshot.

"Oh, my." Bob notices that the human head—its pulpy concavity on one side already hectic with maggots—sports a bristly, jarhead haircut, as if it once belonged to a soldier or marine.

"This here's Penny . . . she's an only child," the Governor explains as he shoves the dripping severed head within range of the chained cadaver. "We came from a small town called Waynesboro. Penny's mother—my sweet wife, Sarah—was killed in a car crash before the Turn."

The child feeds.

Bob watches from the doorway, at once appalled and riveted, as the diminutive zombie slurps and chews the soft matter of the cranial passage as though ferreting out the meat of a lobster.

The Governor watches the feeding. The slurping noises fill the air. "My brother Brian and I—along with a few friends of mine—we set out to find greener pastures with Penny here. Made our way west, crashed in Atlanta for a spell, hooked up with some people, lost some people. Kept moving west."

The little corpse settles down, leaning against the wall with tiny, greasy, scarlet-stained fingers burrowing deep into the hollowed-out skull for morsels.

The Governor's voice drops an octave. "Had a run-in with some dirtbags at an orchard not far from here." His words falter for a moment. No tears but his voice crumbles a little. "Put my brother in charge of Penny while I fended 'em off . . . and one thing led to another."

Bob cannot move. He cannot speak in this airless chamber of stained tiles, exposed plumbing, and mold-darkened grout. He watches the tiny abomination, her ghastly face content now, stringers of brain matter hanging from her little tulip lips, her fish-belly eyes rolling back in her head as she leans back.

"My brother fucked up big-time, got my baby killed," the Governor explains now, his head down, his chin on his chest. His voice gets thick with emotion. "Brian was weak and that's all there is to it. I could not let it go, though." He looks at Bob through raw, wet eyes. "I know you can relate, Bob. I could not let go of my baby girl."

Bob can relate. His chest seizes up with sorrow for Brenda.

"I blame myself for Penny getting killed and comin' back." The Governor stares at the floor. "I kept her going with scraps and we kept headin' west. By the time we got to Woodbury my brother Brian was ape-shit crazy with guilt."

The thing that was once a little girl drops the skull as though discarding an oyster shell. She gazes around the room through her milky eyes as if awakening from a dream.

"I had to put Brian down like a sick dog," the Governor utters, almost to himself. He takes a step closer to the little thing that used to be a child. His voice becomes almost toneless. "I still see my Penny in there sometimes . . . when she's calm like this."

Bob swallows hard. Contrary emotions swirl and eddy inside him—repulsion, sadness, fear, bone-deep longing, even sympathy for this deranged individual—and he hangs his head. "You been through a lot."

"Look at that, Bob." The Governor nods toward the little zombie. The child-thing cocks its head, staring at the Governor with a vexed expression. The thing blinks its eyes. A faint trace of Penny Blake glimmers behind its eyes. "My baby's still in there. Aren't ya, honey?"

The Governor goes over to the chained creature, kneels and strokes its livid cheek.

Bob stiffens, starts to say, "Be careful, you don't want to be—"

"Here's my beautiful baby girl." The Governor strokes the thing's matted hair. The tiny zombie blinks. The pallid face changes, eyes narrowing, blackened lips peeling away from rotten baby teeth.

Bob steps forward. "Look out—"

The Penny-thing snaps its jaws at the exposed flesh of the Governor's wrist, but the Governor pulls away just in time. "Whoopsy!"

The little zombie strains at its chain, scuttling to its feet and reaching at the air . . . as the Governor backs away. He speaks in baby talk. "Wascally Wabbit . . . almost got Daddy that time!"

Bob gets woozy. He can feel his gorge rising, the bile threatening to come up.

"Bob, do me a favor and reach into that loose bundle the head came out of."

"Huh?"

"Do me a favor and grab that last little goodie in that bag over there."

Bob holds his vomit in and turns and finds the bundle on the floor and looks inside. A pale human finger, apparently male, lies at the bottom of the bag in a clot of drying blood. Hair sprouts from the knuckles, and from the ragged end protrudes a small nodule of white bone.

Something loosens inside Bob—as sudden as a rubber band snapping—as he pulls a handkerchief from his pocket, bends down, and retrieves the finger.

"Why don't *you* do the honors, my friend," the Governor suggests, standing proudly over the snapping zombie-child, his hands on his hips.

Bob feels as though his body has begun to move on its own, with a *mind* of its own. "Yeah . . . sure."

"Go ahead."

Bob stands within inches of the chain's limit, as the Penny-thing snarls and sputters noisily at him, clanging against the U-bolt. "Yeah . . . why not?"

Holding the finger out at arm's length, Bob feeds it to the creature.

The little corpse gobbles the thing, falling to its knees, two-handing the finger into her ravenous little pit of a mouth. The nauseating wet noises fill the laundry room.

The two men stand side by side, watching now. The Governor puts his arm around his new friend.

By the end of that week the men on the wall have reached the edge
of the third block, along Jones Mill Road, where the U.S. Post Office
sits boarded and defaced with graffiti. Along the brick wall adjacent
to the parking lot some joker with a few years of college lit classes
has spray-painted the words THIS IS HOW THE WORLD ENDS NOT WITH
A BANG BUT WITH A WALKER, a constant reminder of the end of society and government services as we know them.

On Saturday Josh Lee Hamilton ends up on a work crew, hauling
dollies loaded with scrap lumber from one end of the sidewalk to
the other, bartering his muscles for food so that he and Lilly can
continue to eat. He has run out of valuables to trade, and for the last
couple of days Josh has been doing menial tasks such as emptying
latrines and cleaning animal carcasses in the smokehouse. But he
gladly does the work for Lilly.

Josh has fallen so deeply for the woman that he secretly lets the
tears come at night, in the desolate darkness of the walk-up apartment, after Lilly has drifted off in his arms. Josh finds himself beset
with the ironies of finding love among the wreckage of this plague.
Filled with a kind of reckless hope, as well as the dreamy side ef-
fects of the first true intimate relationship of his life, Josh barely
notices the absence of the other members of his group.

The little clique seems to have scattered to the winds. Occasionally Josh will get a glimpse of Megan at night, creeping along the
balustrades of residential buildings, scantily clad and stoned. Josh
has no idea whether she is still with Scott. In fact, Scott has vanished. No one seems to know where he is, and the sad truth is, nobody seems to care. Business seems to be brisk for Megan. Out of
the fifty or so residents of Woodbury, less than a dozen are women,
and out of those only about four are premenopausal.

Far more troubling is Bob's apparent ascendancy to town mascot.
Evidently the Governor—Josh trusts this sociopath as a leader about
as much as he trusts one of the walkers to coach a Little League
team—has taken an interest in old Bob, and has been plying the
man with good whiskey, barbiturates, and social status.

On Saturday afternoon, however, Josh puts all this out of his mind
as he unloads a pallet of siding at the end of the temporary wall.
Other workmen move along the flanks of the barricade, nailing

planks into place. Some use hammers, others nail guns connected to gas-powered generators. The noise is troublesome if not unmanageable.

"Just stack it over there by the sandbags, cousin," Martinez says with a neighborly nod, an M1 assault rifle on his hip.

Clad in his trademark do-rag and sleeveless camo shirt, Martinez continues to be the hail-fellow-well-met. Josh cannot quite figure the man out. He seems to be the most even-tempered of the Woodbury bunch, but the bar here is not that high. Charged with supervising the ever-changing shift of guards on the walls, Martinez rarely fraternizes with the Governor, although the two of them seem to be joined at the hip. "Just try and keep the noise down to a minimum, bro," he adds with a wink, "if at all possible."

"Gotcha," Josh says with a nod and starts off-loading the four-by-six sheets of particleboard onto the ground. He sheds his lumberjack coat—the sweat has broken out on his neck and back, the winter sun high in the sky today—and he finishes the stacking in mere minutes.

Martinez comes over. "Why don't you go ahead and grab one more load before lunch."

"Roger that," Josh says, and pulls the empty dolly free of the stack, then turns and heads back down the walk, leaving his jacket—as well as his snub-nosed .38 police special—hanging on a fence post.

Josh sometimes forgets that the gun is tucked into his jacket pocket. He has yet to use the thing since coming to Woodbury; the guards have the place pretty much covered.

Over the last week, in fact, only a few attacks have occurred along the edges of the woods, or on the side roads, which have been easily and promptly quelled by the well-armed band of weekend warriors. According to Martinez, the powers that be in Woodbury have discovered a cache of weapons at a National Guard station within walking distance of the town—an entire arsenal of military-grade weaponry—which the Governor has put to good use.

The truth is, walker attacks are the least of the Governor's problems. The human population of Woodbury seems to be curdling under the pressure of postplague life. Tempers are stretched thin. People are starting to lash out at each other.

Josh crosses the two-block distance between the construction site and the warehouse in less than five minutes, thinking about Lilly and his future with her. Lost in his thoughts, he does not notice the odor wafting around him as he approaches the wood-frame building on the edge of the railroad tracks.

The warehouse once stood as a storage shed for the southern terminus of the Chattooga and Chickamauga Railway. Throughout the twentieth century tobacco farmers would ship their bundles of raw leaves up north on this line to Fayetteville for processing.

Josh trudges up to the long narrow building and parks the dolly outside the door. The edifice rises up at least thirty-five feet at the highest pitch of its weathered, gabled roof. The siding is ancient, chipped, and scarred with neglect. The single tall window by the door is broken out and boarded. The place looks like a ruined museum, a relic of the old South. Workmen have been using the building to keep the lumber dry and stash building materials.

"Josh!"

Josh pauses at the entrance when he hears the familiar voice drifting on the breeze behind him. He turns just in time to see Lilly scurrying up in her trademark funky attire—floppy hat, multicolored scarves, and a coyote coat she acquired in trade from an older woman in town—a weary smile on her slender face.

"Babygirl, you are a sight for sore eyes," Josh says, grabbing her and gently pulling her into a bear hug. She hugs him back—not exactly with unbridled abandon, more of a platonic hug—and once again Josh wonders if he has come on too strong with her. Or perhaps their lovemaking has changed some complex dynamic between them. Or maybe he has not lived up to her expectations. She seems to be holding back her affection slightly. Just slightly. But Josh puts it out of his mind. Maybe it's just the stress.

"Can we talk?" she says, looking up into his eyes with a heavy, somber gaze.

"Sure . . . you want to give me a hand?"

"After you," she says, gesturing toward the entrance. Josh turns and pries the door open.

The smell of dead flesh—mingling with the moldy, airless dark inside the storage shed—does not register at first. Nor do they notice the gap between two petrified sections of drywall in the rear of the shed, or the fact that the backside of the building is perilously exposed to a wild section of forest. The building stretches at least a hundred feet back in the darkness, draped in cobwebs and cast-off rail sections so rusted and corroded they are the color of the earth.

"What's on your mind, babydoll?" Josh crosses the cinder floor to a pile of wooden siding. The four-by-six panels look as though they came from a barn, their grooves of deep red paint chipped and scabrous with mud.

"We gotta move on, Josh, we gotta get outta this town . . . before something terrible happens."

"Soon, Lilly."

"No, Josh. Seriously. Listen to me." She tugs his arm and pulls him around so they are face-to-face. "I don't care if Megan and Scott and Bob stay . . . we gotta ditch this place. It looks all cozy and Mayberry RFD on the surface but it's rotting underneath."

"I know . . . I just have to—"

He stops when a shadow blurs outside the slats of the boarded window in his peripheral vision.

"Oh, my God, Josh, did you—"

"Get behind me," he says, realizing several things all at once. He smells the odor permeating the musk of the moldy shed, he hears the low guttural vibrations of growls coming from the rear of the building, and he sees a slice of daylight blooming through a gap in the corner.

Worst of all, Josh realizes he left his pistol in his jacket.

TEN

Right then, a burst of automatic gunfire echoes outside the storage shed.

Lilly jerks in the darkness of the shed, and Josh whirls toward the pile of lumber, when the boarded window near the front door bursts inward.

Three snarling zombies—the pressure of their collective weight forcing the ancient lumber to give way—start climbing into the shed. Two males and a female, each with deep wounds in their faces, their cheeks torn away from exposed gums and teeth like rows of dull ivory, tumble into the darkness. A chorus of snarls fills the building.

Josh barely has time to register this fact when he hears shuffling coming toward him from the rear of the dark shed. He spins and sees the enormous walker in dungarees, most likely a former farmer, his lower intestines hanging out like slimy prayer beads, shambling toward him through the shafts of dust motes, bumping drunkenly into stacks of crates and piles of old railroad ties.

"LILLY, GET BEHIND ME!"

Josh lurches toward the stack of lumber and lifts a huge panel of wood up and in front of them like a shield. Lilly presses against his back, her lungs heaving now, hyperventilating with terror. Josh raises the panel and starts toward the big walker with the inertia of a middle linebacker going into the backfield to sack a quarterback.

The walker lets out a drooling groan as Josh slams the panel into it.

The force of the blow drives the huge corpse backward and to the cinder floor. Josh slams the lumber down on top of the thing. Lilly tumbles onto the pileup. The weight of their bodies pins the giant to the cinders, its dead limbs squirming beneath the panel, its black-ened fingers sticking out the sides of the wood, clawing at the air.

Outside, in the wind, the sound of an emergency bell clangs.

"MOTHERFUCK!"

Josh loses control for a moment and starts slamming the panel down on top of the enormous dead farmer. Lilly is thrown off Josh's back, as Josh rises up and starts stomping his work boot down on the panel, which is crushing the zombie's skull. Josh starts jumping up and down on the panel, letting out a series of garbled, bellowing cries, the rage contorting his face.

Brain matter gushes and spurts out from under the top of the panel, as the sick crunch of dead cranial bones gives way, the farmer going still. Huge rivulets of black fluid spread from under the wood.

All this transpires within a matter of seconds, as Lilly is backing away in horror. All at once the sound of a voice rings out from the street in front of the shed, a familiar voice, calm and collected, de-spite its volume—"GET DOWN, FOLKS!! GET DOWN ON THE FLOOR"—and somewhere in the back of Josh's brain he recognizes the voice of Martinez, and Josh also remembers, simultaneously, that the other three walkers are closing in from the front of the shed.

Josh jumps off the panel, spins around, and sees the three walkers approaching Lilly, reaching out for her with spastic lifeless arms. Lilly screams. Josh lurches toward her, scrambling for a weapon. Only scrap metal and sawdust litter the floor.

Lilly backs away screaming, and the din of her shriek blends with a booming, authoritative voice coming from outside the entrance: "GET DOWN ON THE FLOOR, FOLKS! DOWN ON THE FLOOR NOW!!"

Josh instantly gets it, and he grabs Lilly and yanks her to the cinders.

The three dead things loom over them, mouths gaping and

drooling, so close now Josh can smell the hideous stench of their fetid breath.

The front wall lights up—a fusillade of automatic gunfire punching a pearl necklace of holes along the drywall, each hole blooming a pinpoint of daylight. The volley strafes the midsections of the three upright cadavers, making them dance a macabre Watusi in the darkness.

The noise is tremendous. Wood shards and plaster shrapnel and bits of rotting flesh rain down on Josh and Lilly, who cover their heads.

Josh catches glimpses of the macabre dancing out of the corner of his eye, the walkers jerking and spasming to some arrhythmic drumbeat, as threads of brilliant light crisscross the darkness.

Skulls erupt. Particles fly. The dead figures deflate and collapse one at a time. The barrage continues. Thin shafts of daylight fill the shed with a cat's cradle of deadly luminous sunlight.

Silence descends. Outside the shed, the muffled noise of spent shells ringing off the pavement reaches Josh's ears. He hears the faint clanging of bolts reloading, breeches refilling, collective breaths of exertion drowned by the wind.

A moment passes

He turns to Lilly, who lies next to him, clinging to him, clutching handfuls of his shirt. She looks almost catatonic for a moment, her face pressed against the cinders. Josh hugs her close, strokes her back.

"You okay?"

"Fabulous . . . just peachy." She seems to awaken from the terror, looking down at the spreading puddle of cranial fluid. The bodies lie riddled and eviscerated only inches away. Lilly sits up.

Josh rises and helps her to her feet and starts to say something else when the creak of old wood draws his attention to the entrance. What remains of the door, its top half perforated with bullet holes, squeaks open.

Martinez peers in. He speaks hurriedly, purposefully: "You two good?"

"We're good," Josh tells him, and then hears a noise in the

distance. Voices rising in anger, echoing on the wind. A muffled crash.

"We got another fire to put out," Martinez says, "if you folks are okay."

"We're okay."

With a terse nod, Martinez wheels away from the door and vanishes into the overcast daylight.

Two blocks east of the railroad tracks, near the barricade, a fight has ensued. Fights are commonplace in the new Woodbury. Two weeks ago a couple of the butcher's guards came to blows over the rightful ownership of a well-thumbed issue of *Barely Legal* magazine. Doc Stevens had to set one fighter's dislocated jaw and patch the other boy's hemorrhaging left eye socket before that day was out.

Most of the time these brawls occur in semiprivate—either indoors or late at night—and break out over the most trivial matters imaginable: somebody looks at somebody else the wrong way, somebody tells a joke that offends somebody else, somebody just irritates somebody else. For weeks now, the Governor has been concerned about the growing frequency of serious brawls.

But until today, most of these little rumbles have been private affairs.

Today, the latest melee breaks out in broad daylight, right outside the food center, in front of at least twenty onlookers . . . and the crowd seems to fuel the intensity of the fight. At first the onlookers watch with revulsion as the two young combatants pummel each other with bare fists in the freezing wind, their inelegant blows full of spit and fury, their eyes ablaze with unfocused rage.

But soon something changes in the crowd. Angry shouts turn to whoops and hollers. Bloodlust sparks behind the eyes of the gallery. The stress of the plague comes out in angry hyena yells, psychotic cheers, and vicarious fist pumping from some of the younger men.

Martinez and his guards arrive right at the height of the fight.

Dean Gorman, a redneck farm kid from Augusta dressed in torn denim and heavy-metal tattoos, kicks the legs out from under Johnny

Pruitt, a fat, doughy pothead from Jonesboro. Pruitt—who had the temerity to criticize the Augusta State Jaguars football team—now tumbles to the sandy ground with a gasp.

"Hey! Dial it down!" Martinez approaches from the north side of the street, his M1 on his hip, still warm from the fracas at the railroad shed. Three guards follow on his heels, their guns also braced against their midsections. As he crosses the street it's hard for Martinez to see the fighters behind the semicircle of cheering onlookers.

All that's visible is a cloud of dust, flailing fists, and milling onlookers.

"HEY!!"

Inside the circle of spectators Dean Gorman slams a steel-toed work boot into Johnny Pruitt's ribs, and the fat man keens with agony, rolling away. The crowd jeers. Gorman jumps on the kid but Pruitt counters by slamming a knee up into Gorman's groin. The witnesses howl. Gorman tumbles to his side holding his privates and Pruitt lashes out with a series of sidelong blows to Gorman's face. Blood flings across the sand in dark stringers from Gorman's nose.

Martinez starts pushing bystanders aside, forcing his way into the fray.

"Martinez! Hold up!"

Martinez feels a vise grip tighten on his arm and he whirls around to see the Governor.

"Hold up a second," the wiry man says under his breath with a spark of interest glittering in his deep-set eyes. His handlebar mustache has come in dark and thick, giving his face a predatory cast. He wears a long, black duster over his chambray shirt, jeans, and stovepipe engineer boots, the tails flapping majestically in the wind. He looks like a degenerate paladin from the nineteenth century, a self-styled gunslinger-pimp. "I want to see something."

Martinez lowers his weapon, tilts his head toward the action. "Just worried somebody's gonna go and get his ass killed."

By this point Big Johnny Pruitt has his pudgy fingers around Dean Gorman's throat, and Gorman begins to gasp and blanch. The fight goes from savage to deadly in a matter of seconds. Pruitt will not let go. The crowd erupts in ugly, garbled cheers. Gorman flails and convulses. He runs out of air, his face turning the color of eggplant. His eyes bulge, bloody saliva spraying.

"Stop worrying, grandma," the Governor murmurs, watching intently with those hollowed-out eyes.

Right then Martinez realizes the Governor is not watching the fight per se. Eyes shifting all around the semicircle of shouting spectators, the Governor is *watching the watchers.* He seems to be absorbing every face, every jackal-like howl, every hoot and holler.

Meantime, Dean Gorman starts to fade on the ground, in the stranglehold of Johnny Pruitt's sausage fingers. Gorman's face turns the color of dry cement. His eyes roll back in his head and he stops struggling.

"Okay, that's enough . . . pull him off," the Governor tells Martinez.

"EVERYBODY BACK OFF!"

Martinez forces his way into the huddle with his gun in both hands.

Big fat Johnny Pruitt finally lets go at the urging of the M1's muzzle, and Gorman lies there convulsing. "Go get Stevens," Martinez orders one of his guards.

The crowd, still agitated by all the excitement, lets out a collective groan. Some of them grumble, and some launch a few boos, frustrated by the anticlimax.

Standing off to the side, the Governor takes it all in. When the onlookers begin to disperse—wandering away, shaking their heads— the Governor goes over to Martinez, who still stands over the writhing Gorman.

Martinez looks up at the Governor. "He'll live."

"Good." The Governor glances down at the young man on the ground. "I think I know what to do with the guardsmen."

At that same moment, under the sublevels of the racetrack complex, in the darkness of a makeshift holding cell, four men whisper to each other.

"It'll never work," the first man utters skeptically, sitting in the corner in his piss-sodden boxer shorts, gazing at the shadows of his fellow prisoners gathered around him on the floor.

"Shut the fuck up, Manning," hisses the second man, Barker, a rail-thin twenty-five-year-old, who glowers at his fellow detainees through long strands of greasy hair. Barker had once been Major Gene Gavin's star pupil at Camp Ellenwood, Georgia, bound for special ops duty with the 221st Military Intelligence Battalion. Now, thanks to that psycho Philip Blake, Gavin is gone and Barker has been reduced to a ragged, seminude, groveling lump in the basement of some godforsaken catacomb, left to subsist on cold oatmeal and wormy bread.

The four guardsmen have been under "house arrest" down here for over three weeks, ever since Philip Blake had shot and killed their commanding officer, Gavin, in cold blood, right in front of dozens of townspeople. Now the only things they have going for them are hunger, pure rage, and the fact that Barker is chained to the cinder-block wall to the immediate left of the locked entrance door, a spot from which one could conceivably get a jump on somebody entering the cell . . . like Blake, for example, who has been regularly coming down here to drag prisoners out, one by one, to meet some hellish fate.

"He's not stupid, Barker," a third man named Stinson wheezes from the opposite corner. This man is older, more heavyset, a good old boy with bad teeth who once ran a requisition desk at the National Guard station.

"I agree with Stinson," Tommy Zorn says from the back wall where he slumps in his underwear, his malnourished body covered with a significant skin rash. Zorn once worked as a delivery clerk at the Guard station. "He's gonna see right through this stunt."

"Not if we're careful," Barker counters.

"Who the hell is gonna be the one plays dead?"

"Doesn't matter, I'll be the one kicks his ass when he opens the door."

"Barker, I think this place has put a zap on your head. Seriously. You want to end up like Gavin? Like Greely and Johnson and—"

"YOU COCK-SUCKING COWARD!! WE'RE ALL GONNA END UP LIKE THEM YOU DON'T DO SOMETHING ABOUT IT!!"

The volume of Barker's voice—stretched as thin as high-tension wire—cuts off the conversation like a switch. For a long stretch, the four guardsmen sit in the dark without saying a word.

At last Barker says, "All we need is one of you faggots to play dead. That's all I'm asking. I'll coldcock him when he comes in."

"Making it convincing is the trouble," Manning says.

"Rub shit on yourself."

"Hardy-har-har."

"Cut yourself and rub blood on your face, and then let it dry, I don't know. Rub your eyes until they bleed. You want to get out of here?"

Long silence now.

"You're fucking guardsmen, for Chrissake. You want to rot in here like maggots?"

Another long silence, and then Stinson's voice in the darkness says, "Okay, I'll do it."

Bob follows the Governor through a secure door at one end of the racetrack, then down a narrow flight of iron stairs, and then across a narrow cinder-block corridor, their footsteps ringing and echoing in the dim light. Emergency cage lights—powered by generators—burn overhead.

"Finally it hit me, Bob," the Governor is saying, fiddling with a ring of skeleton keys clipped to his belt on a long chain. "Thing this place needs . . . is entertainment."

"Entertainment?"

"The Greeks had their theater, Bob . . . Romans had their circuses."

Bob has no idea what the man is talking about but he follows along obediently, wiping his dry mouth. He needs a drink badly. He unbuttons his olive-drab jacket, pearls of sweat breaking out on his weathered brow due to the airless, fusty dampness of the cavernous cement underground beneath the racetrack.

They pass a locked door, and Bob can swear he hears the muffled, telltale noises of reanimated dead. The trace odors of rotting flesh mingle with the mildewy stench of the corridor. Bob's stomach lurches.

The Governor leads him over to a metal door with a narrow window at the end of the corridor. A shade is pulled down over the meshed safety glass.

"Gotta keep the citizens happy," the Governor mutters as he pauses by the door, searching for the proper key. "Keep folks docile, manageable . . . pliable."

Bob waits as the Governor inserts a thick metal key into the door's bolt. But just as he is about to jack open the lock, the Governor turns and looks at Bob. "Had some trouble a while back with the National Guard in town, thought they could lord it over the people, push people around . . . thought they could carve out a little kingdom for themselves."

Confused, dizzy, nauseous, Bob gives a nod and doesn't say anything.

"Been keeping a bunch of them on ice down here." The Governor winks as though discussing the location of a cookie jar with a child. "Used to be seven of them." The Governor sighs. "Only four of them left now . . . been going through them like Grant went through Richmond."

"Going through them?"

The Governor sniffs, suddenly looking guiltily at the floor. "They've been serving a higher purpose, Bob. For my baby . . . for Penny."

Bob realizes with a sudden rush of queasiness what the Governor is talking about.

"Anyway . . ." The Governor turns to the door. "I knew they would come in handy for all sorts of things . . . but now I realize their true destiny." The Governor smiles. "Gladiators, Bob. For the common good."

Right then several things happen at once: The Governor turns and snaps up the shade, while simultaneously flipping a light switch . . . and through the safety glass a row of overhead fluorescent tubes suddenly flicker on, illuminating the inside of a three-hundred-square-foot cinder-block cell. A huge man clad only in tattered skiv-vies lies on the floor, twitching, covered with blood, his mouth black and peeled away from his teeth in a hideous grimace.

"That's a shame." The Governor frowns. "Looks like one of 'em turned."

Inside the cell—the noises muffled by the sealed door—the other prisoners are screaming, yanking at their chains, begging to be res-cued from this freshly turned biter. The Governor reaches inside the folds of his duster and draws his pearl-handled .45 caliber Colt. He checks the clip and mumbles, "Stay out here, Bob. This'll just take a second."

He snaps the lock open, and he steps inside the cell, when the man behind the door pounces.

Barker lets out a garbled cry as he tackles the Governor from be-hind, the chain attached to Barker's ankle giving slightly, reaching its limit, tearing its anchor bolt from the wall. Taken by surprise, the Governor stumbles, drops the .45, topples to the deck, gasping, the gun clattering to the floor, spinning several feet.

Bob fills the doorway, yelling, as Barker crabs toward the Gover-nor's ankles, latching on to them, digging his filthy untrimmed fin-gernails into the Governor's flesh. Barker tries to snag the skeleton keys, but the ring is wedged under the Governor's legs.

The Governor bellows as he madly crawls toward the fallen pistol.

The other men cry out as Barker loses what is left of his sanity and goes for the Governor's ankles and growls with feral white-hot killing rage and opens his mouth and bites down on the tender area around the Governor's Achilles' heel, and the Governor howls.

Bob stands paralyzed behind the half-ajar door, watching, thun-derstruck.

Barker draws blood. The Governor kicks at the prisoner and claws for the pistol. The other men try to tear themselves free, hollering inarticulate warnings, while Barker rips into the Governor's legs. The Governor reaches for the gun, which lies only centimeters out of his reach . . . until finally the Governor's long, sinewy fingers get themselves around the Colt's grip.

In one quick continuous motion the Governor spins and aims the single-action semiautomatic pistol at Barker's face and empties the clip.

A series of dry, hot booms flash in the cell. Barker flings backward like a puppet yanked by a cable, the slugs perforating his face, exiting out the back of his skull in a plume of blood mist. The dark crimson matter sprays the cinder-block wall beside the door, some of it getting on Bob, who jerks back with a start.

Across the cell the other men call out—a garble of nonsense words, a frenzy of begging—as the Governor rises to his feet.

"Please, please, I ain't turned—I AIN'T TURNED!" Across the room, Stinson, the big man, sits up, shielding his bloodstained face as he cries out. His quivering lips have been made up with mildew from the wall and grease from the door hinges. "It was a trick! A trick!"

The Governor thumbs the empty clip out of the Colt, the magazine dropping to the floor. Breathing hard and fast, he pulls another clip from his back pocket and palms it into the hilt. He cocks the slide and calmly aims the muzzle at Stinson, while informing the big man, "You look like a fucking biter to me."

Stinson shields his face. "It was Barker's idea, it was stupid, please, I didn't want to go along with it, Barker was nuts, please . . . PLEASE!"

The Governor squeezes off half a dozen successive shots, the blasts making everybody jump.

The far wall erupts in a fireworks display just above Stinson's head, the puffs of cinder-block plaster exploding in sequence, the noise a tremendous, earsplitting barrage, the sparks blossoming and some of the bullets ricocheting up into the ceiling.

The single cage light explodes in a torrent of glass particles that drives everybody to the floor.

At last the Governor lets up and stands there, catching his breath, blinking, and addressing Bob in the doorway. "What we got here, Bob, is a learning opportunity."

Across the room, on the floor, Stinson has pissed himself, mortified and yet unharmed. He buries his face in his hands and weeps softly.

The Governor limps toward the big man, leaving a thin trail of blood droplets. "You see, Bob . . . the very thing that burns inside these boys—makes 'em try stupid shit like this—is gonna make them superstars in the arena."

Stinson looks up with snot on his face now as the Governor looms over him.

"They don't realize it, Bob." The Governor aims the muzzle at Stinson's face. "But they just passed the first test of gladiatorial school." The Governor gives Stinson a hard look. "Open your mouth."

Stinson hiccups with sobs and terror, squeezing out a breathless, "C'mon, *pleeease* . . ."

"Open your mouth."

Stinson manages to open his mouth. Across the room, in the doorway, Bob Stookey looks away.

"See, Bob," the Governor says, slowly penetrating the big man's mouth with the barrel. The room falls stone silent as the other men watch, horrified and rapt. "Obedience . . . courage . . . stupidity. Isn't that the Boy Scout motto?"

Without warning the Governor lets up on the trigger, pulls the muzzle free of the weeping man's mouth, whirls around, and limps toward the exit. "What did Ed Sullivan used to say . . . ? Gonna be a really big sssshooooow!"

The tension goes out of the room like a bladder deflating, replaced by a ringing silence.

"Bob, do me a favor . . . will ya?" the Governor mutters as he passes the bullet-riddled body of Master Gunnery Sergeant Trey Barker on his way out. "Clean this place up . . . but don't take this cocksucker's remains over to the crematorium. Bring him over to the infirmary." He winks at Bob. "I'll take care of him from there."

The next day, early in the morning, before dawn, Megan Lafferty lies nude and cold and supine on a broken-down cot in the darkness of a squalid studio apartment—the private quarters of some guard whose name she can't remember. Denny? Daniel? Megan was too stoned last night to file the name away. Now the skinny young man with the cobra tattoo between his shoulder blades thrusts himself into her with rhythmic abandon, making the cot groan and squeak.

Megan places her thoughts elsewhere, staring at the ceiling, focusing on the dead flies collected in the bowl of an overhead light fixture, trying to withstand the horrible, painful, sticky friction of the man's erection pumping in and out of her.

The room consists of the cot, a ramshackle dresser, flea-bitten curtains drawn over the open window—through which a December wind whistles sporadically—and piles and piles of crates filled with supplies. Some of these supplies have been promised to Megan in return for sex. She notices a stringer of ragged fleshy objects hanging off a hook on the door, which she first misidentifies as dried flowers.

Upon closer scrutiny, though, the flowers reveal themselves in the darkness to be human ears, most likely trophies severed off walkers.

Megan tries to block out thoughts of Lilly's last words to her, spoken just last night around the flaming light of a burning oil drum. *"It's my body, girlfriend, these are fucking desperate times,"* Megan had rationalized, trying to justify her behavior. Lilly had responded with disgust. *"I'd rather starve than do tricks for food."* And then Lilly had officially ended their friendship right then, once and for all. *"I don't care anymore, Megan, I'm done, it's over, I don't want anything to do with you."*

Now the words echo in the huge, empty chasm in Megan's soul. The hole inside her has been there for years, a gigantic vacuum of sorrow, a bottomless pit of self-loathing carved out when she was young. She has never been able to fill this well of pain, and now the Plague World has opened it up like a festering, sucking wound.

She closes her eyes and thinks about drowning in a deep, dark ocean, when she hears a noise.

Her eyes pop open. The sound is unmistakable, coming from just outside the window. Faint and yet clearly audible in the windy hush of the predawn December air, it echoes up over the rooftops: *two pairs of furtive footsteps, a couple of citizens sneaking through the darkness.*

By this point, Cobra Boy has grown weary of his druggy copulation and has slipped off Megan's body. He smells of dried semen and bad breath and urine-impregnated sheets, and he starts snoring the moment the back of his head hits the pillow. Megan levers herself out of bed, careful not to awaken the catatonic customer.

She pads silently across the cool floor to the window and looks out.

The town slumbers in the gray darkness. The vent stacks and chimneys on top of buildings stand silhouetted against the dull light. Two figures are barely visible in the gloom, creeping toward the far corner of the west fence, their breaths puffing vapor in the cold wee-hour light. One of the figures towers over the other.

Megan recognizes Josh Lee Hamilton first, and then Lilly, as the two ghostly figures pause near the corner of the barricade a hundred and fifty yards away. Waves of melancholy course through Megan.

As the twosome disappears over the fence, the sense of loss drives Megan to her knees, and she silently cries in the reeking darkness for what seems like an eternity.

"Toss it down, babydoll," Josh whispers, gazing up at Lilly, as she balances on the crest of the fence, one foot over, one foot on the ledge behind her. Josh is hyperaware of the dozing night guard a hundred yards to the east, slumped on the seat of a bulldozer, his sight line blocked by the massive girth of a live oak.

"Here comes." Lilly awkwardly shrugs the knapsack off one shoulder and then tosses it over the fence to Josh. He catches it. The pack weighs at least ten pounds. It contains Josh's .38 caliber police special, a pick hammer with a collapsible handle, a screwdriver, a couple of candy bars, and two plastic bottles of tap water.

"Be careful now."

Lilly climbs down and hops onto the hard earth outside the fence.

They waste no time hanging around the periphery of town. The sun is coming up, and they want to be well out of sight of the night guard before Martinez and his men get up and return to their posts. Josh has a bad feeling about the way things are going in Woodbury. It seems as though his services are becoming less and less valuable in terms of trade. Yesterday he must have hauled three tons of fencing panels and still Sam the Butcher claims that Josh is behind in his debt, that he's taking advantage of the barter system, and that he's not working off all the slab bacon and fruit he's been going through.

All the more reason for Josh and Lilly to sneak out of town and see if they can't find their own supplies.

"Stick close, babygirl," Josh says, and leads Lilly along the edge of the woods.

They keep to the shadows as the sun comes up, skirting the edge of a vast cemetery on their left. Ancient willows hang down over Civil War–era markers, the spectral predawn light giving the place a haunted, desolate feel. Many of the headstones lie on their sides, some of the graves gaping open. The boneyard makes the flesh on the back of Josh's neck prickle, and he hurries Lilly along toward the intersection of Main and Canyon Drive.

They turn north and head into the pecan groves outside of town.

"Keep your eyes peeled for reflectors along the side of the road," Josh says as they begin to ascend a gentle slope rising into the wooded hills. "Or mailboxes. Or any kind of private drive."

"What if we don't find anything but more trees?"

"Gotta be a farmhouse . . . something." Josh keeps scanning the trees on either side of the narrow blacktop road. Dawn has broken, but the woods on either side of Canyon Drive are still dark and hectic with swaying shadows. Noises blend into each other, and skittering leaves in the wind start to sound like shuffling footsteps behind the trees. Josh pauses, digs in the knapsack, pulls his gun out, and checks the chamber.

"Something wrong?" Lilly's eyes take in the gun, then shift to the woods. "You hear something?"

"Everything's fine, babydoll." He shoves the pistol behind his belt and continues climbing the hill. "As long as we keep quiet, keep moving . . . we'll be fine."

They walk another quarter mile in silence, staying single file, hyperalert, their gazes returning every few moments to the swaying boughs of the deeper woods, and the shadows behind the shadows. The walkers have left Woodbury alone since the incident at the train shed, but Josh has a feeling they are due. He starts to get nervous about straying this far from town, when he sees the first sign of residential property.

The enormous tin mailbox, shaped like a little log cabin, stands at the end of an unmarked private drive. Only the letters L. HUNT reveal the identity of its owner, the numbers 20034 stamped into the rust-pocked metal.

About fifty yards beyond that first mailbox they find more mailboxes. They find over a dozen of them—a cluster of six at the foot of one drive—and Josh begins to sense they have hit the jackpot. He pulls the pick hammer from the knapsack and hands it to Lilly. "Keep this handy, baby. We'll follow this drive, the one with all the mailboxes."

"I'm right behind you," she says, and then follows the big man up the winding gravel path.

The first monstrosity becomes visible like a mirage in the early-morning light, behind the trees, planted in a clearing as though it landed from outer space. If the home were nestled in some tree-lined boulevard in Connecticut or Beverly Hills it would not seem so out of place, but here in the ramshackle rural nether-region the place practically takes Josh's breath away. Rising over three stories above the weed-whiskered lawn, the deserted mansion is a modern architectural wonder, all cantilevers and jutting balustrades and chockablock with roof pitches. It looks like one of Frank Lloyd Wright's lost masterpieces. An infinity pool is partially visible in the backyard, lousy with leaves. Neglect shows on the massive balconies, where icicles hang down and patches of filthy snow cling to the decks. "Must be some tycoon's summer home," Josh surmises.

They follow the road higher into the trees and find more abandoned homes.

One of them looks like a Victorian museum, with gigantic turrets that rise out of the pecan trees like some Moorish palace. Another one is practically all glass, with a veranda that thrusts out over a breathtaking hill. Each stately home features its own private pool, coach house, six-car garage, and sprawling lawn. Each is dark, closed down, boarded, as dead as a mausoleum.

Lilly pauses in front of the dark glass-encased wonder and gazes up at the galleries. "You think we can get inside?"

Josh grins. "Hand me that clawhammer, babydoll . . . and stand back."

They find a treasure trove of supplies—despite all the spoiled food, as well as signs of past break-ins, probably courtesy of the Governor and his goons. In some of the homes they find partially stocked pantries, wet bars, and linen closets brimming with fresh bedding. They find workrooms with more tools than small hardware stores. They find guns and liquor and fuel and medicine. They marvel that the Governor and his men have not yet scoured these places clean. The best part is the complete absence of walkers.

Later, Lilly stands in the foyer of an immaculate Cape Cod, gazing around at the elaborate Tiffany-style light fixtures. "You thinking what I'm thinking?"

"I don't know, girlfriend, what are you thinking?"

She looks at him. "We could *live* in one of these places, Josh."

"I don't know."

She looks around. "Keep to ourselves, stay under the radar."

Josh thinks about it. "Maybe we ought to take this one step at a time. Play dumb for a while, see if anybody else is wise to it."

"That's the best part, Josh, they've been here already . . . they'll leave it alone."

He lets out a sigh. "Let me think about it, babygirl. Maybe talk to Bob."

After searching the garages, they find a few luxury vehicles under tarps, and they begin making plans for the future, discussing the possibility of hitting the road. As soon as they get a chance to talk to Bob, they will make a decision.

They return to town that evening, slipping into the walled area unnoticed through the construction zone along the southern edge of the barricade.

They keep their discovery to themselves.

Unfortunately, neither Josh nor Lilly has noticed the one critical drawback to the luxury enclave. Most of the backyards extend about thirty yards to the edge of a steep precipice, beyond which a rocky slope plunges down into a deep canyon. Down in the winter-seared valley of that canyon, along a dry riverbed, shrouded in tangled dead vines and limbs, a pack of zombies at least a hundred strong wander aimlessly back and forth, bumping into each other.

It will take the creatures less than forty-eight hours—once the noise and smell of humans draw them out—to crawl, inch by inch, up that slope.

ELEVEN

"I still don't see why we can't just live here for a while," Lilly persists that next afternoon, flopping down on a buttery leather sofa positioned against a massive picture window inside one of the glass-encased mansions. The window wraps around the rear of the home's first floor, and overlooks the kidney-shaped pool in the backyard, covered now with a snow-crusted tarp. Winter winds rattle the windows, a fine icy sleet hissing against the glass.

"I'm not saying it's not a possibility," Josh says from across the room, where he is selecting utensils from a drawer of fine silver and putting them into a duffel bag. Evening is closing in on their second day of exploring the enclave, and they have gathered enough supplies to stock a home of their own. They have hidden some of the provisions outside Woodbury's wall, in sheds and barns. They have stashed firearms and tools and canned goods in Bob's camper, and have made plans to get one of the vehicles in working order.

Now Josh lets out a sigh and goes over to the sofa and sits down next to Lilly. "Still not convinced these places are safe," he says.

"C'mon . . . dude . . . these houses are like fortresses, the owners locked them up tight as drums before taking off in their private jets. I can't take one more night in that creepy town."

Josh gives her a sorrowful look. "Baby, I promise you . . . one day all this shit will be over."

"Really? You think?"

"I'm sure of it, babygirl. Somebody's gonna figure out what went wrong . . . some egghead at the CDC's gonna come up with an antidote, keep folks in their graves."

Lilly rubs her eyes. "I wish I had that kind of confidence."

Josh touches her hand. " 'This too shall pass,' baby. It's like my mama always used to say, 'Only thing you can depend on in this world is that you can't depend on nothin' to stay the same, everything changes.' " He looks at her and smiles. "Only thing ain't never gonna change, baby, is how I feel about *you*."

They sit there for a moment, listening to the silent house tick and settle, the wind strafing the home with bursts of sleet, when something moves outside, across the backyard. The tops of several dozen heads slowly rise up behind the edge of the distant precipice, a row of rotting faces, unseen by Lilly and Josh—their backs turned to the window now—as the pack of zombies emerge from the shadows of the ravine.

Oblivious to the imminent threat, lost in her thoughts, Lilly puts her head on Josh's massive shoulder. She feels a twinge of guilt. Each day she senses Josh falling deeper and deeper for her, the way he touches her, the way his eyes light up each morning when they awaken on the cold pallet of that second-floor apartment.

Part of Lilly hungers for such affection and intimacy . . . but a part of her still feels removed, detached, guilty that she's allowed this relationship to blossom out of fear, out of convenience. She feels a sense of duty to Josh. But that's no basis for a relationship. What she's doing is wrong. She owes him the truth.

"Josh . . ." She looks up at him. "I have to tell you . . . you're one of the most wonderful men I have ever met."

He grins, not quite registering the sadness in her voice. "And you're pretty damn fine yourself."

Outside, plainly visible now through the rear window, at least fifty creatures scrabble up and over the ledge, crabbing onto the lawn, their clawlike fingers digging into the turf, tugging their dead weight along in fits and starts. Some of them struggle to their feet and begin lumbering toward the glass-enclosed edifice with mouths gaping hungrily. A dead geriatric dressed in a hospital smock, his long gray hair flagging like milkweed, leads the pack.

Inside the lavish home, behind panes of safety glass, unaware of the encroaching menace, Lilly measures her words. "You've been so good to me, Josh Lee . . . I don't know how long I could have survived on my own . . . and for that I will always be grateful."

Now Josh cocks his head at her, his grin fading. "Why do I all of a sudden get the feeling there's a 'but' in here somewhere?"

Lilly licks her lips thoughtfully. "This plague, this epidemic, whatever it is . . . it does things to people . . . makes them do things they wouldn't dream of doing any other time."

Josh's big brown face falls. "What are you sayin,' babydoll? Something's bothering you."

"I'm just saying . . . maybe . . . I don't know . . . maybe I've let this thing between us go a little too far."

Josh looks at her, and for a long moment he seems to grope for words. He clears his throat. "Ain't sure I'm following you."

By this point the walkers have overrun the backyard. Unheard through the thick glass, their atonal chorus of snarling, moaning vocalizations drowned under the drumming of sleet, the enormous regiment closes in on the house. Some of them—the old long-haired hospital patient, a limping woman without a jaw, a couple of burn victims—have closed the distance to within twenty yards. Some of the monsters stupidly stumble over the lip of the swimming pool, falling through the snow-matted tarp, while others follow the leaders with bloodlust radiating from their cue-ball eyes.

"Don't get me wrong," Lilly is saying inside the hermetically sealed environment of the stately glass house. "I will always love you, Josh . . . always. You are amazing. It's just . . . this world we're in, it twists things. I never want to hurt you."

His eyes moisten. "Wait. Hold up. You're saying being with me is something you would never dream of doing at any other time?"

"No . . . God, no. I love being with you. I just don't want to give the wrong impression."

"The wrong impression about what?"

"That our feelings for each other . . . that they're—I don't know—coming from a healthy place."

"What's unhealthy about our feelings?"

"I'm just saying . . . the fear fucks you up. I haven't been in my right mind since all this shit went down. I don't ever want you to think I'm just using you for protection . . . for survival, is what I mean."

The tears well up in Josh's eyes. He swallows hard and tries to think of something to say.

Ordinarily he would notice the telltale stench seeping into the circulatory systems of the house, the odors of rancid meat braised in shit. Or he would hear the muffled basso profundo drone outside the walls of the house—coming from outside the front and sides of the building now, not just the backyard—so resonant and low it seems to be vibrating the very foundation. Or he would see the teeming movement out of the corner of his eye, through the lozenge windows across the front foyer, behind the drawn drapes in the living room, coming at them from all directions. But he doesn't notice a thing beyond the assault on his heart.

He clenches his fists. "Why the hell would I ever think something like that, Lil?"

"Because I'm a coward!" She burns her gaze into him. "Because I fucking left you to die. Nothing will ever change that."

"Lilly, please don't—"

"Okay . . . listen to me." She gets her emotions under control. "All I'm saying is, I think we should take it down a notch and give each other—"

"OH, NO—OH, SHIT—SHIT *SHIT*!!"

In a single instant, the sudden alarm on Josh's face drives all other thoughts from Lilly's mind.

The intruders first make themselves known to Josh in a reflection on the surface of a framed family photograph across the room—a stiffly smiling assemblage of the previous owners, including a standard poodle with ribbons in its hair, the framed portrait mounted above a spinet piano—the ghostly silhouettes moving across the picture like spirit images. The faint double image reveals the house's panoramic rear window, the one behind the sofa, through which a battalion of zombies is now visible pushing toward the house.

Josh springs to his feet and whirls around just in time to see the rear window cracking.

The closest zombies—their dead faces mashed up against the glass, squashed by the slow-motion stampede behind them—trail black bile and drool across the window. It all happens very quickly. The hairline fissures spreads like time-lapse spiderwebs spinning toward each corner, as dozens of additional reanimated corpses press against the throng, exerting tremendous pressure on the window.

The glass collapses just as Josh grabs Lilly and yanks her off the sofa.

A terrific crack, like a lightning bolt striking the room, accompanies the birthing of hundreds and hundreds of arms, thrusting forward, jaws snapping, bodies tumbling over the back of the sofa on a wave of broken glass, the wet wind rushing into the gracious family room.

Josh moves without thinking, dragging Lilly with one hand across the arched hall toward the front of the house, as the hell choir of dead vocal cords chirr and grind behind them, filling the stately home with zoo noises and the stench of death. Insensate, twitching in their hunger, the zombies take very little time regaining their legs, rising back up from where they had fallen and quickly trundling forward, flailing and growling, lumbering toward their fleeing prey.

Crossing the front vestibule in a flash, Josh rips open the front door.

A wall of the undead greets him.

He flinches and Lilly shrieks, jerking back with a start, as the battery of dead arms and pincerlike fingers reach for them. Behind the arms, a mosaic of dead faces snarl and sputter, some of them drooling blood as black as motor oil, others flayed open and glistening with the pink sinew and musculature of their damaged facial tissue. One of the curled hands hooks a gob of Lilly's jacket, and Josh tears it away while letting out a booming howl—"FUCKERS!!"—and then on a jolt of adrenaline Josh gets his free hand around the edge of the door.

He slams the door on half a dozen flailing arms, and the impact—

combined with Josh's strength, as well as the deluxe quality of the heavy-duty door—severs each of the six appendages.

Flopping limbs of varying lengths splatter and quiver across the rich Italian tile.

Josh grabs Lilly and starts back toward the center of the house, but pauses at the foot of the spiral staircase when he sees the place is flooding with moving corpses. They have entered through the screen door in the mudroom on the east side of the house, and they've climbed in through the dog door on the west side, and they've wriggled in through cracks in the solarium on the north side of the kitchen. Now they surround Josh and Lilly at the base of the stairs.

Grabbing Lilly by the nape of her jacket, Josh pulls her up the steps.

On their way up the circular staircase, Josh draws his .38 and starts shooting. The first shot flashes and misses its mark entirely, chipping a divot out of the lintel along the archway. Josh's aim is off because he is dragging Lilly up the stairs one riser at a time, as the growling, gnashing, flailing horde awkwardly follows.

Some of the walkers cannot negotiate the stairs and slide back down, while others topple to their hands and knees and manage to keep crawling. Halfway up the spiral, Josh fires again and hits a dead skull, sending wet matter across the newel posts and chandelier. Some of the zombies tumble back down the steps like bowling pins. But now, so many of them are on the risers that they begin to clamber *over each other*, inching up the stairs with the frenzied hunger of salmon spawning. Josh fires again and again. Black fluids bloom in the thunder cracks, but it's futile, there are too many, far too many to fight off, and Josh knows it, and Lilly knows it.

"THIS WAY!"

Josh hollers at her the moment they reach the landing on the second floor.

The idea occurs to Josh fully formed, all at once, as he drags Lilly down the hallway toward the last door at the end of the corridor. Josh remembers checking the master bedroom the previous day, finding some useful pharmaceuticals in the medicine cabinet, and admiring the view from the second-floor bay window. He also remembers the enormous live oak standing sentry next to the window.

"IN HERE!"

The walkers reach the top of the stairs. One of them bumps the banister and stumbles backward, bowling over half a dozen other zombies, sending three of them toppling. The threesome skids down the curvature of the stairs, leaving slime trails of oily blood.

Meanwhile, at the far end of the hall, Josh reaches the bedroom door, throws it open, and pulls Lilly inside the spacious room. The door slams behind them. The silence and calm of the bedroom—with its Louis XIV furnishings, immense four-poster bed, luxurious Laura Ashley duvet, and mountain of frilly, ruffled pillows—provide surreal contrasts to the reeking, noisy menace coming down the hall outside the door. The shuffling footsteps loom. The stench grips the air.

"Get over by the window, babydoll! Be right back!!" Josh whirls and makes a beeline for the bathroom, while Lilly goes over by the huge bay window with its velveteen window treatments. She crouches down, breathlessly waiting.

Josh tears the bathroom door open and lurches into the deluxe, soapy-smelling chamber of Italian tile, chrome, and glass. There amid the Swedish sauna and enormous Jacuzzi tub he throws open the vanity cabinet under the sink. He finds the economy-sized brown bottle of rubbing alcohol.

Within seconds he has the bottle open and is back in the main room, dousing everything, flinging the clear liquid on the curtains and bedding and antique mahogany furniture. The pressure of dead weight making wooden seams creak—the noise of moving corpses piling up against the bedroom door—spurs Josh on.

He tosses the empty bottle and lunges toward the window in a single leap.

Outside the beautifully etched and leaded-glass panorama, framed in delicate ruffled curtains, a gigantic old oak stands over the roof pitches, its twisting limbs, bare in the winter light, reaching up past the weather vane at the crest of the roof. One of the gnarled limbs reaches across the second-floor window, coming within inches of the bedroom.

Josh muscles open the center window on wrought-iron hinges. "C'mon, girlfriend, time to abandon ship!" He kicks out the screen, reaches for Lilly, pulls her up and over the sill, shoves her through the gap, and out into the freezing winds. "Climb across the limb!"

Lilly awkwardly reaches out for the spiraling limb, which is the width of a ham hock, with bark as rough as cement stucco, and she holds on with a desperate vise grip. She starts shimmying her way out across the limb. The wind whistles. The twenty-foot drop seems to stretch away as though glimpsed through a backward telescope. The coach house roof wavers in and out of focus below—barely within jumping distance—as Lilly inches toward the center of the tree.

Behind her, Josh ducks back into the bedroom just as the door collapses.

Zombies pour into the room. Many of them tumble over each other, drunkenly reaching and snarling. One of them—a male missing an arm, with one eye socket cratered out as black and empty as cancer—trundles quickly toward the big black man, who stands by the window, digging frantically in his pocket. The air fills with a groaning cacophony. Josh finds his Zippo cigar lighter.

Just as the eyeless walker pounces, Josh sparks the butane and flings the lighter at the alcohol-dampened skirt around the bed. Flames blossom immediately, as Josh kicks out at the attacking zombie, sending the cadaver stumbling back across the floor.

The walker bounces across the burning bed and sprawls to the alcohol-sodden carpet as the fire licks up the pilasters. More corpses move in, agitated by the flaring light and heat and noise.

Josh wastes no time spinning around and vaulting back toward the window.

It takes less than fifteen minutes for the second floor of the glass house to go up, another five minutes for the infrastructure to collapse into itself on a tidal wave of sparks and smoke, the second floor plunging down onto the first, catching the staircase and gobbling through the warren of antiques and expensive floor coverings. The throngs of walkers inside the home are immolated by geysers of flames, the conflagration fueled by the methane of decay oozing off all the reanimated corpses. Within twenty minutes, more than eighty percent of the swarm from the ravine is vanquished in the firestorm, reduced to charred crisps inside the smoking ruins of the stately home.

Oddly, over the course of those twenty minutes, the nature of the house—with its spectacular enclosure of wraparound windows—acts as a chimney, accelerating the blaze but also burning it out quickly. The hottest part of the fire goes straight up, singeing the tops of the trees but containing the damage. The other homes in the area are spared. No sparks are carried on the winds, and the telltale cloud of smoke remains obscured behind the wooded hills, unseen by the citizens of Woodbury.

In the time it takes for the house to burn itself out, Lilly finds enough nerve to vault from the lowest limb of the oak to the roof of the coach house and then climb down the back wall to the rear door of the garage. Josh follows. By that point only a few walkers remain outside the home, and Josh easily dispatches them with the remaining three slugs in the .38's cylinder.

They get into the garage and find the duffel bag, in which they had stashed some of their previous day's take for safekeeping. The heavy canvas carryall contains a five-gallon jug of gasoline, a sleeping bag, a drip coffee machine, two pounds of French Roast, winter scarves, a box of pancake mix, writing tablets, two bottles of kosher wine, batteries, ballpoint pens, expensive red current jam, a box of matzo, and a coil of mountain-climbing rope.

Josh reloads the police special with the last six slugs in his speed loader. Then they sneak out the back door with the duffel bag over Josh's shoulder, and they creep along the outer wall. Crouching in the weeds near the corner of the garage, they wait until the last moving corpse has drifted toward the light and noise of the fire before darting across the property and into the adjacent woods.

They weave their way through the trees without exchanging a word.

The access road to the south lies deserted in the waning daylight. Josh and Lilly keep to the shadows of a dry creek bed running parallel to the winding blacktop. They head east, down the long sloping landscape, back toward town.

They cover a little more than a mile without speaking, acting like an old married couple in the aftermath of a quarrel. By this point, the fear and adrenaline have finally drained out of them, replaced by a shaky kind of exhaustion.

The near miss of the home attack and ensuing fire has left Lilly in a state of panic. She jumps at noises on either side of the path, and she cannot seem to get enough air into her lungs. She keeps smelling walker stink on the wind, and she thinks she hears shuffling sounds behind the trees, which may or may not be mere echoes of their own weary footsteps.

At last, as they turn the corner at the bottom of Canyon Road, Josh says, "Just let me get one thing straight: Are you saying you're just using me?"

"Josh, I didn't—"

"For protection? And that's it? That's as far as your feelings go?"

"Josh—"

"Or . . . are you saying you just don't want me to *feel* like you're doing that?"

"I didn't say that."

"Yeah, baby, I'm afraid you did, that's exactly what you said."

"This is ridiculous." Lilly puts her hands in the pockets of her corduroy jacket as she walks. A layer of grime and ash has turned the fabric of the coat soot gray in the late-afternoon light. "Let's just drop it. I shouldn't have said anything."

"No!" Josh is slowly shaking his head as he walks. "You don't get to do that."

"What are you talking about?"

He shoots a glance at her. "You think this is like a passing thing?"

"What do you mean?"

"Like this is summer camp? Like we're all gonna go home at the end of the season after losing our virginity and getting poison ivy." His voice has an edge. Lilly has never heard this tone before in Josh

Lee Hamilton's voice. His deep baritone skirts the fringes of rage, his jutting chin belying the hurt slicing through him. "You don't get to plant this little bomb and walk away."

Lilly lets out an exasperated sigh and cannot think of what to say, and they walk in silence for a while. The Woodbury wall materializes in the distance, the far western edge of the construction site coming into view, where the bulldozer and small crane sit idle in the waning light. The construction crew has learned the hard way that zombies—like game fish—bite more in the twilight hours.

At last Lilly says, "What the hell do you want me to say, Josh?"

He stares at the ground as he walks and ruminates. The duffel bag rattles, banging on his hip as he trudges along. "How about you're sorry? How about you've been thinking it over, and maybe you're just scared of gettin' close to somebody because you don't want to get hurt, because you've been hurt yourself, and you take it all back, what you said, you take it back and you really love me as much as I love you? How about that, huh?"

She looks at him, her throat burning from the smoke and terror. She is so thirsty. Tired and thirsty and confused and scared. "What makes you think I've been hurt?"

"Just a lucky guess."

She looks at him. Anger tightens in her belly like a fist. "You don't even know me."

He looks down at her, his eyes wide and stung. "Are you shittin' me?"

"We hooked up—what?—barely two months ago. Bunch of people scared out of their wits. Nobody knows *anybody*. We're all just . . . making do."

"You gotta be kidding me. All we been through? And I don't even *know* you?"

"Josh, that's not what I—"

"You're putting me on the same level as Bob and the stoner? Megan and them folks at the camp? Bingham?"

"Josh—"

"All them things you said to me this week—what are you saying?—you been lying? You said them things just to make me feel better?"

"I meant what I said," she murmurs softly. The guilt twists in her. For a brief instant she thinks back to that terrible moment she lost little Sarah Bingham, the undead swarming all over the little girl on those godforsaken grounds outside the circus tent. The helplessness. The paralytic terror that seized Lilly that day. The loss and the grief and the sorrow as deep as a well. The fact is, Josh is correct. Lilly has said things to him in the throes of late-night lovemaking that aren't exactly true. On some level she loves him, cares for him, has strong feelings . . . but she's projecting something sick deep within her, something that has to do with fear.

"That's just fine and dandy," Josh Lee Hamilton says finally, shaking his head.

They are approaching the gap in the wall outside town. The entranceway—a wide spot between two uncompleted sections of barricade—has a wooden gate secured at one end with cable. About fifty yards away, a single guard sits on the roof of a semitrailer, gazing in the opposite direction with an M1 carbine on his hip.

Josh marches up to the gate and angrily loosens the cable, throwing it open. The rattling noise echoes. Lilly's flesh crawls with panic. She whispers, "Josh, be careful, they're gonna hear us."

"I don't give a rat's ass," he says, swinging the gate open for her. "Ain't a prison. They can't keep us from comin' and goin'."

She follows him through the gate and down a side road toward Main Street.

Few stragglers walk the streets at this hour. Most of the denizens of Woodbury are tucked away indoors, having dinner or drinking themselves into oblivion. The generators provide an eerie thrum behind the walls of the racetrack, some of the overhead stadium lights flickering. The wind trumpets through the bare trees of the square, and dead leaves skitter down the sidewalks.

"You have it your way," Josh says as they turn right and head east down Main Street, trudging toward their apartment building. "We'll just be fuck buddies. Quick pop every now and then to relieve the tension. No muss, no fuss . . ."

"Josh, that's not—"

"You could get the same thing from a bottle of rotgut and a vibrator . . . but hey. Warm body's nice every now and then, right?"

"Josh, c'mon. Why does it have to be this way? I'm just trying to—"

"I don't want to talk about it anymore." He bites down on his words as they approach the food center.

A cluster of men gather around the front of the store, warming their hands over a flaming brazier of trash burning in an oil drum. Sam the Butcher is there, a ratty overcoat covering his blood-spackled apron. His gaunt face puckers with distaste, his diamond-chip blue eyes narrowing as he sees the two figures approaching from the west.

"Fine, Josh, whatever." Lilly thrusts her hands deeper into her pockets as she strides alongside the big man, slowly shaking her head. "Whatever you say."

They pass the food center.

"Hey! Green Mile!" Sam the Butcher's voice calls out, flinty, terse, a knife scraping a whetstone. "C'mere a minute, big fella."

Lilly pauses, her hackles up.

Josh walks over to the men. "I got a name," he says flatly.

"Well, excuse the hell outta me," the butcher says. "What was it— Hamilburg? Hammington?"

"Hamilton."

The butcher offers a vacuous smile. "Well, well. Mr. Hamilton. Esquire. Might I have a moment of your valuable time, if you aren't too busy?"

"What do you want?"

The butcher's cold smile remains. "Just outta curiosity, what's in the bag?"

Josh stares at him. "Nothing much . . . just some odds and ends."

"Odds and ends, huh? What kind of odds and ends?"

"Things we found along the way. Nothin' that would interest anybody."

"You do realize you ain't covered your debt on them *other* odds and ends I gave y'all couple days ago."

"What are you talking about?" Josh keeps staring. "I've been on the crew every day this week."

"You ain't covered it yet, son. That heating oil don't grow on trees."

"You said forty hours would cover it."

The butcher shrugs. "You misunderstood me, hoss. It happens."

"How so?"

"I said forty hours on *top* of what you logged already. Got that?"

The staring match goes on for an awkward moment. All conversation around the flaming trash barrel ceases. All eyes are on the two men. Something about the way Josh's beefy shoulder blades are tensing under his lumberjack coat makes Lilly's flesh crawl.

Josh finally gives the man a shrug. "I'll keep on workin', then."

Sam the Butcher tilts his lean, chiseled face toward the duffel bag. "And I'll thank you to hand over whatever you got tucked away in that bag for the cause."

The butcher makes a move toward the duffel bag, reaching out for it.

Josh snaps it back and away from his grasp.

The mood changes with the speed of a circuit firing. The other men—mostly older loafers with hound-dog eyes and stringy gray hair in their faces—begin to instinctively back away. The tension ratchets up. The silence only adds to the latent violence brewing—the soft snapping of the fire the only sound beneath the wind.

"Josh, it's okay." Lilly steps forward and attempts to intercede. "We don't need any—"

"No!" Josh jerks the duffel away from her, his gaze never leaving the dark, bloodshot eyes of the butcher. "Nobody's taking this bag!"

The butcher's voice drops an octave, going all slippery and dark. "You better think long and hard about fucking with me, big boy."

"The thing is, I'm not fucking with you," Josh says to the man in the bloody apron. "Just stating a fact. The stuff in this bag is ours fair and square. And nobody's taking it from us."

"Finders keepers?"

"That's right."

The old men back away farther until it feels to Lilly like she's standing in some flickering, ice-cold fighting ring with two cornered animals. She gropes for some way to ease back the tension but her words get stuck in her throat. She reaches for Josh's shoulder but he pulls away from her as though shocked. The butcher flicks his gaze at Lilly. "You better tell your beau here he's making the mistake of his life."

"Leave her out of this," Josh tells him. "This is between you and me."

The butcher sucks the inside of his cheek thoughtfully. "Tell you what . . . I'm a fair man . . . I'll give you one more chance. Hand over the goodies and I'll wipe the debt clean. We'll pretend this little tiff never happened." Something approximating a smile creases the lines around the butcher's weathered face. "Life's too short. Know what I mean? Especially around here."

"C'mon, Lilly," Josh says without moving his gaze from the butcher's lifeless eyes. "We got better things to do, stand around here flapping our jaws."

Josh turns away from the storefront and starts down the street.

The butcher goes after the duffel. "GIVE ME THAT GODDAMN BAG!"

Lilly jerks forward as the two men come together in the middle of the street.

"JOSH, NO!"

The big man spins and drives the brunt of his shoulder into the butcher's chest. The move is sudden and violent, and harkens back to Josh's gridiron years when he would clear the field for a running back. The man in the blood-stippled apron flings backward, his breath gasping out of him. He trips over his own feet and goes down hard on his ass, blinking with shock and outrage.

Josh turns and continues on down the street, calling over his shoulder. "Lilly, I said c'mon, let's go!"

Lilly doesn't see the butcher suddenly contorting his body against the ground, struggling to dig something out of the back of his belt under his apron. Lilly doesn't see the glint of blue steel filling the butcher's hand, nor does she hear the telltale snap of a safety being thumbed off a semiautomatic, nor does she see the madness in the butcher's eyes, until it's too late.

"Josh, wait!"

Lilly gets halfway down the sidewalk—coming to within ten feet of Josh—when the blast cracks open the sky, the roar of the 9-millimeter so tremendous it seems to rattle the windows half a block down the street. Lilly instinctively dives for cover, hitting the macadam hard, the impact knocking the breath out of her.

She finds her voice then, and she shrieks as a flock of pigeons erupts off the roof of the food center—the swarm of carrion birds spreading across the darkening sky like black needlepoint.

TWELVE

Lilly Caul would remember things about that day for the rest of her life. She would remember seeing the red rosette of blood and tissue—like a tuft in upholstery—blooming from the back of Josh Lee Hamilton's head, the wound appearing a nanosecond before the booming report of the 9-millimeter Glock fully registered in Lilly's ears. She would remember tripping and falling to the pavement six feet behind Josh, one of her molars cracking, another incisor biting through her tongue. She would remember her ears ringing then, a fine spangle of blood droplets on the backs of her hands and lower arms.

But most of all, Lilly would remember the sight of Josh Lee Hamilton folding to the street as though he were swooning, his enormous legs going soft and wobbly like those of a rag doll. That was perhaps the strangest part: The way the giant man seemed to instantly lose his substance. One would expect such a person to not easily give up the ghost, to fall like a great redwood or old landmark building under the wrecking ball, literally shaking the earth on impact. But the fact is, that day, in the waning blue winter light, Josh Lee Hamilton would fade out without even a whimper.

He would simply keel over and land in a silent heap on the cold pavement.

In the immediate aftermath Lilly feels her entire body seize up with chills, gooseflesh pouring down over her flesh, everything going blurry and also crystal clear at the same time, as though her spirit were separating from her earthbound self. She loses control of her actions. She finds herself rising to her feet without even being aware of it.

She finds herself moving toward the fallen man with numb, involuntary steps, the strides of an automaton. "No, wait . . . no, no, wait, wait, wait," she gibbers as she approaches the dying giant. Her knees hit the ground. Her tears run across the front of her as she reaches down and cradles his huge head and babbles, "Somebody . . . get a doctor . . . no . . . get . . . *somebody* . . . get a . . . GET A FUCKING DOCTOR, SOMEBODY!!"

Nestled in Lilly's hands, the blood getting on her sleeves, Josh's face twitches in its death throes, seeming to undulate and pass from one expression to another. His eyes rolling back, he blinks his last blinks, somehow finding Lilly's face and locking on to it with his final spark of life. "Alicia . . . close the window."

A synapse fires, a memory of an older sister fading away in his traumatized brain like a dying ember.

"Alicia, close the . . ."

His face grows still, eyes freezing and hardening in their sockets like marbles.

"Josh, Josh . . ." Lilly shakes him as though trying to kick-start an engine back to life. He's gone. She cannot see through her tears, everything going milky. She feels the wetness on her wrists from his breached skull, and she feels something tightening around the nape of her neck.

"Leave him be," a gravelly voice intones from behind her, thick with rage.

Lilly realizes someone is pulling her away from the body, a large male hand, fingers clutching a hank of her collar, tugging her back.

Something deep within her snaps.

The passage of time seems to elongate and corrupt, like that of a dream, as the butcher yanks the girl away from the body. He drags her back against the curb and she flops against the barrier, banging the back of her head, lying still now, staring up at the lanky man in the apron. The butcher stands over her, breathing hard, shaking

188 | Kirkman & Bonansinga

with adrenaline. Behind him, the old geezers stand back against the storefront, shrinking into their baggy, ragged clothes, their rheumy eyes pinned wide.

Down the block, others materialize in the twilight, peering out of doorways and around corners.

"Look what you two have gone and done now!" the butcher accuses Lilly, shoving the pistol in her face. "I tried to be reasonable!"

"Get it over with." She closes her eyes. "Get it over with . . . go ahead."

"You stupid bitch, I ain't gonna kill ya!" He slaps her with his free hand. "Are you listening? Do I have your attention?"

Footsteps echo in the distance—someone running this way— which goes unheard at first. Lilly opens her eyes. "You're a murderer." She utters this over bloody teeth. Her nose is bleeding. "You're worse than a fucking walker."

"That's your opinion." He slaps her again. "Now I want you to listen to me."

The sting is bracing to Lilly. It wakes her up. "What do you want?"

Voices call out a block away, the charging footsteps closing in, but the butcher doesn't hear anything but his own voice. "Gonna take the rest of Green Mile's debt from you, little sister."

"Fuck you."

The butcher leans down and grabs her by the scruff of her jacket collar. "You're gonna work that skinny little ass until you're—"

Lilly's knee comes up hard enough to drive the man's testicles up into his pelvic bone. The butcher staggers and lets out a startled gasp that sounds like steam escaping from a broken vent.

Lilly springs to her feet, and she claws at the butcher's face. Her nails are chewed to the quicks, so they don't do much damage, but it drives the man back farther. He swings at her. She flinches away from the blow, which grazes her shoulder. She kicks him in the balls again.

The butcher staggers, reaching for his pistol.

By this point, Martinez is half a block away, running toward the scene, followed by two of his guards. He calls out, "WHAT THE FUCK?"

The butcher has gotten his Glock out of his belt and spins toward the oncoming men.

The burly, coiled Martinez pounces immediately, slamming the butt end of his M1 down on the butcher's right wrist, the sound of delicate bones crunching audible above the wind. The Glock flies out of the butcher's hand and the butcher lets out a mucusy howl.

One of the other guards—a black kid in an oversized hoodie—arrives in time to grab Lilly, pulling her away from the action. She writhes and squirms in the young man's arms as the guard holds her at bay.

"Stand down, asshole!" Martinez booms, pointing the assault rifle at the staggering butcher, but almost instantly, before Martinez can react, the butcher gets his hands around the shaft of the carbine.

The two men grapple for the gun, their inertia driving them back into the flaming barrel. The barrel spills its contents, a swirl of sparks going up, as the twosome careens toward the storefront. The butcher slams Martinez into the glass door, glass cracking in hairline fractures as Martinez slams the gun up into the butcher's face.

The butcher rears back in pain, clawing the M1 out of Martinez's grip. The assault rifle flies off across the sidewalk. The old men scatter in terror, while other townspeople arrive from all directions, some of them already sending up a frenzy of angry shouts. The second guard—an older man in aviator glasses and ratty down vest—holds the crowd back.

Martinez delivers a hard right to the butcher's jaw and sends the man in the apron crashing through the broken glass pane of the door.

The butcher lands inside the store's vestibule, sprawling to the tile floor, which is littered with glass shards now. Martinez climbs in after him.

A barrage of punishing blows from Martinez keeps the butcher pinned to the floor, his spittle and blood flinging off in pink threads. Frantically shielding his face, flailing impotently, the butcher tries to fight back but Martinez overpowers the man.

The final blow—a roundhouse punch to the butcher's jaw—knocks the man unconscious.

An awkward moment of silence follows, as Martinez catches

his breath. He stands over the man in the apron, rubbing his knuckles, trying to get his bearings. The noise of the crowd outside the food center has grown to a dull roar—most of them cheering for Martinez—like a demented pep rally.

Martinez cannot figure out what just happened. He never much cared for Sam the Butcher, but on the other hand he cannot imagine what would have gotten into this prick to make him draw on Hamilton.

"What the fuck got into you?" Martinez asks the man on the floor, speaking somewhat rhetorically, not really expecting an answer.

"The man obviously wants to be a star."

The voice comes from the gaping, jagged entrance behind Martinez.

Martinez whirls and sees the Governor standing in the doorway. Sinewy arms crossed against his chest, the long tails of his duster flapping in the breeze, the man has an enigmatic expression on his face, a mixture of bemusement and contempt and baleful curiosity. Gabe and Bruce stand behind the man like sullen totems.

Martinez is more confused than ever. "He wants to be a what?"

The Governor's expression transforms—his dark eyes glittering with inspiration, his handlebar mustache fully grown in now and twitching around the corners of a frown—which tells Martinez to step lightly. "First," the Governor says in a flat, impassive tone, "tell me exactly what happened."

"He didn't suffer, Lilly . . . remember that . . . no pain . . . he just went out like a light." Bob crouches near the curb next to Lilly, who is slumped with her head down, the tears dripping onto her lap. Bob has his first-aid kit open on the sidewalk next to her, and he is dabbing a swab of iodine on her cut face. "That's more than most of us can hope for in this shithole of a world."

"I should have stopped it," Lilly utters in a bloodless, sapped voice that sounds like a pull-string doll on its last legs. She has burned out her tear ducts. "I could have, Bob, I could have stopped it."

The silence stretches, the wind rattling in the eaves and high-tension wires. Practically the entire population of Woodbury has gathered along Main Street to gawk at the aftermath.

Josh lies supine under a sheet next to Lilly. Someone covered the body with the makeshift shroud only minutes earlier, the folds of which now soak with red blotches of blood from Josh's head wounds. Lilly tenderly strokes his leg, compulsively squeezing and massaging as though she might wake him up. Tendrils of hair are knocked loose from Lilly's ponytail, blowing across her scarred, crestfallen features.

"Hush now, honey," Bob says, placing the bottle of Betadine back into the kit. "There was nothing y'all could do, nothing at all." Bob shoots a worried glance up at the jagged, broken glass of the food center entrance. He can barely see the Governor and his men inside the vestibule, talking with Martinez. The butcher's unconscious body lies in the shadows. The Governor gestures expansively toward the body, explaining something to Martinez. "Goddamn shame is what it is," Bob says, looking away. "Goddamn crying shame."

"He didn't have a mean bone in his body," Lilly says softly, looking at the bloodstain soaking the head end of the sheet. "I wouldn't be alive, wasn't for him . . . he saved my life, Bob, all he wanted was—"

"Miss . . . ?"

Lilly looks up at the sound of an unfamiliar voice, and sees an older man in eyeglasses and white lab coat standing behind Bob. A fourth person, a twenty-something girl with blond braids, stands behind the man. She also wears a tattered lab coat and has a stethoscope and blood pressure cuff dangling around her neck.

"Lilly, this is Doc Stevens," Bob says with a nod toward the man. "And that there is Alice, his nurse."

The girl gives Lilly a respectful nod while unwinding the cuff.

"Lilly, you mind if I take a quick peek at those facial bruises?" the doctor says, kneeling next to her, putting the earbuds of his stethoscope in his ears. Lilly says nothing, just turns her gaze back to the ground. The doctor gently touches the scope to her neck, her sternum, her pulse points. He inspects her wounds, softly palpates her ribs. "Very sorry for your loss, Lilly," the doctor murmurs.

Lilly says nothing.

"Some of them wounds are old," Bob comments, rising to his feet, backing away.

"Looks like hairline fractures to number eight and nine, also to the clavicle," he says, gently nudging his fingers through her fleece jacket. "All of them pretty much healed up. Lungs sound clear." He takes the scope out of his ears, winds it around his neck. "Lilly, if you need anything you let us know."

She manages a nod.

The doctor measures his words. "Lilly, I just want you to know . . ." He pauses for a moment, groping for the right words. "Not everybody in this town is . . . like this. I know it's not much in the way of consolation right now." He looks up at Bob, then gazes at the ruined food center window, than back at Lilly. "I guess what I'm saying is, if you ever need somebody to talk to, if something is bothering you, if you need anything whatsoever . . . don't hesitate to come down to the clinic."

Seeing no reaction from Lilly, the doctor lets out a sigh and rises to his feet. He exchanges nervous glances with Bob and Alice.

Bob moves back to Lilly's side, kneels down, and says very softly, "Lilly, honey, we're gonna have to go ahead and move the body now."

At first she barely hears him, in fact doesn't even register what he's saying.

She simply continues staring at the pavement and stroking the dead man's leg and feeling empty. In anthropology class at Georgia Tech she learned about the Algonquin Indians and their belief that the spirit of the dead must be appeased. After a hunt they would literally breathe in the last breaths of a dying bear in order to honor it and accept it into their own bodies and pay homage to it. But Lilly feels only desolation and loss coming into her now from the cooling corpse of Josh Lee Hamilton.

"Lilly?" Bob's voice sounds as though it's coming from a distant solar system. "Is it okay, honey, if we go ahead and move the body?"

Lilly is silent.

Bob nods at Stevens. The doctor nods at Alice, and Alice turns and signals to two men standing their distance with a collapsible stretcher. The two men—both middle-aged cronies of Bob's from the tavern crowd—move in. Unfolding the stretcher, they come within inches of Lilly and kneel down by the body. The first man starts to gently lever the massive body onto the stretcher, when Lilly snaps her gaze up at them, blinking back tears.

"Leave him alone," she mutters, the words coming out in barely a whisper.

Bob puts a hand on her shoulder. "Lilly, honey—"

"I SAID LEAVE HIM ALONE! DON'T TOUCH HIM!! GET THE FUCK AWAY FROM HIM!!!"

Her anguished cry pierces the windswept stillness of the street, getting everyone's attention. Onlookers halfway down the block pause in their conversations and look up. People in doorways peer around corners to see what's going on. Bob waves off the two cronies, and Stevens and Alice back away in awkward silence.

The commotion has drawn several figures out of the food center. They now stand in the jagged opening of the entrance, staring at the sad state of affairs.

Bob gazes up and sees the Governor standing there, arms crossed against his chest on the glass-littered threshold, assessing the situation with his cunning, dark eyes. Bob walks sheepishly over to the entrance.

"She'll be okay," Bob says confidentially to the Governor. "She's just a little torn up right now."

"Who can blame her?" the Governor muses. "Lose your meal ticket like that." He chews the inside of his cheek for a moment, thinking. "Leave her alone for a while. We'll clean up the mess later." He thinks some more, not taking his gaze off the dead body lying next to the curb. At last he calls over his shoulder, "Gabe—c'mere!"

The stocky man in the turtleneck and flattop haircut comes over.

The Governor speaks softly. "I want you to wake up that piece-of-shit butcher, take him down to the holding cells, and throw him in with the Guard."

Gabe gives a nod, whirls, and slips back inside the food center.

"Bruce!" the Governor calls to his second in command. The black man with the shaved head and Kevlar vest comes over with an AK-47 on his hip.

"Yeah, boss."

"I want you to round everybody up, take them over to the square." The black man cocks his head incredulously. "Everybody?"

"You heard me—everybody." The Governor gives him a wink. "Gonna have a little town hall meeting."

"We live in violent times. We're all under tremendous pressure. Every day of our lives."

The Governor barks into a megaphone that Martinez found in the defunct firehouse, the gravelly, smoky voice carrying up over the bare trees and torches. The sun has set on the town, and now the entire population mills about the darkness on the edge of the gazebo in the center of the square. The Governor stands on the stone steps of the structure, addressing his subjects with the stentorian authority of a politician crossed with a wild-eyed motivational speaker.

"I understand the pressures," he goes on, pacing across the steps, milking the moment for all it's worth. His voice echoes across the square, slapping back against the boarded-up storefronts across the street. "We've all dealt with the grief, last few months . . . losing somebody close to us."

He pauses for effect, and he sees many of the faces turning downward, eyes shimmering in the light of torches. He senses the weight of pain pressing down. He smiles inwardly, waiting patiently for the moment to pass.

"What happened at the store today didn't have to happen. You live by the sword . . . I get that. But it didn't have to happen. It was a symptom of a greater sickness. And we're gonna treat that sickness."

For a brief instant he glances back to the east, and he sees the slumped figures gathered over the shrouded body of the black man. Bob kneels behind the girl named Lilly, stroking her back, as he stares trancelike at the fallen giant under the bloody sheet.

The Governor turns back to his audience. "Starting tonight we're gonna inoculate ourselves. From now on, things are gonna be different around here. I promise you . . . things are gonna be different. Gonna be some new rules."

He paces some more, burning his gaze into each and every onlooker.

"The thing that separates us from these monsters out there is *civilization!*" He punches the word "civilization" so hard it bounces off the rooftops. "Order! Laws! The ancient Greeks had this shit down. They knew about tough love. 'Catharsis' they used to call it."

Some of the faces gaze up at him with jittery, expectant expressions.

"You see that racetrack up yonder?" he says into the bullhorn. "Take a good look!"

He turns and gives a signal to Martinez, who stands in the shadows at the base of the gazebo. Martinez thumbs a button on a two-way, and he whispers something to somebody on the other end. This is the part that the Governor insisted be carefully timed.

"Starting tonight," the Governor goes on, watching many of the heads turn toward the big, dark flying saucer planted in the clay west of town, its huge bowl-like rim rising in silhouette against the stars. "Starting right now! That's gonna be our new Greek theater!"

With the pomp and circumstance of a fireworks display, the great xenon spots above the track suddenly flare to life in sequence— making audible metallic snapping noises—sending giant blooms of silver light down on the arena. The gag gets an audible, collective sigh from many of those gathered around the gazebo, some spontaneously applauding.

"Admission is free!" The Governor feels the energy rising, crackling like static electricity, and he bears down on them. "Auditions are ongoing, folks. You want to fight in the ring? All you gotta do is break the rules. That's all you gotta do. Break the law."

He looks at them as he paces, daring them to respond. Some of them look at each other, some of them nod, while others look as though they're about to give him a "Hallelujah."

"Anyone breaks the law is gonna fight! That simple. You don't know what the laws are, all you gotta do is ask. Read the fucking Constitution. Check the Bible. Do unto others. Golden rule. All that. But hear what I'm saying. You do *unto* somebody a little too much . . . you're gonna fight."

A few voices holler out their consent, and the Governor feeds off the energy, stoking the flames. "From now on, you fuck with somebody—you break the law—you're gonna fight!"

A few more voices add to the din, the noise carrying up into the sky.

"You steal from somebody, you're gonna fight!"

Now the crowd hollers its approval, a chorus of righteous howls.

"You bang somebody's old lady, you're gonna fight!"

More voices join in, all the fear and frustration boiling over now.

"You kill somebody, you're gonna fight!"

The cheering starts to corrupt into a cacophony of angry shouts.

"You mess with somebody in any way—especially, you get somebody killed—you're gonna fight. In the arena. In front of God. To the death."

The clamor deteriorates into a mishmash of applause and whooping and hollering. The Governor waits for it to subside like a wave rolling away.

"It starts tonight," he says in barely a whisper, the megaphone crackling. "It starts with this nutcase, guy that runs the general store—Sam the Butcher. Thinks he's judge, jury, and executioner."

All at once the Governor points at the arena and calls out suddenly in a voice that would not be out of place at a charismatic church service: "Who's ready for some payback? *WHO'S READY FOR SOME LAW AND ORDER?*"

The voices erupt.

Lilly gazes up and sees the abrupt exodus of nearly forty people half a block away. The crowd disperses in a noisy mass, moving almost as one—a giant human amoeba of excited fist pumping and inarticulate, angry cheering—charging across the street toward the racetrack arena, which sits in a vast penumbra of silver light two hundred yards to the west. The sight of it turns Lilly's stomach.

She looks away and mutters, "You can take the body away now, Bob."

Standing over her, Bob leans down and tenderly strokes her shoulder. "We'll take good care of him, honey."

She gazes into the distance. "Tell Stevens I want to make the arrangements."

"You got it."

"We'll bury him tomorrow."

"That sounds fine, honey."

Lilly watches the mob of citizens in the distance filing into the arena. For one terrible instant she recalls scenes from old horror movies, angry throngs of townspeople with torches and primitive weapons, closing in on Frankenstein's castle, lusting for the monster's blood.

She shudders. She realizes they are all monsters now—all of them—Lilly and Bob included. Woodbury is the monster now.

THIRTEEN

Curiosity gets the better of Bob Stookey. After escorting Lilly back to her apartment above the dry cleaner, and giving her ten milligrams of alprazolam for sleep, he checks in with Stevens. Arrangements are made to move Josh's body to its temporary resting place in the makeshift morgue under the racetrack. Afterward Bob makes his way back to his camper and grabs a fresh bottle of whiskey from the back. Then he returns to the arena.

By the time he arrives at the south entrance, the crowd noises are swelling and ringing inside the structure like waves crashing against a shore, magnified by the metallic baffles of the arena. Bob creeps through the dark, fetid tunnel toward the light. He pauses just inside the south gate and takes a healthy pull off the bottle of hooch, girding himself, buffering his nerves. The whiskey burns and makes his eyes water.

He steps into the light.

At first all he sees are blurry, indistinct shapes down on the infield, obscured behind massive cyclone fences rising up in front of the spectators. The bleachers on either side of him are mostly empty. The citizens sit above him, scattered across the upper decks, clapping and whooping and craning their necks to see the action. The harsh brilliance of the arc light shining down makes Bob blink. The air smells of old burned rubber and gasoline, and Bob has to squint to identify what's going on down on the track.

He takes a step closer, leans toward the fence, and peers through the chain link.

Two large men grapple with each other in the center of the muddy infield. Sam the Butcher, seminude in his blood-spattered athletic trunks, his bare chest sagging, and his belly hanging over his belt, swings a jury-rigged wooden club at Stinson, the big, lumpy middle-aged guardsman. Stinson, his camo pants dark with bodily fluids, staggers and jerks back, trying to dodge the onslaught, an eighteen-inch machete in his greasy hand. The end of the butcher's club—sprouting rusty nails on one side—catches the side of Stinson's doughy face, gouging flesh.

Stinson rears backward, throwing spittle and strands of thick blood.

The crowd issues a salvo of yelps and angry cheers as Stinson topples over his own feet. Dust rises up into the sodium light as the portly guardsman hits the ground, the machete flying out of his grip and landing in the dirt. The butcher pounces with the club. Nails puncture Stinson's jugular and left pectoral before the man has a chance to roll away. The audience yowls.

Bob turns away for a moment, feeling nauseous and dizzy. He takes another huge gulp of whiskey and lets the burn soothe his terror. He takes another, and another, and finally works up enough nerve to gaze back at the action. The butcher is pummeling Stinson, sending gouts of blood—as black as tar in the sodium lights—spraying across the matted brown turf of the infield.

The wide dirt track circling the infield has armed guards at each gate, intently watching the fracas, their assault rifles cradled at the ready. Bob swallows more whiskey and averts his gaze from the grisly slaughter, focusing on the upper regions of the racetrack. The diamond-vision screen is blank, powerless, probably inoperable. The glass enclosures of VIP boxes lining one side of the arena are mostly deserted and dark . . . all except for one.

The Governor and Martinez stand behind the window of the center box, looking down on the spectacle with unreadable expressions on their faces.

Bob chugs another few fingers of whiskey—he's already halfway through the bottle—and finds himself avoiding eye contact with the crowd. In his peripheral vision he can see the faces of young and old, male and female, all riveted to the bloody skirmish. Many faces contort with a kind of manic delight. Some of the onlookers rise to their feet, hands waving as though they are finding Jesus.

Down on the field the butcher delivers one last savage blow to Stinson's kidney, the nails sinking into the guardsman's fleshy lower back. Blood bubbles and gushes, and then Stinson sags in the dirt, convulsing, twitching in his death throes. Breathing hard, drooling with psychotic glee, the butcher raises the club and faces the crowd. The spectators respond with a surge of howls.

Repulsed, woozy, going numb with horror, Bob Stookey chugs more whiskey and looks down.

"I THINK WE HAVE A WINNER!"

The amplified voice coming through the public address system echoes and feeds back with harsh, electronic squealing noises. Bob gazes up and sees the Governor behind the center box window casually speaking into a microphone. Even from this great distance, Bob can see the weird pleasure glimmering behind the Governor's eyes like two pinpoints of starlight. Bob looks back down.

"HOLD ON! HOLD ON!! LADIES AND GENTLEMEN, I THINK WE HAVE A COMEBACK!!"

Bob looks up.

On the infield, the big lump on the ground has come back to life. Lurching toward the machete, Stinson gets his blood-slick hand around the hilt and twists back toward the butcher, who has his back turned. Stinson pounces with every last ounce of strength. The butcher turns and tries to shield his face as the machete slashes.

The blade sinks into the butcher's neck deep enough to get stuck.

The butcher staggers and falls backward with the machete still planted in his jugular. Stinson moves in with drunken rage, the blood loss making him lumber and weave with eerie resemblance to a zombie. The crowd jeers and roars. Stinson pulls the machete loose and delivers another devastating blow to the butcher's neck, severing the gaunt man's head between the fifth and sixth cervical vertebrae.

The spectators cheer as the butcher's neck floods the ground with its lifeblood.

Bob looks away. He falls to his knees, one hand still clutching the chain link. His stomach lurches and he vomits on the cement floor of the mezzanine. The bottle falls but does not break. Bob pukes out the entire contents of his stomach in heaving gasps—the noise of the crowd going all watery, everything getting blurry and indistinct in his watery vision. He vomits and vomits until there is nothing left but thin strands of bile hanging off his lips. He falls back against the first row of empty bleachers. He retrieves the bottle and sucks down the rest of its contents.

The amplified voice echoes: "AND THAT, FOLKS, IS WHAT WE CALL JUSTICE!"

Outside the arena, at that moment, the streets of Woodbury could be confused with any other deserted ghost ship of a village in the Georgia countryside—abandoned and scoured clean in the advent of the plague.

At first glance, every last inhabitant appears to be missing in action—the entire population still gathered in the stadium, riveted to the final moments of the battle royale. Even the sidewalk in front of the food center has been cleared, any lingering evidence of murder mopped away by Stevens and his men, Josh's body carted off to the morgue.

Now, in the darkness, as the muffled echoes of the crowd swirl on the wind, Lilly Caul wanders the sidewalk in her fleece, torn jeans, and tattered high-tops. She cannot sleep, cannot think, cannot stop crying. The noise from the arena feels like insects crawling on her. The Xanax Bob gave her has done nothing but dull the pain, like a layer of gauze over her racing thoughts. She shivers in the cold and pauses in a dark vestibule in front of a boarded drugstore.

"It's none of my business," a voice says from the shadows. "But a young lady like yourself shouldn't be out alone on these streets."

Lilly turns and sees the glint of metal-rimmed glasses on a dark face. She sighs, wipes her eyes, and looks down. "What difference does it make?"

Dr. Stevens steps into the flickering light of torches. He stands with his hands in his pockets, his lab coat buttoned to the collar, a scarf around his neck. "How are you holding up, Lilly?"

She looks at him through her tears. "Holding up? I'm just grand."

She tries to breathe but her lungs feel as though they're full of sand. "Next stupid question."

"You might think about resting." He comes over to her and inspects her bruises. "You're still in shock, Lilly. You need sleep."

She manages a pallid smile. "I'll sleep when I'm dead." She cringes and looks down, the tears burning her eyes. "Funny thing is, I hardly knew him."

"He seemed like a good man."

She looks up, focusing on the doctor. "Is that even possible anymore?"

"Is what possible?"

"Being a good person."

The doctor lets out a sigh. "Probably not."

Lilly swallows and looks down. "I have to get out of this place." She winces at another sob building in her. "I can't deal with it anymore."

Stevens looks at her. "Join the club."

A moment of awkward silence passes.

Lilly rubs her eyes. "How do you do it?"

"Do what?"

"Stay here . . . put up with this shit. You seem like a semisane person to me."

The doctor shrugs. "Looks can be deceiving. Anyway . . . I stay for the same reason they all stay."

"And that is . . . ?"

"Fear."

Lilly looks at the paving stones. She doesn't say anything. What is there to say? The torchlight across the street dwindles, the wicks burning down, the shadows deepening in the nooks and crannies between the buildings. Lilly fights the dizziness washing over her. She doesn't want to sleep ever again.

"They're going to be coming out of there pretty soon," the doctor says with a nod toward the racetrack in the distance. "Once they've had their fill of the little horror show Blake has concocted for them."

Lilly shakes her head. "Place is a fucking madhouse, and that dude is the craziest one of all."

"Tell you what." The doctor gestures toward the opposite end of town. "Why don't we take a little walk, Lilly . . . avoid the crowds."

She exhales a pained breath, then shrugs and mutters, "Whatever . . ."

That night, Dr. Stevens and Lilly walk for over an hour in the cold, bracing air, meandering back and forth along the far fence on the east side of town, and then down along the abandoned railroad tracks inside the security fence. While they walk and talk, the crowd slowly files out of the arena, wandering back to their dwellings, bloodlust satiated. The doctor does most of the talking that night, speaking softly, ever mindful of the listening ears of guards, who are positioned at strategic corners along the barricade, equipped with guns, binoculars, and walkie-talkies.

The guards are in constant contact with Martinez, who has cautioned his men to pay close attention to the weak areas along the ramparts, and especially the wooded hills to the south and west. Martinez worries that the noise of the gladiatorial matches will very likely draw walkers.

Strolling along the outskirts, Stevens gives Lilly a lecture about the perils of conspiring against the Governor. Stevens warns her to watch her tongue, and he speaks in analogies that make Lilly's head spin. He talks of Caesar Augustus and he speaks of Bedouin dictators through history and how the hardships of desert communities spurred brutal regimes and coups and violent insurrection.

Eventually Stevens brings the conversation full circle to the unfortunate realities of the zombie plague, and suggests that bloodthirsty leaders are very likely a necessary evil now, a side effect of survival.

"I don't want to live like that," Lilly says at last, walking slowly alongside the doctor through a palisade of bare trees. The wind spits a light sleet in their faces, which stings their flesh and coats the forest with a delicate rime of ice. Christmas is only twelve days off, not that anybody would notice.

"No choice in the matter, Lilly," the doctor mutters, head down, scarf across his chin. He stares at the ground as he walks.

"You always have a choice."

"You think? I don't know, Lilly." They walk in silence for a moment. The doctor slowly shakes his head as he walks. "I don't know."

She looks at him. "Josh Hamilton never went bad. My dad sacrificed his life for me." Lilly takes a breath and struggles with her tears. "It's just an excuse. A person is *born* bad. The shit we're dealing with now . . . it's just a fucking trigger. Brings out the real person."

"Then God help us," the doctor murmurs, almost more to himself than to Lilly.

The next day, under a low, steel-gray sky, a small contingent buries Josh Lee Hamilton in a makeshift casket. Lilly, Bob, Stevens, Alice, and Megan are joined by Calvin Deets, one of the workmen, who had grown fond of Josh over the last couple of weeks.

Deets is an older man, an emaciated chain-smoker—probably in the late stages of emphysema—who has a face like an old saddlebag left out in the sun. He stands respectfully back behind the front row of friends, his Caterpillar cap in his gnarled hands, as Lilly says a few words.

"Josh grew up in a religious family," Lilly says in a choked voice, her face turned down as though addressing the frozen ground on the edge of a playground. "He believed we all go to a better place."

Other recent graves spread across the small park, some with homemade crosses or carefully stacked cairns of polished stones. The mound of dirt over Josh's grave rises up at least four feet above ground level. They had to enclose his remains in a piano case that Deets found in a warehouse—the only container big enough to accommodate the fallen giant—and it took Bob and Deets several hours to carve out a suitable hole in the icebound earth.

"Here's hoping Josh is right, because we all . . ." Lilly's voice falters, crumbles. She closes her eyes and the tears seep through her eyelids. Bob takes a step closer, puts an arm around her. Lilly lets out a sob that shudders through her. She cannot continue.

Bob says softly, "Father . . . Son and . . . Holy Spirit. Amen." The others murmur likewise. Nobody moves. The wind kicks up and blows a sheet of powdery-dry snow across the playground, nipping their faces.

Bob gently urges Lilly away from the grave. "C'mon, darlin' . . . let's get you inside."

Lilly puts up little resistance, shuffling alongside Bob as the others turn away silently, heads down, faces crestfallen. For a moment, it looks as though Megan—dressed in a worn leather jacket, which some anonymous benefactor gave her in a druggy post-coitus afterglow—is about to hurry after Lilly, maybe say something to her. But the corkscrew-haired woman with the dishwater-green eyes just lets out an anguished sigh and keeps her distance.

Stevens gives Alice a nod, and the two of them turn and head back down the side road toward the racetrack complex, turning up the collars of their lab coats against the wind. They get halfway to the main drag—safely out of earshot of the others—when Alice says to the doctor, "Did you smell it?"

He nods. "Yep . . . it's on the wind . . . it's coming from the north."

Alice sighs, shaking her head. "I knew these idiots would draw a crowd with all that noise. Should we tell somebody?"

"Martinez already knows." The doctor indicates the guard tower behind them. "Lots of saber rattling going on, God help us."

Alice lets out another sigh. "Gonna be busy next few days, aren't we?"

"That guardsman used up half our whole blood supply, gonna need some more donors."

"I'll do it," Alice says.

"Appreciate the thought, sweetheart, but we got enough A positive to last us until Easter. Besides, I take any more out of you I'll have to plant you next to the big guy."

"Should we keep searching for an O positive?"

The doctor shrugs. "Like looking for a very small needle in a very small haystack."

"I haven't checked Lilly or that other new kid, what's his name."

"Scott? The stoner?"

"Yeah."

The doctor shakes his head. "Nobody's seen hide nor hair of him in days."

"You never know."

The doctor keeps shaking his head, hands deep in his pockets, as he hastens toward the shadows of concrete archways in the distance. "Yeah . . . you never know."

That night, back in her squatter's flat above the boarded-up dry cleaner, Lilly feels numb. She's thankful that Bob has chosen to stay with her for a while. He makes her dinner—his special beef jerky Stroganoff courtesy of Hamburger Helper—and they share enough of Bob's single-malt Scotch and generic Ambien to ease Lilly's racing thoughts.

The noises outside the second-story window grow fainter and farther away—although they seem to be making Bob nervous as he tucks Lilly in. Something is going on down on the streets. Maybe trouble. But Lilly cannot focus on the distant commotion of voices and running footsteps.

She feels as though she's floating, and the moment she lays her head on the pillow she sinks into semiconsciousness. The bare floors and sheet-covered windows of the apartment blur away into a white oblivion. But right before she sinks into the void of dreamless sleep, she sees Bob's weathered face looming over her.

"Why won't you leave with me, Bob?"

The question hangs there for a moment. Bob shrugs. "Haven't really thought about it."

"There's nothing for us here anymore."

He looks away. "Governor says things are gonna get better soon."

"What's the deal with you and him?"

"Whattya talkin' about?"

"He's got a hold on you, Bob."

"That ain't true."

"I just don't get it." Lilly fades. She can barely see the weathered man sitting on the side of her bed. "He's trouble, Bob."

"He's just trying to—"

Lilly barely hears the knock on the door. She tries to keep her eyes open. Bob goes to the door, and Lilly tries to stay awake long enough to identify the visitor. "Bob . . . ? Who is it . . . ?

Footsteps. Two figures come into view over her bed like ghosts. Lilly struggles to see through the shade descending over her eyes.

Bob stands next to a gaunt, lean, dark-eyed man with a carefully trimmed Fu Manchu mustache and coal-black hair. The man smiles as Lilly sinks into unconsciousness.

"Sleep tight, girlfriend," the Governor says. "You've had a long day."

The behavior patterns of the walkers continue to baffle and enthrall the deeper thinkers among Woodbury's inhabitants. Some believe the undead move as bees in a hive, driven by something far more complex than mere hunger. Some theories involve invisible pheromonelike signals passing among zombies, producing behaviors that depend upon the chemical makeup of their prey. Others believe in dog-whistle sensory responses above and beyond mere attraction to sound or smell or movement. No single hypothesis has stuck, but most of Woodbury's residents feel certain about one aspect of zombie behavior: The advent of a herd of any size is to be dreaded and feared and treated with respect. Herds tend to grow spontaneously and take on troubling ramifications. A herd—even a small one, like the cluster of dead forming at this very moment north of town, drawn by the noise of the gladiatorial match the previous night— can overturn a truck, snap fence posts like kindling, or topple even the highest wall.

For the last twenty-four hours Martinez has been marshaling forces in order to suppress the imminent attack. Guards posted on crow's nests at the northwest and northeast corners of the wall have been keeping tabs on the progress of the flock, which first began to morph into a herd about a mile away. The guards have been sending word down the chain of command that the size of the herd has grown from a dozen or so to nearly fifty, and the pack has been moving in a lumbering zigzag through the trees along Jones Mill Road, covering the distance between the deep woods and the outskirts of town at a speed of about two hundred yards an hour, growing in number as they come. Apparently the herds move even slower, collectively, than individual walkers. It has taken this herd fifteen hours to close the distance to four hundred yards.

Now some of them begin to emerge from the leading edge of the forest, shambling out into the open fields bordering the woods and the town. They look like broken toys in the hazy, distant twilight, like windup soldiers bumping into each other, running on the fumes of malfunctioning engines, their blackened mouths contracting and expanding like irises. Even at this distance the rising moon reflects off their milky eyes in shimmering coins of light.

Martinez has three Browning .50 caliber machine guns—courtesy of the ransacked National Guard depot—placed at key junctures along the wall. One sits on the bonnet of a backhoe at the west corner of the wall. Another one is situated on top of a cherry picker at the east corner. The third is positioned on the roof of a semitrailer on the edge of the construction site. Each of the three machine guns already has an operator in place, each man equipped with a headset.

Long gleaming bandoliers of incendiary armor-piercing tracer bullets dangle from the stock of each weapon, with extras in steel boxes sitting nearby.

Other guards take positions along the wall—on ladders and bull-dozer scoops—armed with semiautomatics and long-range sniper rifles loaded with 7.62-millimeter slugs that will penetrate drywall or sheet metal. These men do not wear headsets, but each know to watch for hand signals from Martinez, who positions himself at the top of a crane gantry in the center of the post office parking lot with a two-way. Two enormous klieg lights—scavenged from the town theater—are wired up to the generator chugging in the shadows of the post office loading dock.

A voice crackles on Martinez's radio: "Martinez, you there?"

Martinez thumbs the talk button. "Copy that, chief, go ahead."

"Bob and I are on our way up there, gonna need to harvest some fresh meat."

Martinez frowns, his brow furrowing under his bandanna. "Fresh meat?"

The voice sizzles through the tiny speaker: "How much time we got before all the fun and games start?"

Martinez gazes out at the darkening horizon, the closest zombies still about three hundred and fifty yards away. He thumbs the switch. "Probably won't be within head-shot range for another hour, maybe a little less than that."

"Good," says the voice. "We'll be there in five minutes."

Bob follows the Governor down Main Street toward a wagon train of semi trucks parked in a semicircle outside the looted Menards home and garden center. The Governor walks briskly through the wintry evening air, a bounce to his step, his boot heels clicking on the paving stones. "Times like these," the Governor comments to Bob as they march along, "must feel like you're back in the shit in Afghanistan."

"Yes, sir, I have to admit it does sometimes. I remember one time I got a call to drive down to the front, pick up some marines coming off their watch. It was nighttime, cold as a well digger's ass, just like this. Air raid sirens screaming, everybody hopped up for a firefight. Drove the APC down to this godforsaken trench in the sand, and what do I find? Bunch of whores from the local village giving out blow jobs to the grunts."

"No shit."

"I shit you not." Bob shakes his head in dismay as he walks alongside the Governor. "Right in the middle of an air raid. So I tell them to can it and get in before I leave them there. One of the whores gets in the APC with the men, and I'm like, what the hell. Whatever. Just get me out of this fucking place."

"Understandable."

"So I take off with the gal still going at it in the back of the APC. But you'll never guess what happened then."

"Don't keep me in suspense, Bob," the Governor says with a grin.

"All of a sudden I hear a crash in the back, and I realize that bitch is an insurgent, and she brought an IED in with her, set it off in the cargo bay." Bob shakes his head again. "Firewall protected me, but it was a mess. Took off one of the boys' legs."

"Un-fucking-believable," the Governor marvels as he approaches the circle of eighteen-wheelers. Full darkness has fallen, and light from a torch illuminates the side of a Piggly Wiggly truck on which a grinning pig leers down at them in the dim light. "Hold that thought a second, Bob." The Governor pounds his fist on the trailer. "Travis! You in there? Hey! Anybody home?"

In a cloud of cigar smoke, the rear door springs up on rusty hinges. A heavyset black man sticks his head out of the cargo hold. "Hey, boss . . . what can I do you for?"

"Take one of the empty trailers down to the north wall, on the double. We'll meet you there with further instructions. Got that?"

"Got it, boss."

The black man hops off the rear rail and vanishes around the side of the truck. The Governor takes a deep breath and then leads Bob around the circle of trucks, and then north along a side road toward the barricade. "Pretty goddamn amazing what a man will do for nookie," the Governor muses as they stride along the dirt road.

"Ain't it?"

"These girls you came in with, Bob, Lilly and . . . what's-her-name?"

"Megan?"

"That's the one. That little thing's a firecracker. Am I right?"

Bob wipes his mouth. "Yeah, she's a cute little gal."

"Kinda flirty . . . but hey. Who am I to judge?" Another lascivious grin. "We do what we do to get by. Am I right, Bob?"

"Right as rain." Bob walks along for a moment. "Just between you and me . . . I'm kinda sweet on her."

The Governor looks at the older man with an odd mixture of surprise and pity. "This Megan gal? Well, that's great, Bob. No shame in that."

Bob looks down as he walks. "Love to spend the night with her just once." Bob's voice goes soft. "Just once." He looks up at the Governor. "But, hell . . . I know that's just a pipe dream."

Philip cocks his head at the older man. "Maybe not, Bob . . . maybe not."

Before Bob can muster a response a series of explosive clanging noises go off ahead of them. Brilliant sunbursts from the klieg lights suddenly tear open seams in the distant darkness from opposite corners of the wall, the silver beams sweeping out across the adjacent fields and tree lines, illuminating the oncoming horde of walking corpses.

The Governor leads Bob across the post office lot to the crane gantry, on which Martinez now prepares to give the order to open fire.

"Hold your fire, Martinez!" The Governor's booming voice gets everybody's attention.

Martinez gazes nervously down at the two men. "You sure about this, chief?"

The rumble of a Kenworth cab rises up behind the Governor, accompanied by the telltale beeping noises of a semi moving in reverse. Bob glances over his shoulder and sees an eighteen-wheeler backing into position by the north gate. Exhaust vapors pulse from the truck's vertical stack, and Travis leans out the driver's side window, chewing a cigar and wrestling the steering wheel.

"Gimme your walkie!" The Governor gestures at Martinez, who is already descending the metal ladder affixed to the side of the crane. Bob watches all this from a respectable distance behind the Governor. Something about all this mysterious business makes the older man uneasy.

Outside the wall the meandering mass of zombies closes the distance to two hundred yards.

Martinez reaches the bottom of the ladder and hands over the two-way. The Governor thumbs the switch and barks into the mouthpiece. "Stevens! Can you hear me? You got your radio on?"

After a beat of crackling static the doctor's voice replies, "Yes, I hear you and I don't appreciate—"

"Shut up for a second. I want you to bring that tub-of-lard guardsman, Stinson, to the north wall."

The voice crackles: "Stinson is still recovering, the man has lost a lot of blood in your little—"

"Don't fucking argue with me, Stevens . . . *JUST FUCKING DO IT NOW!*"

The Governor clicks the radio off and throws it back to Martinez.

"Open the gate!" the Governor shouts at two workmen, who stand nearby with pickaxes and anxious expressions, awaiting orders.

The two workmen look at each other.

"You heard me!" the Governor bellows. "Open the goddamn gate!"

The workmen follow orders, throwing the bolt at one end of the gate. The gate swings open, letting in a gust of cold, rancid wind.

"You ask me, we're pushing our luck with this routine," Martinez mutters under his breath, slamming an ammo magazine into his assault rifle.

The Governor ignores the comment and hollers, "Travis! Back it into position!"

The truck shudders and beeps and rattles backward into the opening.

"Now put the ramp down!"

Bob watches, completely vexed by the proceedings, as Eugene hops out of his cab with a grunt and marches around behind the truck. He throws open the vertical door and lowers the ramp to the pavement.

In the glare of spotlights the zombie contingent approaches to within a hundred yards.

Shuffling footsteps draw Bob's attention back over his shoulder.

From the shadowy center of town, in the flicker of burning trash barrels, Dr. Stevens emerges with his arm around the wounded guardsman, who hobbles along with the lethargic gait of a stroke victim.

"Watch this, Bob," the Governor says, throwing a glance over his shoulder at the older man, and then, with a wink, adds, "Beats the hell outta the Middle East."

FOURTEEN

The screams inside the empty trailer, amplified by the corrugated metal floor and steel walls, build and build, an aria of agony, which compels Bob, standing behind the crane, to look away, as the moving cadavers shamble toward the opening, drawn to the noise and smell of fear. Bob needs a drink more than ever now. He needs a lot of drinks. He needs to soak in the booze until he's blind.

At least ninety percent of the herd—all shapes and sizes, in varying degrees of disintegration, faces contorted with scowling bloodlust—press toward the rear of the trailer. The first one trips on the foot of the ramp, falling face-first with a wet splat on the tread. Others follow closely, pushing their way up the incline, as Stinson shrieks inside the enclosure, his sanity torn to shreds.

The portly guardsman, bound to the front wall of the trailer with packing straps and chains, pisses himself, as the first walkers shuffle in for the feeding.

Outside the trailer, Martinez and his men keep an eye on the stragglers along the barricade, most of them milling about aimlessly in the glare of tungsten spotlights, cocking their gray faces and glazed eyes up at the night sky as though the screaming noises might be coming from the heavens. Only about a dozen of the dead miss this opportunity to feed. The men on the 50-calibers take aim, awaiting orders to blow the stragglers away.

The trailer fills up with specimens—the Governor's growing collection of lab rats—until nearly three dozen walkers have swarmed Stinson. The unseen feeding frenzy ensues, and the screaming corrupts into watery, gagging death cries, as the last zombie staggers up the ramp and vanishes inside the mobile abattoir. The noises issuing out the back of the trailer now become almost feral, Stinson reduced to a mewling, squealing head of stock in a slaughterhouse, rendered by the ragged teeth and nails of the dead.

Out in the cold darkness Bob feels his soul contracting inward like an iris closing down. He needs a drink so badly his skull throbs. He barely hears the booming voice of the Governor.

"All right, Travis! Go ahead and pull trap now! Go ahead and close it down!"

The truck driver cautiously creeps around behind the vibrating death trailer and grabs for the rope hanging down from the lip of the door. He yanks it hard and fast, and the vertical gate slams down with a rusty squeak. Travis quickly latches the lock, and then backs away from the trailer as if from a time bomb.

"Take it back to the track, Travis! I'll meet you there in a minute!"

The Governor turns and walks over to Martinez, who stands waiting on the lower rails of the crane. "All right, you can have your fun now," the Governor says.

Martinez thumbs the radio send button. "Okay, guys—take the rest of them out."

Bob jumps at the sudden roar of heavy artillery, the noise and sparks from the .50-calibers lighting up the night. Tracer bullets streak hot pink in the dark, crisscrossing the beams of magnesium-bright klieg lights, engaging their targets in plumes of black, oily blood mist. Bob turns away once again, not interested in seeing the walkers taken apart. The Governor, however, feels differently.

He climbs halfway up the crane ladder so he can see the festivities.

In short order the armor-piercing tracers eviscerate the stragglers. Skulls blossom, florets of brain matter spitting up into the night air, teeth and hair and cartilage and bone chips shattering. Some of the zombies remain upright for many moments, as the rounds spin them in macabre death jigs, arms flailing in the stage light. Bellies burst. Glistening tissue ejaculates in the glare.

The salvo ceases as abruptly as it had begun, the silence slamming hard in Bob's ears.

For a moment the Governor savors the aftermath, the dripping sounds fading on the distant echoes of gunfire dying in the trees. The last few walkers still standing sink to the earth in heaps of bloody pulp and dead flesh, some of them now unrecognizable masses of vaguely human meat. Some of these mounds exude vapors in the chill air, mostly from the friction of the bullets and not from any kind of body heat. The Governor climbs down from his perch.

As the Piggly Wiggly truck pulls away with its load of moving cadavers, Bob swallows the urge to vomit. The ghastly noises from inside the trailer have diminished somewhat, Stinson reduced to a hollowed-out trough of flesh and bone. Now only the muffled smacking sounds of zombies feeding inside the enclosure fade away as the truck rattles toward the racetrack lot.

The Governor comes over to Bob. "Looks like you could use a drink."

Bob cannot muster a reply.

"C'mon, let's go have a cool one," the Governor suggests, slapping the man on the back. "I'm buying."

By the next morning, the north lots have been cleaned up and all evidence of the massacre has been erased. People go about their business as though nothing ever happened, and the rest of that week passes uneventfully.

Over the next five days a few walkers drift into the range of the .50-calibers—drawn by the commotion of the hordes—but mostly things remain quiet. Christmas comes and goes with very little ceremony. Most of the inhabitants of Woodbury have given up on following the calendar.

A few feeble attempts at holiday cheer seem to exacerbate the grim proceedings. Martinez and his men decorate a tree in the courthouse lobby, and they put some tinsel on the gazebo in the square, but that's about it. The Governor pipes Christmas music through the racetrack PA system, but it's more of an annoyance than anything else. The weather stays fairly mild—no snow to speak of, with temperatures remaining in the upper forties.

On Christmas Eve, Lilly goes to the infirmary to have some of her injuries checked out by Dr. Stevens, and after the examination, the doctor invites Lilly to stick around for a little impromptu holiday party. Alice joins them, and they open cans of ham and sweet potatoes—and they even break out a case of Cabernet, which Stevens has been hiding in the storage closet—and they toast things like the old days, better times, and Josh Lee Hamilton.

Lilly senses that the doctor is watching her closely for signs of post-traumatic stress, maybe depression or some other kind of mental disturbance. But ironically, Lilly has never felt more focused and grounded in her life. She knows what she has to do. She knows that she cannot live like this much longer, and she is biding her time until an opportunity to escape presents itself. But maybe on some deeper level it is *Lilly* who is doing the observing.

Maybe she is subconsciously looking for allies, accomplices, collaborators.

Halfway through the evening, Martinez shows up—Stevens invited the young man earlier that day to stop by for a drink—and Lilly learns that she is not the only one here who wants out. After a few cocktails, Martinez gets talkative, and reveals that he fears the Governor will eventually lead them off a cliff. They argue about which is the lesser of two evils—tolerating the Governor's madness or drifting out in the world without a safety net—and they come to zero conclusions. They drink some more.

At length, the evening deteriorates into a drunken bacchanal of off-key caroling and reminiscences of holidays past—all of which depresses everyone even further. The more they drink, the worse they feel. But amid all the lubricating Lilly learns new things—both trivial and important—about these three lost souls. She notices that Dr. Stevens has the worst singing voice she has ever heard, and that Alice has a major crush on Martinez, and that Martinez pines for an ex-wife in Arkansas.

Most importantly, though, Lilly gets a sense that the four of them are bonding in their collective misery, and that bond might serve them well.

The next day, at first light—after spending the night passed out on a gurney in the infirmary—Lilly Caul drags herself outside, blinking at the harsh winter sunshine hammering down on the deserted town. It's Christmas morning, and the pale blue sky seems to punctuate Lilly's sense of being trapped in purgatory. Lilly's skull throbs painfully as she buttons her fleece jacket up to her chin and then makes her way eastward down the sidewalk.

Very few residents are up at this hour, the advent of Christmas morning keeping everybody hunkered inside. Lilly feels compelled to visit the playground on the east edge of the town. The desolate patch of bare ground lies behind a grove of denuded crab apples.

Lilly finds Josh's grave, the sandy dirt still freshly packed in a large mound next to his cairn. She kneels on the edge of the grave and lowers her head. "Merry Christmas, Josh," she utters into the wind, her voice hungover, thick and rusty with sleep.

Only the rustle of branches serves as a response. She takes a deep breath. "Some of the things I've done . . . the way I treated you . . . I'm not proud of." She swallows the urge to cry, the sorrow rising up in her. She bites off her tears. "I just wanted you to know . . . you didn't die in vain, Josh. . . . You taught me something important . . . you made a difference in my life."

Lilly looks down at the dirty white sand beneath her knees and she refuses to cry. "You taught me not to be scared anymore." She mutters this to herself, to the ground, to the cold wind. "We don't have that luxury these days . . . so from now on . . . I'm ready."

Her voice trails off, and she kneels there for the longest time, unaware that her right hand has been digging into the side of her leg through her jeans, hard enough to break the skin and draw blood.

"I'm ready . . ."

The turning of the New Year closes in.

Late one night, beset with the melancholy mood of the season, the man known as the Governor locks himself into the back room of his second-floor apartment with a bottle of expensive French champagne and a galvanized pail brimming with an assortment of human bodily organs.

The tiny zombie chained to the wall across the laundry room sputters and snarls at the sight of him. Her once cherubic face now chiseled with rigor mortis, her flesh as yellow as rotten Stilton, she peels her lips back away from rows of blackened baby teeth. The laundry room with its bare bulbs hanging down and exposed fiberglass insulation—impregnated now with her stench—reeks of foul, infected oils and molds.

"Calm down, sweetheart," the man with several names murmurs softly as he sits down on the floor in front of her, setting the bottle down on one side of him and the bucket on the other. He pulls a latex surgical glove from his pocket and works his right hand into it. "Daddy's got some more goodies for you, keep your tummy full."

He fishes a slimy, purplish-brown lobe from the bucket of entrails and tosses it to her.

Little Penny Blake pounces on the human kidney that has landed with a wet splat on the floor in front of her, her chain stretching to its limit with a clank. She clutches the organ with both of her little hands and gobbles the human tissue with feral abandon until the bloody bile runs between her tiny fingers and paints her face with a stain the consistency of chocolate sauce.

"Happy New Year, sweetheart," the Governor says and pries at the champagne cork. The cork resists. He worries at it with his thumbs until the thing pops, and a stream of golden bubbly percolates over the rim and onto the worn tiles. The Governor has no idea if it is actually New Year's Eve. He knows it's imminent . . . might as well be tonight.

He stares at the puddle of champagne spreading on the floor, the tiny foam of carbonation vanishing into the seams of grout. He finds himself casting his thoughts back to New Year's celebrations of his childhood.

In the old days he looked forward to New Year's Eve for months. Back in Waynesboro he and his buddies would get a whole pig delivered on the thirtieth and start it slow-roasting in the ground behind his parents' place, lining the hole with bricks—Hawaiian luau style—and they would have a two-day feast. The local bluegrass band, the Clinch Mountain Boys, would play all night long, and Philip would get really good weed, and they would party through the first and Philip would get laid and have a grand old time with—

The Governor blinks. He cannot remember if *Philip* Blake used to do this on New Year's Eve or if it was *Brian* Blake who did this. He cannot remember where one brother ends and the other begins. He stares at the floor, blinking, the champagne reflecting a dull, milky, distorted reflection of his own face, the handlebar mustache as dark as lampblack now, the eyes deep set and glinting with cinders of something like madness. He looks at himself and sees Philip Blake staring back. But something is wrong. Philip can also see a ghostly overlay superimposed across his face, an ashen, frightened simulacrum called "Brian."

Penny's watery, garbled feeding noises fade in his ears, drifting far away, and Philip takes his first hit of champagne. The gulp burns his throat as it goes down cold and astringent. The taste of it reminds him of better times. It reminds him of holiday celebrations, family reunions, loved ones coming together after a long estrangement. It tears him apart inside. He knows who he is: He's *the Governor*, he's Philip Blake, *the man who gets things done*.

But.

But . . .

Brian starts to cry. He drops the bottle, and more champagne spills across the tiles, seeping under Penny, who is oblivious to the invisible war going on at the moment within the mind of her caretaker. Brian shuts his eyes, the tears seeping out the corners of his eyelids and tracking down his face in snotty runnels.

He cries for those New Year's Eves gone by, those happy moments between friends . . . and brothers. He cries for Penny, and he cries for her woeful condition, for which he blames himself. He cannot block out the flash-frame image burned into the retina of his mind's eye: *Philip Blake lying in a cold, bloody heap next to a girl on the edge of the woods north of Woodbury.*

While Penny feeds, slurping and smacking her dead lips, and Brian softly sobs, an unexpected noise comes from across the room.

Somebody is knocking on the Governor's door.

It takes a while for the noise to register, the sound of knocking coming in a series of small bursts—hesitant, tentative—and it goes on for quite a while before Philip Blake realizes somebody is out there in the hallway banging on his door.

The identity crisis ceases immediately, the curtain in the Governor's brain sweeping back in place with the abruptness of a power blackout.

It is, in fact, *Philip* who stands, removes his surgical gloves, brushes himself off, wipes his mucusy chin with the sleeve of his sweater, pulls on his stovepipe boots, brushes his long obsidian locks from his eyes, sniffs back his emotion, and exits the laundry room, locking the door behind him.

It is Philip who crosses the living room with his trademark strut. Heart rate slowing, lungs filling with oxygen, his consciousness fully transformed back into the Governor—his eyes clear and sharp—he answers the door on the fifth series of knocks. "What the hell is so goddamn important at this hour that you can't—"

Not fully recognizing the woman standing outside the door, he stops himself. He had expected one of his men—Gabe or Bruce or Martinez—coming to bother him with some minor fire to be put out or some horseshit drama to be settled among the restless townspeople.

"Is this a bad time?" Megan Lafferty purrs with a dreamy tilt of her head, leaning against the doorjamb, the blouse under her denim jacket unbuttoned and showing generous amounts of cleavage.

The Governor pins her with his unwavering gaze. "Honey, I don't know what game you're running down right now but I'm in the middle of something."

"Just thought you might need a little company," she says with faux innocence. She looks like a caricature of a tart, her wine-colored curls mussed and hanging down in suggestive tendrils across her drugged features. She wears too much makeup and appears almost clownlike. "But I totally understand if you're busy."

The Governor lets out a sigh. A smile tugs at the corner of his mouth. "Something tells me you ain't here to borrow a cup of sugar."

Megan throws a glance over her shoulder. The jitters show on her face, in the way her gaze shifts back and forth from the shadows of the empty corridor to the doorway, in the way she holds one of her arms against her side, compulsively stroking the Chinese character tattooed on her elbow. Nobody ever comes up here. The Governor's private quarters are off-limits to even Gabe and Bruce.

"I just—I thought—I—" she stutters.

"No reason to be afraid, darlin'," the Governor says at last.

"I didn't mean to—"

"Might as well c'mon inside," he says and takes her by the arm. "Before you catch your death."

He pulls her inside and secures the door with a click. The sound of the bolt clanking home makes her jump. Her breathing quickens, and the Governor cannot help but notice the rise and fall of her surprisingly fulsome breasts underneath her décolletage, her hourglass figure, her generous hips. This little gal is ripe for breeding. The Governor searches the back of his mind for the last time he used a condom. Did he stock up? Did he have any left in his medicine cabinet? "Get you a drink?"

"Sure." Megan gazes around the spartan furnishings of the living room—the carpet remnants, the mismatched chairs and sofa pulled off the back of a Salvation Army truck. For the briefest instant she frowns, turning up her nose, probably registering the odors permeating the place from the laundry room. "Y'all got any vodka?"

The Governor gives her a grin. "I think we might be able to come up with some." He goes over to the cabinet next to the shuttered front window. He digs out a bottle, pours a few fingers in a couple of paper cups. "Got some orange juice around here somewhere," he murmurs, finding a half-empty can of juice.

He comes back over to her with the drinks. She slugs hers down in one frantic gulp. She looks as though she's been lost in the desert for days and this is her first taste of liquid. She wipes her mouth and lets loose a little belch. "Excuse me . . . sorry."

"You are just the cutest little thing," the Governor says to her with a grin. "You know something, Bonnie Raitt ain't got nothing on you."

She looks at the floor. "Reason I dropped by, I was just wondering . . ."

"Yeah?"

"Guy at the food center told me you might have some weed, Demerol maybe?"

"Duane?"

She nods. "Said you might have some good shit."

The Governor sips his drink. "Now I wonder how Duane would know such a thing."

Megan shrugs. "Anyway, the thing is—"

"Why come to me?" The Governor fixes her with that dark stare. "Why not go to your buddy Bob? He's got a whole medicine chest in that truck of his."

Another shrug. "I don't know, I was just thinking, you and me, we could like . . . make a trade."

Now she looks up at him and bites her lower lip, and the Governor feels the blood rushing to his loins.

Megan rides him in the moonlight darkness of an adjacent room. Completely nude, filmed in a cold sweat, her hair matted to her face, she pistons up and down on his erection with the empty fury of a hobbyhorse on a carousel. She feels nothing other than the painful thrusting. She feels no fear, no emotion, no regret, no shame. Nothing. Just the mechanical gymnastics of sex.

All the lights are off in the room, the only illumination coming from the transom above the drapes, through which the silver light of a wintry moon shines down across the dust motes and dapples the bare wall behind the Governor's secondhand La-Z-Boy recliner.

The man sits sprawled on the armchair, his naked, lanky body writhing beneath Megan, his head tossing backward, the veins in his neck pulsing. But he makes very little sound, shows very little pleasure in the act. Megan can only hear the regular thrumming of his breath, as he thrusts angrily into her again and again.

The La-Z-Boy chair is positioned in a way that draws Megan's peripheral attention to the wall behind her, even as she feels the man's orgasm building, the climax imminent. No pictures hang in the room, no coffee tables, no shaded lamps—only the faint shimmer of rectangular objects lining the wall. At first Megan misidentifies these objects as TV sets, a configuration reminiscent of an electronics-store display. But what would this guy be doing with two dozen TV sets? Soon Megan realizes she's hearing a low burble of white noise issuing from the objects.

"What the hell's the matter?" the Governor grunts beneath her.

Megan has twisted around, her eyes adjusting to the moon shadows. She sees things moving inside the rectangular enclosures. The ghostly movement makes her stiffen, tightening up on his genitals. "Nothing . . . nothing . . . sorry . . . I just . . . I couldn't help but—"

"Goddammit, woman!" He reaches over and flips on a battery-operated camp lantern, which sits on a crate next to the chair.

The light reveals rows of aquariums filled with severed human heads.

Megan lets out a gasp and slips off his cock, tumbling to the floor. She struggles to breathe. Lying prone on the damp carpet, her body rashing with gooseflesh, she gapes at the glass enclosures. In neatly stacked containers of fluid the zombified faces twitch and tic on ragged stumps, mouths palpitating like oxygen-starved fish, their milky eyes rolling around sightlessly in the watery capsules.

"I haven't finished!" The Governor pounces on her, rolls her over, yanks her legs open. He's still hard and enters her violently, the painful friction sending bolts of agony up her spine. "Hold still, goddammit!"

Megan sees a familiar face within the confines of the last tank on the left, and the sight of it turns her to stone. She lies supine on the floor, thunderstruck, her head turned sideways as she gapes in horror at that narrow face engulfed in bubbles in that last aquarium, as the Governor mercilessly plunges into her. She recognizes the peroxide-blond hair suspended in the fluid, forming a seaweedlike corona around the boyish features, the slack mouth, the long lashes, and the pointy button nose.

The recognition of Scott Moon's severed head coincides with the hot gush inside her as the Governor finally finishes his business.

Something deep inside Megan Lafferty crumbles apart as permanently and irreparably as a sand castle collapsing under the weight of a wave.

A moment later the Governor says, "You can get up now, honey . . . clean yourself up."

He says this to the woman without any rancor or contempt, as a proctor might inform a classroom at the end of a test that it's time to put down the pencils.

Then he sees her gaping at the aquarium containing Scott Moon's head, and he realizes this is a moment of truth, an opportunity, a critical juncture in the evening's festivities. A decisive man like Philip Blake always knows when to look for opportunities. He knows when to take advantage of a superior position. He never hesitates, never backs off, never shies away from dirty work.

The Governor reaches down and finds the elastic waistband of his underwear—which is bunched around his ankles—and pulls his briefs back up and over himself. He stands and gazes down at the woman curled into a fetal position on his floor. "C'mon, honey . . . let's go get you cleaned up and have a little talk, you and me."

Megan buries her face in the floor and mutters, "Please don't hurt me."

The Governor leans down and applies a pinch grip to the nape of her neck—nothing intense, just an attention grabber—and says, "I'm not going to ask you again . . . get your ass in the bathroom."

She struggles to her feet, holding herself as though she might burst apart at any moment.

"This way, honey." He roughly clutches her bare arm as he ushers her across the room, out the doorway, and into an adjacent bathroom.

Standing in the doorway, watching her, the Governor feels bad about manhandling her but he also knows Philip Blake would not let up at a time like this. Philip would do what has to be done, he would be strong and resolute; and the part of the Governor that used to be called "Brian" has to follow through with this.

Megan hunches over the sink and picks up the washcloth with trembling hands. She runs water and tentatively wipes herself and trembles. "I swear to God I won't tell anybody," she mutters through her tears. "I just want to go home . . . just want to be alone."

"That's what I want to talk to you about," the Governor says to her from the doorway.

"I won't tell—"

"Look at me, honey."

"I won't—"

"Calm down. Take a deep breath. And look at me. Megan, I said look at me."

She looks up at him, her chin quivering, tears tracking down her cheeks.

He looks at her. "You're with Bob now."

"I'm sorry . . . what?" She wipes her eyes. "I'm what?"

"You're with Bob," he says. "You remember Bob Stookey, guy you came here with?"

She nods.

"You're with him now. You understand? From now on you're with him."

Again she slowly nods.

"Oh and one more thing," the Governor adds softly, almost as an afterthought. "Tell anyone about *any* of this . . . and your pretty little head goes in the tank next to the stoner."

Minutes after Megan Lafferty makes her exit, vanishing into the shadows of the corridor, shivering and hyperventilating as she pulls on her coat, the Governor retires to the side room. He flops down on his La-Z-Boy and sits facing the matrix of fish tanks.

He sits there for quite a while, staring at the tanks, feeling empty. Muffled groans drift through the empty rooms behind him. The thing that was once a little girl is hungry again. Nausea begins to creep up the Governor's gorge, clenching his insides and making his eyes water. He begins to shake. A current of terror over what he's done crackles through him, turning his tendons to ice.

A moment later he lurches forward, slipping off the chair, falling on his knees, and roaring vomit. What is left of his dinner sluices across the filthy carpet. On his hands and knees he upchucks the remaining contents of his stomach, then sits back against the foot of the chair, gasping for breath.

A part of him—that deeply buried part known as "Brian"—feels the tide of revulsion drowning him. He can't breathe. He can't think. And yet he forces himself to keep gazing at the bloated, waterlogged faces staring back at him, bobbing and spewing bubbles in the tanks.

He wants to look away. He wants to flee the room and get away from these twitching, gurgling, dismembered heads. But he knows he must keep staring until his senses are numbed. He needs to be strong.

He needs to be prepared for what is to come.

FIFTEEN

On the west side of town, within the walled area, inside a second-story apartment near the post office, Bob Stookey hears a knock. Sitting up against the headboard of a brass bed, he puts down his dog-eared paperback book—a Louis L'Amour western called *The Outlaws of Mesquite*—and steps into his scuffed loafers. He pulls on his pants. He has some trouble with the zipper, his hands fumbling.

After drinking himself insensate earlier that evening, he still feels wonky and disconnected. The dizziness tugs at his focus and his stomach lurches, as he staggers out of the room and crosses the apartment to the side door, which opens out onto the darkness of a wooden landing at the top of a staircase. Bob belches and swallows bile as he pushes the door open.

"Bob . . . something horrible has . . . *Oh, God, Bob,*" Megan Lafferty sobs from the shadows of the staircase. Her face wet and drawn, her eyes sunken and red, she looks as though she's about to shatter apart like a glass figurine. She trembles in the cold, holding the collar of her denim jacket tight against the bitter winds.

"Come in, darlin', c'mon in," Bob says, pushing the door wider, his heart beating a little faster. "What in God's name happened?"

Megan staggers into the kitchen. Bob takes her by the arms and helps her over to a hard chair canted next to the cluttered dining table. She flops down in her chair and tries to speak but the sobs won't let her. Bob kneels by her chair, stroking her shoulder as she cries. She buries her face in his chest and cries.

Bob holds her. "It's okay, darlin' . . . whatever it is . . . we'll figure it out."

She moans—gut shot with anguish and horror—her tears soaking his sleeveless undershirt. He cradles her head, stroking her damp curls. After an agonizing moment, she looks up at him. "Scott's dead."

"What!"

"I saw him, Bob." She speaks in hitching gasps, her sobs shuddering through her. "He's . . . he's dead and . . . he's turned into one of those things."

"Easy, darlin', take a breath and try to tell me what happened."

"I don't *know* what happened!"

"Where did you see him?"

She sniffs back the gasps and then tells Bob in broken, half-formed sentences about the severed heads bobbing in the darkness.

"Where did you see this?"

She hyperventilates. "In the . . . over in . . . in the Governor's place."

"The Governor's place? You saw Scott at the Governor's place?"

She nods and nods. She tries to explain but the words are caught in her throat.

Bob strokes her arm. "Darlin,' what were you doing in the Governor's place?"

She tries to speak. The sobs return. She buries her face in her hands.

"Let me get you some water," Bob says at last. He hurries over to the sink and runs water into a plastic cup. Half the homes in Woodbury have no utilities, no heat or power or running water. The lucky few who still have these amenities are members of the Governor's inner circle—those to whom the makeshift power structure has bestowed perks. Bob has become a sort of sentimental favorite, and his private quarters reflect this status. Littered with empty bottles and food wrappers, tins of pipe tobacco and girlie magazines, warm blankets and electronic gadgets, the apartment has taken on the look of a shabby man-cave.

Bob brings the water over to Megan, and she gulps it from the plastic cup, some of it seeping out the sides of her mouth and soaking her jacket. Bob gently helps her remove her coat as she finishes the water. He looks away when he sees the front of her blouse buttoned haphazardly, open at the navel, a series of red blotches and deep scratches running down the length of her sternum between her pale breasts. Her bra is askew and one of her nipples shows prominently.

"Here, darlin'," he says, turning toward the linen closet in the front hall. He retrieves a blanket, comes back and tenderly wraps it around her. She gets her crying under control until the sobs have subsided into a series of jerky, shuddering breaths. She stares downward. Her tiny hands lie limp and upturned in her lap, as though she has forgotten how to use them.

"I never should have . . ." she starts to explain and then chokes back the words. Her nose runs and she wipes it. Her eyes close. "What have I done . . . Bob . . . what the fuck is wrong with me?"

"There's nothing wrong with you," he says softly and puts his arm around her. "I'm with you now, honey. I'll take care of you."

She settles down in his arms. Soon she is leaning her head on his shoulder and breathing more regularly. Soon her breaths are coming in low, thick wheezes, as though she might be falling asleep. Bob recognizes the symptoms of shock. Her flesh feels ice-cold in his arms. He wraps the blanket tighter. She nuzzles his neck.

Bob takes deep breaths, waves of emotion slamming through him.

Holding the woman tightly, he gropes for words. His mind races with contrary feelings. He is repulsed by Megan's story of severed heads and Scott Moon's dismembered corpse, as well as the fact that she paid the Governor such a questionable visit in the first place. But Bob is also overcome with unrequited desire. The nearness of her lips, the soft whisper of her breath on his collarbone, and the luster of her wild-strawberry roan curls brushing his chin—all of it intoxicates Bob faster and more profusely than a case of twelve-year-old bourbon. He fights the urge to kiss the top of her head.

"It's gonna be okay," he murmurs softly in her ear. "We'll figure it out."

"Oh, Bob . . ." Her voice sounds fuzzy, maybe still slightly high. "Bob . . ."

"Gonna be okay," he says in her ear, stroking her hair with his greasy, gnarled hand.

She cranes her head up and plants a kiss on his grizzled jawline.

Bob closes his eyes and lets the wave pour over him.

They sleep together that night, and at first Bob panics at the prospect of being in such close and intimate proximity with Megan for such a long period of time. Bob has not had sex with a woman in eleven years, not since he and his late wife, Brenda, stopped having relations. Decades of drink have put the kibosh on Bob's virility. But desire still glows within him like a smoldering ember—and he wants Megan so badly tonight he can taste it like Everclear in the back of his throat, like a finger prodding the base of his spine.

The two of them sleep restlessly in each other's arms, tangled in sweaty blankets on the double bed in the back room. Much to Bob's relief, they do not even remotely come close to having sex.

Throughout the night, Bob's feverish thoughts vacillate between half-formed dreams of making love to Megan Lafferty on a desert island, surrounded by zombie-infested waters, and sudden moments of bleary wakefulness in the shadows of that second-floor bedroom. Bob marvels at the miracle of hearing Megan's arrhythmic breathing next to him, the warmth of her hip nested against his belly, the wonder of her hair in his face, her musky-sweet scent filling his senses. In a strange way he feels whole for the first time since the plague broke out. He feels an oddly invigorating sense of hope. The troubling undercurrents of suspicion and mixed emotions about the Governor melt away in the dark limbo of that bedroom, and the momentary peace that washes over Bob Stookey eventually lulls him into a deep sleep.

Just after dawn he comes awake with a start to a piercing shriek.

At first he thinks he's still dreaming. The scream comes from somewhere outside, and it registers in Bob's ears as a ghostly echo, as if the tail end of a nightmare has just brushed across his waking state. In his half-conscious daze he reaches over for Megan and finds her side of the bed empty. The blankets are bunched at his feet. Megan is gone. He sits up with a jolt.

"Megan, honey?"

He gets out of bed and starts toward the door, the floor like ice on his bare feet, when another shriek pierces the winter winds outside his apartment. He does not notice the overturned chair in the kitchen, the drawers open, the cabinet doors agape, the signs of someone rifling through his belongings.

"Megan?"

He races toward the side door, which is partially ajar and banging in the wind.

"Megan!"

He pushes through the doorway and stumbles out onto the second-floor landing, blinking at the harsh, overcast light and the cold wind in his face.

"MEGAN!!"

At first he cannot take in all the movement and commotion around the building. He sees people gathered down below the stairs, across the street, and along the edge of the post office parking lot—maybe a dozen or so—and they're all pointing at Bob or perhaps at something on the roof. It's hard to tell. Heart hammering, Bob starts down the stairs. He does not notice the coil of towrope wound around the pilasters of the landing until he reaches the bottom of the stairs.

Bob turns and goes as cold and still as granite. "Oh, Lord, no," he utters, gazing up at the body dangling from the landing, swaying in the wind, turning lazily. "Oh, no, no, no, no, no, no, no . . ."

Megan hangs by a makeshift noose around her neck, her face as discolored and livid as antique porcelain.

Lilly Caul hears the commotion outside her window above the dry cleaner, and drags herself out of bed. She throws open the shade and sees townspeople gathered outside their doorways, some of them pointing off toward the post office with anxious expressions, speaking under their breaths. Lilly senses that something terrible has happened, and when she sees the Governor striding quickly along the sidewalk in his long coat with his goons, Gabe and Bruce, at his side, snapping ammo magazines into assault weapons, she dresses quickly.

It takes her less than three minutes to throw on her clothes, hustle down the back stairs, make her way down an alley between two buildings, and cross the two and a half blocks to the post office.

The sky churns with menacing clouds, the wind spitting sleet, and by the time Lilly sees the crowd milling about the base of Bob's stairs, she knows she's seeing the aftermath of something awful. She can tell by the expressions on the faces of the onlookers, and she can tell by the way the Governor is talking to Bob off to the side, each man gazing at the ground as they talk softly to each other, their faces screwed up with anxiety and grim resolve.

Within the circle of onlookers, Gabe and Bruce kneel on the pavement next to a sheet-covered lump, and the sight of that shrouded heap stops Lilly cold. She stands on the periphery, staring, a trickle of icy dread running down her spine. The sight of another pall-covered body on a street corner strums a terrible chord deep within her.

"Lilly?"

She turns and sees Martinez standing next to her, his leather jacket crisscrossed with a bandolier of bullets. He puts a hand on her shoulder. "She was a friend of yours, wasn't she?"

"Who is it?"

"Nobody told you?"

"Is it Megan?" Lilly pushes her way past Martinez, shoving aside several onlookers. "What happened?"

Bob Stookey steps into her path, blocking her progress, gently taking her by the shoulders. "Lil, wait, there's nothing you can do."

"What happened, Bob?" Lilly blinks at the sting in her eyes, the heavy fist in her chest. "Did a walker get her? Let me go!"

Bob holds fast on her shoulders. "No, ma'am. That's not what happened." Lilly notices Bob's eyes, raw and red rimmed, cratered out with grief. His face trembles with anguish. "These fellas will take care of her."

"Is she—"

"She's gone, Lil." Bob looks down and softly shakes his head. "Took her own life."

"What— What happened?"

Still looking down, Bob mumbles something about not being sure.

"Let me go, Bob!" Lilly pushes her way through the row of on-lookers.

"Whoa! Whoa—*slow down there, sister!*" Gabe stands up and blocks Lilly's path. The heavyset man with the bullish neck and flat-top haircut holds on to Lilly's arm. "I know she was a friend of yours—"

"Let me see her!" Lilly yanks her arm free but Gabe grabs her from behind and puts her in a firm shoulder lock. Lilly wriggles furiously. "LET GO OF ME, GODDAMMIT!"

Ten feet away, on the seared brown grass of the parkway, Bruce, the tall black man with the shaved head, kneels by the sheet-draped body, loading a .45 caliber semiautomatic with a fresh magazine. His face grim and set, he breathes deeply, preparing to complete some distasteful task. He ignores the commotion behind him.

"LET GO!" Lilly keeps writhing in the portly man's grip, her gaze locked on the body.

"Calm down," Gabe hisses. "You're making this harder than it has to—"

"Let her go!"

The deep, cigarette-cured voice comes from behind Gabe, and both Lilly and the heavyset man freeze as though startled by an ul-trasonic whistle.

They glance over their shoulders and see the Governor standing inside the circle of onlookers with his hands on his hips, his twin pearl-handled army .45s thrust into either side of his belt, gunslinger-style, his long rock-star hair—as black as India ink—bound in a ponytail and tossing in the wind. The crow's-feet around his eyes, and the lines chiseling his sunken jowls, deepen and crease and grow more prominent as his expression darkens. "It's okay, Gabe . . . let the lady say good-bye to her friend."

Lilly rushes over to the corpse on the ground, kneels, and stares at the shrouded heap, putting her hand to her mouth as though hold-ing in the tide of emotions rising in her. Bruce thumbs the safety down on his semiauto, and awkwardly backs away, standing, gazing down at Lilly as the crowd around them quiets down.

The Governor comes over and stands a respectful five feet away.

Lilly peels back the sheet and clenches her teeth, as she looks at the purplish-gray face of the woman that used to be Megan Lafferty. Eyes swollen shut, jaw set with rigor mortis, the bloodless china-doll face looks as though it has shattered into a million hairline fractures, the dark capillaries apparent now in the early stages of decomposition. The face is ghastly but also excruciatingly poignant to Lilly, wrenching her memories back to those crazy days at Sprayberry High School when the two girls would get high in the restroom and climb up on the school's roof and throw pebbles at the jocks running drills behind the basketball courts. Megan had been Lilly's best gal-pal for years, and despite the girl's faults—and there had been many—Lilly still thinks of her as a best friend. Now Lilly cannot stop staring at this unrecognizable vestige of her feisty friend.

Lilly gasps as Megan's swollen, purple-lidded eyes suddenly pop open, revealing milk-glass pupils.

Lilly does not move as the black man with the shaved head crowds in, the .45 poised to fire a direct blast into the cadaver's head. But before the hammer has a chance to fall, the sound of the Governor's voice calls out: "Hold your fire, Bruce!"

Bruce glances over his shoulder, as the Governor takes a step closer, and then says very softly, "Let her do it."

Lilly looks up at the man in the long coat, blinks, and says nothing. Her heart feels like ash, her blood running cold in her veins. Way off in the distance the sky rumbles with thunder.

The Governor steps closer. "Go ahead, Bruce. Give her the gun."

An endless moment passes, and somehow the gun ends up in Lilly's hand. Beneath her, the thing that was once Megan Lafferty convulses and tenses on the ground, its nervous system dieseling, its mouth peeling away from moldering gray teeth. Lilly can barely see through her tears.

"Put your friend down, Lilly," the Governor urges softly from behind her.

Lilly raises the gun. Megan's neck cranes upward toward her like a fetus emerging from its embryonic fluid, teeth clacking hungrily. Lilly puts the muzzle against the monster's brow.

"Do it, Lilly. Put her out of her misery."

Lilly closes her eyes. The trigger pad burns her finger like an icicle.

When she opens her eyes again the thing on the ground lunges at her, the rancid teeth going for Lilly's jugular.

It happens so quickly it almost fails to register in Lilly's brain.

The blast rings out.

Lilly topples backward, falling on her ass, the .45 slipping out of her hand as the top of Megan's cranium erupts in dark red mist, painting the sidewalk adjacent to the parkway in a spray of brain matter. The reanimated corpse sags and lies still on the tangled shroud—its sharklike eyes fixed on the dark sky.

For a moment Lilly lies supine on the ground, staring at the clouds, gripped in a state of confusion. Who fired the kill shot? Lilly never pulled the trigger. Who did the deed? Lilly blinks away her tears and manages to focus on the Governor standing over her, his grave expression fixed on something to his right.

Bob Stookey stands over the corpse of Megan Lafferty with a .38 police special still clutched in his hand, his shooting arm dangling at his side, a thin wisp of gun smoke still curling out of the barrel.

The desolation on Bob's weathered, deeply lined face is heartbreaking.

Those next few days, nobody pays much attention to the changing weather.

Bob is too busy drinking himself to death to notice anything as trivial as weather fronts, and Lilly occupies herself arranging a proper burial for Megan in a plot next to Josh. The Governor spends most of his time preparing for the next big battle in the racetrack arena. He has big plans for the next round of shows, integrating zombies into the gladiatorial matches.

Gabe and Bruce busy themselves with the nasty job of hacking up the dead guardsmen in an auxiliary warehouse beneath the track. The Governor needs body parts to feed the growing menagerie of zombies being housed in a secret room deep in the cinderblock catacombs. Gabe and Bruce enlist some of the younger men from Martinez's crew to work the chain saws in the festering, cavernous abattoir next to the morgue, rendering human remains into meat.

Meanwhile, the January rains move into the area with slow, insidious menace.

At first, the outer bands of the storm system cause very little alarm—a few scattered showers swelling the storm sewers and icing the streets—with temperatures hovering above freezing. But the distant lightning and roiling black skies on the western horizon begin to worry people. Nobody knows with any degree of certainty— nor will they ever know—why *this* winter turns out to be anomalous for Georgia. The state's relatively mild winters can be occasionally shattered by torrential rains, a nasty snowfall or two, or an ice storm here and there, but no one is prepared for what is about to sweep down across the fruit belt on a low-pressure cell slamming in from Canada.

The National Weather Service out of Peachtree City—still limping along on generators and shortwave radios—issues an early warning that week on as many frequencies as they can spark. But very few listeners benefit from the news. Only a handful of souls hear the frantic voice of the harried meteorologist, Barry Gooden, ranting about the blizzard of '93 and the floods of 2009.

According to Gooden, the bitter cold front that will smash down upon the American South over the next twenty-four hours will collide with the moist, mild, warm surface temperatures of central Georgia and very likely make these other winter storms seem like passing sprinkles. With seventy-mile-an-hour winds in the forecast, as well as dangerous lightning and a mixture of rain and sleet, the storm promises to play unprecedented havoc with the plague-ridden state. Not only will the volatile swings in temperature threaten to turn the gulley washers into blizzards, but—as the state learned only a couple of years earlier, and now with the advent of the plague— Georgians are woefully unprepared for the ravages of flooding.

A few years back, a major storm pushed the Chattahoochee River over its banks and into the highly populated areas around Roswell, Sandy Springs, and Marietta. Mudslides tore homes from their foundations. Highways lay underwater and the catastrophe resulted in dozens of deaths and hundreds of millions of dollars of damage. But *this* year—this monster forming over the Mississippi, unfurling at an alarming rate of speed—promises to be off the charts.

The first signs of extraordinary weather roar into town that Friday afternoon.

By nightfall the rain is coming down at a forty-five-degree angle on fifty-mile-an-hour gusts, falling in sheets against Woodbury's barricade, making defunct high-tension wires across the center of town sing and snap like bullwhips. Volleys of lightning turn the dark alleys to silver flickering photographic negatives, and the gutters spill over across Main Street. Most of Woodbury's inhabitants hunker down inside for the duration . . . leaving the sidewalks and boarded storefronts deserted . . .

. . . mostly deserted, that is, except for a group of four residents, who brave the rains in order to gather surreptitiously in an office beneath the racetrack.

"Leave the light off, Alice, if you don't mind," a voice says from the shadows behind a desk. The dull glimmer of wire-framed spectacles floating in the darkness is the only thing that identifies Dr. Stevens. The muffled drumming of the storm punctuates the silence.

Alice nods and stands near the light switch, nervously rubbing her cold hands against each other. Her lab coat looks ghostly in the gloomy, windowless office that Stevens has been using for a storage room.

"You called this meeting, Lilly," murmurs Martinez from the opposite corner of the room, where he sits on a stool, smoking a cheroot—the slender cigar's glowing tip like a firefly in the darkness. "What are you thinking?"

Lilly paces in the shadows near a row of metal filing cabinets. She wears one of Josh's army surplus raincoats, which is so big on her she looks like a child playing dress-up. "What am I thinking? I'm thinking I'm not going to live like this anymore."

"Meaning what?"

"Meaning this place is rotten to the core, it's sick, and this Governor dude is the sickest one of all, and I don't see things getting any better in the foreseeable future."

"And . . . ?"

She shrugs. "I'm looking at my options."

"Which are?"

She paces some more, choosing her words carefully. "Packing up and taking off by myself seems suicidal . . . but I'd be willing to take my chances out there if it was the only way to get away from this shit."

Martinez looks at Stevens, who is across the room, wiping his eyeglasses with a cloth and listening intently. The two men share an uneasy glance. Finally Stevens speaks up: "You mentioned options."

Lilly stops pacing. She looks at Martinez. "These guys you work with on the fence . . . you trust them?"

Martinez takes a drag off the cheroot, and smoke forms a wreath around his face. "More or less."

"Some more and some less?"

He shrugs. "You could say that, yeah."

"But these guys you trust more than the others, would they back you up in a pinch?"

Martinez stares at her. "What are we talking about here, Lilly?"

Lilly takes a deep breath. She has no idea if she can trust these people, but they also seem like the only sane individuals in Woodbury. She decides to play her hand. After a long pause, she says very softly, "I'm talking about regime change."

Another series of apprehensive glances pass between Martinez, Stevens, and Alice. The edgy silence throbs with the muffled noise of the storm. The winds have kicked up even higher, and thunder rattles the foundation with increasing frequency.

At last the doctor says, "Lilly, I don't think you know what you're—"

"No!" she interrupts him, looking at the floor, speaking in a cold, flat monotone. "No more history lessons, Doc. We're past that now. Past playing it safe. This dude Philip Blake has to go . . . and you know it as well as I do."

Over their heads a volley of thunder reverberates. Stevens lets out an anguished sigh. "You're going to buy yourself a gig in the gladiator ring, you keep talking like that."

Unfazed, Lilly looks up at Martinez. "I don't know you very well, Martinez, but you seem like a fairly even-tempered kind of guy . . . kind of guy who could lead a revolt, get things back on track."

Martinez stares at her. "Slow down, kiddo . . . you're gonna hurt yourself."

"Whatever . . . you don't have to listen to me . . . I don't care anymore." She makes eye contact with each of them, one at a time. "But you all know I'm right. Things are going to get a lot worse around here, we don't do something about this. You want to turn me in for treason, fine, go ahead. Whatever. But we may never get another chance to take this freak down. And I for one am not going to sit on my hands and do nothing while this place goes down in flames and more and more innocent people die. You know I'm right about this." She looks back down at the floor. "The Governor has to go."

Another barrage of thunder rattles the ribs of the building, as the silence in the storage room stretches. Finally Alice speaks up.

"She's right, you know."

SIXTEEN

The next day, the storm—now a constant bombardment of driving rain and freezing sleet—lashes southeastern Georgia with massive force. Telephone poles buckle under the weight of the onslaught, crashing down on highways choked with abandoned cars. Culverts swell and gush, flooding deserted farms, while the higher elevations are coated with treacherous layers of ice. Eleven miles southeast of Woodbury, in a wooded hollow adjacent to Highway 36, the storm hits the largest public cemetery in the southern United States.

The Edward Nightingale Memorial Gardens and Columbarium lines a mile-long bluff just south of Sprewell State Park, and features tens of thousands of historic markers. The Gothic chapel and visitor center stand at the eastern end of the property, within a stone's throw of the Woodland Medical Center—one of the state's largest hospitals. Filled with freshly-turned zombies, abandoned by the staff since the early weeks of the plague, the complex of buildings—including the morgue at Woodland, as well as the enormous labyrinth of funeral parlors underneath the sublevels of Nightingale—teems with reanimated dead, some of them fresh corpses marked for autopsies and burials, others recent DOAs tucked into drawers, all of them trapped, up to this point, in their sealed chambers.

At 4:37 P.M. Eastern Standard Time that Saturday, the nearby Flint River reaches flood levels. In photo-strobe flashes of lightning, the violent currents crash over the banks, razing farms, toppling billboards, and tossing abandoned vehicles across the farm roads like toys scattered by an angry child.

The mudslides start within an hour. The entire northern slope along the borders of the cemetery gives way, sliding toward the Flint on a slimy, brown, mealy wave—ripping graves from the ground, flinging antique caskets across the hill. Coffins break open and spill their ghastly contents into the ocean of mud and sleet and wind. Most of the ragged skeletons break apart like kindling. But many of the non-interred corpses—especially the ones who are still fresh and intact and able to crawl or scrabble—begin slithering toward high, dry land.

Ornate windows along the base of the Nightingale visitor center crack under the pressure of the floodtide, imploding, the gale-force winds doing the rest of the work, tearing sections off Gothic spires and shaving the tops of steeples and decapitating gabled rooftops. A quarter mile to the east, the rushing floodwaters hit the medical center hard, driving debris through weakened entryways and windows.

The zombies trapped inside the morgue pour out of jagged openings, many of them sucked into the currents by the violent wind and air pressure.

By five o'clock that day, a multitude of dead large enough to fill a necropolis—like a vast school of sea creatures washed onto a beach—gets deposited across the neighboring orchards and tobacco fields. They tumble, one over another, on the flood currents, some of them getting caught in trees, others tangling in floating farm implements. Some drift for miles underwater, flailing in the flickering dark with involuntary instinct and inchoate hunger. Thousands of them collect in the moraines and valleys and sheltered areas north of the highway, struggling to climb out of the mud in grotesque pantomimes of primordial man emerging from the Paleolithic soup.

Before the torrential rainstorm has passed—the brunt of it moving on toward the Eastern Seaboard that night—the population of dead now littering the countryside outnumbers the population of living residents, preplague, in the nearby city of Harrington, Georgia—which, according to the sign on Highway 36, totals 4,011 souls.

In the aftermath of this epochal storm, almost a thousand of these wayward corpses begin to coalesce into the largest herd yet witnessed since the advent of the plague. In the rain-swept darkness, the zombies slowly, awkwardly cluster and horde, until a massive throng has formed in the rolling fields between Crest Highway and Roland Road. The herd is so densely packed that from a distance the tops of their putrid heads might be mistaken for a dark, brackish, slow-moving flood tide unfurling across the land.

For no particular reason other than the inexplicable behavior of the dead—be it instinct, scent, pheromones, or random chance—the horde starts churning through the mud in a northwesterly direction, directly toward the closest population center in their path—the town called Woodbury—which lies a little over eight miles away.

The tail end of the storm leaves the farms and fields of southeastern Georgia inundated with vast, black pools of filthy standing water, the shallow sections turning to black ice, the higher areas seizing up in mud.

The weakening band of freezing rain moves through the area, icing the forests and hills around Woodbury in a glassine wonderland of glittering branches, icicle-festooned power lines, and crystalline paths—all of which would be beautiful in another time and place, another context void of plagues and desperate men.

That next day, the residents of Woodbury struggle to get the town back in working order. The Governor orders his work crews to raid a nearby dairy farm for salt blocks, which are brought back on flatbeds and broken into manageable crumbs with chain saws, then spread across roads and sidewalks. Sandbags are positioned on the south side of town, against the flooded railroad tracks, in an effort to keep the standing waters at bay. All day, under a sky the color of soot, the inhabitants mop and salt and shovel and scrape and shore up flooded nooks and crannies.

"The show must go on, Bob," the Governor says late that afternoon, standing on the warning apron of the dirt racetrack, the calcium light blazing down through the mists overhead, the thrumming of generators like a dissonant drone of a bassoon orchestra. The air smells of gas fumes, alkali, and burning garbage.

The surface of the track ripples in the wind, a sea of mud as thick as porridge. The rains hit the arena hard, and now the infield shimmers in the stadium lights with two feet of murky standing water. The ice-filmed bleachers are mostly deserted, except for a small crew of workmen who toil with squeegees and shovels.

"Huh?" Bob Stookey sits slumped on a bleacher twenty feet behind the Governor.

Belching absently, his head lolled in a drunken stupor, Bob looks like a lost little boy. An empty bottle of Jim Beam lies on the ice-rimed steel bench next to him, another one—half full—loosely gripped in his greasy, numb hand. He has been drinking steadily for the past five days, ever since he ushered Megan Lafferty out of this world.

An incorrigible drunk can maintain intoxication better than the average person. Most casual drinkers reach their optimum level of drunkenness—that painless, numbed, convivial buzz that gives shy people the strength to socialize—for only fleeting moments before edging over into complete inebriation. Bob, on the other hand, can reach oblivion after about a quart of whiskey and maintain it for days.

But now, this moment, Bob Stookey has reached the twilight of his binge. After drinking a gallon a day, he has begun to regularly nod off, to lose his grip on reality, to hallucinate and black out for hours.

"I said the show must go on," the Governor says a little louder, coming over to the chain-link fence separating himself and Bob. "These people are getting cabin fever, Bob. They need catharsis."

"Damn straight," Bob slurs in a spittle-clogged grunt. He can barely hold his head up. He gazes down through steel waffling at the Governor, who now stands only a couple of feet away, looking balefully up at Bob through the links of the cyclone fence.

In Bob's feverish gaze, the Governor looks demonic in the cold Lucolux stadium lights, a silver halo appearing around the man's slicked-back hair with its raven-feather ponytail. His breath comes out in puffs of white vapor, his Fu Manchu mustache twitching at the edges as he expounds, "Little winter storm's not gonna keep us down, Bob. I got something in mind, gonna blow these people away. You just wait. You ain't seen nothing yet."

"Sounds . . . good," Bob utters, his head lolling forward, a dark shade drawing down over his vision.

"Tomorrow night, Bob." The Governor's face floats in Bob's faltering vision, a ghostly spirit. "This is a teaching moment. From now on, things are gonna be different around here. Law and order, Bob. This'll be the greatest learning opportunity ever. And a great show to boot. Gonna rock their fucking world. It's all gonna come together in here, in this mud and shit. Bob? You with me? Bob, you okay? Stay with me, old fella."

As Bob slips off the bleacher, crumbling to the ground in another blackout, the last image burned into his mind's eye is the Governor's face, fractured by the rusty geometric diamonds of the chain-link fence.

"Where the hell is Martinez, anyway?" The Governor glances over his shoulder. "Haven't seen a trace of that asshole in hours."

"Listen to me," Martinez says, welding his gaze into the eyes of each conspirator, one by one, in the dim light of the railroad shed. The five men crouch down in a loose semicircle around Martinez, huddling in the back corner, the cobweb-draped shed as dark as a tomb. Martinez lights a cigarillo and smoke engulfs his handsome, cunning face. "You don't ease a trap over a fucking cobra—you strike as fast as possible, as hard as possible."

"When?" utters the youngest one, the one named Stevie. Crouched next to Martinez, the tall, lanky kid of mixed race wears a black silk roadie jacket and has a peach-fuzz mustache, and nervously blinks his long-lashed earnest eyes. Stevie's outward innocence is belied by his ferocious aptitude at destroying zombies.

"Soon." Martinez puffs his stogie. "I'll let you know tonight."

"Where?" asks another conspirator, an older man in a peacoat and scarf, who goes by the name of the Swede. His wild mop of blond hair, leathery face, and barrel chest, which is perpetually crossed with ammo bandoliers, give him the air of a French Resistance fighter in World War II.

Martinez looks at him. "I'll let you know."

The Swede lets out an exasperated sigh. "We're putting our asses on the line here, Martinez. Seems like you could give us a few details, what we're getting into."

Another one speaks up, a black man in a down vest named Broyles. "There's a reason he's not giving us the details, Swede."

"Yeah? Why is that?"

The black man levels his gaze on the Swede. "Margin of error."

"Come again?"

The black man looks at Martinez. "Too much to lose, somebody gets nabbed before the thing goes down, gets tortured and shit."

Martinez nods, smoking his cheroot. "Something like that . . . yeah."

A fourth man, a former mechanic from Macon named Taggert, chimes in: "What about the bookends?"

"Bruce and Gabe?" Martinez says.

"Yeah . . . you think we'll be able to flip them?"

Martinez takes another drag off the stogie. "What do *you* think?"

Taggert shrugs. "I don't think they'll ever go along with anything like this. Blake's got them so far up his ass they gargle for him at night."

"Exactly." Martinez takes a deep breath. "That's why we gotta take them out first."

"You ask me," Stevie mumbles, "most of the folks in this town got no complaints about the Governor."

"He's right," the Swede concurs with a nervous nod. "I'd say ninety percent of these people actually *like* the son of a bitch, and they're just fine with the way things are run around here. Just so the pantry stays full, the wall stays up, the show goes on . . . it's like the Germans in the 1930s when fucking Adolf Hitler—"

"Okay, put a sock in it!" Martinez tosses his cigar to the cinder-strewn floor and snubs it out with the toe of his jackboot. "Listen to me . . . everybody." He meets each man's gaze as he speaks in a low monotone shot through with nervous tension. "This thing's gonna happen, and it's gonna happen quickly and decisively . . . otherwise we're gonna end up in that slaughterhouse room getting chopped up for zombie food. He's gonna have an accident. That's all you need to know at this point. You want out, there's the door. No hard feelings. Now's your chance." He softens a little. "You guys have been good workers, honest men . . . and trust don't come easy around this place. You want to shake hands and pass on this thing, I got no problem with you. But do it now. Because once this thing goes down it ain't gonna have no reboot button on it."

Martinez waits.

Nobody says anything, nobody leaves.

That night, the temperature plummets, the winds kicking up out of the north. Chimneys spume with wood smoke across Woodbury's main drag, the generators working overtime. To the west, the great arc lights over the racetrack remain burning, the final preparations being made for the big world premiere the next evening.

Alone in her place above the dry cleaner, Lilly Caul lays a pair of handguns and extra ammunition across her bedspread—two .22 caliber Ruger Lite semiautomatics, along with an extra magazine and a carton of 32-grain Stingers. Martinez gave her the weapons, along with a quick lesson on how to reload the clips.

She stands back and stares at the gold-plated pistols with a narrowing of her eyes. Her heart quickens, her throat drying with those old familiar feelings of panic and self-doubt. She pauses. She closes her eyes and wills the fear back down her throat. She opens her eyes and holds her right hand up and ponders it as though it belongs to someone else. Her hand does not shake. It is rock steady.

She will not get a minute of sleep this night or perhaps the next.

Pulling a large knapsack from beneath the bed, she packs the weapons, the ammunition, a machete, a flashlight, nylon cord, sleeping pills, duct tape, a can of Red Bull, a cigarette lighter, a roll of plastic tarp, fingerless gloves, binoculars, and an extra down vest. She zips the knapsack shut and shoves it back under the bed.

Less than twenty-four hours remain until the mission that will change the course of her life.

Lilly bundles up in a down coat, insulated boots, and a stocking cap. She checks her windup clock on her bedside table.

Five minutes later, at 11:45 p.m., she locks up her apartment and heads outside.

The town lies deserted in the late-night chill, the air acrid with the odors of sulfur and frozen salt. Lilly has to step gingerly over the iced sidewalks, her boot steps crunching loudly. She glances over her shoulder. The streets are empty. She makes her way around the post office building to Bob's condo.

The wooden staircase from which Megan hung herself, ice-bound since the storm has passed, cracks and snaps as Lilly carefully climbs the risers.

She knocks on Bob's door. No answer. She knocks again. Nothing. She whispers Bob's name but gets no reply, no sound issuing from within. She tries the door and finds it unlocked. She lets herself in.

The dark kitchen sits in silence, the floor littered with broken dishes and crockery, puddles of spilled liquids. For a moment Lilly wonders if she should have brought a firearm. She scans the living room to her right, sees the overturned furniture and mounds of dirty laundry.

She finds a battery-operated lantern on a counter, grabs it, and flips it on. She walks deeper into the apartment and calls out, "Bob?"

The lantern light glistens off broken glass on the hallway floor. One of Bob's medical satchels lies on the carpet, overturned, its contents spilled across the floor. The wall shimmers with something sticky. Lilly gulps down the fear and moves on.

"Anybody home?"

She peers into the bedroom at the end of the hall and finds Bob on the floor, in a sitting position, leaning against the unmade bed, his head lolled forward. Clad in a stained wifebeater and boxer shorts, his skinny legs as white as alabaster, he sits stone-still and for the briefest instant Lilly mistakes him for dead.

But then she sees his chest slowly rising and falling, and she notices the half-empty bottle of Jim Beam loosely clutched in his limp right hand.

"Bob!"

She rushes over to him and gently raises his head, leaning it against the bed. His greasy, thinning hair askew, his heavy-lidded eyes bloodshot and glassy, he mumbles something like, "Too many of 'em . . . they're gonna—"

"Bob, it's Lilly. Can you hear me? Bob? It's me, it's Lilly."

His head lolls. "They're gonna die . . . we don't triage the worst of 'em . . ."

"Bob, wake up. You're having a nightmare. It's okay, I'm here."

"Crawlin' with maggots . . . too many . . . horrible . . ."

She rises to her feet, turns, and hurries out of the room. Across the hall, in the filthy bathroom, she runs some water in a dirty cup, and returns with the water. She gently takes the booze from Bob's hand and throws it across the room, the bottle shattering against the wall, splattering the cabbage-rose wallpaper. Bob jerks at the noise.

"Here, drink this," she says, and gives him a little. He coughs it down. His hands flail impotently as he coughs. He tries to focus on her but his eyes won't cooperate. She strokes his feverish brow. "I know you're hurting, Bob. It's going to be okay. I'm here now. C'mon."

She lifts him by the armpits, heaving the deadweight of his body up and onto the bed. She lays his head on the pillow. She positions his legs under the covers, then pulls the blanket up to his chin, speaking softly to him. "I know how hard it was on you, losing Megan and all, but you just have to hang in there."

His brow furrows, a look of agony contorting his pale, deeply lined, drawn face. His eyes search the ceiling. He looks like a person who has been buried alive and is trying to breathe. He slurs his words. "I never wanted to . . . never . . . it wasn't my idea to—"

"It's okay, Bob. You don't have to say anything." She strokes his brow and speaks in a low, soft tone. "You did the right thing. It's all gonna be okay. Things are gonna change around here, things are gonna get better." She strokes his cheek, the grizzled flesh cold beneath her fingertips. She begins to softly sing. She sings Joni Mitchell's "The Circle Game" to him, just like old times.

Bob's head settles back into the sweat-damp pillow, his breathing beginning to calm. His eyelids droop. Just like old times. He begins to snore. Lilly keeps singing long after he has drifted off.

"We're taking him down," Lilly says very softly to the sleeping man.

She knows he cannot hear a thing she is saying anymore, if he ever could. Lilly is speaking to herself now. Speaking to some deeply buried part of her psyche.

"It's too late to turn back now . . . we're gonna take him down . . ."

Lilly's voice trails off, and she decides to find herself a blanket and spend the rest of that night at Bob's bedside, waiting for the fateful day to dawn.

SEVENTEEN

The next morning, the Governor gets an early start on the last-minute preparations for the big show. He's up before dawn, quickly getting dressed, making coffee, and feeding Penny the last of his supply of human entrails. By seven o'clock he is out on the street, on his way to Gabe's apartment. The salt crew is already up and working on the sidewalks, the weather surprisingly mild considering the events of the last week. The mercury has risen into the lower fifties, and the sky has lightened, perhaps even stabilized, now overcast with a pale gray ceiling of clouds the color of cement. Very little wind disturbs the morning air, and the burgeoning day strikes the Governor as picture-perfect for an evening of new and improved gladiator matches.

Gabe and Bruce supervise the transfer of zombies held captive in the holding rooms beneath the track. It takes several hours to move the things into the staging areas up above, not only because the walkers are unruly beasts but also because the Governor wants to do it in secret. The unveiling of the Ring of Death has gotten the Governor's show biz juices flowing and he wants the evening's revelations to dazzle the crowd. He spends the bulk of that afternoon inside the arena, checking and double-checking the curtain drops, the public address system, the music cues, the lights, the gates, the locks, the security, and last but certainly not least, the competitors.

The two surviving guardsmen, Zorn and Manning, still wasting away in their underground holding cell, have lost most of their body fat and muscle tissue. Subsisting on scraps, stale crackers, and water for months, chained to the wall 24–7, they look like living skeletons and have very little of their sanity left intact. The only saving grace is their military training—as well as their rage—which, over the weeks of their torturous captivity, has festered and deepened and turned them into wild-eyed revenants hungry for vengeance.

In other words, if they can't rip into the throats of their captors, then they'll happily do the next best thing and rip into each other.

The guardsmen are the final piece to the puzzle, and the Governor waits until the last minute to move them. Gabe and Bruce enlist three of their beefiest workmen to go into the holding cell and inject the soldiers with sodium thiopenthol in order to soften them up for travel. They don't have far to go. Dragged along with leather restraints around their necks, mouths, wrists, and ankles, the two guardsmen are led up a series of iron stairs to the concourse level.

Once upon a time, race fans wandered these cement corridors buying T-shirts and corn dogs and beers and cotton candy. Now these tunnels lie in perpetual darkness, boarded up, padlocked, and used as temporary warehouse space for everything from fuel tanks to sealed cartons of valuables pilfered off the dead.

By six-thirty that night everything is ready. The Governor orders Gabe and Bruce to station themselves at opposite ends of the arena, inside the exit tunnels, in order to guard against any wayward contestants—or errant zombies, for that matter—attempting to flee. Satisfied with all his preparations, the Governor heads back home to change into his show garb. He dresses all in black—black leather vest, leather pants, leather motorcycle boots—and puts a leather stay in his ponytail. He feels like a rock star. He finishes off his ensemble with his trademark duster.

Shortly after seven the forty-plus residents of Woodbury begin filing into the stadium. All the posters tacked up on telephone poles and taped across store windows earlier in the week advertise the start time as seven-thirty, but everybody wants to get a good seat down in the center-front of the bleachers, get settled in, get something to drink, get their blankets and cushions situated.

The mild weather has everybody buzzing excitedly as the start time looms.

At 7:28 P.M. a hush falls over the spectators crowded around the front of the bleachers, some of them standing on the warning track, their faces pressed up against the chain-link barrier. The youngest of the men are down front, while the women and couples and older residents sit scattered across the higher rows, blankets wrapped around themselves to ward off the chill. Each and every face reflects the desperate dope hunger of a junkie in withdrawal—gaunt, wrung out, jittery. They sense something extraordinary about to occur. They smell blood on the wind.

The Governor will not disappoint.

At 7:30 on the nose—according to the Governor's self-winding Fossil wristwatch—the music in the stadium begins to sneak under the ceaseless moaning of the wind. It starts out soft and faint through the PA horns—a low chord as deep as a subterranean tremor—the overture familiar to many, even though few would be able to name the actual symphonic poem: *Also sprach Zarathustra* by Richard Strauss. Most know the piece as the theme from *2001: A Space Odyssey*, the booming horn notes coming one at a time, building on a dramatic fanfare.

A light veil of snow becomes visible up in the arc lights, a brilliant beam hitting the center of the muddy infield, a magnesium-bright pool the size of a moon crater. The crowd lets out a collective holler as the Governor strides out into the cone of light.

He raises a hand—a regal, melodramatic gesture, as the music builds to its big climactic finale—the wind tossing the tails of his duster. His boots sink six inches into the muck, the infield a mire of rain-sodden earth. He believes the mud will only add to the drama.

"Friends! Fellow residents of Woodbury!" he booms into a microphone hardwired to a PA stack behind him. His baritone rises up into the night sky, the echo slapping back across the empty stands at either end of the arena. "You've worked hard to keep this town up and running! You are about to be rewarded!"

Three and a half dozen voices—their vocal cords, as well as their sanity, stretched thin—can make a hell of a racket. The caterwauls swirl on the wind.

"Are you ready for some hard-hitting action tonight?"

The gallery lets out a cacophony of hyena yelps and wild cheers.

"Bring on the contestants!"

On cue, huge follow spots flare on across the upper decks, the noise like giant match tips striking—the beams sweeping down across the arena. One by one, the silver pools of light land on enormous black canvas curtains, each of which drapes one of the five gangways around the concourse.

At the far end of the stadium, a garage-style door rolls up and Zorn, the younger of the two guardsmen, appears in the shadows of the gangway. Clad in makeshift shoulder pads and shin guards, he holds a large machete and trembles with latent madness. He starts across the track toward the center of the infield with a feral expression on his face, moving stiffly, jerkily, a prisoner of war off the leash for the first time in many weeks.

Almost simultaneously, like a mirror image of Zorn's entrance, the garage door at the opposite end of the stadium jerks upward, and from the shadows comes Manning, the older soldier, the one with the wild gray hair and bloodshot eyes. Manning carries an enormous battle-axe and trudges through the mud not unlike a zombie himself.

As the two combatants approach each other in the center of the ring, the Governor bellows into the mike, "Ladies and gentlemen, it is with great pride that I give you the Ring of Death!"

The crowd lets out a collective gasp as the curtains around the periphery—once again, on cue—suddenly drop away, revealing clusters of snarling, decomposing, hungry zombies. Some of the spectators in the stands spring to their feet, instinctively wanting to flee, as the biters start lumbering out of their archways, arms reaching for human meat.

The biters get halfway across the infield, their awkward, shuffling steps mired in the mud, before reaching the end of their chains. Some of them—surprised by the limit of their freedom—are yanked off their feet, landing in comic fashion in the mud. Others growl angrily, flailing dead arms at the crowd and the overall injustice of their leashed captivity. The crowd jeers.

"LET THE BATTLE BEGIN!"

At the center of the infield Zorn pounces on Manning before Manning is ready—in fact, before the Governor has even had a chance to make a safe exit—and the older soldier barely has time to block the slashing blow with his weapon.

The machete comes down and grazes the axe head in a gout of sparks.

The crowd cheers as Manning careens backward into the mud, sliding through the muck, coming to within inches of the closest zombie. The walker, wild-eyed with bloodlust, snaps its jaws at Manning's ankles, the chain barely holding the creature. Manning scrambles to get back on his feet, his face ablaze with terror and madness.

The Governor smiles to himself as he walks off the infield, exiting through one of the gates.

The crowd noises echo through the dark tunnel all around him as he walks through the cement-encased shadows, chuckling to himself, thinking about how amazing it would be if one of the guardsmen got bit before the crowd's eyes and actually turned during the course of the battle. Now *that* would be entertainment.

He turns a corner and sees one of his men loading a clip into an AK-47 near a deserted food stand. The young man—an overgrown farm kid from Macon dressed in a ratty down coat and stocking cap—looks up from his weapon. "Hey, Gov . . . how's it going out there?"

"Thrills and chills, Johnny, thrills and chills," the Governor says with a wink as he passes. "Gonna go check on Gabe and Bruce at the exits . . . you make sure those walkers stay inside the infield and don't wander back toward the gates."

"Will do, boss."

The Governor moves on, turning another corner and striding down a deserted tunnel.

The muffled noise of the crowd echoes in waves down the dark passageway as he makes his way toward the east exit. He starts whistling, feeling on top of the world, when all at once he stops whistling and slows down, instinctively reaching for the .38 snubbie in his belt. Something feels wrong all of a sudden.

He comes to an abrupt halt in the middle of the tunnel. The east exit, just visible around a corner twenty feet ahead of him, sits there completely deserted. No sign of Gabe anywhere. The outer gate— a vertical door made of wooden slats, pulled down across the opening—leaks thin strands of bright light from the headlamps of an idling vehicle.

At that point the Governor notices the muzzle of an M1 assault rifle on the floor, poking around the corner—Gabe's gun—lying unattended.

"Son of a bitch!" the Governor blurts, drawing his gun and spinning around.

The blue spark of a Taser crackles in his face, knocking him backward.

Martinez moves in quickly, the Taser in one hand, a heavy leather sap in the other—as the fifty-kilovolt punch sends the Governor reeling backward, slamming into the wall, his .38 flying out of his hand.

Martinez brings the sap down hard on the Governor's temple, the dull slapping noise like a tuneless bell ringing. The Governor convulses against the wall, swinging wildly, refusing to go down. He cries out with the garbled rage of a stroke victim, the veins in his neck and temples bulging, as he kicks out at Martinez.

The Swede and Broyles stand behind Martinez on each flank, ready to move in with the rope and tape. Martinez hits the Governor again with the sap, and this time the blunt object does its work.

The Governor stiffens and slides to the floor, his eyes rolling back in his head. The Swede and Broyles close in on the quivering, twitching body curled into a fetal position on the cement.

They get the Governor tied, bound, and gagged with duct tape in less than sixty seconds. Martinez signals the men outside the gate with a quick whistle, and the slatted door suddenly jumps up.

"On three," Martinez mutters, holstering his Taser, shoving the sap behind his belt. He grabs the man's rope-bound ankles. "One, two . . . *three!*"

Broyles takes the Governor by the shoulders, Martinez lifting the legs, and the Swede leads them out through the gate into the cold wind and around the back of the idling panel van.

The rear hatch is already gaping open. They slide the body in.

Within seconds, the men have climbed into the windowless van, and all the doors have slammed, and the vehicle is lurching backward, away from the gate.

The panel van slams to a stop, then the transmission wrenches down into drive and it roars away.

Within seconds all that's left outside the entrance to the racetrack is a fading cloud of carbon monoxide.

"Wake up, you sick fuck!" Lilly slaps the Governor, the man's eyes fluttering open on the floor of the crowded van as it rumbles out of town.

Gabe and Bruce are bound and gagged near the front of the cluttered payload bay, their mouths covered with duct tape. The Swede holds a .45 Smith & Wesson on the men, their eyes wide and searching. Cartons of military ordnance line the sides of the cargo bay, everything from armor-piercing shells to incendiary bombs.

"Take it easy, Lilly," Martinez cautions, crouching near the front, a walkie-talkie clutched in his gloved hand. His face tight with nervous tension, a heretic rebelling against the church, Martinez turns away and thumbs the switch and says in a low voice, "Just follow the Jeep, and keep the lights off, and let me know when you see a roamer."

The Governor regains consciousness in stages, blinking and scanning his surroundings, testing the strength of his bonds—the elastic shackles, nylon rope, and duct tape tight around his mouth.

"You need to hear this, Blake," Lilly says to the man on the corrugated floor. " 'Governor' . . . 'President' . . . 'King Shit' . . . whatever you call yourself. You think you're some kind of benevolent dictator?"

The Governor's eyes still shift around the confines of the van, not focusing on any one thing—an animal boxed in on the killing floor.

"My friends did not have to *die*," Lilly goes on, looming over the

Governor. Her eyes mist over for a moment and she hates herself for it. "You could have built this place into something great . . . a place where people could live in safety and harmony . . . instead of this twisted, sick freak show that it's become."

Near the front, Martinez thumbs the switch. "Stevie, you see anything yet?"

Through the speaker crackles the younger man's voice. "Negative . . . nothing yet . . . wait!" The sound of static, then rustling noises. Stevie's voice is heard off mike: "What the fuck is that?"

Martinez thumbs the switch. "Stevie, say again, I didn't copy that."

Static . . . rustling noises.

"Stevie! You copy? I don't want to get too far from town!"

Through the static Stevie's voice intermittently sizzles through the noise: "Stop, Taggert. . . . Stop! . . . What the fuck! WHAT THE FUCK!"

In back, Lilly wipes her eyes and latches her gaze on the eyes of the Governor. "Sex for food? Really? Seriously? That's your great society—"

"Lilly!" Martinez barks at her. "Stop it! We got a situation!" He thumbs the send button. "Broyles, stop the van!"

By this point the Governor's eyes have found Lilly's, and the man is fully awake, staring at her with a silent fury that burns holes in her soul, and she doesn't care, she doesn't even notice it.

"All the fighting and the suicides and the fear driving everyone into catatonic stupors . . . ?" She feels like spitting at him. "This is your idea of a fucking COMMUNITY—"

"Lily! Goddammit!" Martinez turns and faces her. "Would you please—"

The truck screeches to a stop, throwing Martinez backward against the firewall and tossing Lilly forward across the Governor and into a stack of ammo boxes. The cartons topple as Lilly sprawls across the floor. The walkie-talkie spins against a duffel bag. The Governor rolls from one side to the other, the duct tape coming loose from his mouth.

The crackle of Broyles's voice squawks out of the speaker. "Got a visual on a walker!"

Martinez crawls toward the two-way, snatching it up and thumb-ing the button. "What the hell's going on, Broyles? What's the idea of slamming on the—"

"Got another one!" the voice squawks out of the tiny speaker. "Got a couple, coming out of the . . . Oh, fuck . . . oh, fuck . . . OH, FUCK!"

Martinez thumbs the switch. "Broyles, what the hell is going on?"

Through the radio: "There's more than we—"

Static washes over the voice for a moment, and then Stevie's voice cuts through the noise: "Jesus Christ, there's a whole bunch of them coming out of the—" Static crackles for a moment. "They're coming out of the woods, man, they keep coming—"

Martinez yells into the mike, "Stevie, talk to me! Should we dump them and come back?"

More static.

Martinez screams, "Stevie! Do you copy? Should we turn around?"

Broyles's voice now: "Too many, boss! Never seen this many in one—"

A burst of static and the sound of a gunshot and glass breaking—echoing outside the walls of the van—all of it gets Lilly to her feet. She realizes what's happening, and she reaches behind her belt for the Ruger. She pulls it out and cocks the slide, glancing over her shoulder. "Martinez, call your men back, get 'em outta here!"

Martinez thumbs the button: "Stevie! Can you hear me?! Get outta here, pull back! Turn around! We'll find another place! Can you hear me? STEVIE!"

The sound of Stevie's anguished cry spurts out of the speaker, right before another barrage of automatic gunfire rattles the air . . . followed by a terrific wrenching of metal . . . and then an enormous crash.

Broyles's voice: "Hold on! They turned it over! There's too god-damn many! Hold on! We're fucked, y'all! WE ARE TOTALLY FUCKED!!"

The van shudders as the engine revs into reverse, rocketing back-ward, the centripetal force throwing everybody forward against the firewall. Lilly slams her shoulder against the gun rack, knocking half a dozen carbines to the floor like kindling. Gabe and Bruce roll, slamming into each other. Unbeknownst to the others, Gabe has his fingers under Bruce's shackle now and he starts wrenching at it. Bruce's gag has come loose and he booms a garbled cry: "YOU MOTHERFUCKERS, NOW WE'RE ALL GONNA DIE!"

The van bumps over an object, and then another, and another— the wet, muffled thumps rocking the chassis—and Lilly holds on to the side brace with her free hand, scanning the cargo hold.

Martinez scrambles on hands and knees toward the fallen walkie-talkie while the black man spits and curses, and Swede aims the muzzle of his .45 at the bald black man. "SHUT THE FUCK UP!"

"YOU MOTHERFUCKERS DON'T EVEN—"

The rear of the van slams into an unknown object and bogs down, the rear wheels spinning on something slick and gooey on the road, the g-forces flinging everybody into the corner. Guns fly off across the hold, and the Governor rolls against a stack of cartons that fall on him. He lets out an angry cry—the duct tape hanging from his chin now—and then he gets quiet.

Everybody gets quiet as the van sits there for a moment, very still.

Then the entire vehicle shudders. The sideways jerk gets every-body's attention. Broyles's voice crackles from the fallen two-way, something about *"too many"* or *"getting out,"* when all at once the roar of Broyles's AK-47 from the cab pierces the silence, followed by an eruption of broken glass and a human shriek.

Then things get quiet again. And still. Except for the low, droning, mucusy moans of hundreds of dead voices, which, coming through the walls of the windowless van, sound like a giant turbine engine rumbling outside the van. Something bumps the vehicle again, jerk-ing it sideways with a violent convulsion.

Martinez grabs an assault rifle off the wall, jacks the lever back, lurches toward the rear hatch, and grasps the handle, when he hears a deep, whiskey-cured voice come from behind him.

"Wouldn't do that if I were you."

Lilly glances down at the floor and sees the Governor—his gag loose—struggling into a sitting position against the wall, his dark eyes smoldering. Lilly holds her Ruger on him. "You're not giving orders anymore," she informs him through clenched teeth.

The van jerks sideways again. The rumbling silence stretches.

"Your little plan's gone all to hell," the Governor says with sadistic glee. His facial features tic with residual trauma.

"Shut up!"

"Thought you'd leave us out here, feed us to the biters, and nobody would be the wiser."

Lilly puts the muzzle of the .22 against his forehead. "I said shut the fuck up!"

The van shudders again. Martinez stands frozen with indecision. He turns, and he starts to say something to Lilly, when a sharp blur of movement near the front takes everybody by surprise.

Bruce has managed to free his hands and suddenly lashes out at the Swede, knocking the gun out of the older man's grip. The .45 goes off as it clatters to the floor, the boom so loud it ruptures eardrums, the blast chinking metal out of the floor and grazing the Swede's left boot, making the older man cry out and slam against the back wall.

In one smooth movement, before Martinez or Lilly can fire, the big black man scoops up the hot .45 and empties three rounds into the Swede's chest. Blood sprays across the corrugated side wall behind the older man as he gasps and writhes and slides to the floor.

From the rear, Martinez spins toward the black man and fires two quick, controlled bursts in his general direction, but by that point Bruce is already diving for cover behind piles of cartons, and the bullets are chewing through cardboard, metal, and fiberglass, setting off a series of muffled blasts inside the boxes, which send puffs of wood shards, sparks, and paper into the air like meteors—

—and everybody dives to the floor—and Bruce gets his hands on his bowie knife—a weapon he had hidden on his ankle—and he's going for Gabe's shackles—and things are happening very quickly now all around the cargo bay—as Lilly swings her Ruger toward the two thugs near the front—while Martinez leaps toward Bruce—and the Governor screams something like "DON'T KILL THEM!—and Gabe is loose now and scrambling for one of the fallen carbines—and Bruce slashes the knife at Martinez, who dodges the blow, and then stumbles against Lilly, sending her slamming against the rear doors—

—and the impact of Lilly's body against the double-doors springs the latch.

The doors suddenly and unexpectedly burst open, letting a swarm of moving corpses into the van.

EIGHTEEN

A large, putrefied biter in a shredded medical smock goes for Lilly, and it nearly gets its rotten teeth into her neck, when Martinez manages to get off a burst that takes off the top of the thing's skull.

Rancid, black blood fountains up across the ceiling, spitting across Lilly's face, as she backs away from the open doorway. More biters scuttle in through the gaping hatch. Lilly's ears go deaf—ringing from the noise—as she backs toward the front wall.

The Governor, still shackled, scoots backward, away from the onslaught, as Gabe gets a loaded carbine rifle up and barking, the barrage punching through dead tissue and rotting skulls. Brain matter blossoms like black chrysanthemums, as the interior of the van smokes and teeters and floods with death stench. More and more biters swarm the opening, despite the blazing gunfire.

"BRUCE, CUT ME LOOSE!"

The Governor's voice—nearly drowned by the din, barely audible to Lilly's ringing eardrums—gets Bruce moving with the knife. Meanwhile Martinez and Lilly unleash a salvo of gunfire, muzzles flashing, the noise enormous, entire clips being emptied, the successive blasts hitting eye sockets and mandibles and slimy bald pates and putrid foreheads, sending black tissue and blood and fluids spurting and flinging across the open hatch.

Bruce's knife slices down on the Governor's shackles, and within seconds the Governor is free and has a carbine in his hands.

The air blazes with gunfire, and soon the five surviving human occupants of the van are clustered together against the cab's firewall, each of them blasting away at will, spraying a hell storm across the rear hatch. The sound is gargantuan, ear-piercing, amplified by the metal fuselage of the van. Some of the rounds miss their targets, ricocheting off the door frame in daisy chains of sparks.

Mangled zombies drop to the floor of the van, dominoes falling, some of them slipping off the slimy back edge of the hatch, others caught in the pile. The barrage continues another ten seconds, during which time the back spray of blood and bodily matter cover the humans in layers of gore. A splinter of steel strikes Lilly's thigh, embedding itself, a wasp sting of pain waking her up.

Over the course of a single minute—an interminable sixty seconds of elapsed time that feels to Lilly like a lifetime—each and every last ammo magazine is emptied into dead flesh, and every last zombie crowding the doorway drops and slides to the pavement outside the van, leaving leech trails of blood on the corrugated ledge.

The last remaining bodies get stuck in the hatchway, and in the horrible, ear-ringing silence that ensues, as Gabe and Martinez and the Governor reload, Bruce lunges toward the hatch. He kicks the stragglers off the rear parapet, the bodies falling to the asphalt with a splat. Lilly thumbs her spent magazine out of her Ruger, the clip clattering to the floor, the metallic clunk unheard by her deafened ears. Her face and arms and clothing are covered in blood and bile. She reloads, her pulse throbbing in her traumatized ears.

In the meantime Bruce wrenches the double doors shut, the damaged hinges making a loud squeak that barely penetrates the ringing in Lilly's ears.

The latch clicks, sealing them back inside the blood-drenched death chamber, but the worst part, the part that has everybody's attention now, is the half-glimpsed landscape beyond the van, the forest on either side of the road, and the switchback way up on the plateau in the distance, draped in darkness and crawling with moving shadows.

What they glimpse before the doors bang shut challenges comprehension. They've all seen herds before, some of them huge, but this one defies description—a mass of dead the likes of which no one has seen since the plague broke out months ago. Nearly a thousand moving corpses in every imaginable state of decomposition stretch as far as the eye can see. Throngs of snarling zombies, so thick one could walk across their shoulders, line the edges of the hill on either side of Highway 85. Moving slowly and lethargically, their sheer number threatening mass destruction, they bring to mind a black glacier aimlessly cutting through the trees and slicing across the fields and roads. Some of them barely have flesh left on their bones, their ragged burial clothing hanging mosslike in the darkness. Others snap at the air with the involuntary twitching of snakes stirred from their nests. The length and breadth of the multitude, each face as pale white as mother-of-pearl, gives the impression of a vast, moving flood tide of infected pus.

Inside the van, the primordial terror touched off by this sight stiffens the spines of everyone present. Gabe raises his carbine at Martinez. "You stupid fucking son of a bitch! Look at what you've done! Look at what you've gotten us into!!"

Before anybody can react Lilly swings her Ruger up and trains it on Gabe. Ears ringing, she cannot hear exactly what he says in reply but she knows he means business. "I will fucking blow you away if you don't back off, asshole!"

Bruce pounces on Lilly with his buck knife, putting it around her neck. "Bitch, you got about three seconds to drop that motherfucking—"

"BRUCE!" The Governor aims his carbine at Bruce. "Back off!"

Bruce doesn't move. The blade stays pressed against Lilly's throat, and Lilly keeps her gun leveled on Gabe, and Martinez trains his assault rifle on the Governor. "Philip, listen to me," Martinez says softly, "I promise you I will drop you first before I go down."

"Everybody just calm the fuck down!" The Governor's knuckles are white on the carbine's hilt. "Only way we're gonna get outta this mess is together!"

The van shudders again as more zombies close in, making everybody jerk.

"What are you thinking?" Lilly says.

"First of all, get those fucking guns out of everybody's face."

Martinez burns his gaze into Bruce. "Bruce, get away from her."

"Do what he says, Bruce." The Governor keeps the muzzle on Bruce. A single pearl of sweat rolls down the bridge of the Governor's nose. "PUT THE FUCKING KNIFE DOWN OR I WILL PUT YOUR BRAINS ON THAT WALL!"

Reluctantly, the rage blazing in his dark almond eyes, Bruce lowers the knife.

The van trembles again, as the guns slowly tilt down, one at a time, away from their targets.

Martinez is the last to lower his rifle. "If we can get to the cab, we can plough our way outta here."

"Negative!" The Governor looks at him. "We'll lead this fucking stampede back to Woodbury!"

"What do you suggest?" Lilly asks the Governor with cold acid running through her veins. She feels the horrible sensation of giving over to the madman again, her soul shrinking into a tiny black hole inside her. "We can't just sit here on our thumbs."

"How far are we from town? Like less than mile?" The Governor asks this almost rhetorically as he gazes around the van's blood-sodden interior, glancing from carton to carton. He sees the spare parts of gun mounts, shell casings, military-grade ammunition. "Lemme ask you something," he says, turning to Martinez. "You seem to have thought through this big coup d'état like a real military man. You got any RPGs in this crate? Anything with a little more punch than a simple grenade?"

It takes them less than five minutes to find the ordnance and load the RPG and lay out the strategy and get into position, and throughout that time the Governor gives most of the orders, keeping everybody moving, as the horde surrounds the van like bees swarming a hive. By the time the survivors are ready to launch their countermeasure, the number of dead pressing in on the vehicle is so high the van nearly tips over.

The muffled sound of the Governor's voice, coming from inside the van, counting down . . . *"three, two, one"* . . . is incomprehensible to the dead, their putrid ears brushing the outer shell of the vehicle.

The first blast blows the rear doors off the van as if they were on explosive bolts.

The eruption catapults half a dozen walkers into the air, the rocket-propelled grenade punching through the dense crowd of corpses clustered outside the hatch like a hot poker ramming through butter. The projectile goes off ten yards away from the van.

The explosion immolates at least a hundred—maybe more—in the general vicinity of the vehicle. The sound of it rivals a sonic boom from a passing jet, the report shaking the ground, arcing up into the heavens, and echoing out across the tops of trees.

The back draft shoots up and out—a convection of flame the size of a basketball court—turning night to day and transforming the closest zombies into flaming human debris, some of them practically vaporized, others becoming dancing columns of fire. The inferno razes an area of fifty square yards around the van.

Gabe leaps out of the van first, a scarf around his mouth and nose to filter the acrid fumes of dead flesh cooking in the napalmlike maelstrom. He is followed closely by Lilly, who covers her mouth with one hand, and fires off three quick shots with her Ruger in the other hand, taking down a few stray zombies in their path.

They make it to the cab, throw the door open, and climb in—pushing Broyles's contorted, bloody remains aside—and within seconds the rear wheels are digging in, and the vehicle is launching out of there.

The van bulldozes through files of zombies, turning the upright cadavers into putrefied jelly on the pavement, cutting a swath toward a hairpin turn that looms ahead of them. And when they reach the tight curve, Gabe executes the last phase of the escape.

He yanks the wheel, and the van careens off the road and up the side of a wooded hill.

The rough terrain taxes the tires and suspension, but Gabe keeps the foot feed pinned, and the rear-wheel drive churns through the soft muddy floor of the hill, fishtailing wildly, nearly dumping the other three men out the gaping, jagged opening in the rear.

When they reach the crest of the hill, Gabe slams on the brakes and the van skids to a stop.

It takes a minute to aim the mortar launcher, a squat iron cylinder that Martinez hastily jury-rigged to a machine-gun mount. The muzzle is pointed upward at a forty-five-degree angle. By the time they're ready to fire, at least two hundred zombies have started shambling up the hill toward the van, drawn to the noise and head-lights.

Martinez primes the launcher and touches off the ignition button.

The mortar booms, the projectile rocketing skyward, arcing out over the valley, the tracery of its tail like a glowing neon contrail. The explosive shell lands smack-dab in the middle of the sea of walking dead. At least four hundred yards from the van, the mini mushroom cloud of flame is seen a few milliseconds before the *FFOOOMP* of its impact is heard, and the flash that follows turns the underbelly of the night sky a deep, hot DayGlo orange.

Flaming particles blossom into the heavens, a mixture of dirt, debris, and dead tissue, the shock wave of fire rolling at least a hundred yards in all directions, burning hundreds of biters into ash. A vast autoclave could not cremate the dead faster or more thoroughly.

The remaining walkers, drawn away from the hill by the fiery spectacle, awkwardly turn and drag themselves toward the light.

Away from Woodbury.

They return to town on hobbling wheels, a cracked rear transaxle, shattered windows, and blown doors. They keep gazing out the back for indications of the phenomenal herd, signs of being followed, but other than a few wayward stragglers stumbling along the edges of the orchards, only the orange glow on the western horizon reflects the aftermath of the swarm.

Nobody sees Gabe silently pass the Governor a pearl-handled .45 semiautomatic behind Martinez's back until it's too late. "We got unfinished business, you and me," the Governor blurts suddenly, pressing the muzzle against the back of Martinez's neck as the van rumbles around a corner.

Martinez lets out one long, anguished sigh. "Get it over with."

"You got a short memory, son," the Governor says. "This is the kind of shit happens outside these walls. I'm not gonna waste you, Martinez . . . not yet, at least . . . right now we need each other."

Martinez says nothing, just looks down at the iron corrugations of the floor and waits for his life to come to an end.

They enter the village from the west, and Gabe pulls around in front of the arena and slides into a parking place reserved for service vehicles. Crowd noises still echo from the stands, although from the sound of the catcalls and whistles, the fights have probably deteriorated into chaos. The show's eccentric emcee has been missing in action for over an hour . . . but nobody has had the wherewithal to leave.

Gabe and Lilly get out of the cab and walk around to the rear hatch. Filmed in a layer of gore, her face spackled with blood spray, Lilly feels a skin-prickling sense of unease, and she puts her hand on the grip of her Ruger, which is wedged behind her belt. She's not thinking straight. She feels as though she's half asleep, sluggish with shock, groggy and breathless.

When she turns the corner at the rear of the van she sees Martinez standing without a weapon, his arms soot-covered from the mortar blowback, his sad chiseled face stippled with blood, the Governor directly behind him, pressing the muzzle of the .45 against his neck.

Lilly instinctively draws her Ruger, but before she can even aim it, the Governor issues a warning.

"You shoot that thing, your boyfriend's going down," the Governor hisses at her. "Gabe, take her little peashooter from her."

Gabe snatches the gun out of Lilly's hands, and Lilly just stares at the Governor. A voice rings out in the night air, coming from above them.

"Hey!"

The Governor ducks down. "Martinez, tell your guy on the upper deck everything's okay."

Way up on the crest of the arena roof, on one corner of the upper deck, a machine-gun turret is mounted. A long perforated barrel angles down at the dirt parking lot, behind which stands a young cohort of Martinez's—a tall black kid from Atlanta, name of Hines—a young man who is not privy to the secret overthrow attempt.

"What the hell's going on?" he yells down at them. "Folks look like y'all been in a war!"

"Everything's cool, Hines!" Martinez calls up to him. "Had to deal with a few biters is all!"

The Governor keeps his .45 out of sight, the muzzle prodding the small of Martinez's back. "Hey, kid!" The Governor jerks his head, indicating the dark grove of trees on the other side of the main road. "You want to do me a favor and take out those stragglers we got coming up behind us through the trees!" Then the Governor points at the van. "When you're done with that, there's two bodies in the van need shooting in the head, then take 'em to the morgue."

The machine-gun turret squeaks, and the barrel swings up, and everybody whirls to see movement across the street, a pair of lumbering silhouettes emerging from the trees, the last of the stragglers.

The muzzle roars off the arena roof, the flare of sparks coming one millisecond before the booming report, as the Governor urges Martinez forward toward the building, everybody jerking at the noise.

Armor-piercing rounds strafe the walkers stumbling out of the forest, the zombies dancing upright for a moment like string puppets in an earthquake, blood mist issuing out the backs of their heads— red steam venting. Hines empties an entire bandolier of .762 millimeter cartridges into the walkers for good measure. When they finally go down in pulpy, steaming gut heaps, the kid named Hines lets out a little victory yelp and then looks back across the grounds.

The Governor, Martinez, and the rest of their party have vanished.

NINETEEN

"You people think this is a fucking democracy?" The Governor's blood-spattered duster sweeps the floor, as his angry, smoky voice bounces off the cinder-block walls of the private room underneath the concession area.

Once designated an accounting office and vault for the track's cash receipts, the room has been picked clean, the old iron safe on one side blown apart. Now only a long, scarred conference table, a few girlie calendars on the wall, a couple of accountants' desks, and some overturned swivel chairs litter the space.

Martinez and Lilly sit on folding chairs against one wall, silent and shell-shocked, while Bruce and Gabe stand nearby with guns at the ready. The tension in the room crackles and sparks like a lit fuse.

"You people seem to have forgotten this place works for one reason and one reason only." The Governor's speech is punctuated by facial tics and residual twitching from the Taser trauma. Dried blood clings to his face, his clothes, and his hair in matted crusts. "It works because I'm the one makes it work! You see what's out there? That's what's on the menu, you want to eat out! You want some kind of utopian paradise, some kind of oasis of warm and fuzzy fellowship? Call Norman Fucking *Rockwell*! This is fucking war!"

He pauses to let it sink in, and the silence presses down on the room.

"You ask any motherfucker out there in the stands, do they want a democracy? Do they want warm and fuzzy? Or do they just want somebody to fucking *manage* things . . . keep them from being some biter's *lunch!*" His eyes blaze. "You seem to have forgotten what it was like when Gavin and his guardsmen were in charge! We got this place back! We got things—"

A knock on the outer door interrupts the rant. The Governor spins toward the sound. *"WHAT!"*

The doorknob clicks, the door cracking open a few inches. The sheepish face of the farm kid from Macon peers in, his AK-47 on a strap at his side. "Boss, the natives are getting restless out there."

"What?"

"Lost both fighters ages ago, nothing but dead bodies and biters on chains out there. Nobody's leaving, though . . . they're just getting wasted on their BYOBs and throwin' shit at the zombies."

The Governor wipes his face, smooths down his Fu Manchu. "Tell 'em there's gonna be an important announcement in a minute."

"But what about—"

"JUST TELL 'EM!"

The farm kid gives a meek nod and turns away, latching the door behind him.

The Governor shoots a look across the room at the big black man in gore-splattered denim. "Bruce, go get Stevens and his little lap-dog. I don't care what they're doing, I want their asses in here right now! On the double!"

Bruce gives a nod, shoves his pistol in his belt, and hurries out of the room.

The Governor turns to Martinez. "I know exactly where you got that fucking stun gun . . ."

The time it takes Bruce to go fetch the doctor and Alice is interminable for Lilly. Sitting next to Martinez, a slimy layer of zombie spoor drying on her skin, the wound in her leg throbbing, she expects a bullet to come smashing through her skull at any moment. She can feel Gabe's body heat behind her, only inches away. She can smell his BO and hear his thick breathing, but he doesn't say a word the whole time they're waiting.

Nor does Martinez speak.

272 | Kirkman & Bonansinga

Nor does the Governor, who continues to pace across the front of the room.

Lilly doesn't care about dying anymore. Something inexplicable has happened to her. She thinks of Josh rotting in the ground and she feels nothing. She thinks about Megan hanging by that make-shift noose and it stirs zero emotion. She thinks of Bob sinking into oblivion.

None of it matters anymore.

The worst part is, she knows the Governor is right. They need a Rottweiler on these walls. They need a monster to stanch the blood tide.

Across the room, the door clicks and Bruce returns with Stevens and Alice. The doctor enters in his wrinkled lab coat, walking a few feet in front of Bruce's gun. Alice brings up the rear.

"Come on in and join the party," the Governor greets them with an icy smile. "Have a seat. Relax. Take a load off, sit a spell."

Without a word the doctor and Alice cross the room and sit down on folding chairs next to Martinez and Lilly like children sent to their rooms. The doctor says nothing, just stares at the floor.

"So the whole gang's here now," the Governor says, coming over to the foursome. He stands inches away, a coach about to give a halftime chalk talk. "Here's the thing, we're gonna strike a little agreement . . . a verbal contract. Very simple. Look at me, Martinez."

It requires herculean effort for Martinez to look up at the dark-eyed man.

The Governor latches his gaze on to Martinez. "The agreement is this. As long as I keep the fucking wolves from the door, keep the gravy boats full around here . . . you don't ask questions about how I do it."

He pauses, standing in front of them, waiting, his hands on his hips, his blood-caked features grim and set, his gaze meeting each of their traumatized stares.

Nobody says anything. Lilly sees herself springing to her feet and kicking her chair over and screaming at the top of her lungs and grabbing one of the rifles and cutting the Governor down in a storm of gunfire.

She stares at the floor.

The silence stretches.

"One more thing," the Governor says, smiling at them, his eyes dead and mirthless. "Anybody breaches this contract, sticks their nose in my business, Martinez dies and the rest of you get banished to the sticks. You got that?" He waits in silence. "Answer me, you cocksuckers! You understand the stipulations of our contract? Martinez?"

The reply comes on a haggard breath. "Yeah."

"I can't hear you!"

Martinez looks at him. "Yeah . . . I understand."

"How about you, Stevens?"

"Yes, Philip." The doctor's voice drips with contempt. "Great closing argument. You should be a lawyer."

"Alice?"

She gives him a quick, jittery nod.

The Governor looks at Lilly. "How about you? Are we clear on this?"

Lilly looks at the floor, says nothing.

The Governor presses in closer. "I'm not getting a consensus here. I'll ask you again, Lilly. You understand the agreement?"

Lilly refuses to speak.

The Governor draws his pearl-handled .45 army Colt, snaps back the slide, and presses the muzzle to her head. But before he can say another word, or send a bullet into her brain, Lilly looks up at him.

"I understand."

"LADIES AND GENTLEMEN!" The nasally voice of the farm kid crackles through the arena's PA system, echoing out over the chaotic scene behind the chain-link barrier. The tight knot of spectators has scattered across the stands, although not a single audience member has departed the stadium. Some of them lie on their backs, drunk, staring at the moonless night sky. Others pass bottles of hooch back and forth, attempting to numb the horrors of the mayhem they have just witnessed across the infield.

Some of the drunker patrons are throwing trash and empty bottles into the arena, tormenting the captive biters, who flail impotently on their chains, their rotting lips dripping with black drool. The two dead combatants lie in heaps just out of reach of the zombies, as the crowd jeers and catcalls. This has been going on for almost an hour.

The amplified voice crackles: "*WE HAVE A SPECIAL AN-NOUNCEMENT FOR YOU FROM THE GOVERNOR!*"

This news gets their attention, and the cacophony of yelps and whoops and whistles dies down. The forty or so spectators awkwardly return to their front-row seats, some of them tripping on drunken feet. Within minutes the entire crowd has coalesced down front, behind the cyclone-fence barricade that once protected race fans from spinouts and flaming tires flying off the track.

"*PUT YOUR HANDS TOGETHER FOR OUR FEARLESS LEADER, THE GOVERNOR!*"

From the middle gangway, like a ghost, the long-coated figure emerges from the shadows into the cold vapor of calcium lights, blood stippled and muddy, his coattails flagging in the wind, a Trojan commander returning from the siege of Troy. Striding out to the center of the infield, standing amid the expired guardsmen, he whips the mike cord behind him, raises the mike, and booms into it: "*FRIENDS, YOU ARE ALL HERE BECAUSE OF FATE . . . FATE HAS BROUGHT US TOGETHER . . . AND IT IS OUR FATE TO SURVIVE THIS PLAGUE TOGETHER!*"

The crowd, most of them drunk, lets out an intoxicated cheer.

"*IT IS ALSO MY FATE TO BE YOUR LEADER . . . AND I ACCEPT THAT ROLE WITH PRIDE! AND ANY SON OF A BITCH WHO DOESN'T LIKE IT CAN COME TAKE IT AWAY! ANYTIME! YOU KNOW WHERE TO FIND ME! ANY TAKERS OUT THERE? ANYBODY GOT ENOUGH SAND TO KEEP THIS TOWN SAFE?*"

The drunken voices fade. The faces behind the chain link go slack. He's got their attention now. The wind in the high gantries punctuates the silence.

"*EACH AND EVERY ONE OF YOU TONIGHT SHALL BEAR WITNESS TO A NEW DAY IN WOODBURY! TONIGHT THE BARTER SYSTEM OFFICIALLY COMES TO AN END!*"

Now the silence grips the arena like a pall. The spectators do not expect this, their heads cocked as though hanging on every word.

"FROM NOW ON, SUPPLIES WILL BE GATHERED FOR THE GOOD OF ALL! AND THEY WILL BE DISTRIBUTED EQUALLY! THIS IS HOW PEOPLE WILL EARN THEIR WAY INTO OUR COMMUNITY! BY GATHERING SUPPLIES! BY BENEFITING THE COMMON GOOD!"

One older gentleman a few rows above the others stands on wobbly knees, his Salvation Army topcoat buffeting in the wind, and he begins to clap, nodding his head, his grizzled jaw jutting proudly.

"THESE POLICY CHANGES WILL BE STRICTLY ENFORCED! ANYONE CAUGHT TRADING FAVORS OF ANY SORT IN RETURN FOR GOODS WILL BE FORCED TO FIGHT IN THE RING OF DEATH AS PUNISHMENT!" The governor pauses, scanning the crowd, letting this sink in. *"WE ARE NOT BARBARIANS! WE TAKE CARE OF OUR OWN! WE! ARE! OUR BROTHERS' KEEPERS!!"*

Now more and more of the onlookers stand and begin to applaud, some of them spontaneously sobering up, finding their voices, cheering as though in a church service responding to a hallelujah.

The Governor's sermon strikes a climactic chord: *"THIS WILL BE A NEW ERA OF WOODBURY WORKING TOGETHER! TO FORM A HAPPIER, HEALTHIER, MORE COHESIVE COMMUNITY!!"*

By this point, nearly every spectator has risen to their feet, and the roar of their voices—a sound not unlike an old-fashioned tent revival meeting—reverberates up into the upper tiers and echoes across the night sky. People are clapping, hollering their approval, and exchanging glances of relief and pleasant surprise . . . and perhaps even hope.

The fact is, from this distance, behind the cyclone fence, most of them glassy-eyed from drinking all night, the spectators do not notice the bloodthirsty glint behind the dark eyes of their benevolent leader.

The next morning, the slender young woman in the ponytail finds herself down in the fetid, reeking atmosphere of the abattoir under the stadium.

Clad in her bulky Georgia Tech sweatshirt, antique jewelry, and ripped jeans, Lilly does not shake, does not feel compelled to chew her fingernails, does not in fact feel *any* nervous tension or repulsion at the disgusting task to which she's been assigned as a sort of slap on the wrist for her complicity in the coup attempt.

She in fact feels nothing but a low simmering rage as she crouches in the dim light of the subterranean chamber, wielding the eighteen-inch Teflon-coated axe.

She brings the axe down hard and true, chopping the gristle of the Swede's severed leg, which is stretched across the floor drain. Making a wet popping noise like a pressurized lid opening, the blade slices through the knee joint as a chef's knife might notch a raw drumstick from a chicken thigh. The backsplash of blood spits up at Lilly, stippling her collar and chin. She barely notices it as she tosses the two sections of human limb into the plastic garbage bin next to her.

The bin contains parts of the Swede, Broyles, Manning, and Zorn—a caldron of single-serving-sized entrails, organs, hairy scalps, slimy white ball joints, and severed limbs—collected and stored on ice to keep the games running, keep the arena zombies complacent.

Lilly wears rubber garden gloves—which have turned a dark shade of purple over the course of the last hour—and she has allowed her anger to fuel her axe blows. She has dismantled three bodies with the greatest of ease, barely noticing the other two men—Martinez and Stevens—laboring in opposite corners of the filthy, windowless, gore-stained cinder-block chamber.

No words are exchanged among the shunned, and the work goes on unabated for another half an hour when, sometime around noon, the sound of muffled steps coming from out in the corridor on the other side of the door registers in Lilly's deafened ears. The lock clicks, and the door opens.

"Just wanted to check on your progress," the Governor announces, coming into the room in a smart leather vest, a pistol holstered on his thigh, and his hair pulled back and away from his chiseled features. "Very impressive work," he says, coming over to Lilly's bin and glancing down at the gelatinous contents. "Might need to procure a few morsels later for feeding purposes."

Lilly doesn't look up. She keeps chopping, tossing, and wiping the edge of her blade on her jeans. At last she pulls an entire upper body cavity, which still has the cadaver's head attached, across her chopping area.

"Carry on, troops," the Governor says with an approving nod, before turning and heading for the door. As he slips out of the room, Lilly murmurs something under her breath that no else can hear.

The voice in her head—firing across the synapses in her brain—reaches her lips on barely a whisper, directed at the Governor.

"Soon . . . when you're not needed . . . this will be *you*."

She brings the axe down again and again.